Love
Doug + Caroline

The Best War Stories

The Best War Stories

Authors Include

AMBROSE BIERCE

JAMES M. CAIN

RUDYARD KIPLING

GEOFFREY HOUSEHOLD

JAMES A. MICHENER

IRWIN SHAW

MALLARD PRESS

An Imprint of BDD Promotional Book Company, Inc.
666 Fifth Avenue
New York, NY 10103
Manufactured in Great Britain

This edition first published in the United States of America in 1990
by The Mallard Press

By arrangement with The Octopus Group Limited

'Mallard Press and its accompanying design and logo are trademarks
of BDD Promotional Book Company, Inc.'

Copyright © 1990 Arrangement by The Octopus Group Limited

ISBN 0 792 45247 X

Printed in Great Britain at The Bath Press, Avon

CONTENTS

Naomi Mitchison

Black Sparta

THAT steep road went on and up, narrow and stony, going back to Sparta, Sparta again worse than ever it was, that freedom they'd promised him gone down the wind – oh, a Spartan promise! He was tied to the end of an ox-cart with a raw hide rope that had dried and tightened in the sun till his wrists were bleeding and his hands swollen; he ached all the time under a load of grain sacks. Far away, behind him now, was Megalopolis, the new city, the city with the fine name where bonds were free at last, the city of the folk that hated Sparta; he would never get there. It was his own fault ever to have trusted a Spartan promise, fought for her, suffered for her. If he fell down the oxen wouldn't stop and the rope would drag him over the stones after them; he must keep up. If only there was water anywhere. If only the rope would stay slack, not tighten suddenly on his sore, burning wrists when the cart jerked. Now one of the sacks had shifted and was rubbing the skin off his shoulder.

The road got steeper and stonier still. Up in front, the Spartans with spears shouldered were singing as they went. Four were ordered back to hurry the baggage carts. They wanted to be over the pass, back again in their own hollow valley of Sparta by nightfall. Already they thought how sweet their fair-haired wives would be after so long away. The ox-teams were goaded on, the helot baggage carriers shouted at till they hurried; the four Spartans went forward along the ranks to their places again, and he cowered, expecting to be hit. One of them checked himself and walked slower; he kept pace with the slave at the cart tail. 'Tragon,' he said, then repeated it, louder.

The man took his eyes off the ground and looked round and said 'Phylleidas,' then, hardly raising his voice above the creaking of the cart wheel, 'get me away.' The Spartan, still keeping pace, drew his sword and cut the rope between hands and cart; the loose end trailed over the stones and Tragon almost lost his balance for a moment. Then, still saying nothing, he cut through the knots at the wrists: the hide was so stuck into the cuts it had made that it did not fall away when he pulled.

When that was done they went on walking side by side behind the cart, but the helot had a hand free to shift the sacks. Even now he was the first to speak: 'They got you safe back?'

Phylleidas took a deep breath, glad to have no more than that to answer. 'I'd lost so much blood I couldn't speak for ten days. Chilon was killed. But I'm not even lame now; a year is a long time.'

He was questioning Tragon all the time with his eyes, but the man would say nothing till the question was put to him straight. Then he burst out: 'Why am I here now? It's you who should answer that! It's your State that promised me freedom if I served her well as a soldier! Didn't I? Didn't I?'

'You were taken prisoner.'

'So would you have been if they hadn't got you back in time! I was wounded, I was wounded twice more after you had gone. You'd see the scars now if I was clean. I couldn't even stand.'

'And then?'

'They asked for a ransom. Not very much, but I hadn't the money and no one offered it!' He turned his head and looked straight at the Spartan; his face was cut and bruised and dirty; only the eyes, thought Phylleidas, were the same, and, under that stare, he had to face again that most disturbing memory, which he had hoped was quite smothered; the message coming about the ransom for a helot soldier. They had the name wrong; but he had never tried to find out if there was a mistake. Only he was too ill then, and too unhappy – and he was not rich. He tried to face out the stare from Tragon, but felt he was blushing – oh, it was not the part of a good citizen to go filling Sparta with these freed slaves! Tragon went on: 'No, the ransom never came. So when I was better I was sold in Corinth. It's not too bad being a slave there. Most of the others were barbarians; my master had no great wish to keep a slave who was a Hellene – even my sort. He hadn't been bred up to kill them from behind in the dark like you, Phylleidas!' He looked round again, half expecting a blow, but when it did not come he went on again: 'He offered to sell me my freedom and gave me a chance of earning the money; then I was going to Megalopolis.'

'Why?'

'You don't think I loved Sparta then, do you? But it didn't happen. I'll tell you why. My master was a friend of your proxenos; I was sent there one day with a letter. There were two – of them' – he nodded forward towards the singing of the Spartan soldiers – 'in the courtyard. They asked me who I was. Like a fool I told. Because: well, seeing them made me suddenly think I wanted to be with you all again. If they put it right – it would have been so easy for them and I thought somehow they were going to – I'd be back where I was, where I should be, and

Megalopolis nothing! Oh, I was ready to believe in you again, I was, Phylleidas—'

'Don't talk so much!' said Phylleidas, trying not to speak as angrily as he felt with all those hot, loose words jumping like pebbles against his shining mind. 'What happened?'

'This!' said Tragon, holding out his wrists where the creeping blood drops had begun to settle and thicken. 'This! I was back in the trap. Whether they believed me or not, they laughed at me. And they bought me from my master and the painted temples and kind girls of Corinth, they bought me, laughing, and even then I thought – I thought they might have remembered back a year! I thought so till we got clear of the city; I was going to be grateful to them – by the Twins I was! But – but— And then, when I tried to speak, tried to tell them how I'd fought, and about you – oh, don't be angry with me, Phylleidas, they didn't believe me! – and when I tried to say the Amyclæ God was my God too, then it all came down on me again, pain and darkness, black Sparta like my fathers told me it was!'

Phylleidas frowned, trying to sift the core of plain fact out of the voice that shifted him about between past and present like a bird in the wind – like that hawk quartering, slipping suddenly across the sky, over the shadows in the dusky pass ahead, between them and Sparta . . . Hastily he drew back his eyes from too far, too vague lookings, steadied his mind: 'And now?'

For once Tragon spoke shortly: 'Now it's for you, Phylleidas.'

But what, what? The rest of today had been water-clear before: over the pass, home, the wagons for him and Idaios to get stacked while the others cooked supper, and then, before supper was quite over, to slip away barefoot, the cool, rough turf pressing up against his skin with that amazing, tingling texture of wild things, and down and over the wall, the stones that would have lost their heat at nightfall, the ditch to jump, the thin boughs of the nut tree just swaying in the moonlight, the dizzy brushing by herb borders in the garden, and then to call three times close to the shutters and know that in the dark inside one girl would hear and wake and be struck through all her sweet body by the same hard and lovely heart beats as his own! Now this other thing was rippling the clearness, breaking the image, this voice he knew better than hers.

'Tell me how you are getting me out of the trap, Phylleidas!'

'Wait,' he said, 'wait,' and walked on, keeping pace with this intolerable stumbling of slaves and oxen.

From half under the sacks the voice went on: 'When you said Chilon was killed I couldn't believe you at once. That beauty broken clean. I knew how he loved you, Phylleidas, how the flame in him caught you up, burning, flaring. I remember him coming to you the day before, when we knew it was to be a hard fight, in clear day with his hands full of flowers.'

'Oak leaves,' said Phylleidas. It hurt him, it tore him, and yet he wanted Tragon to go on. None of the others would talk about Chilon, not really – only like someone in a song of old wars – when a year ago Chilon had been so much alive! 'Oak leaves and quince flowers, wild quince – oh God!'

'And he said you should both wear them in sunlight: in sunlight you had been lovers: in the hills: in full air. And he took off his breastplate because there would be no attack yet, and he had on his old shirt. He took that off and put on the new one, the red one with short sleeves, while you made the wreath, looking at him all the time, knocking off the quince petals because your hand shook. And I said I would mend the old shirt that evening, and he laughed and said better not: let luck in at the holes. So I didn't. And he asked me to drink with you both.'

'Yes,' said Phylleidas, 'and I never saw him, Tragon, not after he was dead. They got me away. I didn't know till afterwards. I saw him fighting and shouting and happy. I never saw him dead.' They were still walking up, but the hills and the shadows had heightened faster still at each side, and all round them; soon there would be a star; soon the pass would dip towards Sparta. He thought quickly, then spoke again: 'Stay walking as you are for a little, Tragon; I shall get you out very soon!' And he leapt forward, running up to the others, his spear in his hand low and balanced.

But when he came to them and they looked round at him, Idaios and the rest, there was something surprising in their faces that stopped him saying what he meant to say. And yet, when they smiled at him and he smiled back at them, not speaking, what had he thought he would see? They were the same as they had always been. And suddenly it came into his mind with a faint horror, that perhaps he himself was not the same any longer. So he must speak, must try it on them and know if there was the least difference! 'Those helots who fought for us last year,' he said, 'did you know any of them?'

Idaios spat a dark, star-shaped mess into the grey glistening dust of the road: 'Know them!'

'But they were brave enough!' said Phylleidas. 'I'm sure of that: quick, brave soldiers.'

'If we were there to see!' said Idaios. 'And it's that sort we get walking about now, freed: as if it was their country!' He swung his arm out, low against the hillside as if he could sweep it all in and hold it against his breast and mouth. And he had been in the same battles, in another brigade, but still – mightn't he know as much? – as much and more, be less blinded by something, whatever it was, friendship – oh no, not friendship, not with a helot! 'Six feet of earth,' said Idaios, 'I would give them that!' And the others laughed and nodded, and the single first stars nodded in the evening over their spear heads.

Phylleidas dropped behind again, letting the oxen and the loaded carts go by him, the slinking, cowering drivers shoving at the wheels as they caught in ruts, or suddenly holding back as the downward slope at the far side began and the yoke-blocks butted forward and bumped against the swinging horns. Sharply he wished he could have the courage not to see Tragon, not to speak to him, to let the past bury its dead, bury him as Chilon had been buried, till just now, under a blue, far-off mountain of memory. And even at this minute, couldn't he get out of it, get back to the others again and not be different? No good: he had cut the rope. Now, he and Tragon were walking level. 'You know the Green Cave?' he said. 'Can you get there in the dark?'

'I can follow the water up.'

'Good. I'll give those two behind something else to look at, then you can go.'

'But what then, Phylleidas? How long shall I stay there? I've no food, no weapons! I shall be missed – they'll follow me – they'll get me again!'

It came thundering into his head to say: 'Look out for yourself, that's all I shall do!' and then go back to his own real friends and let the world go on. But where would Tragon go? To Megalopolis, to be an enemy. Unless he died first. If one starts a thing one has to finish it. He said, 'You'll have to get right away. A hundred miles from Sparta. In case anything happens. You should keep up near the cliffs and go south, and so to the sea. If I get you new clothes no one will know you. But you must take the first ship you can. I'll bring you money and food and a sword.'

'When?'

'Tomorrow night late, about the time the Swan dips. Here's my ration to take with you for now. Drop the sacks in a bush.' As Tragon caught hold of the bread their fingers touched and Phylleidas shivered as if somehow this had sealed him to something. His head flung back with nostrils stretched and eyes wide against the night. But surely he had done nothing against his honour? Not yet, he thought, but most certainly against something else, something even more a part of him than his honour. But he could not tell, it was no use watching his own mind like this! 'Is that clear?' he said.

'Yes,' said Tragon, 'and oh – Phylleidas, when I thought Sparta so black, I'd forgotten you!'

But Phylleidas hadn't waited for that; the moment he felt the voice rise to emotion he had jumped back and was suddenly letting himself go, clearing out the anger and irritation in a splendid bursting river of curses, the sort of thing he only did once or twice in a year. And the two drivers, as surprised as they were terrified, never noticed one shadow the less or heard the bushes rustling at the side of the road.

And then Phylleidas went back to the others. They were singing and he joined in, drowning himself for a time in the music that accented the beat of their half-tired, half-eager feet on the downward road. And if that could have gone on for ever with the night getting no later and home no nearer and yet no further, he would have kept his peace of heart, stayed still a part of something, Sparta, black Sparta, velvet black in the great hollows cupped and spread below them, Sparta that would be green again in the daytime, the greenest place in Hellas, green and sunny as it was in the days when he and Chilon had both been alive and loving one another so that the sunshine followed them about and golden, golden grew the air in the shadows under the oak leaves.

They halted and set the slaves to gathering wood and lighting fires from the little braziers they carried. The wagons were lined up for him and Idaios to count and see to. He began slowly, wondering what to say when Idaios found out – it was his end – about the missing helot. His peace was quite gone again. He kept on thinking about what he had done. But it was not only that; it was remembering the shifting voice, the too many, too piercing words, the way the man moved suddenly, all over, with his untaught body and mind that did not know clearness and beauty and discipline. He felt jarred on as if he had been made to listen to a harp played out of tune. Idaios shouted for him: 'There's a slave got away! One of these swine cut the rope!' He had the two drivers from behind by the neck, his broad, fierce hands bearing down on them, gripping at the base of their skulls ready for a kill, shoving them over at last into two heaps at Phylleidas's feet for him to kick as hard as he could. By the time he and Idaios had finished beating the helots he had almost stopped being so unhappy. But, of course, there was nothing to be got out of them. 'Didn't *you* see when you went by last time?' asked Idaios. But 'No,' he said sharply, aware of the number of lies that would have to be told sooner or later. Some of them came at once, round the camp fire when the others questioned him about what had happened, very angry that it should happen to be just their Mess that the loss would fall on! The glow of their fire had been a signal for one or two other Spartiates who had been up hunting near the pass to come over and join them, with a delicious wild sucking-pig for the pot. They offered their hounds for tracking the runaway, but it was impossible to say just where his trail could be picked up from among all the others, so that was no use.

They ate the sucking-pig with the good little balls of oatmeal and herbs that their Mess cook knew by this time always to make for them when there was half an hour to spare. The moon rose over the hills, big and pale golden, and sailed up, seeming to get littler and littler and brighter silver, putting out the stars round it, but not the warm, gay fire of pine boughs. One of the newcomers was playing a reed whistle at the far side, sharp leaping tunes of the midsummer dances that twirled up with the smoke and out on to the spreading air. Below in the valley was the lovely tangled din of nightingales singing against one another, and now and then an owl. Sometimes the tethered oxen rattled the carts, but there was little sound from any of the helots, only once or twice a laugh or an angry voice hastily shut down again, or from time to time, a deep moaning breath or a fit of sobbing from one of the beaten drivers. Phylleidas had been gnawing gently at a soft marrowy rib bone, spitting out the sharp bits and exploring the hollows with his tongue. Now he put it down and backed out of the circle, was gone before any of them saw. Idaios laughed and told the newcomers that his friend was just married. Before the night had gone on much longer two of the others were away as well; the Mess was just at the right age for marrying then.

Tragon was still following up the stream-bed, now, in late Spring, nearly dry and full of loose ankle-bruising stones, to the Green Cave. For a time he had just been terrified, sure he would be followed, caught again, hurt, so that he could only think of going very quickly and silently. Where there was any light he would run, tripping over branches, knocking against things that made terribly loud noises, then hiding under jutting rocks, hardly able to listen for the pounding of his heart like feet chasing him. And again he would come into heavy shadows and must feel his way under oak boughs. But by moon-rise everything was still and he knew he must be near the cave that he and Phylleidas had played in as boys; and at last he began to realize that he was free, that this wasn't a dream, that perhaps he would never be tied to a cart tail, never be whipped and laughed at any more. He could think it out clearly and wonderfully for a moment or two, but then he would get lost and not know what was real. All this year, ever since the unanswered message to Phylleidas, everything had been wrong. He had been horribly sure that no Spartan friendship or promise was worth anything; and not only that. He saw them as evil, a black rotting on the face of life. He had believed them once to his ruin; if ever he was free to fight again it would be on the other side! And now the impossible thing had happened and he had got free. And he was believing it all over again! Now the sideways crack in the rock that was the beginning of the cave shone with a dripping of wet moss; he squeezed through carefully so that it should look undisturbed, felt his way across the cold pool and over to the stone ledge at the back. He had not been there since he was grown-up. But it was dry and broad enough to lie along; he ate half the bread, then fell suddenly asleep with a piece still half chewed in his mouth.

Further down from the pass the night was warmer and stiller. In the moonlight Phylleidas could see every crack in the flat face of the house, the deep shadow under the tiles where the swallows were all asleep in their nests, even the green paint lions ramping on the shutters. He had given his third call and now stood back, pressing into a bush of mallow, in case her mother or nurse were to wake and look out with Theano.

The thin petals and pointed buds of the mallow patted against his cheek, shaken by the quickening of his breathing. The shutter on the left creaked and a hand came round the edge, shoving it open. Theano knelt upright on the sill for a full minute, peering out, with a long and lovely smile. Her hair was short still from the cutting at marriage; the clipped ends frilled out level with her shoulders; she smoothed it back out of her eyes, passing her hands across it till it lay sleek over her head, and then pressed down a band of soft leather over it, one he knew, with plaited ends that were nice to bite. She wore a girl's dress of white stuff, with a deep, close-fitting sash, so short that when she knelt up in it like this it was clear of her knees. She could not see Phylleidas, only knew he was there, and suddenly unpinned her dress on the right shoulder so that it fell clear of her breast. Then quickly, before he could look enough, leant over on one hand and vaulted clear of the flowers on to the turf, and turned and pushed back the shutters. From behind she was like a boy; he could guess at the movements of her shoulder and leg muscles with her arms up and knees stiff getting the wood into place.

As she faced him he came out of the shadows and their arms opened to one another, and they were trembling and hid their faces in the hollows of the other's shoulder, and pressed against each other till the trembling quieted into the warmth and tension, the pain waiting to turn into pleasure that both their bodies knew so well, that their minds answered to with murmuring and faint delicious laughter and sharpening of all their senses, so that the dew brushing against their bare arms was brilliant and exciting as their own kisses. They stood away then, only just touching fingers, looking into one another's eyes, staring freely and fearlessly because they were lawful lovers, man and wife, equal sharers in the same delight. He leant over quickly and kissed the tip of her bare breast, and she threw her head back and laughed and jumped with both feet like a child, and then tugged his hand so that they both started running.

They ran together, through two fields and an orchard, sometimes hand-in-hand, sometimes loose with Phylleidas racing round her, or she round him, bounding into the cool air that yet did not make them less warm, jumping over shadows, at stars, across each other's tracks! By and by they came to a cornfield, pale under the high moon, and still running they snatched at the soft, milky corn ears and bit at them. At the top of the field a bank sloped up with tangly trees growing on it, thorn and pomegranate and spiky evergreens. Theano looked round at him, with the sweet laughter hovering about her lips, and Phylleidas knew she was ready to play at hunter and hunted, and leapt out after her suddenly and very quickly.

Already the moon was lower in the sky when they looked about them again, lying loose on the turf, half sleepy and half full of awareness, so that everything took on some very special life of its own, a twig with three leaves on it, nodding to itself in a stray current of air, the bright haze round the moon, Theano's little finger-nail held up at eye-level. Suddenly Phylleidas turned half over as well as he could with her head still snuggling down on to his arm. 'I want to tell you something,' he said.

'Tell,' said Theano sleepily, with one ear close over the solid and lovely throbbing of the blood in the bend of his elbow.

'Today,' he said, 'I found a helot who had fought beside me and Chilon last year; he was filthy with sores and dirt on his back and head; he was tied to a cart tail. I cut the rope and helped him to get away.'

Theano sat up straight in one movement: 'You didn't!'

'I sent him to the Green Cave. Tomorrow night I shall take him food and money and my other sword. I've known him since we were boys.'

'Known him!' said Theano, reminding him for the moment of Idaios. 'What do you mean?'

'Well, he was on father's farm. I suppose – no, we weren't friends, of course; but he was brave and good-hearted. And Chilon liked him.'

'But this – Phylleidas, it's no business of yours, surely! You'll get yourself into trouble over it, my dear.' She frowned, her face close up to his.

He took her hand, he wanted her close, he felt very little and helpless and knew she was right about the trouble he would be in, and suddenly he saw his State as a vast, menacing black thing that he could never even try to appeal to if his rights were not its. 'I couldn't not,' he said.

And she: 'But if the State had not freed him there must have been some reason against it that you don't know.'

'I ought to have paid his ransom. The Ephors don't free them unless it's very clear.'

Theano shook herself. 'They're right! It's not those dogs we want for our lovers, not their children we want to bear!'

She rubbed her rumpled fair hair against Phylleidas, but he looked out over it, troubled, not sure if he could tell her properly. 'But he ought to have been freed. He fought for us. He talked about Chilon just now. He oughtn't to be dragged back and whipped and kicked! He hates us. When he gets out he may still hate us. He may go to Megalopolis.'

'And you're helping him! Oh, my dear love, don't.'

'But I must. I mustn't think of what's to come. Only of now and – and justice.'

'Justice isn't in one time only.'

'Mine's for now, and last year.'

'Justice isn't ours! It can't be any one man's – it's not justice any longer then.'

'Where is it, Theano?'

'With the State. Surely. We can't know, we can't see the whole. If we take it into our own hands – oh my dear, it puts the whole thing wrong! And that's more than any life or judgment of ours.'

Phylleidas picked up her hand that was lying on his knee and began straightening the fingers, one after the other. 'But this – why wasn't I right, Theano?'

'How can I tell? I'm only a little bit of the whole thing, too. If I had to say, perhaps it would be that there are so few of us and so many of them; we can't afford to go the least out of our way. But you're not happy about what you've done, are you?'

'No,' he said, and suddenly she caught hold of him and began kissing him deeply and fiercely, because she could not bear her own husband to be unhappy.

After a time he looked up, happier. 'Dear, I must go,' he said, 'back to the others. Don't mind what I've been saying.'

She nodded, her mouth shut against any words that might keep him with her still. This going back to camp was all part of it, the wholeness that she had tried to make clear to herself and him. It would have happened in no other state in Hellas. But yet it worked out in the arithmetic of love; her mother said so, and the older women. And she knew at least that it kept her brave. They ran together again, till she was in sight of the house, and kissed quickly and ran once more, but each their own way. He did not think much more about Tragon; when he got back to camp he threw himself down and slept solidly till morning when Idaios woke him at last, after letting him sleep long after the others.

But Theano did not sleep for a long time. She was turning his story over and over and that last 'no' admitting his unhappiness. Unhappiness surely, and what else? Perhaps guilt. The more she looked at it, the more it seemed to her that he had done wrong in some subtle way which neither of them knew but which troubled them both, not a clear human wrong you could either leave or put right, but like some ill word in a temple, something cast against a holiness that she could only dimly know. Towards dawn she slept on her uneasiness and dreamt of her lover running down a long, blazing hot road, looking back over his shoulder, with something chasing him, while she called to him to come over to her, in the green grass, but it seemed as if he could not hear. And the thing after him, whatever its final dreadfulness would be, was coming nearer and nearer. She woke with the taste of that in her mouth and the fear of that in the back of her head. She made up her mind what was the good thing to do. She wrapped a veil of heavy grey stuff, woven at home, that she wore now with a queer pride to show that she was a grown woman, married, over her head and round her shoulders, and went out and down to Sparta, and stood in the market-place, waiting for the Ephors to go by on their way to the Council.

One or two friends spoke to her, an uncle whom she liked, her old nurse, and her youngest brother running past, very important, with a message from his Iren. She leant on her long ash stick, not moving even when the sun shifted round full on her. And they saw by her quietness that she had business of her own, and did not question her. It was nearly midday before the Ephors came into the market-place of Sparta. She waited until they had been to the Temple and made their vows for the safety and good counsel of the State. Then she moved out, so that she stood in their path and could see their faces. She let the first two go by, but caught the third one by the edge of his cloak and knelt. He took her hand in his. 'Your asking?' he said. Now it was not so easy to speak; she felt choking and blind and very young; she began once and then stopped. He waited; there was a space clear about them where men and women turned out of their way to leave room for shy Truth to come to the speaker. At last she said, 'I have to tell you of a helot escaped from bonds the State laid on him and likely to be a danger. He is in the Green Cave, and will be till late tonight. Send the Krypteia.'

'Who told you?' the Ephor said, bending nearer.

She shook her head.

'Follow me,' he said, and kept hold of her hand.

She went in to the Council House between him and another; as the door shut behind them she turned her head quickly and was dreadfully afraid: this was the thing in her dream. She had never been inside before: it was quite a little room, and, after all, just seven men sitting round on chairs, some quite old and some not, with combed beards and bright still eyes. Two of them she had seen in her father's house as guests of honour. She had led the singing of the hymn to the luck of the house when they were listening – or not listening: why should she be frightened? There was also, she saw, one rather young man, standing, with his hand and cloak up over the lower part of his face, so that she could not see who he was. 'Where is this man?' asked the Ephor she had spoken to in the market. 'Say clearly.'

'In the hills to the right of the Western Pass. The road turns – like this – and there is a big pointed rock, covered with vines.'

Suddenly she realized, from the way he was following her words, who the standing man was, and began speaking directly to him: 'You know it? Follow up the river-bed till just before it clears the trees.

There are low cliffs with ferns in the cracks that close in on both sides. Go between them. A few paces on, to the right again, there is a sloping split in the rocks with a little spring trickling out of it. He is there. Go before night.'

She turned from him – the head of the Krypteia – out of breath as if she had been running, back to the Ephors. 'I have said.'

'When did you see this cave?'

'Just after I was married, we – I – I saw it.'

The Ephor stuck out his beard at her suddenly. 'How do you know about the helot, my girl?'

All at once the whole seven had their eyes on her! 'Artemis help me,' she said, 'it is true!' The Ephor got up and began coming towards her quite slowly; he lifted his hands for a grip and she was nearly screaming. He pounced on her wrist and she gasped, stiffening and steadying. 'He will get away in the night!' she said. 'Send today!'

'Who is helping him?' said the Ephor.

She looked up at his face, then down at his hands, tightening, tightening over hers. 'No one.'

Suddenly she was let loose again and another Ephor spoke from behind her: 'You are Theano, daughter of Euboidas, married to Phylleidas, whose farm is up the road to the Western Pass.' She said nothing at all; this seemed to be a statement, not a question. Besides, she was badly frightened, and not for herself alone now. But if one is part of a whole one can have no secrets. 'I see,' said the same man, and as he spoke she saw the door opening again.

She did what she could; she turned to the Ephor who had spoken and said slowly: 'I don't think you *do* see.' And then sprang for the open door, half expecting it to catch her before she was through. But they let her go. She had dropped her ash stick; it didn't matter. She screwed her hands tight into the grey veil and ran through the market and up the road for home.

In the morning the question of the missing slave had come up again. Phylleidas had tried to make as little as possible of it, and so had Idaios, backing him. But the rest decided they must report it, and sent Phylleidas to do that. Two of the others were to follow with the oxen and carts and everything else, checked and counted. Those who were left would have a good day of it, bathing in the pools of the lazy Eurotas, warming and shrinking already at the first touch of summer, or they would be seeing their fathers and mothers and friends, and paying the vows they made before they went. The married ones perhaps could steal another word or two with their wives, and one whose father was dead had to go and get leave to set up house on his own. The Mess cook came in too, to buy salt and a new iron cooking pot. There was tanned leather

wanted, besides, for shoe soling. One of the helot drivers was limping
badly that morning from a kick on the kneecap.

Phylleidas went off down the road at a quick walk, sometimes half
a run. If only he could have bought Tragon and then freed him himself!
He had been in other States and knew the practice. But Sparta was
different. One did not own things that way. The helots belonged to all
the citizens, no one of them to any single master; the only way to free
Tragon was through all these citizens in council. And that was no good.
So Phylleidas must go outside the law. All the way towards the city he
was looking very carefully at the faces of everyone he met – every
Spartiate. Had this one or that ever gone outside the law? Had he
become different from the others? Surely not. And how lovely, how
beautiful to stay always the same without doubt or conflict, with
everything resolved and happy and open! When he got to the city he
would have to find some gold or silver money; not much. He thought his
mother would have some, the remains of old hoardings. And there was
a cousin who had travelled. The clothes would be easy enough, and the
food; though he would feel rather a fool buying them. If only there was
someone he could talk to about it! But it had to be a secret now and in
the future. Well, it was good discipline for the mind to have secrets
which must be kept.

And then suddenly he saw someone he could speak to. She was
going slowly along the side of the road, with her head bent under the
grey shawl. He had not even recognized her till she was quite near, and
she was not looking his way at all, but fixedly on the ground, unlike
herself. He touched her on the shoulder and said, 'My wife!'

She stopped and lifted her head and drew in her breath on a tearing
cry. 'You!' she said. 'Oh – what are you doing? Where are you going?'

'I have to get the things I told you of: food, clothes and money. You
know why. Can you help me about the money, Theano?'

She let him go and stood back a pace. Between them the dry mud on
the edge of the cart rut flaked and powdered. He heard a corn-crake in
the field behind him. She said: 'I have helped you.'

And he said: 'What have you done?'

And she said: 'I have done my duty, and yours.'

He looked past her down the Sparta road. 'You told them?'

'The Ephors. Yes.'

'How much?'

'Where he is hidden. Only that. Not about you. Oh, my dear, you
said you were unhappy!'

'What are they doing?'

'Sending: before night.'

'And it's midday now. Sending, sending. You said—'

'The Krypteia.'

He faced towards her again. She meant to tell him how dreadful it had been, show him the bruises where the bones of the old man's fingers had stuck into her hand and arm. But he was looking like a stranger. He said, very low, 'I must hurry.' And he lifted his hand and hit her on the side of the head and sent her staggering across the road. Then he went on.

She lay on the stones at the road edge with her arms wrapped round her head. While he was in hearing she must not scream, must not even cry out loud. She choked on dry grass and dust. She was too surprised to have any feeling at all about him, love or hate or fear, not for a long time. Slowly she sat up, lifting her aching, dazed head, and looked along the road. After some minutes she found she was looking the wrong way; it cost her infinite pains to turn. He was out of sight. She crawled under the shadow of an olive and fell through deep and painful gulfs of dizzying, cracking darkness. When she sat up again, and at last stood, she could tell by the sun it was much later in the day.

Actually, Phylleidas had never been on Krypteia himself; but his friends had. Chilon had done it three years before. It was a normal happening, exciting and interesting in its way, and part of a good citizenship, one of the things one did when one was told. But today it did not seem like that. Because of Tragon. This same Tragon who talked so maddeningly, who was not by any right standards the sort of man that men should be. Up to now he had not been quite sure how the State would judge it; he had hoped that perhaps the State might in some obscure way be brought to give him, if not approval, at least consent. But now the judgment had been made. The Krypteia would be there before nightfall. Yes. So he must go against everything now, with even fuller knowledge of what he was doing. She made him. She forced him to be different. He had done with her, done with everything beautiful and peaceful. Because he had chosen to go his own way.

He bought the clothes and the food, quickly, then went to his mother's house and found, as he thought, that she still had some Persian money, kept for the mere magpie pleasure of it, not for use. She gave it to him, though, and his old sword that he had lent to his next brother. The brother was away, but the sword was in his room. He took it without arguing. That was lucky. Before he had time to think any more he was on the road to the Pass again and the sun was dropping half-way towards evening.

Tragon sat on the ledge at the back of the cave, gripping the edge of it with his hands. His eyes were accustomed to the dim green light, so that he could scarcely believe he was not visible from outside. The sloping crack between the stones was blinking bright, the little ferns and mosses were edged and dripping with sunlight. The day had been going on now – how long? The strain of it was beginning to spread down from his eyes and mind into his finger-tips. And then there would be most of the night. He wished he could have slept again, got strong for his day and night – he thought he must reckon it as that – of getting to the coast, when he would need all his courage and endurance in the hills, all his wits when he got down to the plain. But sleep was nowhere near. He was hungry too, but that he was used to. Half a day more perhaps: the slow dimming of the crack, just as it had slowly lightened that morning. The cave would be quite black again till moonrise; so much the better. When it was all thick dark he could think he was not there at all. But a day and most of a night for Phylleidas to change his mind, for a Spartan promise to be broken! No, no, he thought to himself, it couldn't be another trap! Why should it be? But Phylleidas might so easily come to think differently by now, and then – what would it matter what he had said to a helot! For a time Tragon simply sat there raging over this unalterable slavery that was fixed into him, blood and bone, so that, however much he tried to be like the others, tried to make their virtues his – as he had during the fighting – it was yet no use, and a promise to him *was* different. He knew he was a man too, he knew that he could even understand some things and do some things better and quicker than they; he knew he could have bought his freedom in Corinth, or any other Hellene state, perhaps even by luck, skill and bravery grown worthy of citizenship, at least been respected and safe, able to talk as an equal with the rest! But that was a knowledge got with the outside of himself, through his intelligence. Deep below he felt his slavery, here in Sparta. And where else mattered? It was his own Sparta. Tonight, if all went well, he would set about leaving it for ever. Suddenly he realized that if he had gone to Megalopolis, as he wanted, it was simply to be fighting Sparta, to be in this way if in no other violently aware of Sparta still. He got up and walked about the cave, touching the damp walls with the palms of his hands. Wherever he went he would still in his heart be a helot of Sparta.

Surely it was beginning to get a little less light! He went over to the crack, and then stayed tense, listening. That must be footsteps. A long way off still, but the echo carried them up between the cliffs. Was it some shepherd or swineherd – one of his own people? But there was no sound of beasts. Was it Phylleidas twelve hours before his time? Or was it – was it – for a dreadful moment the Pan-flutes too shrill to hear but not to feel were dinning round his head; his sight dimmed and cleared and dimmed again; his muscles twitched him about, uncontrolled. Then he got free and listened again. It was only one man coming, either a stranger or Phylleidas: not them. The ravine was all in shadow now, though there was sun in the tops of the pines on the far side. He lay on his face and peered through the fern curtain at the very bottom, warily, in case it was not Phylleidas. The steps got nearer and nearer; he fought to keep himself calm. They must be near the bend. Yes, it was Phylleidas – hurrying. He climbed to his feet, slowly, holding on to the juts of the cave wall; he was sweating all over.

Phylleidas shoved through into the cave, burning and gasping with the pace he had come up that difficult bed of stone; he threw the clothes down. 'Change, quick!' he said and dropped to the ground and drank with his head and shoulders right in the pool. When he sat up, getting used to the dark, Tragon was in his new clothes and buckling on the sword. 'Now eat,' he said, 'and get the money stowed safe. You'll have to hurry.'

'Why?' said Tragon, biting into the bread and sausage.

Phylleidas waited till he had a mouthful down, then said, 'The Krypteia are after you.'

Tragon made a queer little moan and gave at the knees, collapsed on to the floor of the cave.

'They won't be here yet,' said Phylleidas, trying not to show either anger or disgust. 'And you'll be all right if you keep steady.'

And Tragon said: 'Did you change your mind, Phylleidas?'

'No,' said Phylleidas heavily.

'Then why?'

'They found out. What does it matter how! You've got to get up clear of the wood and cross the road higher than they'll come. Eat a little, you fool!'

Tragon ate obediently. 'They'll know I've crossed the road,' he said, 'when they find me gone. Will they have hounds?'

'I don't know!' said Phylleidas. 'And don't be so frightened, for God's sake. Remember the battles we've been in together, Tragon!'

Tragon said, 'I shall be alone,' and got up. He looked quite decent in the new clothes. Then: 'Has anyone ever escaped?'

'Dozens, I expect,' said Phylleidas, startled at this and beginning to see what the name of the Krypteia meant to the hunted ones. 'If only you can keep your head! Can you?'

But Tragon said: 'If they get me I shan't say it was you who helped me!'

Phylleidas couldn't bear answering that in its own emotion; he said: 'They'll know my sword.' He turned Tragon round and saw that the purse was twisted safely through his belt, then said: 'Now go. You'll get a ship. Good luck, Tragon!' And he went over to the crack.

Tragon came over too, eating his last mouthful, and suddenly said: 'Do you hear anything?'

'Phylleidas listened too. He said: 'They're before their time. Go!'

And Tragon shook and said, 'I shall never do it!'

'Yes, you will!' said Phylleidas; then: 'I'll stay and cover you.'

'Oh!' said Tragon, and suddenly kissed him and took a breath and turned and ran up the ravine.

When he was out of sight, Phylleidas sat down; he thought he had easily another minute or two. And he had to reckon up just where he was. He had never meant to say the last thing; he thought that when Tragon was off, he would be clear again, be able to take his own real place and not be different any more. Now he was going to do something very terrible and very open, so that he would never be able to get away from it; he dared not quite face that. They were taking a long time. He supposed some were going up-stream a little so as to get to the cave mouth from every side at once. But that was all right: however much they went up-stream Tragon would be much further up, and anyhow they would not see him because they would not be looking for him there. He began to wonder whether it would be possible to argue with them, to show them quite plainly his and Tragon's Right, so that they would stop. But that was out of the question: even if he could explain everything, making clear what was so tangled in his own mind, they were under orders from the Ephors and could not do anything but carry out those orders. He would have himself, in the old days. Then how to delay them? Best perhaps to get right into the cave, so that they would think for a long time that he was Tragon. Perhaps they would shoot in at random, but he thought not, and anyhow he must chance it; they were more likely to try and smoke him out. He sat on the ledge and swung one foot over the other. It was a game, the sort of game the boys played.

There were quite a lot of noises outside now; it was beginning. He laughed to himself rather happily, with the play idea all through him. But then he heard the short, muffled, snapping bark of a hound. That certainly lessened Tragon's chance of escape. Unless he could do something; he thought hard. There was silence outside for long enough to make anyone strained with listening, then suddenly a horrid long yell that set his heart beating very fast; it made him think: If I was a helot that might have bolted me. Rather quickly the play feeling got swamped by the much less pleasant feeling of how it would be if— A big if, of course, but there it was. There were two of them at the edge of the crack now, whispering, then listening. He could not help moving a little, making a slight noise. He heard one say: 'There he is!' They moved away and he could hear them dragging branches over the stones for the fire to smoke him out. He thought this was a bad game and going on much too long. The hound barked again, nastily. He drew his sword, quite clear that he would get out before there was a fire and before they expected him. Suddenly he wondered whether, if he was a helot, if it was really true, not all a game, he would not rather stay and be smothered by the smoke and not go out to face certain death in the ravine.

He tiptoed to the crack and looked out as well as he could. There were three of them up to the right pulling along a young oak tree with plenty of green leaves for smoke. One of them at least was a man he knew. The fourth stood lower down in the bed of the ravine on the other side, holding two hounds on a leash. He had never noticed before what terrible great beasts they were, with enormous depth of chest, leaning forward, towards him, from all four legs, tugging at their collars. He thought of them racing after Tragon – almost at once – and looked for a flat stone to jump on to. It was not a game after all, not with those brutes.

As he leapt for the stone, the bloodhounds of the Krypteia were loosed on him, both together. He could only deal with one of them. The other knocked him over and he and it rolled in the stones, its horrible baying right in his ears, its stinking breath in his face, its claws tearing his side as he kept it off him with both hands on its throat under the jaw-bone. Then sheer weight told and it got a grip on his left arm and he yelled with pain and terror trying desperately to knock it off before it was through to the bone. It was pulled off him and he got half up, clinging to a rock, and saw swords all round. 'Who are you?' they said, but he did not answer at once. His arm was dreadfully torn and hurting so that he could hardly stand. One of them said: 'You're not the same man!' and another, 'You're Phylleidas!' As he stood upright and then moved a step or two among the lowered swords, the hound started baying again and straining towards him and the blood it could smell so thick. He got his sword out of the body of the first hound; the Krypteia stood all around him. He said: 'The man's escaped.'

'God, we can trail him!' said one of them.

But Phylleidas struck down into the neck of the hound with all the quickness and strength he had left. 'You won't!' he said. All four of the men were on to him at once, their hands on his arms and throat; he fought them instinctively, biting and kicking and throwing himself back to drag them over. Then they got him down and it was finished.

He did not go on struggling; he let one of them hold him while another bandaged his arm. The hound he had stabbed was still kicking a little, but for yards down the shrunk pools of the river were trickling fresh and red with the beast's blood; he would never bay like that after Tragon now. The eldest of the four men was standing in front of him, looking down at him with eyes all troubled by something he had never met before. 'Do you know what you have done?' he said.

'Yes,' Phylleidas said, 'I know. I have saved Tragon from you.'

'But' – the man knelt down on the stone beside him, as if closer sight

could somehow bring him understanding – 'we are the Krypteia! And
you've killed our hounds!'

'You loosed them on me. Get that bandage tighter. You might look
at my side, too.'

'But we couldn't tell you were one of us! What were you doing
hiding in that cave?'

'I didn't want you to kill Tragon.'

'But the Ephors sent us!'

Phylleidas looked up, smiling, easier now that the pressure of the
bandage was keeping his torn flesh together. 'That's why. You wouldn't
have stopped in the name of any God, if I could have made you know
it was not just!'

'No! Are you a better judge than the state?'

And, 'Yes!' said Phylleidas. The man stared at him once more, then
got up and beckoned to one of the others. Phylleidas watched them
quite happily for a moment or two; they were in a different world. But
then he saw them pointing up-stream, and one of them looking carefully
along the cliffs at each side, for places where anyone could climb. He
got on to his feet. 'Oh, what are you doing?' he said.

The older man spoke over his shoulder: 'What we were ordered.
Killing a helot.' And he laughed.

'Oh no!' said Phylleidas. 'You can't! That's finished—' and he
stumbled towards him, horridly feeling that his own voice was somehow
odd as if it had picked up new tones and sharpnesses from the helot! He
caught at them anyhow, their hands, their knees: 'Oh by all the Gods!'
he said, 'stop! You don't understand! He was my friend!'

But one after another they got away from him, till only the older
man was left. Phylleidas sat down on a stone and began to cry. After a
time the man spoke: 'I think you must be mad, Phylleidas. But, mad or
not, you have tried to stop the Krypteia and you have killed the hounds
of the Krypteia. You have said you are a friend to a helot whom the
State has judged to death. You have cried and screamed like a woman,
before men younger than yourself. What are you going to do?'

Phylleidas said: 'I don't know.' He was not really much interested in
what he had been doing.

'You have gone against the State, you have disowned your citizenship,' the man went on, and suddenly stooped and shook him. 'Listen in
the name of the Twins, Phylleidas! Look at me! We shall have to tell
the Ephors; you will be disgraced; you can't stay a citizen after this; no
one will speak to you!'

'Well?' said Phylleidas. It was all going over his head like cloud
shadows.

The man was finding it very hard to speak. At last he picked up the
sword from where it lay by the second hound. 'I offer you honour,' he

said, 'if you choose to kill yourself now, we can make a story. No one but the Ephors need know. I have sent the young men away. I will help you.' Phylleidas took the sword: 'What am I to do with it?'

'Put the point over your heart – so: between the bones. Fall forward on to it. It is very quick and hurts less than dishonour. I will see it goes true, Phylleidas.'

But suddenly Phylleidas began to laugh, as violently as he had been crying before. 'I can't help it,' he said, 'Don't look like that! It tickled. Oh why are you all so different from me?'

The man said nothing for about a minute, then, very slowly: 'Phylleidas, you are trying to make me think you are really mad. But the Ephors won't take that. They'll judge you for what you have done, not what you are. It's no use.'

Phylleidas sheathed the sword with a click; he seemed to be feeling his hurt arm again. 'I'm not mad,' he said, 'but I'm very sleepy.' He stumbled over to the edge of the river-bed under the cliffs where there was a strip of fine shingle and weeds, and lay down all in a piece and was asleep before his loose hand had slipped off his knee on to the ground.

The sunlight slid up the trees and up the sky and away; it was nearly night. Theano came up into the ravine and saw her husband lying in the river-bed and the other man watching beside him. She had been coming slowly because of her headache, but now she broke into a kind of miserable run. 'What have you done?' she said.

'Nothing,' said the man, rather grimly.

'Then – has he?'

'Look at him, girl, whoever you are! Look at him, the pig!'

'Oh,' said Theano, 'he's asleep, not dead!' And she began to laugh with her hands up at her temples. 'Oh, he's asleep!'

'Yes,' said the man, and kicked him as hard as he could.

Theano screamed, but Phylleidas only moved a little in his sleep and seemed to smile. 'So!' said Theano, and picked up a stone in both hands and swung it back shoulder-high for the throw.

'Wait till you hear!' said the Spartiate quickly, his hands up to guard himself, all the same. 'You are his wife?' Theano nodded, but still held the stone ready. 'Well, then: the man wasn't there, but *he* was' – and he nodded towards Phylleidas – 'and he killed our bloodhounds – look. And he tried to stop us, though he knew what orders we were under. He will lose his citizenship for that. I offered him the way out; I would have held the sword for him. But he would not take it – he laughed!'

Theano went over to Phylleidas and sat down beside him, screwing up her eyes and saying nothing yet. She picked up his bandaged arm, heavy with the depth of his sleep. 'Was that you?' she said.

'The hound – before we could get it off. Is he mad?'

'He is not mad,' said Theano, 'but he is singing a song of his own, against ours.'

'I don't understand. If he had killed himself you would be left in honour now.'

Theano shivered. 'He knows what I want better than you do.'

'And your children?'

'Will they be less good than they would have been?'

He shrugged his shoulders. 'If you choose to refuse them the best thing in life—! But what are you going to do, Theano, daughter of Euboidas?'

'Nothing. If all this was so true for him that he' – she hesitated a moment with her hand against her forehead – 'that he took these risks, then it is real, isn't it? As real as our things. And we have to accept it.' She took off her thick veil and threw it over Phylleidas, tucking it in at the sides, for the dew was beginning to fall heavily, and hunched herself up with her arms crossed over her breasts to keep as warm as she could. The Spartiate had a long stick and was using it to lever up roots and stones and make a hole to bury the hounds. When he had done that he came and sat down on a flat stone at the foot of the cliff opposite Theano.

The stars came out through the pine-tops and swung round and over; the moon followed and climbed to a high chilly midnight, and slid slowly down, dimming whatever stars she passed. Theano drowsed and woke and drowsed again, stiffly and painfully. Her feet and legs and the outsides of her arms got so cold that she could feel nothing else. Phylleidas slept on without moving the tiniest muscle anywhere; his slow even breath made no sound till she leant right over to him, anxiously, and laid her head just by his.

The Spartiate looked up and spoke to her across the river-bed in the stillness: 'I think they're coming back.'

She blinked herself wide awake and took a deep cold breath of moon-grey air.

'If they killed, there will be no need to tell the Ephors.'

But there was no answer to this.

After a time the other three came trailing back, one of them limping. The elder man and Theano got up and stood together in the middle of the ravine to meet them. When they were all there he asked: 'Well?'

The next eldest answered: 'We've lost him. We beat all over the woods for him, we've been up into the dry hills. But we'd not much chance without the hounds. Then Kalokleinas fell over a root and hurt his foot. If we could get another hound—'

'No good. He'll have fouled his trail by now, got on to stone most likely or else among the goats.'

'We did everything we could have done.'

'It's the first time for years we've failed.'

They all glared at Phylleidas sleeping through it all. Theano stood in front of him. 'It's my loss as well as yours!' she said rather shakily. 'I wanted the kill. But the Gods aren't always with one.'

'This was one man, not the Gods,' said Kalokleinas, the limping one, and stared at Theano.

'He was possessed by something: not himself, not man-like. I know him.' She felt she was fighting now.

'It wasn't the work of any Gods I know – some Stranger perhaps! Did he rape a priestess in Argos?' said the older man, spitting.

And then the other: 'Or was it some helot mud-God he's been paying vows to?'

'And who's to pay us for this night and a shame on the Krypteia?'

'Yes, who?' said Kalokleinas, and caught Theano by the wrist.

She stood still, wondering very quickly whether to call Phylleidas, whether if she did she would be able to wake him out of this queer sleep. No, she would not call yet. 'What good will it be if I pay?' she said. 'It will be a bigger shame on the Krypteia then!' He had her wrist just where the Ephor had held it and bruised it in the morning: she clenched her hand and went on in a low voice, trying to keep her knees tense against the trembling that was running down them. 'We are all Spartiate here; need you mind that I saw you come back with clean swords? Nobody not of us will know.' She looked up, over the cliff top, keeping her eyes from any meeting with the shining eyes of the young men. She felt them closing in on her, the warmth of them brushing her cold arm.

'Nobody need know anything that happens tonight!' said Kalokleinas.

'But it's not night any longer!' she said with his breath on her cheek. 'Look, look, there's dawn fighting against the moon!' As she spoke a light wind came blowing down the ravine and all the leaves on the trees whispered; some tension seemed to relax round her among the Krypteia. 'You're tired,' she said, 'all tired. Sleep, I will keep watch.'

And, 'Sleep,' said the older man, 'the sun will be warm soon.'

One by one they fell away from her, with sleep coming on to them, and curled themselves up wherever the stones left a space, and slept.

Theano sat down again beside her husband and began weaving rushes together to keep herself from falling asleep too. The moon sank through the trees. Gradually she began to see what she was doing. Some way off, in the wood, a bird woke and chirped, then another. Colours crept back into the world. She leant over to Phylleidas and felt his hand; it was not very warm and he stirred a little to her touch. Across the river bed, the elder man was awake and looking at her, with his cloak wrapped thickly over his arms and shoulders. Theano spoke very suddenly, every word darting like a little bird through the still air between them: 'How are you saving the honour of your Krypteia?'

Taken unawares, the man stared back at her and answered heavily: 'I must speak the truth to the Ephors.'

'And about my husband?'

'The truth.'

'And about me?'

'There's nothing to say.'

'But suppose I tell them – well, a little more than the truth, about last night and your young men?'

'They won't believe you.'

'I can make them believe me.'

'They won't care.'

'Oh, but they will! When I tell them that I, Theano, daughter of Euboidas, was lured here—'

The man shifted uncomfortably. 'Anyway, it won't save *him*!'

'No. But it will hurt you – you and the others – badly.'

The man got up and came over to her. 'What do you want, Theano, daughter of Euboidas?'

She made room for him beside her, at Phylleidas' feet. 'I want you to tell a lie for me. Say you killed the helot and he killed your hounds. After all it was because of him. And say nothing about my husband.'

'That's a big lie you're asking me for.'

'Well, is it?' she said. 'You see, it's for good every way. The helot will be out of the country; he's not one to stay and lead revolts. Phylleidas will come back and be one of us – not different any more. And he and I will have our children and stay part of the whole, and the song will not be broken.'

'But – suppose he's still mad?'

'It was only about this one thing; and now it's over.' She lifted her eyes to his. 'Well, here's a bargain. Wait till he wakes; if he's still mad you shall say what you like – the truth if you must. If not, give me my lie.'

'But my young men: suppose they don't agree?' He clutched on to that, because he found that, quite against his will, he appeared to have agreed to something he never meant!

'I'll talk to them myself,' said Theano. 'Don't you think so?' She laughed rather quiveringly.

'You're a little wench and a half!' said the man. 'I wish you were my wife, not his! Give me a kiss.'

Theano crooked her fingers together tightly and looked down at Phylleidas. 'Very well,' she said and turned her face round to be kissed.

The sun tilted over the edge of the ravine, pushing the shadow down the low cliff and the mouth of the cave. Immediately the damp chill of night fled out of the air; Theano stretched out her arms, turning them this way and that to it. She began to smell the pines, more and more strongly every moment. Kalokleinas woke and then the other two young men. And at last, when the sun had covered him, had soaked him head to foot with warmth, Phylleidas woke too, and yawned and heaved himself lazily up. Theano stood away a little under a holm oak that stretched branches right across the river-bed; she clung on to the biggest with stiff pricked fingers, praying, vowing quickly to Artemis and the Twins, because in a minute she would know. At first he only saw the others. He looked at them unblinkingly for quite a long time. 'You didn't get him,' he said. No one answered, and he nodded. 'You won't now. He's too clever. Once he told Chilon and me—' And then he checked himself, looking round. 'It's day,' he said. 'I've slept a long time. Will one of you tie this bandage again?' He held out his arm. The elder man was whispering to Kalokleinas, but one of the others came and did it. Theano wanted to, but she had to stay hidden; still she did not know, either way.

'Has anyone got any food?' he said again. 'I had nothing much yesterday. I'm hungry now.'

'I've not,' said the man who was doing the bandage, shortly, and made the knot firm with teeth and fingers.

He picked up a stone with his other hand and shied it casually across the ravine; then he looked downstream, towards the holm oak. 'You're here,' he said, 'after all.' And he held out his hands to her. She let go of the tree and came to him with her vows answered. They stood together, facing Krypteia. He said, 'It's finished!'

And she said to them: 'You see; he's back.'

And the older man said: 'Yes. I do see. I think you're right.'

She went back to the place where Phylleidas had lain, and picked up her veil. Some of it had dried in the sun and some was still dewy and cold in its roughness. She was very, very tired and her head ached again. But Phylleidas was borrowing a little oil from Kalokleinas to wash with; no one had a comb. He laughed, and after a minute or two she saw that Kalokleinas was laughing too. They both went past her to the flat green pool that was made by the water dripping from the cave, and knelt down and began dabbling in it with their hands and arms. An end of the bandage dropped into the water, and Kalokleinas reached over and tucked it away. The other two young ones joined them. Theano leant against the bank. She wondered, without hate, without much interest even, where the helot was now; she wondered how long it would be before rain would come and wash away the stains of the hounds' blood; she wondered when she could get home and what everyone would say; she hoped they wouldn't ask her too many questions before she could go away and sleep; she wished she could

BLACK SPARTA

go and dabble in the wet pool with the men. It would be hot and dusty walking back, even by the field path. The elder man had a piece of black bread in the fold of his cloak. He took it out and began slowly cutting it up on a flat stone: a piece for each of the Krypteia, a piece for Phylleidas, and a piece for her.

W. H. Prescott

The Battle of Lepanto, 1571

(From *The History of Philip II, King of Spain*)

ON the third of October, Don John put to sea, and stood for the gulf of
Lepanto. As the fleet swept down the Ionian Sea, it passed many a spot
famous in ancient story. None, we may imagine, would be so likely to
excite an interest at this time as Actium, on whose waters was fought
the greatest naval battle of antiquity. But the mariner, probably, gave
little thought to the past, as he dwelt on the conflict that awaited him at
Lepanto. On the fifth, a thick fog enveloped the armada, and shut out
every object from sight. Fortunately the vessels met with no injury, and
passing by Ithaca, the ancient home of Ulysses, they safely anchored off
the eastern coast of Cephalonia. For two days their progress was
thwarted by head-winds. But on the seventh, Don John, impatient of
delay, again put to sea, though wind and weather were still unfavourable.

It was two hours before dawn, on Sunday, the memorable seventh of
October, when the fleet weighed anchor. The wind had become lighter;
but it was still contrary, and the galleys were indebted for their progress
much more to their oars than their sails. By sunrise they were abreast
of the Curzolari, – a cluster of huge rocks, or rocky islets, which on the
north defends the entrance of the gulf of Lepanto. The fleet moved
laboriously along, while every eye was strained to catch the first glimpse
of the hostile navy. At length the watch on the foretop of the *Real*
called out 'A sail!' and soon after declared that the whole Ottoman fleet
was in sight. Several others, climbing up the rigging, confirmed his
report; and in a few moments more, word was sent to the same effect by
Andrew Doria, who commanded on the right. There was no longer any
doubt; and Don John, ordering his pennant to be displayed at the
mizzen-peak, unfurled the great standard of the League, given by the
pope, and directed a gun to be fired, the signal for battle. The report,
as it ran along the rock shores, fell cheerily on the ears of the
confederates, who, raising their eyes towards the consecrated banner,
filled the air with their shouts.

The principal captains now came on board the *Real*, to receive the last orders of the commander-in-chief. Even at this late hour, there were some who ventured to intimate their doubts of the expediency of engaging the enemy in a position where he had a decided advantage. But Don John cut short the discussion. 'Gentlemen,' he said, 'this is the time for combat, not for counsel.' He then continued the dispositions he was making for the attack.

He had already given to each commander of a galley written instructions as to the manner in which the line of battle was to be formed in case of meeting the enemy. The armada was now disposed in that order. It extended on a front of three miles. Far on the right, a squadron of sixty-four galleys was commanded by the Genoese admiral, Andrew Doria, – a name of terror to the Moslems. The centre, or *battle*, as it was called, consisting of sixty-three galleys, was led by John of Austria, who was supported on the one side by Colonna, the captain-general of the pope, and on the other by the Venetian captain-general, Veniero. Immediately in the rear was the galley of the Grand-Commander Requesens who still remained near the person of his former pupil; though a difference which arose between them on the voyage, fortunately now healed, showed that the young commander-in-chief was wholly independent of his teacher in the art of war.

The left wing was commanded by the noble Venetian, Barbarigo, whose vessels stretched along the Aetolian shore, to which he approached as near as, in his ignorance of the coast, he dared to venture, so as to prevent his being turned by the enemy. Finally, the reserve, consisting of thirty-five galleys, was given to the brave marquis of Santa Cruz, with directions to act in any quarter where he thought his presence most needed. The smaller craft, some of which had now arrived, seem to have taken little part in the action, which was thus left to the galleys.

Each commander was to occupy so much space with his galley as to allow room for manoeuvring it to advantage, and yet not enough to allow the enemy to break the line. He was directed to single out his adversary, to close with him at once, and board as soon as possible. The beaks of the galleys were pronounced to be a hindrance rather than a help in action. They were rarely strong enough to resist a shock from an antagonist, and they much interfered with the working and firing of the guns. Don John had the beak of his vessel cut away. The example was followed throughout the fleet, and, as it is said, with eminently good effect. It may seem strange that this discovery should have been reserved for the crisis of a battle.

When the officers had received their last instructions, they returned to their respective vessels; and Don John, going on board of a light frigate, passed rapidly through the part of the armada lying on his right, while he commanded Requesens to do the same with the vessels on his left. His object was to feel the temper of his men, and to rouse their mettle by a few words of encouragement. The Venetians he reminded of their recent injuries. The hour for vengeance, he told them, had arrived. To the Spaniards and other confederates he said: 'You have come to fight the battle of the Cross; to conquer or to die. But whether you are to die or conquer, do your duty this day, and you will secure a glorious immortality.' His words were received with a burst of enthusiasm which went to the heart of the commander, and assured him that he could rely on his men in the hour of trial. On returning to his vessel, he saw Veniero on his quarter-deck; and they exchanged salutations in as friendly a manner as if no difference had existed between them. At this solemn hour both these brave men were willing to forget all personal animosity in a common feeling of devotion to the great cause in which they were engaged.

The Ottoman fleet came on slowly and with difficulty. For, strange to say, the wind, which had hitherto been adverse to the Christians, after lulling for a time, suddenly shifted to the opposite quarter, and blew in the face of the enemy. As the day advanced, moreover, the sun, which had shone in the eyes of the confederates, gradually shot its rays into those of the Moslems. Both circumstances were of good omen to the Christians, and the first was regarded as nothing short of a direct interposition of Heaven. Thus ploughing its way along, the Turkish armament, as it came more into view, showed itself in greater strength than had been anticipated by the allies. It consisted of nearly two hundred and fifty royal galleys, most of them of the largest class, besides a number of smaller vessels in the rear, which, like those of the allies, appear scarcely to have come into action. The men on board, of every description, were computed at not less than a hundred and twenty thousand. The galleys spread out, as usual with the Turks, in the form of a regular half-moon, covering a wider extent of surface than the combined fleets, which they somewhat exceeded in number. They presented, indeed, as they drew nearer, a magnificent array, with their gilded and gaudily-painted prows, and their myriads of pennons and streamers, fluttering gaily in the breeze; while the rays of the morning sun glanced on the polished scymitars of Damascus, and on the superb aigrettes of jewels which sparkled in the turbans of the Ottoman chiefs.

In the centre of the extended line, and directly opposite to the station occupied by the captain-general of the League, was the huge galley of Ali Pasha. The right of the armada was commanded by Mahomet Sirocco, viceroy of Egypt, a circumspect as well as courageous leader; the left, by Uluch Ili, dey of Algiers, the redoubtable corsair of the Mediterranean. Ali Pasha had experienced a difficulty like that of Don John, as several of his officers had strongly urged the inexpediency of engaging so formidable an armament as that of the allies. But Ali, like his rival, was young and ambitious. He had been sent by his master to fight the enemy; and no remonstrances, not even those of Mahomet Sirocco, for whom he had great respect, could turn him from his purpose.

He had, moreover, received intelligence that the allied fleet was much inferior in strength to what it proved. In this error he was fortified by the first appearance of the Christians; for the extremity of their left wing, commanded by Barbarigo, stretching behind the Aetolian shore, was hidden from his view. As he drew nearer and saw the whole extent of the Christian lines, it is said his countenance fell. If so, he still did not abate one jot of his resolution. He spoke to those around him with the same confidence as before, of the result of the battle. He urged his rowers to strain every nerve. Ali was a man of more humanity in his nature than often belonged to his nation. His galley-slaves were all, or nearly all, Christian captives; and he addressed them in this brief and pithy manner: 'If your countrymen are to win this day, Allah give you the benefit of it: yet if I win it, you shall certainly have your freedom. If you feel that I do well by you, do then the like by me.'

As the Turkish admiral drew nearer, he made a change in his order of battle, by separating his wings farther from his centre, thus conforming to the dispositions of the allies. Before he had come within cannon-shot, he fired a gun by way of challenge to this enemy. It was answered by another from the galley of John of Austria. A second gun discharged by Ali was as promptly replied to by the Christian commander. The distance between the two fleets was now rapidly diminishing. At this solemn moment a death-like silence reigned throughout the armament of the confederates. Men seemed to hold their breath, as if absorbed in the expectation of some great catastrophe. The day was magnificent. A light breeze, still adverse to the Turks, played on the waters, somewhat fretted by the contrary winds. It was nearly noon; and as the sun, mounting through a cloudless sky, rose to the zenith, he seemed to pause, as if to look down on the beautiful scene, where the multitude of galleys, moving over the water, showed like a holiday spectacle rather than a preparation for mortal combat.

The illusion was soon dispelled by the fierce yells which rose on the air from the Turkish armada. It was the customary war-cry with which the Moslems entered into battle. Very different was the scene on board of the Christian galleys. Don John might be there seen, armed *cap-à-pie*, standing on the prow of the *Real*, anxiously awaiting the conflict. In this conspicuous position, kneeling down, he raised his eyes to Heaven, and humbly prayed that the Almighty would be with his people on that day. His example was followed by the whole fleet. Officers and men, all prostrating themselves on their knees, and turning their eyes to the consecrated banner which floated from the *Real*, put up a petition like that of their commander. They then received absolution from the priests, of whom there were some in every vessel; and each man, as he rose to his feet, gathered new strength, as he felt assured that the Lord of Hosts would fight on his side.

When the foremost vessels of the Turks had come within cannon-shot, they opened their fire on the Christians. The firing soon rang along the whole of the Turkish line, and was kept up without interruption as it advanced. Don John gave orders for trumpet and atabal to sound the signal for action; which was followed by the simultaneous discharge of such of the guns in the combined fleet as could be brought to bear on the enemy. The Spanish commander had caused the *galeazzas*, those mammoth warships, to be towed half a mile ahead of the fleet, where they might intercept the advance of the Turks. As the latter came abreast of them, the huge galleys delivered their broadsides right and left, and their heavy ordnance produced a startling effect. Ali Pasha gave orders for his galleys to open their line and pass on either side, without engaging these monsters of the deep, of which he had had no experience. Even so their heavy guns did considerable damage to several of the nearest vessels, and created some confusion in the pacha's line of battle. They were, however, but unwieldy craft, and having accomplished their object, seem to have taken no further part in the combat.

The action began on the left wing of the allies, which Mahomet Sirocco was desirous of turning. This had been anticipated by Barbarigo, the Venetian admiral, who commanded in that quarter. To prevent it, as we have seen, he lay with his vessels as near the coast as he dared. Sirocco, better acquainted with the soundings, saw there was space enough for him to pass, and darting by with all the speed that oars could give him, he succeeded in doubling on his enemy. Thus placed between two fires, the extreme of the Christian left fought at terrible disadvantage. No less than eight galleys went to the bottom, and several others were captured. The brave Barbarigo, throwing himself into the heat of the fight, without availing himself of his defensive armour, was pierced in the eye by an arrow, and, reluctant to leave the glory of the field to another, was borne to his cabin. The combat still continued with unabated fury on the part of the Venetians. They fought like men who felt that the war was theirs, and who were animated not only by the thirst for glory, but for revenge.

Far on the Christian right a manoeuvre similar to that so successfully executed by Sirocco was attempted by Uluch Ali, the dey of Algiers. Profiting by his superiority in numbers, he endeavoured to turn the right wing of the confederates. It was in this quarter that Andrew Doria commanded. He had foreseen this movement of his enemy, and he succeeded in foiling it. It was a trial of skill between the two most accomplished seamen in the Mediterranean. Doria extended his line so far to the right indeed, to prevent being surrounded, that Don John was obliged to remind him that he left the centre too much exposed. His dispositions were so far unfortunate for himself, that his own line was thus weakened, and afforded some vulnerable points to his assailant. These were soon detected by the eagle eye of Uluch Ali; and, like the king of birds swooping on his prey, he fell on some galleys separated by a considerable interval from their companions, and, sinking more than one, carried off the great *Capitana* of Malta in triumph as his prize.

While the combat opened thus disastrously to the allies both on the right and on the left, in the centre they may be said to have fought with doubtful fortune. Don John had led his division gallantly forward. But the object on which he was intent was an encounter with Ali Pasha, the foe most worthy of his sword. The Turkish commander had the same combat no less at heart. The galleys of both were easily recognized, not only from their position, but from their superior size and richer decoration. The one, moreover, displayed the holy banner of the League; the other, the great Ottoman standard. This, like the ancient standard of the caliphs, was held sacred in its character. It was covered with texts from the Koran, emblazoned in letters of gold, and had the name of Allah inscribed upon it no less than twenty-eight thousand nine hundred times. It was the banner of the sultan, having passed from father to son since the foundation of the imperial dynasty, and was never seen in the field unless the grand seigneur or his lieutenant was there in person.

Both the chiefs urged on their rowers to the top of their speed. Their galleys soon shot ahead of the rest of the line, driven through the boiling surges as by the force of a tornado, and closed with a shock that made every timber crack, and the two vessels to quiver to their very keels. So powerful, indeed, was the impetus they received, that the pacha's galley, which was considerably the larger and loftier of the two, was thrown so far upon his opponent, that the prow reached the fourth bench of rowers. As soon as the vessels were disengaged from each other, and those on board had recovered from the shock, the work of death began. Don John's chief strength consisted in some three hundred Spanish arquebusiers, culled from the flower of his infantry. Ali, on the other hand, was provided with an equal number of janizaries. He was followed by a smaller vessel, in which two hundred more were stationed as a *corps de reserve*. He had, moreover, a hundred archers on board. The bow was still as much in use with the Turks as with the other Moslems.

The pacha opened at once on his enemy a terrible fire of cannon and musketry. It was returned with equal spirit and much more effect; for the Turks were observed to shoot over the heads of their adversaries. The Moslem galley was unprovided with the defences which protected the sides of the Spanish vessels; and the troops, crowded together on the lofty prow, presented an easy mark to their enemy's balls. But though numbers of them fell at every discharge, their places were soon supplied by those in reserve. They were enabled, therefore, to keep up an incessant fire, which wasted the strength of the Spaniards; and as both Christian and Mussulman fought with indomitable spirit, it seemed doubtful to which side victory would incline.

The affair was made more complicated by the entrance of other parties into the conflict. Both Ali and Don John were supported by some of the most gallant captains in their fleets. Next to the Spanish commander, as we have seen, were Colonna and the veteran Veniero, who, at the age of seventy-six, performed feats of arms worthy of a paladin of romance. In this way a little squadron of combatants gathered round the principal leaders, who sometimes found themselves assailed by several enemies at the same time. Still the chiefs did not lose sight of one another; but, beating off their inferior foes as well as they could, each, refusing to loosen his hold, clung with mortal grasp to his antagonist.

Thus the fight raged along the whole extent of the entrance to the gulf of Lepanto. The volumes of vapour rolling heavily over the waters effectually shut out from sight whatever was passing at any considerable distance, unless when a fresher breeze dispelled the smoke for a moment, or the flashes of the heavy guns threw a transient gleam on the dark canopy of battle. If the eye of the spectator could have penetrated the cloud of smoke that enveloped the combatants, and have embraced the whole scene at a glance, he would have perceived them broken up into small detachments, separately engaged one with another, independently of the rest, and indeed ignorant of all that was doing in other quarters. The contest exhibited few of those large combinations and skilful manoeuvres to be expected in a great naval encounter. It was rather an assemblage of petty actions, resembling those on land. The galleys, grappling together, presented a level arena, on which soldier and galley-slave fought hand to hand, and the fate of the engagement was generally decided by boarding. As in most hand-to-hand contests, there was an enormous waste of life. The decks were loaded with corpses, Christian and Moslem lying promiscuously together in the embrace of death. Instances are recorded where every man on board was slain or wounded. It was a ghastly spectacle, where blood flowed in rivulets down the sides of the vessels, staining the waters of the gulf for miles around.

It seemed as if a hurricane had swept over the sea, and covered it with the wreck of the noble armaments which a moment before were so proudly riding on its bosom. Little had they now to remind one of their late magnificent array, with their hulls battered, their masts and spars gone or splintered by the shot, their canvas cut into shreds and floating wildly on the breeze, while thousands of wounded and drowning men were clinging to the floating fragments, and calling piteously for help. Such was the wild uproar which succeeded the Sabbath-like stillness that two hours before had reigned over these beautiful solitudes.

The left wing of the confederates, commanded by Barbarigo, had been sorely pressed by the Turks, as we have seen, at the beginning of the fight. Barbarigo himself had been mortally wounded. His line had been turned. Several of his galleys had been sunk. But the Venetians gathered courage from despair. By incredible efforts they succeeded in beating off their enemies. They became the assailants in their turn. Sword in hand, they carried one vessel after another. The Capuchin was seen in the thickest of the fight, waving aloft his crucifix, and leading the boarders to the assault. The Christian galley-slaves, in some instances, broke their fetters, and joined their countrymen against their masters. Fortunately, the vessel of Mahomet Sirocco, the Moslem admiral, was sunk; and though extricated from the water himself, it was only to perish by the sword of his conqueror, Giovanni Contarini. The Venetian could find in his heart no mercy for the Turk.

The fall of their commander gave the final blow to his followers. Without further attempt to prolong the fight they fled before the avenging swords of the Venetians. Those nearest the land endeavoured to escape by running their vessels ashore, where they abandoned them as prizes to the Christians. Yet many of the fugitives, before gaining the land, perished miserably in the waves. Barbarigo, the Venetian admiral, who was still lingering in agony, heard the tidings of the enemy's defeat, and, uttering a few words expressive of his gratitude to Heaven, which had permitted him to see this hour, he breathed his last.

During this time the combat had been going forward in the centre between the two commanders-in-chief, Don John and Ali Pasha, whose galleys blazed with an incessant fire of artillery and musketry, that enveloped them like 'a martyr's robe of flames.' The parties fought with equal spirit, though not with equal fortune. Twice the Spaniards had boarded their enemy, and both times they had been repulsed with loss. Still their superiority in the use of fire-arms would have given them a decided advantage over their opponents, if the loss they had inflicted had not been speedily repaired by fresh reinforcements. More than once the contest between the two chieftains was interrupted by the arrival of others to take part in the fray. They soon, however, returned to each other, as if unwilling to waste their strength on a meaner enemy. Through the whole engagement both commanders exposed themselves to danger as freely as any common soldier. In such a contest even Philip must have admitted that it would be difficult for his brother to find, with honour, a place of safety. Don John received a wound in the foot. It was a slight one, however, and he would not allow it to be dressed till the action was over.

Again his men were mustered, and a third time the trumpets sounded to the attack. It was more successful than the preceding. The Spaniards threw themselves boldly into the Turkish galley. They were met with the same spirit as before by the janizaries. Ali Pasha led them on. Unfortunately, at this moment, he was struck in the head by a musket-ball, and stretched senseless in the gangway. His men fought worthily of their ancient renown. But they missed the accustomed voice of their commander. After a short but ineffectual struggle against the fiery impetuosity of the Spaniards, they were overpowered and threw down their arms. The decks were loaded with the bodies of the dead and the dying. Beneath these was discovered the Turkish commander-in-chief, severely wounded, but perhaps not mortally. He was drawn forth by some Castilian soldiers, who, recognizing his person, would at once have dispatched him. But the disabled chief, having rallied from the first effects of his wound, had sufficient presence of mind to divert them from their purpose, by pointing out the place below where he had deposited his money and jewels; and they hastened to profit by the disclosure, before the treasure should fall into the hands of their comrades.

Ali was not so successful with another soldier, who came up soon after, brandishing his sword, and preparing to plunge it into the body of the prostrate commander. It was in vain that the latter endeavoured to turn the ruffian from his purpose. He was a convict, one of those galley-slaves whom Don John had caused to be unchained from the oar and furnished with arms. He could not believe that any treasure would be worth so much as the head of the pacha. Without further hesitation, he dealt him a blow which severed it from his shoulders. Then, returning to his galley, he laid the bloody trophy before Don John. But he had miscalculated on his recompense. His commander gazed on it with a look of pity mingled with horror. He may have thought of the generous conduct of Ali to his Christian captives, and have felt that he deserved a better fate. He coldly inquired 'of what use such a present could be to him'; and then ordered it to be thrown into the sea. Far from the order being obeyed, it is said the head was stuck on a pike, and raised aloft on board of the captured galley. At the same time the banner of the Crescent was pulled down; while that of the Cross, run up in its place, proclaimed the downfall of the pacha.

The sight of the sacred ensign was welcomed by the Christians with a shout of 'Victory!' which rose high above the din of battle. The tidings of the death of Ali soon passed from mouth to mouth, giving fresh heart to the confederates, but falling like a knell on the ears of the Moslems. Their confidence was gone. Their fire slackened. Their efforts grew weaker and weaker. They were too far from shore to seek an asylum there, like their comrades on the right. They had no resource but to prolong the combat or to surrender. Most preferred the latter. Many vessels were carried by boarding, others were sunk by the victorious Christians. Ere four hours had elapsed, the centre, like the right wing, of the Moslems might be said to be annihilated.

Still the fight was lingering on the right of the confederates, where, it will be remembered, Uluch Ali, the Algerine chief, had profited by Doria's error in extending his line so far as greatly to weaken it. Uluch Ali, attacking it on its most vulnerable quarter, had succeeded, as we have seen, in capturing and destroying several vessels, and would have inflicted still heavier losses on his enemy had it not been for the seasonable succour received from the Marquis of Santa Cruz. This brave officer, who commanded the reserve, had already been of much service to Don John when the *Real* was assailed by several Turkish galleys at once during his combat with Ali Pasha; for at this juncture the marquis of Santa Cruz arriving, and beating off the assailants, one of whom he afterwards captured, enabled the commander-in-chief to resume his engagement with the pacha.

No sooner did Santa Cruz learn the critical situation of Doria, than, supported by Cardona, 'general' of the Sicilian squadron, he pushed forward to his relief. Dashing into the midst of the *mêlée*, the two commanders fell like a thunderbolt on the Algerine galleys. Few attempted to withstand the shock. But in their haste to avoid it, they were encountered by Doria and his Genoese galleys. Thus beset on all sides, Uluch Ali was compelled to abandon his prizes and provide for his own safety by flight. He cut adrift the Maltese *Capitana*, which he had lashed to his stern, and on which three hundred corpses attested the desperate character of her defence. As tidings reached him of the discomfiture of the centre, and of the death of Ali Pasha, he felt that nothing remained but to make the best of his way from the fatal scene of action, and save as many of his own ships as he could. And there were no ships in the Turkish fleet superior to his, or manned by men under more perfect discipline. For they were the famous corsairs of the Mediterranean, who had been rocked from infancy on its waters.

Throwing out his signals for retreat, the Algerine was soon to be seen, at the head of his squadron, standing towards the north, under as much canvas as remained to him after the battle, and urged forward through the deep by the whole strength of his oarsmen. Doria and Santa Cruz followed quickly in his wake. But he was borne on the wings of the wind, and soon distanced his pursuers. Don John, having disposed of his own assailants, was coming to the support of Doria, and now joined in the pursuit of the viceroy. A rocky headland, stretching far into the sea, lay in the path of the fugitive; and his enemies hoped to intercept him there. Some few of his vessels were stranded on the rocks. But the rest, near forty in number, standing more boldly out to sea, safely doubled the promontory. Then, quickening their flight, they gradually faded from the horizon, their white sails, the last thing visible, showing in the distance like a flock of Arctic seafowl on their way to their native homes. The confederates explained the inferior sailing of their own galleys on this occasion by the circumstances of their rowers, who had been allowed to bear arms in the fight, being crippled by their wounds.

The battle had lasted more than four hours. The sky, which had been almost without a cloud through the day, began now to be overcast, and showed signs of a coming storm. Before seeking a place of shelter for himself and his prizes, Don John reconnoitred the scene of action. He met with several vessels too much damaged for further service. These, mostly belonging to the enemy, after saving what was of any value on board, he ordered to be burnt. He selected the neighbouring port of Petala, as affording the most secure and accessible harbour for the night. Before he had arrived there, the tempest began to mutter and darkness was on the water. Yet the darkness rendered only more visible the blazing wrecks, which, sending up streams of fire mingled with showers of sparks, looked like volcanoes on the deep.

Sir Walter Raleigh

The Last Fight of the *Revenge*

A Report of the Truth of the Fight about the Isles of The Azores this last Summer [1591] *betwixt the* Revenge, *one of Her Majesty's ships, and an Armada of the King of Spain*

BECAUSE the rumours are diversely spread, as well in England as in the Low Countries and elsewhere, of this late encounter between Her Majesty's ships and the Armada of Spain; and that the Spaniards, according to their usual manner, fill the world with their vainglorious vaunts, making great appearance of victories: when on the contrary, themselves are most commonly and shamefully beaten and dishonoured; thereby hoping to possess the ignorant multitude by anticipating and forerunning false reports. It is agreeable with all good reason, for manifestation of the truth to overcome falsehood and untruth, that the beginning, continuance and success of this late honourable encounter of Sir Richard Grenville, and other Her Majesty's Captains, with the Armada of Spain, should be truly set down and published without partiality or false imaginations.

The Lord Thomas Howard, with six of Her Majesty's ships, six victuallers of London, the barque *Ralegh*, and two or three pinnaces riding at anchor near unto Flores, one of the Westerly Islands of the Azores, the last of August in the afternoon, had intelligence by one Captain Middleton, of the approach of the Spanish Armada. Which Middleton being in a very good sailer, had kept them company three days before, of good purpose, both to discover their forces the more, as also to give advice to my Lord Thomas of their approach. He had no sooner delivered the news but the Fleet was in sight. Many of our ship's company were on shore in the Island; some providing ballast for their ships; others filling of water and refreshing themselves from the land with such things as they could either for money, or by force recover. By reason whereof our ships being all disordered and rummaging everything out of order, very light for want of ballast. And that which was most to our disadvantage, the one half part of the men of every ship sick, and utterly unserviceable. For in the *Revenge* there were ninety diseased: in the *Bonaventure*, not so many in health as could handle her mainsail. For had not twenty men been taken out of a barque of Sir George Carys, his being commanded to be sunk, and those appointed to her, she had hardly ever recovered England. The rest for the most part were in little better state.

The names of Her Majesty's ships were these as followeth: the *Defiaunce*, which was Admiral, the *Revenge* Vice-Admiral, the *Bonaventure* commanded by Captain Cross, the *Lion* by George Fenner, the *Foresight* by Thomas Vavisour, and the *Crane* by Duffield. The *Foresight* and the *Crane* being but small ships; only the other were of the middle size. The rest, besides the barque *Ralegh*, commanded by Captain Thin, were victuallers, and of small force or none.

The Spanish fleet, having shrouded their approach by reason of the Island, were now so soon at hand, as our ships had scarce time to weigh their anchors, but some of them were driven to let slip their cables and set sail. Sir Richard Grenville was the last weighed, to recover the men that were upon the Island, which otherwise had been lost. The Lord Thomas with the rest very hardly recovered the wind, which Sir Richard Grenville not being able to do, was persuaded by the master and others to cut his mainsail, and cast about, and to trust to the sailing of his ship: for the squadron of Seville were on his weather bow. But Sir Richard utterly refused to turn from the enemy, alleging that he would rather choose to die, then to dishonour himself, his country, and ship, persuading his company that he would pass through the two Squadrons, in despite of them: and enforce those of Seville to give him way. Which he performed upon divers of the foremost, who, as the mariners term it, sprang their luff, and fell under the lee of the *Revenge*. But the other course had been the better, and might right well have been answered in so great an impossibility of prevailing. Notwithstanding out of the greatness of his mind, he could not be persuaded.

In the meanwhile, as he attended those which were nearest him, the great *San Felipe* being in the wind of him, and coming towards him, becalmed his sails in such sort, as the ship could neither way nor feel the helm: so huge and high charged was the Spanish ship, being of a thousand and five hundred tons, who after laid the *Revenge* aboard [alongside]. When he was thus bereft of his sails, the ships that were under his lee luffing up, also laid him aboard: of which the next was the Admiral of the Biscaines, a very mighty and puissant ship commanded by Britan Dona. The said *Felipe* carried three tier of ordinance on a side, and eleven pieces in every tier. She shot eight forth right out of her chase, besides those of her stern ports.

After the *Revenge* was entangled with the *Felipe*, four other boarded her; two on her larboard, and two on her starboard. The fight thus beginning at three of the clock in the afternoon, continued very terrible all that evening. But the great *San Felipe* having received the lower tier of the *Revenge*, discharged with crossbar shot, shifted herself with all diligence from her sides, utterly misliking her first entertainment. Some say that the ship foundered, but we cannot report it for truth, unless we were assured. The Spanish ships were filled with companies of soldiers, in some two hundred besides the mariners; in some five, in others eight hundred. In ours there were none at all, beside the mariners, but the servants of the commanders and some few voluntary gentlemen only. After many interchanged volleys of great ordinance and small shot, the Spaniards deliberated to enter the *Revenge*, and made divers attempts, hoping to force her by the multitudes of their armed soldiers and musketeers, but were still repulsed again and again, and at all times beaten back, into their own ships, or into the seas.

In the beginning of the fight, the *George Noble* of London, having received some shot through her by the Armadas, fell under the lee of the *Revenge*, and asked Sir Richard what he would command him, being but one of the victuallers and of small force. Sir Richard bid him save himself, and leave him to his fortune. After the fight had thus, without intermission, continued while the day lasted and some hours of the night, many of our men were slain and hurt, and one of the great galleons of the Armada, and the Admiral of the Hulks both sunk, and in many other of the Spanish ships great slaughter was made. Some write that Sir Richard was very dangerously hurt almost in the beginning of the fight, and lay speechless for a time ere he recovered. But two of the *Revenge*'s own company, brought home in a ship of lime from the Islands, examined by some of the Lords, and others: affirmed that he was never so wounded as that he forsook the upper deck, till an hour before midnight; and then being shot into the body with a Musket as he was dressing, was again shot into the head, and withal his surgeon wounded to death. This agreeth also with an examination taken by Sir Francis Godolphin, of four other mariners of the same ship being returned, which examination the said Sir Francis sent unto master William Killigrue of Her Majesty's privy Chamber.

But to return to the fight, the Spanish ships which attempted to board the *Revenge*, as they were wounded and beaten off, so always others came in their places, she having never less than two mighty galleons by her sides, and aboard her. So that ere the morning from three of the clock the day before, there had fifteen several Armadas assailed her; and all so ill approved their entertainment, as they were by the break of day, far more willing to hearken to a composition, then hastily to make any more assaults or entries. But as the day increased, so our men decreased: and as the light grew more and more, by so much more grew our discomforts. For none appeared in sight but enemies, saving one small ship called the *Pilgrim*, commanded by Jacob Whiddon, who hovered all night to see the success: but in the morning bearing with the *Revenge*, was huntcd like a hare amongst many ravenous hounds but escaped.

All the powder of the *Revenge* to the last barrel was now spent, all her pikes broken, forty of her best men slain, and the most part of the rest hurt. In the beginning of the fight she had but one hundred free from sickness, and fourscore and ten sick, laid in hold upon the ballast. A small troop to man such a ship, and a weak garrison to resist so mighty an army. By those hundred all was sustained, the volleys, boardings, and enterings of fifteen ships of war, besides those which beat her at large. On the contrary, the Spanish were always supplied with soldiers brought from every squadron: all manner of arms and powder at will. Unto ours there remained no comfort at all, no hope, no supply either of ships, men, or weapons. The masts all beaten over board, all her tackle cut asunder, her upper work altogether razed, and in effect evened she was with the water, but the very foundations or bottom of a ship, nothing being left over head either for flight or defence.

Sir Richard finding himself in this distress, and unable any longer to make resistance, having endured in this fifteen hours fight the assault of fifteen several Armadas, all by turns aboard [alongside] him, and by estimation eight hundred shot of great artillery, besides many assaults and entries. And that himself and the ship must needs be possessed by the enemy, who were now all cast in a ring round about him. The *Revenge* not able to move one way or other, but as she was moved with the waves and billow of the sea. [Sir Richard] commanded the master gunner, whom he knew to be a most resolute man, to split and sink the ship, that thereby nothing might remain of glory or victory to the Spaniards, seeing in so many hours fight, and with so great a navy they were not able to take her, having had fifteen hours time, fifteen thousand men, and fifty and three sail of men of war to perform it withal. And persuaded the company, or as many as he could induce, to yield themselves unto God, and to the mercy of none else; but as they had like valiant resolute men, repulsed so many enemies, they should not now shorten the honour of their nation by prolonging their own lives for a few hours, or a few days.

The master gunner readily condescended and divers others; but the Captain and the Master were of an other opinion, and besought Sir Richard to have care of them alleging that the Spaniard would be as ready to entertain a composition [compromise] as they were willing to offer the same: and that there being divers sufficient and valiant men yet living, and whose wounds were not mortal, they might do their country and prince acceptable service hereafter. And (that where Sir Richard had alleged that the Spaniards should never glory to have taken one ship of Her Majesty's, seeing that they had so long and so notably defended themselves) they answered, that the ship had six foot [of] water in hold, three shot under water which were so weakly stopped, as with the first working of the sea, she must needs sink, and was besides so crushed and bruised, as she could never be removed out of the place.

And as the matter was thus in dispute, and Sir Richard refusing to hearken to any of those reasons: the master of the *Revenge* (while the Captain won unto him the greater part) was conveyed aboard the General Don Alfonso Bassan. Who finding none over-hasty to enter the *Revenge* again, doubting least Sir Richard would have blown them up and himself, and perceiving by the report of the master of the *Revenge* his dangerous disposition: yielded that all their lives should be saved, the company sent for England, and the better sort to pay such reasonable ransom as their estate would bear, and in the mean season to be free from galley or imprisonment. To this he so much the rather condescended as well as I have said for fear of further loss and mischief to themselves, as also for the desire he had to recover Sir Richard Grenville; whom for his notable valour he seemed greatly to honour and admire.

When this answer was returned, and that safety of life was promised, the common sort being now at the end of their peril, the most drew back from Sir Richard and the master gunner, being no hard matter to dissuade men from death to life. The master gunner finding himself and Sir Richard thus prevented and mastered by the greater number, would have slain himself with a sword, had he not been by force withheld and locked into his cabin. Then the general sent many boats aboard the *Revenge*, and divers of our men fearing Sir Richard's disposition, stole away aboard the general and other ships. Sir Richard thus overmatched, was sent unto by Alfonso Bassan to remove out of the *Revenge*, the ship being marvellous unsavoury, filled with blood and bodies of dead and wounded men like a slaughterhouse. Sir Richard answered that he might do with his body what he list, for he esteemed it not, and as he was carried out of the ship he swooned, and reviving again desired the company to pray for him. The general used Sir Richard with all humanity, and left nothing unattempted that tended to his recovery, highly commending his valour and worthiness, and greatly bewailed the danger wherein he was, being unto them a rare spectacle, and a resolution seldom approved, to see one ship turn toward so many enemies, to endure the charge and boarding of so many huge Armadas, and to resist and repel the assaults and entries of so many soldiers. All which and more, is confirmed by a Spanish captain of the same Armada, and a present actor in the fight, who being severed from the rest in a storm, was by the *Lyon* of London a small ship taken, and is now prisoner in London.

The general commander of the Armada was Don Alfonso Bassan, brother to the Marquess of Santa Cruz. The Admiral of the Biscaine squadron, was Britan Dona. Of the squadron of Seville, Marques of Arumburch. The hulks and flyboats were commanded by Luis Cutino. There were slain and drowned in this fight well near two thousand of the enemy, and two especial commanders Don Luis de San Juan and Don Jorge de Prunaria de Malaga, as the Spanish Captain confesseth, besides divers others of special account, whereof as yet report is not made.

The Admiral of the hulks and the *Asunción* of Seville, were both sunk by the side of the *Revenge*; one other recovered the road of San Miguel, and sunk also there; a fourth ran herself with the shore to save her men.

Sir Richard died as it is said, the second or third day aboard the General, and was by them greatly bewailed. What became of his body, whether it were buried in the sea or on the land we know not. The comfort that remaineth to his friends is, that he hath ended his life honourably in respect of the reputation won to his nation and country, and of the same to his posterity, and that being dead, he hath not outlived his own honour.

A few days after the fight was ended, and the English prisoners dispersed into the Spanish and Indies ships, there arose so great a storm from the West and Northwest, that all the fleet was dispersed, as well the Indian fleet which were then come unto them as the rest of the Armada that attended their arrival, of which fourteen sail together with the *Revenge*, and her 200 Spaniards, were cast away upon the Isle of San Miguel. So it pleased them to honour the burial of that renowned ship the *Revenge*, not suffering her to perish alone for the great honour she achieved in her lifetime.

Robert Southey

Trafalgar

(From *The Life of Nelson*)

THE station which Nelson had chosen was some fifty or sixty miles to the west of Cadiz, near Cape St Mary. At this distance he hoped to decoy the enemy out, while he guarded against the danger of being caught with a westerly wind near Cadiz, and driven within the Straits. The blockade of the port was rigorously enforced, in hopes that the combined fleets might be forced to sea by want. The Danish vessels therefore, which were carrying provisions from the French ports in the bay, under the name of Danish property, to all the little ports from Ayamonte to Algeziras, from whence they were conveyed in coasting boats to Cadiz, were seized. Without this proper exertion of power the blockade would have been rendered nugatory by the advantage thus taken of the neutral flag. The supplies from France were thus effectually cut off. There was now every indication that the enemy would speedily venture out; officers and men were in the highest spirits at the prospect of giving them a decisive blow – such, indeed, as would put an end to all further contests upon the seas.

On the 9th Nelson sent Collingwood what he called in his diary the 'Nelson touch'. 'I send you,' said he, 'my plan of attack, as far as a man dare venture to guess at the very uncertain position the enemy may be found in; but it is to place you perfectly at ease respecting my intentions, and to give full scope to your judgment for carrying them into effect. We can, my dear Coll, have no little jealousies. We have only one great object in view, that of annihilating our enemies, and getting a glorious peace for our country. No man has more confidence in another than I have in you, and no man will render your services more justice than your very old friend, Nelson and Bronte.'

The order of sailing was to be the order of battle – the fleet in two lines, with an advanced squadron of eight of the fastest sailing two-deckers. The second in command, having the entire direction of his line, was to break through the enemy, about the twelfth ship from their rear; he would lead through the centre, and the advanced squadron was to cut off three or four ahead of the centre. This plan was to be adapted to the strength of the enemy, so that they should always be one-fourth superior to those whom they cut off. Nelson said that 'his admirals and captains, knowing his precise object to be that of a close and decisive action, would supply any deficiency of signals and act accordingly. In case signals cannot be seen or clearly understood, no captain can do wrong if he places his ship alongside that of an enemy.'

About half-past nine in the morning of the 19th the *Mars*, being the nearest to the fleet of the ships which formed the line of communication with the frigates inshore, repeated the signal that the enemy were coming out of port. The wind was at this time very light, with partial breezes, mostly from the S. S. W. Nelson ordered the signal to be made for a chase in the south-east quarter. About two the repeating ships announced that the enemy were at sea. All night the British fleet continued under all sail, steering to the south-east. At daybreak they were in the entrance of the Straits, but the enemy were not in sight. About seven, one of the frigates, made signal that the enemy were bearing north. Upon this the *Victory* hove to, and shortly afterwards Nelson made sail again to the northward. In the afternoon the wind blew fresh from the south-west, and the English began to fear that the foe might be forced to return to port.

A little before sunset, however, Blackwood, in the *Euryalus*, telegraphed that they appeared determined to go to the westward. 'And that,' said the Admiral in his diary, 'they shall not do, if it is the power of Nelson and Bronte to prevent them.' Nelson had signified to Blackwood that he depended upon him to keep sight of the enemy. They were observed so well that all their motions were made known to him, and as they wore twice, he inferred that they were aiming to keep the port of Cadiz open, and would retreat there as soon as they saw the British fleet; for this reason he was very careful not to approach near enough to be seen by them during the night. At daybreak the combined fleets were distinctly seen from the *Victory*'s deck, formed in a close line of battle ahead, on the starboard tack, about twelve miles to leeward, and standing to the south. Our fleet consisted of twenty-seven sail of the line and four frigates; theirs of thirty-three and seven large frigates. Their superiority was greater in size and weight of metal than numbers. They had four thousand troops on board, and the best riflemen that could be procured, many of them Tyrolese, were dispersed through the ships.

Soon after daylight Nelson came upon deck. The 21st of October was a festival in his family, because on that day his uncle, Captain Suckling, in the *Dreadnought*, with two other line-of-battle ships, had beaten off a French squadron of four sail of the line and three frigates.

Nelson, with that sort of superstition from which few persons are entirely exempt, had more than once expressed his persuasion that this was to be the day of his battle also, and he was well pleased at seeing his prediction about to be verified. The wind was now from the west – light breezes, with a long heavy swell. Signal was made to bear down upon the enemy in two lines, and the fleet set all sail. Collingwood, in the *Royal Sovereign*, led the lee line of thirteen ships; the *Victory* led the weather line of fourteen. Having seen that all was as it should be, Nelson retired to his cabin, and wrote the following prayer –

'May the great God whom I worship, grant to my country, and for the benefit of Europe in general, a great and glorious victory, and may no misconduct in any one tarnish it, and may humanity after victory be the predominant feature in the British fleet! For myself individually, I commit my life to Him that made me, and may His blessing alight on my endeavours for serving my country faithfully! To Him I resign myself and the just cause which is entrusted to me to defend. Amen, Amen, Amen.'

Blackwood went on board the *Victory* about six. He found him in good spirits, but very calm; not in that exhilaration which he felt upon entering into battle at Aboukir and Copenhagen; he knew that his own life would be particularly aimed at, and seems to have looked for death with almost as sure an expectation as for victory. His whole attention was fixed upon the enemy. They tacked to the northward, and formed their line on the larboard tack; thus bringing the shoals of Trafalgar and St Pedro under the lee of the British, and keeping the port of Cadiz open for themselves. This was judiciously done; and Nelson, aware of all the advantages which he gave them, made signal to prepare to anchor.

Villeneuve was a skilful seaman, worthy of serving a better master and a better cause. His plan of defence was as well conceived and as original as the plan of attack. He formed the fleet in a double line, every alternate ship being about a cable's length to windward of her second ahead and astern. Nelson, certain of a triumphant issue to the day, asked Blackwood what he should consider as a victory. That officer answered that, considering the handsome way in which battle was offered by the enemy, their apparent determination for a fair trial of strength, and the situation of the land, he thought it would be a glorious result if fourteen were captured. He replied: 'I shall not be satisfied with less than twenty.' Soon afterwards he asked him if he did not think there was a signal wanting. Captain Blackwood made answer that he thought the whole fleet seemed very clearly to understand what they were about. These words were scarcely spoken before that signal was made which will be remembered as long as the language or even the memory of England shall endure – 'ENGLAND EXPECTS EVERY MAN WILL DO HIS DUTY!' It was received throughout the fleet with a shout of answering acclamation, made sublime by the spirit which it breathed and the feeling which it expressed. 'Now,' said Lord Nelson, 'I can do no more. We must trust to the great Disposer of all events and the justice of our cause. I thank God for this great opportunity of doing my duty.'

He wore that day, as usual, his admiral's frock-coat, bearing on the left breast four stars of the different orders with which he was invested. Ornaments which rendered him so conspicuous a mark for the enemy were beheld with ominous apprehension by his officers. It was known that there were riflemen on board the French ships, and it could not be doubted but that his life would be particularly aimed at. They communicated their fears to each other, and the surgeon, Mr Beatty, spoke to the chaplain, Dr Scott, and to Mr Scott, the public secretary, desiring that some person would entreat him to change his dress or cover the stars; but they knew that such a request would highly displease him. 'In honour I gained them,' he had said when such a thing had been hinted to him formerly, 'and in honour I will die with them.' Mr Beatty, however, would not have been deterred by any fear of exciting his displeasure from speaking to him himself upon a subject in which the weal of England, as well as the life of Nelson, was concerned; but he was ordered from the deck before he could find an opportunity. This was a point upon which Nelson's officers knew that it was hopeless to remonstrate or reason with him; but both Blackwood and his own captain, Hardy, represented to him how advantageous to the fleet it would be for him to keep out of action as long as possible, and he consented at last to let the *Leviathan* and the *Temeraire*, which were sailing abreast of the *Victory*, be ordered to pass ahead.

Yet even here the last infirmity of this noble mind was indulged, for these ships could not pass ahead if the *Victory* continued to carry all her sail; and so far was Nelson from shortening sail, that it was evident he took pleasure in pressing on, and rendering it impossible for them to obey his own orders. A long swell was setting into the Bay of Cadiz. Our ships, crowding all sail, moved majestically before it, with light winds from the south-west. The sun shone on the sails of the enemy, but their well-formed line, with their numerous three-deckers, made an appearance which any other assailants would have thought formidable, but the British sailors only admired the beauty and the splendour of the spectacle, and in full confidence of winning what they saw, remarked to each other what a fine sight yonder ships would make at Spithead!

The French admiral, from the *Bucentaure*, beheld the new manner in which his enemy was advancing – Nelson and Collingwood, each leading his line; and pointing them out to his officers, he is said to have exclaimed that such conduct could not fail to be successful. Yet Villeneuve had made his own dispositions with the utmost skill, and the fleets under his command waited for the attack with perfect coolness. Ten minutes before twelve they opened their fire. Eight or nine of the ships immediately ahead of the *Victory*, and across her bows, fired single guns at her to ascertain whether she was yet within their range. As soon as Nelson perceived that their shot passed over him, he desired Blackwood and Captain Prowse, of the *Sirius*, to repair to the respective frigates, and on their way to tell all the captains of the line-of-battle ships that he depended on their exertions, and that, if by the prescribed mode of attack they found it impracticable to get into action immediately, they might adopt whatever they thought best, provided it led them quickly and closely alongside an enemy. As they were standing on the poop, Blackwood took him by the hand, saying he hoped soon to return and find him in possession of twenty prizes. He replied, 'God bless you, Blackwood; I shall never see you again.'

Nelson's column was steered about two points more to the north than Collingwood's, in order to cut off the enemy's escape into Cadiz. The lee line, therefore, was first engaged. 'See,' cried Nelson, pointing to the *Royal Sovereign*, as she steered right for the centre of the enemy's line, cut through it astern of the *Santa Anna*, three-decker, and engaged her at the muzzle of her guns on the starboard side; 'see how that noble fellow Collingwood carries his ship into action!' Collingwood, delighted at being first in the heat of the fire, and knowing the feelings of his commander and old friend, turned to his captain and exclaimed: 'Rotherham, what would Nelson give to be here!' Both these brave officers, perhaps, at this moment thought of Nelson with gratitude for a circumstance which had occurred on the preceding day. Admiral Collingwood, with some of the captains, having gone on board the *Victory* to receive instructions, Nelson inquired of him where his captain was, and was told in reply that they were not upon good terms with each other. 'Terms!' said Nelson; 'good terms with each other!' Immediately he sent a boat for Captain Rotherham, led him, so soon as he arrived to Collingwood, and saying, 'Look, yonder are the enemy!' bade them shake hands like Englishmen.

The enemy continued to fire a gun at a time at the *Victory* till they saw that a shot had passed through her main-topgallant sail; then they opened their broadsides, aiming chiefly at her rigging, in the hope of disabling her before she could close with them. Nelson as usual had hoisted several flags, lest one should be shot away. The enemy showed no colours till late in the action, when they began to feel the necessity of having them to strike. For this reason the *Santissima Trinidad*,

Nelson's old acquaintance, as he used to call her, was distinguishable only by her four decks, and to the bow of this opponent he ordered the *Victory* to be steered. Meantime an incessant raking fire was kept up upon the *Victory*. The Admiral's secretary was one of the first who fell; he was killed by a cannon shot while conversing with Hardy. Captain Adair, of the marines, with the help of a sailor, endeavoured to remove the body from Nelson's sight, who had great regard for Mr Scott, but he anxiously asked, 'Is that poor Scott that's gone?' and being informed that it was indeed so, exclaimed, 'Poor fellow!'

Presently a double-headed shot struck a party of marines who were drawn up on the poop, and killed eight of them, upon which Nelson immediately desired Captain Adair to disperse his men round the ship, that they might not suffer so much from being together. A few minutes afterwards a shot struck the fore-brace bits on the quarter-deck, and passed between Nelson and Hardy, a splinter from the bit tearing off Hardy's buckle and bruising his foot. Both stopped, and looked anxiously at each other: each supposed the other to be wounded. Nelson then smiled, and said: 'This is too warm work, Hardy, to last long.'

The *Victory* had not yet returned a single gun; fifty of her men had by this time been killed or wounded, and her maintopmast, with all her studding sails and their booms, shot away. Nelson declared that in all his battles he had seen nothing which surpassed the cool courage of his crew on this occasion. At four minutes after twelve she opened her fire from both sides of her deck. It was not possible to break the enemy's lines without running on board one of their ships; Hardy informed him of this, and asked him which he would prefer. Nelson replied: 'Take your choice, Hardy; it does not signify much.' The master was ordered to put the helm to port, and the *Victory* ran on board the *Redoubtable* just as her tiller-ropes were shot away. The French ship received her with a broadside, then instantly let down her lower-deck ports for fear of being boarded through them, and never afterwards fired a great gun during the action. Her tops, like those of all the enemy's ships, were filled with riflemen. Nelson never placed musketry in his tops; he had a strong dislike to the practice, not merely because it endangers setting fire to the sails, but also because it is a murderous sort of warfare, by which individuals may suffer and a commander now and then be picked off, but which never can decide the fate of a general engagement.

Captain Harvey, in the *Temeraire*, fell on board the *Redoubtable* on the side; another enemy was in like manner on board the *Temeraire*; so that these four ships formed as compact a tier as if they had been moored together, their heads all lying the same way. The lieutenants of the *Victory* seeing this, depressed their guns of the middle and lower decks, and fired with a diminished charge, lest the shot should pass through and injure the *Temeraire*; and because there was danger that the *Redoubtable* might take fire from the lower deck guns, the muzzles of which touched her side when they were run out, the fireman of each gun stood ready with a bucket of water, which, as soon as the gun was discharged, he dashed into the hole made by the shot. An incessant fire was kept up from the *Victory* from both sides, her larboard guns playing upon the *Bucentaure* and the huge *Santissima Trinidad*.

It had been part of Nelson's prayer that the British fleet should be distinguished by humanity in the victory he expected. Setting an example himself, he twice gave orders to cease firing upon the *Redoubtable*, supposing that she had struck, because her great guns were silent; for, as she carried no flag, there was no means of instantly ascertaining the fact. From this ship, which he had thus twice spared, he received his death. A ball fired from her mizzen-top, which in the then situation of the two vessels was not more than fifteen yards from that part of the deck where he was standing, struck the epaulette on his left shoulder, about a quarter after one, just in the heat of action. He fell upon his face, on the spot which was covered with his poor secretary's blood. Hardy, who was a few steps from him, turning round, saw three men raising him up. 'They have done for me at last, Hardy!' said he. 'I hope not!' cried Hardy. 'Yes,' he replied, 'my backbone is shot through!'

Yet even now, not for a moment losing his presence of mind, he observed as they were carrying him down the ladder, that the tiller-ropes, which had been shot away, were not yet replaced, and ordered that new ones should be rove immediately. Then, that he might not be seen by the crew, he took out his handkerchief and covered his face and his stars. Had he but concealed these badges of honour from the enemy, England perhaps would not have cause to receive with sorrow the news of the battle of Trafalgar. The cockpit was crowded with wounded and dying men, over whose bodies he was with some difficulty conveyed, and laid upon a pallet in the midshipman's berth. It was soon perceived, upon examination, that the wound was mortal. This, however, was concealed from all except Captain Hardy, the chaplain, and the medical attendants. He himself being certain, from the sensation in his back and the gush of blood he felt momently within his breast, that no human care could avail him, insisted that the surgeon should leave him, and attend to those to whom he might be useful, 'for,' said he, 'you can do nothing for me.'

All that could be done was to fan him with paper, and frequently give him lemonade to alleviate his intense thirst. He was in great pain, and expressed much anxiety for the event of the action, which now began to declare itself. As often as a ship struck, the crew of the

Victory hurrahed, and at every hurrah a visible expression of joy gleamed in the eyes and marked the countenance of the dying hero. But he became impatient to see Captain Hardy, and as that officer, though often sent for, could not leave the deck, Nelson feared that some fatal cause prevented him, and repeatedly cried, 'Will no one bring Hardy to me? He must be killed! He is surely dead!'

An hour and ten minutes elapsed from the time when Nelson received his wound before Hardy could come to him. They shook hands in silence; Hardy in vain struggling to express the feelings of the most painful and yet sublimest moment. 'Well, Hardy,' said Nelson, 'how goes the day with us?' – 'Very well,' replied Hardy: 'ten ships have struck, but five of the van have tacked, and show an intention to bear down upon the *Victory*. I have called two or three of our fresh ships round, and have no doubt of giving them a drubbing.' – 'I hope,' said Nelson, 'none of our ships have struck.' Hardy answered, 'There was no fear of that.' Then, and not till then, Nelson spoke of himself. 'I am a dead man, Hardy,' said he; 'I am going fast; it will be all over with me soon. Come nearer to me.' Hardy observed that he hoped Mr Beatty could yet hold out some prospect of life. 'Oh no!' he replied, 'it is impossible; my back is shot through. Beatty will tell you so.' Captain Hardy then once more shook hands with him, and with a heart almost bursting hastened upon deck.

By this time, all feeling below the breast was gone; and Nelson, having made the surgeon ascertain this, said to him: 'You know I am gone. I know it. I feel something rising in my breast' – putting his hand on his left side – 'which tells me so.' And upon Beatty's inquiring whether his pain was very great, he replied, 'So great that he wished he was dead.' 'Yet,' said he in a lower voice, 'one would like to live a little longer too!' Captain Hardy, some fifty minutes after he had left the cockpit, returned, and again taking the hand of his dying friend and commander, congratulated him on having gained a complete victory. How many of the enemy were taken he did not know, as it was impossible to perceive them distinctly; but fourteen or fifteen at least. 'That's well!' cried Nelson – 'but I bargained for twenty.' And then in a stronger voice he said, 'Anchor, Hardy, anchor.' Hardy upon this hinted that Admiral Collingwood would take upon himself the direction of affairs. 'Not while I live, Hardy,' said the dying Nelson, ineffectually endeavouring to raise himself from the bed; 'Do you anchor.'

His previous order for preparing to anchor had shown how clearly he foresaw the necessity of this. Presently calling Hardy back, he said to him in a low voice: 'Don't throw me overboard'; and he desired that he might be buried by his parents, unless it should please the king to order otherwise. Then turning to Hardy: 'Kiss me, Hardy,' said he.

Hardy knelt down and kissed his cheek, and Nelson said: 'Now I am satisfied. Thank God, I have done my duty!' Hardy stood over him in silence for a moment or two, then knelt again and kissed his forehead. 'Who is that?' said Nelson; and being informed, he replied: 'God bless you, Hardy.' And Hardy then left him for ever.

Nelson now desired to be turned upon his right side, and said: 'I wish I had not left the deck, for I shall soon be gone.' Death was indeed rapidly approaching. He said to the chaplain: 'Doctor, I have *not* been a *great* sinner.' His articulation now became difficult, but he was distinctly heard to say: 'Thank God, I have done my duty!' These words he repeatedly pronounced. And they were the last words that he uttered. He expired at thirty minutes after four, three hours and a quarter after he had received his wound.

Leo Tolstoy

Pierre a Prisoner

(Chapters IX–XIII, Book XII, of War and Peace.
Translated by Louise and Aylmer Maude.)

THE officer and soldiers who had arrested Pierre treated him with hostility but yet with respect, in the guard-house to which he was taken. In their attitude towards him could still be felt both uncertainty as to who he might be – perhaps a very important person – and hostility as a result of the recent personal conflict with him. But when the guard was relieved next morning, Pierre felt that for the new guard – both officers and men – he was not as interesting as he had been to his captors; and in fact the guard of the second day did not recognize in this big, stout man in a peasant coat the vigorous person who had fought so desperately with the marauder and the convoy and had uttered those solemn words about saving a child; they saw in him only No. 17 of the captured Russians, arrested and detained for some reason by order of the Higher Command. If they noticed anything remarkable about Pierre, it was only his unabashed meditative concentration and thoughtfulness, and the way he spoke French, which struck them as surprisingly good. In spite of this he was placed that day with the other arrested suspects, as the separate room he had occupied was required by an officer.

All the Russians confined with Pierre were men of the lowest class and, recognizing him as a gentleman, they all avoided him, more especially as he spoke French. Pierre felt sad at hearing them making fun of him.

That evening he learnt that all these prisoners (he, probably, among them) were to be tried for incendiarism. On the third day he was taken with the others to a house where a French general with a white moustache sat with two colonels and other Frenchmen with scarves on their arms. With the precision and definiteness customary in addressing prisoners, and which is supposed to preclude human frailty, Pierre like the others was questioned as to who he was, where he had been, with what object, and so on.

PIERRE A PRISONER

These questions, like questions put at trials generally, left the essence of the matter aside, shut out the possibility of that essence being revealed, and were designed only to form a channel through which the judges wished the answers of the accused to flow so as to lead to the desired result, namely a conviction. As soon as Pierre began to say anything that did not fit in with that aim, the channel was removed and the water could flow to waste. Pierre felt, moreover, what the accused always feel at their trial, perplexity as to why these questions were put to him. He had a feeling that it was only out of condescension or a kind of civility, that this device of placing a channel was employed. He knew he was in these men's power that only by force had they brought him there, that force alone gave them a right to demand answers to their questions, and that the sole object of that assembly was to inculpate him. And so, as they had the power and wish to inculpate him, this expedient of an inquiry and trial seemed unnecessary. It was evident that any answer would lead to conviction. When asked what he was doing when he was arrested, Pierre replied in a rather tragic manner that he was restoring to its parents a child he had saved from the flames. Why had he fought the marauder? Pierre answered that he 'was protecting a woman', and that 'to protect a woman who was being insulted, was the duty of every man; that' . . . They interrupted him, for this was not to the point. Why was he in the yard of a burning house where witnesses had seen him? He replied that he had gone out to see what was happening in Moscow. Again they interrupted him: they had not asked where he was going, but why he was found near the fire? Who was he? they asked, repeating their first question, which he had declined to answer. Again he replied that he could not answer it.

'Put that down, that's bad . . . very bad,' sternly remarked the general with the white moustache and red flushed face.

On the fourth day fires broke out on the Zúbovski rampart.

Pierre and thirteen others were moved to the coach-house of a merchant's house near the Crimean Bridge. On his way through the streets Pierre felt stifled by the smoke which seemed to hang over the whole city. Fires were visible on all sides. He did not then realize the significance of the burning of Moscow, and looked at the fires with horror.

He passed four days in the coach-house near the Crimean Bridge and during that time learnt, from the talk of the French soldiers, that all those confined there were awaiting a decision which might come any day from the marshal. What marshal this was, Pierre could not learn from the soldiers. Evidently for them 'the marshal' represented a very high and rather mysterious power.

These first days, before the 8th of September when the prisoners were had up for a second examination, were the hardest of all for Pierre.

CHAPTER X

ON the 8th of September an officer – a very important one judging by the respect the guards showed him – entered the coach-house where the prisoners were. This officer, probably some one on the staff, was holding a paper in his hand, and called over all the Russians there, naming Pierre as 'the man who does not give his name'. Glancing indolently and indifferently at all the prisoners, he ordered the officer in charge to have them decently dressed and tidied up before taking them to the marshal. An hour later a squad of soldiers arrived and Pierre with thirteen others was led to the Virgin's Field. It was a fine day, sunny after rain, and the air was unusually pure. The smoke did not hang low as on the day when Pierre had been taken from the guardhouse on the Zúbovski Rampart, but rose through the pure air in columns. No flames were seen, but columns of smoke rose on all sides, and all Moscow as far as Pierre could see was one vast charred ruin. On all sides there were waste spaces with only stoves and chimney stacks still standing, and here and there the blackened walls of the brick houses. Pierre gazed at the ruins and did not recognize districts he had known well. Here and there he could see churches that had not been burnt. The Kremlin, which was not destroyed, gleamed white in the distance with its towers and the belfry of Iván the Great. The domes of the New Convent of the Virgin glittered brightly and its bells were ringing particularly clearly. These bells reminded Pierre that it was Sunday, and the feast of the Nativity of the Virgin. But there seemed to be no one to celebrate this holiday: everywhere were blackened ruins, and the few Russians to be seen were tattered and frightened people, who tried to hide when they saw the French.

It was plain that the Russian nest was ruined and destroyed, but in place of the Russian order of life that had been destroyed, Pierre unconsciously felt that a quite different, firm French order had been established over this ruined nest. He felt this in the looks of the soldiers who, marching in regular ranks briskly and gaily, were escorting him and the other criminals; he felt it in the looks of an important French official in a carriage and pair driven by a soldier, whom they met on the way. He felt it in the merry sounds of regimental music he heard from the left side of the field, and felt and realized it especially from that list of prisoners the French officer had read out when he came that morning. Pierre had been taken by one set of soldiers and led first to one and then to another place with dozens of other men, and it seemed that they might have forgotten him, or confused him with the others. But no: the answers he had given when questioned had come back to him in his designation as 'the man who does not give his name', and under the appellation, which to Pierre seemed terrible, they were now leading him somewhere with unhesitating assurance on their faces that he and all the other prisoners were exactly the ones they wanted and that they were being taken to the proper place. Pierre felt himself to be an insignificant chip fallen among the wheels of a machine whose action he did not understand but which was working well.

He and the other prisoners were taken to the right side of the Virgin's Field, to a large white house with an immense garden not far from the convent. This was Prince Sheherbátov's house, where Pierre had often been in other days, and which, as he learnt from the talk of the soldiers, was now occupied by the marshal, the Duke of Eckmühl (Davoût).

They were taken to the entrance, and led into the house one by one. Pierre was the sixth to enter. He was conducted through a glass gallery, an ante-room, and a hall, which were familiar to him, into a long low study at the door of which stood an adjutant.

Davoût, spectacles on nose, sat bent over a table at the further end of the room. Pierre went close up to him, but Davoût, evidently consulting a paper that lay before him, did not look up. Without raising his eyes he said in a low voice:

'Who are you?'

Pierre was silent because he was incapable of uttering a word. To him, Davoût was not merely a French general, but a man notorious for his cruelty. Looking at his cold face, as he sat like a stern schoolmaster who was prepared to wait a while for an answer, Pierre felt that every instant of delay might cost him his life; but he did not know what to say. He did not venture to repeat what he had said at his first examination, yet to disclose his rank and position was dangerous and embarrassing. So he was silent. But before he had decided what to do, Davoût raised his head, pushed his spectacles back on his forehead, screwed up his eyes, and looked intently at him.

'I know that man,' he said in a cold, measured tone, evidently calculated to frighten Pierre.

The chill that had been running down Pierre's back now seized his head as in a vice.

'You cannot know me, General, I have never seen you . . .'

'He is a Russian spy,' Davoût interrupted, addressing another general who was present, but whom Pierre had not noticed.

Davoût turned away. With an unexpected reverberation in his voice Pierre rapidly began:

'No, Monseigneur,' he said, suddenly remembering that Davoût was a Duke. 'No, Monseigneur, you cannot have known me. I am a militia officer and have not quitted Moscow.'

'Your name?' asked Davoût.

'Bezúkhov.'

'What proof have I that you are not lying?'

'Monseigneur!' exclaimed Pierre not in an offended but in a pleading voice.

Davoût looked up and gazed intently at him. For some seconds they looked at one another, and that look saved Pierre. Apart from conditions of war and law, that look established human relations between the two men. At that moment an immense number of things passed dimly through both their minds, and they realized that they were both children of humanity and were brothers.

At the first glance, when Davoût had only raised his head from the paper where human affairs and lives were indicated by numbers, Pierre was merely a circumstance and Davoût could have shot him without burdening his conscience with an evil deed, but now he saw in him a human being. He reflected for a moment.

'How can you show me that you are telling the truth?' said Davoût coldly.

Pierre remembered Ramballe, and named him and his regiment and the street where the house was.

'You are not what you say,' returned Davoût.

In a trembling, faltering voice Pierre began adducing proofs of the truth of his statements.

But at that moment an adjutant entered and reported something to Davoût.

Davoût brightened up at the news the adjutant brought and began buttoning up his uniform. It seemed that he had quite forgotten Pierre.

When the adjutant reminded him of the prisoner, he jerked his head in Pierre's direction with a frown and ordered him to be led away. But where they were to take him Pierre did not know: back to the coach-house or to the place of execution his companions had pointed out to him as they crossed the Virgin's Field.

He turned his head and saw that the adjutant was putting another question to Davoût.

'Yes, of course!' replied Davoût, but what this 'yes' meant, Pierre did not know.

Pierre could not afterwards remember how he went whether it was far, or in which direction. His faculties were quite numbed, he was stupefied, and noticing nothing around him went on moving his legs as the others did till they all stopped and he stopped too. The only thought in his mind at that time was: Who was it that had really sentenced him to death? Not the men on the Commission that had first examined him – not one of them had wished to or, evidently, could have done it. It was not Davoût, who had looked at him in so human a way. In another moment Davoût would have realized that he was doing wrong, but just then the adjutant had come in and inter-rupted him. The adjutant, also, had evidently had no evil intent though he might have refrained from coming in. Then who was executing him, killing him, depriving him of life – him, Pierre, with all his memories, aspirations, hopes, and thoughts? Who was doing this? And Pierre felt that it was no one.

It was a system – a concurrence of circumstances.

A system of some sort was killing him – Pierre – depriving him of life, of everything, annihilating him.

CHAPTER XI

FROM Prince Sheherbátov's house the prisoners were led straight down the Virgin's Field, to the left of the nunnery, as far as a kitchen-garden in which a post had been set up. Beyond that post a fresh pit had been dug in the ground, and near the post and the pit a large crowd stood in a semi-circle. The crowd consisted of a few Russians and many of Napoleon's soldiers who were not on duty – Germans, Italians, and Frenchmen in a variety of uniforms. To the right and left of the post stood rows of French troops in blue uniforms with red epaulettes and high boots and shakos.

The prisoners were placed in a certain order, according to the list (Pierre was sixth), and were led to the post. Several drums suddenly began to beat on both sides of them, and at that sound Pierre felt as if part of his soul had been torn away. He lost the power of thinking or understanding. He could only hear and see. And he had only one wish – that the frightful thing that had to happen, should happen quickly. Pierre looked round at his fellow-prisoners and scrutinized them.

The two first were convicts with shaven heads. One was tall and thin, the other dark, shaggy, and sinewy, with a flat nose. The third was a domestic serf, about forty-five years old, with grizzled hair and a plump well-nourished body. The fourth was a peasant, a very handsome man with a broad light-brown beard and black eyes. The fifth was a factory hand, a thin, sallow-faced lad of eighteen in a loose cloak.

Pierre heard the French consulting whether to shoot them separately or two at a time. 'In couples,' replied the officer in command in a calm cold voice. There was a stir in the ranks of the soldiers and it was evident that they were all hurrying – not as men hurry to do something they understand, but as people hurry to finish a necessary but unpleas-ant and incomprehensible task.

A French official wearing a scarf came up to the right of the row of prisoners, and read out the sentence in Russian and in French.

Then two pairs of Frenchmen approached the criminals, and at the officer's command took the two convicts who stood first in the row. The convicts stopped when they reached the post and, while sacks were being brought, looked dumbly around as a wounded beast looks at an approaching huntsman. One crossed himself continually, the other scratched his back and made a movement of the lips resembling a smile. With hurried hands the soldiers blindfolded them, drawing the sacks over their heads, and bound them to the post.

Twelve sharpshooters with muskets stepped out of the ranks with a firm regular tread, and halted eight paces from the post. Pierre turned away to avoid seeing what was about to happen. Suddenly a cracking rolling noise was heard which seemed to him louder than the most terrific thunder, and he looked round. There was some smoke, and the Frenchmen were doing something near the pit with pale faces and trembling hands. Two more prisoners were led up. In the same way, and with similar looks, these two glanced vainly at the onlookers with only a silent appeal for protection in their eyes, evidently unable to understand or believe what was going to happen to them. They could not believe it because they alone knew what their life meant to them, and so they neither understood nor believed that it could be taken from them.

Again Pierre did not wish to look, and again turned away; but again the sound as of a frightful explosion struck his ear, and at the same moment he saw smoke, blood, and the pale scared faces of the Frenchmen who were again doing something by the post, their trembling hands impeding one another. Pierre, breathing heavily, looked round as if asking what it meant. The same question was expressed in all the looks that met his.

On the faces of all the Russians, and of the French soldiers and officers without exception, he read the same dismay, horror, and conflict that were in his own heart. 'But who, after all, is doing this? They are all suffering as I am. Who then is it? Who?' flashed for an instant through his mind.

'Sharpshooters of the 86th, forward!' shouted someone. The fifth prisoner, the one next to Pierre, was led away – alone. Pierre did not understand that he was saved, that he and the rest had been brought there only to witness the execution. With ever-growing horror, and no sense of joy or relief, he gazed at what was taking place. The fifth man was the factory lad in the loose cloak. The moment they laid hands on him, he sprang aside in terror and clutched at Pierre. (Pierre shuddered and shook himself free.) The lad was unable to walk. They dragged him along holding him up under the arms, and he screamed. When they got him to the post he grew quiet, as if he had suddenly understood something. Whether he understood that screaming was useless, or whether he thought it incredible that men should kill him, at any rate he took his stand at the post, waiting to be blindfolded like the others, and like a wounded animal looked around him with glittering eyes.

Pierre was no longer able to turn away and close his eyes. His curiosity and agitation, like that of the whole crowd, reached the highest pitch at this fifth murder. Like the others this fifth man seemed calm; he wrapped his loose cloak closer and rubbed one bare foot with the other.

When they began to blindfold him he himself adjusted the knot which hurt the back of his head; then when they propped him against the bloodstained post, he leaned back and, not being comfortable in that position, straightened himself, adjusted his feet, and leaned back again more comfortably. Pierre did not take his eyes from him and did not miss his slightest movement.

Probably a word of command was given and was followed by the reports of eight muskets; but try as he would Pierre could not afterwards remember having heard the slightest sound of the shots. He only saw how the workman suddenly sank down on the cords that held him, how blood showed itself in two places, how the ropes slackened under the weight of the hanging body, and how the workman sat down, his head hanging unnaturally and one leg bent under him. Pierre ran up to the post. No one hindered him. Pale frightened people were doing something around the workman. The lower jaw of an old Frenchman with a thick moustache trembled as he untied the ropes. The body collapsed. The soldiers dragged it awkwardly from the post and began pushing it into the pit.

They all plainly and certainly knew that they were criminals who must hide the traces of their guilt as quickly as possible.

Pierre glanced into the pit, and saw that the factory lad was lying with his knees close up to his head and one shoulder higher than the other. That shoulder rose and fell rhythmically and convulsively, but spadesful of earth were already being thrown over the whole body. One of the soldiers, evidently suffering, shouted gruffly and angrily at Pierre to go back. But Pierre did not understand him, and remained near the post, and no one drove him away.

When the pit had been filled up a command was given. Pierre was taken back to his place, and the rows of troops on both sides of the post made a half turn and went past it at a measured pace. The twenty-four sharp-shooters with discharged muskets, standing in the centre of the circle, ran back to their places as the companies passed by.

Pierre gazed now with dazed eyes at these sharp-shooters who ran in couples out of the circle. All but one rejoined their companies. This one, a young soldier, his face deadly pale, his shako pushed back, and his musket resting on the ground, still stood near the pit at the spot from which he had fired. He swayed like a drunken man, taking some steps forwards and back to save himself from falling. An old, non-commissioned officer ran out of the ranks and taking him by the elbow dragged him to his company. The crowd of Russians and Frenchmen began to disperse. They all went away silently and with drooping heads.

'That will teach them to start fires,' said one of the Frenchmen.

Pierre glanced round at the speaker and saw that it was a soldier who was trying to find some relief after what had been done, but was not able to do so. Without finishing what he had begun to say he made a hopeless movement with his arm and went away.

CHAPTER XII

AFTER the execution Pierre was separated from the rest of the prisoners and placed alone in a small, ruined, and befouled church.

Towards evening a non-commissioned officer entered with two soldiers and told him that he had been pardoned and would now go to the barracks for the prisoners-of-war. Without understanding what was said to him, Pierre got up and went with the soldiers. They took him to the upper end of the field, where there were some sheds built of charred planks, beams, and battens, and led him into one of them. In the darkness some twenty different men surrounded Pierre. He looked at them without understanding who they were, why they were there, or what they wanted of him. He heard what they said, but did not understand the meaning of the words and made no kind of deduction from or application of them. He replied to questions they put to him, but did not consider who was listening to his replies, nor how they would understand them. He looked at their faces and figures, but they all seemed to him equally meaningless.

From the moment Pierre had witnessed those terrible murders committed by men who did not wish to commit them, it was as if the mainspring of his life, on which everything depended and which made everything appear alive, had suddenly been wrenched out and every-thing had collapsed into a heap of meaningless rubbish. Though he did not acknowledge it to himself, his faith in the right ordering of the universe, in humanity, in his own soul and in God, had been destroyed. He had experienced this before, but never so strongly as now. When similar doubts had assailed him before, they had been the result of his own wrongdoing, and at the bottom of his heart he had felt that relief from his despair and from those doubts was to be found within himself. But now he felt that the universe had crumbled before his eyes and only meaningless ruins remained, and this not by any fault of his own. He felt that it was not in his power to regain faith in the meaning of life.

Around him in the darkness men were standing, and evidently something about him interested them greatly. They were telling him something and asking him something. Then they led him away somewhere, and at last he found himself in a corner of the shed among men who were laughing and talking on all sides.

'Well, then, mates . . . that very Prince *who* . . .' some voice at the other side of the shed was saying, with a strong emphasis on the word *who*.

Sitting silent and motionless on a heap of straw against the wall, Pierre sometimes opened and sometimes closed his eyes. But as soon as he closed them he saw before him the dreadful face of the factory lad – especially dreadful because of its simplicity – and the faces of the murderers, even more dreadful because of their disquiet. And he opened his eyes again and stared vacantly into the darkness around him.

Beside him in a stooping position sat a small man, of whose presence he was first made aware by a strong smell of perspiration which came from him every time he moved. This man was doing something to his legs in the darkness, and though Pierre could not see his face he felt that the man continually glanced at him. On growing used to the darkness Pierre saw that the man was taking off his legbands, and the way he did it aroused Pierre's interest.

Having unwound the string that tied the band on one leg, he carefully coiled it up and immediately set to work on the other leg, glancing up at Pierre. While one hand hung up the first string, the other was already unwinding the band on the second leg. In this way, having carefully removed the legbands by deft circular motions of his arm following one another uninterruptedly, the man hung the legbands up on some pegs fixed above his head. Then he took out a knife, cut something, closed the knife, placed it under the head of his bed, and seating himself more comfortably, clasped his arms round his lifted knees and fixed his eyes on Pierre. The latter was conscious of something pleasant, comforting, and well rounded in these deft movements, in the man's well-ordered arrangements in his corner, and even in his very smell, and he looked at the man without taking his eyes from him.

'You've seen a lot of trouble, sir, eh?' the little man suddenly said.

And there was so much kindliness and simplicity in his sing-song voice, that Pierre tried to reply, but his jaw trembled and he felt tears rising to his eyes. The little fellow, giving Pierre no time to betray his confusion, instantly continued in the same pleasant tones:

'Eh, lad, don't fret!' said he, in the tender sing-song caressing voice old Russian peasant women employ. 'Don't fret, friend – "suffer an hour, live for an age!" that's how it is, my dear fellow. And here we live, thank Heaven, without offence. Among these folk, too, there are good men as well as bad,' said he, and, still speaking, he turned on his knees with a supple movement, got up, coughed, and went off to another part of the shed.

'Eh, you rascal!' Pierre heard the same kind voice saying at the other end of the shed. 'So you've come, you rascal? She remembers . . . Now, now, that'll do!'

And the soldier, pushing away a little dog that was jumping up at him, returned to his place and sat down. In his hands he had something wrapped in a rag.

'Here, eat a bit, sir,' said he, resuming his former respectful tone as he unwrapped and offered Pierre some baked potatoes. 'We had soup for dinner and the potatoes are grand!'

Pierre had not eaten all day, and the smell of the potatoes seemed extremely pleasant to him. He thanked the soldier and began to eat.

'Well, are they all right?' said the soldier with a smile. 'You should do like this.'

He took a potato, drew out his clasp knife, cut the potato into two equal halves on the palm of his hand, sprinkled some salt on it from the rag, and handed it to Pierre.

'The potatoes are grand!' he said once more. 'Eat some like that!'

Pierre thought he had never eaten anything that tasted better.

'Oh, I'm all right,' said he, 'but why did they shoot those poor fellows? The last one was hardly twenty.'

'Tss, tt . . .!' said the little man. 'Ah, what a sin . . . what a sin!' he added quickly, and as if his words were always waiting ready in his mouth and flew out involuntarily he went on: 'How was it, sir, that you stayed in Moscow?'

'I didn't think they would come so soon. I stayed accidentally,' replied Pierre.

'And how did they arrest you, dear lad? At your house?'

'No, I went to look at the fire, and they arrested me there, and tried me as an incendiary.'

'Where there's law there's injustice,' put in the little man.

'And have you been here long?' Pierre asked as he munched the last of the potato.

'I? It was last Sunday they took me, out of a hospital in Moscow.'

'Why are you a soldier then?'

'Yes, we are soldiers of the Ápsheron regiment. I was dying of fever. We weren't told anything. There were some twenty of us lying there. We had no idea, never guessed at all.'

'And do you feel sad here?' Pierre inquired.

'How can one help it, lad? My name is Platón, and the surname is Karatáev,' he added, evidently wishing to make it easier for Pierre to address him. 'They call me "little falcon" in the regiment. How is one to help feeling sad? Moscow – she's the mother of cities. How can one see all this and not feel sad? But "the maggot gnaws the cabbage, yet dies first"; that's what the old folk used to tell us,' he added rapidly.

'What? What did you say?' asked Pierre.

'Who? I?' said Karatáev. 'I say things happen not as we plan but as God judges,' he replied, thinking that he was repeating what he had said before, and immediately continued:

'Well, and you, have you a family estate, sir? And a house? So you have abundance, then? And a housewife? And your old parents, are they still living?' he asked.

And though it was too dark for Pierre to see, he felt that a suppressed smile of kindliness puckered the soldier's lips as he put these questions. He seemed grieved that Pierre had no parents, especially that he had no mother.

'A wife for counsel, a mother-in-law for welcome, but there's none as dear as one's own mother!' said he. 'Well, and have you little ones?' he went on asking.

Again Pierre's negative answer seemed to distress him, and he hastened to add:

'Never mind! You're young folks yet, and please God may still have some. The great thing is to live in harmony . . .'

'But it's all the same now,' Pierre could not help saying.

'Ah, my dear fellow!' rejoined Karatáev, 'never decline a prison or a beggar's sack!'

He seated himself more comfortably, and coughed, evidently preparing to tell a long story.

'Well, my dear fellow, I was still living at home,' he began. 'We had a well-to-do homestead, plenty of land, we peasants lived well and our house was one to thank God for. When father and we went out mowing there were seven of us. We lived well. We were real peasants. It so happened . . .'

And Platón Karatáev told a long story of how he had gone into someone's copse to take wood, how he had been caught by the keeper, had been tried, flogged, and sent to serve as a soldier.

'Well, lad,' and a smile changed the tone of his voice, 'we thought it was a misfortune but it turned out a blessing! If it had not been for my sin, my brother would have had to go as a soldier. But he, my younger brother, had five little ones, while I, you see, only left a wife behind. We had a little girl, but God took her before I went as a soldier. I come home on leave and I'll tell you how it was. I look and see that they are living better than before. The yard full of cattle, the women at home, two brothers away earning wages, and only Michael, the youngest, at home. Father, he says, "All my children are the same to me: it hurts the same whichever finger gets bitten. But if Platón hadn't been shaved for a soldier, Michael would have had to go." He called us all to him and, will you believe it, placed us in front of the icons. "Michael," he says, "come here and bow down to his feet; and you, young woman, you bow down too; and you, grandchildren, also bow down before him! Do you understand?" he says. That's how it is, dear fellow. Fate looks for a head. But we are always judging, "that's not well – that's not right!" Our luck is like water in a drag-net: you pull at it and it bulges, but when you've drawn it out it's empty! That's how it is.'

And Platón shifted his seat on the straw.

After a short silence he rose.

'Well, I think you must be sleepy,' said he, and began rapidly crossing himself and repeating:

'Lord Jesus Christ, holy Saint Nicholas, Frola and Lavra! Lord Jesus Christ, holy Saint Nicholas, Frola and Lavra![1] lord Jesus Christ, have mercy on us and save us!' he concluded, then bowed to the ground, got up, sighed, and sat down again on his heap of straw. 'That's the way. Lay me down like a stone, O God, and raise me up like a loaf,' he muttered as he lay down, pulling his coat over him.

'What prayer was that you were saying?' asked Pierre.

'Eh?' murmured Platón, who had almost fallen asleep. 'What was I saying? I was praying. Don't you pray?'

'Yes, I do,' said Pierre. 'But what was that you said: Frola and Lavra?'

'Well, of course,' replied Platón quickly, 'the horses' saints. One must pity the animals too. Eh, the rascal! Now you've curled up and got warm, you daughter of a bitch!' said Karatáev, touching the dog that lay at his feet, and again turning over he fell asleep immediately.

Sounds of crying and screaming came from somewhere in the distance outside, and flames were visible through the cracks of the shed, but inside it was quiet and dark. For a long time Pierre did not sleep, but lay with eyes open in the darkness listening to the regular snoring of Platón, who lay beside him, and he felt that the world that had been shattered was once more stirring in his soul with a new beauty and on new and unshakable foundations.

[1] Florus and Laurus, brothers who were martyred under Diocletian, are numbered among the saints of the Russo-Greek church and are accounted the patron saints of horses by the peasants, who mispronounce their names.

CHAPTER XIII

TWENTY-THREE soldiers, three officers, and two officials, were confined in the shed in which Pierre had been placed and where he remained for four weeks.

When Pierre remembered them afterwards they all seemed misty figures to him except Platón Karatáev, who always remained in his mind a most vivid and precious memory and the personification of everything Russian, kindly, and round. When Pierre saw his neighbour next morning at dawn, the first impression of him, as of something round, was fully confirmed: Platón's whole figure – in a French overcoat girdled with a cord, a soldier's cap, and bast shoes – was round. His head was quite round, his back, chest, shoulders, and even his arms, which he held as if ever ready to embrace something, were rounded, his pleasant smile and his large gentle brown eyes were also round.

Platón Karatáev must have been fifty judging by his stories of campaigns he had been in, told as by an old soldier. He did not himself know his age and was quite unable to determine it. But his brilliantly white, strong teeth, which showed in two unbroken semicircles when he laughed – as he often did – were all sound and good, there was not a grey hair in his beard or on his head, and his whole body gave an impression of suppleness and especially of firmness and endurance.

His face, despite its fine, rounded wrinkles, had an expression of innocence and youth, his voice was pleasant and musical. But the chief peculiarity of his speech was its directness and appositeness. It was evident that he never considered what he had said or was going to say, and consequently the rapidity and justice of his intonation had an irresistible persuasiveness.

His physical strength and agility during the first days of his imprisonment were such that he seemed not to know what fatigue and sickness meant. Every night, before lying down, he said: 'Lord, lay me down as a stone and raise me up as a loaf!' and every morning on getting up he said: 'I lay down and curled up, I get up and shake myself.' And indeed he only had to lie down, to fall asleep like a stone, and he only had to shake himself, to be ready without a moment's delay for some work, just as children are ready for play directly they awake. He could do everything, not very well but not badly. He baked, cooked, sewed, planed, and mended boots. He was always busy, and only at night allowed himself conversation – of which he was fond – and songs. He did not sing like a trained singer who knows he is listened to, but like the birds, evidently giving vent to the sounds in the same way that one stretches oneself, or walks about to get rid of stiffness, and the sounds were always high-pitched, mournful, delicate, and almost feminine, and his face at such times was very serious.

Having been taken prisoner and allowed his beard to grow, he seemed to have thrown off all that had been forced upon him – everything military and alien to himself – and had returned to his former peasant habits.

'A soldier on leave – a shirt outside the breeches,'[1] he would say.

He did not like talking about his life as a soldier, though he did not complain, and often mentioned that he had not been flogged once during the whole of his army service. When he related anything it was generally some old and evidently precious memory of his 'Christian'[2] life, as he called his peasant existence. The proverbs, of which his talk was full, were for the most part not the coarse and indecent saws soldiers employ, but those folk-sayings which taken without a context seem so insignificant, but when used appositely suddenly acquire a significance of profound wisdom.

He would often say the exact opposite of what he had said on a previous occasion, yet both would be right. He liked to talk and he talked well, adorning his speech with terms of endearment and with folk-sayings which Pierre thought he invented himself, but the chief charm of his talk lay in the fact that the commonest events – sometimes just such as Pierre had witnessed without taking notice of them – assumed in Karatáev's speech a character of solemn fitness. He liked to hear the folk-tales one of the soldiers used to tell of an evening (they were always the same), but most of all he liked to hear stories of real life. He would smile joyfully when listening to such stories, now and then putting in a word or asking a question to make the moral beauty of what was told clear to himself. Karatáev had no attachments, friendships, or love, as Pierre understood them, but loved and lived affectionately with everything life brought him in contact with, particularly with man – not any particular man, but those with whom he happened to be. He loved his dog, his comrades, the French, and Pierre who was his neighbour, but Pierre felt that in spite of Karatáev's affectionate tenderness for him (by which he unconsciously gave Pierre's spiritual life its due) he would not have grieved for a moment at parting from him. And Pierre began to feel in the same way towards Karatáev.

To all the other prisoners Platón Karatáev seemed a most ordinary soldier. They called him 'little falcon' or 'Platósha', chaffed him good-naturedly, and sent him on errands. But to Pierre he always remained

[1] The peasants wear their shirts fastened by a girdle at the waist and hanging loose outside their breeches, whereas a soldier's shirt is tucked inside.

[2] In Russian the words *Christian* and *peasant* are very similar, the one being derived from the other, and Karatáev's pronunciation identified them.

what he had seemed that first night: an unfathomable, rounded, eternal personification of the spirit of simplicity and truth.

Platón Karatáev knew nothing by heart, except his prayers. When he began to speak he seemed not to know how he would conclude.

Sometimes Pierre, struck by the meaning of his words, would ask him to repeat them, but Platón could never recall what he had said a moment before, just as he never could repeat to Pierre the words of his favourite song: *Native* and *birch-tree* and *my heart is sick* occurred in it, but when spoken and not sung no meaning could be got out of it. He did not, and could not, understand the meaning of words apart from their context. Every word and action of his was the manifestation of an activity unknown to him, which was his life. But his life, as he regarded it, had no meaning as a separate thing. It had meaning only as part of a whole of which he was always conscious. His words and actions flowed from him as evenly, inevitably, and spontaneously, as fragrance exhales from a flower. He could not understand the value or significance of any word or deed taken separately.

Joseph Conrad

The Warrior's Soul

THE old officer with long white moustaches gave rein to his indignation.

'Is it possible that you youngsters should have no more sense than that! Some of you had better wipe the milk off your upper lip before you start to pass judgment on the few poor stragglers of a generation which has done and suffered not a little in its time.'

His hearers having expressed much compunction the ancient warrior became appeased. But he was not silenced.

'I am one of them – one of the stragglers, I mean,' he went on patiently. 'And what did we do? What have we achieved? He – the great Napoleon – started upon us to emulate the Macedonian Alexander, with a ruck of nations at his back. We opposed empty spaces to French impetuosity, then we offered them an interminable battle so that their army went at last to sleep in its positions lying down on the heaps of its own dead. Then came the wall of fire in Moscow. It toppled down on them.

'Then began the long rout of the Grand Army. I have seen it stream on, like the doomed flight of haggard, spectral sinners across the innermost frozen circle of Dante's Inferno, ever widening before their despairing eyes.

'They who escaped must have had their souls doubly riveted inside their bodies to carry them out of Russia through that frost fit to split rocks. But to say that it was our fault that a single one of them got away is mere ignorance. Why! Our own men suffered nearly to the limit of their strength. Their Russian strength!

'Of course our spirit was not broken; and then our cause was good – it was holy. But that did not temper the wind much to men and horses.

'The flesh is weak. Good or evil purpose, Humanity has to pay the price. Why! in that very fight for that little village of which I have been telling you we were fighting for the shelter of those old houses as much as victory. And with the French it was the same.

'It wasn't for the sake of glory, or for the sake of strategy. The

French knew that they would have to retreat before morning and we knew perfectly well that they would go. As far as the war was concerned there was nothing to fight about. Yet our infantry and theirs fought like wild cats, or like heroes if you like that better, amongst the houses – hot work enough – while the supports out in the open stood freezing in a tempestuous north wind which drove the snow on earth and the great masses of clouds in the sky at a terrific pace. The very air was inexpressibly sombre by contrast with the white earth. I have never seen God's creation look more sinister than on that day.

'We, the cavalry (we were only a handful), had not much to do except turn our backs to the wind and receive some stray French round shot. This, I may tell you, was the last of the French guns and it was the last time they had their artillery in position. Those guns never went away from there either. We found them abandoned next morning. But that afternoon they were keeping up an infernal fire on our attacking column; the furious wind carried away the smoke and even the noise but we could see the constant flicker of the tongues of fire among the French front. Then a driving flurry of snow would hide everything except the dark red flashes in the white swirl.

'At intervals when the line cleared we could see away across the plain to the right a sombre column moving endlessly; the great rout of the Grand Army creeping on and on all the time while the fight on our left went on with a great din and fury. The cruel whirlwind of snow swept over that scene of death and desolation. And then the wind fell as suddenly as it had arisen in the morning.

'Presently we got orders to charge the retreating column; I don't know why unless they wanted to prevent us from getting frozen in our saddles by giving us something to do. We changed front half right and got into motion at a walk to take that distant dark line in flank. It might have been half-past two in the afternoon.

'You must know that so far in this compaign my regiment had never been on the main line of Napoleon's advance. All these months since the invasion the army we belonged to had been wrestling with Oudinot in the north. We had only come down lately driving him before us to the Beresina.

'This was the first occasion then that I and my comrades had a close view of Napoleon's Grand Army. It was an amazing and terrible sight. I had heard of it from others; I had seen the stragglers from it; small bands of marauders, parties of prisoners in the distance. But this was the very column itself! A crawling, stumbling, starved, half-demented mob. It issued from the forest a mile away and its head was lost in the murk of the fields. We rode into it at a trot, which was the most we could get out of our horses, and we stuck in that human mass as if in a moving bog. There was no resistance. I heard a few shots, half a dozen perhaps. Their very senses seemed frozen within them. I had time for a good look while riding at the head of my squadron. Well, I assure you, there were men walking on the outer edge so lost to everything but their misery that they never turned their heads to look at our charge. Soldiers!

'My horse pushed over one of them with his chest. The poor wretch had a dragoon's blue cloak, all torn and scorched, hanging from his shoulders and he didn't even put his hand out to snatch at my bridle and save himself. He just went down. Our troopers were pointing and slashing; well, and of course at first I myself . . . What would you have! An enemy is an enemy. Yet a sort of sickening awe crept into my heart. There was no tumult – only a low deep murmur dwelt over them interspersed with louder cries and groans while that mob kept on pushing and surging past us, sightless and without feeling. A smell of scorched rags and festering wounds hung in the air. My horse staggered in the eddies of swaying men. But it was like cutting down galvanized corpses that didn't care. Invaders! Yes . . . God was already dealing with them.

'I touched my horse with the spurs to get clear. There was a sudden rush and a sort of angry moan when our second squadron got into them on our right. My horse plunged and somebody got hold of my leg. As I had no mind to get pulled out of the saddle I gave a back-handed slash without looking. I heard a cry and my leg was let go suddenly.

'Just then I caught sight of the subaltern of my troop at some little distance from me. His name was Tomassov. That multitude of resurrected bodies with glassy eyes was seething round his horse as if blind, growling crazily. He was sitting erect in his saddle, not looking down at them and sheathing his sword deliberately.

'This Tomassov, well, he had a beard. Of course we all had beards then. Circumstances, lack of leisure, want of razors, too. No, seriously, we were a wild-looking lot in those unforgotten days, which so many, so very many of us did not survive. You know our losses were awful, too. Yes, we looked wild. *Des Russes sauvages* – what!

'So he had a beard – this Tomassov I mean; but he did not look *sauvage*. He was the youngest of us all. And that meant real youth. At a distance he passed muster fairly well, what with the grime and the particular stamp of that campaign on our faces. But directly you were near enough to have a good look into his eyes, that was where his lack of age showed, though he was not exactly a boy.

'Those same eyes were blue, something like the blue of autumn skies, dreamy and gay, too – innocent, believing eyes. A topknot of fair hair decorated his brow like a gold diadem in what one would call normal times.

THE WARRIOR'S SOUL

'You may think I am talking of him as if he were the hero of a novel. Why, that's nothing to what the adjutant discovered about him. He discovered that he had a "lover's lips" – whatever that may be. If the adjutant meant a nice mouth, why, it was nice enough but of course it was intended for a sneer. That adjutant of ours was not a very delicate fellow. "Look at those lover's lips," he would exclaim in a loud tone while Tomassov was talking.

'Tomassov didn't quite like that sort of thing. But to a certain extent he had laid himself open to banter by the lasting character of his impressions which were connected with the passion of love and, perhaps, were not of such a rare kind as he seemed to think them. What made his comrades tolerant of his rhapsodies was the fact that they were connected with France, with Paris!

'You of the present generation, you cannot conceive how much prestige there was then in those names for the whole world. Paris was the centre of wonder for all human beings gifted with imagination. There we were, the majority of us young and well connected, but not long out of our hereditary nests in the provinces; simple servants of God; mere rustics, if I may say so. So we were only too ready to listen to the tales of France from our comrade Tomassov. He had been attached to our mission in Paris the year before the war. High protections very likely – or maybe sheer luck.

'I don't think he could have been a very useful member of the mission because of his youth and complete inexperience. And apparently all this time in Paris was his own. The use he made of it was to fall in love, to remain in that state, to cultivate it, to exist only for it in a manner of speaking.

'Thus it was something more than a mere memory that he had brought with him from France. Memory is a fugitive thing. It can be falsified, it can be effaced, it can be even doubted. Why! I myself come to doubt sometimes that I, too, have been in Paris in my turn. And the long road there with battles for its stages would appear still more incredible if it were not for a certain musket ball which I have been carrying about my person ever since a little cavalry affair which happened in Silesia at the very beginning of the Leipsic campaign.

'Passages of love, however, are more impressive perhaps than passages of danger. You don't go affronting love in troops as it were. They are rarer, more personal and more intimate. And remember that with Tomassov all that was very fresh yet. He had not been home from France three months when the war began.

'His heart, his mind were full of that experience. He was really awed by it, and he was simple enough to let it appear in his speeches. He considered himself a sort of privileged person, not because a woman had looked at him with favour, but simply because, how shall

I say it, he had had the wonderful illumination of his worship for her, as if it were heaven itself that had done this for him.

'Oh yes, he was very simple. A nice youngster, yet no fool; and with that, utterly inexperienced, unsuspicious, and unthinking. You will find one like that here and there in the provinces. He had some poetry in him too. It could only be natural, something quite his own, not acquired. I suppose Father Adam had some poetry in him of that natural sort. For the rest *un Russe sauvage* as the French sometimes call us, but not of that kind which, they maintain, eats tallow candle for a delicacy. As to the woman, the French woman, well, though I have also been in France with a hundred thousand Russians, I have never seen her. Very likely she was not in Paris then. And in any case hers were not the doors that would fly open before simple fellows of my sort, you understand. Gilded salons were never in my way. I could not tell you how she looked, which is strange considering that I was, if I may say so, Tomassov's special confidant.

'He very soon got shy of talking before the others. I suppose the usual camp-fire comments jarred his fine feelings. But I was left to him and truly I had to submit. You can't very well expect a youngster in Tomassov's state to hold his tongue altogether; and I – I suppose you will hardly believe me – I am by nature a rather silent sort of person.

'Very likely my silence appeared to him sympathetic. All the month of September our regiment, quartered in villages, had come in for an easy time. It was then that I heard most of that – you can't call it a story. The story I have in my mind is not in that. Outpourings, let us call them.

'I would sit quite content to hold my peace, a whole hour perhaps, while Tomassov talked with exaltation. And when he was done I would still hold my peace. And then there would be produced a solemn effect of silence which, I imagine, pleased Tomassov in a way.

'She was of course not a woman in her first youth. A widow, maybe. At any rate I never heard Tomassov mention her husband. She had a salon, something very distinguished; a social centre in which she queened it with great splendour.

'Somehow, I fancy her court was composed mostly of men. But Tomassov, I must say, kept such details out of his discourses wonderfully well. Upon my word I don't know whether her hair was dark or fair, her eyes brown or blue; what was her stature, her features, or her complexion. His love soared above mere physical impressions. He never described her to me in set terms; but he was ready to swear that in her presence everybody's thoughts and feelings were bound to circle round her. She was that sort of woman. Most wonderful conversations on all sorts of subjects went on in her salon: but through them all there flowed unheard like a mysterious strain of music the assertion, the power, the tyranny of sheer beauty. So apparently the woman was beautiful. She detached all these talking people from their life interests, and even from vanities. She was a secret delight and a secret trouble. All the men when they looked at her fell to brooding as if struck by the thought that their lives had been wasted. She was the very joy and shudder of felicity and she brought only sadness and torment to the hearts of men.

'In short, she must have been an extraordinary woman, or else Tomassov was an extraordinary young fellow to feel in that way and to talk like this about her. I told you the fellow had a lot of poetry in him and observed that all this sounded true enough. It would be just about the sorcery a woman very much out of the common would exercise, you know. Poets do get close to truth somehow – there is no denying that.

'There is no poetry in my composition, I know, but I have my share of common shrewdness, and I have no doubt that the lady was kind to the youngster, once he did find his way inside her salon. His getting in is the real marvel. However, he did get in, the innocent, and he found himself in distinguished company there, amongst men of considerable position. And you know what that means: thick waists, bald heads, teeth that are not – as some satirist puts it. Imagine amongst them a nice boy, fresh and simple, like an apple just off the tree; a modest, good-looking, impressionable, adoring young barbarian. My word! What a change! What a relief for jaded feelings! And with that, having in his nature that dose of poetry which saves even a simpleton from being a fool.

'He became an artlessly, unconditionally devoted slave. He was rewarded by being smiled on and in time admitted to the intimacy of the house. It may be that the unsophisticated young barbarian amused the exquisite lady. Perhaps – since he didn't feed on tallow candles – he satisfied some need of tenderness in the woman. You know, there are many kinds of tenderness highly civilized women are capable of. Women with heads and imagination, I mean, and no temperament to speak of, you understand. But who is going to fathom their needs or their fancies? Most of the time they themselves don't know much about their innermost moods, and blunder out of one into another, sometimes with catastrophic results. And then who is more surprised than they? However, Tomassov's case was in its nature quite idyllic. The fashionable world was amused. His devotion made for him a kind of social success. But he didn't care. There was his one divinity, and there was the shrine where he was permitted to go in and out without regard for official reception hours.

'He took advantage of that privilege freely. Well, he had no official duties, you know. The Military Mission was supposed to be more complimentary than anything else, the head of it being a personal friend of our Emperor Alexander; and he, too, was laying himself out for successes in fashionable life exclusively – as it seemed. As it seemed.

'One afternoon Tomassov called on the mistress of his thoughts earlier than usual. She was not alone. There was a man with her, not one of the thick-waisted, bald-headed personages, but a somebody all the same, a man over thirty, a French officer who to some extent was also a privileged intimate. Tomassov was not jealous of him. Such a sentiment would have appeared presumptuous to the simple fellow.

'On the contrary he admired that officer. You have no idea of the French military men's prestige in those days, even with us Russian soldiers who had managed to face them perhaps better than the rest. Victory had marked them on the forehead – it seemed for ever. They would have been more than human if they had not been conscious of it; but they were good comrades and had a sort of brotherly feeling for all who bore arms, even if it was against them.

'And this was quite a superior example, an officer of the major-general's staff, and a man of the best society besides. He was powerfully built, and thoroughly masculine, though he was as carefully groomed as a woman. He had the courteous self-possession of a man of the world. His forehead, white as alabaster, contrasted impressively with the healthy colour of his face.

'I don't know whether he was jealous of Tomassov, but I suspect that he might have been a little annoyed at him as at a sort of walking absurdity of the sentimental order. But these men of the world are impenetrable, and outwardly he condescended to recognize Tomassov's existence even more distinctly than was strictly necessary. Once or twice he had offered him some useful worldly advice with perfect tact and delicacy. Tomassov was completely conquered by that evidence of kindness under the cold polish of the best society.

'Tomassov, introduced into the *petit salon*, found these two exquisite people sitting on a sofa together and had the feeling of having interrupted some special conversation. They looked at him strangely, he thought; but he was not given to understand that he had intruded. After a time the lady said to the officer – his name was De Castel – "I wish you would take the trouble to ascertain the exact truth as to that rumour."

' "It's much more than a mere rumour," remarked the officer. But he got up submissively and went out. The lady turned to Tomassov and said: "You may stay with me."

'This express command made him supremely happy, though as a matter of fact he had had no idea of going.

'She regarded him with her kindly glances, which made something glow and expand within his chest. It was a delicious feeling, even though it did cut one's breath short now and then. Ecstatically he drank in the sound of her tranquil, seductive talk full of innocent gaiety and of spiritual quietude. His passion appeared to him to flame up and envelope her in blue fiery tongues from head to foot and over her head, while her soul reposed in the centre like a big white rose . . .

'H'm, good this. He told me many other things like that. But this is the one I remember. He himself remembered everything because these were the last memories of that woman. He was seeing her for the last time though he did not know it then.

'M. De Castel returned, breaking into that atmosphere of enchantment Tomassov had been drinking in even to complete unconsciousness of the external world. Tomassov could not help being struck by the distinction of his movements, the ease of his manner, his superiority to all the other men he knew, and he suffered from it. It occurred to him that these two brilliant beings on the sofa were made for each other.

'De Castel sitting down by the side of the lady murmured to her discreetly, 'There is not the slightest doubt that it's true,'' and they both turned their eyes to Tomassov. Roused thoroughly from his enchantment he became self-conscious; a feeling of shyness came over him. He sat smiling faintly at them.

'The lady without taking her eyes off the blushing Tomassov said with a dreamy gravity quite unusual to her:

' "I should like to know that your generosity can be supreme – without a flaw. Love at its highest should be the origin of every perfection.'

'Tomassov opened his eyes wide with admiration at this, as though her lips had been dropping real pearls. The sentiment, however, was not uttered for the primitive Russian youth but for the exquisitely accomplished man of the world, De Castel.

'Tomassov could not see the effect it produced because the French officer lowered his head and sat there contemplating his admirably polished boots. The lady whispered in a sympathetic tone:

' "You have scruples?"

'De Castel, without looking up, murmured: "It could be turned into a nice point of honour."

'She said vivaciously: "That surely is artificial. I am all for natural feelings. I believe in nothing else. But perhaps your conscience . . ."

'He interrupted her: "Not at all. My conscience is not childish. The fate of those people is of no military importance to us. What can it matter? The fortune of France is invincible."

' "Well then . . ." she uttered, meaningly, and rose from the couch.

The French officer stood up, too. Tomassov hastened to follow their example. He was pained by his state of utter mental darkness. While he was raising the lady's white hand to his lips he heard the French officer say with marked emphasis:

' "If he has the soul of a warrior (at that time, you know, people really talked in that way), if he has the soul of a warrior he ought to fall at your feet in gratitude.'

'Tomassov felt himself plunged into even denser darkness than before. He followed the French officer out of the room and out of the house; for he had a notion that this was expected of him.

'It was getting dusk, the weather was very bad, and the street was quite deserted. The Frenchman lingered in it strangely. And Tomassov lingered, too, without impatience. He was never in a hurry to get away from the house in which she lived. And besides, something wonderful had happened to him. The hand he had reverently raised by the tips of its fingers had been pressed against his lips. He had received a secret favour! He was almost frightened. The world had reeled – and it had hardly steadied itself yet. De Castel stopped short at the corner of the quiet street.

' "I don't care to be seen too much with you in the lighted thoroughfares, M. Tomassov," he said in a strangely grim tone.

' "Why?" asked the young man, too startled to be offended.

' "From prudence," answered the other curtly. "So we will have to part here; but before we part I'll disclose to you something of which you will see at once the importance."

'This, please note, was an evening in late March of the year 1812. For a long time already there had been talk of a growing coolness between Russia and France. The word war was being whispered in drawing rooms louder and louder, and at last was heard in official circles. Thereupon the Parisian police discovered that our military envoy had corrupted some clerks at the Ministry of War and had obtained from them some very important confidential documents. The wretched men (there were two of them) had confessed their crime and were to be shot that night. Tomorrow all the town would be talking of the affair. But the worst was that the Emperor Napoleon was furiously angry at the discovery, and had made up his mind to have the Russian envoy arrested.

'Such was De Castel's disclosure; and though he had spoken in low tones Tomassov was stunned as by a great crash.

' "Arrested," he murmured, desolately.

' "Yes, and kept as a state prisoner – with everybody belonging to him . . ."

'The French officer seized Tomassov's arm above the elbow and pressed it hard.

' "And kept in France," he repeated into Tomassov's very ear, and then letting him go stepped back a space and remained silent.

' "And it's you, you, who are telling me this!" cried Tomassov in an extremity of gratitude that was hardly greater than his admiration for the generosity of his future foe. Could a brother have done for him more! He sought to seize the hand of the French officer, but the latter remained wrapped up closely in his cloak. Possibly in the dark he had not noticed the attempt. He moved back a bit and in his self-possessed voice of a man of the world, as though he were speaking across a card table or something of the sort, he called Tomassov's attention to the fact that if he meant to make use of the warning the moments were precious.

' "Indeed they are," agreed the awed Tomassov. "Good-bye then. I have no word of thanks to equal your generosity; but if ever I have an opportunity, I swear it, you may command my life . . ."

'But the Frenchman retreated, had already vanished in the dark lonely street. Tomassov was alone, and then he did not waste any of the precious minutes of that night.

'See how people's mere gossip and idle talk pass into history. In all the memoirs of the time if you read them you will find it stated that our envoy had a warning from some highly placed woman who was in love with him. Of course it's known that he had successes with women, and in the highest spheres, too, but the truth is that the person who warned him was no other than our simple Tomassov – an altogether different sort of lover from himself.

'This then is the secret of our Emperor's representative's escape from arrest. He and all his official household got out of France all right – as history records.

'And amongst that household there was our Tomassov of course. He had, in the words of the French officer, the soul of a warrior. And what more desolate prospect for a man with such a soul than to be imprisoned on the eve of war; to be cut off from his country in danger, from his military family, from his duty, from honour, and – well – from glory, too.

'Tomassov used to shudder at the mere thought of the moral torture he had escaped; and he nursed in his heart a boundless gratitude to the two people who had saved him from that cruel ordeal. They were wonderful! For him love and friendship were but two aspects of exalted perfection. He had found these fine examples of it and he vowed them indeed a sort of cult. It affected his attitude towards Frenchmen in general, great patriot as he was. He was naturally indignant at the invasion of his country, but this indignation had no personal animosity in it. His was fundamentally a fine nature. He grieved at the appalling amount of human suffering he saw around him. Yes, he was full of compassion for all forms of mankind's misery in a manly way.

'Less fine natures than his own did not understand this very well. In the regiment they had nicknamed him the Humane Tomassov.

'He didn't take offence at it. There is nothing incompatible between humanity and a warrior's soul. People without compassion are the civilians, government officials, merchants and such like. As to the ferocious talk one hears from a lot of decent people in war time – well, the tongue is an unruly member at best, and when there is some excitement going on there is no curbing its furious activity.

'So I had not been very surprised to see our Tomassov sheathe deliberately his sword right in the middle of that charge, you may say. As we rode away after it he was very silent. He was not a chatterer as a rule, but it was evident that this close view of the Grand Army had affected him deeply, like some sight not of this earth. I had always been a pretty tough individual myself – well, even I . . . and there was that fellow with a lot of poetry in his nature! You may imagine what he made of it to himself. We rode side by side without opening our lips. It was simply beyond words.

'We established our bivouac along the edge of the forest so as to get some shelter for our horses. However, the boisterous north wind had dropped as quickly as it had sprung up, and the great winter stillness lay on the land from the Baltic to the Black Sea. One could almost feel its cold, lifeless immensity reaching up to the stars.

'Our men had lighted several fires for their officers and had cleared the snow around them. We had big logs of wood for seats; it was a very tolerable bivouac upon the whole, even without the exultation of victory. We were to feel that later, but at present we were oppressed by our stern and arduous task.

'There were three of us round my fire. The third one was that adjutant. He was perhaps a well-meaning chap but not so nice as he might have been had he been less rough in manner and less crude in his perceptions. He would reason about people's conduct as though a man were as simple a figure as, say, two sticks laid across each other; whereas a man is much more like the sea whose movements are too complicated to explain, and whose depths may bring up God only knows what at any moment.

'We talked a little about that charge. Not much. That sort of thing does not lend itself to conversation. Tomassov muttered a few words about a mere butchery. I had nothing to say. As I told you I had very soon let my sword hang idle at my wrist. That starving mob had not even *tried* to defend itself. Just a few shots. We had two men wounded. Two! . . . and we had charged the main column of Napoleon's Grand Army.

THE WARRIOR'S SOUL

'Tomassov muttered wearily: "What was the good of it?" I did not wish to argue, so I only just mumbled: "Ah, well!" But the adjutant struck in unpleasantly:

' "Why, it warmed the men a bit. It has made me warm. That's a good enough reason. But our Tomassov is so humane! And besides he has been in love with a French woman, and thick as thieves with a lot of Frenchmen, so he is sorry for them. Never mind, my boy, we are on the Paris road now and you shall soon see her!" This was one of his usual, as we believed them, foolish speeches. None of us but believed that the getting to Paris would be a matter of years – of years. And lo! less than eighteen months afterwards I was rooked of a lot of money in a gambling hell in the Palais Royal.

'Truth, being often the most senseless thing in the world, is sometimes revealed to fools. I don't think that adjutant of ours believed in his own words. He just wanted to tease Tomassov from habit. Purely from habit. We of course said nothing, and so he took his head in his hands and fell into a doze as he sat on a log in front of the fire.

'Our cavalry was on the extreme right wing of the army, and I must confess that we guarded it very badly. We had lost all sense of insecurity by this time; but still we did keep up a pretence of doing it in a way. Presently a trooper rode up leading a horse and Tomassov mounted stiffly and went off on a round of the outposts. Of the perfectly useless outposts.

'The night was still, except for the crackling of the fires. The raging wind had lifted far above the earth and not the faintest breath of it could be heard. Only the full moon swam out with a rush into the sky and suddenly hung high and motionless overhead. I remember raising my hairy face to it for a moment. Then, I verily believe, I dozed off, too, bent double on my log with my head towards the fierce blaze.

'You know what an impermanent thing such slumber is. One moment you drop into an abyss and the next you are back in the world that you would think too deep for any noise but the trumpet of the Last Judgment. And then off you go again. Your very soul seems to slip down into a bottomless black pit. Then up once more into a startled consciousness. A mere plaything of cruel sleep one is, then. Tormented both ways.

'However, when my orderly appeared before me, repeating: 'Won't your Honour be pleased to eat? . . . Won't your Honour be pleased to eat? . . . I managed to keep my hold of it – I mean that gaping consciousness. He was offering me a sooty pot containing some grain boiled in water with a pinch of salt. A wooden spoon was stuck in it.

'At that time these were the only rations we were getting regularly. Mere chicken food, confound it! But the Russian soldier is wonderful.

Well, my fellow waited till I had feasted and then went away carrying off the empty pot.

'I was no longer sleepy. Indeed, I had become awake with an exaggerated mental consciousness of existence extending beyond my immediate surroundings. Those are but exceptional moments with mankind, I am glad to say. I had the intimate sensation of the earth in all its enormous expanse wrapped in snow, with nothing showing on it but trees with their straight stalk-like trunks and their funeral verdure; and in this aspect of general mourning I seemed to hear the sighs of mankind fal ing to die in the midst of a nature without life. They were Frenchmen. We didn't hate them; they did not hate us; we had existed far apart – and suddenly they had come rolling in with arms in their hands, without fear of God, carrying with them other nations, and all to perish together in a long, long trail of frozen corpses. I had an actual vision of that trail: a pathetic multitude of small dark mounds stretching away under the moonlight in a clear, still, and pitiless atmosphere – a sort of horrible peace.

'But what other peace could there be for them? What else did they deserve? I don't know by what connection of emotions there came into my head the thought that the earth was a pagan planet and not a fit abode for Christian virtues.

'You may be surprised that I should remember all this so well. What is a passing emotion or half-formed thought to last in so many years of a man's changing, inconsequential life? But what has fixed the emotion of that evening in my recollection so that the slightest shadows remain indelible was an event of strange finality, an event not likely to be forgotten in a life-time – as you shall see.

'I don't suppose I had been entertaining those thoughts more than five minutes when something induced me to look over my shoulder. I can't think it was a noise; the snow deadened all the sounds. Something it must have been, some sort of signal reaching my consciousness. Anyway, I turned my head, and there was the event approaching me, not that I knew it or had the slightest premonition. All I saw in the distance were two figures approaching in the moonlight. One of them was our Tomassov. The dark mass behind him which moved across my sight were the horses which his orderly was leading away. Tomassov was a very familiar appearance, in long boots, a tall figure ending in a pointed hood. But by his side advanced another figure. I mistrusted my eyes at first. It was amazing! It had a shining crested helmet on its head and was muffled up in a white cloak. The cloak was not as white as snow. Nothing in the world is. It was white more like mist, with an aspect that was ghostly and martial to an extraordinary degree. It was as if Tomassov had got hold of the God of War himself. I could see at once that he was leading this resplendent vision by the arm. Then I

saw that he was holding it up. While I stared and stared, they crept on
– for indeed they were creeping – and at last they crept into the light
of our bivouac fire and passed beyond the log I was sitting on. The
blaze played on the helmet. It was extremely battered and the frost-
bitten face, full of sores, under it was framed in bits of mangy fur. No
God of War this, but a French officer. The great white cuirassier's
cloak was torn, burnt full of holes. His feet were wrapped up in old
sheepskins over remnants of boots. They looked monstrous and he
tottered on them, sustained by Tomassov who lowered him most
carefully on to the log on which I sat.

'My amazement knew no bounds.

' "You have brought in a prisoner," I said to Tomassov, as if I could
not believe my eyes.

'You must understand that unless they surrendered in large bodies
we made no prisoners. What would have been the good? Our Cossacks
either killed the stragglers or else let them alone, just as it happened.
It came really to the same thing in the end.

'Tomassov turned to me with a very troubled look.

' "He sprang up from the ground somewhere as I was leaving the
outpost," he said. "I believe he was making for it, for he walked
blindly into my horse. He got hold of my leg and of course none of
our chaps dared touch him then."

' "He had a narrow escape," I said.

' "He didn't appreciate it," said Tomassov, looking even more
troubled than before. "He came along holding to my stirrup leather.
That's what made me so late. He told me he was a staff officer; and
then talking in a voice such, I suppose, as the damned alone use, a
croaking of rage and pain, he said he had a favour to beg of me. A
supreme favour. Did I understand him, he asked in a sort of fiendish
whisper.

' "Of course I told him that I did. I said: *oui, je vous comprends*."

' "Then," said he, "do it. Now! At once – in the pity of your heart."

'Tomassov ceased and stared queerly at me above the head of the
prisoner.

'I said, "What did he mean?"

' "That's what I asked him," answered Tomassov in a dazed tone,
"and he said that he wanted me to do him the favour to blow his
brains out. As a fellow soldier," he said. "As a man of feeling – as –
as a humane man."

'The prisoner sat between us like an awful gashed mummy as to
the face, a martial scarecrow, a grotesque horror of rags and dirt, with
awful living eyes, full of vitality, full of unquenchable fire, in a body
of horrible affliction, a skeleton at the feast of glory. And suddenly
those shining unextinguishable eyes of his became fixed upon Tomas-

sov. He, poor fellow, fascinated, returned the ghastly stare of a suffering soul in that mere husk of a man. The prisoner croaked at him in French.

' "I recognize, you know. You are her Russian youngster. You were very grateful. I call on you to pay the debt. Pay it, I say, with one liberating shot. You are a man of honour. I have not even a broken sabre. All my being recoils from my own degradation. You know me."

'Tomassov said nothing.

' "Haven't you got the soul of a warrior?" the Frenchman asked in an angry whisper, but with something of a mocking intention in it.

' "I don't know," said poor Tomassov.

'What a look of contempt that scarecrow gave him out of his unquenchable eyes. He seemed to live only by the force of infuriated and impotent despair. Suddenly he gave a gasp and fell forward writhing in the agony of cramp in all his limbs; a not unusual effect of the heat of a camp-fire. It resembled the application of some horrible torture. But he tried to fight against the pain at first. He only moaned low while we bent over him so as to prevent him rolling into the fire, and muttered feverishly at intervals: "*Tuez moi, tuez moi . . .*" till, vanquished by the pain, he screamed in agony, time after time, each cry bursting out through his compressed lips.

'The adjutant woke up on the other side of the fire and started swearing awfully at the beastly row that Frenchman was making.

' "What's this? More of your infernal humanity, Tomassov," he yelled at us. "Why don't you have him thrown out of this to the devil on the snow?"

'As we paid no attention to his shouts, he got up, cursing shockingly, and went away to another fire. Presently the French officer became easier. We propped him up against the log and sat silent on each side of him till the bugles started their call at the first break of day. The big flame, kept up all through the night, paled on the livid sheet of snow, while the frozen air all round rang with the brazen notes of cavalry trumpets. The Frenchman's eyes, fixed in a glassy stare, which for a moment made us hope that he had died quietly sitting there between us two, stirred slowly to right and left, looking at each of our faces in turn. Tomassov and I exchanged glances of dismay. Then De Castel's voice, unexpected in its renewed strength and ghastly self-possession, made us shudder inwardly.

' "*Bonjour, Messieurs.*"

'His chin dropped on his breast. Tomassov addressed me in Russian.

' "It is he, the man himself . . ." I nodded and Tomassov went on in a tone of anguish: "Yes, he! Brilliant, accomplished, envied by men, loved by that woman – this horror – this miserable thing that cannot die. Look at his eyes. It's terrible."

'I did not look, but I understood what Tomassov meant. We could do nothing for him. This avenging winter of fate held both the fugitives and the pursuers in its iron grip. Compassion was but a vain word before that unrelenting destiny. I tried to say something about a convoy being no doubt collected in the village – but I faltered at the mute glance Tomassov gave me. We knew what those convoys were like: appalling mobs of hopeless wretches driven on by the butts of Cossacks' lances, back to the frozen inferno, with their faces set away from their homes.

'Our two squadrons had been formed along the edge of the forest. The minutes of anguish were passing. The Frenchman suddenly struggled to his feet. We helped him almost without knowing what we were doing.

' "Come," he said, in measured tones. "This is the moment." He paused for a long time, then with the same distinctness went on: "On my word of honour, all faith is dead in me."

'His voice lost suddenly its self-possession. After waiting a little while he added in a murmur: "And even my courage . . . Upon my honour."

'Another long pause ensued before, with a great effort, he whispered hoarsely: "Isn't this enough to move a heart of stone? Am I to go on my knees to you?"

'Again a deep silence fell upon the three of us. Then the French officer flung his last word of anger at Tomassov.

' "Milksop!"

'Not a feature of the poor fellow moved. I made up my mind to go and fetch a couple of our troopers to lead that miserable prisoner away to the village. There was nothing else for it. I had not moved six paces towards the group of horses and orderlies in front of our squadron when . . . but you have guessed it. Of course. And I, too, I guessed it, for I give you my word that the report of Tomassov's pistol was the most insignificant thing imaginable. The snow certainly does absorb sound. It was a mere feeble pop. Of the orderlies holding our horses I don't think one turned his head round.

'Yes. Tomassov had done it. Destiny had led that De Castel to the man who could understand him perfectly. But it was poor Tomassov's lot to be the predestined victim. You know what the world's justice and mankind's judgment are like. They fell heavily on him with a sort of inverted hypocrisy. Why! That brute of an adjutant, himself, was the first to set going horrified allusions to the shooting of a prisoner in cold blood! Tomassov was not dismissed from the service of course. But after the siege of Dantzig he asked for permission to resign from the army, and went away to bury himself in the depths of his province, where a vague story of some dark deed clung to him for years.

'Yes. He had done it. And what was it? One warrior's soul paying its debt a hundredfold to another warrior's soul by releasing it from a fate worse than death – the loss of all faith and courage. You may look on it in that way. I don't know. And perhaps poor Tomassov did not know himself. But I was the first to approach that appalling dark group on the snow: the Frenchman extended rigidly on his back, Tomassov kneeling on one knee rather nearer to the feet than to the Frenchman's head. He had taken his cap off and his hair shone like gold in the light drift of flakes that had begun to fall. He was stooping over the dead in a tenderly contemplative attitude. And his young, ingenuous face, with lowered eyelids, expressed no grief, no sternness, no horror – but was set in the repose of a profound, as if endless and endlessly silent, meditation.'

Arthur Conan Doyle

How the Brigadier was Tempted by the Devil

THE spring is at hand, my friends. I can see the little green spear-heads breaking out once more upon the chestnut trees, and the café tables have all been moved into the sunshine. It is more pleasant to sit there, and yet I do not wish to tell my little stories to the whole town. You have heard my doings as a lieutenant, as a squadron officer, as a colonel, as the chief of a brigade. But now I suddenly become something higher and more important. I become history.

If you have read those closing years of the life of the Emperor which were spent in the Island of St Helena, you will remember that, again and again, he implored permission to send out one single letter which should be unopened by those who held him. Many times he made this request, and even went so far as to promise that he would provide for his own wants and cease to be an expense to the British Government if it were granted to him. But his guardians knew that he was a terrible man, this pale, fat gentleman in the straw hat, and they dared not grant him what he asked. Many have wondered who it was to whom he could have had anything so secret to say. Some have supposed that it was to his wife, and some that it was to his father-in-law; some that it was to the Emperor Alexander, and some to Marshal Soult. What will you think of me, my friends, when I tell you it was to me – to me, the Brigadier Gerard – that the Emperor wished to write? Yes, humble as you see me, with only my 100 francs a month of half-pay between me and hunger, it is none the less true that I was always on the Emperor's mind, and that he would have given his left hand for five minutes' talk with me. I will tell you tonight how this came about.

It was after the Battle of Fére-Champenoise where the conscripts in their blouses and their sabots made such a fine stand, that we, the more long-headed of us, began to understand that it was all over with us. Our reserve ammunition had been taken in the battle, and we were left with silent guns and empty caissons. Our cavalry, too, was in a deplorable condition, and my own brigade had been destroyed in the charge at Craonne. Then came the news that the enemy had taken Paris, that the citizens had mounted the white cockade; and finally, most terrible of all, that Marmont and his corps had gone over to the Bourbons. We looked at each other and asked how many more of our generals were going to turn against us. Already there were Jourdan, Marmont, Murat, Bernadotte, and Jomini – though nobody minded much about Jomini, for his pen was always sharper than his sword. We had been ready to fight Europe, but it looked now as though we were to fight Europe and half of France as well.

We had come to Fontainebleau by a long, forced march, and there we were assembled, the poor remnants of us, the corps of Ney, the corps of my cousin Gerard, and the corps of Macdonald: twenty-five thousand in all, with seven thousand of the guard. But we had our prestige, which was worth fifty thousand, and our Emperor, who was worth fifty thousand more. He was always among us, serene, smiling, confident, taking his snuff and playing with his little riding-whip. Never in the days of his greatest victories have I admired him as much as I did during the Campaign of France.

One evening I was with a few of my officers, drinking a glass of wine of Suresnes. I mention that it was wine of Suresnes just to show you that times were not very good with us. Suddenly I was disturbed by a message from Berthier that he wished to see me. When I speak of my old comrades-in-arms, I will, with your permission, leave out all the fine foreign titles which they had picked up during the wars. They are excellent for a Court, but you never heard them in the camp, for we could not afford to do away with our Ney, our Rapp, or our Soult – names which were as stirring to our ears as the blare of our trumpets blowing the reveille. It was Berthier, then, who sent to say that he wished to see me.

He had a suite of rooms at the end of the gallery of Francis the First, not very far from those of the Emperor. In the ante-chamber were waiting two men whom I knew well: Colonel Despienne, of the 57th of the line, and Captain Tremeau, of the Voltigeurs. They were both old soldiers – Tremeau had carried a musket in Egypt – and they were also both famous in the army for their courage and their skill with weapons. Tremeau had become a little stiff in the wrist, but Despienne was capable at his best of making me exert myself. He was a tiny fellow, about three inches short of the proper height for a man – he was exactly three inches shorter than myself – but both with the sabre and with the small-sword he had several times almost held his own against me when we used to exhibit at Verron's Hall of Arms in the Palais Royal. You may think that it made us sniff something in the wind when we found three such men called together into one room. You cannot see the lettuce and dressing without suspecting a salad.

'Name of a pipe!' said Tremeau, in his barrack-room fashion. 'Are we then expecting three champions of the Bourbons?'

To all of us the idea appeared not improbable. Certainly in the whole army we were the very three who might have been chosen to meet them.

'The Prince of Neufchâtel desires to speak with the Brigadier Gerard,' said a footman, appearing at the door.

In I went, leaving my two companions consumed with impatience behind me. It was a small room, but very gorgeously furnished. Berthier was seated opposite to me at a little table, with a pen in his hand and a note-book open before him. He was looking weary and slovenly – very different from that Berthier who used to give the fashion to the army, and who had so often set us poorer officers tearing our hair by trimming his pelisse with fur one campaign, and with grey astrakhan the next. On his clean-shaven, comely face there was an expression of trouble, and he looked at me as I entered his chamber in a way which had in it something furtive and displeasing.

'Chief of Brigade Gerard!' said he.

'At your service, your Highness!' I answered.

'I must ask you, before I go further, to promise me, upon your honour as a gentleman and a soldier, that what is about to pass between us shall never be mentioned to any third person.'

My word, this was a fine beginning! I had no choice but to give the promise required.

'You must know, then, that it is all over with the Emperor,' said he, looking down at the table and speaking very slowly, as if he had a hard task in getting out the words. 'Jourdan at Rouen and Marmont at Paris have both mounted the white cockade, and it is rumoured that Talleyrand has talked Ney into doing the same. It is evident that further resistance is useless, and that it can only bring misery upon our country. I wish to ask you, therefore, whether you are prepared to join me in laying hands upon the Emperor's person, and bringing the war to a conclusion by delivering him over to the allies?'

I assure you that when I heard this infamous proposition put forward by the man who had been the earliest friend of the Emperor, and who had received greater favours from him than any of his followers, I could only stand and stare at him in amazement. For his part he tapped his pen-handle against his teeth, and looked at me with a slanting head.

'Well?' he asked.

'I am a little deaf on one side,' said I, coldly. 'There are some things which I cannot hear. I beg that you will permit me to return to my duties.'

'Nay, but you must not be headstrong,' rising up and laying his hand upon my shoulder. 'You are aware that the Senate has declared against Napoleon, and that the Emperor Alexander refuses to treat with him.'

'Sir,' I cried, with passion, 'I would have you know that I do not care the dregs of a wine-glass for the Senate or for the Emperor Alexander either.'

'Then for what do you care?'

'For my own honour and for the service of my glorious master, the Emperor Napoleon.'

'That is all very well,' said Berthier, peevishly, shrugging his shoulders. 'Facts are facts, and as men of the world, we must look them in the face. Are we to stand against the will of the nation? Are we to have civil war on the top of all our misfortunes? And besides, we are thinning away. Every hour comes the news of fresh desertions. We have still time to make our peace, and, indeed, to earn the highest regard, by giving up the Emperor.'

I shook so with passion that my sabre clattered against my thigh.

'Sir,' I cried, 'I never thought to have seen the day when a Marshal of France would have so far degraded himself as to put forward such a proposal. I leave you to your own conscience; but as for me, until I have the Emperor's own order, there shall always be the sword of Etienne Gerard between his enemies and himself.'

I was so moved by my own words and by the fine position which I had taken up, that my voice broke, and I could hardly refrain from tears. I should have liked the whole army to have seen me as I stood with my head so proudly erect and my hand upon my heart proclaiming my devotion to the Emperor in his adversity. It was one of the supreme moments of my life.

'Very good,' said Berthier, ringing a bell for the lackey. 'You will show the Chief of Brigade Gerard into the salon.'

The footman led me into an inner room, where he desired me to be seated. For my own part, my only desire was to get away, and I could not understand why they should wish to detain me. When one has had no change of uniform during a whole winter's campaign, one does not feel at home in a palace.

I had been there about a quarter of an hour when the footman opened the door again, and in came Colonel Despienne. Good heavens, what a sight he was! His face was as white as a guardsman's gaiters, his eyes projecting, the veins swollen upon his forehead, and every hair of his moustache bristling like those of an angry cat. He was too angry to speak, and could only shake his hands at the ceiling and make a gurgling in his throat. 'Parricide! Viper!' those were the words that I could catch as he stamped up and down the room.

Of course it was evident to me that he had been subjected to the same infamous proposals as I had, and that he had received them in the same spirit. His lips were sealed to me, as mine were to him, by the promise which we had taken, but I contented myself with muttering 'Atrocious! Unspeakable!' – so that he might know that I was in agreement with him.

Well, we were still there, he striding furiously up and down, and I seated in the corner, when suddenly a most extraordinary uproar broke out in the room which we had just quitted. There was a snarling, worrying growl, like that of a fierce dog which has got his grip. Then came a crash and a voice calling for help. In we rushed, the two of us, and, my faith, we were none too soon.

Old Tremeau and Berthier were rolling together upon the floor, with the table upon the top of them. The Captain had one of his great, skinny yellow hands upon the Marshal's throat, and already his face was lead-coloured, and his eyes were starting from their sockets. As to Tremeau, he was beside himself, with foam upon the corners of his lips, and such a frantic expression upon him that I am convinced, had we not loosened his iron grip, finger by finger, that it would never have relaxed while the Marshal lived. His nails were white with the power of his grasp.

'I have been tempted by the devil!' he cried, as he staggered to his feet. 'Yes, I have been tempted by the devil!'

As to Berthier, he could only lean against the wall, and pant for a couple of minutes, putting his hands up to his throat and rolling his head about. Then, with an angry gesture, he turned to the heavy blue curtain which hung behind his chair.

The curtain was torn to one side and the Emperor stepped out into the room. We sprang to the salute, we three old soldiers, but it was all like a scene in a dream to us, and our eyes were as far out as Berthier's had been. Napoleon was dressed in his green-coated chasseur uniform, and he held his little, silver-headed switch in his hand. He looked at us each in turn, with a smile upon his face – that frightful smile in which neither eyes nor brow joined – and each in turn had, I believe, a pringling on his skin, for that was the effect which the Emperor's gaze had upon most of us. Then we walked across to Berthier and put his hand upon his shoulder.

'You must not quarrel with blows, my dear Prince,' said he; 'they are your title to nobility.' He spoke in that soft, caressing manner which he could assume. There was no one who could make the French tongue sound so pretty as the Emperor, and no one who could make it more harsh and terrible.

'I believe he would have killed me,' cried Berthier, still rolling his head about.

'Tut, tut! I should have come to your help had these officers not heard your cries. But I trust that you are not really hurt!' He spoke with earnestness, for he was in truth very fond of Berthier – more so than of any man, unless it were of poor Duroc.

Berthier laughed, though not with a very good grace.

'It is new for me to receive my injuries from French hands,' said he.

'And yet it was in the cause of France,' returned the Emperor. Then, turning to us, he took old Tremeau by the ear. 'Ah, old grumbler,' said he, 'you were one of my Egyptian grenadiers, were you not, and had your musket of honour at Marengo. I remember you very well, my good friend. So the old fires are not yet extinguished! They still burn up when you think that your Emperor is wronged. And you, Colonel Despienne, you would not even listen to the tempter. And you, Gerard, your faithful sword is ever to be between me and my enemies. Well, well, I have had some traitors about me, but now at last we are beginning to see who are the true men.'

You can fancy, my friends, the thrill of joy which it gave us when the greatest man in the whole world spoke to us in this fashion. Tremeau shook until I thought he would have fallen, and the tears ran down his gigantic moustache. If you had not seen it, you could never believe the influence which the Emperor had upon those coarse-grained, savage old veterans.

'Well, my faithful friends,' said he, 'if you will follow me into this room, I will explain to you the meaning of this little farce which we have been acting. I beg, Berthier, that you will remain in this chamber, and so make sure that no one interrupts us.'

It was new for us to be doing business, with a Marshal of France as sentry at the door. However, we followed the Emperor as we were ordered, and he led us into the recess of the window, gathering us around him and sinking his voice as he addressed us.

'I have picked you out of the whole army,' said he, 'as being not only the most formidable but also the most faithful of my soldiers. I was convinced that you were all three men who would never waver in your fidelity to me. If I have ventured to put that fidelity to the proof, and to watch you while attempts were at my orders made upon your honour, it was only because, in the days when I have found the blackest treason amongst my own flesh and blood, it is necessary that I should be doubly circumspect. Suffice it that I am well convinced now that I can rely upon your valour.'

'To the death, sire!' cried Tremeau, and we both repeated it after him.

Napoleon drew us all yet a little closer to him, and sank his voice still lower.

'What I say to you now I have said to no one – not to my wife or my brothers; only to you. It is all up with us, my friends. We have come to our last rally. The game is finished, and we must make provision accordingly.'

My heart seemed to have changed to a nine-pounder ball as I listened to him. We had hoped against hope, but now when he, the man who was always serene and who always had reserves – when he, in the quiet, impassive voice of his, said that everything was over, we realized that the clouds had shut for ever, and the last gleam gone. Tremeau snarled and gripped at his sabre, Despienne ground his teeth, and for my own part I threw out my chest and clicked my heels to show the Emperor that there were some spirits which could rise to adversity.

'My papers and my fortune must be secured,' whispered the Emperor. 'The whole course of the future may depend upon my having them safe. They are our base for the next attempt – for I am very sure that these poor Bourbons would find that my footstool is too large to make a throne for them. Where am I to keep these precious things? My belongings will be searched – so will the houses of my supporters. They must be secured and concealed by men whom I can trust with that which is more precious to me than my life. Out of the whole of France, you are those whom I have chosen for this sacred trust.

'In the first place, I will tell you what these papers are. You shall not say that I have made you blind agents in the matter. They are the official proof of my divorce from Josephine, of my legal marriage to Marie Louise, and of the birth of my son and heir, the King of Rome. If we cannot prove each of these, the future claim of my family to the throne of France falls to the ground. Then there are securities to the value of forty millions of francs – an immense sum, my friends, but of no more value than this riding-switch when compared to the other papers of which I have spoken. I tell you these things that you may realize the enormous importance of the task which I am committing to your care. Listen, now, while I inform you where you are to get these papers, and what you are to do with them.

'They were handed over to my trusty friend, the Countess Walewski, at Paris, this morning. At five o'clock she starts for Fontainebleau in her blue berline. She should reach here between half-past nine and ten. The papers will be concealed in the berline, in a hiding-place which none know but herself. She has been warned that her carriage will be stopped outside the town by three mounted officers, and she will hand the packet over to your care. You are the younger man, Gerard, but you are of the senior grade. I confide to your care this amethyst ring, which you will show the lady as a token of your mission, and which you will leave with her as a receipt for her papers.

'Having received the packet, you will ride with it into the forest as far as the ruined dove-house – the Colombier. It is possible that I may meet you there – but if it seems to me to be dangerous, I will send my body-servant, Mustapha, whose directions you may take as being mine. There is no roof to the Colombier, and tonight will be a full moon. At the right of the entrance you will find three spades leaning against the wall. With these you will dig a hole three feet deep in the north-eastern corner – that is, in the corner to the left of the door, and nearest to Fontainebleau. Having buried the papers, you will replace the soil with great care, and you will then report to me at the palace.'

These were the Emperor's directions, but given with an accuracy and minuteness of detail such as no one but himself could put into an order. When he had finished, he made us swear to keep his secret as long as he lived, and as long as the papers should remain buried. Again and again he made us swear it before he dismissed us from his presence.

Colonel Despienne had quarters at the 'Sign of the Pheasant,' and it was there that we supped together. We were all three men who had been trained to take the strangest turns of fortune as part of our daily life and business, yet we were all flushed and moved by the extraordinary interview which we had had, and by the thought of the great adventure which lay before us. For my own part, it had been my fate three several times to take my orders from the lips of the Emperor himself, but neither the incident of the Ajaccio murderers nor the famous ride which I made to Paris appeared to offer such opportunities as this new and most intimate commission.

'If things go right with the Emperor,' said Despienne, 'we shall all live to be marshals yet.'

We drank with him to our future cocked hats and our bâtons.

It was agreed between us that we should make our way separately to our rendezvous, which was to be the first milestone upon the Paris road. In this way we should avoid the gossip which might get about if three men who were so well known were to be seen riding out together. My little Violette had cast a shoe that morning, and the farrier was at work upon her when I returned, so that my comrades were already there when I arrived at the trysting-place. I had taken with me not only my sabre, but also my new pair of English rifled pistols, with a mallet for knocking in the charges. They had cost me a hundred and fifty francs at Trouvel's, in the Rue de Rivoli, but they would carry far further and straighter than the others. It was with one of them that I had saved old Bouvet's life at Leipzig.

The night was cloudless, and there was a brilliant moon behind us, so that we always had three black horsemen riding down the white road in front of us. The country is so thickly wooded, however, that we could not see very far. The great palace clock had already struck ten, but there was no sign of the Countess. We began to fear that something might have prevented her from starting.

And then suddenly we heard her in the distance. Very faint at first were the birr of wheels and the tat-tat-tat of the horses' feet. Then they grew louder and clearer and louder yet, until a pair of yellow lanterns swung round the curve, and in their light we saw the two big brown horses tearing along, the high, blue carriage at the back of them. The postilion pulled them up panting and foaming within a few yards of us. In a moment we were at the window and had raised our hands in a salute to the beautiful pale face which looked out at us.

'We are the three officers of the Emperor, madame,' said I, in a low voice, leaning my face down to the open window. 'You have already been warned that we should wait upon you.'

The Countess had a very beautiful, cream-tinted complexion of a sort which I particularly admire, but she grew whiter and whiter as she looked up at me. Harsh lines deepened upon her face until she seemed, even as I looked at her, to turn from youth into age.

'It is evident to me,' she said, 'that you are three impostors.'

If she had struck me across the face with her delicate hand she could not have startled me more. It was not her words only, but the bitterness with which she hissed them out.

'Indeed, madame,' said I. 'You do us less than justice. These are the Colonel Despienne and Captain Tremeau. For myself, my name is Brigadier Gerard, and I have only to mention it to assure anyone who has heard of me that—'

'Oh, you villains!' she interrupted. 'You think that because I am only a woman I am very easily to be hoodwinked! You miserable impostors!'

I looked at Despienne, who had turned white with anger, and at Tremeau, who was tugging at his moustache.

'Madame,' said I, coldly, 'when the Emperor did us the honour to entrust us with this mission, he gave me this amethyst ring as a token. I had not thought that three honourable gentlemen would have needed such corroboration, but I can only confute your unworthy suspicions by placing it in your hands.'

She held it up in the light of the carriage lamp, and the most dreadful expression of grief and of horror contorted her face.

'It is his!' she screamed, and then, 'Oh, my God, what have I done? What have I done?'

I felt that something terrible had befallen. 'Quick, madame, quick?' I cried. 'Give us the papers!'

'I have already given them.'

'Given them! To whom?'

'To three officers.'

'When?'

'Within the half-hour.'

'Where are they?'

'God help me, I do not know. They stopped the berline, and I handed them over to them without hesitation, thinking that they had come from the Emperor.'

It was a thunder-clap. But those are the moments when I am at my finest.

'You remain here,' said I, to my comrades. 'If three horsemen pass you, stop them at any hazard. The lady will describe them to you. I will be with you presently.' One shake of the bridle, and I was flying into Fontainebleau as only Violette could have carried me. At the palace I flung myself off, rushed up the stairs, brushed aside the lackeys who would have stopped me, and pushed my way into the Emperor's own cabinet. He and Macdonald were busy with pencil and compasses over a chart. He looked up with an angry frown at my sudden entry, but his face changed colour when he saw that it was I.

'You can leave us, Marshal,' said he, and then, the instant the door was closed: 'What news about the papers?'

'They are gone!' said I, and in a few curt words I told him what had happened. His face was calm, but I saw the compasses quiver in his hand.

'You must recover them, Gerard!' he cried. 'The destinies of my dynasty are at stake. Not a moment is to be lost! To horse, sir, to horse!'

'Who are they, sire?'

'I cannot tell. I am surrounded with treason. But they will take them to Paris. To whom should they carry them but to the villain Talleyrand? Yes, yes, they are on the Paris road, and may yet be overtaken. With the three best mounts in my stables and—'

I did not wait to hear the end of the sentence. I was already clattering down the stairs. I am sure that five minutes had not passed before I was galloping Violette out of the town with the bridle of one of the Emperor's own Arab chargers in either hand. They wished me to take three, but I should have never dared to look my Violette in the face again. I feel that the spectacle must have been superb when I dashed up to my comrades and pulled the horses on to their haunches in the moonlight.

'No one has passed?'

'No one.'

'Then they are on the Paris road. Quick! Up and after them!'

They did not take long, those good soldiers. In a flash they were upon the Emperor's horses, and their own left masterless by the roadside. Then away we went upon our long chase, I in the centre, Despienne upon my right, and Tremeau a little behind, for he was the heavier man. Heavens, how we galloped! The twelve flying hoofs roared and roared along the hard, smooth road. Poplars and moon, black bars and silver streaks, for mile after mile our course lay along the same chequered track, with our shadows in front and our dust behind. We could hear the rasping of bolts and the creaking of shutters from the cottages as we thundered past them, but we were only three dark blurs upon the road by the time that the folk could look after us. It was just striking midnight as we raced into Corbail; but an hostler with a bucket in either hand was throwing his black shadow across the golden fan which was cast from the open door of the inn.

'Three riders!' I gasped. 'Have they passed?'

'I have just been watering their horses,' said he. 'I should think they—'

'On, on, my friends!' and away we flew, striking fire from the cobblestones of the little town. A gendarme tried to stop us, but his voice was drowned by our rattle and clatter. The houses slid past, and we were out on the country road again, with a clear twenty miles between ourselves and Paris. How could they escape us, with the finest horses in France behind them? Not one of the three had turned a hair, but Violette was always a head and shoulders to the front. She was going within herself too, and I knew by the spring of her that I had only to let her stretch herself, and the Emperor's horses would see the colour of her tail.

'There they are!' cried Despienne.

'We have them!' growled Tremeau.

'On, comrades, on!' I shouted, once more.

A long stretch of white road lay before us in the moonlight. Far away down it we could see three cavaliers, lying low upon their horses' necks. Every instant they grew larger and clearer as we gained upon them. I could see quite plainly that the two upon either side were wrapped in mantles and rode upon chestnut horses, whilst the man between them was dressed in a chasseur uniform and mounted upon a grey. They were keeping abreast, but it was easy enough to see from the way in which he gathered his legs for each spring that the centre horse was far the fresher of the three. And the rider appeared to be the leader of the party, for we continually saw the glint of his face in the moonshine as he looked back to measure the distance between us. At first it was only a glimmer, then it was cut across with a moustache, and at last when we began to feel their dust in our throats I could give a name to my man.

'Halt, Colonel de Montluc!' I shouted. 'Halt, in the Emperor's name!'

I had known him for years as a daring officer and an unprincipled rascal. Indeed, there was a score between us, for he had shot my friend, Treville, at Warsaw, pulling his trigger, as some said, a good second before the drop of the handkerchief.

Well, the words were hardly out of my mouth when his two comrades wheeled round and fired their pistols at us. I heard Despienne give a terrible cry, and at the same instant both Tremeau and I let drive at the same man. He fell forward with his hands swinging on each side of his horse's neck. His comrade spurred on to Tremeau, sabre in hand, and I heard the crash which comes when a strong cut is met by a stronger parry. For my own part I never turned my head, but I touched Violette with the spur for the first time and flew after the leader. That he should leave his comrades and fly was proof enough that I should leave mine and follow.

He had gained a couple of hundred paces, but the good little mare set that right before we could have passed two milestones. It was in vain that he spurred and thrashed like a gunner driver on a soft road. His hat flew off with his exertions, and his bald head gleamed in the moonshine. But do what he might, he still heard the rattle of the hoofs growing louder and louder behind him. I could not have been twenty yards from him, and the shadow head was touching the shadow haunch, when he turned with a curse in his saddle and emptied both his pistols, one after the other, into Violette.

I have been wounded myself so often that I have to stop and think before I can tell you the exact number of times. I have been hit by musket balls, by pistol bullets, and by bursting shells, besides being pierced by bayonet, lance, sabre, and finally by a brad-awl, which was the most painful of any. Yet out of all these injuries I have never known the same deadly sickness as came over me when I felt the poor, silent, patient creature, which I had come to love more than anything in the world except my mother and the Emperor, reel and stagger beneath me. I pulled by second pistol from my holster and fired point-blank between the fellow's broad shoulders. He slashed his horse across the flank with his whip, and for a moment I thought that I had missed him. But then on the green of his chasseur jacket I saw an ever-widening black smudge, and he began to sway in his saddle, very slightly at first, but more and more with every bound, until at last over he went, with his foot caught in the stirrup, and his shoulders thud-thud-thudding along the road, until the drag was too much for the tired horse, and I closed my hand upon the foam-spattered bridle-chain. As I pulled him up it eased the stirrup leather, and the spurred heel clinked loudly as it fell.

'Your papers!' I cried, springing from my saddle. 'This instant!'

But even as I said it, the huddle of the green body and the fantastic sprawl of the limbs in the moonlight told me clearly enough that it was all over with him. My bullet had passed through his heart, and it was only his own iron will which had held him so long in the saddle. He had lived hard, this Montluc, and I will do him justice to say that he died hard also.

But it was the papers – always the papers – of which I thought. I opened his tunic and I felt in his shirt. Then I searched his holsters and his sabre-tasche. Finally I dragged off his boots, and undid his horse's girth so as to hunt under the saddle. There was not a nook or crevice which I did not ransack. It was useless. They were not upon him.

When this stunning blow came upon me I could have sat down by the roadside and wept. Fate seemed to be fighting against me, and that is an enemy from whom even a gallant hussar might not be ashamed to flinch. I stood with my arm over the neck of my poor wounded Violette, and I tried to think it all out, that I might act in the wisest way. I was aware that the Emperor had no great respect for my wits, and I longed to show him that he had done me an injustice. Montluc had not the papers. And yet Montluc had sacrificed his companions in order to make his escape. I could make nothing of that. On the other hand, it was clear that, if he had not got them, one or other of his comrades had. One of them was certainly dead. The other I had left fighting with Tremeau, and if he escaped from the old swordsman he had still to pass me. Clearly, my work lay behind me.

I hammered fresh charges into my pistols after I had turned this over in my head. Then I put them back in the holsters, and I examined my little mare, she jerking her head and cocking her ears the while, as if to tell me that an old soldier like herself did not make a fuss about a scratch or two. The first shot had merely grazed her off-shoulder, leaving a skin-mark, as if she had brushed a wall. The second was more serious. It had passed through the muscle of her neck, but already it had ceased to bleed. I reflected that if she weakened I could mount Montluc's grey, and meanwhile I led him along beside us, for he was a fine horse, worth fifteen hundred francs at the least, and it seemed to me that no one had a better right to him than I.

Well, I was all impatience now to get back to the others, and I had just given Violette her head, when suddenly I saw something glimmering in a field by the roadside. It was the brass-work upon the chasseur hat which had flown from Montluc's head; and at the sight of it a thought made me jump in the saddle. How could the hat have flown off? With its weight, would it not have simply dropped? And here it lay, fifteen paces from the roadway! Of course, he must have thrown it off when he had made sure that I would overtake him. And if he threw it off – I did not stop to reason any more, but sprang from the mare with my heart beating the *pas-de-charge*. Yes, it was all right this time. There, in the crown of the hat was stuffed a roll of papers in a parchment wrapper bound round with yellow ribbon. I pulled it out with the one hand and, holding the hat in the other, I danced for joy in the moonlight. The Emperor would see that he had not made a mistake when he put his affairs into the charge of Etienne Gerard.

I had a safe pocket on the inside of my tunic just over my heart, where I kept a few little things which were dear to me, and into this I thrust my precious roll. Then I sprang upon Violette, and was pushing forward to see what had become of Tremeau, when I saw a horseman riding across the field in the distance. At the same instant I heard the sound of hoofs approaching me, and there in the moonlight was the Emperor upon his white charger, dressed in his grey overcoat and his three-cornered hat, just as I had seen him so often upon the field of battle.

'Well!' he cried, in the sharp, sergeant-major way of his. 'Where are my papers?'

I spurred forward and presented them without a word. He broke the ribbon and ran his eyes rapidly over them. Then, as we sat our horses head to tail, he threw his left arm across me with his hand upon my shoulder. Yes, my friends, simple as you see me, I have been embraced by my great master.

'Gerard,' he cried, 'you are a marvel!'

I did not wish to contradict him, and it brought a flush of joy upon my cheeks to know that he had done me justice at last.

'Where is the thief, Gerard?' he asked.

'Dead, sire.'

'You killed him?'

'He wounded my horse, sire, and would have escaped had I not shot him.'

'Did you recognize him?'

'De Montluc is his name, sire – a Colonel of Chasseurs.'

'Tut,' said the Emperor. 'We have got the poor pawn, but the hand which plays the game is still out of our reach.' He sat in silent thought for a little, with his chin sunk upon his chest. 'Ah, Talleryand, Talleyrand,' I heard him mutter, 'if I had been in your place and you in mine, you would have crushed a viper when you held it under your heel. For five years I have known you for what you are, and yet I have let you live to sting me. Never mind, my brave,' he continued, turning to me, 'there will come a day of reckoning for everybody, and when it arrives, I promise you that my friends will be remembered as well as my enemies.'

'Sire,' said I, for I had had time for thought as well as he, 'if your plans about these papers have been carried to the ears of your enemies, I trust you do not think that it was owing to any indiscretion upon the part of myself or of my comrades.'

'It would be hardly reasonable for me to do so,' he answered, 'seeing that this plot was hatched in Paris, and that you only had your orders a few hours ago.'

'Then how—?'

'Enough,' he cried, sternly. 'You take an undue advantage of your position.'

HOW THE BRIGADIER WAS TRIED BY THE DEVIL

That was always the way with the Emperor. He would chat with you as with a friend and a brother, and then when he had wiled you into forgetting the gulf which lay between you, he would suddenly, with a word or with a look, remind you that it was as impassable as ever. When I have fondled my old hound until he has been encouraged to paw my knees, and I have then thrust him down again, it has made me think of the Emperor and his ways.

He reined his horse round, and I followed him in silence and with a heavy heart. But when he spoke again his words were enough to drive all thought of myself out of my mind.

'I could not sleep until I knew how you had fared,' said he. 'I have paid a price for my papers. There are not so many of my old soldiers left that I can afford to lose two in one night.'

When he said 'two' it turned me cold.

'Colonel Despienne was shot, sire,' I stammered.

'And Captain Tremeau cut down. Had I been a few minutes earlier, I might have saved him. The other escaped across the fields.'

I remembered that I had seen a horseman a moment before I had met the Emperor. He had taken to the fields to avoid me, but if I had known, and Violette been unwounded, the old soldier would not have gone unavenged. I was thinking sadly of his sword-play, and wondering whether it was his stiffening wrist which had been fatal to him, when Napoleon spoke again.

'Yes, Brigadier,' said he, 'you are now the only man who will know where these papers are concealed.'

It must have been imagination, my friends, but for an instant I may confess that it seemed to me that there was a tone in the Emperor's voice which was not altogether one of sorrow. But the dark thought had hardly time to form itself in my mind before he let me see that I was doing him an injustice.

'Yes, I have paid a price for my papers,' he said, and I heard them crackle as he put his hand up to his bosom. 'No man has ever had more faithful servants – no man since the beginning of the world.'

As he spoke we came upon the scene of the struggle. Colonel Despienne and the man whom we had shot lay together some distance down the road, while their horses grazed contentedly beneath the poplars. Captain Tremeau lay in front of us upon his back, with his arms and legs stretched out, and his sabre broken short off in his hand. His tunic was open, and a huge blood-clot hung like a dark handkerchief out of a slit in his white shirt. I could see the gleam of his clenched teeth from under his immense moustache.

The Emperor sprang from his horse and bent down over the dead man.

'He was with me since Rivoli,' said he, sadly. 'He was one of my old grumblers in Egypt.'

And the voice brought the man back from the dead. I saw his eyelids shiver. He twitched his arm, and moved the sword-hilt a few inches. He was trying to raise it in salute. Then the mouth opened, and the hilt tinkled down on to the ground.

'May we all die as gallantly,' said the Emperor, as he rose, and from my heart I added 'Amen.'

There was a farm within fifty yards of where we were standing, and the farmer, roused from his sleep by the clatter of hoofs and the cracking of pistols, had rushed out to the roadside. We saw him now, dumb with fear and astonishment, staring open-eyed at the Emperor. It was to him that we committed the care of the four dead men and of the horses also. For my own part, I thought it best to leave Violette with him and to take De Montluc's grey with me, for he could not refuse to give me back my own mare, whilst there might be difficulties about the other. Besides, my little friend's wound had to be considered, and we had a long return ride before us.

The Emperor did not at first talk much upon the way. Perhaps the deaths of Despienne and Tremeau still weighed heavily upon his spirits. He was always a reserved man, and in those times, when every hour brought him the news of some success of his enemies or defection of his friends, one could not expect him to be a merry companion. Nevertheless, when I reflected that he was carrying in his bosom those papers which he valued so highly, and which only a few hours ago appeared to be for ever lost, and when I further thought that it was I, Etienne Gerard, who had placed them there, I felt that I had deserved some little consideration. The same idea may have occurred to him, for when we had at last left the Paris high road, and had entered the forest, he began of his own accord to tell me that which I should have most liked to have asked him.

'As to the papers,' said he, 'I have already told you that there is no one now, except you and me, who knows where they are to be concealed. My Mameluke carried the spades to the pigeon-house, but I have told him nothing. Our plans, however, for bringing the packet from Paris have been formed since Monday. There were three in the secret, a woman and two men. The woman I would trust with my life; which of the two men has betrayed us I do not know, but I think that I may promise to find out.'

We were riding in the shadow of the trees at the time, and I could hear him slapping his riding-whip against his boot, and taking pinch after pinch of snuff, as was his way when he was excited.

'You wonder, no doubt,' said he, after a pause, 'why these rascals did not stop the carriage at Paris instead of at the entrance to Fontaine-bleau.'

In truth, the objection had not occurred to me, but I did not wish to appear to have less wits than he gave me credit for, so I answered that it was indeed surprising.

'Had they done so they would have made a public scandal, and run a chance of missing their end. Short of taking the berline to pieces, they could not have discovered the hiding-place. He planned it well – he could always plan well – and he chose his agents well also. But mine were the better.'

It is not for me to repeat to you, my friends, all that was said to me by the Emperor as we walked our horses amid the black shadows and through the moon-silvered glades of the great forest. Every word of it is impressed upon my memory, and before I pass away it is likely that I will place it all upon paper, so that others may read it in the days to come. He spoke freely of his past, and something also of his future; of the devotion of Macdonald, of the treason of Marmont, of the little King of Rome, concerning whom he talked with as much tenderness as any bourgeois father of a single child; and, finally, of his father-in-law, the Emperor of Austria, who would, he thought, stand between his enemies and himself. For myself, I dared not say a word, remembering how I had already brought a rebuke upon myself; but I rode by his side, hardly able to believe that this was indeed the great Emperor, the man whose glance sent a thrill through me, who was now pouring out his thoughts to me in short, eager sentences, the words rattling and racing like the hoofs of a galloping squadron. It is possible that, after the word-splittings and diplomacy of a Court, it was a relief to him to speak his mind to a plain soldier like myself.

In this way the Emperor and I – even after years it sends a flush of pride into my cheeks to be able to put those words together – the Emperor and I walked our horses through the Forest of Fontainebleau, until we came at last to the Colombier. The three spades were propped against the wall upon the right-hand side of the ruined door, and at the sight of them the tears sprang to my eyes as I thought of the hands for which they were intended. The Emperor seized one and I another.

'Quick!' said he. 'The dawn will be upon us before we get back to the palace.'

We dug the hole, and placing the papers in one of my pistol holsters to screen them from the damp, we laid them at the bottom and covered them up. We then carefully removed all marks of the ground having been disturbed, and we placed a large stone upon the top. I dare say that since the Emperor was a young gunner, and helped to train his pieces against Toulon, he had not worked so hard with his hands. He was mopping his forehead with his silk handkerchief long before we had come to the end of our task.

The first grey cold light of morning was stealing through the tree trunks when we came out together from the old pigeon-house. The Emperor laid his hand upon my shoulder as I stood ready to help him to mount.

'We have left the papers there,' said he, solemnly, 'and I desire that you shall leave all thought of them there also. Let the recollection of them pass entirely from your mind, to be revived only when you receive a direct order under my own hand and seal. From this time onwards you forget all that has passed.'

'I forget it, sire,' said I.

We rode together to the edge of the town, where he desired that I should separate from him. I had saluted, and was turning my horse, when he called me back.

'It is easy to mistake the points of the compass in the forest,' said he. 'Would you not say that it was in the north-eastern corner that we buried them?'

'Buried what, sire?'

'The papers, of course,' he cried, impatiently.

'What papers, sire?'

'Name of a name! Why, the papers that you have recovered for me.'

'I am really at a loss to know what your Majesty is talking about.'

He flushed with anger for a moment, and then burst out laughing.

'Very good, Brigadier!' he cried. 'I begin to believe that you are as good a diplomatist as you are a soldier, and I cannot say more than that.'

So that was my strange adventure in which I found myself the friend and confident agent of the Emperor. When he returned from Elba he refrained from digging up the papers until his position should be secure, and they still remained in the corner of the old pigeon-house after his exile to St Helena. It was at this time that he was desirous of getting them into the hands of his own supporters, and for that purpose he wrote me, as I afterwards learned, three letters, all of which were intercepted by his guardians. Finally, he offered to support himself and his own establishment – which he might very easily have done out of the gigantic sum which belonged to him – if they would only pass one of his letters unopened. This request was refused, and so, up to his death in '21, the papers still remained where I have told you. How they came to be dug up by Count Bertrand and myself, and who eventually obtained them, is a story which I would tell you, were it not that the end has not yet come.

Some day you will hear of those papers, and you will see how, after

HOW THE BRIGADIER WAS TRIED BY THE DEVIL

he has been so long in his grave, that great man can still set Europe shaking. When that day comes, you will think of Etienne Gerard, and you will tell your children that you have heard the story from the lips of the man who was the only one living of all who took part in that strange history – the man who was tempted by Marshal Berthier, who led that wild pursuit upon the Paris road, who was honoured by the embrace of the Emperor, and who rode with him by moonlight in the Forest of Fontainebleau. The buds are bursting and the birds are calling, my friends. You may find better things to do in the sunlight than listening to the stories of an old, broken soldier. And yet you may well treasure what I say, for the buds will have burst and the birds sung in many seasons before France will see such another ruler as he whose servants we were proud to be.

Ambrose Bierce

One of the Missing

JEROME SEARING, a private soldier of General Sherman's army, then confronting the enemy at and about Kenesaw Mountain, Georgia, turned back upon a small group of officers, with whom he had been talking in low tones, stepped across a light line of earthworks, and disappeared in a forest. None of the men in line behind the works had said a word to him, nor had he so much as nodded to them in passing, but all who saw understood that this brave man had been entrusted with some perilous duty. Jerome Searing, though a private, did not serve in the ranks; he was detailed for service at division headquarters, being borne upon the rolls as an orderly. 'Orderly' is a word covering a multitude of duties. An orderly may be a messenger, a clerk, an officer's servant – anything. He may perform services for which no provision is made in orders and army regulations. Their nature may depend upon his aptitude, upon favour, upon accident. Private Searing, an incomparable marksman, young – it is surprising how young we all were in those days – hardy, intelligent, and insensible to fear, was a scout. The general commanding his division was not content to obey orders blindly without knowing what was in his front, even when his command was not on detached service, but formed a fraction of the line of the army; nor was he satisfied to receive his knowledge of his *vis-à-vis* through the customary channels; he wanted to know more than he was apprised of by the corps commander and the collisions of pickets and skirmishers. Hence Jerome Searing – with his extraordinary daring, his woodcraft, his sharp eyes and truthful tongue. On this occasion his instructions were simple: to get as near the enemy's lines as possible and learn all that he could.

In a few moments he had arrived at the picket line, the men on duty there lying in groups of from two to four behind little banks of earth scooped out of the slight depression in which they lay, their rifles protruding from the green boughs with which they had masked their small defences. The forest extended without a break toward the front, so solemn and silent that only by an effort of the imagination could it be conceived as populous with armed men, alert and vigilant – a forest formidable with possibilities of battle. Pausing a moment in one of the rifle pits to apprise the men of his intention, Searing crept stealthily forward on his hands and knees and was soon lost to view in a dense thicket of underbrush.

'That is the last of him,' said one of the men; 'I wish I had his rifle; those fellows will hurt some of us with it.'

Searing crept on, taking advantage of every accident of ground and growth to give himself better cover. His eyes penetrated everywhere, his ears took note of every sound. He stilled his breathing, and at the cracking of a twig beneath his knee stopped his progress and hugged the earth. It was slow work, but not tedious; the danger made it exciting, but by no physical signs was the excitement manifest. His pulse was as regular, his nerves were as steady, as if he were trying to trap a sparrow.

'It seems a long time,' he thought, 'but I cannot have come very far; I am still alive.'

He smiled at his own method of estimating distance, and crept forward. A moment later he suddenly flattened himself upon the earth and lay motionless, minute after minute. Through a narrow opening in the bushes he had caught sight of a small mound of yellow clay – one of the enemy's rifle pits. After some little time he cautiously raised his head, inch by inch, then his body upon his hands, spread out on each side of him, all the while intently regarding the hillock of clay. In another moment he was upon his feet, rifle in hand, striding rapidly forward with little attempt at concealment. He had rightly interpreted the signs, whatever they were; the enemy was gone.

To assure himself beyond a doubt before going back to report upon so important a matter, Searing pushed forward across the line of abandoned pits, running from cover to cover in the more open forest, his eyes vigilant to discover possible stragglers. He came to the edge of a plantation – one of those forlorn, deserted homesteads of the last years of the war, upgrown with brambles, ugly with broken fences, and desolate with vacant buildings having blank apertures in place of doors and windows. After a keen reconnaissance from the safe seclusion of a clump of young pines, Searing ran lightly across a field and through an orchard to a small structure which stood apart from the other farm buildings, on a slight elevation, which he thought would enable him to overlook a large scope of country in the direction that he supposed the enemy to have taken in withdrawing. This building, which had originally consisted of a single room, elevated upon four posts about ten feet high, was now little more than a roof; the floor had fallen away, the joists and planks loosely piled on the ground below or resting on end at various angles, not wholly torn from their fastenings above. The supporting posts were themselves no longer vertical. It looked as if the whole edifice would go down at the touch of a finger. Concealing himself in the débris of joists and flooring, Searing looked across the open ground between his point of view and a spur of Kenesaw Mountain, a half mile away. A road leading up and across this spur was crowded with troops – the rear guard of the retiring enemy, their gun barrels gleaming in the morning sunlight.

Searing had now learned all that he could hope to know. It was his duty to return to his own command with all possible speed and report his discovery. But the grey column of infantry toiling up the mountain road was singularly tempting. His rifle – an ordinary 'Springfield', but fitted with a globe sight and hair trigger – would easily send its ounce and a quarter of lead hissing into their midst. That would probably not affect the duration and result of the war, but it is the business of a soldier to kill. It is also his pleasure if he is a good soldier. Searing cocked his rifle and 'set' the trigger.

But it was decreed from the beginning of time that Private Searing was not to murder anybody that bright summer morning, nor was the Confederate retreat to be announced by him. For countless ages events had been so matching themselves together in that wondrous mosaic to some parts of which, dimly discernible, we give the name of history, that the acts which he had in will would have marred the harmony of the pattern.

Some twenty-five years previously the Power charged with the execution of the work according to the design had provided against that mischance by causing the birth of a certain male child in a village at the foot of the Carpathian Mountains, had carefully reared it, supervised its education, directed its desires into a military channel, and in due time made it an officer of artillery. But the concurrence of an infinite number of favouring influences and their preponderance over an infinite number of opposing ones, this officer of artillery had been made to commit a breach of discipline and fly from his native country to avoid punishment. He had been directed to New Orleans (instead of New York), where a recruiting officer awaited him on the wharf. He was enlisted and promoted, and things were so ordered that he now commanded a Confederate battery some three miles along the line from where Jerome Searing, the Federal scout, stood cocking his rifle. Nothing had been neglected – at every step in the progress of both these men's lives, and in the lives of their ancestors and contemporaries, and of the lives of the contemporaries of their ancestors – the right thing had been done to bring about the desired result. Had anything in all this vast concatenation been overlooked, Private Searing might have fired on the retreating Confederates that morning, and would perhaps have missed. As it fell out, a captain of artillery, having nothing better to do while awaiting his turn to pull out and be off, amused himself by sighting a field piece obliquely to his right at what he took to be some Federal officers on the crest of a hill, and discharged it. The shot flew high of its mark.

As Jerome Searing drew back the hammer of his rifle, and, with his eyes upon the distant Confederates, considered where he could plant his shot with the best hope of making a widow or an orphan or a childless mother – perhaps all three, for Private Searing, although he had repeatedly refused promotion, was not without a certain kind of ambition – he heard a rushing sound in the air, like that made by the wings of a great bird swooping down upon its prey. More quickly than he could apprehend the gradation, it increased to a hoarse and horrible roar, as the missile that made it sprang at him out of the sky, striking with a deafening impact one of the posts supporting the confusion of timbers above him, smashing it into matchwood, and bringing down the crazy edifice with a loud clatter, in clouds of blinding dust!

Lieutenant Adrian Searing, in command of the picket guard on that part of the line through which his brother Jerome had passed on his mission, sat with attentive ears in his breastwork behind the line. Not the faintest sound escaped him; the cry of a bird, the barking of a squirrel, the noise of the wind among the pines – all were anxiously noted by his overstrained sense. Suddenly, directly in front of his line, he heard a faint, confused rumble, like the clatter of a falling building translated by distance. At the same moment an officer approached him on foot from the rear and saluted.

'Lieutenant,' said the aide, 'the colonel directs you to move forward your line and feel the enemy if you find him. If not, continue the advance until directed to halt. There is reason to think that the enemy has retreated.'

The lieutenant nodded and said nothing; the other officer retired. In a moment the men, apprised of their duty by the non-commissioned officers in low tones, had deployed from their rifle pits and were moving forward in skirmishing order, with set teeth and beating hearts. The lieutenant mechanically looked at his watch. Six o'clock and eighteen minutes.

When Jerome Searing recovered consciousness, he did not at once understand what had occurred. It was, indeed, some time before he opened his eyes. For a while he believed that he had died and been buried, and he tried to recall some portions of the burial service. He thought that his wife was kneeling upon his grave, adding her weight to that of the earth upon his chest. The two of them, widow and earth, had crushed his coffin. Unless the children should persuade her to go home, he would not much longer be able to breathe. He felt a sense of wrong.

'I cannot speak to her,' he thought; 'the dead have no voice; and if I open my eyes I shall get them full of earth.'

He opened his eyes – a great expanse of blue sky, rising from a fringe of the tops of trees. In the foreground, shutting out some of the trees, a high, dun mound, angular in outline and crossed by an intricate, patternless system of straight lines; in the centre a bright ring of metal – the whole an immeasurable distance away – a distance so inconceivably great that it fatigued him, and he closed his eyes. The moment that he did so he was conscious of an insufferable light. A sound was in his ears like the low, rhythmic thunder of a distant sea breaking in successive waves upon the beach, and out of this noise, seeming a part of it, or possibly coming from beyond it, and intermingled with its ceaseless undertone, came the articulate words: 'Jerome Searing, you are caught like a rat in a trap – in a trap, trap, trap.'

Suddenly there fell a great silence, a black darkness, an infinite tranquillity, and Jerome Searing, perfectly conscious of his rathood, and well assured of the trap that he was in, remembered all, and nowise alarmed, again opened his eyes to reconnoitre, to note the strength of his enemy, to plan his defence.

He was caught in a reclining posture, his back firmly supported by a solid beam. Another lay across his breast, but he had been able to shrink a little way from it so that it no longer oppressed him, though it was immovable. A brace joining it at an angle had wedged him against a pile of boards on his left, fastening the arm on that side. His legs, slightly parted and straight along the ground, were covered upward to the knees with a mass of débris which towered above his narrow horizon. His head was as rigidly fixed as in a vice; he could move his eyes, his chin – no more. Only his right arm was partly free. 'You must help us out of this,' he said to it. But he could not get it from under the heavy timber athwart his chest, nor move it outward more than six inches at the elbow.

Searing was not seriously injured, nor did he suffer pain. A smart rap on the head from a flying fragment of the splintered post, incurred simultaneously with the frightfully sudden shock to the nervous system, had momentarily dazed him. His term of unconsciousness, including the period of recovery, during which he had had the strange fancies, had probably not exceeded a few seconds, for the dust of the wreck had not wholly cleared away as he began an intelligent survey of the situation.

With his partly free right hand he now tried to get hold of the beam which lay across, but not quite against, his breast. In no way could he do so. He was unable to depress the shoulder so as to push the elbow beyond that edge of the timber which was nearest his knees; failing in that, he could not raise the forearm and hand to grasp the beam. The brace that made an angle with it downward and backward prevented him from doing anything in that direction, and between it and his body the space was not half as wide as the length of his forearm. Obviously he could not get his hand under the beam nor over it; he could not, in fact, touch it at all. Having demonstrated his inability, he desisted, and began to think if he could reach any of the débris piled upon his legs.

In surveying the mass with a view to determining that point, his attention was arrested by what seemed to be a ring of shining metal immediately in front of his eyes. It appeared to him at first to surround some perfectly black substance, and it was somewhat more than a half an inch in diameter. It suddenly occurred to his mind that the blackness was simply shadow, and that the ring was in fact the muzzle of his rifle protruding from the pile of débris. He was not long in satisfying himself that this was so – if it was a satisfaction. By closing either eye he could look a little way along the barrel – to the point where it was hidden by the rubbish that held it. He could see the one side, with the corresponding eye, at apparently the same angle as the other side with the other eye. Looking with the right eye, the weapon seemed to be directed at a point to the left of his head, and *vice versá*. He was unable to see the upper surface of the barrel, but could see the under surface of the stock at a slight angle. The piece was, in fact, aimed at the exact centre of his forehead.

In the perception of this circumstance, in the recollection that just previously to the mischance of which this uncomfortable situation was the result, he had cocked the gun and set the trigger so that a touch would discharge it, Private Searing was affected with a feeling of uneasiness. But that was as far as possible from fear; he was a brave man, somewhat familiar with the aspect of rifles from that point of view, and of cannon, too; and now he recalled, with something like amusement, an incident of his experience at the storming of Missionary Ridge, where, walking up to one of the enemy's embrasures from which he had seen a heavy gun throw charge after charge of grape among the assailants, he thought for a moment that the piece had been withdrawn; he could see nothing in the opening but a brazen circle. What that was he had understood just in time to step aside as it pitched another peck of iron down that swarming slope. To face firearms is one of the commonest incidents in a soldier's life – firearms, too, with malevolent eyes blazing behind them. That is what a soldier is for. Still, Private Searing did not altogether relish the situation, and turned away his eyes.

After groping, aimless, with his right hand for a time, he made an ineffectual attempt to release his left. Then he tried to disengage his head, the fixity of which was the more annoying from his ignorance of what held it. Next he tried to free his feet, but while exerting the powerful muscles of his legs for that purpose it occurred to him that a disturbance of the rubbish which held them might discharge the rifle; how it could have endured what had already befallen it he could not understand, although memory assisted him with various instances in point. One in particular he recalled, in which, in a moment of mental abstraction, he had clubbed his rifle and beaten out another gentleman's brains, observing afterward that the weapon which he had been diligently swinging by the muzzle was loaded, capped, and at full cock – knowledge of which circumstance would doubtless have cheered his antagonist to longer endurance. He had always smiled in recalling that blunder of his 'green and salad days' as a soldier, but now he did not smile. He turned his eyes again to the muzzle; it seemed somewhat nearer.

Again he looked away. The tops of the distant trees beyond the bounds of the plantation interested him; he had not before observed how light and feathery they seemed, nor how darkly blue the sky was, even among their branches, where they somewhat paled it with their green; above him it appeared almost black. 'It will be uncomfortably hot here,' he thought, 'as the day advances. I wonder which way I am looking.'

Judging by such shadows as he could see, he decided that his face was due north; he would at least not have the sun in his eyes, and north – well, that was toward his wife and children.

'Bah!' he exclaimed aloud, 'what have they to do with it?'

He closed his eyes. 'As I can't get out, I may as well go to sleep. The rebels are gone, and some of our fellows are sure to stray out here foraging. They'll find me.'

But he did not sleep. Gradually he became sensible of a pain in his forehead – a dull ache, hardly perceptible at first, but growing more and more uncomfortable. He opened his eyes and it was gone – closed them and it returned. 'The devil!' he said irrelevantly, and stared again at the sky. He heard the singing of birds, the strange metallic note of the meadow lark, suggesting the clash of vibrant blades. He fell into pleasant memories of his childhood, played again with his brother and sister, raced across the fields, shouting to alarm the sedentary larks, entered the sombre forest beyond, and with timid steps followed the faint path to Ghost Rock, standing at last with audible heart-throbs before the Dead Man's Cave and seeking to penetrate its awful mystery. For the first time he observed that the opening of the haunted cavern was encircled by a ring of metal. Then all else vanished, and left him gazing into the barrel of his rifle as before. But whereas before it had seemed nearer, it now seemed an inconceivable distance away, and all the more sinister for that. He cried out, and, startled by something in his own voice – the note of fear – lied to himself in denial: 'If I don't sing out I may stay here till I die.'

He now made no further attempt to evade the menacing stare of the gun barrel. If he turned away his eyes an instant it was to look for assistance (although he could not see the ground on either side the ruin), and he permitted them to return, obediently to the imperative fascination. If he closed them, it was from weariness, and instantly the poignant pain in his forehead – the prophecy and menace of the bullet – forced him to reopen them.

The tension of nerve and brain was too severe; nature came to his relief with intervals of unconsciousness. Reviving from one of these, he became sensible of a sharp, smarting pain in his right hand, and when he worked his fingers together, or rubbed his palm with them, he could feel that they were wet and slippery. He could not see the hand, but he knew the sensation; it was running blood. In his delirium he had beaten it against the jagged fragments of the wreck, had clutched it full of splinters. He resolved that he would meet his fate more manly. He was a plain, common soldier, had no religion and not much philosophy; he could not die like a hero, with great and wise last words, even if there were someone to hear them, but he could die 'game', and he would. But if he could only know when to expect the shot!

Some rats which had probably inhabited the shed came sneaking and scampering about. One of them mounted the pile of débris that held the rifle; another followed, and another. Searing regarded them at first with indifference, then with friendly interest; then, as the thought flashed into his bewildered mind that they might touch the trigger of his rifle, he screamed at them to go away. 'It is no business of yours,' he cried.

The creatures left; they would return later, attack his face, gnaw away his nose, cut his throat – he knew that, but he hoped by that time to be dead.

Nothing could now unfix his gaze from the little ring of metal with its black interior. The pain in his forehead was fierce and constant. He felt it gradually penetrating the brain more and more deeply, until at last its progress was arrested by the wood at the back of his head. It grew momentarily more insufferable; he began wantonly beating his lacerated hand against the splinters again to counteract that horrible ache. It seemed to throb with a slow, regular, recurrence, each pulsation sharper than the preceding, and sometimes he cried out, thinking he felt the fatal bullet. No thoughts of home, of wife and children, of country, of glory. The whole record of memory was effaced. The world had passed away – not a vestige remained. Here, in this confusion of timbers and boards, is the sole universe. Here is immortality in time – each pain an everlasting life. The throbs tick off eternities.

Jerome Searing, a man of courage, the formidable enemy, the strong, resolute warrior, was as pale as a ghost. His jaw was fallen; his eyes protruded; he trembled in every fibre; a cold sweat bathed his entire body; he screamed with fear. He was not insane – he was terrified.

In groping about with his torn and bleeding hand he seized at last a strip of board, and, pulling, felt it give way. It lay parallel with his body, and by bending his elbow as much as the contracted space would permit, he could draw it a few inches at a time. Finally it was altogether loosened from the wreckage covering his legs; he could lift it clear of the ground its whole length. A great hope came into his mind: perhaps he could work it upward, that is to say backward, far enough to lift the end and push aside the rifle; or, if that were too tightly wedged, so hold the strip of board as to deflect the bullet. With this object he passed it backward inch by inch, hardly daring to breath, lest that act somehow defeat his intent, and more than ever unable to remove his eyes from the rifle, which might perhaps now hasten to improve its waning opportunity. Something at least had been gained; in the occupation of his mind in this attempt at self-defence he was less sensible of the pain in his head and had ceased to scream. But he was still dreadfully frightened, and his teeth rattled like castanets.

The strip of board ceased to move to the suasion of his hand. He tugged at it with all his strength, changed the direction of its length all he could, but it had met some extended obstruction behind him, and the end in front was still too far away to clear the pile of débris and reach the muzzle of the gun. It extended, indeed, nearly as far as the trigger-guard, which, uncovered by the rubbish, he could imperfectly see with his right eye. He tried to break the strip with his hand, but had no leverage. Perceiving his defeat, all his terror returned, augmented tenfold. The black aperture of the rifle appeared to threaten a sharper and more imminent death in punishment of his rebellion. The track of the bullet through his head ached with an intenser anguish. He began to tremble again.

Suddenly he became composed. His tremor subsided. He clinched his teeth and drew down his eyebrows. He had not exhausted his means of defence; a new design had shaped itself in his mind – another plan of battle. Raising the front end of the strip of board, he carefully pushed it forward through the wreckage at the side of the rifle until it pressed against the trigger guard. Then he moved the end slowly outward until he could feel that it had cleared it, then, closing his eyes, thrust it against the trigger with all his strength! There was no explosion; the rifle had been discharged as it dropped from his hand when the building fell. But Jerome Searing was dead.

A line of Federal skirmishes swept across the plantation toward the mountain. They passed on both sides of the wrecked building, observing nothing. At a short distance in their rear came their Commander, Lieutenant Adrian Searing. He cast his eyes curiously upon the ruin and sees a dead body half buried in boards and timbers. It is so covered with dust that its clothing is Confederate grey. Its face is yellowish white; the cheeks are fallen in, the temples sunken, too, with sharp ridges about them, making the forehead forbiddingly narrow; the upper lip, slightly lifted, shows the white teeth, rigidly clinched. The hair is heavy with moisture, the face as wet as the dewy grass all about. From his point of view the officer does not observe the rifle; the man was apparently killed by the fall of the building.

'Dead a week,' said the officer curtly, moving on, mechanically pulling out his watch as if to verify his estimate of time. Six o'clock and forty minutes.

Joseph Conrad

The Tale

OUTSIDE the large single window the crepuscular light was dying out slowly in a great square gleam without colour, framed rigidly in the gathering shades of the room.

It was a long room. The irresistible tide of the night ran into the most distant part of it, where the whispering of a man's voice, passionately interrupted and passionately renewed, seemed to plead against the answering murmurs of infinite sadness.

At last no answering murmur came. His movement when he rose slowly from his knees by the side of the deep, shadowy couch holding the shadowy suggestion of a reclining woman revealed him tall under the low ceiling, and sombre all over except for the crude discord of the white collar under the shape of his head and the faint, minute spark of a brass button here and there on his uniform.

He stood over her a moment, masculine and mysterious in his immobility, before he sat down on a chair near by. He could see only the faint oval of her upturned face and, extended on her black dress, her pale hands, a moment before abandoned to his kisses and now as if too weary to move.

He dared not make a sound, shrinking as a man would do from the prosaic necessities of existence. As usual, it was the woman who had the courage. Her voice was heard first – almost conventional while her being vibrated yet with conflicting emotions.

'Tell me something,' she said.

The darkness hid his surprise and then his smile. Had he not just said to her everything worth saying in the world – and that not for the first time!

'What am I to tell you?' he asked, in a voice creditably steady. He was beginning to feel grateful to her for that something final in her tone which had eased the strain.

'Why not tell me a tale?'

'A tale!' He was really amazed.

'Yes. Why not?'

THE TALE

These words came with a slight petulance, the hint of a loved woman's capricious will, which is capricious only because it feels itself to be a law, embarrassing sometimes and always difficult to elude.

'Why not?' he repeated, with a slightly mocking accent, as though he had been asked to give her the moon. But now he was feeling a little angry with her for that feminine mobility that slips out of an emotion as easily as out of a splendid gown.

He heard her say, a little unsteadily with a sort of fluttering intonation which made him think suddenly of a butterfly's flight:

'You used to tell – your – your simple and – and professional – tales very well at one time. Or well enough to interest me. You had a – a sort of art – in the days – the days before the war.'

'Really?' he said, with involuntary gloom. 'But now, you see, the war is going on,' he continued in such a dead, equable tone that she felt a slight chill fall over her shoulders. And yet she persisted. For there's nothing more unswerving in the world than a woman's caprice.

'It could be a tale not of this world,' she explained.

'You want a tale of the other, the better world?' he asked, with a matter-of-fact surprise. 'You must evoke for that task those who have already gone there.'

'No. I don't mean that. I mean another – some other – world. In the universe – not in heaven.'

'I am relieved. But you forget that I have only five days' leave.'

'Yes. And I've also taken a five days' leave from – from my duties.'

'I like that word.'

'What word?'

'Duty.'

'It is horrible – sometimes.'

'Oh, that's because you think it's narrow. But it isn't. It contains infinities, and – and so—'

'What is this jargon?'

He disregarded the interjected scorn. 'An infinity of absolution, for instance,' he continued. 'But as to this "another world" – who's going to look for it and for the tale that is in it?'

'You,' she said, with a strange, almost rough, sweetness of assertion.

He made a shadowy movement of assent in his chair, the irony of which not even the gathered darkness could render mysterious.

'As you will. In that world, then, there was once upon a time a Commanding Officer and a Northman. Put in the capitals, please, because they had no other names. It was a world of seas and continents and islands—'

'Like the earth,' she murmured, bitterly.

'Yes. What else could you expect from sending a man made of our common, tormented clay on a voyage of discovery? What else could he find? What else could you understand or care for, or feel the existence of even? There was comedy in it, and slaughter.'

'Always like the earth,' she murmured.

'Always. And since I could find in the universe only what was deeply rooted in the fibres of my being there was love in it, too. But we won't talk of that.'

'No. We won't,' she said, in a neutral tone which concealed perfectly her relief – or her disappointment. Then after a pause she added: 'It's going to be a comic story.'

'Well—' he paused, too. 'Yes. In a way. In a very grim way. It will be human, and, as you know, comedy is but a matter of the visual angle. And it won't be a noisy story. All the long guns in it will be dumb – as dumb as so many telescopes.'

'Ah, there are guns in it, then! And may I ask – where?'

'Afloat. You remember that the world of which we speak had its seas. A war was going on in it. It was a funny world and terribly in earnest. Its war was being carried on over the land, over the water, under the water, up in the air, and even under the ground. And many young men in it, mostly in wardrooms and messrooms, used to say to each other – pardon the unparliamentary word – they used to say, "It's a damned bad war, but it's better than no war at all." Sounds flippant, doesn't it?'

He heard a nervous, impatient sigh in the depths of the couch while he went on without a pause.

'And yet there is more in it than meets the eye. I mean more wisdom. Flippancy, like comedy, is but a matter of visual first-impression. That world was not very wise. But there was in it a certain amount of common working sagacity. That, however, was mostly worked by the neutrals in diverse ways, public and private, which had to be watched; watched by acute minds and also by actual sharp eyes. They had to be very sharp indeed, too, I assure you.'

'I can imagine,' she murmured, appreciatively.

'What is there that you can't imagine?' he pronounced, soberly. 'You have the world in you. But let us go back to our commanding officer, who, of course, commanded a ship of a sort. My tales if often professional (as you remarked just now) have never been technical. So I'll just tell you that the ship was of a very ornamental sort once, with lots of grace and elegance and luxury about her. Yes, once! She was like a pretty woman who had suddenly put on a suit of sackcloth and stuck revolvers in her belt. But she floated lightly, she moved nimbly, she was quite good enough.'

'That was the opinion of the commanding officer?' said the voice from the couch.

'It was. He used to be sent out with her along certain coasts to see

– what he could see. Just that. And sometimes he had some preliminary information to help him, and sometimes he had not. And it was all one, really. It was about as useful as information trying to convey the locality and intentions of a cloud, of a phantom taking shape here and there and impossible to seize, would have been.

'It was in the early days of the war. What at first used to amaze the commanding officer was the unchanged face of the waters, with its familiar expression, neither more friendly nor more hostile. On fine days the sun strikes sparks upon the blue; here and there a peaceful smudge of smoke hangs in the distance, and it is impossible to believe that the familiar clear horizon traces the limit of one great circular ambush.

'Yes, it is impossible to believe, till some day you see a ship not your own ship (that isn't so impressive), but some ship in company, blow up all of a sudden and plop under almost before you know what has happened to her. Then you begin to believe. Henceforth you go out for the work to see – what you can see, and you keep on at it with the conviction that some day you will die from something you have not seen. One envies the soldiers at the end of the day, wiping the sweat and blood from their faces, counting the dead fallen to their hands, looking at the devastated fields, the torn earth that seems to suffer and bleed with them. One does, really. The final brutality of it – the taste of primitive passion – the ferocious frankness of the blow struck with one's hand – the direct call and the straight response. Well, the sea gave you nothing of that, and seemed to pretend that there was nothing the matter with the world.'

She interrupted, stirring a little.

'Oh, yes. Sincerity – frankness – passion – three words of your gospel. Don't I know them!'

'Think! Isn't it ours – believed in common?' he asked, anxiously, yet without expecting an answer, and went on at once: 'Such were the feelings of the commanding officer. When the night came trailing over the sea, hiding what looked like the hypocrisy of an old friend, it was a relief. The night blinds you frankly – and there are circumstances when the sunlight may grow as odious to one as falsehood itself. Night is all right.

'At night the commanding officer could let his thoughts get away – I won't tell you where. Somewhere where there was no choice but between truth and death. But thick weather, though it blinded one, brought no such relief. Mist is deceitful, the dead luminosity of the fog is irritating. It seems that you *ought* to see.

'One gloomy, nasty day the ship was steaming along her beat in sight of a rocky, dangerous coast that stood out intensely black like an India-ink drawing on gray paper. Presently the second in command spoke to his chief. He thought he saw something on the water, to seaward. Small wreckage, perhaps.

'"But there shouldn't be any wreckage here, sir," he remarked.

'"No," said the commanding officer. "The last reported submarined ships were sunk a long way to the westward. But one never knows. There may have been others since then not reported nor seen. Gone with all hands."

'That was how it began. The ship's course was altered to pass the object close; for it was necessary to have a good look at what one could see. Close, but without touching; for it was not advisable to come in contact with objects of any form whatever floating casually about. Close, but without stopping or even diminishing speed; for in those times it was not prudent to linger on any particular spot, even for a moment. I may tell you at once that the object was not dangerous in itself. No use in describing it. It may have been nothing more remarkable than, say, a barrel of a certain shape and colour. But it was significant.

'The smooth bow-wave hove it up as if for a closer inspection, and then the ship, brought again to her course, turned her back on it with indifference, while twenty pairs of eyes on her deck stared in all directions trying to see – what they could see.

'The commanding officer and his second in command discussed the object with understanding. It appeared to them to be not so much a proof of the sagacity as of the activity of certain neutrals. This activity had in many cases taken the form of replenishing the stores of certain submarines at sea. This was generally believed, if not absolutely known. But the very nature of things in those early days pointed that way. The object, looked at closely and turned away from with apparent indifference, put it beyond doubt that something of the sort had been done somewhere in the neighbourhood.

'The object in itself was more than suspect. But the fact of its being left in evidence roused other suspicions. Was it the result of some deep and devilish purpose? As to that all speculation soon appeared to be a vain thing. Finally the two officers came to the conclusion that it was left there most likely by accident, complicated possibly by some unforeseen necessity; such, perhaps, as the sudden need to get away quickly from the spot, or something of that kind.

'Their discussion had been carried on in curt, weighty phrases, separated by long, thoughtful silences. And all the time their eyes roamed about the horizon in an everlasting, almost mechanical effort of vigilance. The younger man summed up grimly:

'"Well, it's evidence. That's what this is. Evidence of what we were pretty certain of before. And plain, too."

'"And much good it will do to us," retorted the commanding officer. "The parties are miles away; the submarine, devil only knows where, ready to kill; and the noble neutral slipping away to the eastward, ready to lie!"

'The second in command laughed a little at the tone. But he guessed that the neutral wouldn't even have to lie very much. Fellows like that, unless caught in the very act, felt themselves pretty safe. They could afford to chuckle. That fellow was probably chuckling to himself. It's very possible he had been before at the game and didn't care a rap for the bit of evidence left behind. It was a game in which practice made one bold and successful, too.

'And again he laughed faintly. But his commanding officer was in revolt againt the murderous stealthiness of methods and the atrocious callousness of complicities that seemed to taint the very source of men's deep emotions and noblest activities; to corrupt their imagination which builds up the final conceptions of life and death. He suffered—'

The voice from the sofa interrupted the narrator.

'How well I can understand that in him!'

He bent forward slightly.

'Yes. I, too. Everything should be open in love and war. Open as the day, since both are the call of an ideal which it is so easy, so terribly easy, to degrade in the name of Victory.'

He paused; then went on:

'I don't know that the commanding officer delved so deep as that into his feelings. But he did suffer from them – a sort of disenchanted sadness. It is possible, even, that he suspected himself of folly. Man is various. But he had no time for much introspection, because from the southwest a wall of fog had advanced upon his ship. Great convolutions of vapours flew over, swirling about masts and funnel, which looked as if they were beginning to melt. Then they vanished.

'The ship was stopped, all sounds ceased, and the very fog became motionless, growing denser and as if solid in its amazing dumb immobility. The men at their stations lost sight of each other. Footsteps sounded stealthy; rare voices, impersonal and remote, died out without resonance. A blind white stillness took possession of the world.

'It looked, too, as if it would last for days. I don't mean to say that the fog did not vary a little in its density. Now and then it would thin out mysteriously, revealing to the men a more or less ghostly present-ment of their ship. Several times the shadow of the coast itself swam darkly before their eyes through the fluctuating opaque brightness of the great white cloud clinging to the water.

'Taking advantage of these moments, the ship had been moved cautiously nearer the shore. It was useless to remain out in such thick weather. Her officers knew every nook and cranny of the coast along their beat. They thought that she would be much better in a certain cove. It wasn't a large place, just ample room for a ship to swing at her anchor. She would have an easier time of it till the fog lifted up.

'Slowly, with infinite caution and patience, they crept closer and closer, seeing no more of the cliffs than an evanescent dark loom with a narrow border of angry foam at its foot. At the moment of anchoring the fog was so thick that for all they could see they might have been a thousand miles out in the open sea. Yet the shelter of the land could be felt. There was a peculiar quality in the stillness of the air. Very faint, very elusive, the wash of the ripple against the encircling land reached their ears, with mysterious sudden pauses.

'The anchor dropped, the leads were laid in. The commanding officer went below into his cabin. But he had not been there very long when a voice outside his door requested his presence on deck. He thought to himself: "What is it now?" He felt some impatience at being called out again to face the wearisome fog.

'He found that it had thinned again a little and had taken on a gloomy hue from the dark cliffs which had no form, no outline, but asserted themselves as a curtain of shadows all round the ship, except in one bright spot, which was the entrance from the open sea. Several officers were looking that way from the bridge. The second in command met him with the breathlessly whispered information that there was another ship in the cove.

'She had been made out by several pairs of eyes only a couple of minutes before. She was lying at anchor very near the entrance – a mere vague blot on the fog's brightness. And the commanding officer by staring in the direction pointed out to him by eager hands ended by distinguishing it at last himself. Indubitably a vessel of some sort.

' "It's a wonder we didn't run slap into her when coming in," observed the second in command.

' "Send a boat on board before she vanishes," said the commanding officer. He surmised that this was a coaster. It could hardly be anything else. But another thought came into his head suddenly. 'It is a wonder,' he said to his second in command, who had rejoined him after sending the boat away.

'By that time both of them had been struck by the fact that the ship so suddenly discovered had not manifested her presence by ringing her bell.

' "We came in very quietly, that's true," concluded the younger officer. "But they must have heard our leadsmen at least. We couldn't have passed her more than fifty yards off. The closest shave! They may even have made us out, since they were aware of something coming in. And the strange thing is that we never heard a sound from her. The fellows on board must have been holding their breath."

' "Aye," said the commanding officer, thoughtfully.

THE TALE

'In due course the boarding-boat returned, appearing suddenly alongside, as though she had burrowed her way under the fog. The officer in charge came up to make his report, but the commanding officer didn't give him time to begin. He cried from a distance:

' "Coaster, isn't she?"

' "No, sir. A stranger – a neutral," was the answer.

' "No. Really! Well, tell us all about it. What is she doing here?"

'The young man stated then that he had been told a long and complicated story of engine troubles. But it was plausible enough from a strictly professional point of view and it had the usual features: disablement, dangerous drifting along the shore, weather more or less thick for days, fear of a gale, ultimately a resolve to go in and anchor anywhere on the coast, and so on. Fairly plausible.

' "Engines still disabled?" inquired the commanding officer.

' "No, sir. She has steam on them."

'The commanding officer took his second aside. "By Jove!" he said, "you were right! They were holding their breaths as we passed them. They were."

'But the second in command had his doubts now.

' "A fog like this does muffle small sounds, sir,' he remarked. 'And what could his object be, after all?"

' "To sneak out unnoticed," answered the commanding officer.

' "Then why didn't he? He might have done it, you know. Not exactly unnoticed, perhaps. I don't suppose he could have slipped his cable without making some noise. Still, in a minute or so he would have been lost to view – clean gone before we had made him out fairly. Yet he didn't."

'They looked at each other. The commanding officer shook his head. Such suspicions as the one which had entered his head are not defended easily. He did not even state it openly. The boarding officer finished his report. The cargo of the ship was of a harmless and useful character. She was bound to an English port. Papers and everything in perfect order. Nothing suspicious to be detected anywhere.

'Then passing to the men, he reported the crew on deck as the usual lot. Engineers of the well-known type, and very full of their achievement in repairing the engines. The mate surly. The master rather a fine specimen of a Northman, civil enough, but appeared to have been drinking. Seemed to be recovering from a regular bout of it.

' "I told him I couldn't give him permission to proceed. He said he wouldn't dare to move his ship her own length out in such weather as this, permission or no permission. I left a man on board, though."

' "Quite right."

'The commanding officer, after communing with his suspicions for a time, called his second aside.

' "What if she were the very ship which had been feeding some infernal submarine or other?" he said in an undertone.

'The other started. Then, with conviction:

' "She would get off scot-free. You couldn't prove it, sir."

' "I want to look into it myself."

' "From the report we've heard I am afraid you couldn't even make a case for reasonable suspicion, sir."

' "I'll go on board all the same."

'He had made up his mind. Curiosity is the great motive power of hatred and love. What did he expect to find? He could not have told anybody – not even himself.

'What he really expected to find there was the atmosphere, the atmosphere of gratuitous treachery, which in his view nothing could excuse; for he thought that even a passion of unrighteousness for its own sake could not excuse that. But could he detect it? Sniff it? Taste it? Receive some mysterious communication which would turn his invincible suspicions into a certitude strong enough to provoke action with all its risks?

'The master met him on the after-deck, looming up in the fog amongst the blurred shapes of the usual ship's fittings. He was a robust Northman, bearded, and in the force of his age. A round leather cap fitted his head closely. His hands were rammed deep into the pockets of his short leather jacket. He kept them there while he explained that at sea he lived in the chart-room, and led the way there, striding carelessly. Just before reaching the door under the bridge he staggered a little, recovered himself, flung it open, and stood aside, leaning his shoulder as if involuntarily against the side of the house, and staring vaguely into the fog-filled space. But he followed the commanding officer at once, flung the door to, snapped on the electric light, and hastened to thrust his hands back into his pockets, as though afraid of being seized by them either in friendship or in hostility.

'The place was stuffy and hot. The usual chart-rack overhead was full, and the chart on the table was kept unrolled by an empty cup standing on a saucer half-full of some spilt dark liquid. A slightly nibbled biscuit reposed on the chronometer-case. There were two settees, and one of them had been made up into a bed with a pillow and some blankets, which were now very much tumbled. The Northman let himself fall on it, hands still in his pockets.

' "Well, here I am," he said, with a curious air of being surprised at the sound of his own voice.

'The commanding officer from the other settee observed the handsome, flushed face. Drops of fog hung on the yellow beard and moustaches of the Northman. The much darker eyebrows ran together in a puzzled frown, and suddenly he jumped up.

THE TALE

' "What I mean is that I don't know where I am. I really don't," he burst out, with extreme earnestness. "Hang it all! I got turned around somewhere. The fog has been after me for a week. More than a week. And then my engines broke down. I will tell you how it was."

'He burst out into loquacity. It was not hurried, but it was insistent. It was not continuous for all that. It was broken by the most queer, thoughtful pauses. Each of these pauses lasted no more than a couple of seconds, and each had the profoundity of an endless meditation. When he began again nothing betrayed in him the slightest consciousness of these intervals. There was the same fixed glance, the same unchanged earnestness of tone. He didn't know. Indeed, more than one of these pauses occurred in the middle of a sentence.

'The commanding officer listened to the tale. It struck him as more plausible than simple truth is in the habit of being. But that, perhaps, was prejudice. All the time the Northman was speaking the commanding officer had been aware of an inward voice, a grave murmur in the depth of his very own self, telling another tale, as if on purpose to keep alive in him his indignation and his anger with that baseness of greed or of mere outlook which lies often at the root of simple ideas.

'It was the story that had been already told to the boarding officer an hour or so before. The commanding officer nodded slightly at the Northman from time to time. The latter came to an end and turned his eyes away. He added, as an afterthought:

' "Wasn't it enough to drive a man out of his mind with worry? And it's my first voyage to this part, too. And the ship's my own. Your officer has seen the papers. She isn't much, as you can see for yourself. Just an old cargo-boat. Bare living for my family."

'He raised a big arm to point at a row of photographs plastering the bulkhead. The movement was ponderous, as if the arm had been made of lead. The commanding officer said, carelessly:

' "You will be making a fortune yet for your family with this old ship.'

' "Yes, if I don't lose her,' said the Northman, gloomily.

' "I mean – out of this war," added the commanding officer.

'The Northman stared at him in a curiously unseeing and at the same time interested manner, as only eyes of a particular blue shade can stare.

' "And you wouldn't be angry at it," he said, "would you? You are too much of a gentleman. We didn't bring this on you. And suppose we sat down and cried. What good would that be? Let those cry who made the trouble," he concluded, with energy. "Time's money, you say. Well – *this* time *is* money. Oh! isn't it!"

'The commanding officer tried to keep under the feeling of immense disgust. He said to himself that it was unreasonable. Men were like that – moral cannibals feeding on each other's misfortunes. He said aloud:

' "You have made it perfectly plain how it is that you are here. Your log-book confirms you very minutely. Of course, a log-book may be cooked. Nothing easier."

'The Northman never moved a muscle. He was gazing at the floor; he seemed not to have heard. He raised his head after a while.

' "But you can't suspect me of anything," he muttered, negligently.

'The commanding officer thought: "Why should he say this?"

'Immediately afterwards the man before him added: "My cargo is for an English port."

'His voice had turned husky for the moment. The commanding officer reflected: "That's true. There can be nothing. I can't suspect him. Yet why was he lying with steam up in this fog – and then, hearing us come in, why didn't he give some sign of life? Why? Could it be anything else but a guilty conscience? He could tell by the leadsmen that this was a man-of-war."

'Yes – why? The commanding officer went on thinking: "Suppose I ask him and then watch his face. He will betray himself in some way. It's perfectly plain that the fellow *has* been drinking. Yes, he has been drinking; but he will have a lie ready all the same." The commanding officer was one of those men who are made morally and almost physically uncomfortable by the mere thought of having to beat down a lie. He shrank from the act in scorn and disgust, which were invincible because more temperamental than moral.

'So he went out on deck instead and had the crew mustered formally for his inspection. He found them very much what the report of the boarding officer had led him to expect. And from their answers to his questions he could discover no flaw in the log-book story.

'He dismissed them. His impression of them was – a picked lot; have been promised a fistful of money each if this came off; all slightly anxious, but not frightened. Not a single one of them likely to give the show away. They don't feel in danger of their life. They know England and English ways too well!

'He felt alarmed at catching himself thinking as if his vaguest suspicions were turning into a certitude. For, indeed, there was no shadow of reason for his inferences. There was nothing to give away.

'He returned to the chart-room. The Northman had lingered behind there; and something subtly different in his bearing, more bold in his blue, glassy stare, induced the commanding officer to conclude that the fellow had snatched at the opportunity to take another swig at the bottle he must have had concealed somewhere.

'He noticed, too, that The Northman on meeting his eyes put on an elaborately surprised expression. At least, it seemed elaborated. Nothing could be trusted. And the Englishman felt himself with astonishing conviction faced by an enormous lie, solid like a wall, with no way round to get at the truth, whose ugly murderous face he seemed to see peeping over at him with a cynical grin.

' "I dare say," he began, suddenly, "you are wondering at my proceedings, though I am not detaining you, am I? You wouldn't dare to move in this fog?"

' "I don't know where I am," the Northman ejaculated, earnestly. "I really don't."

'He looked around as if the very chart-room fittings were strange to him. The commanding officer asked him whether he had not seen any unusual objects floating about while he was at sea.

' "Objects! What objects? We were groping blind in the fog for days."

' "We had a few clear intervals," said the commanding officer. "And I'll tell you what we have seen and the conclusion I've come to about it."

'He told him in a few words. He heard the sound of a sharp breath indrawn through closed teeth. The Northman with his hand on the table stood absolutely motionless and dumb. He stood as if thunderstruck. Then he produced a fatuous smile.

'Or at least so it appeared to the commanding officer. Was this significant, or of no meaning whatever? He didn't know, he couldn't tell. All the truth had departed out of the world as if drawn in, absorbed in this monstrous villainy this man was – or was not – guilty of.

' "Shooting's too good for people that conceive neutrality in this pretty way," remarked the commanding officer, after a silence.

' "Yes, yes, yes," the Northman assented, hurriedly – then added an unexpected and dreamy-voiced "Perhaps."

'Was he pretending to be drunk, or only trying to appear sober? His glance was straight, but it was somewhat glazed. His lips outlined themselves firmly under his yellow moustache. But they twitched. Did they twitch? And why was he drooping like this in his attitude?

' "There's no perhaps about it," pronounced the commanding officer sternly.

'The Northman had straightened himself. And unexpectedly he looked stern, too.

' "No. But what about the tempters? Better kill that lot off. There's about four, five, six million of them," he said, grimly; but in a moment changed into a whining key. "But I had better hold my tongue. You have some suspicions."

' "No, I've no suspicions," declared the commanding officer.

'He never faltered. At that moment he had the certitude. The air of the chart-room was thick with guilt and falsehood braving the discovery, defying simple right, common decency, all humanity of feeling, every scruple of conduct.

'The Northman drew a long breath. "Well, we know that you English are gentlemen. But let us speak the truth. Why should we love you so very much? You haven't done anything to be loved. We don't love the other people, of course. They haven't done anything for that either. A fellow comes along with a bag of gold . . . I haven't been in Rotterdam my last voyage for nothing."

' "You may be able to tell something interesting, then, to our people when you come into port," interjected the officer.

'I might. But you keep some people in your pay at Rotterdam. Let them report. I am a neutral – am I not? . . . Have you ever seen a poor man on one side and a bag of gold on the other? Of course, I couldn't be tempted. I haven't the nerve for it. Really I haven't. It's nothing to me. I am just talking openly for once."

' "Yes. And I am listening to you," said the commanding officer, quietly.

'The Northman leaned forward over the table. "Now that I know you have no suspicions, I talk. You don't know what a poor man is. I do. I am poor myself. This old ship, she isn't much, and she is mortgaged, too. Bare living, no more. Of course, I wouldn't have the nerve. But a man who has nerve! See. The stuff he takes aboard looks like any other cargo – packages, barrels, tins, copper tubes – what not. He doesn't see it work. It isn't real to him. But he sees the gold. That's real. Of course, nothing could induce me. I suffer from an internal disease. I would either go crazy from anxiety – or – or – take to drink or something. The risk is too great. Why – ruin!"

' "It should be death." The commanding officer got up, after this curt declaration, which the other received with a hard stare oddly combined with an uncertain smile. The officer's gorge rose at the atmosphere of murderous complicity which surrounded him, denser, more impenetrable, more acrid than the fog outside.

' "It's nothing to me," murmured the Northman, swaying visibly.

' "Of course not," assented the commanding officer, with a great effort to keep his voice calm and low. The certitude was strong within him. "But I am going to clear all you fellows off this coast at once. And I will begin with you. You must leave in half an hour."

'By that time the officer was walking along the deck with the Northman at his elbow.

' "What! In this fog?" the latter cried out, huskily.

' "Yes, you will have to go in this fog."

' "But I don't know where I am. I really don't."

'The commanding officer turned round. A sort of fury possessed him.

The eyes of the two men met. Those of the Northman expressed a profound amazement.

' "Oh, you don't know how to get out." The commanding officer spoke with composure, but his heart was beating with anger and dread. "I will give you your course. Steer south-by-east-half-east for about four miles and then you will be clear to haul to the eastward for your port. The weather will clear up before very long."

' "Must I? What could induce me? I haven't the nerve."

' "And yet you must go. Unless you want to—"

' "I don't want to," panted the Northman. "I've enough of it."

'The commanding officer got over the side. The Northman remained still as if rooted to the deck. Before his boat reached his ship the commanding officer heard the steamer beginning to pick up her anchor. Then, shadowy in the fog, she steamed out on the given course.

' "Yes," he said to his officers, "I let him go." '

The narrator bent forward towards the couch, where no movement betrayed the presence of a living person.

'Listen,' he said, forcibly. 'That course would lead the Northman straight on a deadly ledge of rock. And the commanding officer gave it to him. He steamed out – ran on it – and went down. So he had spoken the truth. He did not know where he was. But it proves nothing. Nothing either way. It may have been the only truth in all his story. And yet . . . He seems to have been driven out by a menacing stare – nothing more.'

He abandoned all pretence.

'Yes, I gave that course to him. It seemed to me a supreme test. I believe – no, I don't believe. I don't know. At the time I was certain. They all went down; and I don't know whether I have done stern retribution – or murder; whether I have added to the corpses that litter the bed of the unreadable sea the bodies of men completely innocent or basely guilty. I don't know. I shall never know.'

He rose. The woman on the couch got up and threw her arms around his neck. Her eyes put two gleams in the deep shadow of the room. She knew his passion for truth, his horror of deceit, his humanity.

'Oh, my poor, poor—'

'I shall never know,' he repeated, sternly, disengaged himself, pressed her hands to his lips, and went out.

'Taffrail'

The Night Patrol

THE night was intensely dark, with every indication of rain in the low, heavy-looking clouds and the damp, chilly feeling in the air. The young moon had long since set, but no stars twinkled overhead, for from horizon to horizon the arch of the heavens was shrouded in an impenetrable canopy of velvety, smoky black, with here and there the inkier blackness of bunches and wisps of scattered nimbus trailing lazily to the north-eastward on the wings of some freakish upper air-current.

On the surface it was quite calm, what little breeze there had been during the day having died away at sundown. And now, soon after midnight, the oiliness of the sea was only ruffled in little patches by occasional errant cat's-paws, as gentle breaths of air came stealing fitfully seaward from the direction of the coast.

To the east and the south-east, where lay the land, the undersides of the clouds on the horizon flickered and glowed spasmodically with a dull ruby light reflected from the gleam of distant and invisible gun-flashes. In the same direction, white balls of fire from star-shell and flares soared ceaselessly skywards, now in twos and threes, sometimes in sudden batches of a dozen. They curved over and down, shedding areas of bluish-white light, misty, but very brilliant, until, waning gradually, they fell slowly to earth, to be followed by others. And though those flares were fired ashore in the trenches many miles away, their illumination would have permitted those in the destroyer patrol watching off the coast to read moderate-sized print without difficulty. The trenches themselves must have been bathed in a glare as bright as daylight.

From somewhere on land, far away behind those leaping balls of fire, the narrow, misty beam of a searchlight, terminating abruptly where it met the clouds, wandered uneasily across the low sky. Another, nearer at hand on the coast, wakened into being at intervals, and sent its ray sweeping slowly to and fro across the sea, searching for it knew not what, like a great watching eye.

The still air throbbed in the insistent murmur of heavy gun-fire, now loud like thunder as the offshore breeze freshened, now hushed to a sound like the far-away rolling of many drums, or the soft rumble of a distant goods-train passing through a culvert. It was the song of the Western Front, the ceaseless song which had continued for nearly four years.

To those in the destroyers it was no novelty. No great offensive was in progress. Affairs ashore were in their normal condition, each side holding its own trench-lines, and contenting itself with nightly raids and uninterrupted bombardments of the opposing trenches and black areas. Those whose duty lay afloat had long since become accustomed to the sounds of strife, regarding them, indeed, as being quite in the order of things. Sometimes, when the firing seemed to quicken in its fury, they rather pitied the men fighting in the trenches, wondering vaguely how 'them pore blokes' were getting on, and secretly rather envious at not being able to lend them more of a helping hand in the common cause. But when the wind rose, and the short, curling sea made life a misery and a burden; when, in the bitter winter gales, the driving spray froze as it fell and glued men's mufflers to their necks, covered the always slippery decks with sheet-ice until it was barely possible to stand upright when the ship rolled, and choked the muzzles of the guns with blocks of solid ice, which had to be thawed out with hot water – then it was that the men at sea were jealous of those who fought on land, and had nothing whatsoever to do with that most unstable and unsympathetic element, the sea.

The work of the patrolling destroyers was certainly no sinecure. They had occasional spells off, but sometimes for a fortnight or more they were at it night after night in all weathers, taking what rest they could in the day-time. There had been many 'scraps' with German torpedo-craft – short, sharp, desperate encounters in the blackness of the night, when the combatants, rushing practically alongside each other at high speed, pumped shell at their opposite numbers at point-blank range, and dodged and twisted madly in their efforts to ram and to use their torpedoes. They were always breathless, rather nerve-racking experiences, these battles in the darkness. They began so suddenly, and when one least expected them. Events succeeded each other with nightmare rapidity, while the element of chance entered hugely into them. One might make up one's mind what to do in fifty different combinations of circumstances, but it was always the fifty-first that happened. The Germans, moreover, though it is true they generally sought safety in flight when once engaged, were desperate fighters when it came to the point, and frequently gave as many hard knocks as they got.

The enemy always had the advantage in that they could emerge from their ports at their own chosen time. There was no knowing when or where they might appear, and the watchers, spread out in groups over a large area, had always to be ready. When, as it sometimes happened, month after month passed without incident, the work of the patrols, always arduous, seemed rather purposeless and monotonous. The inactivity – to call it that for want of a better word, for they were always busy – might have lulled some people into a sense of false security, encouraged them to relax their efforts, to take things a little more easily.

But not so these men. There was hardly a destroyer working in the area which, at one time or another, had not been blooded in close-quarter conflict with the Boche. Every officer and man knew his work. Each one of them realized that the ship which sighted the enemy before the enemy sighted her, and was thus enabled to get in the first salvo of shell, or the first torpedo, generally had the opponent at her mercy. Even if the foe appeared in superior strength it mattered little. Again and again it had been proved by actual experience that these night destroyer actions normally ended in close-range *mêlées*, in which, before very long, the ships of both sides became hopelessly mixed. So superiority in numbers was usually countered by surprise. In other words, the side which struck first, and struck hard, generally won.

Moreover, and what was far more important, these outlying destroyers were the advanced sentries for a complicated system of other patrols behind them, not to mention an army of other craft – auxiliary patrol-vessels engaged in their usual task of hunting and harrying submarines, transports and hospital-ships passing to and fro across the Channel, merchantmen – ships of every possible persuasion and calling.

There had been regrettable incidents in the past, when German destroyers, favoured by mist and low visibility, had slipped through the cordon of watchers to bombard towns, to sink and destroy ships, and had succeeded in making their escape without being brought to action. Such things did not happen through any defect in organization, or through any lack of zeal or energy on the part of the patrols. They were merely the outcome of bad luck, the ever-changing fortune of war.

Nevertheless, when such incidents took place, certain sections of the public press raised their voices and clamoured mercilessly for somebody's blood, inquiring, in terms both impolite and acid, what the navy was thinking about to permit such goings-on.

They little knew the conditions in which the patrols worked, did not realize a tithe of their responsibility, or that, to any seaman, it was manifestly impossible for every square mile of sea in the Strait to be watched and guarded constantly. They forgot that the hostile raids, regrettable though they might be, were only part and parcel of the ebb and flow of war. It is impossible to make omelets without breaking eggs, impossible to make war without loss; while, after all, the sallies with the

Germans occasionally indulged in with varying success were only comparable to those nightly raids in the trenches.

No; some people ashore who had the satisfaction of sleeping in their beds every night of their lives forgot that there had been no appreciable tightening of their belts, and quite omitted to remember to what and to whom this was due.

And the navy, when attacked by the Scribes and the Pharisees, its own countrymen, those whom it fed and defended, merely shrugged its shoulders and said nothing. It had been pilloried in the past, and would doubtless be pilloried in the future. It knew the fickleness of public opinion; recollected, with some little bitterness, that at one port men wounded at the battle of Jutland had been hissed and execrated while being carried ashore on their blood-stained stretchers.

Such things should not be, but unhappily are; so the Sea Service, being wise in its generation and too proud to explain, smiled, said nothing, and – continued to do its duty without the plaudits of the multitude.

The watchers continued to watch.

II

On board the *Minx*, the third destroyer in the line, M'Call, the first lieutenant, was keeping the first two hours of the middle watch. He stood close to the bridge-screens, using his glasses continually to sweep the horizon, with an ever-watchful eye upon the black smudge and the dim trail of phosphorescent water which showed the position of the ship next ahead, a cable distant. Occasionally, as the ship crept up or dropped astern of her station, or sheered a little out of the line, he flung an order over his shoulder to the man at the revolution telegraph, or to the helmsman twiddling his wheel as he peered into the dimly lit compass-bowl, the men repeating the orders word for word, to show they had been heard and understood.

Besides M'Call himself, the quartermaster, and the man at the engine-room telegraphs, space had also to be found on the small bridge for a couple of A.B.s, who had nothing to do but keep a constant look-out to port and to starboard, a leading signalman, the messenger, and two more men, whose duty was to attend to the instruments and the voice-pipes communicating with the guns and the torpedo-tubes. There was hardly room to move, no space whatsoever to walk up and down.

At the first lieutenant's feet, coiled up in an impossible attitude in a deck-chair tucked in under the chart-table, lay Langlands, the lieutenant-commander, seemingly asleep. He and his second in command invariably spent the entire night on the bridge when the ship was on patrol, relieving each other every couple of hours for the doubtful comfort of the deck-chair. It was a miserable sleeping-billet at the best of times, and bitterly cold; while as often as not one or both of the officers spent the hours of darkness without a wink of actual sleep. But neither would dare trust himself off the bridge for a moment when there was the least possibility of the enemy being sighted. It was their station in action.

The sub., lucky fellow, spent his watch below, slumbering more or less peacefully on the settee in the charthouse, a concession he generally made up for by keeping extra watch in the day-time. As for the gunner and the midshipman, R.N.V.R., the latter a young gentleman who was still at a public school in 1916, they, fully dressed, were sleeping, or pretending to sleep, in some hole or corner near the stations they would occupy in action, the 'snotty' somewhere in the forepart of the ship, near the foremost 4-inch gun, and the gunner by his beloved torpedo-tubes. The engineer-lieutenant and the surgeon-probationer were the only officers who could turn in in their clothes with really clear consciences, though the former had elected to make himself a bivouac on deck with blankets, a rug, and an air-pillow within six feet of the hatch leading to his engine-room. He was a wise man, was the engineer officer, and a married man with a large family. He had once been in the wardroom of a destroyer when a mine exploded under the stern, and since that distressing experience he preferred being on deck. The surgeon-probationer either did not know of, or did not care for, such things. He lay stretched out on a settee in the stuffy wardroom, snoring blissfully.

Men, some dozing, but the majority wide awake, lay clustered round the guns, the torpedo-tubes, or the searchlight, prepared for an instant summons. Shell and cartridges were piled in all the gun-positions, where the loading numbers could find them easily in the dark; while at various places on deck were bundles of cutlasses, and rifles with magazines charged and scabbarded bayonets fixed, ready for immediate use in the event of running alongside an enemy and boarding. All the officers and some of the men carried automatic pistols or revolvers in belts strapped round their thick lammy coats; while two unshaven gentlemen, one an ex-grocer's assistant from Bermondsey, and the other a Glasgow newspaper-boy, presided drowsily over a couple of machine-guns.

In a word, the ship was prepared for action. A single touch on the bell-push on the bridge by the first lieutenant's elbow would set the alarm-gongs jangling and bring the men jumping to their feet.

The night, except for that constant rumble of gun-fire in the east, was very still. There was no whistling of wind through the rigging, nothing but the hiss, gurgle, and liquid splutter of the bow-wave as the ship moved through the water, the deep humming of the stokehold fans, and the occasional shrill, protesting cry of a startled and indignant diver disturbed in his beauty-sleep on the water and scuttering clumsily for safety.

The sub., in the charthouse, awakened by the conversation of the gun's crew sitting on deck outside, was softly anathematizing them.

'I met 'er at the cinema last time I was on long leaf,' said a voice. 'Fine, strappin' gal she was. Reg'lar little bit of all right. She takes a fancy to me the minute—'

'Go hon, you ruddy old Bluebeard!' came a gruff interjection. 'What about that other gurl I used to see you walkin' out with?'

'Can't 'elp the other gal,' was the rather indignant reply. 'She played me false. I found out she was bein' courted by a lance-corpril belongin' to a bantam reg'ment. I 'ad a dust-up with 'im about it; but she weren't worth fightin' over, so I just said 'e could bloomin' well 'ave 'er. This one I'm tellin' you about takes a fancy to me the moment she claps eyes on me.'

'She can't know much about you, Shiner.'

'What d'you mean? Can't know much about me!' with some acerbity. 'What d'you mean, speakin' like that? Why should she want to know about me? She loves me at first sight, I tells you!'

'Go hon, you old liar!' was the polite retort.

'S'welp me, she did! She takes me 'om to see 'er pa and ma, and they likes me, too, 'cos they asks me to stay and 'ave a bit o' supper. 'Er pa works in Pompey dockyard. 'E and 'is missus likes their drop o' gargle now and then, so the nex' night I does the polite and treats 'em all to seats at the 'Ippodrome, and a bit o' somethin' t'eat at a restorong afterwards. Cost me more'n 'arf-a-quid, that did. And now it's all fixed up proper, and me and Lucy gets married nex' time I goes on long leaf. Fine, strappin' bit o' fluff, she is. Got a bit o' money in the bank, too!'

'Can't you fellers let a bloke get a drop o' sleep, 'stead o' chawin' your fat all the bloomin' night?' growled a new and very irritated voice. ' 'Oo wants to hear about your love conquests, Shiner?'

'I'll 'ave you know I'm engaged to the young lady,' came the dignified answer. 'Any bloke what says a word agin' 'er gets a punch on the nose! See?'

'Well, you might let other blokes get a bit o' sleep, anyhow.'

'Oh, go to 'ell!' said Shiner wrathfully. 'You don't know what bein' in love feels like. 'Oo's goin' to fall in love with a bloke with a face like yourn?'

'Ssh!' hissed someone. 'Don't get having a barging-match, you two. You'll wake Little Jimmy in a minute. He's asleep in the charthouse.'

'Oh, go to 'ell!' retorted the amorous one.

The sub-lieutenant, rather pleased that his newly discovered lower-deck nickname was not 'Dirty Dick' or 'Sweaty Sam', chuckled softly to himself, examined his wrist-watch, discovered he had still over an hour before he was due on the bridge, and rolled over and went to sleep again.

III

Presently, as the destroyers reached the limit of their patrol, M'Call, on the bridge, saw the long, dark shadow of the leader swinging out of the line as she altered course to starboard to proceed in the opposite direction.

'Captain, sir,' he said, bending down to shake the recumbent figure in the deck-chair by the shoulder, 'they're altering course.'

'Right!' grunted the lieutenant-commander, sitting up and fumbling for his pipe. 'Follow 'em round. Are we up to time?'

'To the minute, sir. The tide's been against us during the last run.'

'Right! Let's see. High-water's at 1.42, our time, isn't it?'

'Yes, sir.'

'So, if we have to go skiboosting about over those blessed banks after the Huns, there'll be water enough for us up till about half three – what?'

'There or thereabouts, sir. We might say four o'clock at a pinch.'

'That be blowed for a yarn!' smiled the C.O. 'Not in these trousers! What about that fellow who smashed up his rudder and propellers the other day by leaving it a bit too late? The Court of Inquiry had his blood, all right; and I'll be shot if you'll persuade me to become a burnt-offering!'

'You mean the *Galeka*, sir?' laughed the first lieutenant, watching the next ahead as her helm went over. 'Of course! It's become a habit with her. Sheds propellers by the dozen, and is always in dock expectin' other people to do her dirty work. Damn stoopid, I call it. What sort of ship goes messin' about on an eight-foot bank, and she drawin' ten and a bit? *We* don't do silly things like that, thank the Lord! Not often, anyhow. Port fifteen, quartermaster!'

The lieutenant-commander seemed rather amused.

'The *Galeka* made a mistake of an hour over this beastly B.S.T. business,' he pointed out. 'I don't wonder at it, personally; but if I were you, Number One, I shouldn't say too much. She's not the only one who's slipped up, not by a very long chalk. What about the time you—'

'Port twenty!' M'Call interrupted, anxious to avoid a question which he had every reason to know would be awkward. 'Ease to ten!' as the ship swung round after her leader. ' 'Midships! Meet her starboard! Steady! What was it you were going to say, sir?' he inquired.

'I've forgotten now,' Langlands yawned. 'But let me know when we turn again, and if I find you astern of a station you'll be hanged, drawn, and blooming well quartered.'

THE NIGHT PATROL

'I will bear it in mind, sir,' replied Number One, quite unperturbed.

It must have been about twenty minutes later that M'Call, who was intently watching the horizon through his glasses, grunted with surprise. Was his imagination at fault, or had he really seen something – something vaguely white and indistinct – far away in the darkness?

'Starboard look-out,' he asked, lowering his binoculars to wipe the object-glasses, 'did you see anything fine on the starboard bow just now?'

'Thought I saw a sort o' sudden splash,' the man answered. 'Thought maybe 'twas a fish jumpin', or a breakin' sea, sir.'

'Can't have been a sea,' said M'Call, rather puzzled; 'it's flat calm.'

'That's what it looked like to me, sir,' the seaman protested, rather annoyed at being doubted. 'There, sir!' after a pause; 'there it is again!' He pointed at a glimmer of white with a triumphant forefinger.

The officer's glasses flew to his eyes, and the briefest inspection satisfied him that the man was right, for there slowly crept into his field of vision a ghostly looking streak of whitened, splashing water. He did not linger an instant, but shouting, 'Action!' pressed the bell-push in front of him.

The time was twelve and a half minutes to two.

The alarm-gongs whirred and jangled throughout the ship, and even as their strident chatter died away he could hear the men be-stirring themselves on deck, and the shuffling of feet as they closed up round their guns.

'Action stations!' roared a voice. 'Show a leg, boys! Look lively now!'

'What is it?' asked Langlands, already on his feet.

'Bow-waves on the starboard bow, sir!'

'All right,' the skipper answered, seemingly quite unmoved by the information, but feeling his heart fluttering with excitement. 'I'll take the ship. You look after the gunnery.'

'Ay, ay, sir. Hicks!'

'Sir?'

'Pass down: All guns load with lyddite; bearing – green,[1] three, five; range – one, four, double o; deflection – one, five, right.'

'That's them all right!' murmured the captain, with his glasses to his eyes, as the dim flicker of a flaming funnel broke out of the darkness. 'Damn bad stoking, too! Is the sub. up here?'

'Yes, sir.'

---

[1] the side on which a target happens to be is always passed down as 'green' or 'red', to avoid possible confusion between the words 'starboard' and 'port'. The order 'Green – three, five', would mean that the guns were to be laid on an object on the starboard side, 35 degrees from right ahead. Similarly, 'Red – one, two, o', would signify that the target was to port, 120 degrees from right ahead.

'Warn the tubes to be ready to starboard. Don't fire until you get orders.'

'Increasing speed, sir!' sang out a signalman, as the lumped-up water in the wake of the destroyer ahead grew whiter and more distinct. 'Leader altering course to starboard, sir!'

Langlands, his glasses still levelled on the approaching enemy, flung an order over his shoulder to the man at the telegraph, and the *Minx*, throbbing to the increased thrust of her turbines, darted forward.

The glimmering bow-waves were now clearly visible to the naked eye, and even as the commanding officer watched them, he saw first the whitened trails of water in the wake of several fast-moving vessels, and then the long, blurred smudges of the ships themselves, dimly silhouetted against a lighter patch on the horizon. They were something over a mile distant.

'How many d'you make out, Number One?' he asked.

'Three or four, sir,' said M'Call, putting his lips to a voice-pipe to pass another order to the guns.

'They don't seem to have spotted us,' the captain went on. 'Perhaps they can't see us against the dark background to the west'ard. Are you all ready?'

'Yes, sir. Quite ready.'

The natural sound of his own voice comforted him, for Langlands, though certainly no coward, was not one of those abnormal men who could saunter through the very gates of hell without trepidation in their hearts. In such people heroism and calmness in the face of danger is a natural habit which can cost them little. They actually do not know what fear is, and hence have no difficulty in combating it.

Another species of bravery altogether is shown by those who feel fear, but can manage to stifle it – can make their will triumph over the perfectly natural desire for personal safety.

And Langlands had this quality. He had been in action many times; but always, before the firing began, his sensations were the same – a ghastly dread of the unexpected, a sickly feeling of apprehension, and an apparent loss of control of his body and limbs, as if his muscles were suddenly made of jelly. But his mind was ever active in such conditions. His brain worked fast and clearly, and outwardly his demeanour was just the same as usual. The fear he felt in his innermost heart never made itself manifest. He had trained himself to conceal it, and went so far as to smoke a pipe in action to convince others that he was in no way perturbed. Artificiality perhaps, but his men noticed it, and took courage.

It was the suspense that was so intolerable, the awful period of waiting between the time the enemy were sighted and the firing of the first shot. It might be seconds or it might be minutes; but it always seemed hours – hours of mental anguish and nerve-racking anxiety. Once under fire, however, these sensations left him altogether, and all thoughts of his own personal safety, all terror of the unknown, were brushed aside. He became cool and alert. Then followed the period of wild exultation when his chief desire was ever the same – to get to close quarters; to fight, if need be, with his bare fists. Realization, he found, was never quite so bad as anticipation. It was the thinking beforehand of what might happen that was so maddeningly unnerving.

The orders for the destroyers on patrol were very simple and elastic, and all the commanding officers knew exactly what was expected of them. They knew the exact speed at which the leader intended to fight, and that, until they came into close action, they had only to conform to his movements. Complications really began when the engagement became general and the formation was broken, for then it was a case of each ship for herself, her duty to single out an opponent, and, if possible, to stick to him until he was crippled or sunk.

They were at liberty to use their own initiative, taking what chances they were offered of ramming or of using their torpedoes, and utilizing their gun-fire to the best possible advantage. Beyond that, nothing else much mattered; and if, in the *mêlé* which was almost bound to ensue, any friendly vessel had the ill-fortune to be stopped or sunk, it was an understood thing that her crew would have to take their chance until the close of the engagement. Their mates could not break off the action to succour them. The orders were very definite on one point – that while a British ship could steam and a British gun could fire, the raiders were to be pursued, hotly engaged, and reported.

By this time the enemy was at a distance of little more than a thousand yards, and, still steaming fast on a roughly parallel and opposite course, seemed quite oblivious of the presence of the British. It was scarcely possible that he had not sighted them, for even with the naked eye Langlands could clearly see the humped-up, unfamiliar shapes of the German destroyers, with their two squat funnels standing nearly upright, the tall mast aft, and the shortest ones forward. There was no mistaking them.

Perhaps they took the British for friends. Maybe they were merely reserving their fire, or were trusting to their speed to slip past without giving battle, for not a light twinkled down their line, not a gun roared out. They still steamed steadily on, grim, menacing, and silent. There were five of them.

The flotillas must have been drawing together at a combined speed of fifty knots, possibly more, and if both continued their courses they would flash by each other at a distance of about four hundred yards. And at fifty knots, one thousand yards is covered in thirty-six seconds; but still the British leader held steadily on his course. The seconds dragged – the enemy came nearer and nearer – the suspense became maddening. Langlands felt his heart thumping like a sledge-hammer. Was the leader missing his opportunity? It seemed as if in another few seconds it would be too late!

But the senior officer was an old hand at the business, and knew what he was about, and at exactly the right moment his helm went over, and Langlands was the leading destroyer swerving abruptly to starboard until she was heading straight for the centre of the hostile line. It was evidently the senior officer's intention to attempt to ram the fourth or fifth ship, leaving those ahead to the other destroyers under his orders. It was the plan agreed upon, the plan they all knew by heart.

There came a blaze of greenish-golden flame and the crash of a ragged salvo as the leader's guns opened the ball. A little cluster of spray fountains, white and shimmering, leapt out of the dark sea close to the leading German, and almost before they had tumbled out of sight the guns were flashing all down the hostile line. In another instant every British ship replied and the firing became general.

The time was 1.49.20.

The guns were firing at point-blank range, so that careful aiming, even if it had been possible, was unnecessary. The din became deafening as the loading numbers crammed projectiles and cartridges home, the breeches of the guns slammed to, and the gun-layers pressed their triggers and fired. The air thudded and shook. Intermingled with the deep roaring of the heavier weapons came the unmistakable stutter of the two-pounder pom-poms as they fell to work to sweep the opposing bridges and decks, and the shriller stammering of the Lewis guns and Maxims. Projectiles screeched and whinnied overhead, burst with a dull, crashing explosion, and sent their fragments humming and hissing through the air to strike funnels, hull, and deck fittings with an insistent jangling clatter like pebbles in a tin can. Machine-gun bullets sprayed past in droves, swishing and crackling as they came like raindrops through foliage.

Langlands, all but blinded by the brilliant flares of the *Minx's* guns, held steadily on his course. The water round the ship seemed to be spouting and boiling with falling shell, and all he could see of the enemy was the flashes of their guns bursting out redly through a leaping curtain of shell-geysers, and clouds of dense, rolling smoke. The Germans seemed to be altering course a little, for the ship the *Minx* was making for, the third in the line, was drawing slightly across the bows.

'Port ten!' he ordered breathlessly, intent on running her down.

'Port ten it is, sir,' came the deep voice of the coxswain, as he twirled the wheel.

' 'Midships! Steady so, Baker!'

'Steady it is, sir!'

THE NIGHT PATROL

A searchlight from some ship in the German line flickered into brilliance, illuminated the scene for an instant in its sickly glare, and then was suddenly extinguished.

There came a crash, an explosion, and a momentary blaze of reddish fire from amidships, as a shell drove home by the *Minx*'s after-funnel; but Langlands paid little heed, for the ship still sped on. Another projectile detonated on the water close under the bow, and a signalman on the bridge sat down with a grunt of stupefied astonishment, and began cursing softly to himself. The coxswain, with his right arm broken by a piece of the same shell, groaned audibly as he tried to use the limb and felt the jagged ends of the bone grating horribly together. He suffered excruciating torment, for, unknown to himself, another sliver of red-hot steel had penetrated the muscles of his back. He was in agony, but he still watched the captain, waiting for his next order, and casting an occasional glance at the compass before him to keep the ship on her course.

A red Very light, soaring aloft, bathed the scene in a momentary flush of crimson before, curving over, it fell hissing into the water. The crashing, thudding medley still went on, but above the din M'Call could be heard passing orders like an automaton, and without a tremor in his voice. He passed his orders, but he little knew that the man below whose duty it was to transmit them to the guns was stretched out on deck, slowly sobbing his life away.

'Can I fire, sir?' suddenly screamed the sub., hoarse with excitement.

'Yes!' the captain shouted back, without turning his head.

And a moment later, when the boy saw the flame-spouting silhouette of the enemy's leader in line with the sights of his instrument, he pressed an ebonite knob, shouted through a voice-pipe, and looked anxiously aft. He was rewarded, for he saw the dull bluish flash and the silvery streak of a torpedo as it leapt from its tube and plunged with a splash into the water. Where that particular torpedo went he never knew, for there was no resultant explosion.

But an instant or two later, when the second German came in line, he pressed another knob. The range at the time seemed absurdly short, and the enemy flashed by in an instant, but the weapon went home. It seemed to strike her fairly amidships, for there came a lurid blast of flame and a cloud of greyish smoke and spray, followed by the roar of an explosion which for a moment completely drowned the sound of the guns.

'Got her, by George!' the sub. muttered softly to himself, watching her as the turmoil subsided and he caught a glimpse of the dripping bow and stern of the enemy's ship lifting themselves out of the water, with the middle portion sagging horribly. 'Clean in halves!'

He had never seen the effect of a torpedo before, and could hardly believe his eyes.

Then several things seemed to happen all at once.

A torpedo fired by the enemy, travelling on the surface in a flutter of spray, suddenly shot past within ten feet of the *Minx*'s bows, and almost at the same moment the destroyer astern of the one which had been torpedoed crashed into her helpless consort with a grinding splintering thud which could almost be felt. The firing from both ships ceased abruptly, and a chorus of shouts and screams came out of the darkness.

The collision occurred within about two hundred feet of the *Minx*'s bows, so close and on such a bearing that Langlands could hardly avoid the tangle.

'Hard a-starboard!' he yelled, however, unwilling to risk damaging his own vessel by running down an enemy which must already be helpless through having been collided with by a friend. 'Hard a-starboard, Baker!'

The coxswain flung the wheel over with all his strength, but it was too late.

The ship slewed, but a moment later Langlands caught a hasty glimpse of the black hull of his enemy right under the bows. He found himself looking down on her deck; could see the blurred, white faces of her men as they stared up at him; heard their frightened screams as they saw this new monster bearing down upon them to complete their destruction. It must have been a terrifying sight, the towering, V-shaped bow tearing remorselessly towards them at over twenty knots, with the twin bow-waves leaping and playing on each side of the sharp stem.

A gun roared off from somewhere close at hand, and with the orange flash of it Langland felt his cap whirled off his head and something strike him across the forehead. A warm gush streamed down his face; but in the excitement of the moment he scarcely noticed it.

The next instant the ship struck.

There was a rendering, shuddering thud, the shrill, protesting sound of riven steel, and then a sudden cessation of speed. The hostile destroyer, struck in the stern, twisted round with the force of the blow, and heeled bodily over until the water poured over the farther edge of her deck. Then the *Minx*'s bows tore their way aft, splintering, grinding, and crunching – enlarging the enormous wound, wrenching off the side plating, and allowing the water to pour in. The stern of the enemy slid free, and it could be heard slithering along the starboard side as the *Minx* still drove ahead.

The time was exactly 1.52. Four and a half minutes since the enemy had been sighted; two and a half since the first gun had been fired. It had seemed an eternity.

THE NIGHT PATROL

Out of the corner of his eye Langlands caught sight of the shape of one of his friends, spouting flame, driving past to starboard and circling madly across the *Minx*'s bows; while another shadow, vague and indistinct in a smoke-cloud, and with guns silent, flashed past, travelling to the north-eastward at high speed. It was the German leader escaping.

For a while the flashes of guns still broke out of the darkness from the direction in which the scattered remnant of the enemy, pursued and hotly engaged, were flying for their lives. The flashes gleamed golden and ruby, while an occasional shell-burst showed up as a flicker of smoky scarlet. The flashes receded farther and farther towards the horizon, and the sobbing, pulsating thunder waned gradually, fainter and fainter, as the combatants streamed away. Then the rolling thud of a distant heavy explosion, and save for the dull mutter of the guns ashore the night was still.

About an hour later, when the pursuers returned, they found nothing but an area of sea strewn with the wreckage of sunken ships, the unmistakable flotsam of battle. They lingered on the spot to rescue several badly wounded and half-drowned Germans who cried piteously for help; but of the *Minx* there was no trace.

'*Minx!* Oh, *Minx!*' they asked by wireless. '*Minx*, where are you?'

But the *Minx* did not answer, and it was with a touch of sadness in their triumphant hearts that the victors picked their way back over the rippling sandbanks towards the anchorage in the golden-grey of the dawn.

IV

The rain-clouds had cleared away, but with the advent of daylight a dense sea-fog lay close and thick upon the water; and through it three battle-scarred destroyers steamed wearily but proudly home towards a certain English port whither they had been ordered for necessary repairs.

All three exhibited plain traces of the fight. One, with an enormous gash on the water-line in the engine-room, caused by a bursting shell which had put the port turbine out of action, limped painfully along at a bare ten knots, with her pumps working to keep down the flow of water, and a collision-mat plastered over the orifice. Another, the leader, had her bridge wrecked, her foremost 4-inch gun useless, and a number of jagged holes through the forecastle; while the grey hulls, upper works, and funnels of all three were torn and perforated by shell-splinters, and mottled here and there by the unmistakable yellow splashes and charred paint where projectiles had struck and detonated. They looked as if they had undergone a severe gruelling, as indeed they had; but their casualties were remarkably light – no more than seven killed and thirteen wounded.

It was nearly noon when, with new White Ensigns fluttering gaily from their mizzens, they steamed jauntily into harbour through the entrance between the well-known grey stone breakwaters, each crowned with its white lighthouse.

The fog had cleared a little. The time of their arrival had been reported by wireless, and as they entered a bunch of signal-flags went up to the truck of the admiral's flagstaff ashore. An instant later the men-of-war at their moorings seemed suddenly to swarm with men.

'Oh lor!' grunted the senior officer of the incoming destroyers, realizing what was about to happen as he conned his ship from the battered bridge. 'Hell and scissors! I always feel such a damned idiot on these occasions! Never know what to do.'

And a few moments afterwards, as the leader passed within a hundred feet of a huge, blister-sided monitor, the signal ashore came down with a rush, and the monitor's men, waving their caps, broke into a roar of frenzied and uncontrolled cheering, which was taken up by ship after ship. It was no ordinary three cheers. It was a noise like the yelling of the crowd when a goal is scored at a popular football match, a deep-throated bellow which reverberated across the water and echoed and re-echoed from the cliffs. It was an encouraging sound, a sound of good-feeling and good-fellowship, very genuine and spontaneous; and nobody can make more din than the sailorman when he is happy and really puts his heart into it.

The sea-front was densely packed with civilian spectators, who had heard vague rumours of a naval engagement, and even they shouted themselves hoarse and waved parasols, hats, and handkerchiefs as the three destroyers slid up to their buoys.

'I'm glad they're pleased,' murmured the senior officer, blushing a rosy red and rubbing his unshaven chin. 'I do feel a sanguinary fool, though, and I wish to Heaven they'd stop their beastly row! I can't hear myself think.'

'Signal, sir,' said the yeoman of signals, who had been busy with his telescope. ' "Vice-admiral to division. Well done. Congratulate you most heartily on your success. Admiral would like to see commanding officers when convenient. *Minx* reports—'

'*Minx!*' shouted the S.O. in delighted astonishment. 'Has she got back, then?'

'Seems so, sir,' said the yeoman, looking round with his telescope. 'Yes, sir,' after a pause. 'That's her! They're just putting her into the floating dock. Her bows are smashed up somethin' crool, and her topmast has gone over the side.'

'Ah, that accounts for our getting no answer to our wireless signals,' murmured the commander. 'Thank Heaven, she's in, though!'

He meant it.

THE NIGHT PATROL

'On the night of the 28th–29th four of our destroyers on patrol met five enemy craft on their way to take part in a raid in the Channel. A hot engagement ensued, in the course of which three of the enemy were sunk. The other two, hit repeatedly and hotly pursued to their base, succeeded in escaping in a badly damaged condition, though from aerial reconnaissance it is believed that one of them subsequently foundered. We lost no ships, and our casualties, considering the close range at which the action was fought, were very slight. All the next of kin have been informed.' – *Official Communiqué*.

'Sea-Wrack'

The Day's Work

SUB-LIEUTENANT Andrew Carr crouched in the basket of the kite-balloon, his numbed fingers gripping the telephone receiver – the headphone of which he pressed against his ear. With the other hand he clutched the edge of the gyrating gondola, as squalls of icy wind swooped down on the balloon.

'Blazes!' he muttered, glancing first at the snow-laden wrack in the north-western sky, then down at the deck of the kite-balloon depot-ship some thousand feet below him. 'Blazes!' he repeated, 'when *are* they going to give the signal "Haul Down"?'

A feeling of exasperated impotence filled his soul. Up here he could see the urgency: down there they were fussing with the depot-ship's boats. Oh, he knew there was a blizzard threatening – more than threatening; for its first icy messengers were then screaming through the wickerwork of the basket and drumming through the gondola-stays. Above his head – though he dared not glance up too frequently, for it made him giddy – the balloon was swooping and pitching in a manner he did not care to see.

'Boats!' he stormed suddenly, as he stamped deadened feet on the frail platform. 'Boats! why worry about boats? Why not get the damned balloon down to its night stowage before this blasted storm really breaks?' He dropped the telephone suddenly and grabbed at a stay, for a terrific gust had listed the balloon-envelope and thrown it bodily to one side: with a frightening jerk the basket was yanked sideways so that for a moment the platform was angled at forty-five degrees. Cold fear gripped Andrew Carr as the stay in his right hand grew suddenly slack. The gondola began to droop at one end. Instinctively he shuffled up to the higher end. 'Gosh!' he muttered, his eyes full of fear, 'the port for'ard stay's been torn out of its basket joint – there are only three more – oh, why *don't* they give the order for "Haul Down"?'

He grabbed the telephone-receiver again and shouted down the mouthpiece. 'Depot-ship! Depot-ship! Below there: why'n hell don't you haul me down? One of the basket-stays has parted: it's blowing like stink up here – oh, get a move on, why the . . .'

Andrew broke off. For the first time in his young life, panic threatened to obliterate every sense he had. Although he was numbed to the core, sweat beaded on his face, trickling down his nose, falling from under his woollen helmet and freezing on his cheeks and lips. He felt, somehow, abandoned, lost, inhumanly forgotten: none of those devils down there, mucking about with boats, seemed to care a hoot what happened to him. Frenziedly he struggled against the waves of panic. He was only nineteen years old: a sense of unfairness assailed him. 'Mucking about with boats!' he muttered bitterly – and, suddenly reckless, he leant far out over the side of the wildly swaying basket, holding his balance only because he had a knee jammed under a projection. Through the darkness of the gathering night he peered down at the deck of the depot-ship below. Unconsciously, he noted the angle of the bar-taut steel wire that led downwards from the balloon to the winch of the ship. He had never realized before how frail it looked. But his eyes were concentrating through the gloom on the half-submerged picket-boat and the running figures of the seamen below moving about like ants at some desperate work.

'Something's gone wrong,' he muttered, and, taking another grip with his knee, he focused with one hand his binoculars on the scene. In and out of his constricted field of vision there appeared now, when he managed to steady the glasses, a magnified view of the picket-boat as she dipped and jumped wildly alongside. Her funnel was stowed, and the stoker petty officer and two seamen-crew staggered and swung about her reeling deck in their attempts to hook the heavy ring of her slings on to the vast steel hook of the main-derrick hoist.

'Gosh!' said Andrew suddenly, as a sea broke over the boat's bows and the figures were hidden in whirling spray. 'Gosh! if they don't get a move on, she'll founder alongside before they get her hoisted!' He could sympathize with that sweating, struggling crew; he had been midshipman of a boat himself when she bucked and cavorted and strong men were thrown about by a huge leaden ball just above the main derrick hook.

A new high note in the humming wind attracted Andrew's attention. He withdrew his straining eyes from the glasses and took a wider look at the vast harbour below. The sea was a medley of spume and scud, the smoky grey waves marbled into a seething white cauldron by the shrieking squall. In a moment, Andrew saw, it would reach the depot-ship, between which and the nor'-western shore of the low-lying island everything was now blurred. Away beyond the depot-ship, plumes and eddies of smoke flew horizontally to leeward from the waking titans whose bulk loomed dim and monstrous – line after line. Battleships, cruisers, destroyers – the fleet was raising steam. The worst gale of the worst year's weather was breaking over the harbour.

Numbed, almost deafened, his frozen feet, hands and face leaden and blue, Andrew Carr crouched in his flimsy basket and peered through watery, narrowed eyes at the desolation below. His momentary panic had gone. Something of the majesty and sheer elemental destructiveness of the great gale that boomed and roared round his eyrie and blotted out distance and landmarks aroused an answering paean in his heart. The great frozen wind spoke with the certainty of a mighty organ prelude, with a force and a passion that tore through the flimsy sense of civilized convention like a mastodon in full and resistless stride. Dimly, Andrew felt nerved up for great events. The brotherhood and support of countless generations of seamen seemed suddenly to close around him. Almost, in the hum and screech of the wind, he heard their strong deep voices overriding the roar of the gale. Andrew braced his young body, and the lines of his mouth grew taut and hard, as a kind of nervous exultation gripped him. If only he could get down, he felt, and find some time to think: to sit in a comfortable chair in front of the wardroom stove, and be able to say with the airiness of nineteen years, slowly, gravely, 'Yes, it *was* a bit thick . . . damn it all, they might have hauled me down before . . . I mean . . .' and knowing all the while in his inmost mind that he had been scared to death, had been feeling panic-stricken, and cold and miserable. It would be an experience to hug to himself with a kind of relish, somehow, and the implications and reactions of which – with a mystery all their own – could be explored tentatively and truthfully, but with a certain caution, in the five minutes as he lay in his bunk at night before switching off the cabin-light.

A loud crack, startling, unexpected, galvanized Andrew into sudden life, so that he gripped the edge of the basket and peered fearfully upwards. But the underside of the rolling, plunging balloon-envelope was in dark shadow, where night seemed already to have fallen. Though he looked up and thought he could see a waving end of thick wire, he could not be sure – only the suspicion lingered that something else in the rigging had parted.

As if remembering, he leant over the edge of the basket again and peered down at his floating home. The squall had shrieked on down harbour, and a huge rising sea had gathered in its wake. Big hummocks, razor-edged and grey-white, and deep hollows loomed significantly.

Andrew focused his glasses on the depot-ship and, tense for a moment, stared unbelievingly down. The picket-boat had gone. Moving the glasses frantically he caught at last a passing but steady look at the boat's empty crutches on the depot-ship's high deck.

His faced paled.

'Gone!' he whispered – and as if in reply his own sense of

dependability vanished. That chair in front of the wardroom fire; that snug little cabin housing warm changes of clothing: all suddenly seemed to fade; they grew evanescent as hope itself. No longer could he depend on them. The depot-ship, that solid ten-thousand ton vessel, their parent-ship, was not so certain, not so solid after all. She could not even guarantee the safety of her own picket-boat alongside. What chance, then, for him? In this tremendous storm she might drag her anchors . . . she might . . . the wardroom fire seemed all at once a picture from the past: that cabin a strange memory; in neither had he a confident stake now.

Andrew slumped down on the slanting platform and stared with unseeing eyes at the bearing indicator within a foot of his head. Then, dully, he noticed that its tarpaulin cover had gone, blown to shreds by the roaring gusts that still whistled over the edge and through the wickerwork of the basket.

As he crouched in a lethargy, almost comatose, the telephone-bell rang shrilly, urgently, through the basket – its pitiful little tinkle whipped away by the wind almost as soon as it sounded.

But Andrew had heard it. Kneeling low in the basket, he held the receiver against his frozen ear and shouted down the mouthpiece—

'Hullo! Hullo! At last! What the . . .'

He broke off and listened to the urgent voice the other end.

'Carr, Carr; are you all right? Listen: we've had several kinds of trouble. Lost the picket-boat . . . swamped being hoisted in, and the coxwain's . . . no, we couldn't lower a boat; wouldn't have lived a moment in the sea that's running . . .'

'Yes, yes; that's all very well,' Andrew's voice broke in. 'But d'you realize this perishing basket I'm in's only hanging by a thread. Yes, one of the stays has gone. What . . .' Andrew burst into profanity. 'Hell, man; I've been roaring down this blasted mouthpiece till I'm blue in the face . . . !'

'That'll do, Carr . . .' Andrew grinned as he listened. 'This is "on service". Because we're friends, no reason why you should fly off the handle like this. I've been pretty busy down here. Now, listen, old man: take this in. Can you hear?'

Andrew spoke soothingly. 'All right, old boy: I'm listening.'

The voice of twenty-one spoke again crisply, authoritatively—

'We may have to let the balloon go – to get *you*, see? We're ready – double-blanked this end – only chance's to heave down and quick and steady – so once we start, hold tight, and look out – and remember these instructions – if a red light's flashed continuously from the winch aft – keep your eye on it, for heaven's sake – that's a signal to pull the rip-cord and scupper the balloon. Remember, after that, you've got about sixty seconds to get aboard. If you have to sink her – it may be your only chance – nip over the side and come down the wire hand over hand: we'll have a net ready for you, and . . . well, we'll be ready anyhow . . .'

Andrew Carr shivered. The emergency escape! The last resort of the kite-balloonists! Gosh, he thought, things must be bad if old Jimmy considered it was the only chance – and his balloons were the apple of his eye. A harsh jerk, like a badly-started lift, threw him in a heap on the bottom of the car. Bruised, he scrambled to his feet and glanced downwards at the wire. It was pulsing and vibrating. The winch had begun to heave-in.

The new strain on the wire and the downward motion somewhat steadied the gondola, though above his head Andrew heard with uneasy ears the rasping of the rigging and the straining fabric.

But the kite-balloon was coming in fast. Jimmy was taking the chance of heaving-in full speed. Andrew glanced at the dial. 900 feet . . . 850–800–750–700 . . . yes, he was coming down fast. Under his feet, the depot-ship was growing bigger and bigger. He could now recognize expressions on the features of the white faces peering up at him from the decks below: they seemed anxious. The men in oilskins round the winch looked now and again over their shoulders. Andrew shifted his position and threw a glance that way too. As he did so, his eyes widened, and, unconsciously, his hands took a fresh, convulsive grip of the gondola-cage. Another squall was sweeping towards the depot-ship: not half a mile away, the sea vanished in a smoking smother of rain and whitened water that eddied and boiled.

Andrew glanced at the height-indicator. 500 feet now. It seemed the last straw; when he was so near safety.

With a moaning hiss, the squall burst over the depot-ship – the sub-lieutenant catching a last look at the white faces below. He saw Jimmy, his CO, frantically urging the last ounce out of the winchman; then, with a scream, the wind struck the balloon. The stays and rigging hummed: the basket seemed to jerk sideways and upwards with a wild, horrifying motion that struck intense fear into Andrew's heart. Peering out through the driving rain, he could not see any envelope above as the squall roared past. There came a sudden jarring crack, and Andrew groaned. At once, he sensed the free, lifting motion as if he were soaring skywards on a mighty swing. His chest and stomach all at once appeared to have been left hundreds of feet below him. Wedged in the corner of t..e careening basket he threw a horrified look downwards. The depot-ship had disappeared – lost in the welter of the squall. But he had seen enough. His face grew grey, as the realization came that he was utterly lost now, with no possibility, even, of trying out the emergency plan outlined by his CO.

Below the basket, the parted winch-wire whipped and snaked and vibrated as if exulting in its utter freedom, while the wind, as if screaming its final triumph, howled as it battered the reeling torpedo-shaped envelope – howled and died away. Dazed, Andrew crouched below the edge of the car. The motion was worse than anything he had ever experienced. The awesome swoops and sickening side-plunges of the driven balloon made him feel as if he were tethered to the tail of a playful comet that gambolled in quarter-mile circles. But the atmosphere round the soaring car grew lighter, though the swiftness of his motion still made him gasp. Soon, with one frantic eye, he pierced the gloom below. The untethered kite-balloon had risen a thousand feet. A mile away to the nor'-west'ard, he saw the depot-ship.

'First the picket-boat, now me,' yelled Andrew, anger choking him. 'What a ship!' But his fury was short-lived. He noted the rapid, urgent flash of her masthead signalling light – and he realized that in ten minutes it would be dark. His thoughts cleared. With quick, practised eye, he took a snap-bearing of the fast-vanishing depot-ship, then drew out from its locker the powerful electric signalling lamp. But before using it, he fired six charges downwards, from the brass Very pistol, and the sight of their trailing, red lights cutting brilliantly through the darkness towards the fleet brought a badly-needed comfort to his young heart. Then he trained the lamp over the edge and followed the Very emergency signals with a crisp morse message, repeated over and over again:

'Adrift. Course south-east. Speed sixty knots. Balloon damaged. Am going to use rip-cord middle harbour. SOS SOS.'

Andrew was putting the signal-lamp away in the locker, his eye already on the rip-cord, when a cross-current of wind swooped down like an eddy of the gale. The balloon-envelope lurched away to the south-west – the gondola jerked off to the east. Andrew's feet were swung away off the platform: his balance lost, he fell in a heap on the edge of the car. For a moment, the wind knocked out of him, he trembled in the balance, then slumped down into the basket. Winded, he fell heavily, and his head met the solid bearing-indicator. In the bottom of the basket he lay still; from under the woollen helmet a trickle of blood slowly spread . . .

On the bare, wet deck of the duty destroyer, a big man in oilskins struggled aft. Arriving at the wardroom hatch, he panted for breath, then clattered down the iron ladder. As he twitched the curtain of the door aside, the captain glanced up sharply. 'What is it, torpedo cox'n?' he asked.

'Kite-balloon adrift, sir – half-way across the harbour. There's –' the torpedo cox'n took another breath, 'there's somebody aloft in her, sir.'

The tall, hook-nosed lieutenant-commander was already on his feet, struggling into the oilskin lying handy on the nearby chair. He was rather expecting something like this. As he settled the scarf round his neck, the yeoman of signals came down the ladder with a signal. 'Priority, sir!' he reported, holding out the pad.

'Very good.' The captain read it swiftly, then put it in his pocket. 'Cox'n,' he ordered. 'My compliments to the first lieutenant on the bridge. Stand-by to slip at once – cable and all – at the first shackle, yes. We can retrieve it later. Chief' – the captain turned to another figure – 'we're at five minutes' notice I know, but – I want to slip in a minute and a half from now. Sub!'

'Sir!' the young sub-lieutenant was making fast a length of spunyarn round the waist of his oilskins. 'Sir?'

'Chart of the harbour – and the Pentland Firth – to start with. Up on the bridge with you. See if you can pick up the kite-balloon. If you find her – hold her. Get bearings, and check up on her course. Yeoman, make a signal: "Am slipping at once in accordance with instructions received." '

A rumbling noise came from forward. The first lieutenant had slipped the cable. The captain nodded his head appreciatively and ran from the ladder to the upper-deck. He had two hundred feet to travel to the bridge, and, in the weather prevailing, he knew the wire slip-rope would not last long.

On the bridge the special sea-dutymen stood by at their stations. The captain leant over the compass and took a quick glance round – a glance almost perfunctory, for all the salient points of the anchorage had long since been deeply etched in memory.

Figures loomed on the long, wet forecastle from which hoarse voices sounded, their insistent tones seeming to swirl disembodied, errant, without ownership, in the blast of the wind, now appearing close up, and with something of urgency, against the bridge-screens, then fading away, lost, in the darkness – as if they had been projected into the night-murk and surrendered to the overpowering, enveloping voice of the gale.

The captain, his shoulders hunched up, leant over the rails. 'Slip!' he roared through a megaphone, and, like a faint echo, the order came back from the forecastle-head: 'Slip, sir! all gone for'ard, sir!'

'Hard-a-port: half ahead port, slow astern starboard.' The captain's order came just one minute and twenty-five seconds after he had jumped to his feet in the wardroom.

The long, scarce-distinguishable shape of the destroyer shuddered gently, then, like a vibrating wraith, she moved, mysterious, responsive, slowly at first, then faster. 'Ten knots,' the captain ordered, his eye piercing the gloom aft, his mind cognizant of the exact position of the invisible poop to which led the twin strips of gleaming corticine decks on either side of the funnels. At the wheel, the torpedo cox'n slanted a look at the yeoman of signals. 'We're going to get wet soon,' he muttered.

The man holding the telescope made an impatient movement by way of reply. He was looking round the harbour for relevant signals in the swift, instinctive exercise of his craft, his flitting eye reading, rejecting, selecting, the twinkling morse messages as a post-office sorter deals with a multitude of letters. As the destroyer swung round, he moved continually across the bridge in the background, appearing suddenly alongside the port look-out one moment only to materialize the next at the sub-lieutenant's elbow. In his ceaseless, restless search for vantage points, where visibility was good, he had the air of an oil-skinned jack-o-lantern. The torpedo cox'n's remark was relegated to a corner of his mind whence it could be extracted when things were less pressing.

The destroyer was swinging fast now – seeming to spin round the hub of her bows, and the gusts of wind swirled through the bridge. Forcibly, at that moment, pitted against the blast of the wind and the assault of steep-pitched waves, the long dark boat seemed to present in her swift responsive obedience, eager, satisfying, the crystallization of some long-thought-out purpose of her distant designer – to entrust to the trained seamen who stood on her bridge, in control, a vastly powerful, yet delicate, engine of tremendous potentialities: a racing, lithe ship crammed full of mechanical perfection of detail, with the speed of a racehorse and the bite of a tarantula.

As if her lean shape were peculiarly adapted to crowded anchorages and constricted waters, the destroyer snaked her way easily, at fifteen knots, through the narrow channel. 'Yes,' replied the yeoman at last as he paused by the torpedo cox'n, 'you're right; we're going to get wet.' Out of the corner of his eye the cox'n caught a gleam of light and heard the sharp snap as the telescope extension was shot home. Though he did not see it, he knew the yeoman had tucked the instrument under his arm. He always did when they reached that part of the channel.

More than spray was coming over the flared bows now; for the fierce, steep waves had travelled over seven miles across the wide harbour before they broke heavily against the destroyer's questing stem. In the angle of the bridge, just forward of the ready-use chart-table, the captain stood jammed into his favourite corner. 'You'd better get out of that,' the first lieutenant had warned a new sub-lieutenant; 'that's the owner's pet nook.' And so it had always remained. Near by, the sub. kept an eye on the ship's course – more as a matter of routine than of necessity, for the torpedo cox'n was eminently dependable. The shrouded glow from the binnacle light shone upwards, lending an air of snugness to the enclosed bridge. As the cox'n moved the spokes of the wheel with sensitive, firm hands, the telemotor-gear sounded faintly, a low-pitched chatter of protest, against the whistle of the wind and the drumming of spray on the bridge-screens.

The captain, without taking his eyes off the darkness ahead, held a muttered conversation with the sub.

'I know him,' the latter said. 'Yes, sir; you could just see the balloon through glasses . . . about the middle of the Firth, and going, well, just like the wind. Wonder why'n earth he didn't rip her and come down here?'

'May have got damaged.' The captain spoke tersely, frowning into the night. 'Has the answer to that signal come yet, yeoman?'

'Just coming through now, sir.'

The captain grunted. 'Just as well; I never did like the idea of charging a boom in a gale – and three of 'em . . .'

Night had fallen completely as the duty destroyer bore down on the first of the booms. The gate-ship's lights shone out brightly, but they wallowed and plunged in the rising sea. The kite-balloon had disappeared into the south-east'ard.

'Golly, sir,' the sub. breathed, looking ahead with wide-opened eyes, 'there'll be some sea running in Pentland Firth.'

The captain nodded. 'It'll be a following sea, fortunately. I wouldn't care to try the Old Man of Hoy tonight – not after seeing what he can do to a full-blown battleship.'

The sub's features grew suddenly grave, and a little disquieted, for he also had seen the spectacle alluded to: a grey, battered ship slowly steaming into harbour with her upper-works and superstructure looking as if she had been in action – as indeed she had, but the opponent in this case had been Nature, whose onslaughts are more terrifying than anything yet invented by the puny hand of mankind.

'It was a kind of wall of water, wasn't it, sir?' suggested the sub. in subdued tones. The captain waved a hand at a dim figure on the tiny bridge of the gate-ship.

'Yes,' he replied. 'When you get a ten-knot current piling up against a contrary gale of wind with an uneven sea-bed in a constricted channel – well, curious things in waves result. You may run suddenly into a hole in the sea – and on the other side of the hole maybe there's a vertical wave of water sixty feet high waiting to welcome you . . .'

The sub. shuddered, glad they were bound east'ard, not westward.

The destroyer slipped through the third boom gate. She cleared the narrow channel and came out into the Firth. The captain eased her away from the island and watched the white-flecked mountains that rolled up in disarray ahead. His lips tightened and he gripped the rails as he gave the order 'starboard ten'. The cox'n was frowning with concentration at the wheel, his legs wide-straddled on the grating, his hands gripping the spokes more firmly. He muttered to himself as the fierce current took the boat in its swirling stride. The captain glanced quickly at the compass and looked out through his glasses. 'Steady her head three points to port,' he ordered as the boat lurched up on the shoulder of a huge following sea and yawed points away off her course.

'Ay, ay, sir,' the cox'n replied. 'Steady she is, sir, course south-east.'

The sub. staggered to the chart-table, and lifting the canvas flap disappeared, as to the upper half of his body, into the gloomy recess. Switching on the tiny lamp, he entered up time and alteration of course in the navigator's notebook. As he leant there, temporarily cut off from the whistling hum of the wind, he muttered to himself fervently, 'I'll be glad when the old hooker's out of this damned spot'; then, as he kept his feet with difficulty, an urgent need for human companionship gripped him, so that he struggled backwards out of the canvas flap and reeled to a friendly rail. After a moment, he noticed a new figure looming near. 'What a night, No. 1!' he bawled. The newcomer nodded his sou'wester vigorously. 'Be glad . . . when we . . . get out of the Firth.'

The sub., glancing at the captain, wondered suddenly what that sphinx-like figure was thinking of so deeply. Then he saw that the torpedo cox'n was keeping his feet only with considerable difficulty. The wind roared after the reeling destroyer as if in a malicious frenzy that she was escaping: black clouds of smoke, greasy, pungent with the heavy smell of oil, swept forward from the squat funnels and enveloped the bridge; for the 'Chief' was hotting-up his boilers, ready for any call for increased speed.

Aft, out of the welter of foam and driving spray, enormous heavy seas roared up, carrying in their mountainous bulk a strange impression every now and again of perpetual motion, so that the observer is persuaded they are only half-way on their thunderous journey round the world, immutable, permanent, and, as long as the ship can keep ahead of them, on a more or less fixed course, not particularly hostile.

Something of this impression came to the first lieutenant as he peered aft through narrowed eyes – though he was not looking so much at the vast following sea as at the clean-swept decks, and double-lashed gear, for which he was responsible. Then out of the murk astern his eye caught sight suddenly of a dark-looming mountain of a height so incredible that he jumped across the bridge and caught the captain's arm. At the head of the bridge-ladder, together, a few seconds later, they gripped the after-rails and looked out astern where the low poop, wet, wave-swept, and glistening, appeared all at once to be supremely and absurdly near the water and vulnerable. Rearing high above it, topped by ten feet of yellow roaring spume, the personification of implacable and dangerous threat, the vast wave dwarfed the destroyer so that the first lieutenant stared at it as with a sudden revelation. Never had he realized before how narrow was the beam, how low the freeboard, of his ship.

The captain whistled once through pursed lips, then jumped to the revolution-indicator. He revolved the latter until the whirring point of the handle seemed to coruscate in a glittering circle of light – like an enormous catherine-wheel. Years after, when the wind of a westerly gale drove spattering rain against the windows in winter, and the house shook with the shock of the gusts, the first lieutenant would suddenly remember that moment. He would see again the captain's tall figure bent in fierce concentration over the revolution-indicator, and the rotary motion of his hand – as if he were winding up a huge clockwork-machine with only ten vital seconds in which to do it. Then, with the roar and hum of the gale once more drumming round him, he saw the captain leap back to his side and point a steady finger aft where the vast wave seemed to be ready to engulf the ship, drawing inexorably nearer, growing steeper, with an implacable detachment more nerve-racking than outright anger because it was the personification of Nature at her wildest. It is at moments like this that men cluster together and the individual becomes part of the tribe banded in company, conjointly, unitedly, to face and repel the danger at the cave-door. And because the ocean is so vast, so universal, and her challenge so frequent and unmistakable, the phenomenon is more common at sea. There are no mutinies in a gale, no complaints, and the bad-hat of the mess-deck is first aloft and last down.

A curious idea came to the first lieutenant as he stood gripping the after-rails of the reeling bridge. He drew closer to his captain, who, as he noticed with surprise, was pointing aft and presumably speaking, for his lips were moving. The full force of the following gale caught at their bodies in that exposed position, tearing and flapping at their oilskins, snatching at their sou'westers. The first lieutenant bent nearer. He caught a few words before they were swept away, engulfed, by the wind.

'. . . Twenty knots . . .' the captain was bellowing. 'I think she'll stand it for a few minutes . . . this wave . . . biggest I've ever seen . . . passing over a ledge . . . too near the Skerries . . . must keep ahead as much as . . . can . . . If fall back, get pooped sure as eggs . . . eggs . . .'

The first lieutenant nodded vigorously, then suddenly clutched his sou'wester and swayed. Putting his mouth near the captain's ear he shouted back: 'Huge . . . father and mother of all waves, chasing us . . . look! seems quite flat at the ridge, and high, high . . .' He looked again at the wave, and there suddenly came to him an absurd fancy that in height and appearance it resembled strangely the long, clean-cut nave of a cathedral with a ten-foot line of snow left on the roof-ridge. He was about to convey his idea to the captain when he felt the ship under his feet writhe suddenly and shake. Simultaneously a hand gripped his arm.

'We're running ahead of it!' the captain was shouting in his ear. 'Look! it's dropping back! Thank God! We're over the ledge . . . passed it . . . twenty knots . . . risky – but done the trick . . . must reduce soon . . . though out of the Firth now.'

Incredulously, the first lieutenant stared aft. The captain, he saw, was right: the huge mass of the wave appeared to be diminishing in size, its white, horizontal ridge was undoubtedly lower. The destroyer, as if exulting in her escape, was burrowing her way zealously along the floor of a deep, dark valley, and even as the first lieutenant glanced sharply for'ard over his shoulder he felt her bows rise. Out of the corner of his eye he noted that the captain was still looking fixedly aft, his gloved hands clenched on the rails, and in his whole appearance there was something irresistibly reminiscent of the victorious boxer who stands fixedly but watchfully while his opponent is counted out. Then, as if all at once tired, the captain let go his grasp, and turning, staggered forward to his usual place at the bridge-rails, where the sub., one arm hooked round a stanchion, legs widely straddled, peered out over the smoking bows through binoculars at the sea ahead. The first lieutenant, after a quick glance along the decks, followed.

'We'll have to ease her down again,' the captain said, and No. 1 nodded. The latter bent nearer. 'Fifteen?' he shouted. The captain made a gesture of assent.

The first lieutenant lurched to the revolution-indicator and rang down the revolutions to the equivalent of fifteen knots. His leather sea-boots appeared to be getting very heavy, his oilskin a burden. From his position at the rails, the captain was making signs which No. 1 easily interpreted. He touched the torpedo cox'n's arm. 'All right, cox'n; turn over to the quartermaster now, then go below. On the way for'ard tell the P.O. of the watch to have a look at the grips of the motorboat and whaler – and take in any slack. When we alter course to the east'ard, there'll be some heavy seas coming aboard in the waist.'

The torpedo cox'n, having turned over to the quarter-master, saluted. 'Ay, ay, sir,' he said, and his voice sounded hoarse. He stepped down stiffly from the grating, and the lines of his gaunt face showed deep, grim, in the glow of the binnacle light.

Two hours later – watches forgotten – the captain, the first lieutenant, and the sub. still held the bridge. The destroyer's course had been altered to east; and her motion for an hour was frightful; heavy seas stormed her port quarter, breaking green on her lower upper-deck and cascading through gun platforms and torpedo tubes. The three officers, except for an occasional remark, were silent. They found talking too difficult. Once the sub. had pointed aft and shouted into the first lieutenant's ear: 'The wardroom hatch's gone again, No. 1!' and the latter had smiled grimly and replied: 'More than that would have gone if that big one had pooped us – and, anyhow, we could do with a new hatch; we wanted one badly.'

Now and again the skipper had struggled down to the charthouse and made rough calculations in regard to course and speed. He was keeping a close watch on the wind, for the direction of the wind – or its opposite – was the course that the unfortunate kite-balloon must perforce follow.

A curious phenomenon of those northern waters – of which the skipper was well aware – is that though a gale may be raging round the Orkneys and Shetlands, a placid calm may be holding only a hundred miles away in the North Sea. Therefore, the captain watched the wind, and at the end of two hours his scrutiny was rewarded; he was sure the wind was not only drawing aft, but also he began to suspect that there were signs the weather was about to moderate. On reaching this conclusion he raised his head and stared thoughtfully into the sky. The first lieutenant, observing him, came-to alongside.

'Backing a bit,' the latter said, indicating the sea.

'Yes,' the captain agreed, gripping No. 1's arm. 'If it continues to draw round to the west'ard, that means our young friend aloft – who is ahead of us – will be blown first sou'east then east'sou'-east, and finally east . . .' The wind swept away the last words, so that the first lieutenant drew closer. He saw, however, the trend of his captain's thought.

'Good thing, then, sir,' he suggested. 'We'll be able to cut off a bit of the corner?'

The captain nodded his head vigorously. 'Yes.'

The first lieutenant settled his sou'wester more firmly on his head and sent a thought after the unfortunate young officer in the balloon. Their own lot might not be so uncomfortable compared with his . . . driven helplessly before the gale away to the south-east over the open sea.

The first watch passed, and the captain was able to increase speed, for they were running out of the worst of the weather: the wind, which had backed to west, now blew in blustery squalls – those vicious blasts that often accompany the tail-end of a cyclone. The first lieutenant looked gloomily along the port side of the boat, noting the heavy damage she had sustained. As he stood gripping the bridge rails, fragments of torn canvas, ripped from the dodgers, blew and pecked at his legs. Quite near and below him the remains of the whaler rattled eerily in the davits, round which the dim figures of the watch on deck moved cautiously. Every now and again voices reached him, and there was the intermittent sound of hammering. The first lieutenant sighed and turned away. She had been a good boat, and he had won a sailing race in her.

A signalman staggered up the bridge-ladders from the battered galley with a bowl of cocoa that he shielded from the swooping wind as if he were bearing the Crown Regalia. It was welcome: that thick ship's cocoa that no-one who has drunk it in a January gale in the North Sea will ever forget.

The middle watch dragged its stubborn hours through the night to the accompaniment of all sorts of new and strange groans and rattles from protesting beams and loosened cordage. The sub. had been sent down to the charthouse for a stand-easy, but the captain and the first-lieutenant still stood leaden-footed on the bridge, the salt caking their faces, from which gleamed blood-shot eyes irritated by the greasy, pungent oil-fuel smoke; and neither was without painful bruises occasioned by sudden and violent contact with unyielding objects.

Dawn came at last to disclose wide, yellow waste of waters, uneasy, sullen. The wind had dropped considerably, but it now blew in fitful gusts from the south. A long, hollow swell rolled up from the south-west. The destroyer looked bare as a flagstaff, her burnt funnels grey and dirty-white with caked salt. Aft, both wardroom and cabin-flat shelters had been swept away, and no-one but a seaman would have suspected that the few wisps of splintered wood on the port side had once been a whaler.

On the bridge anxious eyes searched the sea and horizon – but in vain: nothing was in sight. The skipper, moving one heavy sea-boot after the other with a kind of obdurate persistence, went down to the charthouse; came back.

'We'll alter course two points to starboard,' he said. 'Quartermaster, port ten.'

'Port ten, sir – on, sir.'

'Meet her; midships; steady!'

'Midships! Steady, sir!'

The bare, gleaming forecastle-head – visible at last – seemed to bore its powerful stem into the shoulder of a swell as the long, grey boat obediently swung to her new course; a lazy dollop of water, weighing perhaps five tons, came in over the starboard bow, brown, dirty-looking, and burst suddenly and surprisingly into a cataract of purest white and green that swirled aft and surrounded the forecastle gun until the latter looked like an island fortress – but the snap and power had gone out of its punch. Wildly flapping signal-halliards – unnoticed during the night – suddenly sounded unnaturally loud. At the rails the captain's brows drew together in a frown. He beckoned the first lieutenant.

A moment later a seaman made his way cautiously aloft, clinging with sure hands to the ratlines of the swaying Jacob's ladder that ascended to the foreyard. Arriving at the head of the ladder, he hooked one arm firmly, and stared out at the horizon. Suddenly, he extended his hand, pointing, then looked down at the upturned faces on the bridge; his mouth opened, and the first lieutenant, glancing upwards with a strained attention to catch his message, noticed the flash of his teeth white against the black of his cowl-like sou'wester. 'Kite-balloon away to the south'ard!' the look-out man roared, and his stentorian hail fell upon the bridge with the urgent import of vital discovery. 'Two points on the starboard bow – 'bout four miles away!'

The captain gave a terse order; the bows of the destroyer bumped round to the point indicated; the revolution-indicator tinkled suddenly with a continuous whirr as accompaniment. In five minutes the derelict kite-balloon could be plainly seen. The captain's eyes narrowed as he observed her.

'She's down,' he muttered, 'probably been down for some time; otherwise . . . we shouldn't have overhauled her.' The captain turned abruptly. 'First lieutenant, see to the boat; get the crew all ready with lifebelts; warn the doctor to stand by, blankets, brandy – he'll know.'

A sense of urgency descended on the occupants of the bridge, for the captain had increased speed as high as he dared – and more. The long, storm-battered ship seemed to the first lieutenant, as he felt the deep-seated throb under his feet enlarge, to grow more sonorous, to lay herself out like a lithe animal of the chase when the quarry is sighted. She stormed through the seas, propellers racing as the stern lifted over the yellow, rolling swell, sharp stem diving suddenly into the trough with a jarring thud, then, staggered, reeling forward with a violent roll while the flying spray rattled hard against the bridge-screens, stinging the tense faces peering out from above them. Soon they were quite close. The captain's hands gripped the rails with unconscious force, his grim-looking expression seeming to accentuate the prominent curve of the dominating hook-nose, and draw even deeper the two furrows that ran vertically from cheek to jaw. At half-speed, the commanding officer brought his boat round on the shoulder of a long, hollow roller; the engine-room telegraphs rang out suddenly, cleaving across the waste of yellow silence with an emphasis almost startling; at once the propellers thrashed madly astern, raising great boiling mounds of seething white water round the poop that piled up against the sheer of the stern.

'Where is he?' the captain was muttering, taking hasty glances through his binoculars.

There was no time to lose; the basket was awash, swept by waves, as the balloon careened drunkenly, precariously, on the surface of the sea. At one of his favourite vantage points the yeoman stood as if clamped in some extraordinary manner to the very texture of the ship's frame, so tense his concentration, so intent the whole of his being projected through the telescope in the effort of observation.

The captain glanced sharply aft, and a gleam came to his bloodshot eyes; there was no time being wasted there. He saw the destroyer's dinghy take the water, one hand bailing as a confused sea broke over her. But she got away and pulled slowly over towards the balloon. The captain withdrew his gaze and turned round, for the yeoman had made a sudden exclamation as he stood leaning over the starboard rails, his hand stretched out, a flush of excitement rising in his sallow cheeks.

'There! sir! There he is! Look! He's took to the basket-stays; fifteen feet above the for'ard end, almost hidden; under that bulge!'

With a swift, instinctive movement, as if to lend corroboration to his report, the yeoman whipped up the telescope again and peered once more through it. But the captain was satisfied; he had seen that small huddle of clothing lashed to the upper end of one of the stays. For a fleeting moment a look of relief flashed across the weatherbeaten features. He looked again towards the destroyer's boat. There was, he saw at once, little time to lose. The balloon was growing more flabby; the storm and sea-battered envelope was failing there before his eyes; it had done well, the captain reflected, to last so long. Suddenly he drew in his breath: 'Ah!' he muttered – and, as he opened his mouth, the yeoman closed up his telescope suddenly with a metallic snap. It was a symbolic movement, timed to the exact second – though the signalman was unaware of any relevancy in his action, for it was instinctive. The balloon, almost emptied of gas, had flopped on the water; like a dying fish, it moved spasmodically; then spread slowly. Somewhere under its convoluting, silvery folds was the basket.

The destroyer's boat was near now. In the sternsheets the cox'n, holding his balance by a miracle, was leaning forward, half on his feet, half crouched down. The oarsmen kept their eyes on his face. The latter was working strangely, the jaw convulsively chewing, the eyes gleaming. It seemed as if he were about to discharge at his crew some inspiriting message – but when, after what seemed a vast effort at self-expression, it came, it appeared strangely commonplace, for the cox'n, shifting his quid of tobacco, said simply and hoarsely: 'What say now, lads, shall we shake her up?'

The crew seemed to read into that simple message of exhortation a species of magic, however; for they 'shook her up' to some effect, laying back on their oars and putting the whole weight of their strong bodies into their strokes. The cox'n, relapsing into his habitual taciturnity, regarded their efforts with an approving eye. It was only the second time in the whole of the commission that he had urged his crew to greater endeavour, and they, accordingly, judged rightly that the matter was pressing.

From the bridge of the destroyer the captain shouted through a megaphone: 'Pull round the other side – get a move on! I'm coming closer.'

The destroyer got too close. The greater part of the envelope was now floating, deflated, on the surface. Swept across by the southerly set, the forward end of the envelope drifted under the ship's hull. The skipper jumped to the engine-room 'phone and rang down a warning. 'Right under the ship!' he muttered to the first lieutenant, who had returned to the bridge. 'If we don't look out, we'll get the condenser-inlets scuppered – and full of the fabric.'

In the boat, which had now reached the balloon, the bowman was frantically pulling away the debris to get at the basket, and beyond that, the stays. The cox'n let go his tiller and came forward to help. He was up to his knees in water as he went. 'Bail – and keep on bailing,' he grunted to the crew. The bowman was holding on like grim death to what he had. With the cox'n's help he hauled in more. The small boat was listing madly, riding drunkenly over the long, hollow swells – almost awash. From under a ten-foot high tuck in the balloon envelope the gondola suddenly surged out into the open; beyond it, and only two feet above the surface, appeared a huddle of clothing. The bowman caught sight of it. 'There he is!' he cried. 'He's there!'

'Heave now!' the cox'n grunted, his sinews creaking. 'One, two – six!'

With a sudden swirl the basket came aft along the gunwale. The cox'n hauled in on the stay with one hand; produced, like a conjurer, a knife with the other. With sure, deft slashes, he cut adrift the rough lashing with which Andrew Carr had buttressed his failing strength as the balloon came down. The entire boat's crew swarmed round and drew the unconscious figure safely over the gunwale.

'Trim the boat – or you'll be swamped!' the captain's peremptory hail echoed over the water. The latter stood at the bridge-rails, condenser-inlets temporarily forgotten, his haggard face lightening. He turned to the first lieutenant, who had just arrived on the bridge. 'I want to get away as soon as possible, No. 1,' he said. 'Put him in my day-cabin; get the boat hoisted; meanwhile, I want a volunteer to go over the side and examine and clear the condenser-inlets.'

'Ay, ay, sir.' The first lieutenant saluted and turned, brushing past the chief engineer on his way and giving the latter a commiserating grin as he noted his despondent face.

Five minutes later the first lieutenant was standing in the waist of the ship regarding with a certain concern the figure of the torpedo cox'n as that tall, hatchet-faced individual secured round his waist a length of lifeline. 'Trained as a diver,' the latter had said, putting forward his claim to do the work required. 'Can hold my breath if I get foul of anything, for the best part of two minutes, sir . . .'

'Yes,' the captain had said briefly, 'let him try, No. 1.' And so the first lieutenant stood doubtfully, because if anything happened to him . . . well, it would be unfortunate, to say the least of it – he was the best man in the ship.

The saturnine features of the torpedo cox'n, however, expressed no kind of doubt about the work in hand as he joked with the men around. The only concession he had accorded was in the laying aside of his heavy sea-boots. 'Get a better grip with me stockinged feet, sir,' he had remarked tersely. The first lieutenant, on his part, had rove a line right under the hull and secured it taut at each end, so that the man over the side would not be hopelessly inconvenienced by the heavy roll of the ship.

Thus, while Andrew Carr was being safely and snugly tucked up in blankets by the young doc., the torpedo cox'n took his chance and slithered down an angled slimy hull, with a long, dangerous-looking knife, like a pirate of old, clenched in his teeth.

With his heart in his mouth, and soaked to the skin, the first lieutenant gripped the rails and leant over them, directing the work. It was perilous enough on account of the confused sea, which had made it difficult to afford the man a good lee in which to work. But with the aid of the close-rove endless line round the hull the torpedo cox'n was enabled to cling close, like a gigantic fly, to the side of the ship. Once a big yellow roller, coming in suddenly, completely immersed him, and the first lieutenant heaved a sigh of relief when it rolled away to disclose a half-drowned cox'n still on the job.

On his second trip he took with him a sharp hook on the end of another length of rope. When he had secured this firmly as low down as he could place it, the men on deck hauled away, and ripped bodily out of the condenser-inlet a great mass of crumpled and torn balloon fabric. For the best part of twenty minutes, off and on, coming inboard for a breather occasionally, the man over the side carried on, stoically and doggedly, with the job for which he had volunteered. He came aboard for the last time, and the first lieutenant clapped him on the back, glancing anxiously at the drawn and lined features, at the torn fingers. 'Go aft at once, cox'n,' he ordered, 'before the chill penetrates any farther; get a tot of brandy from the wardroom steward.'

'It wasn't so cold,' said the tall man, panting, 'the sea's warmer than the air, maybe.' He grinned suddenly, and fingered the fabric, bits of which had got mixed up with his oilskins. 'Make a good baccy pouch, sir,' he said diffidently.

The first lieutenant laughed, and in his voice there sounded a note of relief. 'Time to think of that, cox'n, when we get home again, and you've had that brandy and a darned good rub down.'

As the duty destroyer turned and shaped her course homewards, the chief engineer paused at the engine-room hatch and cast a long look at the scarce distinguishable remains of the fast-sinking kite-balloon. The glance was not approving. 'I should like,' he muttered vindictively, 'to have a word with the blasted cove who invented them . . . just a quiet word, in some quiet place . . .'

It was late afternoon and dusk was gathering round the gate-ships as the skipper jerked a thumb at the long-grey ship that slipped through the boom defences at fifteen knots. With puckered-up, experienced eyes the old trawlerman cast a slow, grave look along her decks. 'She's had a dusting and all,' he said to his assistant. 'Wireless gone, whaler smashed up, both after-hatch shelters gone. Ay, she's been through it . . .'

'I wonder,' said the mate. 'I wonder if – here she comes now; she may give us a hail.' The speaker put a vast mahogany fist against his ear. He held on with the other as the gate-ship rolled.

Across the water, distinct above the roar of the forced draught and the swish of the bow-wave, came the destroyer's hail: 'Many thanks; good night; weather poor, but fishing excellent!'

The gate-skipper grinned and dug his mate in the ribs with a calloused elbow. He was only an onlooker. He watched battleships, cruisers, destroyers, and all manner of craft through his gate, but his own job was far from a sinecure. In bad weather – and in fog – especially fog – his crew, and himself often stood in imminent danger of total and sudden extinction. But like many onlookers, he saw much of the game – and more of the players. 'Excellent fishing,' he repeated and grinned again. 'Then they got him all right.'

Night was falling as the duty destroyer retrieved her shackle of cable at the buoy and moored up again. Andrew Carr was safely in the hospital ship, his young mind clearing gradually from what seemed a nightmare of recollection. On the bridge the captain rang down 'Finished with engines', and walked stiffly to the bridge-ladder, where he paused. 'Make up the log, sub.; put away your charts and gear, then meet me in the wardroom.'

The young figure engaged in casting off a length of spun-yard from its middle, straightened up, and saluted. 'Ay, ay, sir.'

On the now silent bridge the yeoman of signals paused near the wheel, which the torpedo cox'n was just leaving. 'Well, we got wet, mate, as we thought, but – you got wetter than usual; find it cold taking a dip over the side?'

THE DAY'S WORK

The torpedo cox'n stepped down from the grating and smiled. 'I been warm,' he said in a hoarse whisper, 'ever since. You had ought to've seen the tot of brandy I gets served out with. Good?' The speaker smacked his lips and smiled again. 'It would ha' give a battleship a kick.'

The yeoman made a sudden dive for the side, his telescope flashing up to inspect a distant winking light. 'Here, mate,' he grunted, 'take this down, quick. "Commodore F—",' he started to read.

In the wardroom, aft, there was an air of snug restfulness. The steward had brought a tray of drinks. A card-table stood ready for a game of bridge. Overhead there came a sound of sea-boots, and down the iron ladder clattered the yeoman of signals. The captain glanced up with an apprehensive eye. 'What now?' he muttered, taking the proffered pad. Slowly his expression turned to one of pleased surprise. The signal was from Commodore of Flotillas, and the captain read it aloud. 'Congratulations. Revert to eight hours' notice for steam. Report on board at 10 a.m. tomorrow.'

The captain handed back the pad. 'Thank you, yeoman. Have a copy put up on the mess-deck notice-boards.'

'Ay, ay, sir.' The yeoman withdrew. Just outside the door he encountered the steward. 'Congratulated by Commodore F—,' he hissed into the other's ear. 'Oh, we're a tiddly boat all right—' The speaker hurried on, leaving a puzzled steward scratching his head doubtfully. He was not sure what 'tiddly' meant, but finally came to the conclusion it was complimentary.

Inside the mess the captain yawned and stretched luxuriously in his chair. 'A bath,' he murmured; 'a red-hot bath, then a game of bridge, and a spot of dinner – and a whole night in.' The speaker looked reflectively at the roaring stove, and noticed that the dull corner of brightwork had been cleaned up, as directed after the previous Sunday's inspection. His glance travelled on, resting in turn on his grimy, unshaven officers, then stopped at the clock secured to the white-painted bulkhead.

'Twenty-three hours,' the captain murmured, and raised his glass. 'The Day's Work,' he added the words slowly, thoughtfully, then got stiffly to his feet, putting down the glass with an air of finality that had in it a vague suggestion that the captain found cause neither for regret nor for pleasure in the previous twenty-three hours, but only a species of mild satisfaction which was unimportant. He looked round the mess. 'Now for that bath. See you in half an hour for that rubber – and mind you're not late, sub.'

'Bartimeus'

The Survivor

'. . . And regrets to report only one survivor.' –
Admiralty Announcement

THE glass dropped another point, and the captain of the cruiser glanced
for the hundredth time from the lowering sky to the two destroyers
labouring stubbornly in the teeth of the gale on either beam. Then he
gave an order to the yeoman of signals, who barked its repetition to the
shelter-deck where the little group of signalmen stamped their feet and
blew on their numbed fingers in the lee of the flag-lockers. Two of the
group scuffled round the bright-coloured bunting: the clips of the
halliards snapped a hoist together, and vivid against the grey sky the
signal went bellying and fluttering to the masthead.

The figures on the bridges of the destroyers wiped the stinging spray
from their swollen eyelids and read the message of comfort.

'Return to base. Weather conditions threatening.'

They surveyed their battered bridges and forecastles, their stripped,
streaming decks and the guns' crews; they thought of hot food, warm
bunks, dry clothing, and all the sordid creature comforts for which soul
and body yearn so imperiously after three years of North Sea warfare.
Their answering pendants fluttered acknowledgement, and they swung
round on the path for home, praising Allah who had planted in the
brain of the cruiser captain a consideration for the welfare of his
destroyer screen.

'If this is what they call "threatening",' observed the senior officer of
the two boats, as his command clove shuddering through the jade-green
belly of a mountainous sea, flinging the white entrails broadcast, 'if this
is merely threatening I reckon it's time someone said, Home, James!'

His first lieutenant said nothing. He had spent three winters in these
grey wastes, and he knew the significance of that unearthly clear
visibility and the inky clouds banked ahead to the westward. But
presently he looked up from the chart and nodded towards the menace
in the western sky. 'That's snow,' he said. 'It ought to catch us about the
time we shall make Scaw Dhu light.'

'We'll hear the fog buoy all right,' said the captain.

'If the pipes ain't frozen,' was the reply. 'It's perishing cold.' He ran a gauntletted hand along the rail and extended a handful of frozen spray. 'That's salt – *and* frozen . . .'

The snow came as he had predicted, but rather sooner. It started with great whirling flakes like feathers about a gull's nesting-place, a soundless ethereal vanguard of the storm, growing momentarily denser. The wind, from a temporary lull, reawakened with a roar. The air became a vast witch's cauldron of white and brown specks, seething before the vision in a vertible Bacchanal of Atoms. Sight became a lost sense: time, space, and feeling were overwhelmed by that shrieking fury of snow and frozen spray thrashing pitilessly about the homing grey hulls and the bowed heads of the men who clung to the reeling bridges.

The grey, white-crested seas raced hissing alongside and, as the engine-room telegraphs rang again and again for reduced speed, overtook and passed them. Out of the welter of snow and spray the voices of the leadsmen chanting soundings reached the ears of those inboard as the voice of a doctor reaches a patient in delirium, fruitlessly reassuring . . .

Number Three of the midship gun on board the leading destroyer turned for the comfort of his soul from the contemplation of the pursuing seas to the forebridge, but snow-flakes blotted it from view. Providence, as he was accustomed to visualize it in the guise of a red-cheeked lieutenant-commander, had vanished from his ken. Number Three drew his hands from his pockets, and raising them to his mouth leaned towards the gunlayer. The gunlayer was also staring forward as if his vision had pierced that whirling grey curtain and was contemplating something beyond it, infinitely remote . . . There was a concentrated intensity in his expression not unlike that of a dog when he raises his head from his paws and looks towards a closed door.

' 'Ere,' bawled Number Three, seeking comradeship in an oppressive, indefinable loneliness. ' 'Ow about it – eh? . . .' The wind snatched at the meaningless words and beat them back between his chattering teeth.

The wind backed momentarily, sundering the veil of whirling obscurity. Through this rent towered a wall of rock, streaked all about with driven snow, at the foot of which breakers beat themselves into a smoking yeast of fury. Gulls were wailing overhead. Beneath their feet the engine room gongs clanged madly.

Then they struck.

The foremost destroyer checked on the shoulder of a great roller as if incredulous: shuddered: struck again and lurched over. A mountainous sea engulfed her stern and broke thundering against the after-funnel. Steam began to pour in dense hissing clouds from the engine-room hatchways and exhausts. Her consort swept past with screeching siren, helpless in the grip of the backwash for all her thrashing propellers that strove to check her headlong way. She too struck and recoiled: sagged in the trough of two stupendous seas, and plunged forward again ... Number Three, clinging to the greasy breech-block of his gun, clenched his teeth at the sound of that pitiless grinding which seemed as if it would never end ...

Of the ensuing horror he missed nothing, yet saw it all with a wondering detachment. A wave swept him off his feet against a funnel stay, and receding, left him clinging to it like a twist of waterlogged straw. Hand over hand he crawled higher, and finally hung dangling six feet above the highest wave, legs and arms round about the wire stay. He saw the forecastle break off like a stick of canteen chocolate and vanish into the smother. The other destroyer had disappeared. Beneath him, waist deep in boiling eddies, he saw men labouring about a raft, and had a vision of their upturned faces as they were swept away. The thunder of the surf on the beaches close at hand drowned the few shouts and cries that sounded. The wire from which he dangled jarred and twanged like a banjo-string, as the triumphant seas beat the soul out of the wreck beneath him.

A funnel-stay parted, and amid clouds of smoke and steam the funnel slowly began to list over the side. Number Three of the midship gun clung swaying like a wind-tossed branch above the maelstrom of seething water till a wave drove over the already-unrecognizable hull of the destroyer, leaped hungrily at the dangling human figure and tore him from his hold.

Bitterly cold water and a suffocating darkness engulfed him. Something clawed at his face and fastened on to his shoulder; he wrenched himself free from the nerveless clutch without ruth or understanding; his booted heel struck a yielding object as he struggled surfaceward, kicking wildly like a swimming frog ... the blackness became streaked with grey light and pinpoints of fire. Number Three had a conviction that unless the next few strokes brought him to the surface it would be too late. Then abruptly the clamour of the wind and sea, and the shriek of the circling gulls smote his ears again. He was back on the surface once more, gulping greedy lungfuls of air.

A wave caught him and hurled him forward on its crest, spread-eagled, feebly continuing the motions of a swimmer. It spent itself, and to husband his strength the man turned on his back, moving his head from side to side to take in his surroundings.

He was afloat (he found it surprisingly easy to keep afloat) inside a narrow bay. On both sides the black cliffs rose, all streaked with snow, out of a thunderous welter of foam. The tide sobbed and lamented in the hollows of unseen caverns, or sluiced the length of a ledge to splash in cascades down the face of the cliff.

THE SURVIVOR

The snow had abated, and in the gathering dusk the broken water showed ghostly white. To seaward the gale drove the smoking rollers in successive onslaughts against the reef where the battered remains of the two destroyers lay. All about the distorted plating and tangle of twisted stanchions the surf broke as if in a fury of rapine and destruction . . .

Another wave gripped him and rushed him shoreward again. The thunder of the surf redoubled. 'Hi! hi! hi! hi!' screeched the storm-tossed gulls. Number Three of the midships gun abandoned his efforts to swim and covered his face with his soggy sleeve. It was well not to look ahead. The wave seemed to be carrying him towards the cliffs at the speed of an express train. He wondered if the rocks would hurt much, beating out his life . . . He tried desperately to remember a prayer, but all he could recall was a sermon he had once listened to on the quarter-deck, one drowsy summer morning at Malta . . . About coming to Jesus on the face of the waters . . . 'And Jesus said "come." . . .' Fair whizzing along, he was . . .

Again the wave spent itself, and the man was caught in the backwash, drawn under, rolled over and over, spun round and round, gathered up in the watery embrace of another roller and flung up on all fours on a shelving beach. Furiously he clawed at the retreating pebbles, lurched to his feet, staggered forward a couple of paces, and fell on hands and knees on the fringe of a snow-drift. There he lay awhile, panting for breath.

He was conscious of an immense amazement, and, mingled with it, an inexplicable pride. He was still alive! It was an astounding achievement, being the solitary survivor of all those officers and men. But he had always considered himself a bit out of the ordinary . . . Once he had entered for a race at the annual sports at the Naval Barracks, Devonport. He had never run a race before in his life, and he won. It seemed absurdly easy. 'Bang!' went the pistol: off they went, helter-skelter, teeth clenched, fists clenched, hearts pounding, spectators a blur, roaring encouragement . . .

He won, and experienced the identical astonished gratification that he felt now.

'You runs like a adjective 'are, Bill,' his chum had admitted, plying the hero with beer at the little pub halfway up the cobbled hill by the dockyard.

Then he remembered other chums, shipmates, and one in particular called Nobby. He rose into a sitting position, staring seaward. Through the gloom the tumult of the seas, breaking over the reef on which they had foundered, glimmered white. The man rose unsteadily to his feet; he was alone on the beach of a tiny cove with his back to forbidding cliffs. Save where his own footsteps showed black, the snow was unmarked, stretching in an unbroken arc from one side of the cove to the other. The solitary figure limped to the edge of the surf and peered through the stinging scud. Then, raising his hands to his mouth, he called for his lost mate.

'Nobby!' he shouted, and again and again, 'Nobby! Nobby! . . . Nobbee-e!' . . .

'Nobby,' echoed the cliffs behind, disinterestedly.

'Hi! Hi! Hi!' mocked the gulls.

The survivor waded knee-deep into the froth of an incoming sea.

'Ahoy!' he bawled to the driving snowflakes and spindrift. His voice sounded cracked and feeble. He tried to shout again, but the thunder of the waves beat the sound to nothing.

He retraced his steps and paused to look round at the implacable face of the cliff, at the burden of snow that seemed to overhang the summit, then started again to seaward. A wave broke hissing about his feet: the tide was coming in.

Up to that moment fear had passed him by. He had been in turn bewildered, incredulous, cold, sick, bruised, but sustained throughout by the furious animal energy which the body summons in a fight for life. Now, however, with the realization of his loneliness in the gathering darkness, fear smote him. In fear he was as purely animal as he had been in his moments of blind courage. He turned from the darkling sea that had claimed chum and shipmates, and floundered through the snow-drifts to the base of the cliff. Then, numbed with cold, and well-nigh spent, he began frantically to scale the shelving surfaces of the rock.

Barnacles tore the flesh from his hands and the nails from his fingertips as he clawed desperately at the crevices for a hold. Inch by inch, foot by foot he fought his way upwards from the threatening clutch of the hungry tide, leaving a crimson stain at every niche where the snow had gathered. Thrice he slipped and slithered downwards, bruised and torn, to renew his frantic efforts afresh. Finally he reached a broad shelf of rock, halfway up the surface of the cliff, and there rested awhile, whimpering softly to himself at the pain of his flayed hands.

Presently he rose again and continued the dizzy ascent. None but a sailor or an experienced rock-climber would have dreamed of attempting such a feat single-handed, well-nigh in the dark. Even had he reached the top he could not have walked three yards in the dense snow-drifts that had gathered all along the edge of the cliffs. But the climber knew nothing about that; he was in search of *terra firma*, something that was not slippery rock or shifting pebbles, somewhere out of the reach of the sea.

He was within six feet of the summit when he lost a foothold, slipped, grabbed at a projecting knob of rock, slipped again, and so slipping and bumping and fighting for every inch, he slid heavily down on to his ledge again.

He lay bruised and breathless where he fell. That tumble came near to finishing matters; it winded him – knocked the fight out of him. But a wave, last and highest of the tide, sluiced over the ledge and immersed his shivering body once more in icy water; the unreasoning terror of the pursuing tide that had driven him up the face of the cliff whipped him to his feet again.

He backed against the rock, staring out through the driving spindrift into the menace of the darkness. There ought to be another wave any moment: then there would be another: and after that perhaps another. The next one then would get him. He was too weak to climb again . . .

The seconds passed and merged into minutes. The wind came at him out of the darkness like invisible knives thrown to pin him to a wall. The cold numbed his intelligence, numbed even his fear. He heard the waves breaking all about him in a wild pandemonium of sound, but it was a long time before he realized that no more had invaded his ledge, and a couple of hours before it struck him that the tide had turned . . .

Towards midnight he crawled down from his ledge and followed the retreating tide across the slippery shale, pausing every few minutes to listen to the uproar of sea and wind. An illusion of hearing human voices calling out of the gale mocked him with strange persistence. Once or twice he stumbled over a dark mass of weed stranded by the retreating tide, and each time bent down to finger it apprehensively.

Dawn found him back in the shelter of his cleft, scraping limpets from their shells for a breakfast. The day came slowly over a grey sea, streaked and smeared like the face of an old woman after a night of weeping. Of the two destroyers nothing broke the surface. It was nearly high water, and whatever remained of their battered hulls was covered by a tumultuous sea. They were swallowed. The sea had taken them – them and a hundred-odd officers and men, old shipmates, messmates, townies, raggies – just swallowed the lot . . . He still owed last month's mess-bill to the caterer of his mess . . . He put his torn hands before his eyes and strove to shut out the awful grey desolation of that hungry sea.

During the forenoon a flotilla of destroyers passed well out to seaward. They were searching the coast for signs of the wrecks, and the spray blotted them intermittently from sight as they wallowed at slow speed through the grey seas.

The survivor watched them and waved his jumper tied to a piece of drift-wood; but they were too far off to see him against the dark rocks. They passed round a headland, and the wan figure, half frozen and famished, crawled back into his cleft like a stricken animal, dumb with cold and suffering. It was not until the succeeding low water, when the twisted ironwork was showing black above the broken water on the reef, that another destroyer hove in sight. She too was searching for her lost sisters, and the castaway watched her alter course and nose cautiously towards the cove. Then she stopped and went astern.

The survivor brandished his extemporized signal of distress and emitted a dull croaking sound between his cracked lips. A puff of white steam appeared above the destroyer's bridge, and a second later the reassuring hoot of a siren floated in from the offing. They had seen him.

A sudden reaction seized his faculties. Almost apathetically he watched a sea-boat being lowered, saw it turn and come towards him, rising and falling on the heavy seas, but always coming nearer . . . he didn't care much whether they came or not – he was that cold. The very marrow of his bones seemed to be frozen. They'd have to come and fetch him if they wanted him. He was too cold to move out of his cleft.

The boat was very near. It was a whaler, and the bowman had boated his oar, and was crouching in the bows with a heaving-line round his forearm. The boat was plunging wildly, and spray was flying from under her. The cliffs threw back the orders of the officer at the tiller as he peered ahead from under his tarpaulin sou'wester with anxiety written on every line of his weather-beaten face. He didn't fancy the job, that much was plain; and indeed, small blame to him. It was no light undertaking, nursing a small boat close in to a dead lee shore, with the aftermath of such a gale still running.

They came still closer, and the heaving line hissed through the air to fall at the castaway's feet.

'Tie it round your middle,' shouted the lieutenant. 'You'll have to jump for it – we'll pull you inboard all right.'

The survivor obeyed dully, reeled to the edge of his ledge and slid once more into the bitterly cold water.

Half a dozen hands seemed to grasp him simultaneously, and he was hauled over the gunwale of the boat almost before he realized he had left his ledge. A flask was crammed between his chattering teeth; someone wound fold upon fold of blanket round him.

'Any more of you, mate?' said a voice anxiously; and then, 'Strike me blind if it ain't old Bill!'

The survivor opened his eyes and saw the face of the bowman contemplating him above his cork lifebelt. It was a vaguely familiar face. They had been shipmates somewhere once. Barracks, Devonport, p'raps it was. He blinked the tears out of his eyes and coughed as the raw spirit ran down his throat.

'Any more of you, Bill, old lad?'

The survivor shook his head.

'There's no one,' he said, ' 'cept me. I'm the only one what's lef' outer two ships' companies.' Again the lost feeling of bewildered pride crept back.

THE SURVIVOR

'You always was a one, Bill!' said the bowman in the old familiar accent of hero-worship.

The survivor nodded confirmation. 'Not 'arf I ain't,' he said appreciatively. 'Sole survivor I am!' And held out his hand again for the flask. 'Christ! look at my 'ands!'

James M. Cain

The Taking of Montfaucon

I

I BEEN asked did I get a DSC in the late war, and the answer is no, but
I might of got one if I had not run into some tough luck. And how that
was is pretty mixed up, so I guess I better start at the beginning, so you
can get it all straight and I will not have to do no backtracking. On the
26th of September, 1918, when the old 79th Division hopped off with
the rest of the AEF on the big drive that started that morning, the big
job ahead of us was to take a town named Montfaucon, and it was the
same town where the Crown Prince of Germany has his PC [Post of
Command] in 1916, when them Dutch was hammering on Verdun and
he was watching his boys fight by looking up at them through a
periscope. And our doughboys was in two brigades, the 157th and
158th, with two regiments in each, and the 157th Brigade was in front.
But they ain't took the town because it was up on a high hill, and on the
side of the hill was a whole lot of pillboxes and barbed wire what made
it a tough job. Only I ain't seen none of that, because I spent the whole
day on the water wagon, along with another guy name of Armbruster,
and we was driving it up from the Division PC what we left to the
Division PC where we was going. And that there weren't so good,
because neither him, me, nor the horse hadn't had no sleep, account of
the barrage shooting off all night, and every time we come to one of
them sixteen-inch guns going through the woods and a Frog would
squat down and pull the cord, why the horse would pretty near die and
so would we. But sometime we seen a little of what was going on, like
when a Jerry aviator come over and shot down four of our balloons and
then flew over the road where we was and everybody tooken a shot at
him, only I didn't because I happen to look at my gun after I pulled the
bolt and it was all caked up with mud and I kind of changed my mind
about taking a shot.

So after a while we come to a place in a trench and they said it was
the new Division PC, and Ryan, who was the stable sergeant, come
along and took the horse, and we got something to eat and there was

still plenty shelling going on, but not bad like it was, and we figured we could get some sleep. So then it was about six o'clock in the evening. But pretty soon Captain Madeira, he come to me and says I was to go on duty. And what I was to do was to go with another guy, name of Shepler, to find the PC of the 157th Brigade, what was supposed to be one thousand yards west of where we was, and then report back. And why we was to do that was so we could find the Brigade PC in the night and carry messages to it. Because us in the Headquarters Troops, what we done in the fighting was act as couriers and all like of that, and what we done in between the fighting was curry horse belly. So me and Shepler started out. And as the Brigade PC was supposed to be one thousand yards west, and where we was was in a trench, and the trench run east and west, it looked like all we had to do was to follow the trench right into where the sun was setting and it wouldn't be no hard job to find what we was looking for.

And it weren't. In about ten minutes we come to the Brigade PC and there was General Nicholson [Brigadier General William J. Nicholson, commanding 157th Infantry Brigade] and his aides, and a bunch of guys what was in Brigade Headquarters, all setting around in the trench. But they was moving. They was all set to go forwards somewheres, and had their packs with them.

'Well,' says Shep, 'we ain't got nothing to do with that. Let's go back.'

'Right,' I says. But then I got to thinking. 'What the hell good is it,' I says, 'for us to go back and tell them we found this PC when in a couple of minutes there ain't going to be nobody in it?'

'What the hell good is the war?' says Shep. 'We was told to find this PC and we've found it. Now we go back and let them figure out what the hell good it is.'

'This PC,' I says, 'soon as the General clears out, is same as a last year's bird nest.'

'That's jake with me,' says Shep. 'In this man's army you do what you're told to do, and we've done it. We ain't got nothing to do with what kind of a bird's nest it is.'

'No,' I says, 'we ain't done it. We was told to find a PC. And soon as Nick gets out this ain't going to be no PC, but only a dugout. We got to go with him. We got to find where his new PC is at, and then we go back.'

'Well, if we ain't done it,' says Shep, 'that's different.'

So in a couple of minutes Nick started off, and we went with him, and a hell of a fine thing we done for ourself that we ain't went back in the first place, like Shep wanted to do. Because where we went, it weren't over no road and it weren't through no trench. It was straight up toward the front line over No Man's Land, and a worse walk after supper nobody ever took this side of Hell. How we went was single file, first Nick, and then them aides, and then them headquarters guys, and then us. About every fifty yards, a runner would pick us up, and point the way, and then fall back and let us pass. And what we was walking over was all shell holes and barbed wire, and you was always slipping down and busting your shin, and then all them dead horses and things was laying around, and you didn't never see one till you had your foot in it, and then it made you sick. And dead men. The first one we seen was in a trench, kind of laying up against the side, what was on a slant. And he was sighting down his gun just like he was getting ready to pull the trigger, and when you come to him you opened your mouth to beg his pardon for bothering him. And then you didn't.

Well, we went along that way for a hell of a while. And pretty soon it seemed like we wasn't nowheres at all, but was slugging along through some kind of black dream what didn't have no end, and them goddam runners look like ghosts what was standing there to point, only we wasn't never going to get where they was pointing nor nowheres else.

But after a while we come to a road and on the side of the road was a piece of corrugated iron. And Nick, soon as he come to that, unslung his musette bag and sat down on it. And then all them other guys sat down too. So me and Shep, we figured on that awhile, because at first we thought they was just taking a rest, but then Shep let on it looked like to him they was expecting to stay awhile. So then we went up to Nick.

'Sir,' I says, 'is this the new Brigade PC?'

'Who are you?' he says.

'We're from Division Headquarters,' I says. 'We was ordered to find the Brigade PC and report back.'

'This is the new PC,' he says.

'This piece of iron?' I says.

'Yes,' says he.

'Thank you, sir,' I says, and me and Shep saluted and left him.

'A hell of a looking PC,' says Shep, soon as we got where he couldn't hear us.

'A hell of a looking PC all right,' I says, 'but it's pretty looking alongside of that trip we got going back.'

'I been thinking about that,' he says.

So then we sat down by the road a couple of minutes.

'Listen,' he says. 'I ain't saying I like that trip none. But what I'm thinking about is suppose we get lost. I don't mind telling you I can't find my way back over them shell holes.'

'I got a idea,' I says.

'Shoot,' he says.

'This here road we're setting on,' I says, 'must go somewheres.'

'They generally do,' he says.

'If we can find someplace what's on the end of it,' I says, 'I can take you back if you don't mind a little walking. Because I know all these roads around here like a book.' And how that was, was because I had been on observation post before the drive started, and had to study them maps, and even if I hadn't never been on the roads I knowed how they run.

'I'll walk with you to sunup,' he says, 'if it's on a road and we know where we're going. But I ain't going to try to get back over that No Man's Land, boy, I'll tell you that. Because I just as well try to fly.'

So we asked a whole lot of guys did they know where the road run, and not none of them knowed nothing about it. But pretty soon we found a guy in the engineers, what was fixing the road, and he said he thought the road run back to Avocourt.

'Let's go,' I says to Shep. 'I know where we're at now.'

So we started out, and sure enough after a while we come to Avocourt. And I knowed there was a road run east from Avocourt over the ridge to Esnes, if we could only figure out which the hell way was east. So the moon was coming up about then, and we remembered the moon came up in the east, and we headed for it, and hit the road. And a bunch of rats come outen a trench and began going up the road in front of us, hopping along in a pretty good line, and Shep said they was trench camels, and that give us a laugh, and we felt better. And pretty soon, sure enough we come to Esnes, and turned left, and in a couple minutes we was right back in the Division PC what we had left after supper, and it weren't much to look at, but it sure did feel like home.

II

Well, we weren't no sooner there than a bunch of guys begun to holler out to Captain Madeira that here we was, and he came a-running, and if we had of been a letter from home he couldn't of been more excited about us.

'Thank God, you've come,' he says.

'Sure we've come,' says Shep; 'you wasn't really worried about us, was you?'

But I seen it was more than us the Captain was worrying about, so I says:

'What's the matter?'

'General Nicholson has broken liaison,' he says, 'and we've got not a way on earth to reach him unless you fellows can do it.'

'Well, I guess we can, hey kid?' I says to Shep.

But Shep shook his head. 'Maybe you can,' he says, 'but I ain't got no more idea where we been than a blind man. I'll keep you company, though, if you want.'

'Company hell,' says the Captain. 'Here,' he says to me, 'you come in and see the General.'

So he brung me into the dugout what was the PC to see General Kuhn [Major General Joseph E. Kuhn, commanding general, 79th Division]. And most of the time, the General was a pretty snappy-looking soldier. He was about medium size, and he had a cut to his jaw and a swing to his back what look like them pictures you see in books. But he weren't no snappy-looking soldier that night. He hadn't had no shave, and his eyes was all sunk in, and no wonder. Because when the Division ain't took Montfaucon that day, like they was supposed to, it balled everything up like hell. It put a pocket in the American advance, a kind of a dent, what was holding up the works all along the line. And the General was getting hell from Corps, and he had lost a lot of men, and that was why he was looking like he was.

'Do you know where General Nicholson is?' he says to me, soon as Captain Madeira had told him who I was.

'Yes, sir,' I says, 'but I don't think *he* does.'

Now what the General said to that I ain't sure, but he mumbled something to hisself what sound like he be damned if he did either.

'I want you to take a message to him,' he says.

'Yes, sir,' I says.

So he commenced to write the message. And while I was standing there I was so sleepy everything look like it was turning around, like them things you see in a dream. It was a couple of aides in there, and maybe an orderly, and Captain Madeira, and it was in behind a lot of blankets, what they wet and hang over the door of a dugout to keep out gas. And in the middle of it was General Kuhn, writing on a pad in lead pencil, and I remember thinking how old he looked setting there, and then that would blank out and I couldn't see nothing but his whiskers, and then that would blank out and I would be thinking it was pretty tough on him, and I would do my best to help him out. It weren't no more than a minute, mind. Why I was thinking all them things jumbled up together was because I hadn't had no sleep.

'All right,' he says to me; 'listen now while I read it to you.'

And why they read it to you is so if you lose it you can tell them what was in it and you ain't no worse off. And he hadn't no sooner started to read it then I snapped out of that dream pretty quick. Because it was short and sweet. It said that Nick was to attack right away soon as he got it. And I knowed a little about this Montfaucon stuff from hearing them brigade guys talk while we was going over No Man's Land, so I knowed I weren't carrying no message what just said good morning.

'Is that clear to you?' he says.

'Yes, sir,' I says.

'Captain, give this man a horse. As good a horse as you've got.'

'Yes, sir,' says the Captain.

'You better ride pretty lively. And report back to me here.'

'Yes, sir.'

'No, wait a minute. I'm moving my PC to Malancourt in the next hour. Do you know where Malancourt is?'

'Yes, sir.'

'Hunh,' he says, like he meant thank God there was somebody in the outfit what knowed right from left and I was glad I had studied them maps good like I had and could be some use to him.

'Then report to me in Malancourt.' And me and the Captain saluted and went out.

So the Captain took me to Ryan, and Ryan saddled me a horse, and while he was doing it Shep came up and begun to talk about the argument we had about whether we was going with Nick or not, and he handed it to me for figuring out the right thing to do, and the Captain said he was goddam proud of us both for carrying out orders with some sense when everybody else act like they had went off their nut and things was all shot to hell, and I felt pretty good. So pretty soon Ryan come with the horse, and I started out, and after I had went about a couple of miles it was commencing to get light, so I dug my heels in, because I knowed I didn't have much time.

III

Well, in another five minutes I come to Avocourt. And soon as I rode around the bend I got a funny feeling in my stomach. Because I seen something I had forgot when me and Shep was there, and that was that there was two roads what run from Avocourt up to the front line, one of them running north and the other running northeast, and they kind of forked off from each other in such a way that when you was coming down one of them like we done you wouldn't notice the other one at all. And I knowed as soon as I looked at them that I didn't have no idea which one we had come over and it weren't no way to find out.

So I pulled in and figured. And I closed my eyes and tried to remember how that road had looked when we was coming back down it into Avocourt with the moon rising on our left before we hit the road to Esnes, and that was damn hard, because I was so blotto from not having no sleep that soon as I closed my eyes all I got was a bellering in my ears. But I squinted them up good, and pretty soon it jumped in front of me, how that road looked, and right near Avocourt was a bunch of holes in the middle of it, what look like a tank had got stuck there and dug them up trying to get out. So I opened my eyes and was all set to hit for them holes. But then I knowed I was in for it good. Because in between while we had been over the road, them engineers had surfaced it, and it weren't no holes, because they was all covered up with stone.

But it weren't doing no good setting on top of the horse figuring, so I picked the right-hand road and started up it. I figured I would go about as far as me and Shep had come, and then maybe I would run into Nick, or somebody that could tell me where he was at, or what the right road was to take, and that the main thing was to get a move on. But that there sounds easier than it was. Because once you start out somewheres, and get to wondering are you headed right or not, you're bad off, and you might just as well be standing still for all you're going to get there.

'I kept pushing the horse on, and every step he took I would look around to see if I could see something that me and Shep had seen, and about all I seen was tanks and engineers forking stone, what was what we had saw the night before, but it didn't prove nothing because you could see tanks and engineers on any road. And them engineers wasn't no help, because engineers is dumb as hell and then they ain't got nothing to do with fighting outfits and 157th Brigade sounds just the same to them as any other brigade, and a hell of a wonder me and Shep had found one the night before that could even tell us which way the road run.

Well, after I had went a ways, about as far as I thought me and Shep had come, and ain't seen a thing that I could say for certain we had saw the night before, and no sign of Nick or his piece of corrugated iron, what might be covered up with stone too for all I knowed, I figured I was on the wrong road sure as hell, and I got a awful feeling that I would have to go back to Avocourt and start over again. Because that order in my pocket, it weren't getting no cooler, I'm here to tell you. It was damn near burning a hole in my leg, and a funny hiccuppy noise would come up out of my neck every time I thought of it.

But I went a little bit further, just to make sure, and then I come to something that I thought straightened me all out. It was kind of a crossroads, bearing off to the left. And I couldn't remember that we had passed it the night before, so I figured I must of gone wrong when I tooken the right-hand fork at Avocourt. But this road, I thought, will put me right, because it leads right acrost to the other one and I won't have to lose all that time going back to Avocourt. So I helloed down it, and for the first time since I left Avocourt I felt I was going right. And sure enough, pretty soon I come to the other road, and it weren't no new stone on it at that place, so I turned right, toward the front, and started up it. And I worked on the horse a little bit, because without no loose stone under his foot he could go better, and kind of patted him on the neck and talked to him, because he hadn't had no sleep neither and he was tired as hell by this time, and then I lifted him along so he went in a good run. And it weren't quite light yet, and I thought thank God I'll be in time.

So pretty soon I come to some soldiers what wasn't engineers. So I pulled up and hollered out:

'What way to the Hundred and fifty-seventh Brigade PC?'

'The what?' they say.

'The Hundred and fifty-seventh Brigade PC,' I says. 'General Nicholson's PC.'

'Never hear tell of it,' they says.

'The hell you say,' I says. 'And you're a hell of a goddam comical outfit, ain't you?'

Because that was one of them gags they had in the army. They would ask a guy what his outfit was, and then when he told them they would say they never hear tell of it.

So I rode a little further and come to another bunch. 'Which way is the Hundred and fifty-seventh Brigade PC?' I says. 'General Nicholson's PC?'

But they never said nothing at all. Because they was doughboys going up in the lines, and when you hear somebody talk about doughboys singing when they're going to fight, you can tell him he's a damn liar and say I said so. Doughboys when they're going up in the lines they look straight in front of them and they swaller every third step and they don't say nothing.

So pretty soon I come to another bunch what wasn't doughboys and I asked them. 'Search me, buddy,' they says, and I went on. And I done that a couple of times, and I ain't found out nothing. So then I figured it weren't no use asking for the Brigade PC no more, because a lot of them guys they wouldn't never of hear tell of the Hundred and fifty-seventh Brigade even if they was in it, so I figured I would find out what outfit they was in and then I could figure out from that about where I was at. So that's what I done.

'What outfit, buddy?' I says to the next bunch I come to. But all they done was look dumb, so I didn't waste no more time on them, but went on till I come to another bunch, and I asked them.

'AEF,' a guy sings out.

'What the hell,' I says. 'You think I'm asking for fun?'

'YMCA,' says another, and I went on. And then all of a sudden I knowed why them guys was acting like that, and why it was was this: Ever since they come to France, they had been told if somebody up in the front lines asks you what your outfit is, don't you tell him because maybe he's a German spy trying to find out something. Because of course they wasn't really worried none that I was a German spy. What they was worried about was that maybe I was a MP or something what was going around finding out how they was minding the rule, and they wasn't taking no chances. Later on, when a whole hell of a lot of couriers had got lost and the American Army didn't know was it coming or going, they changed that rule. They marked all the PC's good so you could see them, and had arrows pointing to them a couple miles away so you couldn't get lost. But the rule hadn't been changed that morning, and that was why them guys wouldn't say nothing.

Well, was you ever in a lunatic asylum? That was what it was like for me from that time on. I would ask and ask, and all I ever got was 'YMCA', or 'Company B', or something like that, and it getting later all the time, and me with that order in my pocket. And after a while I thought well I got to pretend to be an officer and scare somebody into telling me where I'm at. So the first ones I come to was a captain and a lieutenant setting by the side of the road, and they was wearing bars. But me not having no bars didn't make no difference, because up at the front some officers wore bars but most of them didn't, and if you take the bars off, one guy without a shave looks pretty much like another. So I went up to them and saluted and spoke sharp, like I had been bawling out orders all my life.

'Which way is General Nicholson's PC?' I says, and the captain jumped up and saluted.

'General Nicholson?' he says. 'Not around here, I'm pretty sure, sir,' he says.

'Hundred and fifty-seventh Brigade?' I says, pretty short, like he must be asleep or something if he didn't know where that was.

'Oh, no,' he says. 'That wouldn't be in this Division. This is all Thirty-seventh.'

So then I knowed I was sunk. The 37th Division, it was on our left, and that meant I had been on the right road all the time when I left Avocourt, as I seen many a time since by checking it up on the maps, and had went wrong by wondering about that fork. And it weren't nothing to do but cut across again, and hope I might bump into General Nicholson somehow, and if I didn't to keep on beating to Malancourt, so I could report to General Kuhn like I had been told to do. And what I done from then on I ain't never figured out, even from them maps, because I was thinking about that order all the time, and how it ought to been delivered already if it was going to do any good, and I got a little wild. I put the horse over the ditch and went through the woods, and never went back to the crossroads at all. And them woods was all full of shell holes, so you couldn't go straight, and the day was still cloudy, so you couldn't tell by the sun which way you was headed, and it weren't long before I didn't know which the hell way I was going. One time I must of been right up with the fighting, because a guy got up out

of a shell hole and yelled at me for Christ sake not go over the top of
that hill with the horse, because there was a sniper a little ways away,
and I would get knocked off sure as hell. But by that time a sniper, if he
only knowed where the hell he was sniping from, would of looked like
a brother, so I went over. But it weren't no sniper, because I didn't get
knocked off.

And another time I come to the rim of a shell hole what was so big
you could of dropped a two-storey house in it, and right new, but it
weren't no dirt around it and you couldn't see no place the dirt had
went. And right then the horse he wheeled and began to cut back
toward where he had come from. Because he was so tired by then he
was stumbling every step and didn't want to go on. So I had to fight
him. And then I got off and begun to beat him. And then I begun to
blubber. And then I begun to blubber some more on account of how I
was treating the horse, because he ain't done nothing and it was up to
me to make him go.

And while I was standing there blubbering, near as I can figure out,
the 313th, what was part of the 157th Brigade, was taking Montfaucon.
Because General Kuhn he ain't sat back and waited for me. Soon as I
left him he got on a horse and rode up to the front line hisself, there in
the dark, and passed the word over they was to advance, and then
relieved a general what didn't seem to be showing no signs of life, and
put a colonel in command at that end of the line, and pretty soon things
were moving. So Nick, he got the order that way and went on, and the
boys, if they had Nick in command, they would take the town. So they
took it.

v

It must of been after eleven o'clock when I got in to Malancourt. And
there by the side of the road was General Kuhn, all smeared up with
mud and looking like hell. And I went up to him and saluted.

'Did you deliver that message?' he says.

'No, sir,' I says.

'What!' he says. 'Then what are you doing coming in here at this
hour?'

'I got lost,' I says.

He never said nothing. He just looked at me, starting in from my
eyes and going clear down to my feet, and that there was the saddest
look I ever seen one man turn on another. And it weren't nothing to do
but stand there and hold on to the reins of the goddam horse, and wish
to hell the sniper had got me.

But just then he looked away quick, because somebody was saluting
in front of him and commencing to talk. And it was Nick. And what he

was talking about was that Montfaucon had been took. But he didn't no more than get started before General Kuhn started up hisself.

'What do you mean!' he says, 'by breaking liaison with me? And where have you been anyway?'

'Where have I been?' says Nick. 'I've been taking that position, that's where I've been. And I did not break liaison with you!'

So come to find out, them runners what had showed us the way over No Man's Land was supposed to keep liaison only it was their first day of fighting, same as it was everybody else's, and what they done was keep liaison with that last year's bird nest what Nick had left, and didn't get it straight they was supposed to space out a little bit till they reached to the Division PC.

'And, anyway,' says Nick, 'there was a couple of your own runners that knew where I was. Why didn't you use them?'

So of course that made me feel great.

So they began to cuss at each other, and the generals can outcuss the privates, I'll say that for them. So I kind of saluted and went off, and then Captain Madeira, he come to me.

'What's the matter?' he says.

'Nothing much,' I says.

'You didn't make it, hey?'

'No. Didn't make it.'

'Don't worry about it. You did the best you could.'

'Yeah, I done the best I could.'

'You're not the only one. It's been a hell of a night and a hell of a day.'

'Yeah, it sure has.'

'Well – don't worry about it.'

'Thanks.'

So that is how I come not to get no DSC in the late war. If I had of done what I was sent to do, maybe they would of given me one, because Shep, he got cited, and they sure needed me bad. But I never done it, and it ain't no use blubbering over how things might be if only they was a little different.

P. C. Wren

The Coward of the Legion

JEAN JACQUES DUBONNET had distinguished himself that day, and he lay on his bed that night and cried. His companion, old Jean Boule, in that little hut of sticks and banana-leaves, had just been congratulating him on the fact that he had almost certainly won himself the *croix de guerre* or the *médaille militaire* for his distinguished bravery. And he had burst into tears, his body shaken with great rending sobs.

John Bull was not only a gentleman; he was a person of understanding and sympathy, and he had suffered enough, and seen enough of suffering, to feel neither surprise, disgust, nor contempt.

'God! Oh, God! I am a coward. I am a branded coward!' blubbered the big man on the creaking bed of boughs and boxes.

Was this fever, reaction, drink, *le cafard*, or what?

Certainly Dubonnet had played the man, and shown great physical courage that day against the Sakalaves, the brave Malagasy savages who have given Madame la République a good deal of trouble and annoyance, and filled many a shallow grave with the unconsidered carcases of *Marsouins*[1] and Légionnaires in the red soil of Madagascar. As the decimated Company had slowly fallen back from the ambush in the dense plantations of the lovely Boueni palms, Lieutenant Roberte had fallen, shot through the body by a plucky Sakalave who had deliberately rested his prehistoric musket on his thigh and discharged it at a dozen yards range, himself under heavy fire. With insulting howls of '*Taim-poory taim-poory*,' half a dozen of the enemy had sprung at the fallen man, when Dubonnet, rushing from cover, had shot two in quick succession, bayoneted two others, kicked violently in the face a fifth, who stooped over the Lieutenant with a *coupe-coupe*, and then, swinging his Lebel by the butt, had put up so good a fight that he had driven the savages back and had then partly dragged and partly carried his officer with him, to where the Company could rally, re-form, and make their stand to await reinforcements. Undeniably Dubonnet had

[1] Colonel Infantry (Infanterie de la Marine).

risked his life to save that of his officer, and had fought with very great courage and determination or he could never have reached the rallying-place with an unconscious man, when so many of his comrades could not reach it at all.

Yet there he lay, weeping like a child, and calling upon his Maker to ease his guilty bosom of the burden it had borne so long – the knowledge that he was a 'branded' coward.

It was terribly, cruelly hot in the tiny hut, and, to John Bull, who arose from his camp-bed of packing-case boards, it seemed even hotter outside, as he went to fetch the hollow bamboo water-'bottle' which hung from the tree under which the hut was built. Was it possible that the Madagascan moon gave out heat-rays of its own, or reflected those of the sun as it did the rays of light? It really seemed hotter in the moonlight than out of it . . . Carrying the bamboo water-receptacle, a cylinder as tall as himself – really a pipe with one end sealed with gum, wax, or clay, when a joint of the stem does not serve the purpose – the Englishman passed in through the doorless doorway and delivered an ultimatum.

'Whatever may be the trouble, *mon ami*, weeping will not help it. Enough! . . . Sit up and tell me all about it, or I'll wash you off that bed like the insect you're pretending to be . . . Now then – drink or a drenching?'

'Give me a drink for the love of God!' said Dubonnet, sitting up. 'Absinthe, rum, cognac – anything,' and he clutched at the breast of his canvas shirt as though he feared it might open and expose his breast.

'Yes. Good cold water,' replied John Bull.

'Cold water!' mocked the other between sobs. 'Cold Englishman! *Cold water!*' and he bowed his head on his knees and groaned and wept afresh.

The old soldier carefully poured water from the open end of the great pipe into a *gamelle* and offered it to the other, who drank feverishly. 'Are you wounded in the chest, there?' he asked.

This *cafard*, the madness that comes upon soldiers who eat out their hearts in the monotony of exile and wear out their stomachs and brains in the absinthe-shop, takes strange forms and reduces its victims to queer plights. How should le Légionnaire Jean Jacques Dubonnet, *Soldat première classe*, recommended for decoration for bravery in the field, be a coward?

'Oh, merciful God – help me to bear it. I am a Coward – a branded Coward!' wailed the huddled figure on the rickety, groaning bed.

'See here, comrade,' said John Bull, overcoming a certain slight, but perceptible, repugnance, and placing an arm across the bowed and quivering shoulders, 'I am no talker, as you are aware. If it would give you any relief to tell me all about it – rest assured that no word of it will ever be repeated by me. It may ease you. I may be able to help or comfort. Many Légionnaires, some on their death-beds, have felt the better for telling me of their troubles . . . But do not think I want to pry.'

Swiftly the wretched man turned, flung his arms about the Englishman's neck, and kissed him.

John Bull forbore to shudder. (Heavens! How different is the excellent French *poilu* from the British Tommy!) But if he could bring peace and the healing, soothing sense of confession, if not of anything approaching absolution, to this tortured soul, the night would have been well spent – better spent than in sleep, though he was very, very tired.

'I *will* tell you, *mon ami*, and will pray to you then to give me comfort or a bullet in the temple. A little accident as you clean your rifle! *I* cannot do it. I *dare* not do it – and no bullet will touch me in battle – as you have seen today. I live to die, and am too big a coward to take my life. . . I am a branded coward. . . . See! See!' and he tore open the breast of his shirt. At once he closed it again, and hugged himself.

'No, no! I will tell you first,' he cried.

The madness of *le cafard*, no doubt. The man had only recently been drafted to the VIIth Company from the depôt, and had appeared a morose, surly, and unattractive person, friendless and undesirous of friends. Accident had made him the stable-companion of the Englishman in his little damp fever-stricken hell in the reeking corner of the Betsimisarake district, in which the remains of the Company were pinned . . .

The deplorable and deploring Dubonnet thrust his grimy fists into his eyes and across the end of his amorphous nose, as, with a sniff which militated against the romantic effect of the declaration, he said, 'I swear I loved her. I loved her madly. It was my unfortunate and uncontrollable love that caused the trouble in the first place . . . But it was her fault too, mind you! Why couldn't she have *told* me she had a husband, away at Lyons, finishing his military service – a husband whom she had not seen for six months, and whom she would not see for another six? . . . Too late the fool confessed it – a month before he was coming, and a couple of months before something else was coming! And he famous, as I learned too late, for having all the jealous hate of Hell in his heart, if she so much as looked at another man. He, a porter of the Halles, notorious for his quarrelsomeness and for his fearful strength and savage temper. She hated him nearly as much as she feared him – and me, me she loved to distraction. And I her . . . Believe me, she was the loveliest flower-seller in Paris – with a foot and ankle, an eye, a figure, ravishing, I tell you . . . and he would break her neck when he saw how she was and stab me to the heart. *She* would never have told him it was I she loved, but those others would – for dozens knew that she was my *amie*, and many in my gang did not love me. I am not of those whom men love – but women, ah! – and there were jealous ones in our *ruelle* who would have gone far to see her beauty spoiled and my throat cut . . . It was all her fault, I say! Did she not deceive me in hiding the fact that she had a husband? She deceived us all. But when this *scélérat* should turn up from Lyons, and find her at her pitch or in the flower-market, would any of them have held their tongues? . . . Can you not see it? . . . The crowd at the door, the screams as he entered and dragged her out into the gutter by the hair, his foot on her throat . . . and, afterwards – his knife at my breast . . . Would any of the gang have stood by me? No, they would have licked their chops and goaded him on . . . and, oh God, I am a *coward*. . . . I can fight when my blood is up and I have to struggle for my life . . . I can fight as one of a regiment, a company, a crowd, all fighting side by side, each defending the other by fighting the common foe . . . I can take my part in a mêlée and I can do deeds then that I do not know I have done till afterwards . . . I can fight when the tiger in me is aroused and has smelt blood – but I am a *coward* if I am alone. I, alone, dare not fight one man alone . . . Were I being tracked alone through the jungle here by but one of the six men I attacked today, my knees would knock together and my legs would refuse to bear me up. I should flee if they would carry me, flee shrieking, but they would not bear me a hundred metres. They would collapse, and I should lie shuddering with closed eyes, awaiting the blow. I can hunt – with the pack – but I cannot be hunted. No. When our band waylaid the greasy bourgeois as he lurched homeward from his restaurant in the Place Pigalle or his Montmartre cabaret, I was as good an *apache* as any in the gang, and struck my blow with the best; but if it was a case of a row with the *agents de police*, and we were being individually shadowed, my heart turned to water, and I lay in bed for days. In a fair fight between about equal numbers of anarchists and *apaches* on the one hand, and the *messieurs les agents* on the other, if it came upon us suddenly as they raided our rookery, I could play a brave man's part in the rush for the street; but I cannot be the hunted one – I cannot fight alone with none on either side of me. Oh God, I am a coward,' and the wretch again buried his face in his knees and wept and sobbed afresh.

A common, cowardly gutter-hooligan apparently; an *apache*, a Paris street-wolf, and, like all wolves, braver in the pack than when alone; but in John Bull's gaze there was more of pity than anything. Suppose he, John Bull, had been born in a foul corner of some filthy cellar beneath a Paris slum? Would he have been so different? Was the *man* to blame, or the Fate that gave him the ancestry and environment that had made him precisely what he was?

'You will be called out before the battalion and decorated with the cross or the *médaille, mon ami*, for your heroism today. Put the past behind, and let your life re-date from the day the Colonel pins the decoration on your breast. Begin afresh. You will carry about with you always the visible sign and recognition that you are a hero – there on your breast, I say.' . . .

With a shriek of '*What do I bear on my breast now?*' the ex-*apache* tore open his shirt and exposed two strips of strong linen sticking-plaster, each some ten inches long and two inches wide, that lay stuck horizontally across his broad chest.

What was this? Had he two ghastly gashes beneath the plaster? Had all that he had been saying been merely the delirium of a badly-wounded man? Seizing their ends, the *apache* tore them violently from his skin, and, by the light of the little lamp, John Bull saw, deeply branded and most skilfully tattooed in the ineradicable burns, the following words (in French):

J. J. Dubonnet
Liar and Coward

The Englishman recoiled in horror, and the other thought it was in contempt.

'Where are your fine phrases *now*?' he snarled, with concentrated bitterness. ' "*You will carry about with you always the visible sign and recognition that you are a hero*," ' he mocked. 'I do indeed! . . . Oh God, take it from me. Let me sleep and wake to find it gone, and I will become a monk and wear out my life in prayer' . . . and he threw himself face-downward on the bed and tore the covering of his straw pillow with his teeth.

'See, *mon ami*,' said John Bull, 'the *médaille* will be above that. It will be superimposed. It will bury that beneath it. Let it bury it for ever. That is of the past – the *médaille* is of today and the glorious future. That is man's revenge – the cruel punishment and vengeance of an injured brute. The *médaille* is man's reward – the glad recognition of those who admire courage' . . .

'It is not the husband's work,' growled Dubonnet. 'He never caught me. My own gang did that – my comrades – my *friends*! Think of their loathing and contempt, their hatred and disgust, that they could do that to a man and leave him to live. Think of it! . . . And I dare not kill myself and meet *her*. I am a coward. I fear Death himself, and I fear her reproachful eyes still more . . . I *am* a coward and I *am* a liar. I broke my faith and word and trust to her – and I feared the death that she welcomed because *I* was by her side to share it. She drank the poison in her glass, threw herself into my arms, and bade me drink mine and come with her to the Beyond, where no brutal, hated husband could drag her from me to his own loathed arms . . . And I did not. I could not. She died in my arms with those great reproachful eyes on mine,

and whispered, "Come with me, my Beloved. I am afraid to go alone."
And when I would not, she cursed me and died. And I let her go alone
– I, who had planned our double suicide, our glorious and romantic
suicide in each other's arms – that we might not have to part, might not
have to face her husband's wrath, might be together for all time, though
it were in hell . . . Before she drank, she blessed me. Before she died,
she cursed me – and still I could not drink . . . And now I have not the
courage to go on living, and I have not the courage to take my life . . .
And they are going to brand me as a hero, are they? . . . *That* on my
coat and *this* beneath it!' and peals of hysterical laughter rang out on
the still night.

'Yes – *that* on your coat,' said the Englishman. 'Does it count for
nothing? Let the one balance the other. Put the past behind you and
start afresh . . . Can you bear pain? Physical pain, I mean?'

'Is not all my life a pain? – did I not have to bear the pain of being
branded with a red-hot iron? What is physical pain compared with what
I bear night and day – remorse, self-loathing, the fear of the discovery
of *this* by my comrades? How much longer will it be before some prying
swine sees these strips and refuses to believe they hide wounds – laughs
at my tale of attempted suicide in a fit of *cafard* – *hara-kiri* – self-
mutilation with a knife' . . .

'Because, if you can face the pain, we can obliterate that. We can
remove the record of shame, and you can wear the record of courage
and duty without fear of discovery of the . . .'

'*What* do you say?' cried Dubonnet, as the words penetrated his
anguished and self-centred mind. '*What?* Remove it? *How* – in the
name of God?'

'Burn it out as it was burnt in,' was the cool reply. 'I will do it for you
if you ask me to . . . The pain will be ghastly and the mark hideous – but
it will *be* a mark and nothing else. Anyone seeing it will merely see that
you have been severely burnt – and they'll be about right.'

Dubonnet sat up.

'You could and would do that?' he said.

'Yes. I should make a flat piece of iron red-hot and lay it firmly
across the writing. It would depend on you whether it were successful
or not, and would be a good test of nerve and courage. Have it done –
and make up your mind that cowardice and treachery were burnt out
with the words. Then start life afresh and win another decoration' . . .

'There are anaesthetics,' whimpered Dubonnet. 'Chloroform' . . .

'Not for Legionaries in Madagascar,' was the reply. 'Unless you'd
like to go to Médecin-Major Parme with your story and ask him to
operate, to oblige a young friend?'

Dubonnet shivered, and then spat. '*Médecin-Major Parme!*' he
growled.

'If you like to wait a few weeks or months or years, you may have the opportunity and the money to buy chloroform,' continued the Englishman, 'or the means for making local injections of cocaine or something; but I suggest you make a kind of sacrament of the business – have the damnable thing burnt out precisely as it was burnt in, and as you clench your teeth on the bullet in manly silence and soldierly stoicism, realize it is *the past* that is being burnt also, and that the good fire is burning out all that makes you hate yourself and hate life. Let it be symbolic.'

John Bull knew his man. He had met his type before. Too much imagination; too little ballast; the material for a first-class devil, or a first-class man; swayed and governed by his symbols, shibboleths, and prejudices; the slave and victim of an *idée fixe* . . . If he could get him to undergo this ordeal, he would emerge from it a new man – a saved man. An anaesthetic would spoil the whole moral effect. If he would face the torture and bear it, he would regard himself as a brave man, just as surely as he now regarded himself as a coward. He would recover his self-respect, and he would *be* brave because he believed himself to be brave. It would literally be his regeneration and salvation.

'It would hurt no more in the undoing than it did in the doing,' he continued.

The poor wretch shuddered.

'She had written a few words of farewell to one or two,' he said, 'and told how we were going to die together, and when and where . . . Her mother and some others burst in and found me with her body in my arms and my untasted poison beside me . . . I went mad. I raved. I denounced myself. A vile woman who had once loved me, jeered at me and bade me drink my share and rid the world of myself . . . I could not . . . My own gang bound me on my bed, and one of them brought an old chisel and the half of an iron pipe split lengthways. With the straight edge and the semicircular one, they did their work. I was their prisoner for – ah! *how* long? And then they tattooed the scars – not satisfied with their handiwork as it was . . . Before her husband found me I had fled to the shelter of the Legion . . . I told the surgeon at Fort St Jean that it was done by a rival gang because I had pretended to join them and did not. He gave me a roll of the sticking-plaster and advised me, for my comfort, to hide my '*endossement*' as he brutally called it' . . .

'Well, now get rid of it,' interrupted John Bull.

'The flat iron clamp, binding the corners of that packing-case, would be the very thing. You are *not* a coward. You proved that today. Prove it more highly tonight, and, when they decorate you, let there be a still more honourable decoration beneath – the scars of a great victory . . . Come on' . . .

When old Jean Jacques Dubonnet fell, many years later, at Verdun, the Colonel of his battalion, on hearing the news, remarked, 'I have lost my bravest soldier.'

The marks of a terrible burn on his chest were almost obliterated by German bullets and bayonets.

Rudyard Kipling

The Gardener

One grave to me was given,
  One watch till Judgment Day;
And God looked down from Heaven
  And rolled the stone away.

One day in all the years,
  One hour in that one day,
His Angel saw my tears,
  And rolled the stone away!

EVERY one in the village knew that Helen Turrell did her duty by all her world, and by none more honourably than by her only brother's unfortunate child. The village knew, too, that George Turrell had tried his family severely since early youth, and were not surprised to be told that, after many fresh starts given and thrown away, he, an Inspector of Indian Police, had entangled himself with the daughter of a retired non-commissioned officer, and had died of a fall from a horse a few weeks before his child was born. Mercifully, George's father and mother were both dead, and though Helen, thirty-five and independent, might well have washed her hands of the whole disgraceful affair, she most nobly took charge, though she was, at the time, under threat of lung trouble which had driven her to the South of France. She arranged for the passage of the child and a nurse from Bombay, met them at Marseilles, nursed the baby through an attack of infantile dysentery due to the carelessness of the nurse, whom she had had to dismiss, and at last, thin and worn but triumphant, brought the boy late in the autumn, wholly restored, to her Hampshire home.

All these details were public property, for Helen was as open as the day, and held that scandals are only increased by hushing them up. She admitted that George had always been rather a black sheep, but things might have been much worse if the mother had insisted on her right to keep the boy. Luckily, it seemed that people of that class would do almost anything for money, and, as George had always turned to her in his scrapes, she felt herself justified – her friends agreed with her – in cutting the whole non-commissioned officer connection, and giving the child every advantage. A christening, by the Rector, under the name of Michael, was the first step. So far as she knew herself, she was not, she said, a child-lover, but, for all his faults, she had been very fond of George, and she pointed out that little Michael had his father's mouth to a line; which made something to build upon.

As a matter of fact, it was the Turrell forehead, broad, low, and well-shaped, with the widely spaced eyes beneath it, that Michael had most faithfully reproduced. His mouth was somewhat better cut than the family type. But Helen, who would concede nothing good to his mother's side, vowed he was a Turrell all over, and, there being no one to contradict, the likeness was established.

In a few years Michael took his place, as accepted as Helen had always been – fearless, philosophical, and fairly good-looking. At six, he wished to know why he could not call her 'Mummy,' as other boys called their mothers. She explained that she was only his auntie, and that aunties were not quite the same as mummies, but that, if it gave him pleasure, he might call her 'Mummy' at bedtime, for a pet-name between themselves.

Michael kept his secret most loyally, but Helen, as usual, explained the fact to her friends; which when Michael heard, he raged.

'Why did you tell? *Why* did you tell?' came at the end of the storm.

'Because it's always best to tell the truth,' Helen answered, her arm round him as he shook in his cot.

'All right, but when the troof's ugly I don't think it's nice.'

'Don't you, dear?'

'No, I don't, and' – she felt the small body stiffen – 'now you've told, I won't call you "Mummy" any more – not even at bedtimes.'

'But isn't that rather unkind?' said Helen softly.

'I don't care! I don't care! You've hurted me in my insides and I'll hurt you back. I'll hurt you as long as I live!'

'Don't, oh, don't talk like that, dear! You don't know what—'

'I will! And when I'm dead I'll hurt you worse!'

'Thank goodness, I shall be dead long before you, darling.'

'Huh! Emma says, " 'Never know your luck." (Michael had been talking to Helen's elderly, flat-faced maid.) 'Lots of little boys died quite soon. So'll I. *Then* you'll see!'

Helen caught her breath and moved towards the door, but the wail of 'Mummy! Mummy!' drew her back again, and the two wept together.

At ten years old, after two terms at a prep. school, something or somebody gave him the idea that his civil status was not quite regular.

THE GARDENER

He attacked Helen on the subject, breaking down her stammered defences with the family directness.

' 'Don't believe a word of it,' he said, cheerily, at the end. 'People wouldn't have talked like they did if my people had been married. But don't you bother, Auntie. I've found out all about my sort in English Hist'ry and the Shakespeare bits. There was William the Conqueror to begin with, and – oh, heaps more, and they all got on first-rate. 'Twon't make any difference to you, my being *that* – will it?'

'As if anything could—' she began.

'All right. We won't talk about it any more if it makes you cry.' He never mentioned the thing again of his own will, but when, two years later, he skilfully managed to have measles in the holidays, as his temperature went up to the appointed one hundred and four he muttered of nothing else, till Helen's voice, piercing at last his delirium, reached him with assurance that nothing on earth or beyond could make any difference between them.

The terms at his public school and the wonderful Christmas, Easter, and Summer holidays followed each other, variegated and glorious as jewels on a string; and as jewels Helen treasured them. In due time Michael developed his own interests, which ran their courses and gave way to others; but his interest in Helen was constant and increasing throughout. She repaid it with all that she had of affection or could command of counsel and money; and since Michael was no fool, the War took him just before what was like to have been a most promising career.

He was to have gone up to Oxford, with a scholarship, in October. At the end of August he was on the edge of joining the first holocaust of public-school boys who threw themselves into the Line; but the captain of his O.T.C., where he had been sergeant for nearly a year, headed him off and steered him directly to a commission in a battalion so new that half of it still wore the old Army red, and the other half was breeding meningitis through living overcrowdedly in damp tents. Helen had been shocked at the idea of direct enlistment.

'But it's in the family,' Michael laughed.

'You don't mean to tell me that you believed that old story all this time?' said Helen. (Emma, her maid, had been dead now several years.) 'I gave you my word of honour – and I give it again – that – that it's all right. It is indeed.'

'Oh, *that* doesn't worry me. It never did,' he replied valiantly. 'What I meant was, I should have got into the show earlier if I'd enlisted – like my grandfather.'

'Don't talk like that! Are you afraid of it's ending so soon, then?'

'No such luck. You know what K. says.'

'Yes. But my banker told me last Monday it couldn't *possibly* last beyond Christmas – for financial reasons.'

' 'Hope he's right, but our Colonel – and he's a Regular – says it's going to be a long job.'

Michael's battalion was fortunate in that, by some chance which meant several 'leaves,' it was used for coast-defence among shallow trenches on the Norfolk coast; thence sent north to watch the mouth of a Scotch estuary, and, lastly, held for weeks on a baseless rumour of distant service. But, the very day that Michael was to have met Helen for four whole hours at a railway-junction up the line, it was hurled out, to help make good the wastage of Loos, and he had only just time to send her a wire of farewell.

In France luck again helped the battalion. It was put down near the Salient, where it led a meritorious and unexacting life, while the Somme was being manufactured; and enjoyed the peace of the Armentières and Laventie sectors when that battle began. Finding that it had sound views on protecting its own flanks and could dig, a prudent Commander stole it out of its own Division, under pretence of helping to lay telegraphs, and used it round Ypres at large.

A month later, and just after Michael had written to Helen that there was nothing special doing and therefore no need to worry, a shell-splinter dropping out of a wet dawn killed him at once. The next shell uprooted and laid down over the body what had been the foundation of a barn wall, so neatly that none but an expert would have guessed that anything unpleasant had happened.

By this time the village was old in experience of war, and English fashion had evolved a ritual to meet it. When the postmistress handed her seven-year-old daughter the official telegram to take to Miss Turrell, she observed to the Rector's gardener: 'It's Miss Helen's turn now.' He replied, thinking of his own son: 'Well, he's lasted longer than some.' The child herself came to the front-door weeping aloud, because Master Michael had often given her sweets. Helen, presently, found herself pulling down the house-blinds one after one with great care, and saying earnestly to each: 'Missing *already* means dead.' Then she took her place in the dreary procession that was impelled to go through an inevitable series of unprofitable emotions. The Rector, of course, preached hope and prophesied word, very soon, from a prison camp. Several friends, too, told her perfectly truthful tales, but always about other women, to whom, after months and months of silence, their missing had been miraculously restored. Other people urged her to communicate with infallible Secretaries of organizations who could communicate with benevolent neutrals, who could extract accurate information from the most secretive of Hun prison commandants. Helen did and wrote and signed everything that was suggested or put before her.

Once, on one of Michael's leaves, he had taken her over a munition factory, where she saw the progress of a shell from blank-iron to the all but finished article. It struck her at the time that the wretched thing was never left alone for a single second; and 'I'm being manufactured into a bereaved next of kin,' she told herself, as she prepared her documents.

In due course, when all the organizations had deeply or sincerely regretted their inability to trace, etc., something gave way within her and all sensation – save of thankfulness for the release – came to an end in blessed passivity. Michael had died and her world had stood still and she had been one with the full shock of that arrest. Now she was standing still and the world was going forward, but it did not concern her – in no way or relation did it touch her. She knew this by the ease with which she could slip Michael's name into talk and incline her head to the proper angle, at the proper murmur of sympathy.

In the blessed realization of that relief, the Armistice with all its bells broke over her and passed unheeded. At the end of another year she had overcome her physical loathing of the living and returned young, so that she could take them by the hand and almost sincerely wish them well. She had no interest in any aftermath, national or personal, of the war, but, moving at an immense distance, she sat on various relief committees and held strong views – she heard herself delivering them – about the site of the proposed village War Memorial.

Then there came to her, as next of kin, an official intimation, backed by a page of a letter to her in indelible pencil, a silver identity-disc, and a watch, to the effect that the body of Lieutenant Michael Turrell had been found, identified, and re-interred in Hagenzeele Third Military Cemetery – the letter of the row and the grave's number in that row duly given.

So Helen found herself moved on to another process of the manufacture – to a world full of exultant or broken relatives, now strong in the certainty that there was an altar upon earth where they might lay their love. These soon told her, and by means of time-tables made clear, how easy it was and how little it interfered with life's affairs to go and see one's grave.

'So different,' as the Rector's wife said, 'if he'd been killed in Mesopotamia, or even Gallipoli.'

The agony of being waked up to some sort of second life drove Helen across the Channel, where, in a new world of abbreviated titles, she learnt that Hagenzeele Third could be comfortably reached by an afternoon train which fitted in with the morning boat, and that there was a comfortable little hotel not three kilometres from Hagenzeele itself, where one could spend quite a comfortable night and see one's grave next morning. All this she had from a Central Authority who lived in a board and tar-paper shed on the skirts of a razed city full of whirling lime-dust and blown papers.

'By the way,' said he, 'you know your grave, of course?'

'Yes, thank you,' said Helen, and showed its row and number typed on Michael's own little typewriter. The officer would have checked it, out of one of his many books; but a large Lancashire woman thrust between them and bade him tell her where she might find her son, who had been corporal in the A.S.C. His proper name, she sobbed, was Anderson, but, coming of respectable folk, he had of course enlisted under the name of Smith; and had been killed at Dickiebush, in early 'Fifteen. She had not his number nor did she know which of his two Christian names he might have used with his alias; but her Cook's tourist ticket expired at the end of Easter week, and if by then she could not find her child she should go mad. Whereupon she fell forward on Helen's breast; but the officer's wife came out quickly from a little bedroom behind the office, and the three of them lifted the woman on to the cot.

'They are often like this,' said the officer's wife, loosening the tight bonnet-strings. 'Yesterday she said he'd been killed at Hooge. Are you sure you know your grave? It makes such a difference.'

'Yes, thank you,' said Helen, and hurried out before the woman on the bed should begin to lament again.

Tea in a crowded mauve and blue striped wooden structure, with a false front, carried her still further into the nightmare. She paid her bill beside a stolid, plain-features Englishwoman, who, hearing her inquire about the train to Hagenzeele, volunteered to come with her.

'I'm going to Hagenzeele myself,' she explained. 'Not to Hagenzeele Third; mine is Sugar Factory, but they call it La Rosière now. It's just south of Hagenzeele Three. Have you got your room at the hotel there?'

'Oh yes, thank you. I've wired.'

'That's better. Sometimes the place is quite full, and at others there's hardly a soul. But they've put bathrooms into the old Lion d'Or – that's the hotel on the west side of Sugar Factory – and it draws off a lot of people, luckily.'

'It's all new to me. This is the first time I've been over.'

'Indeed! This is my ninth time since the Armistice. Not on my own account. *I* haven't lost any one, thank God – but, like every one else, I've a lot of friends at home who have. Coming over as often as I do, I find it helps them to have some one just look at the – the place and tell them about it afterwards. And one can take photos for them, too. I get quite a list of commissions to execute.' She laughed nervously and

tapped her slung Kodak. 'There are two or three to see at Sugar Factory
this time, and plenty of others in the cemeteries all about. My system
is to save them up, and arrange them, you know. And when I've got
enough commissions for one area to make it worth while, I pop over
and execute them. It *does* comfort people.'

'I suppose so,' Helen answered, shivering as they entered the little
train.

'Of course it does. (Isn't it lucky we've got window-seats?) It must
do or they wouldn't ask one to do it, would they? I've a list of quite
twelve or fifteen commissions here' – she tapped the Kodak again – 'I
must sort them out tonight. Oh, I forgot to ask you. What's yours?'

'My nephew,' said Helen. 'But I was very fond of him.'

'Ah, yes! I sometimes wonder whether *they* know after death? What
do you think?'

'Oh, I don't – I haven't dared to think much about that sort of thing,'
said Helen, almost lifting her hands to keep her off.

'Perhaps that's better,' the woman answered. 'The sense of loss must
be enough, I expect. Well, I won't worry you any more.'

Helen was grateful, but when they reached the hotel Mrs Scarsworth
(they had exchanged names) insisted on dining at the same table with
her, and after the meal, in the little, hideous salon full of low-voiced
relatives, took Helen through her 'commissions' with biographies of the
dead, where she happened to know them, and sketches of their next of
kin. Helen endured till nearly half-past nine, ere she fled to her room.

Almost at once there was a knock at her door and Mrs Scarsworth
entered; her hands, holding the dreadful list, clasped before her.

'Yes – yes – *I* know,' she began. 'You're sick of me, but I want to tell
you something. You – you aren't married, are you? Then perhaps you
won't . . . But it doesn't matter. I've *got* to tell some one. I can't go on
any longer like this.'

'But please—' Mrs Scarsworth had backed against the shut door,
and her mouth worked dryly.

'In a minute,' she said. 'You – you know about these graves of mine
I was telling you about downstairs, just now? They really *are* commissions. At least several of them are.' Her eye wandered round the room.
'What extraordinary wall-papers they have in Belgium, don't you
think? . . . Yes. I swear they are commissions. But there's *one*, d'you
see, and – and he was more to me than anything else in the world. Do
you understand?'

Helen nodded.

'More than any one else. And, of course, he oughtn't to have been.
He ought to have been nothing to me. But he *was*. He *is*. That's why I
do the commissions, you see. That's all.'

'But why do you tell me?' Helen asked desperately.

'Because I'm *so* tired of lying. Tired of lying – always lying – year in and year out. When I don't tell lies I've got to act 'em and I've got to think 'em, always. *You* don't know what that means. He was everything to me that he oughtn't to have been – the one real thing – the only thing that ever happened to me in all my life; and I've had to pretend he wasn't. I've had to watch every word I said, and think out what lie I'd tell next, for years and years!'

'How many years?' Helen asked.

'Six years and four months before, and two and three-quarters after. I've gone to him eight times, since. Tomorrow'll make the ninth, and – and I can't – I *can't* go to him again with nobody in the world knowing. I want to be honest with some one before I go. Do you understand? It doesn't matter about *me*. I was never truthful, even as a girl. But it isn't worthy of *him*. So – so I – I had to tell you. I can't keep it up any longer. Oh, I can't!'

She lifted her joined hands almost to the level of her mouth, and brought them down sharply, still joined, to full arms' length below her waist. Helen reached forward, caught them, bowed her head over them, and murmured: 'Oh, my dear! My dear!' Mrs Scarsworth stepped back, her face all mottled.

'My God!' said she. 'Is *that* how you take it?'

Helen could not speak, and the woman went out; but it was a long while before Helen was able to sleep.

Next morning Mrs Scarsworth left early on her round of commissions, and Helen walked alone to Hagenzeele Third. The place was still in the making, and stood some five or six feet above the metalled road, which it flanked for hundreds of yards. Culverts across a deep ditch served for entrances through the unfinished boundary wall. She climbed a few wooden-faced earthen steps and then met the entire crowded level of the thing in one held breath. She did not know that Hagenzeele Third counted twenty-one thousand dead already. All she saw was a merciless sea of black crosses, bearing little strips of stamped tin at all angles across their faces. She could distinguish no order or arrangement in their mass; nothing but a waist-high wilderness as of weeds stricken dead, rushing at her. She went forward, moved to the left and the right hopelessly, wondering by what guidance she should ever come to her own. A great distance away there was a line of whiteness. It proved to be a block of some two or three hundred graves whose headstones had already been set, whose flowers were planted out, and whose new-sown grass showed green. Here she could see clear-cut letters at the ends of the rows, and, referring to her slip, realized that it was not here she must look.

A man knelt behind a line of headstones – evidently a gardener, for he was firming a young plant in the soft earth. She went towards him, her paper in her hand. He rose at her approach and without prelude or salutation asked: 'Who are you looking for?'

'Lieutenant Michael Turrell – my nephew,' said Helen slowly and word for word, as she had many thousands of times in her life.

The man lifted his eyes and looked at her with infinite compassion before he turned from the fresh-sown grass toward the naked black crosses.

'Come with me,' he said, 'and I will show you where your son lies.'

When Helen left the Cemetery she turned for a last look. In the distance she saw the man bending over his young plants; and she went away, supposing him to be the gardener.

Geoffrey Household

Tell These Men
to Go Away

MISS TITTERTON was so ashamed of being put inside – as she believed it was now called – and so uneasily certain that she must have committed an offence that it was very difficult to persuade her she was not a criminal. Even the Family could never quite restore her faith in herself.

In the nineteenth century the Family – Miss Titterton always pronounced the word with a coronet over the capital F – owned some five hundred square miles of Hungarian soil; by the twentieth this inheritance had been reduced to fifty. Neither chaperones nor husbands could control the females, and no racecourse, marriage, cabaret or casino was safe from the males. The only hope for the future of the Family and its estates was, their lawyers said – and the Emperor graciously supported the recommendation – an English governess who could inculcate a sense of discipline into the infant generation during the formative years.

The choice fell upon Miss Titterton. Not for a moment did she feel unworthy, but she could not explain it. She had no connections with Nobility or Higher Clergy, and was far too truthful to claim anything but humble birth and a sound education. Though she was never allowed to suspect it, her appointment was simply due to the fact that she had been the fourth candidate to be interviewed. Her prospective employer, the Countess, had languidly remarked that, whether or not English governesses had the inhuman virtues ascribed to them, they were a dying fashion, and nobody could possibly be expected to endure conversing with more than three of them in quick succession.

Miss Titterton settled into the nursery wing, and was immediately adored by her charges. She had never, my dears, felt the necessity for any harsh discipline. At any rate she trained the characters of two generations of the Family with such success that they could without effort appear imperturbably British: a quality which in later life impressed their bank managers and allowed a presumption of innocence in such divorces as were sadly unavoidable.

When Ellen Titterton was sixty-five, the Family, who all loved a generous gesture, pensioned her off and presented to her a gay, distinguished, little doll's house just off the main street of their market town. She had as well enough savings of her own – she never seemed to spend any money except of felicitous presents to the children – to impress local society with her independence, and she earned a trifle of income by giving delicately efficient English lessons.

She was slim, straight, respected and as reasonable as ever. She had no special enthusiasms. She did not occupy herself unduly with priests or pets or worthy causes, content to contribute the graces of etiquette to her little circle of maiden aunts and major's widows. She read and recommended; she played the piano well; she left the proper cards upon her friends on all the correct occasions. The society which Miss Titterton ornamented was exactly that for which Providence and a Victorian girlhood had prepared her. She was also grateful to Providence for a basic training in languages which allowed her to speak Hungarian with a hardly noticeable accent.

In 1938 the Family saw what was coming and removed themselves to London. They could not persuade the beloved nursery governess to accompany them. At her age, she insisted, she did not choose to be uprooted. As she had always told the children, when one has made one's bed one must lie on it.

Her confidence was justified. Nobody thought of interning her when Hungary entered the war on the German side – or, if anybody did, the proposal was rejected as a waste of time and money. She continued to live her miniature social life and comforted herself by the thought that there was no quarrel between her two countries. It was a mere accident of diplomacy that Hungary had become an enemy nation. The Germans are so self-willed, my dear, though very musical of course.

When German base units were stationed in the little town, the social decencies were eased for her by her friends. Should some veteran German officer be invited to coffee, it was understood that Ellen Titterton must be warned. If, in spite of this, she came face to face with the enemy her dignified bow was a satisfaction to all concerned. It apologized so exquisitely for the fact that international differences prevented any personal relations.

The Germans found great difficulty, Miss Titterton said, in distinguishing between allied and conquered territory; she would have thought it could have been explained to them. So she was puzzled – but still charitable – when a German army truck, half loaded with furniture, called at her house. Out of it stepped an officer and six SS men.

The officer saluted and asked if he might be permitted to inspect the house. Miss Titterton realized that the visit was official, not social, and that her distant bow would be out of place. She followed the high, black boots from room to room, and back to the front door. There, on her own doorstep, she was bluntly informed that, since the only occupants of the house were herself and her little dainty-aproned servant, she did not need more than two bedrooms. No doubt she would be glad to make a free gift of the furniture of the other to some suffering family in the Ruhr which had been bombed out.

Miss Titterton did not approve of this method of collection. Giving to the Hungarian troops she understood – and to hospitals, bazaars, all the scores of war charities. Very willingly she played her tiny part, for after all the Hungarians were not in action against British troops. Even if they had been, it would have made no difference to her pity.

She replied to the demand that she was very sorry, but she could not give up her furniture. That third bedroom, unused, and spotless, was specially dear. It was the dream of her retirement that some day one of the Family would come to stay with her.

The officer showed his army authority – German Army – to remove the furniture – Hungarian furniture – and regretted that he had no alternative. He ordered two men up the stairs. They seemed to Miss Titterton rather brutal and large, but she reminded herself that removal men had so much heavy lifting to do. All the same, she was outraged. She took the rational but extraordinary step of telephoning to the town police for protection.

The Family could never find out what had happened at the other end of the line. The police, who knew all about the Herrenvolk's requisitioning, could only recommend prompt obedience. Why they took any action at all was beyond conjecture. It may have been that they wondered if the SS was being impersonated by some band of ordinary, less efficient criminals; it may have been that they were just weary of being ignored. Whatever the reason, Sergeant Bacso, sword, pistol, moustache and all, paced round the corner of the main street and halted in front of Miss Titterton's house.

The dressing-table had got as far as the front door. It could go no farther, since Ellen Titterton, drawn up to her full height, was standing in the doorway. She neither protested nor fluttered. To get the furniture out she herself would first have had to be removed to the army truck, stiff and dignified as a piece of Victorian teak.

Sergeant Bacso was also of an older generation. He and Miss Titterton knew of each other's existence and reputation, but had had no dealings together. For Miss Titterton police were like plumbers – necessary and useful but required only in unpleasant emergencies. For the sergeant she was part of a closed world to which emergencies must not be allowed to happen. That at first was the only common ground.

The Family knew Bacso well – far from a hero and not the sort of man to interfere with his own comfort. He was gorgeous, bumbling, incoherent, and harmless as an old turkey cock. He gobbled at Miss

Titterton and Hitler's SS. While he recovered from the shock of this forcible collection of free gifts.

The sergeant was not at all the modern policeman with a probation order in one hand and a tax demand in the other. He did not think of himself as representing the arbitrary benevolence of the State; he was just the protector of the haves, however humble, against the have-nots. Not a very worthy ideal. But, such as it was, it absolutely prevented him from pointing out quietly to Miss Titterton that a private individual should not argue with the SS. For Sergeant Bacso property was property.

He drew out his notebook and formally asked Miss Titterton whether she was or was not willing to present the furniture of one bedroom to the Reich. She replied decidedly that she was not. He took down her statement, closed his notebook and put it back in his pocket.

The SS men were grinning at him as if he were a circus clown in policeman's uniform. He had a wide-open escape route from the deadlock if he merely pointed out that Miss Titterton was British and that he washed his hands of her. The Family doubted if it ever occurred to him. He was used to thinking of her as one of the town's old ladies. The only officials likely to remember her nationality off-hand were those of the former British Legation where she appeared once a year for the party on the King's Birthday in some astonishing confection twenty years out of date and carefully pressed and ornamented.

Having decided that his customer's complaint was justified, Sergeant Bacso pulled his splendid moustache and awaited an invitation to act. He got it.

'Sergeant,' said Miss Titterton, 'is it not your duty to tell these men to go away?'

It was a gentle inquiry rather than a command. But there was no disobeying. Miss Titterton had developed her confident manner through taking over two generations of spoilt children from dear old peasant nannies who – regrettably but so very naturally – had no idea at all of discipline. Her voice was sufficient. Unlike the SS she had never been compelled to use corporal punishment.

Sergeant Bacso settled his gleaming shako on his head and joined Miss Titterton at the front door. What really bothered him was not so much standing up to a detachment of the most conscienceless thugs in the German Army as giving orders to an officer. Hungarians of his generation had a very great respect for officers.

He saluted and apologized with every second sentence, but he was firm. Miss Titterton's furniture could not be requisitioned without payment, and it was not going to leave her house until he had referred the matter to his superiors.

By this time a small crowd had gathered. They probably did not cheer, but looked as if they wanted to. The two SS men who were still carrying the dressing-table put it down. Their comrades stood by the truck, lounging and contemptuously interested. The unconscious arrogance of an old lady and a town policeman had surpassed their own.

The officer called them to attention and began to storm at Bacso. The foaming, emphatic German was a little too fast for the sergeant, but not for Miss Titterton – though there were words the meaning of which she preferred to ignore. She stopped the flow with a slight gesture of her hand and remarked that in the great days of the German Army the officers she met were always gentlemen. Women had been slung across the street for less. But Miss Titterton's rebukes were always unanswerable. That phrase 'the great days' made any violent retort extremely difficult.

The SS were almost about to climb into their truck and visit other free contributors. Afterwards, of course, they would have returned and had the furniture of the whole house off her. But for the moment they were on the defensive. They were back in school with the copybook maxims of truth, courage and good manners.

Sergeant Bacso, triumphant and peaceable, invited his country's allies to accompany him to the police station; he meant that he was only too willing to refer the question of Miss Titterton's bedroom to higher authority if they would be good enough to come with him. But the SS officer, ready for any excuse to reimpose himself on the situation, pretended to believe that the sergeant was threatening arrest. He nodded to his bullies around the truck who intimidatingly strolled forward.

Bacso in a noble access of Magyar defiance drew his pistol. The illusion of civic law and order was destroyed. By resorting to violence he immediately removed himself from the fantastic world which Miss Titterton had created.

It could easily have been his last act; but the Herrenvolk, relieved of unwelcome memories of civilization and back in their familiar environment, decided that he and his pop-gun were merely comic. They disarmed him and, according to Ellen Titterton, deprived him of his nether garments. She was reluctant to give details. Good manners were as needful as always even if you young people chose to call them inhibitions. It appeared that the SS detachment had hustled Bacso round the corner and launched him into the main street by a kick on the bare backside. He had the sympathy of the whole town, but it was recognized that he never would get over the humiliation, never be so professionally fierce and polished again.

Miss Titterton's respectability, too, was gravely compromised. The police came for her at once, and the local magistrate with them. In spite of being a distant cousin of the Family and a frequent visitor – a highly-strung little boy, she remembered, who had been so unnecessarily afraid of the dark – he would not hold any conversation with her and would not listen. He bundled her off to his court under the eyes of the SS, and promptly gaoled her for insulting glorious allies and creating a disturbance. A common gaol it had been, among common criminals. She had been very glad to see how well the poor women were treated. She was sure that she had been allowed no special privileges beyond permission to decorate her cell with curtains and chintz covers and to invite selected prisoners to coffee. Their moral education had been sadly neglected, and she hoped that her influence on them had been for the good.

Miss Titterton felt that it was very forgiving of the Family to rescue her and fly her back to London immediately after the war. When they explained to her that prison had been the only way of preserving her from a quite certain concentration camp and the very possible attentions of the Gestapo, she tried hard to believe them. But in her experience, she said, justice was always done. She was afraid it stood to reason that she had deserved her sentence – perhaps for not taking enough care with the unruly member, my dear. It was very kind of them all to accept her disgrace so light-heartedly.

Sid Gorrell

Out of the Depths

To the watchers on the Bolts the painted sails of the stricken galleon seemed to lie across her hull like a funeral pall as she settled by the head. The end came quickly as the sea rushed through the last tier of open gun-ports; the open spaces of the forward castle flooded and she slid forward and downward. For moments only the enclosed buoyancy of the state-rooms in the tall after castle held her poised, whilst all that remained was the great gilt crucifix, glinting in the westering sun. Then that too slid beneath the waves as this first casualty of the Invincible Armada sank to her burial in the sands of the Channel.

The young reserve officer remained quietly in his pew as the last of the congregation passed out through the porch. He gazed round the church, quiet except for the whisper of the sea coming through the open west door. The sea, with its many voices, had always been to him a natural background to worship and as a boy he had believed that if, by some cataclysm, the sea-shore had retreated out beyond the Bolts, thrusting their headlands out into the channel, the church would still retain its sea-voices, the gift of the centuries, like a shell to which one puts an ear. His gaze wandered to the list of incumbents on the wall opposite the font. From that of the first priest-in-charge in 1125 the line stretched unbroken to his father's name, thirty-seventh in order. Thirty-seven names in eight hundred years. No wonder the villagers spoke of the sinking of the Armada galleon as a comparatively recent event in local history. To the communicants, the great golden chalice, the only relic to be cast up from the wreck, was a constant reminder. In those days, he mused, England had stood alone against a foe who fought in the name of Christianity. Now in the year of 1940 she stood alone against a tyranny in which mercy and justice were regarded as Christian vices. He sighed as he left the church, hoping that it would soon be all over.

That afternoon his father drove him into Plymouth to take over command of the anti-submarine trawler, engaged in escorting Channel convoys, to which he had been appointed. He found her lying at

Number Eight Wharf in the dockyard, outside the old French battleship *Paris*, which had struggled across the Channel after the fall of France and was now the operational headquarters of the coastal patrols. He slipped quietly aboard and found the three officers in the wardroom. The First Lieutenant apologized for not being on hand to give him a formal welcome at the gangway, but he waved his hand deprecatingly.

'It's all right, Number One,' he smiled, 'I didn't advertise my arrival, and in any case Nelson won't fall off his column.' His manner foreshadowed a homely atmosphere, and his officers relaxed.

Next morning he reported to Commander Auxiliary Patrols aboard the *Paris* and then returned on board to address his ship's company mustered on the foredeck. This formality over he called the cox'n into his cabin.

'They seem to be a very smart crowd, cox'n,' he began.

'Time will tell, sir,' grinned the cox'n. 'I hope we see plenty of action; it will keep them from fighting amongst themselves.' In response to a questioning look on his commanding officer's face he continued, 'Well, it's like this, sir, I've never been shipmates with such a mixed bag before. Out of the forty of us on the mess-decks we have eighteen C of Es, twelve RCs, two Methodists, a Baptist, and two Congregationalists. That lot's all right, of course, but on top of that we have a Jehovah's Witness, a Plymouth Brother, a Christian Scientist – that's some sort of faith-healing practice – and then there are two characters who call themselves atheists.'

'Two atheists, eh! They will have to have some allegiance, on paper at least, just in case we have to bury them.' The Captain thought for a moment. 'Put 'em down as C of E, cox'n. They won't be noticed that way.'

'C of E, sir,' replied the cox'n, as if confirming their size in shoes.

Soon began the tedious days of escort duty. Collecting his convoy in the Sound, he ordered his trawlers to take up their stations one at each corner of the lines of ships, their listening equipment reaching out under water to form a screen to seaward.

Westwards towards the Lizard, picking up more ships from Falmouth as they went, around the Longships and up the coast of Cornwall they steamed till, off Lundy Island, he detached two of the escort with ships bound for Barry and Milford, while he and *Ellesmere* continued with their part of the convoy to Swansea.

Three days later they met again at the rendezvous off Lundy to escort deep-laden ships for Plymouth, Southampton, Portsmouth and points east. Day followed tedious day, with only the destruction of an occasional drifting mine by rifle fire to break the monotony. Down on the mess-deck the lack of real action was beginning to tell.

After Divine Worship on their first Sunday at sea the First Lieutenant came to see him.

'You forgot part of the drill this morning, Cap'n,' he observed.

'Which bit was that?' he asked.

'After Divisions and before prayers you did not say, "Fall out Roman Catholics".'

'I know I didn't; are the Catholics complaining?'

'No; didn't say a thing. I believe that they enjoyed it.'

'Then we will enjoy their company too. If we collect a torpedo we shall go aloft together,' he added with a grin. Two days later he spoke to the cox'n. 'Any reaction to my roping all hands in to Divine Worship on Sunday, cox'n?'

'The RCs were a bit surprised at first, sir, but as they heard that you were going to be a preacher after the war they felt they were not letting the side down. It was the Jehovah's Witness that made the fuss. Said he didn't mind Nonconformists or C of Es, though they were misguided enough, but he didn't like worshipping with idolators who hung crucifixes all over the place.'

'What's he doing in the Service, I wonder? I thought they were conscientious objectors.'

'I believe they are, but this one is trying to make the grade with a little Wren in Plymouth whose old man is a Regimental Sergeant-Major.'

'Then I don't blame him for preferring the prospect of enemy action to tea with father-in-law,' smiled the Captain.

Convoy succeeded convoy and still no sign of the enemy, for his group at least, though other groups seemed to be getting plenty of action. The only fighting *Cornelian*'s crew did was amongst themselves in the various ports after closing time. He mentioned the advisability of asking for a transfer for the man who was the chief cause of the trouble. 'Too late, now, sir,' said the First Lieutenant, 'the whole mess-deck is almost evenly divided. Now the damn fools are quarrelling about miracles. Say they only occur in Catholic countries and that it's a racket to attract tourists. I wish to God they could get a bit of action.' His tone was bitter.

Action, when at last it came, was sudden and violent. Convoy PW 84 was proceeding westwards past the Start, visible abeam in the light of a waning moon. The dark shape of the Bolts could be seen against the stars on the starboard bow. Suddenly a roar, like that of an express train, came over the Asdic repeaters in the wings of the bridge. Tensed, he waited for the torpedo to strike, but it passed down the side and the noise receded up channel. 'Contact bearing green one-five, range four thousand five hundred,' called the Asdic operator from the bridge house. 'Action Stations!' Sub-Lieutenant Crabbe pressed the alarm and within seconds the men were running to their stations, fastening the strings of their life jackets as they ran. 'Charlie Victor to the Commodore, signalman.' Signalman Pole trained his night-signalling lantern on to the leading ship of the starboard column and the letters CV were answered almost immediately by a similar dim blue light. Then on his steam siren the Commodore spelt out the same two letters which were repeated all down the columns of merchant ships. Slowly the leaders of the columns turned outwards and around, each ship following until the whole convoy was headed back up-Channel.

Meanwhile, the First Lieutenant, after a hurried visit to the bridge, had set his depth charges to ten seconds each. 'Instruct *Jasper* to stand by whilst I investigate a contact and tell *Ruby* and *Ellesmere* to remain with the convoy.' Pole clicked out the messages. By now *Cornelian* had worked up to full speed and the range was rapidly closing, the outgoing pinging sound of the Asdic bringing back the hiccuping echoes ever more quickly. Sub-Lieutenant Ryan, at his station beside the Asdic recorder, was adjusting the course to bring the target ahead.

Ping . . . hick, ping . . . hick, ping . . . hick, sang the Asdic repeater, bringing echo and signal closer and closer. Now she was nearly under them, and by the ringing sound of the echo they knew it was a submarine.

'Instantaneous echoes,' called Ryan, excitement shaking his voice.

'First and throwers,' called the Captain over the Navy phones to the First Lieutenant. 'First and throwers going, sir,' came the reply. There was a double sharp rap as the firing charges sent a five-hundred pound canister out on each quarter to fall into the sea twenty yards away. Another rolled out of the racks over the stern. He counted five seconds.

'Fire two.'

'Fire two,' was repeated from aft as another canister rolled over the stern to form a diamond pattern around the target.

'Remove your earphones,' he called to Ryan and the Asdic rating, for the force of the explosions would otherwise crash into their heads to cause permanent damage. It came like the clanging of a mighty anvil struck by a giant of mythology, and the whole sea shimmered around them. Then four great columns of water climbed up into the night.

'Hard-a-port,' he called down the voice pipe to the wheelhouse.

'Hard-a-port, sir,' answered the helmsman and the escort vessel swung around until he steadied her facing up-Channel.

'Star-shell ahead at one thousand,' he called to the cox'n on the fo'c'sle head.

The cox'n repeated the order and a shell left the four-inch gun to explode in the air at a thousand yards ahead, sending an eerie light from its parachute flare to illuminate the seas around. It lit up the dark headlands; it lit up the valley with its ancient church and, to a great cheer from the crew, it lit up the nose of the submarine with its gaping torpedo tubes breaking the surface. 'Bang!' *Jasper*'s gun was ready and her gunners lynx-eyed, for immediately there was the flash of impact followed by a shattering explosion in her torpedo tubes and the submarine disappeared beneath the waves.

'Stop engines, full astern.' The engine room telegraphs clanged and the vessel lost way through the water. He did not want to run in over the sinking submarine for fear of more explosions from her.

Then, in the ghostly light of the now low-lying flare, a great cross arose out of the sea beside them and on the cross a lonely figure which seemed to gaze sadly down on them as slowly it rose higher and higher. The captain ran to the side of the bridge and saw the outlines of the ancient poop, scoured by the sandladen tides of the centuries. None of the crew saw it, for their gaze was fixed with awe upon that sad figure upon the great cross. With a shriek the rating who had scorned all miracles fled from his gun while the others fell to their knees. Slowly the crucifix sank beneath the waves.

H. E. Bates

How Sleep the Brave

I

THE sea moved away below us like a stream of feathers smoothed down
by a level wind. It was grey and without light as far as we could see.
Only against the coast of Holland, in a thin line of trimming that soon
lost itself in the grey coasts of the North, did it break into white waves
that seemed to remain frozen between sea and land. Down towards the
Channel the sun, even from six thousand feet, had gone down at last
below long layers of cloud. They had been orange and blue at first, then
yellow and pale green, and then, as they were now, entirely the colour
of slate. Above them there was nothing but a colourless sky that would
soon be dark altogether.

There had been snow all over England that week. For two nights it
had drifted against the huge wheels of the Stirlings, in scrolls ten feet
high. The wind had partially swept it from the smooth fabric of fuselages
as it fell and then frost had frozen what remained of it into uneven drifts
of papery dust. In the mornings gangs of soldiers worked at the runways,
clearing them to black-white roads edged with low walls of snow, and
lorries drove backwards and forwards along them, taking away like huge
blocks of salt the carved-out drifts. In two more days the thaw came
and yellow pools of snow-water lay in the worn places of the runways.
It froze a little again late at night, leaving a muddy skin of ice on pools
that looked dangerous with the sunlight level and cold on them in the
early morning. It wasn't dangerous really and the wheels of the Stirlings
smashed easily through the ice, splintering it like the silver glass toys on
a Christmas tree. Then in the daytime the pools thawed again and if
you watched the take-off from the control tower through a pair of
glasses you saw the snow-water sparkle up from the wheels like brushes
of silver feathers.

And now, beyond the hazy coast of Holland, with its thin white
trimming that grew less white in the twilight as we flew towards it, we
could see what reports had already told us. There was snow all over
Europe. The day was too advanced to see it clearly. All you could see

was a great hazy field of cotton-wool that had fewer marks on it than a layer of cloud. Far ahead of us, south and south-west and east, it ceased even to be white. It became the misty, colourless distances of all Europe, and suddenly as I looked at it, for almost the last time before darkness hit it altogether, I thought of what it would be like to fly on, southward, to the places I had never seen, the places without flak, the places in sunshine, the places beyond the war and the snow. It was one of those detached ideas that you get when flying, or rather that get you: a lightheaded idea that seems to belong to the upper air and is gone as soon as its futility has played with you.

For a few more minutes the trimming of coast lay dead below us and then, in a moment, was gone past us altogether. For just a few moments longer the misty cotton-wool of the snow over Europe meant something, and then I looked and could see it no longer. Darkness seemed to have floated suddenly between the snow and the Stirling. What was below us was just negative. It was not snow, or land, or Europe. It was just the negative darkness that would flare any moment into hostility.

This darkness was to be ours for five hours or more. I was already cold and the aircraft was bumping like a goods train. The most violent bumps seemed to jerk a little more blood out of my feet. I remembered this sensation from other trips and now tried moving my toes in my boots. But the boots were too thick and my toes were already partially dead. This was my fifteenth trip as flight engineer but even now I could not get rid of two sensations that had recurred on all those trips since the very first: the feeling that I had no feet and the feeling, even more awful than that, that I had swallowed something horribly sour, like vinegar, which had now congealed between my chest and throat. I never thought of it as fear. I was always slightly scared, in a numb way, before the trips began, and before Christmas, before the snow fell, I had been more scared than hell on the Brest daylights. But now I only thought of this sourness as discomfort. It always did something to my power of speech. I always kept the inter-comm. mouthpiece ready, but I rarely used it. I could hear other voices over the inter-comm. but I rarely spoke, unless it was very necessary, in reply. It wasn't that I didn't want to speak, and it had little to do with the fact that Ellis, Captain of K.42, did not encourage talking. I think I was scared that by speaking I might give the impression that I was scared. So I kept my mouth shut and let the sourness bump in my throat and pretended, as perhaps the other six of us pretended, that I was tough and taciturn and did not care.

'A lot of light muck on the port side, skipper.'

'O.K.'

The voice of Osborne, from the rear turret, came over the inter-comm., the Northern accent sharp and cold and almost an order in itself. Ossy, from Newcastle, five feet six, with the lean Newcastle face and grey monkey-wrinkled eyes, was the youngest of us. In battle-dress the wads of pictures in his breast pockets gave him a sort of oblong bust. In his Mae West this bust became quite big and handsome, so that he looked out of proportion, like a pouter pigeon. We always kidded Ossy about giving suck. But in his Mae West there was no room for his photographs; so always, before a trip, Ossy took them out and put them in his flying boots, one in each leg. In one leg of his boots he also carried a revolver, and in the other an American machine spanner. No one knew quite what this spanner was for, except perhaps that it was just one of those things that air-crews begin to carry about with them as foolish incidentals and that in the end become as essential as your right arm. So Ossy never came on trips except he had with him, in the legs of his boots, the things that mattered: the revolver, the spanner, and the pictures of a young girl, light-haired, print-frocked, pretty in a pale Northern way, taken in the usual back-garden attitudes on Tyneside. 'She's a wizard kid,' he said.

As for the spanner, if it was a talisman, I knew that Ed Walker, the second dickey, carried two rabbits' feet. You might have expected the devotion to a good-luck charm from Ossy, who anyway had the good sense to carry a spanner. But it surprised you that Winchester hadn't taught Ed Walker anything better than a belief in rabbits' feet. They were very ordinary rabbits' feet. The tendons had been neatly severed and the hair was quite neat and tidy and smooth. Ed kept them hidden under his shirts in a drawer in his bedroom and he didn't know that anyone knew they were there. I shared the room with him and one day when I opened the wrong drawer by mistake there were the rabbits' feet under the shirts, hidden as a boy might have hidden a packet of cigarettes from his father. Ed was very tall and slow-eyed and limp. He took a long time to dress himself and did not talk much. Between Winchester at eighteen and a Stirling at nineteen there wasn't much life to be filled in. He was so big that sometimes he looked lost; as if he had suddenly found himself grown up too quickly. And sometimes I used to think he didn't talk much solely for the reason that he hadn't much to say. But just because of that, and because of the rabbits' feet and the big lazy helplessness that went with them and because we could lie in bed and not talk much and yet say the right things when we did talk, we were fairly devoted.

Between the coast of Holland and the first really heavy German flak I always felt in a half-daze. I always felt my mind foreshorten its view. It was like travelling on a very long journey in a railway train. You didn't look forward to the ultimate destination, but only to the next station. In this way it did not seem so long. If it were night you could never tell exactly where you were, and sometimes you were suddenly surprised by the lights of a station.

We had no station lights: that was the only difference. We bumped on against the darkness. I don't know why I always felt it was against the darkness, and not in it or through it. Darkness on these long winter trips seemed to solidify. The power we generated seemed to cut it. We had to cut it to get through.

If we got through – but we did not say that except as a joke. At prayer-meeting, in intelligence room, before the trips, the Wing Commander always liked that joke. 'When you come back – *if* you come back.' But he was the only one, I think, who did like it, and most of us had given up laughing now. It might have been rather funnier if, for instance, he had said he hoped we had taken cases of light ale on board, or that we might get drunk on Horlick's tablets and black coffee. Not that this would have been very funny. And the funniest joke in the world, coming from him, wouldn't have given us any more faith than we had.

Faith is a curious thing to talk about. You can't put your hand on it, but there it is. And I think what we and that crew had faith in was not jokes or beam-approach or navigation or the kite itself, but Ellis.

'It's like a duck's arse back here,' Ossy suddenly said. 'One minute I'm in bloody Switzerland and the next I'm up in the North Sea.'

We laughed over the inter-comm.

'It's your ten-ton spanner,' Ellis said.

'What spanner, Skipper, what spanner?'

'Drop it overboard!'

'What spanner, what—'

'Go on, drop it. I can feel the weight of the bloody thing from here. You're holding us back.'

'There's flak coming up like Blackpool illuminations, Skip. Honest, Skip. Take plenty of evasive action—'

'Just drop the bloody spanner, Ossy, and shut up.'

We all laughed again over the inter-comm. There was a long silence, and then Ossy's voice again, now very slow:

'Spanner gone.'

We laughed again, but it was broken by the voice of Ellis. 'What about this Blackpool stuff?'

'It's all Blackpool stuff. Just like the Tower Ball-room on a carnival night.'

They were pumping it up all round us, heavy and light, and for a few minutes it was fairly violent. We were slapped about inside the kite like a collection of loose tools in a case.

Then from the navigation seat came the voice of Mac, the big Canadian from Winnipeg, slow and sardonic:

'Keep the milk warm, Ossy dear. It's baby feed time.' And we laughed again.

After that, for a long time, none of us spoke again. I always noticed that we did not speak much until Ellis started to talk. The voice of Ellis was rather abrupt. The words were shot out and cut off like sections of metal ejected by a machine. I sometimes wondered what I was doing on these trips, in that kite, with Ellis, as flight engineer. He knew more about aero-engines generally, and about these aero-engines particularly, than I should ever know. If ever a man had a ground-crew devoted by the terror of knowledge it was Ellis.

We too were devoted by something of the same feeling. He was a small man of about thirty, a little younger than myself, with those large raw hands that mechanics sometimes have: the large, angular, metallic hands that seem to get their shape and power from the constant handling of tools. These hands, his voice, and finally his eyes were the most remarkable things about him. They were dark eyes that looked at you as impersonally as the lens of a camera. Before them you knew you had better display yourself as you were and not as you hoped you might be.

If Ed Walker had not begun to live, Ellis had lived enough for both of them. For so small a man it was extraordinary how far you had to look up to him, and I think perhaps we looked up at him because of the fullness of that life. A man like Ed would always be insular, clinging to the two neat rabbits' feet of English ideals. The sea, on which Ellis had served for five or six years before the war, had beaten the insularity out of him. It had given him the international quality of a piece of chromium. He was small but he gave out a feeling of compression. You had faith in him because time had tested the pressure his resistances could hold. He did not drink much: hardly at all. Most of us got pretty puce after bad trips, or good trips too if it comes to that, and sometimes people like Ossy got tearful in the bar of the Grenadier and looked wearily into the eyes of strangers and said 'We bloody near got wrapped up. Lost as hell. Would have been if it hadn't been for the Skipper,' and probably in the morning did not remember what they said.

But all of us knew that, and did remember. We knew too why Ellis did not drink. It was because of us. The sea, I think, had taught him something about the cold results of sobriety.

The flak was all the time fairly violent and now and then we dropped into pockets of muck that lifted the sourness acidly into my throat and dragged it down again through my stomach. It was always bad here. We were a good way over now and I remembered the met. reports at prayer-meeting: about seven-tenths over Germany and then clearing over the target. We had many bombers out that night and I hoped it would be clear.

Thinking of the weather, I went for a moment into one of those odd mesmeric dazes that you get on long trips, and thought of myself. I was the eldest of the crew: thirty, with a wife I did not live with now. I had been a successful under-manager in Birmingham and we had at one time a very nice villa on the outskirts. For some reason, I don't know why, we quarrelled a lot about little things like my not cleaning the bath after I'd used it, and the fact that my wife liked vinegar with salmon. We were both selfish in the same ways. We were like two beans that want to grow up the same pole and then strangle each other trying to do so. I had been glad of the war because it gave me the chance to break from her, and now flying had beaten some of the selfishness out of me. My self was no longer assertive. It had lost part of its identity, and I hoped the worst parts of its identity, through being part of the crew. It had done me good to become afraid of losing my skin, and my only trouble really was that I suffered badly from cold. I now could not feel my feet at all.

Suddenly I could not feel anything. Something hit us with a crack that seemed to lift us straight up as if we had been shot through a funnel. The shock tore me sideways. It flung me violently down and up and down again as if I had been a loose nut in a revolving cylinder.

II

'O.K. everybody?'

We had been shaken like that before, on other trips, but never with quite that violent upward force. I lay on the floor of the aircraft and said something in answer to Ellis's voice. I hadn't any idea what it was. I wasn't thinking of myself, but only, at that moment, of the aircraft. I felt the blow had belted us miles upward, like a rocket.

I staggered about a bit and felt a little dazed. It seemed after a few moments that everybody was O.K. I looked at Mac, huge face immobile over the navigator's table, pinning down his charts and papers even harder with a violent thumb. I looked at his table and it was almost level. It did not tilt much with the motion of the aircraft and I knew then we were flying in a straight line. I looked at Allison, the radio operator, and his eyes, framed in a white circle between the earphones, looked back at me. He did not look any paler than usual. He did not look more fixed, more vacant, or more eaten up by trouble than usual. That was just the way he always looked. There had been a kind of cancerous emptiness on his face ever since a blitz had killed his child.

I grinned at him and then the next moment was not thinking of what had happened. The kite was flying well and I heard Ellis's voice again.

'Must be getting near, Mac?'

'About ten minutes, flying time.'

'O.K.'

She bumped violently once or twice as they spoke and seemed to slide into troughs of muck. The sick lump of tension bumped about in my throat and down into my bowels and up again.

'If I see so much as a flea's eyelash I'll feel bloody lucky,' Mac said.

He got up and began to grope his way towards the forward hatch. In those days the navigator did the bomb-aiming. Huge and ponderous and blown out, he looked in the dim light like the man in the adverts for Michelin tyres. I sat down at his table. I felt sick and my head ached. Once as a boy, I had had scarlet fever and my head, as the fever came on, seemed to grow enormous and heavy, many times too large for my body. Now it was the same. It seemed like a colossal lump of helpless pulp on my shoulders. The light above the table seemed to flicker and splinter against my eyes.

I knew suddenly what it was. I wasn't getting my oxygen. It scared me for a moment and then I knew it must have been the fall. I don't quite know what I did. I must have fumbled about with the connexions for a time and succeeded in finding what was wrong at last.

I felt as if I began to filter slowly back into the aircraft. I came back with that awful mental unhappiness, split finally apart by relief, that you get as you struggle out of anaesthesia. I came back to hear the voices of Ellis and Mac, exchanging what I knew must be the instructions over the target. They seemed like disembodied voices. I tried to shake my brain into clarity. It seemed muddy and weak.

At last I got some sense into myself, but it was like exchanging one trouble for another. By the voices over the inter-comm. I knew that we had trouble. The weather was violent and sticky and Mac could not see. Something very dirty and unexpected had come up to change that serene met. forecast at prayer-meeting: clearing over the target. It was not clearing. We were in the middle of something violent, caught up by one of those sinister weather changes that make you hate wind and rain and ice with impotent stupidity.

'Try again, Skip? I can't see a bloody thing.'

'O.K. Again.'

Whether it cleared or not I never knew. Ellis took her in hand and it was something like driving a springless car down a mountain pass half blocked by the blast of rocks. We went in as steadily as that. The flak beat under the body of the aircraft and once or twice seemed to suck it aside. I held myself tense, throttling my whole body back. If all you needed was good insides and no capacity for thought I was only half equipped. I was not thinking, but my emotions had dissolved into my guts like water.

'Bombs gone!'

'O.K.' Ellis said. 'Thank Christ for that.'

A second later I felt the aircraft pull upwards, as if, bombless, she were suddenly more powerful than the weather. The force of that upward surge seemed to pull me together. It seemed to clean the heaving taste of oil and sickness out of my throat. I was glad too of the voice of Ellis, ejecting smoothly the repeated 'O.K. everybody?' We rocked violently, but I did not mind it. Whatever came now must be, I thought, an anti-climax to that moment. We had been in twice and out again. It was all that mattered now.

III

After two days' digging the rescue squad found the body of Allison's child, untouched but dead, pinned down into a cavity by a fallen door; and then Allison himself, his clothes plastered white as a limeworker's from the dust of debris washed by rain, crawled into the ruins and carried out the child in his own arms. She was still in her nightdress and she must have died as she was, the door falling but not striking her, making the little protective cavity, like a triangular coffin, in which she lay until they found her. Allison walked out of the bombed house and then, not knowing what he was doing, began to walk up the street, still carrying the child. He must have walked quite a long way, and quite fast, before anyone could stop him. He did not know what he was doing. He vaguely remembered a policeman and he remembered another man who took the child out of his arms. His idea was to take the child to his wife, who lay in hospital with a crushed shoulder and who had been crying out for the baby constantly for two days. He had an idea that it might help her if she saw the face of the child again.

It was my job among other things to watch the dials of the various engine pressures on the panel before me and to switch over the fuel tanks as and when it became necessary. On me depended, to a large extent, the balance of the aircraft. Sometimes you got a tank hit and the business of transferring the weight of fuel from one wing to another needed skill. There had been records of flight engineers who, in situations of this kind, and by their skill, had really brought an aircraft home.

I had never done anything as important as that and as I sat watching the dials on the panel I was thinking of Allison. You could never tell by his calm, white face what Allison was thinking. After the bomb had destroyed his house and child he had been away from the station for a couple of weeks. His wife got slowly better. He went back to see her quite often, for some days at a time, during the next six months. During this time he had fits of mutinous depression in which he wrote long letters to the boys, myself among them. They were always the same letters: the story of the child. He had nothing else to say because, obviously, there was nothing else in his life. He would always go back, for ever, to that moment; the moment when he carried the child from the house and up the street, himself like a dead person walking, until someone stopped him and took the child away. When he came back to operations with us he never once spoke of this; and none of us ever spoke of it either. I tried to understand for a time what Allison felt. Then I gave it up. I should have been surprised if he had felt anything at all. All that could be felt, whether it was fear or terror or anger or the mutilation of everything normal in you to utter despair, must have already been felt by Allison. He was inoculated for ever against terror and despair.

'Hell, it's the bloodiest night you ever saw,' Mac said.

'I could have told you that,' Thompson said. The voice of the sergeant in the mid-upper turret came over the inter-comm. 'And Skip, they'll have us in a bloody cone any minute.'

'God, it's dirty,' Mac said.

'They're heading for the straight,' Ossy said. 'Arse-end Charlie two lengths behind. Sergeant Thompson well up—'

'Stop nattering!' Ellis said.

We were hit a moment later. It was not so violent as the hit which had forced us upward, earlier, as in a funnel. It seemed like a colossal hand-clap. Terrific and shattering, it beat at us from both port and starboard sides. There was a moment as if you were in a vacuum. Then you were blown out of it. It was like the impact of an enormous and violent wave at sea.

I don't know what happened, but the next moment we were on fire. The flames made a noise like the hiss of a rocket before it leaves the ground. They shot with a slight explosive sound all along the port side of the fuselage, forward from where I sat. I yelled something through the inter-comm. and I heard Mac yelling too. I got hold of the fire extinguisher and began to work it madly. I remember the aircraft bumping so violently that it knocked by hands upward and I shot the extinguisher liquid on the roof. I fell down and got up again, still playing the extinguisher. Then I got the jet straight on to the flames and for a moment it transformed them into smoke, which began to fill the fuselage, so that we could not see. Then the flames shot up again. They blew outward suddenly and violently like the blowback from a furnace. I felt them slap my face, scorching my eyeballs. Then I saw them shoot back and they ran fiercely up the window curtains. At that moment the extinguisher ran dry and I began to tear down the curtains with my bare hands, which were already numb with cold so that I could not feel the flames. I don't know quite what I did with those curtains. I must have beaten the flames out of them by banging them against my boots because I remember once looking down and seeing the sheepskin smouldering, and I remember how the idea of being on fire myself terrified me more than the idea of the plane itself being on fire.

Sometime before this the inter-comm. had gone and suddenly I saw Ellis, who until that moment could not have known much of what we were doing back there, open the door behind the pilot's seat. His face ejected itself and remained for a second transfixed, yellow beyond the smoke. I shall never forget it. I saw the mouth open and move, and I must have yelled something in reply before the door closed again. I had an awful feeling suddenly that Ellis had gone for ever. We were shut off, alone, with the fire, Mac and Allison and myself, and there was nothing Ellis could do.

All this time Allison sat there as if nothing was happening. You hear of wireless operators at sea, when the ship is sinking, having a kind of supernatural power of concentration. Allison had that concentration. Mac and I must have behaved like madmen. We hit the flames with the screwed-up curtains and with our bare hands and once I saw Mac press his huge Michelin body against the fuselage and kill the flames by pressure as he might have killed an insect on his back. The flames had a sort of maddening elasticity. It was like putting back the inner tube of a bicycle tyre. You pushed it back in one place and it leapt out again in another. Several times the aircraft rocked violently and we fell on the floor. When we got up again we fell against each other. All the time Allison sat there. And I knew that although it was amazing it was also right. He had to sit there. Somehow, if it killed us, we had to keep the flames from him. There was no room for three of us in the confined space of the fuselage, and it was the best thing that Allison should sit there, as if nothing had happened, clamped down by his earphones, as if in a world of his own. Allison was our salvation.

It was very hot by this time and suddenly I was very tired. I could not see very clearly. It was as if the blow-back of the flames had scorched the pupils of my eyes. They were terribly raw and painful, and the smoke seemed to soak into them like acid. I had no idea where we were. There were no voices in the inter-comm., but after a time the pilot's door opened and Ed Walker crawled back to Allison, with a written message. Allison read it and nodded. I tried to shout something at Ed, but I began to cough badly and it was useless. Then the flames broke out in two new places; on the port side, aft of where I had been sitting, and in the roof above my head. When I went to lift my hands to beat the flames they would not rise. It was like trying to lift the whole aircraft. I felt sick and the sickness ran weakly and coldly down the arteries of my arms and out of the fingers.

Then suddenly I made a great effort. I had been standing there helplessly for what seemed a long time. It could not have been more than a few seconds but it was like a gap of agony in a dream. I wanted to move but I could not move and so at last because I could not throw my hands against the flames I threw my whole body. I let it fall with outstretched arms against the fuselage and I felt the slight bounce of my Mae West as it hit the metal. I lay there for about a second, very tired. My head was limp against the hot metal of the fuselage, and my eyes were crying from the acid of the smoke. Then I raised my head. I had come to the moment of not caring. The flames were burning my legs and I was too tired to beat them out again. I was going to burn and die and it did not matter.

Then I lifted my eyes. Shrapnel had torn a hole in the fuselage and I could just see at an angle through the gap. It was like looking out of a window and seeing out in the darkness the reflection of the fire in the room. It was only that this fire was magnified. It was like a huge level dish of flame. It was horizontal and the edges of it were torn to violent shreds in the night.

'Oh! Christ,' I said. 'Oh! Christ, Christ Jesus!'

I expected at any moment to see that burning wing tear past my face. It was fantastic to see it riding with us. It did not seem part of us. It was like an enormous orange and crimson torch sailing wildly through the darkness.

All the time I knew that it must split and break, that in a moment now we were at the end. And in some curious way the idea gave me strength. For the first time since the fire began I could think clearly. My hands and my mind were not tired. I thought of my helmet and took it off. The fire must have burnt a hole in the fuselage somewhere forward, for air was now blowing violently in, clearing a gulley through the smoke. I held my helmet and then swung it. The moment was very clear. The flames crawled like big yellow insects up the slope of the fuselage and I began to hit them, with a sort of delirious and final calm, with the helmet. At the same time I saw the faces of Mac and Allison. Mac too must have known about the fire on the wing. His eyes were big and protuberant with desperation. But Allison still sat there as if nothing had happened; thin, pale, his head manacled by the earphones.

Then something happened. It was Ed Walker, coming in through the pilot's door with a message. I saw him go to Allison and again I saw Allison nod his head. Then he beckoned us and we went to Allison's seat. Leaning over, we read the message. 'Over the sea. Take up ditching stations. Stand by for landing.' We were coming down.

I must have put my helmet on my head. I must have strapped it quite carefully in the few seconds' interval between reading the message and beginning to haul out the dinghy. Then Ed Walker came back with Ossy, the rear-gunner and then the mid-upper gunner climbed down. The five of us stood there, braced for about a minute. The fuselage was still burning and through the window the flat plate of flame along the wing had thickened and broadened and looked more fantastic than ever.

I stood braced and ready with the axe. I no longer felt tired and I knew that I might have to hit the door, if it jammed, with all the strength I had. As we came down, throttled back, but the speed violent still, I drew in my insides and held them so taut that they seemed to tie themselves in a single knot of pain.

Next moment we hit the water. And in that moment, as the violence of the impact lifted all of us upward, I looked at Ossy. It was one of these silly moments that remained with me, clear and alive, long after the more confused moments of terror.

Ossy too was clenching something tightly in his hand. It was the spanner.

IV

K.42 went down almost immediately, and except for a second or two when she was caught up in the light of her own fire, we never saw her again. I heard the port wing split with a crack before she went down, and I heard the explosive hiss of the sea beating over the flames. I could smell too the smell of fire and steam, dirty and hot and acid, blown at us on the wind. It remained in my mouth, sharp with the sourness of the sea-water, for a long time.

The next thing I knew was that we were in the dinghy. It was floating; it was right side up; and we were all there. I never knew at all how it happened. It was like a moment when, in a London raid, I had dived under a seat on a railway station. One moment I was standing waiting for the train; the next I was lying under the seat, my head under my arms, with a soldier and a girl. When I finally got up and looked under the seat it did not seem that there was room under it for a dog.

'Everybody O.K.?' Ellis said. 'I can't see you. Better answer your names.'

'I got a torch,' Mac said.

'O.K. Let's have a look at you.'

He shone the torch in our faces. The light burnt my eyes when I looked up.

'O.K. Everybody feel all right?'

'No, sir,' Ossy said. 'I'm bloody wet.'

We all laughed with extra heartiness at that.

'What was the last contact with base?'

'Half an hour before we hit the drink,' Allison said.

'You think they got you?'

'They were getting me then,' Allison said. 'But afterwards we were off course. The transmitter was u.s. after the fix.'

'All right,' Ellis said. 'And listen to me.' He shone the torch on his wrist. 'It's now eleven ten. I'm going to call out the time every half-hour.'

The torch went out. It seemed darker than ever. The dinghy rocked on the sea.

'Remember what the wind was, Mac?'

'She was north north-east,' Mac said. 'About thirty on the ground.'

'Any idea where we should be?'

'We were on course until that bloody fire started. But Jesus, you did some evasive action after that. Christ knows where we went.'

'We ought to be in the North Sea somewhere, just north-west of Holland.'

'I guess so,' said Mac.

'North north-east – that might blow us down-Channel.'

'In time it might blow us to Canada,' Mac said.

'As soon as it gets light we can get the direction of the wind,' Ellis said. 'We'll use the compass and then you'll all paddle like hell.'

I sat there and did not say anything. I knew now that my hands were burnt, but I did not know how badly. I tried putting them in my pockets, but with the rocking of the dinghy I could not balance myself. The pain of my hands all that night was my chief concern. The pain of my eyes, which were scorched too, did not seem so bad. I could shut them against the wind, and for long intervals I did so, riding on the dinghy blindly, the swell of the wave magnified because I could not see. It was better to close my eyes. If I did so the wind, cold and steady but not really strong, could not reach the raw eyeballs. The sea-spray could not hit them and pain them any more.

But I could not shut my hands. Fire seemed to have destroyed the reflex action of the muscles. The fingers stood straight out. It was not so much the pain of burning as the pain of a paralysis in which the nerves had been stripped raw. I had to hold them in one position. In whatever way my body moved my hands remained outstretched and stiff. When the sea broke over the dinghy, as it did at the most unexpected moments, the spray splashed my hands and the salt was like acid on the burns and I could not dry it off. I had to sit there until the wind dried it for me. And then it was as if the wind was freezing every spit of spray into a flake of ice and that the flakes were burning my hands all over again.

I sat there all night, facing the wind. Every half-hour Ellis gave out the time. He said nothing about rations or about the rum. From this I gathered that he was not hopeful about our position. It seemed to mean that he expected us to be a long time in the dinghy and that we must apportion rations for two, three, or perhaps four days. I had noticed too that all through the period of snow, for the last week, the wind rose steadily with the sun. By mid-afternoon, on land, it blew at forty or fifty miles an hour, raising white frozen dust in savage little clouds on the runways. Then it dropped with the sun. So if in the morning the wind strengthened we should, I thought, have a hard job to paddle crossways against it; which was our way to England. We should drift towards the Channel, into the Straits, and then down-Channel. Nothing could stop us. The wind would be strongest when we could paddle best, and weakest when we could not steer well. I saw that we might drift for days and end up, even if we were lucky, far down the French coast, certainly not east of Cherbourg. I did not see how we could reach England.

Perhaps it did me good to think like this. I know that afterwards Ellis thought much like it; except that he had a worse fear – that we might be so near the coast of Europe that, that night before we could realize our position, we might be blown into the shore of Germany or Holland. It was at least better than thinking like Ossy, who seemed so sure he would be in England in the morning and in Newcastle, on crash leave, in the afternoon.

And to think of this kept me from thinking of my hands. My mind, thinking of the possibility of future difficulties, went ahead of my pain. All night, too, there was little danger from the sea. It was very cold but the dinghy rode easily, if rather sluggishly, in the water. Our clothes were very wet and I could feel the water slapping about my boots in the well of the dinghy. We simply road blindly in the darkness, without direction, under a sky completely without stars and on a sea completely without noise except for the flat slapping of waves on the rubber curve of the dinghy.

After a time I managed to bandage my hands very roughly with my handkerchief. The handkerchief was in my left trousers-pocket. I could not stand up or, in the confined space of the well that was full of feet, move my leg more than a few inches. But at last I straightened my thigh downward a little, and then my left hand downward against my thigh. The pain of touching the fabric filled my mouth with sickness. It was like pushing your hand into fire. When I pushed my hand still further down the sickness dried in my mouth and the roof of it and my tongue were dry and contracted, as if with alum. Then I pushed my hand further down. I could just feel the handkerchief between the tips of my fingers. I drew it out very slowly. The opening of the pocket, chafing against my hand, seemed to take off the flesh. The raw pain seemed to split my hand and long afterwards, when my hands were covered by the handkerchief and warm and almost painless, my head was cold with the awful sweat of pain.

I sat like that for the rest of the night, my hands roughly bound together.

v

We were all quite cheerful in the morning. The sky in the east was split into flat yellow bars of wintry light. As they fell on the yellow fabric of the dinghy it looked big and safe and friendly. The wind was not strong and the air no colder. The sea was everywhere the colour of dirty ice.

Ellis then told us what our position was.

'I am dividing the rations for three days,' he said. I knew afterwards that this was not true. He was reckoning on their lasting for six days. 'We eat in the morning. You get a tot of rum at midday. Then a biscuit at night. That's all you'll get.'

We did not say anything.

'Now we paddle in turns, two at a time, fifteen minutes each. If the wind is still north north-east it means steering at right angles across it. We can soon check the wind when the sun comes up. It ought to come almost behind the sun. It means paddling almost north. The risk is that we'll bloody well go down-Channel and never get back.'

None of us said anything again.

'I'll dish the rations out and then we'll start. We'll start with a drop of rum now, because it's the first time. Then Ossy and Ed start paddling; then Mac and Ally; then Thompson and – what's the matter with your hands?' he said to me.

'Burnt a bit,' I said.

'Can you hold anything?'

'They won't reflex or anything,' I said. 'But my wrists are all right. I could hold the paddle with my wrists.'

'Don't talk cock!' he said.

'I can't sit here doing nothing,' I said.

'O.K.' he said, 'you can call out the time. Every hour now. And anyway it'll take us an hour to bandage those hands.'

Ossy and Ed started paddling. They were fresh and paddled rather raggedly at first, over-eager, one long-armed and one short so that the dinghy rocked.

'Take it steady,' Ellis said. 'Keep the sun on your right cheek. Take long strokes. You've got all day.'

'Not if I know it,' Ossy said. 'I got crash-leave coming, so I'll catch the midnight to Newcastle.'

'You've got damn all coming if you don't keep your mouth shut. Do you want your guts full of cold air?'

Ellis got out his first-aid pack and peeled off the adhesive tape. He had changed places with Thompson and was sitting next to me.

'What did you do?' he said. 'Try to fry yourself?'

'I dropped my gloves,' I said.

'Take it easy,' he said. 'I'll take the handkerchief off.'

He took off the handkerchief and for some moments I could not move my hands. The air seemed to burn again the shining swollen blisters. I sat in a vacuum of pain. Oh! Christ, I thought. Oh, Jesus, Jesus! I fixed my eyes on the horizon and held them there, blind to everything except the rising and falling line below the faint yellow bars of sun. I held my hands raw in the cold air and the wind savagely drove white-hot needles of agony down my fingers. Jesus, I thought, please,

Jesus. I knew I could not bear it any more and then I did bear it. The pain came in waves that rose and fell with the motion of the dinghy. The waves swung me sickeningly up and down, my hands part of me for one second and then no longer part of me, the pain stretching away and then driving back like hot needles into my naked flesh.

I became aware after a time of a change of colour in the sea. This colour travelled slowly before my eyes and spewed violently into the dinghy. It was bright violet. I realized that it seemed one moment part of the sea and one moment part of the dinghy because it was, in reality, all over my hands. The motion of the dinghy raised it to the line of sea and spewed it down into the yellow wall of fabric.

I was not fully aware of what was happening now. I knew that the violet colour was the colour of the gentian ointment Ellis was squeezing on my hands; I knew that the pure whiteness that covered it was the white of bandage. For brief moments my mind was awake and fixed. Then violet and white and yellow and the grey of the sea were confused together. They suddenly became black and the blackness covered me.

When I could look at the sea again and not see those violent changes of colour the sun was well above the horizon and Mac and Allison were paddling. I did not then know they were paddling for the second time. I held my hands straight out, the wrists on my knees, and stared at the sea. It was roughened with tiny waves like frosted glass. I did not speak for a long time and the men in the dinghy did not speak to me. There was no pain in my hands now. And in my mind the only pain was the level of negative pain of relief, the pain after pain, that had no violence or change.

I must have sat there all morning, not speaking. We might have drifted into the coast and I shouldn't have known it. I watched the sun clear itself of the low cloud lying above the sea, and then the sky itself clear slowly about the sun. It became a pale wintry blue and as the sun rose the sea was smoothed down, until it was like clean rough ice as far as you could see.

It must have been about midday that I was troubled with the idea that I ought to paddle. From watching the sea I found myself watching the faces of the others. They looked tired in the sun. I realized that I had been sitting there all morning, doing nothing. I did not know till afterwards that I had called out the time, from the watch on my wrist, every hour.

But now I wanted to paddle. I had to paddle. I had to pull my weight. It seemed agonizing and stupid to sit there, not moving or speaking, but only watching with sore and half-dazed eyes that enormous empty expanse of sea and sky. I had to do something to break the level pain of that monotony.

Thinking this, I must have tried to stand up.

'Sit down, you bloody fool! Sit down!' Ellis yelled. 'Sit down!'

The words did not hurt me. I must have obeyed automatically, not knowing it. But in the second that Ellis shouted I was myself again. The stupefaction of pain was broken. For the first time since daybreak I looked at the men about me. They ceased being anonymous. I really saw their faces. They were no longer brown-yellow shapes, vague parts of the greater yellow shape of the dinghy. They were the men I knew, and I was consciously and fully with them, alive again.

'You feel better?' Ellis said.

'I'm all right.'

'I gave you a shot,' he said.

'I'm all right. I could paddle.'

'You could bloody hell,' he said.

'I could do something,' I said. 'I want to do something.'

'O.K. Keep a look-out. Bawl as soon as you see anything that looks like a kite or a sail.'

From that moment I felt better. I could not use my hands, but I had something on which to use my eyes. The situation in the morning had seemed bad. Now I turned it round. There was nothing so bad that it couldn't be worse. Supposing my eyes had been burnt out, and not my hands? I felt relieved and grateful and really quite hopeful now.

At one o'clock exactly we had a small tot of rum. The wind had risen, as I thought it would with the sun. But there was no cloud and no danger, that afternoon, of snow. Visibility was down to two or three miles and in the far distance there was a slight colourless haze on the face of the sea. But it was, as far as you could tell, good flying weather.

'So,' as Ellis said, 'there is a chance of a patrol. The vis. isn't improving, but it ought to be good enough. It all depends anyway on the next two hours.'

No one paddled as we drank the rum. We rested for ten minutes. Then Ossy and Ed began paddling again. Helped by the rest, the rum, and the fact that the sun was so clear and bright on the water, we all felt much more hopeful. Occasionally a little water swilled over into the dinghy, but the next moment Allison, calm and methodical, baled it out again with his hands.

I kept watching the sea and the sky. At two o'clock I called out the time. The hour seemed to have gone very quickly. I realized that we had one more hour in which we could hope to be seen by an aircraft; only two in which we could hope, even remotely, to be picked up. But I was not depressed. I do not think any of us were depressed. It was good that we were together, dependent, as we always had been, on each other. And we were so far only looking forward, not backward. We had no disappointment to feed on, but only the full hope of the afternoon.

None of us knew that Ellis had already prepared himself, as early as one o'clock, for another night in the dinghy.

It must have been about half-past two when Allison shouted. He began waving his hands, too. It was the most excitable Allison I had ever seen, his hands waving, and his head thrown backward in the sun.

'You see it?' he shouted. 'You see it?'

I saw the kite coming from north-westwards, about right angles to the sun. It was black and small, and flying at about six thousand.

'It's a single-engine job,' Ossy said.

'A Spit,' Thompson said.

She came towards us level and straight, not deviating at all. I felt the excitement pump into my throat. She seemed to be about a mile or two away and was coming fast. It was not like the approach of a ship. In a few seconds she would pass over us; she would go straight on or turn. It would be all over in a few seconds. 'Come on, baby,' Mac said. 'For Pete's sake don't you know you got too much altitude? Come on, baby,' he whispered, 'blast and damn you, come on.'

We had ceased paddling. The dinghy rocked slowly up and down. As the Spitfire came dead over us our seven faces must have looked to its pilot, if he had seen us at all, like seven empty white plates on the rim of a yellow table. They must have looked for one second like this before they tilted slowly down, and then finally upside down as we stared at our feet in the well of the dinghy.

'He'll be back,' Ossy said. 'He's bound to come back.'

None of us spoke in answer, and it was some time after I heard the last sound of the plane that Mac and Allison began paddling again.

VI

The plane did not come back and the face of the sea began to darken about four o'clock. From the colour of slate on the western horizon the sunset rose through dirty orange to cold pale green above. The wind had almost dropped with the sun and except for the slap of the paddles hitting the water there was no sound.

Soon Ellis ordered the paddling to cease altogether. Then we sat for about half an hour between light and darkness, the dinghy rocking sluggishly up and down, and ate our evening meal.

To each of us Ellis rationed out one biscuit and one piece, about two inches square, of plain chocolate. I could not hold either the biscuit or the chocolate in my hands, which Ellis had covered with long white muffs of bandage. Ellis therefore held them for me, giving me first a bite of chocolate, then a bite of the biscuit. I ate these very slowly, and in between the mouthfuls Ellis did something to my hands. 'If she comes rough in the night you may get them wet,' he said.

In the morning Ellis had saved the fabric of the first-aid pack and adhesive tape that bound the biscuit tin. Now he undid another pack and put the bandages and the ointment and the line inside his Mae West. Then with the two pieces of fabric he made bags for my hands. I put my hands into these bags and Ellis bound them about my wrists with the adhesive tape. It was a very neat job and I felt like a boxer.

'Now we'll work the night like we did the paddling,' he said. 'We'll split it into one-hour watches with two on a watch.'

He gave me the last of the chocolate before he went on speaking. It clung to the roof of my mouth and I felt very thirsty. Below the taste of the chocolate there was still a faint taste, dry and acrid, of the burning plane.

'Ed and Ossy begin from five o'clock. Then Ally and Mac. Then Thompson and myself.'

'What about me?' I said. 'I'm all right.'

'You've got your work cut out with your hands,' he said.

'I'm O.K.,' I said.

'Look after your hands,' he said. 'And don't go to sleep. You're liable to get bounced off this thing before the night's gone.'

You did not argue with Ellis when the tone of his voice was final. Now it was very final and without answering I sat watching the western sky. It was colourless and clear now, with the first small stars, quite white, beginning to shine in the darker space about the sunset. I don't know how the others felt about these stars or if they noticed them at all, but they gave me a sense of comfort. I was determined not to be downcast. I was even determined not to be hopeful. My hands did not seem very bad now and I felt no colder than I had always been. I knew we should not be picked up that night; or even perhaps the next day. So as darkness came on and the stars increased until they were shining so brightly that I could see the reflection of the largest of them brokenly tossed like bits of phosphorescence in the sea, I did as I had always done on a long trip to Germany. I foreshortened the range of my thoughts. I determined not to think beyond the next hour, when the watch would be changed.

Being in that dinghy, that night, not knowing where we were or where we were going, all of us a little scared but all of us too scared to show it, was rather like having an operation. It smoothed the complications of your life completely. Before the operation the complication from all sorts of causes, small and large, income tax, unanswered letters, people you hated, people who hurt you, bills, something your wife said about your behaviour, seemed sometimes to get your life into an awful mess. Many things looked like small catastrophes. It was a catastrophe if you were late at the office, or if you couldn't pay a bill. Then suddenly you had to have your operation. And in a moment nothing mattered except one thing. The little catastrophes were cancelled out. All your life up to the moment of lying on the stretcher dissolved away, smoothed and empty of all its futilities and little fears. All that mattered was that you came through.

My attitude on the dinghy that night became like that. Before the moment we had taken off, now more than a day ago, and had flown out towards the snows of Europe, there was little of my life that seemed to matter. You hear of people cast away in open boats who dream sadly of their loved ones at home. But I didn't dream of anyone. I felt detached and in a way free. The trouble with my wife – whether we could make a go of it or whether we really hated each other or whether it was simply the strain of the war – no longer mattered. All my life was centred into a yellow circle floating without a direction on a dark sea.

It must have been about midnight when we saw, in what we thought was the east, light fires breaking the sky in horizon level. They were orange in colour and intermittent, like stabs of Morse. We knew that it was light flak somewhere on a coast, but which coast didn't really trouble us. The light of that fire, too far away to be heard or reflected in the dark sea, comforted us enormously.

We watched it for more than two hours before it died away. Looking up from the place where the fire had been and into the sky itself, I realized that the stars had gone. I remember how the sudden absence of all light, first the far-off flak, then the stars, produced an effect of awful loneliness. It must then have been about three o'clock. During the time we were watching the flak we had talked a little, talking of where we thought it was. Now, one by one, we gave up talking. Even Ossy gave up talking, and once again there was no sound except the slapping of the sea against the dinghy.

But about an hour later there was a new sound. It was the sound of the wind rising and skimming viciously off the face of the sea, slicing up glassy splinters of spray. And there was now a new feeling in the air with the rising of the wind.

It was the feeling of ice in the air.

VII

When day broke, about eight o'clock, we were all very cold. Our beards stood out from our faces and under the bristles the skin was shrunk. Mac, who was very big, looked least cold of all; but the face of Allison, thin and quite bloodless, had something of the grey-whiteness of broken edges of foam that split into parallel bars the whole face of the sea. This grey-whiteness made Allison's eyes almost black and they sank deep into his head. In the same way the sea between the bars of foam had a glassy blackness too.

The wind was blowing at about forty miles an hour and driving us fairly fast before it. The sky was a grey mass of ten-tenths cloud, so

thick that it never seemed to move in the wind. Because there was no
sun I could not tell if the wind had changed. I knew only that it drove
at your face with an edge of raw ice that seemed to split the skin away.

Because of this coldness Ellis changed his plans.

'It's rum now and something to eat at midday. Instead of the other
way round.'

As we each took a tot of rum Ellis went on talking.

'We'll paddle as we did yesterday. But it's too bloody cold to sit still
when you're not paddling. So you'll all do exercises to keep warm.
Chest-slapping and knee-slapping and any other damn thing. It's going
to get colder and you've got to keep your circulation.'

He now gave us, after the rum, a Horlick's tablet each.

'And now any suggestions?'

'It's sure bloody thing we won't get to Newcastle at this rate,' Ossy
said.

'You're a genius,' Ellis said.

'Couldn't we fix a sail, Skip?' Ossy said. 'Rip up a parachute, or even
use a whole chute?'

'How are you going to hold your sail?' Ellis said. 'With hay-rakes or
something?'

All of us except Allison made suggestions, but they were not very
good. Allison alone did not speak. He was always quiet, but now he
seemed inwardly quiet. He had scarcely any flesh on his face and his lips
were blue as if bruised with cold.

'O.K., then,' Ellis said. 'We carry on as we did yesterday. Ossy and
Ed start paddling. The rest do exercises. How are your hands?' he said
to me.

'O.K.,' I said. I could not feel them except in moments when they
seemed to burn again with far-off pain.

'All right,' he said. 'Time us again. A quarter of an hour paddling.
And if the sea gets worse there'll have to be relays of baling too.'

When Ossy and Ed started paddling I saw why Ellis had talked of
baling. The dinghy moved fast and irregularly; it was hard to synchronize
the motions of the two paddles when the sea was rough. We were very
buoyant on the sharp waves and sometimes the crests hit us sideways,
rocking us violently. We began to ship water. It slapped about in the
well of the dinghy among our seven pairs of feet. It hit us in the more
violent moments on the thighs and even as far up as our waists. We were
so cold that the waves of spray did not shock us and except when they
hit our faces we did not feel them. Nevertheless I began to be very glad
of the covers Ellis had put on my hands.

Soon all of us were doing something: Ossy and Ed paddling;
Thompson and Ellis baling out the water, Thompson with a biscuit tin,
Ellis with a small tobacco tin. They threw the water forward with the

wind. While these four were working Mac and Allison did exercises, beating their knees and chests with their hands. Mac still looked very like the Michelin tyre advertisement, huge, clumsy, unsinkable. To him the exercises were a great joke. He beat his knees in dance time, drumming his hands on them. It kept all of us except Allison in good spirits. But I began to feel more and more that Allison was not there with us. He slapped his knees and chest with his hands, trying to keep time with Mac, but there was no change in his face. It remained vacant and deathly; the dark eyes seemed driven even deeper into the head. It began to look more and more like a face in which something had killed the capacity for feeling.

We went on like this all morning, changing about, two exercising, two paddling, two baling out. The wind did not rise much and sometimes there were moments when it combed the sea flat and dark. The waves, short and unbroken for a few moments, then looked even more ominous. Then with a frisk of the wind they rose into fresh bars of foam.

It was about midday when I saw the face of the sea combed down into that level darkness for a longer time than usual. The darkness travelled across it from the east, thickening as it came. Then as I watched, it became lighter. It became grey and vaporous, and then for a time grey and solid. This greyness stood for a moment a mile or two away from us, on the sea, and then the wind seemed to fan it to pieces. These millions of little pieces became white and skimmed rapidly over the dark water, and in a moment we could not see for snow.

The first thing the snow did was to shut out the vastness of the empty sea. It closed round us, and we were blinded. The area of visible sea was so small that we might have been on a pond. In a way it was comforting.

Those who were paddling went on paddling and those who were baling went on baling the now snow-thickened water. We did not speak much. The snow came flat across the sea and when you opened your mouth it drove into it. I bent my head against it and watched the snow covering my hands. For the last hour they had begun to feel jumpy and swollen and God knew what state they were in.

It went on snowing like that for more than an hour, the flakes, big and wet and transparent as they fell. They covered the outer curve of the dinghy, on the windward side, with a thick wet crust of white. They covered our bent backs in the same way, so that we looked as if we were wearing white furs down to our waists, and they thickened to a yellow colour the sloppy water in the dinghy.

All the time Allison was the only one who sat upright. At first I thought he was being clever; because he did not bend his back the snow collected only on his shoulders. That seemed a good idea. Then, whenever I looked up at him, I was struck by the fact that whether he was paddling or baling his attitude was the same. He sat stiff, bolt upright, staring through the snow. His hands plunged down at his side automatically, digging a paddle into the water, or scooping the water out of the dinghy and baling it away. His eyes, reflecting the snow, were not dark. They were cold, and colourless. He looked terribly thin and terribly tired, and yet not aware of being tired. I felt he had simply got into an automatic state, working against the sea and the snow, and that he did not really know what he was doing. Still more I felt that he did not care.

I knew the rest of us cared very much. After the first comfortable shut-in feeling of the snow had passed we felt desperate. I hated the snow now more than the sea. It shut out all hope that Air-Sea Rescue would ever see us now. I knew that it might snow all day and I knew that after it, towards sunset, it would freeze. If it snowed all day, killing all chances of rescue, and then froze all night, we should be in a terrible state the next morning, our third day.

The thought of this depressed me, for a time, very much. It was now about half-past twelve. The time seemed crucial. Unless it stopped snowing very soon, so that coastal stations could send out patrols in the early afternoon, we must face another night on the dinghy. I knew that all of us, with the exception of Allison, felt this. We were very tired and cold and stiff from not stretching our bodies, and the snow, whirling and thick and wet, seemed to tangle us up into a circle from which we were never going to get out.

In such moments as this Ellis did the right thing. He had driven us rather hard all morning, getting us out of small depressed moments by saying: 'Come on, we've got to keep going. Come on,' or with a dry joke, 'No fish and chips for Ossy if we don't keep going. It's tough tit for Ossy if he doesn't get his fish and chips.' He knew just when he could drive us no longer. Now he let up.

'O.K.,' he said. 'Give it a rest.'

'Holy Moses,' Mac said. 'I used to love snow. Honest, I used to love the bloody stuff.'

Even Mac looked tired. The snow had collected on his big head, giving him the look of an old man with white hair.

'Jesus,' he said. 'I'll never feel the same way about snow again.'

'What time do you make it?' Ellis said to me.

'Twelve forty-five coming up to six – now,' I said.

'O.K.,' he said. 'Set your watches.'

While we set our watches, synchronizing them, calling out the figures, Ellis got out the rum, the chocolate and the biscuits. Afterwards I looked back and knew it was not so much the food, as Ellis's order to synchronize the watches, that made me feel better at that moment.

Time was our link with the outside world. From setting our watches together we got a sense of unity.

Ellis gave out the chocolate and the biscuits, in the same ration as before.

'Everybody all right? Ossy?'

'I'm a bloody snowball, if that's anything,' Ossy said.

'Good old Ossy.'

Ellis looked at each of us in turn. 'All right, Ally?' he said.

Allison nodded. He still sat bolt upright and he still did not speak.

Ellis did not speak either until it was time to tot out the rum. He used the silver bottom of an ordinary pocket-flask for the rum and this, about a third full, was our ration. He always left himself till last, but this time he did not drink. 'God, I always hate the stuff. It tastes like warm rubber,' he said.

'Drink it, Ally,' he said.

Allison held out his hand. I could see that the fingers were so cold that, like my own after the burning, they would not flex. I saw Ellis bend them and fold them, like a baby's, over the tot. I saw the hand remained outstretched, stiff in the falling snow, until finally Allison raised it slowly to his lips. I think we all expected to see that cup fall out of Allison's hands, and we were all relieved and glad when at last Ellis reached over and took it away.

As we sat there, rocking up and down, there was a slight lessening of the snow. Through the thinning flakes we could see, soon, a little more of the sea. No sooner could I see more of it than I hated it more. I hated the long troughs and the barbarous slits of foam between them and the snow driving, curling and then flat, like white tracer above. I hated the ugliness and emptiness of it and above all the fact of its being there.

VIII

That afternoon a strange thing happened. By two o'clock the snow grew thinner and drew back into a grey mist that receded over the face of the sea. As it cleared away altogether the sky cleared too, breaking in a southerly direction to light patches of watery yellow which spread under the wind and became spaces of bright blue. Across these spaces the sun poured in musty shafts and the inner edges of cloud were whiter than the snow had been. Far off, below them, we saw pools of light on the sea.

We were now paddling roughly in a straight line away from the sun. We were all, with the exception of Allison, quite cheerful. There was something tremendously hopeful about this breaking up of the sky after snow.

Allison alone sat there as if nothing had happened. He had not spoken since morning. He still looked terribly cold and tired and yet as if he did not know he was tired.

Suddenly he spoke.

'Very lights,' he said.

'Hell!' Mac said. 'Where?'

'Look,' Allison said.

He was pointing straight before us. The sky had not broken much to the north and the cloud there was very low.

'I don't see a bloody thing,' Mac said.

'Christ, if it is,' Ossy said. 'Christ, if it is.'

We were all very excited. The paddling and baling stopped, and we rocked in the water.

'Where did you see this?' Ellis said.

'There,' Allison said. He was still pointing, but his eyes were as empty as they had always been.

'You're sure they were Very lights?'

'I saw them.'

'How long were they burning?'

'They just lit up and went out.'

'But where? Where exactly?'

'You see the dark bit of cloud under there? They came out of that.'

We all looked at that point for a long time. I stared until my eyeballs seemed to smart with hot smoke again.

'Ally, boy,' Mac said. 'You must have awful good eyesight.'

'What would Very lights be doing at this time of day?' Ed said.

'I can't think,' Ellis said. 'Probably Air-Sea Rescue. It's possible. They'd always be looking.'

'A kite wouldn't be dropping them unless it saw something.'

'It might. Funny things happen.'

'Hell they do,' Mac said.

'You couldn't expect even Air-Sea Rescue to see us in this muck,' I said.

Ossy and Ed began to paddle again. As we went forward we still kept our eyes on the dark patch of cloud, but nothing happened. Nor did Allison speak again; nor had any of us the heart to say we thought him mistaken.

For a time we hadn't the heart for much at all. The situation in the dinghy now looked messy and discouraging. The melting snow was sloppy in the bottom, a dirty yellow colour; there were too many feet. It was still very cold and when we tried to do exercises – I could only beat my elbows against my sides – we knocked clumsily against each other. We had done that before, in the morning, and once or twice it had seemed mildly funny. Now it was more irritating than the snow, the cold and the disappointment of Allison's false alarm.

All this time the sky was breaking up. In the west and south, through wide blue lakes of cloud, white shafts of sun fell as bright and cold as chromium on the sea. These shiny edges of sunlight sometimes produced a hallucination. They looked in the distances like very white cliffs, jagged and unbelievably real. Staring at them, it was easy to understand why Allison had seen a Very light in a cloud.

So we paddled until three o'clock; and I knew it was hopeless. We had another hour of daylight: the worst of the day. The sea, with the sun breaking on it, looked terribly empty; but with the darkness on it we should at least have nothing to look for. Ellis, as always, was very good at this moment. His face was red and fresh and his eyes, bright blue, did not look very tired. He had managed somehow to keep neater than the rest of us. You felt he had kept back enormous reserves of energy and hope and that he hadn't even begun to think of the worst. And now he suddenly urged us to sing. 'Come on, a sing-song before tea, chaps,' he said. 'Come on.'

So we began singing. We first sang 'Shenandoah' and 'Billy Boy'. Then we sang other songs, bits of jazz, and 'Daisy, Daisy', and then we came back to 'Shenandoah'. We sang low and easy and there was no resonance about it because of the wind. But it was a good thing to sing because you could sing the disappointment out of yourself and it kept you from thinking. We must have gone on singing for nearly an hour and the only one of us who didn't sing much was Allison. From time to time I saw his mouth moving. It simply moved up and down, rather slowly, erratically, out of tune. Whatever he was singing did not belong to us. He was very pale, and the cavity of his mouth looked blue and his eyes were distant and dark as if they were still staring at those Very lights in the distant cloud.

It must have been about four o'clock when he fell into the dinghy. The sea pitched us upward and Allison fell forward on his face. He fell loosely and his head struck the feet crowded in the bottom of the dinghy, which rocked violently with the fall.

Ellis and Mac pulled him upright again. His face was dirty with snow water and his eyes were wide open. Ellis began to rub his hands. The veins on the back of them were big and blue, the colour of his lips, and he began to make a choking noise in his throat. His body was awkward and heavy in the well of the dinghy and it was hard to prevent him from slipping down again. The dinghy rocked badly and I thought we might capsize.

'Put him between my knees,' I said. 'I can hold him like that.'

They propped him up and I locked his body with my knees, keeping it from falling. I held my bandaged hands against his face and he made a little bubbling noise with his mouth, not loud, but as if he was going to be gently sick.

As I held him like that and as we bumped about in the dinghy, badly balanced, swinging and rocking like one of those crazy boats at a fun fair, I looked at the sky.

The sun had suddenly gone down. Already above the sunset the sky was clear and green and I could feel the frost in the air.

IX

I held Allison's body with my knees all that night and his face with my damaged hands. My legs are long and gradually the feeling went out of them. But once I had got into that position it was too complicated to move.

As darkness came down ice began to form like thin rough glass on the outer sides of the dinghy, where the snow had first settled and thawed. Frost seemed to tighten up the rubber, which cracked off the ice as it moved with the waves. It was bitterly cold, very clear and brittle, without much wind. The sky was very clear too and there was a splintering brightness in the stars.

At intervals of about an hour we gave Allison drinks of rum. At these moments he did not speak. He would make the gentle, bubbling noise with his lips and then leave his mouth open, so that a little of the rum ran out again. I would shut his mouth with my hand. Sometimes I put my unbandaged wrists on his face and it was as cold as stone.

All that night, in between these times, I thought a lot. The cold seemed to clear my brain. All the feeling had gone from my hands and from my legs and thighs, and my head seemed almost the only part of me alive. For the first time I thought of what might be happening, or what might yet happen, at home. I thought of base, where they would be wondering about us. I could see the Mess ante-room: the long cream room with the fire at one end, the pictures of Stirlings on the walls, the chaps playing cards, someone drumming to a Duke Ellington record on the lid of the radio. I wondered if they had given us up. I wondered too about the papers. If they had already said anything about us it could only be in the dead phrase: one of our aircraft is missing. Hearing it, did anyone think about it again? We had been drifting for two days on the sea and for a long time we had been on fire in the air. If we didn't come back no one would ever know. If we did come back the boys at the station would be glad, and perhaps the papers would give us a line in a bottom corner. I didn't feel very bitter but that night, as I sat there, holding Allison with my burnt hands, I saw the whole thing very clearly. We had been doing things that no one had ever done before. Almost every week you read of aircraft on fire in the air. You read it in the papers and then you turned over and read the sports news. You heard it on the radio and the next moment you heard a dance band. You sat eating in restaurants and read casually of men floating for days in dinghies. God, I was hungry. I began to think of food, sickly and ravenously, and then put it out of my mind. You read and heard of these things, and they stopped having meaning. Well, they had meaning for me now. I suddenly realized that what we were doing was a new experience in the world. Until our time no one had ever been on fire in the air. Until our time there had never been so many people to hear of such things and then to forget them again.

I wanted to speak. Where my stomach should have been there was a distended bladder of air. I pressed Allison's head against it. I must have moved sharply, not thinking, and he groaned.

'Ally?' I said. 'Are you all right, Ally?'

He did not answer. Ellis gave him a little more rum and then I held his mouth closed again.

I looked at the stars and went on thinking. The stars were very frosty and brittle and green. One of them grew bright enough to be reflected, broken up, in the black water. Did my wife care? This, I thought, is a nice moment to reason it out. Neither of us had wanted to have children. We hadn't really wanted much at all except a flat, a lot of small social show, and a good time. Looking back, I felt we were pretty despicable. We had really been attracted by a mutual selfishness. And then we got to hating each other because the selfishness of one threatened the selfishness of another. A selfishness that surrenders is unselfishness. Neither of us would surrender. We were too selfish to have children; we were too selfish to trouble about obligations. Finally, we were too selfish to want each other.

All this, it seemed, had happened a long time ago. Life in the dinghy had gone on a thousand years. I had never had the use of my hands, and I had never eaten anything but chocolate and biscuit and rum. Curious that they were luxuries. I had never sat anywhere except on the edge of that dinghy, with the sea beating me up and down, the ice cracking on the sides, and my feet in freezing water. I had never done anything except hold Allison with my hands and knees. And now I had held him so long that we seemed frozen together.

Every time we gave Allison the rum that night, I smelled it for a long time in the air, thick and sweet. Once it ran down out of his open mouth over my wrists and very slowly, so as not to disturb him, I raised my wrists and licked it off. My lips were sore with salt and, because it was not like drinking from a cup, the rum burnt the cracks in them. I was cold too and moving my hands was like moving some part of Allison's body, not my own.

Then once more the rum ran out of Allison's mouth and poured over my hands, and suddenly I thought it strange that he could not hold it. I waited for Ellis to crawl back across the dinghy and sit down. Then I tried to find Allison's hands. They were loose and heavy at his sides. I tried to move his head, so that I could speak to him. His face was white in the starlight. I bent down at last and touched it with my own.

'Ally,' I thought. 'Jesus, Ally. Jesus, Jesus.'

His mouth was stiff and open and his face was colder than the frost could ever make it.

x

I held him for the rest of that night, not telling even Ellis he was dead. It was then about three o'clock. I felt that it was not the frost or the sea or the wind that had killed him. He had been dead for a long time. He had been dead ever since he walked out of the bombed house with the child in his arms.

The death of Allison made me feel very small. Until morning, when the others knew, it did not depress me. For the rest of the night, in the darkness, with the frost terribly vicious in the hours up to seven o'clock, my jacket stiff with ice where the spray had frozen and the ice thin and crackling in the well of the dinghy, I felt it was a personal thing between myself and Allison. I had got myself into the war because, at first, it was an escape from my wife. It was an escape from the wrong way of doing the toast in the morning, the way she spilled powder on her dressing-gown, the silly songs she sang in the bathroom. It was an escape from little things that I magnified by selfishness into big things. I think I wanted to show her, too, that I was capable of some sort of bravery; as if I had any idea what that was.

Now, whatever I had done seemed small beside what Allison had done. I remember how Allison and his wife had wanted the baby, how it had come after Allison had joined up, how its responsibilities excited them. I saw now what he must have felt when he walked out of the bombed house with all his excitement, his joy and his responsibilities compressed into a piece of dead flesh in his hands. I understood why he had been dead a long time.

Just before seven o'clock, when it became light enough for us to see each other, I called Ellis and told him Allison was dead. The thing was a great shock to the rest of us and I saw a look of terror on Ossy's face. Then Ellis and Mac took Allison and laid him, as best they could, in the bottom of the dinghy. None of us felt like saying much and it was Mac who covered Allison's face with his handkerchief, which fluttered and threatened to blow away in the wind.

'It's tough tit, Ally boy. It's tough tit,' he said.

I felt very lonely.

XI

The wind blew away the handkerchief about ten minutes later, leaving
the face bare and staring up at us. The handkerchief floated on the sea
and floated away fast on bars of foam that were coming up stronger now
with the morning wind. We stared for a moment at the disappearing
handkerchief, because it was a more living thing than Allison's face
lying in the sloppy yellow ice-water in the dinghy, and then Thompson,
who never spoke much unless he had something real to say, suggested
we should wrap him in his parachute.

'At least we can cover him with it,' he said.

So while Ed and Ossy paddled and Thompson baled what water he
could and I sat there helpless, trying to get some flexibility into the arms
cramped by holding Allison all night, Mac and Ellis wrapped the body
roughly, as best they could, in the parachute. Mac lifted the body in his
arms while Ellis and Thompson baled ice and water from the dinghy,
and then Ellis spread the parachute. Together they wrapped Allison in
it like a mummy.

'Christ, why didn't we think of this before?' Ellis said. 'It would have
kept him warm. I blame myself.'

'He died a long time ago,' I said.

'He what?'

'You couldn't have done anything,' I said.

Soon they finished wrapping him in the parachute and he seemed to
cover almost all the space in the dinghy, so that we had nowhere to put
our feet and we kept pushing them against him. The sun was up now,
pale yellow in a flat sky, but it was still freezing. The sea seemed to be
going past at a tremendous pace, black and white and rough, as if we
were travelling with a current or a tide.

I could see that Ossy and Ed Walker were terribly dejected. We
were all pale and tired, with bluish dark eyes, and stubby beards which
seemed to have sucked all the flesh from our cheek-bones. But Ossy
and Ed, partly through the intense cold, much more through the shock
of Allison's death, seemed to have sunk into that vacant and silent state
in which Allison himself had been on the previous afternoon. They
were staring flatly at the sea.

'O.K., chaps,' Ellis said, 'breakfast now.'

He began to ration out the biscuits and the chocolate. One piece of
chocolate had a piece of white paper round it. As Ellis unwrapped it
the wind tore it overboard. It too, like the handkerchief, went away at
great speed, as if we were travelling on a tide.

Suddenly Ellis stopped in the act of holding a piece of chocolate to
my mouth. I opened my mouth ready to bite it. So we both sat
transfixed, I with my mouth open, Ellis holding the chocolate about
three inches away.

'You see it?' he said. 'You see it? You see?'

'Looks like a floating elephant,' Mac said.

'It's a buoy!' Ellis said. 'Don't you see, it's a buoy!'

'Holy Moses,' Mac said.

'Paddle!' Ellis said. 'For Christ's sake, paddle! All of you, paddle.'

I made a violent grab at the chocolate with my mouth, partly biting it and Ellis's finger before it was snatched away. Ellis swore and we all laughed like hell. The sight of that buoy, rocking about half a mile westwards, like a drunken elephant, encouraged us into a light-hearted frenzy, in which at intervals we laughed again for no reason at all.

'We're going in with the tide,' I said. 'I've been watching it.'

'Paddle like hell!' Ellis said. 'Straight for the buoy. Paddle!'

I paddled with my mind. They said afterwards that I paddled also with my hands. The buoy seemed to go past us, two or three minutes later, at a devil of a speed, though it was we who were travelling. The wind had freshened with the sun and we seemed to bounce on the waves, shipping water. But we had forgotten about baling now. We had forgotten almost about the body of Allison, rolling slightly in the white parachute in the dirty sea-water at our feet. We had forgotten about everything except frantically paddling with the tide.

It was likely that we should have seen land a long time before this, except that it was without cliffs and was a low line of sand unlit by sun. In the far distance there was a slight haze which turned to blue and amber as the sun rose. Then across the mist and the colour the line of land broke like a long wave of brown.

Ten minutes later there was hardly any need to paddle at all. The tide was taking us in fast, in a calmer stretch of water, towards a flat, wide beach of sand. Beyond it there was no town. There were only telegraph wires stretching up and down the empty coast, and soon we were so near that I could see where the snow had beaten and frozen on the black poles, in white strips on the seaward side.

I looked at my watch as we floated in, not paddling now, on the tide. It was about eight o'clock and we had been, as far as I could tell, nearly sixty hours in the dinghy.

Then as we came in, and the exhilaration of beating in towards the coast on that fast tide began to lessen, I became aware of things. I became aware of my hands. They were swollen from lack of attention and stiff from holding Allison. I became aware of hunger. The hollowness of my stomach filled at intervals with the sickness of hunger and then emptied again. I became aware again of Allison, wrapped in the parachute, once very white, now dirty with sea-water and the excited marks of our feet, and I became aware, in one clear moment before the dinghy struck the sand, of Ellis and Mac and Ed and

Thompson and all that they now meant to me. I became aware of Ossy, standing in the dinghy like a crazy person, waving his spanner.

When the dinghy hit the sand and would go no further I jumped overboard. There was no feeling of impact as my legs struck the shore. They seemed hollow and dead. They folded under me as if made of straw and I fell on my face on the wet sand of the beach, helpless, and lay there like a fool.

And as I lay there, the sand wet and cold and yet good on my face, I became aware of a final thing. We had been out a long way, and through a great deal together. We had been through fire and water, death and frost, and had come home.

And soon we should go out again.

William Venables

Survivor's Leave

FIRING a boiler with coal is one of the toughest jobs on earth. Perhaps nowhere else in industry have the effects of mechanization eased the life of the labourer more than in the stokehold of a steamer. Nowadays, boilers are fired by pressurized oil sprayed through a needle-sized orifice; and the fireman's main job is to keep the orifice clean by poking it with a wire every few hours.

How different the fireman's task on a coal-fired steamer. A special breed of man evolved who could face the searing heat of an open furnace and distribute huge shovelfuls of coal with mathematical precision across the glowing bars. Most of these men at one time lived in Liverpool, and were the sons of men who once fired the great Cunarders and White Star liners. This fast-dying breed have their own catarrhal twang and whimsicalities of speech, and a typical mode of ambulation called the Western Ocean roll which consists of short, rapid steps, and a peculiar flexibility of the hips which gives more evidence of agility than the toughness that is their greatest virtue.

Such were the pair who, having dined on a timid cup of tea and soggy Nelson cake in Sugden's Cocoa Rooms, traipsed down Miller's Bridge towards the Liverpool docks. Each pulled a half-smoked 'nicker' from an inside pocket, lit it, and inhaled with relish. It was the second year of the war and both had, a week before, been granted thirty days' survivor's leave after the sinking of the meatship *Cowhide*.

Apart from being obviously 'Liverpool firemen', the two were conspicuous for their incongruity. The larger, Charlie Curtiss, was six feet one and of massive stature. His benign and rubicund features would have looked well over a clerical collar. His companion, Spadger Hollins, barely reached his shoulder and as he tripped beside him with mincing gait, his alert little face, dominated by darting blue eyes, gave an impression of birdlike inquisitiveness indeed, a suggestion of the cocky sparrow from which he derived his nickname.

'Look 'ere, Curtiss,' began Spadger – it was typical of the status between the two that he never used Charlie's Christian name unless he was particularly pleased with him – 'look 'ere, I'm blooming well fed up with this 'ere survivor's leave. Feedin' on wet Nellies at the Coaks-gah! An' the price they charges fer fags, crikey!' Charlie grunted his complete agreement.

'I votes we goes down ter the *Marsupian* an' sees the Sec,' decided Spadger. 'The Sec's a right good scouser. 'Im what was in the *Mardinian* wi' us, 'member?'

Charlie nodded his becapped head and mumbled to indicate that his memory was still as good as ever.

Thus it was that, some twenty minutes later, the pair boarded the freighter *Marsupian* in Alexandra Dock and ambushed Mr Henry Fotheringham, her second engineer. Mr Fotheringham, wearily climbing the engine room ladder in a sweat-soaked boiler-suit, regarded them both with distaste.

'Morning, Sec,' beamed Spadger, touching a coal-scarred finger to his cap. 'Any jobs goin'?'

Mr Fotheringham, gaining time to analyse the problem presented, leaned against a burnished handrail, took out his tobacco box, and rolled his thoughts into a cigarette. It was indeed a problem.

When on shore-leave in foreign ports Hollins and Curtiss were notorious for their ability to nose out the most potent local plonk and imbibe same to more than capacity. Hollins usually started a fight and Curtiss went to gaol with him. Apart from this serious and oft-recurring delinquency, the second engineer knew no two men more capable of keeping the steam on the blood with less smoke from the funnel.

With this pair in the stokehold the *Marsupian* would have at least eight hours a day without incurring the wrath of an irate Commodore of Convoys whose main delight seemed to be the chastising of smoking steamers. That decided him.

'Okay,' he grunted with a scowl. 'Sign on ten in the morning. Shipping office.'

'Ta, Sec,' fawned Spadger. 'Yer a toff.'

Forty-eight hours later the *Marsupian* was one of twenty grey-clad merchantmen waddling down the Mersey Channel line-in-line like a herd of circus elephants. The convoy had been delayed twelve hours while the channel was swept for magnetic mines dropped by Jerry during the previous night's blitz.

Spadger and Charlie were on the Second's watch, the four-to-eight, as the *Marsupian* steamed towards the Bar. Her two boilers had three furnaces each, and of these Spadger tended the low fires and Charlie the high ones, which were a bit on the high side for Spadger. As there were twice as many high fires as low ones this division of labour suited the pair admirably.

Stripped to the waist and glistening with sweat, Charlie was able to exercise his vast reserves of brute strength while Spadger sat on the bilge-valve casing and regaled him with advice and an occasional bawdy song. Having just had an issue of duty-free cigarettes, Spadger was blissfully smoking, and titillating his salivary juices with extravagant visions of the meal that would be his at eight bells.

'Yer know, Char ole boy,' mused Spadger, 'this 'ere cook's a pie-faced, measly hunka meat, but I'll say this fer' 'im, 'e can make a Irish stoo fit fer a king. Ay, yer wouldn't get better in the Savoy 'Otel.'

Just then a husky youth emerged from a gloomy tunnel wheeling a barrow full of coal, one of the many he would have to fill and push before his four-hour watch was over.

'Shuv it over there, Alf,' ordered Spadger, nodding imperiously towards a small pile of coal in front of one of the fires. 'First-tripper, eh?' ruminated Spadger as the trimmer trundled his barrow back into the bunkers. 'Pore li'l bleeder. Wunner why 'is ma let 'im come ter sea. Tell yer what, Char, when yer've sliced that fire, 'ave a smoke an' then yer can give the pore kid a 'and in the bunkers, eh?'

'Sure, Spadge,' grunted Charlie, ramming a nine-foot steel slice into the furnace, bending it as his weight loosened the fiery mass from the bars.

It was about then that the *Marsupian* steamed over a magnetic mine and, not being fitted with degaussing wires, her steel hull triggered off the mine's lethal mechanism. The explosion which followed blasted the bottom out of number two hold. Hatch-boards and cargo screamed into the air in a holocaust of roaring smoke and flame.

On the bridge, Captain Hodgson, the mate, and the helmsman were thrown to the deck by the blast. Bruised and dazed, the Captain staggered to the wheel and altered course to swing his sinking ship out of the line of convoy.

Down in the stokehold the terrific jolt flung Charlie Curtiss onto the butt of his slice, winding him with a heavy blow in the solar plexus. Slumping to the plates, he doubled up, groaning with pain. Spadger Hollins, blissfully eulogizing the cook's flavoursome stew, suddenly found himself floundering in a heap of coal which seemed to have acquired urgent life of its own. For a moment he lay in a daze, every sense numbed by the explosion.

Gradually he became aware of aching limbs, and a head which throbbed like the best morning-after he had ever had. With a groan he staggered to his feet. The stokehold was in darkness except for the glow from the fires. He could hear the scream of escaping steam, and a prolonged rumble as the heaps of coal in the bunkers sought a common level.

With a cry of dismay Spadger limped across the already-listing stokehold and, with a strength belying his meagre frame, tried to force Charlie to his knees.

'Char, wake up! Get up, Char, we're sinkin',' he yelled, slapping Charlie's cheeks. 'Oh, crikey, wake up, Char!'

Stumbling across the stokehold, Spadger turned on the sea-cock and filled a bucket with icy water. He flung it in Charlie's face, and swore with relief as Charlie, spluttering and holding his stomach, struggled to a sitting position.

'Cor lumme, me belly,' moaned Charlie.

'Never mind yer flippin' belly,' screamed Spadger. 'We've gotta get out quick! We're sinkin'.'

While Spadger was trying to heave Charlie to his feet, the second engineer stumbled into the stokehold. 'Anyone hurt in here?' he called, flashing his torch on the two firemen. 'The Old Man's ordered abandon ship. Up the ladder with you, quick! Where's the trimmer?'

'Crikey!' gasped Spadger, staring in consternation at the bunker tunnel. 'Young Alf's trapped in the bunkers!'

By the light of the torch, Spadger and the second engineer peered along the steel tunnel leading into the bunker. The far end was blocked. Somewhere behind that wall of coal if he wasn't already buried and smothered young Alf, on his first day at sea, lay trapped in a sinking ship. For a moment they looked at each other in dismay. Already the stokehold plates were covered by sooty water which swished eerily about their feet.

While Charlie scrambled to his feet, all personal aches forgotten, Spadger grabbed a shovel and darted into the tunnel. Frantically he attacked the sloping wall before him, flinging the coal behind him where Charlie scooped it away to keep the tunnel clear. The second engineer focused his torch so that they could see.

As fast as Spadger excavated a sizeable hole, there came the clatter of slithering coal, and the hole was filled again. It was like trying to dig a hole in quicksand.

'It's no flippin' use,' groaned Spadger, still attacking the dyke of coal. ' 'Ow much coal d'yer reckon there'll be, Sec?'

'Shouldn't be more than four or five feet thick,' answered the Second. 'But God knows how much has slid in from the wings. I'm afraid we'll have to leave the poor chap.'

'Not bleedin' likely!' grunted Spadger, straightening from his shovel and wiping the sweat from his eyes. ' 'Ow about tunnellin', Sec?'

'Not a hope.' The Second pursed his lips and shook his head dejectedly. 'There's no time to rig props. This ship won't float much longer. Feel that?' The ship suddenly lurched to starboard and a roaring torrent swirled about their knees. The rush of water increased and was too much for them. All three were swept from their feet. Then, miraculously it seemed, the settling vessel asserted her dignity and slowly rose to an even keel.

The three men scrambled to their feet, spluttering ashy water, heedless of cuts and bruises, fearful of the maelstrom of icy water which might at any instant pour down upon them from the smothering sea. Lit by the dim glow from the furnace fires, they stared at each other with frightened eyes, then, with one accord, they waded back into the tunnel.

'I've got it, Sec!' cried Spadger, his eyes wide with inspiration. 'Charlie can 'old the trimmin'-plate above 'is 'ead, an' I can tunnel between 'is legs. You can do it, can't yer, Char ole man?'

'Er course,' grunted Charlie.

'It's in the wing!' cried the Second, floundering to the port side and burying his face in the water as he went on all fours, feeling for the six-by-three trimming-plate. 'Here it is.'

He and Spadger carried the thin steel plate into the tunnel, and slid it over Charlie's back as he stooped, hands on knees. The diminutive Spadger scrambled between Charlie's legs and scooped shovelfuls of coal backwards with frantic haste. The Second shovelled the coal clear of the tunnel entrance.

Every few minutes it was found possible to force the steel plate farther into the wall of coal. Shovelful by shovelful Spadger burrowed his way forward towards the trapped trimmer. Fortunately there was not a great height of coal above the tunnel entrance; even so, Charlie was grunting with strain before Spadger shouted out excitedly, 'I think I'm through!' A few minutes later, he called back, 'Pass me the torch, Sec.'

Spadger crawled through into the bunker space. The beam of the torch climbed over the hills of coal which rose against the ship's side to the deck-head, over the dust-blackened lake of water which had penetrated through strained seams from the sea. The light halted on the ashen face of the young trimmer mercifully unconscious as he lay slumped across a heap of coal, his lower body beneath the water.

With a shout of relief that the trimmer wasn't buried, Spadger waded through the water, hoisted Alf to his back, and struggled with him to the tunnel entrance, the torch jammed beneath an armpit to light the way.

Unceremoniously he dumped the unconscious trimmer beneath the arch of Charlie's legs so that the Second could pull him into the comparative safety of the stokehold.

Laying the trimmer on the bilge-valve casing above the surging water, the Second and Spadger were able to relieve the weight on the trimming-plate until Charlie could slip from beneath it. Charlie then swung Alf to his shoulder and climbed the stokehold ladder with him, the other two following, urging him to hurry.

On deck they found that the ship was sinking fast. The rest of her crew were safely in the boats. The Captain was just scrambling into a lifeboat when the four men arrived from below, Charlie carrying Alf like a sleeping babe.

'Good lord!' exclaimed the Captain, 'I thought everyone had abandoned ship!'

'We can now, sir,' said Mr Fotheringham. 'These two wouldn't leave until they'd dug the trimmer out of the bunkers.'

'Good work!' congratulated Captain Hodgson. 'I hope you both enjoy your survivor's leave.'

'Survivor's leave,' grunted Spadger Hollins, as he sat in the lifeboat and glumly watched the *Marsupian* sink until she bottomed on the channel with only her masts remaining above water. 'Survivor's leave again! Flippin' heck, what a bleedin' war!'

George MacDonald Fraser

Wee Wullie

THE duties of a regimental orderly officer cover pretty well everything from inspecting the little iced cakes in the canteen to examining the prisoners in the guard room cells to ensure that they are still breathing. In our battalion, the cells were seldom occupied; the discipline imposed on our volatile mixture of Aberdonians and Glaswegians was intelligent rather than tough, and more often than not trouble was dealt with before it got the length of a charge sheet.

So when I walked into the guardroom for a late night look round and saw one of the cell doors closed and padlocked, and a noise issuing from behind it like the honking of a drowsy seal, I asked McGarry, the provost sergeant, who his guest for the night might be.

'It's yon animal, Wee Wullie,' he said. 'Sharrap, ye Glasgow heathen! He's gey fu' sir, an' half-killed a redcap in the toon. They had to bring him here in a truck wi' his hands tied and a man sittin' on his heid. And afore I could get him in there I had to restrain him, mysel'.'

I realized that McGarry had a swelling bruise on one cheek and that his usually immaculate khaki shirt was crumpled; he was a big man, with forearms like a blacksmith, and the skin on his knuckles was broken. I was glad it wasn't me he had had to restrain.

'He's sleepin' like a bairn noo, though,' he added, and he said it almost affectionately.

'I looked through the grill of the cell. Wee Wullie was lying on the plank, snoring like an organ. Between his massively booted feet at one end, and the bonnet on his grizzled head at the other, there was about six and a half feet of muscular development that would have done credit to a mountain gorilla. One of his puttees was gone, his shirt was in rags, and there was a tear in his kilt; his face, which at the best of times was rugged, looked as though it had been freshly trampled on. On the palm of one outstretched hand still lay a trophy of his evening's entertainment – a Military Police cap badge. In that enormous brown paw it looked about as big as a sixpence.

'You did well to get him inside,' I told McGarry.

'Ach, he's no' bad tae manage when he's puggled,' said the provost. 'A big, coorse loon, but the booze slows him doon.'

I had some idea of what McGarry called 'no' bad tae manage'. I recalled Hogmanay, when Wee Wullie had returned from some slight jollification in the Arab quarter having whetted his appetite for battle on the local hostelries, and erupted through the main gate intent on slaughter. It had been at that moment of the day which, for a soldier, is memorable above all others; the hour when the Last Post is sounded, and everything else is still while the notes float sadly away into the velvet dark; the guard stand stiffly to attention by the main gate with the orderly officer behind, and the guard room lanterns light up the odd little ceremony that has hardly changed in essentials since the Crimea. It is the end of the Army's day, peaceful and rather beautiful.

Into this idyll had surged Wee Wullie, staggering drunk and bawling for McGarry to come out and fight. For a moment his voice had almost drowned the bugle, and then (because he was Wee Wullie with 30 years' service behind him) he had slowly come to attention and waited, swaying like an oak in a storm, until the call was ended. As the last note died away he hurled aside his bonnet, reeled to the foot of the guard room steps, and roared:

'Coom oot, McGarry! Ah'm claimin' ye! Ye've had it, ye big Hielan' stirk! Ye neep! Ye teuchter, ye!'

McGarry came slowly out of the guard room, nipping his cigarette, and calmly regarded the Neanderthal figure waiting for him. It looked only a matter of time before Wee Wullie started drumming on his chest and pulling down twigs to eat, but McGarry simply said,

'Aye, Wullie, ye're here again. Ye comin' quiet, boy?'

Wullie's reply was an inarticulate bellow and a furious fist-swinging charge, and five minutes later McGarry was kneeling over his prostrate form, patting his battered face, and summoning the guard to carry the body inside. They heaved the stricken giant up, and he came to himself just as they were manhandling him into the cooler. His bloodshot eyes rolled horribly and settled on McGarry, and he let out a great cry of baffled rage.

'Let me at 'im! Ah want at 'im!' He struggled furiously, and the four men of the guard clung to his limbs and wrestled him into the cell.

'Wheesht, Wullie,' said McGarry, locking the door. 'Just you lie doon like a good lad. Ye'll never learn; ye cannie fight McGarry when ye're fu'. Now just wheesht, or I'll come in tae ye.'

'You!' yelled Wullie through the bars. 'Oh, see you! Your mither's a Tory!'

McGarry laughed and left him to batter at the door until he was tired. It had become almost a ritual with the two of them, which would be concluded when Wullie had sobered up and told McGarry he was sorry. It was Wullie's enduring problem that he liked McGarry and would fight with him only when inflamed by drink; yet drunk, he could not hope to beat him as he would have done sober.

I thought of these things as I looked into the cell at Wee Wullie asleep. On that wild Hogmanay I should, of course, have used my authority to reprimand and restrain him, and so prevented the unseemly brawl with the provost sergeant, but you don't reprimand a rogue elephant or a snapped wire hawser, either of which would be as open to sweet reason as Wee Wullie with a bucket in him. The fact that he would have been overwhelmed by remorse afterwards for plastering me all over the guard room wall would not really have been much consolation to either of us. So I had remained tactfully in the background while Sergeant McGarry had fulfilled his regimental duty of preserving order and repressing turbulence.

And now it had happened again, for the umpteenth time, but this time it was bad. From what McGarry had told me, Wee Wullie had laid violent hands on a military policeman, which meant that he might well be court-martialled – which, inevitably, for a man with a record like his, would mean a long stretch in the glass-house at Cairo.

'He'll no' get away wi' it this time, poor loon,' said McGarry. 'It'll be outwith the battalion, ye see. Aye, auld Wullie, he'll be the forgotten man of Heliopolis nick if the redcaps get their way.' He added, apparently irrelevantly, 'For a' the Colonel can say.'

I left the guardroom and walked across the starlit parade ground through the grove of tamarisks to the white-walled subalterns' quarters, wondering if this was really the finish of Wee Wullie. If it was, well, the obvious thing to do would be to thank God we were rid of a knave, an even bigger battalion pest than the famous Private McAuslan, the dirtiest soldier in the world, an Ishmael, a menace, a horrible man. At the same time . . .

All that was really wrong with Wee Wullie was his predilection for strong drink and violent trouble. He was drunk the first time I ever saw him, on a desert convoy passing under Marble Arch, that towering monument to Mussolini's vanity which bestrides the road on the Libyan border. I had noticed this huge man, first for his very size, secondly for his resemblance to the late William Bendix, and lastly for his condition, which was scandalous. He was patently tight, but still at the good-humoured stage, and was being helped aboard a truck by half a dozen well-wishers. They dropped him several times, and he lay in the sand roaring. I was a green subaltern, but just experienced enough to know when not to intervene, so I left them to it, and eventually they got him over the tailboard. (It is astonishing just how often an officer's duty seems to consist of looking the other way, or maybe I was just a bad officer.)

In the battalion itself he was a curious mixture. As far as the small change of soldiering went, Wullie was reasonably efficient. His kit at inspections was faultless, his knowledge and deportment exact, so far as they went, which was just far enough for competence. In his early days he had been as high as sergeant before being busted (I once asked the Adjutant when this had been, and he said, 'God knows, about the first Afghan War, I should think'), but in later years the authorities had despaired of promoting him to any rank consistent with his length of service. Occasionally they would make him a lance-corporal, just for variety, and then Wullie would pick a fight with the American Marines, or tip a truck over, or fall in alcoholic stupor into a river and have to be rescued, and off would come his stripe again. He had actual service chevrons literally as long as his arm, but badges of rank and good conduct he had none.

Yet he enjoyed a curiously privileged position. In drill, for example, it was understood that there were three ways of doing this: the right way, the wrong way, and Wee Wullie's way. His movements were that much slower, more ponderous, than anyone else's; when he saluted, his hand did not come up in a flashing arc, but jerked up so far, and then travelled slowly to his right eyebrow. On parade, there was some incongruity in the sight of a platoon of wee Gleska keelies and great-chested Aberdonians (who run to no spectacular height, as a rule) with Gargantua in their midst, his rifle like a popgun in his huge fist, and himself going through the motions with tremendous intensity, half a second behind everyone else. There was almost a challenge in the way he performed, as though he was conscious of being different, and yet there was about him a great dignity. Even the Regimental Sergeant Major recognized it, and excused much.

This was when he was sober and passive. Even then he was withdrawn and monosyllabic; only when he was slightly inebriated could he be described as sociable. Beyond that he was just outrageous, a dangerous, wickedly powerful ruffian whom only the redoubtable McGarry could manage single-handed.

Yet there was in the battalion a curiously protective instinct towards him. It seemed to emanate from the Colonel, who had ordered that Wullie was never to be brought before him for disciplinary action except when it was unavoidable. Thus his crimes and misdemeanours were usually dealt with at company level, and he got off fairly lightly. When the Colonel did have to deal with him he would consign Wullie to the cells and afterwards try to find him a quiet niche where he would be out of trouble, invariably without success. When he was made medical orderly he got at the M.O.'s medicinal brandy and wrecked the place; he lost the job of padre's batman through his unceasing profanity; attached to the motor transport section he got tremendously high and put a three-ton truck through a brick wall ('I always said that particular experiment was sheer lunacy,' said the Adjutant. 'I mean, a truck was all he needed, wasn't it?'). An attempt was even made to get him into the band, and the little pipe-sergeant was scandalized. 'He has no sense of time, colonel sir,' he protested. 'Forbye, look at the size of his feet, and think of that clumph-clumph-clumphing on the great ceremonial parades.'

In the end he was made the M.O.'s gardener, and he seemed to take to it. He did not do any actual gardening himself, but he could address the Arab gardeners in their own language, and got all the plants neatly arranged in columns of threes, dressed by the right, and in order of what he considered their seniority. For in his quiet moments there was a strong military sense in Wullie, as there should have been after 30 years in uniform. This was brought home to me in the only conversation of any duration I ever had with him, one day when I was orderly officer and was inspecting the whitewashed stones which Wullie's Arabs were arranging in the headquarters plot. For some reason I mentioned to Wullie that I was not intending to stay in the Army when my number came up, and he said, with his direct, intent stare, 'Then ye're a fool, sir.' Only Wullie could have called an officer a fool, in a way which carried no disrespect and only Wullie would have added 'sir' to the rebuke.

And on another occasion he did me a great service. It was shortly after his Hogmanay escape, and I was again orderly officer and was supervising the closing of the wet canteen. The joint was jumping and I hammered with my walking-stick on the bar and shouted, 'Last drinks. Time, gentlemen, please,' which was always good for a laugh. Most of them drank and went, but there was one bunch, East End Glaswegians with their bonnets pulled down over their eyes, who stayed at their table. Each man had about three pints in front of him; they had been stocking up.

'Come on,' I said. 'Get it down you.'

There were a few covert grins, and someone muttered about being entitled to finish their drinks – which strictly speaking they were. But there was no question they were trying it on: on the other hand, how does a subaltern move men who don't want to be moved? I know, personality. Try it some time along the Springfield Road.

'You've got two minutes,' I said, and went to supervise the closing of the bar shutters. Two minutes later I looked across; they were still there, having a laugh and taking their time.

I hesitated; this was one of those moments when you can look very silly, or lose your reputation, or both. At that moment Wee Wullie, who had been finishing his pint in a corner, walked past and stopped to adjust his bonnet near me.

'Tak' wan o' them by the scruff o' the neck and heave 'im oot,' he said, staring at me, and then went out of the canteen.

It was astonishing advice. About the most awful crime an officer can commit is to lay hands on another rank. Suppose one of them belted me? It could be one hell of a mess, and a scandal. Then one of them laughed again, loudly, and I strode across to the table, took the nearest man (the smallest one, incidentally) by the collar, and hauled him bodily to the door. He was too surprised to do anything; he was off balance all the way until I dropped him just outside the doorway.

He was coming up, spitting oaths and murder, when Wee Wullie said out of the shadows at one side of the door:

'Jist you stay down, boy, or ye'll stay down for the night.'

I went into the canteen again. The rest were standing, staring. 'Out,' I said, like Burt Lancaster in the movies, and they went, leaving their pints. When I left the canteen Wee Wullie had disappeared.

And now he was probably going to disappear for keeps, I thought that night after seeing him in the cell. How long would he get for assaulting a redcap? Two years? How old was he, and how would he last out two years on the hill, or the wells, or whatever diversions they were using now in the glasshouse? Of course, he was as strong as an ox. And what had McGarry meant, 'For a' the Colonel can say'?

What the Colonel did say emerged a few days later when the Adjutant, entering like Rumour painted full of tongues, recounted what had taken place at Battalion H.Q. when the town Provost Marshal had called. The P.M. had observed that the time had come when Wee Wullie could finally get his come-uppance, and had spoken of general courts-martial and long terms of detention. The Colonel had said, uh-huh, indeed, and suggested that so much was hardly necessary: it could be dealt with inside the battalion. By no means, said the P.M., Wee Wullie had been an offence to the public weal too long; he was glasshouse-ripe; a turbulent, ungodly person whom he, the P.M., was going to see sent where he wouldn't hear the dogs bark. The Colonel then asked, quietly, if the P.M., as a special favour to him, would leave the matter entirely in the Colonel's hands.

Taken aback, the P.M. protested at length, and whenever he paused for breath the Colonel would raise his great bald hawk head and gently repeat his request. This endured for about twenty minutes, after which the P.M. gave way under protest – under strong protest – and stumped off muttering about protecting pariahs and giving Capone a pound out of the poor box. He was an angry and bewildered man.

'So the matter need not go to the General Officer Commanding,' concluded the Adjutant mysteriously. 'This time.' Pressed for details, he explained, in a tone that suggested he didn't quite believe it himself, that the Colonel had been ready, if the P.M. had been obdurate, to go to the G.O.C. on Wee Wullie's behalf.

'All the way, mark you,' said the Adjutant. 'For that big idiot. Of course, if the G.O.C. happens to have been your fag at Rugby, I dare say it makes it easier, but I still don't understand it.'

Nor did anyone else. Generals were big stuff, and Wullie was only one extremely bad hat of a private. The Colonel called him several other names as well, when the case came up at orderly room, and gave him 28 days, which was as much as he could award him without sending him to the military prison.

So Wullie did his time in the battalion cells, expressing repentance while he cleaned out the ablutions, and exactly twenty-four hours after his release he was back inside for drunkenness, insubordination, and assault, in that he, in the cookhouse, did wilfully overturn a cauldron of soup and, on being reprimanded by the cook-sergeant, did strike the cook-sergeant with his fist . . .

And so on. 'I don't know,' said the Adjutant in despair. 'Short of shooting him, what *can* you do with him? What *can* you do?'

He asked the question at dinner, in the Colonel's absence. It was not a mess night, and we were eating our spam informally. Most of the senior officers were out in their married quarters; only the second-in-command, a grizzled major who was also a bachelor, represented the old brigade. He sat chewing his cheroot absently while the Adjutant went on to say that it couldn't last for ever; the Colonel's curious – and misguided – protection of Wee Wullie would have to stop eventually. And when it did, Wee Wullie would be away, permanently.

The second-in-command took out his cheroot and inspected it. 'Well, it won't stop, I can tell you that,' he said.

The Adjutant demanded to know why, and the second-in-command explained.

'Wee Wullie may get his desserts one of these days; it's a matter of luck. But I do know that it will be over the Colonel's dead body. You expressed surprise that the Colonel would go to the G.O.C.; I'm perfectly certain he would go farther than that if he had to.'

'For heaven's sake, why? What's so special about Wee Wullie?'

'Well, he and the Colonel have served together a long time. Since the first war, in fact. Same battalion, war and peace, for most of the time – joined almost the same day, I believe. Wounded together at Passchendaele, that sort of thing.'

'We all know that,' said the Adjutant impatiently. 'But even so, granted the Colonel feels responsible, I'd have said Wee Wullie has overstepped the mark too far and too often. He's a dead loss.'

'Well,' said the second-in-command, 'that's as may be.' He sat for a moment rolling a new cheroot in his fingers. 'But there are things you don't know.' He lit the cheroot and took a big breath. Everyone was listening and watching.

'You know,' said the second-in-command, 'that after the battalion came out of France in 'forty, it was sent to the Far East. Well, Wullie didn't go with it. He was doing time in Sowerby Bridge glasshouse, for the usual offences – drunkenness, assault on a superior, and so on. When he came out the battalion had gone into the bag after Singapore, so Wullie was posted to one of our Terrier battalions in North Africa – it was Tom Crawford's, in fact. I don't suppose Tom was particularly happy to see the regiment's Public Enemy Number One, but he had other things to think about. It was the time when the desert war was going to and fro like ping-pong – first Rommel on top, then us – and his battalion had taken a pretty fair hammering, one way and another.

'Anyway, when Rommel made his big breakthrough, and looked like going all the way to Shepheard's Hotel, Tom's chaps were being pushed back with the rest. There was some messy fighting, and in it they picked up a prisoner – a warrant officer in the German equivalent of the service corps. They learned from him about the existence of one of those petrol dumps that Rommel had put down on an earlier push – you know the sort of thing, we did it, too. When you're on the run you bury all the fuel you can, and when you come back that way, there it is. How they got this chap to spill the beans I don't know, but he did.

'Well, Tom saw at once that if they could scupper this buried dump it might be a telling blow to the Jerry advance, so he went after it. One of his company commanders, fellow called MacLennan, took off with a truck, a couple of Sappers, the German prisoner as a guide, a driver – and Wee Wullie. They took him along because he was big and rough, and just the chap to keep an eye on the Hun. And off they went into the blue to blow the dump sky-high.

'It was away out of the main run, down to the southward, and it was going to be a near thing for them to get there before Rommel's crowd, so they went hell for leather. They didn't make it. Somewhere along the way the truck went over a land-mine, the driver was killed, and MacLennan's knee-cap was smashed. The Sappers and Wullie and the Hun were just shaken, but the truck was a complete write-off. And there they were, miles behind their own retreating brigade, stranded in the middle of God knows where, and no way of getting home but walking.'

The second-in-command's cheroot had gone out. He chewed it out of the side of his mouth, staring at the table-cloth.

'You know what the desert's like. If you haven't got transport, you die. Unless someone finds you. And MacLennan knew the only people who might find them were the Germans, and that was a thin chance at best. If they'd made it to the dump it would have been different. As it

was, they would have to shift for themselves – with about two days'
water and upwards of forty miles to go before they had even a reasonable
chance of being picked up.

'MacLennan couldn't go, of course, with his leg smashed. He got
them to make him comfortable in the lee of the wrecked truck, kept
one water bottle himself, and ordered the four of them to clear out.
One of the Sappers wanted to stay with him, but MacLennan knew
there was no point to it. Barring miracles, he was done for. He just laid
down the law to them, told them to head north, and wished them luck.
Wee Wullie never said anything, apparently – not that that was unusual,
since he was sober.

'MacLennan watched them set off, into that hellish burning waste,
and then settled down to die. He supposed his water might last him
through the next day, and decided that whatever happened, he wouldn't
shoot himself. Cool boy, that one. He's at Staff College now, I believe.
But it didn't come to that; his miracle happened. Up north, although he
didn't know it, Rommel was just coming to a halt near Alamein, and by
sheer chance on the second day one of our long-range group patrols
came on him just as he was drinking the last of his water.'

The second-in-command paused to relight his cheroot, and I noticed
the Adjutant's hand stray towards his glass, and stop half-way.

'Well, they took MacLennan in,' said the second-in-command, 'and
of course he got them on the hunt right away for the other four. It took
them some time. They found one body about twenty miles north of
where MacLennan had been, and another a little farther on. And when
they were on the point of giving up, they found Wee Wullie. He was
walking north, or rather, he was staggering north, and he was carrying
the fourth chap in a fireman's lift.

'He was in a fearful state. His face was black, his tongue and mouth
were horribly dried up, all his gear was gone, of course, and he must
have been on the very edge of collapse. He couldn't see, he couldn't
hear, he couldn't speak – but he could march. God knows how long
he'd been without water, or how long he'd been carrying the other
fellow; he was so done that when they found him they had to stop him,
physically, in his tracks, because they couldn't make him understand.
One of them said afterwards' – the second-in-command hesitated and
drew on his cheroot – 'that he believed Wee Wullie would just have
gone on for ever.'

Knowing Wee Wullie, I could have believed it too. After a moment
the Adjutant said: 'That was pretty good. Didn't he – well, he hasn't
any decorations, has he? You'd have thought, seeing he saved a
comrade's life—'

'It wasn't a comrade,' said the second-in-command. 'He was carrying
the German. And it didn't save his life. He died soon after.'

'Even so,' said the Adjutant. 'It was pretty bloody heroic.'

'I'd say so,' said the second-in-command. 'But Wee Wullie's his own worst enemy. When he was taken back to base and the hospital, he made a splendid recovery. Managed to get hold of drink, somehow, terrified the nursing staff, climbed out on the roof and sang 'The Ball of Kirriemuir' at the top of his voice – all seventy-odd verses, they tell me. They tried to drag him in, and he broke a military policeman's jaw. Then he fell off the roof and got concussion. It isn't easy to hang gongs on a man like that. Although I dare say if it had been, say, MacLennan that he'd been carrying, and not the German, that might have made a difference.'

'Well,' said the Adjutant, 'it would have made our Colonel's attitude . . . well, easier to understand.'

'Maybe that's the point,' said the second-in-command. 'Wee Wullie tried to save an enemy. The German to him was really a nuisance – a dead loss. But he was prepared to risk his own life for him, to go all the way. I don't know. Anyway,' he added, looking as near embarrassment as was possible for him, 'that may explain some of the things you haven't understood about him. Why, as far as the Colonel is concerned, he can set fire to the barracks and murder half the redcaps in the garrison, but the Colonel will still be bound to go all along the line for him. So will I, if it means the G.O.C., and the High Command, the whole lot. And so will the battalion. It's an odd situation. Oh, perhaps Wullie understands it and plays on it. So what? I know the Provost-Marshal's right: he's a drunken, dangerous, disgraceful, useless ruffian. But whenever I see him at his worst, I can't help thinking of him going though that desert, marching, and not falling. Just marching. Now, where's the ludo set? There isn't a subaltern can live with me on the board tonight.'

I have my own view of Wee Wullie, which is naturally coloured by my own experience of him. When I finally left the battalion, he was still there, pottering about the M.O.'s garden and fighting with the guard; they were still protecting him, rightly or wrongly. What is worth protecting? Anyway, his story is as I saw it, and as the second-in-command told it to me. Only the times have changed.

F. J. Salfeld

Fear of Death

WHY did I want to join the Navy and fight? Mostly I wished to test the unknown in myself. As a child I was once accidentally pushed into a park lake on Boxing Day. I must have been terrified, but I cannot recall my fear. All that remains is a memory, bright after thirty years, of lying on my back under the water, looking up as if into a frosted mirror, and seeing a white shadow cross the rippling grey when a swan paddled over me, in hopes that the disturbance meant bread crusts. I was too young to realize death. Later, a youth, I was trapped by the tide on a cliff-bound Devon shore. But I had time to seek ways of escape, and I did not believe I should die. So although I was alone, I was not afraid.

But when I was in the Mediterranean last summer . . . Rommel had crossed the Egyptian border. Alexandria was preparing to defend itself. No British ship expected, in those waters, to escape attack by aircraft, warship or submarine – or any two of these and sometimes all three.

The first day I tasted action was sunny, but a sharp wind blew, making stays and wires hiss. Coming off duty I paused on the gun deck to watch the ship swing through the creamy sea, to count the attending destroyers and the stolid merchantmen smoking along in line ahead like chaperoned dowagers.

Then I went down to my mess deck and began to darn a sock. Three of the relieved watch took their soap and towels to the bathroom. Others dragged the leather seats off the long stools, laid them on the deck and went to sleep. One wrote a letter. Some chatted, an odd mixture of Cockney, Liverpool, Glasgow, Yorkshire, Canadian and other accents.

I had finished the warp of my darn and started on the weft when the alarm sounded: a series of urgent longs on the buzzer. It was also the first time most of my messmates had gone into action – indeed the first time some of them had been to sea. I don't know what I expected our first reactions to be; but not something so entirely unheroic as bad temper. I was annoyed at having to put my sock away half-darned. The sleepers resented being wakened up. The letter-writer flung his pen down with an exclamation of anger. A formerly active service AB, recalled after serving his time, said: '— it! Just like them bastards to wait till we're off watch.' There he spoke for all. He stood on the stool and made a short speech to the canary he had bought ashore and hung in its cage above the mess table. 'Yer've got yer seed,' he said, gravely, 'an 'yer've got yer water. Fill yer belly till I comes back. So long, cock.' The bird hopped sharply on its perch.

Then the unanimous rush for gas masks, tin hats, anti-flash gear, oilskins and sea-boots, the clank of feet up the iron ladder, the crash of the hatch cover shutting off the empty deck, the milling of dozens of men in the narrow alleyways as they sought their stations, petty officers shouting 'Double away there!' in the detached, irritated tones of men already looking inward to their own fate, the steady shuffle-shuffle of rubber and leather on linoleum.

I remembered, as I pushed my way to my magazine, aft, how in war films of infantry advancing their pace seemed as slow as a dream. So with us, until the press thinned out and we could run. Ahead of me, in the engine room flat, I heard a sudden yell of laughter. Two stokers, taking a shower when the buzzer went, had been caught naked. As they shoved frantically against the human stream their towels were snatched from around their waists and the alleyway resounded with the echo of flat hands against bare buttocks. The stokers were grinning. One hadn't had time to dry his body.

The hatchway to my magazine lay just aft the wardroom. I glanced in as I passed. It was empty. Periodicals sprawled on the padded benches and the carpeted deck. On the arm of a chair a book had been placed, covers up, so that the owner need not search for his place when he returned.

Down the vertical ladder to the flooding cabinet, down again to the magazine. The face of one of the damage control party peered at us from above. 'All down?' he shouted. 'All down,' replied the corporal of marines in charge, and the rating, like a dandyish racing motorist in his white anti-flash helmet and long white gloves, descended to the cabinet and closed the armoured, counter-weighted hatch, so heavy that it took his full strength to move. Then, as the weight balanced and started in his favour, it fell with a jar. A pause, as he climbed up again, and then the dropping of the top cover and snick of its clips.

So there we were, a dozen blue-overalled men in this chilly cavern stacked from deck to deckhead with cordite and shells – safe so long as no bomb struck or, if the magazine had to be flooded, we could get out before the water rose; and with some prospect of escape if the ship, supposing her torpedoed, did not sink too quickly. Either the armoured hatch might be raised by the pressure of shoulders, or we might follow each other up the ladder inside the turret. There was just enough room to squeeze in there and haul oneself up the iron rungs, wet with warm oil dripping down from the pump that moved the guns. The pump was pounding now like an excited heart, and the turret slowly swung to meet the bombers, German or Italian, that we knew were coming in. Shut off below in a clamour of sound – the pump, the rattle of steel shell and brass cartridges in the racks, the communicated vibration of the propeller shafts on either side – we should have to guess its progress from the way the turret swung, from the abrupt lift of the deck as the ship heeled in a quick evasive turn to dodge a stick of bombs, from the commander's voice through the loud speaker should a lull allow him to broadcast a commentary. But we could not hear his voice unless we climbed the ladder and held our faces to the speaker.

The telephone rang from above. The corporal pressed his answering buzzer and jammed his ear against the instrument, listened, yelled back a jest I could not catch and told us to stand by. I had unclipped a number of charges and the bar of the first shell rack had been taken down. The shell hoist was loaded and men stood by the cordite lifts, waiting for the automatic doors to open. I held a charge in my arms. We were all ready. There was time to think and I was unsure whether I liked my thought, which was not that I might die but that I wanted to live lest my death should bring sorrow to those who loved me. The idea fascinated. I was filled with a sorrow in which lay no regret for the stopping of my own breath; I felt what I imagined would be the ache and emptiness in *their* hearts.

Masochism or vanity, or both, the notion drew me further. How would A and B adjust their lives, when they could no longer share mine? Would C mind very much, D and E remember me for long? From the desolation of this self-torture I was glad to be freed by what sounded, in the general din, like a couple of polite coughs. Our guns had opened fire. The hoists began to work.

The next hour gave us no time for thought. We were all too busy, lifting the 80lb shells out of the racks, shovelling in the cordite whenever the doors opened, sliding on the greasy grating as the ship rolled, chipping flesh off knuckles and elbows, swearing, sweating and laughing when somebody lurched or fell. And all the time, the remote, irregular cough of the guns, and every now and then a curious thud against the ship's side that shook the magazine – the near misses of the unseen bombs, whistling down in the sunlight.

Then we had our first lull and I the glad relief of not having been too much afraid. The corporal rang up his friend the sergeant in the turret to find out what had happened. A boy of twenty, a clerk in civil life, who had told me once that his ambition was to find a cure for cancer, took out of his overalls a pamphlet on biochemistry. A stout, fat-cheeked youth, who had come into the Navy from a Thames barge, squatted down and began to read an oily, battered copy of *No Orchids for Miss Blandish*. Two others resumed an earlier, giggly wrestling bout. The rest I could not see; the charge cases hid them. I could hear their voices, casual to the point of anti-climax.

Was this all, then? Did the prospect of death mean no more than a check to a clerk's dream, the interruption of a book and the postponement of childish horseplay? I look round at my companions, to divine if I could, behind this extrovert behaviour, some secret speculation. It was than that I noticed the man in the corner. I didn't know his name (it turned out later that none of us did) or anything about him. He might have been thirty; he could have been forty. He never chatted to anyone and seemed to have no friends or interests in the ship, but lived his own withdrawn life. He was sitting now on a sand-filled fire bucket, his hands laid inertly on his knees, his colourless face a stare of strain, as if death had spoken to him already and he knew he was lost. (Which might have been so, for the next day he was removed from the magazine and, at his own request, made an anti-aircraft lookout, and at his post a bullet from a Junkers killed him.)

I wanted to ask him what thoughts he had, to be thus paralysed. Or was his fear without form? Or was he afraid of fear, as most men are until they have tried themselves out. But these questions are not to be asked – and the telephone had rung again, the turret was turning. Again the discreet cough, the choking, the stumbling and the oaths. But this time the atmosphere was new. The constraints were gone. The question mark poised in every brain had vanished. For good or ill, we each had our answer. One man sang as he staggered from the racks with his shells; and I, who suddenly felt happy and free, knew why. He had passed his test; he was on good terms with his spirit.

We all, in more or less degree, shared this strange intoxication – except the corporal of marines, to whom action was ordinary, and the pale man in the corner, who sat on, not watching, seeing nothing. The corporal stumbled over the deck to him. 'Well strike me pink!' he exclaimed. 'What the hell do you think this is, mate? A make-and-mend? Come on then, stand easy's over.' Whereupon the man rose from his bucket, walked over to the turret and began to climb up the escape ladder – not with panic speed but deliberately, as if in obedience to an order. The corporal watched him with dropped jaw, charged after him and pulled him down again by his heels. 'You can't do that there 'ere,' he said, patiently.

The man stood where the corporal had pushed him, against an empty shell rack, his hands by his side, still silent, like a martyr with eyes of pain. And the corporal could find nothing more to say. He put his arms akimbo, then scratched the back of his head with his right hand. But it was beyond him to deal with a man in a trance. He could only point to the fire bucket, and the man returned there and stood like a statue. Thus he was when the second and final action of that day ended, the 'All clear' was broadcast, the armoured hatch was opened from above, and we were free. Nobody spoke to the man whose nerve was gone and nobody looked at him, except that the corporal, who always left the magazine last, said to him with a rough, puzzled gentleness: 'Up you go, mate.'

I found my mess-deck half-wrecked by a heavy bomb which had crashed through without exploding, fractured a water pipe, smashed table and hurled jags of metal through lockers, hammocks and fittings. Most of the lights were out. At the forward end, which was undamaged, grimy men clustered around the tables smoking, talking of the action and of friends who were wounded or dead, and of how they had died. At the end of the table a youngster sat crying openly like the child he had so recently been. He had seen his 'winger', his best friend, decapitated. Grief and shock joined in the tears that drew two pink lanes down his grease-stained cheeks. The old AB was searching among debris for the corpse of his canary. The place had the air of a cemetery chapel.

No consolation, no comfort, was offered. They were inarticulate men, unable to frame the smooth sympathies of a politer life. I think they were more instinctive than men of education, and out of their instinct knew that grief cannot be soothed by those it does not touch. So they talked and argued and boasted around the weeping boy as though he wasn't there.

The AB found his crushed and muddied bird and showed it to us. He leaned across the table, his mouth tight with anger. He had placed the bird in a dirty handkerchief. Somebody spoke the epitaph: 'Poor little bastard! 'E never done nobody no 'arm.' The AB laid a chunk of fractured piping beside the corpse, wrapped it up carefully and tied a reef knot in the handkerchief. Then he left the mess. We knew what he was going to do. Dead men over the side in weighted canvas, a canary in a knotted handkerchief – it seemed no parody. All were victims.

Nobody knew what to say next. We became embarrassed by our own silence. At last the leading hand of that mess stood up. 'Well, what about some eats?' he asked, nervously, uncertain whether the idea was fitting. We consented by moving away so that the table could be laid, with the boy still sobbing at the end of it, and none telling him he was in the way of the cooks as they lifted plates and mugs down from the rack above him.

The food was brought from the galley, the bread dumped on the white American cloth. I was astonished at my hunger. The old AB, the sobbing boy, whose tears had now become hiccups at which even he himself laughed, everybody ate an enormous meal.

Fred Urquhart

The Prisoner's Bike

'WELL, I've got an Italian,' Mr McBride said to his wife when he came back from the Mart one Monday. 'I spoke to the Camp Labour Organizer and he said I could get one to billet.'

'And where are you going to billet him, pray?' Mrs McBride said belligerently.

'Oh, we'll easy get some place riggit up for him,' Mr McBride said. 'What aboot that little roomie at the foot o' the stairs?' There's nothin' intil't just now but boxes and a lot o' auld junk.'

'There's no Italian comin' to bide in this house,' his wife said. 'Do ye want us all to be murdered in oor beds?'

'Dinna be daft, woman,' he said. 'They're quiet, inoffensive souls.'

'Quiet! Inoffensive! Frankie McBride, ha'e ye taken leave o' yer senses?'

'Well, well,' he said. 'If ye dinna want him in the hoose I'll get another place for him. But he's comin' here the morn, anyway. I've got to ha'e another man aboot the place, Italian or no Italian.'

'Can he nae stay at the Camp and come every day wi' the lorry the way the prisoners ging to other farms?' Mrs McBride said. 'That would be the best way. Ye'd ha'e no responsibility for him then.'

'They winna do it. This is too far for the lorry to come. We've got to billet him or do without him.'

'We'll all be murdered in oor beds,' Mrs McBride wailed. 'I tell ye nae good'll come out o' it. Dinna say I didna warn ye when ye find yersel' wi' a knife in yer back. A' thae Italians carry stilettos.'

She nagged about it all evening, but the next morning Mr McBride was up early and away to the Prisoner of War Camp. Mrs McBride and Mary the maid, a glaikit girl of fifteen were preparing the dinner when he came back. They peered out of the kitchen window at the Italian sitting beside Mr McBride in the front seat of the car. 'He's nae feared,' Mrs McBride cried. 'Wi' that villain cockit there aside him. The Tally could easy ha'e grabbed the wheel and coupit them baith oot in the ditch.'

Mr McBride barged into the kitchen, crying: 'Well, well, here he is!' The Italian followed him, grinning shyly. He was a tall, good-looking youth of about twenty-two with dark wavy hair. He bobbed his head amiably to everything Mr McBride said to him, and he kept saying: 'No compree, no compree.'

'I'd no compree him,' Mrs McBride said. 'He comprees fine. I'd like to gi'e him a right guid wallop wi' this dish-clout. I'd soon take the grin off his face!'

'Stop yer antics, Frankie,' she cried to her husband who was trying by pantomine to explain something to the prisoner. 'And get awa' oot o' here and take that grinnin' heathen wi' ye!'

'Get on wi' yer work, girl,' she said to Mary who had run to the window to watch the Italian follow Mr McBride across the court.

Mary went back sulkily to peel potatoes. 'Dinna you glower at me like that, girl,' Mrs McBride said. 'And if I catch ye makin' sheep's-eyes again at that dirty Tally I'll send ye packin' doon the road.'

At lousing-time Mr McBride came in and said: 'What aboot some dinner for the Tally?'

'He's gettin' nothin' to eat in this hoose,' Mrs McBride said firmly. 'If he gets anythin' it'll be ower ma dead body.'

'Well, ye'd better order yer coffin right now,' her husband said. 'He's here to work and he's here to bide, so ye'd better just make the best o' it.'

'He's eatin' nothin' in this hoose,' Mrs McBride said.

'Well, well, he can eat it in the barn. Get somethin' hot for him and I'll take it oot to him.'

Mrs McBride handed him a plate with some mince and potatoes. 'That's plenty for him.'

He handed it back. 'Ye'll put as much as that on again,' he said. 'The man's a guid worker and I'm goin' to see that he's fed properly.'

'Where's he goin' to bide?' Mrs McBride said. 'He's nae comin' here. As soon as he comes in that door I ging oot at the other ane.'

'Ye dinna need to pack yer kist just yet,' Mr McBride said, grinning, 'I've got a room for him wi' Jack Hutcheon. Mrs Hutcheon's nae feared for gettin' a stiletto in her back!'

'Nae that ye should worry yersel' aboot that,' he said as he went out. 'Yer stays make a guid enough armour!'

Jack Hutcheon's cottage was a mile from the steading and he cycled to his work. 'Ye'll ha'e to get a bike for the Tally, too,' he said to Mr McBride. 'Ye canna expect him to walk a' that way.'

The farmer picked his fat big-pored nose and thought for a minute. 'I'll gi'e him mine,' he said after a while, and he looked down at his protruding stomach and chuckled. 'I doot ma ain cyclin' days are ower!'

The Italian grinned more than ever when he was given the bike at the end of the day. 'Beeceecle?' he said. 'Beeceecle!'

'Will he be able to ging it, dae ye think?' Mr McBride said to Jack Hutcheon.

But before Hutcheon could answer the prisoner had jumped on the bike and was pedalling round and round the court. He laughed and shouted, waving first one arm and then the other. Then he took both hands off the handlebars and leaned back, singing at the pitch of his voice. 'Good?' he cried, jumping off. 'Veree good, yes?'

'Very good,' Mr McBride said.

Guiseppe was a barber and came from Bologna. At first he had been scared and unhappy when he was told that he was to be billeted away from the Camp; he had not wanted to leave his friends and go amongst people to whom he could not make himself understood. But in a few days he had settled down on the farm. The Hutcheons were very kind to him. At nights Jack Hutcheon tried to teach him English. He and his wife and two children could not pronounce the Italian's name, so they changed it to Gee-up. The other men on the farm took up this. At first they chaffed him about the war, but in a good-natured way. 'Mussolini no good,' they would say, and Guiseppe would grin and say: 'Churchill no good.' But soon they stopped this. There was no fun in chaffing somebody who did not get angry. They saw that the Italian was a decent man like themselves even though he wore a magenta-coloured uniform with big round blue patches. They saw that he was glad to be out of the war, and that he had not wanted to be a soldier any more than they wanted to be soldiers themselves. In a vague sort of way they felt that there must be many more like him in Italy and that all Italians were not Mussolinis and Cianos.

Guiseppe made friends most quickly with the cottar children, and usually there were two or three of them hanging around him. Like their parents they delighted to tease him, saying 'You no good'. But he would just laugh and repeat this, and soon the children tired of the joke. He taught them the Italian for simple things, pointing at them and repeating the names again and again, laughing at the children's attempts to say them.

Mr McBride bought a small English-Italian dictionary, but he found that it was almost impossible to use it. Whenever he wanted to find a word to explain something to Guiseppe he would find that the dictionary was in the house. Or if he had it in his pocket it was usually much quicker to explain what he wanted by signs. Guiseppe always told him the Italian word for whatever he was wanting, and Mr McBride would repeat it several times, nodding his head and looking ponderous. But in a few minutes he would have forgotten it and the same pantomime would be gone through the next day. The only word he seemed able to remember was 'aqua'. 'And that's funny,' he said to his wife. 'I wasna just what ye'd call very bright at Latin at the school.'

The men, too, tried to learn Italian, but they did not learn nearly as quickly as Guiseppe learned certain Scottish words. Mrs McBride was horrified one day when she heard him speaking in the stable. 'If he was goin' aboot his work he wouldna ha'e time to say things like that,' she said. 'The men ha'e awfa little need to learn him thae words. He'll be sayin' them to the bairns next.'

'Ach, ye're nae needin' to worry yersel' aboot them,' Mr McBride said. 'It was the bairns that taught him maist o' the words, anyway!'

Everybody on the farm was interested in the Catholic medallion which Guiseppe wore on his wrist. It had a picture of the Virgin and Child on it. One day when he went into the Potato Shed Mr McBride found the men having an argument about the Italian word for 'baby'. 'I ken what it is, too,' Jack Hutcheon was saying, scratching his head. 'But I'm damned if I can mind it.'

'Here, Gee-up!' he cried.

The Italian came over grinning. Jack seized his wrist and pulled the medallion from under his sleeve. 'What's that?' he said, pointing to the Child in the Virgin's arms. But before Guiseppe could understand what was wanted of him, Jack suddenly remembered for himself.

'I mind on it now!' he cried. 'It's baboon! Baboon!'

Mr McBride was so amused by this rendering of 'bambino' (which he had not known himself) that he repeated the story everywhere. Only Mrs McBride was not amused. She was the only one on the farm who had not tried to learn Italian. She was quite untouched by the Italian's charm. She went out of her way to find fault with him, and she was always complaining about him to her husband. 'A pure rogue if ever there was one,' she said. 'He's as full of blarney as the very Devil.' When he was working near the house she watched him from the kitchen window, ready to pounce on the slightest fault. But even though there had been anything, her husband would not have listened to her; he was well pleased with the way Guiseppe worked. The only thing that Mrs McBride could get to complain about was the fact that when he was walking from one job to another Guiseppe sometimes took a comb from his pocket and passed it through his thick dark hair. 'D'ye see that, Frankie?' she said. 'If he was right busy he wouldna ha'e time to dae that. The muckle sissy!

'I'm nae complainin',' Mr McBride said. 'I only wish I had a head o' hair like him so that I could use a comb! And anyway, the men are fell pleased wi' him. He's a grand barber. I wouldna be surprised if after the war he didna set up a wee shoppie doon in the village.'

But one day Mrs McBride thought that at last she had found the chance she had been waiting for. She was watching the men coming in from the fields at lousing-time. Guiseppe sitting on his horse's back was singing what she felt was an Italian love-song. Mary the maid was coming from the drying-green with a basket of clothes. Guiseppe smiled and waved to her, and Mary shouted: 'See and nae fall off the horse's back!'

Guiseppe grinned and patted the horse's neck as he slid off at the stable-door. 'Thees veree good horse,' he said, winking at the girl. 'By and by he speak Italian!'

He led the horse into the stable. Mary was loitering at the door, but Mrs McBride rapped angrily on the window. 'Come inside at once, ye shameless besom!' she called. 'If I catch ye at that again I'll send ye packin'.'

'Ach to hell,' Mary said. 'I wasna doin' any harm. I can speak to who I like, can't I?'

Mrs McBride put down the pot she was filling at the tap. 'What's that?' she said, turning off the water. 'Ye can speak to whae ye like, can ye? Well, well! Nae as long as I have anythin' to do wi' it!'

'Well, then, I'm leavin',' Mary said. 'I was for leavin' at the term, onywye. But I'll ging afore then.'

'Ging then,' Mrs McBride snapped. 'Ye can ging right now. I'll be glad to see the back o' ye, ye dirty shameless bitch!'

For the next few minutes Mrs McBride forgot about the Italian, but happening to glance out of the window while she was thinking of something else to say to Mary, who by this time was howling with rage, she saw Guiseppe come out of the stable, and come towards the dairy to get his pitcher of milk. 'Ye're just a dirty slut, onywye,' she said to the girl, though she kept looking out of the window.

She saw Guiseppe stop at the dairy door, take out his knife and begin to scrape the mud off his boots on to the strip of concrete between the dairy and the kitchen doors. 'Go to your room, girl!' Mrs McBride said, turning her back on Mary. 'I'll attend to you later.'

She lifted the curtain a bit, scowling out at the Italian. Now was her chance! Many a battle had she waged with the men about that very same bit of concrete, quarrelling them for bringing their carts over it. And if none of the farmworkers were to be allowed to dirty it, then no lousy heathen of an Italian was going to be allowed either!

'Ging to yer room and pack yer kist, girl,' she said over her shoulder. 'And bide there till I come up.'

'I'll get ma mither to ye,' Mary snivelled.

'Get her!' Mrs McBride said majestically. 'Get her! I'll gi'e her a right guid piece o'ma mind. I'm nane feared for her or for you either. I'll tell her exactly what I think o' ye baith – a dirty pair!'

'I'll get the bobby,' Mary shrieked, making for the back stairs. 'I'll have ye up for slander.'

'Just you daur! Just you daur!' Mrs McBride said, lowering her brows and half-smiling. 'Just you daur, and by the Lord Harry I'll see that there are a lot o' funny things come oot in the court.'

Mary gawked and retreated up the stairs. Mrs McBride wiped her nose on the back of her hand and went to the door. She pulled it open with a flourish and opened her mouth. But what she had been going to shout died away into a mumble.

Guiseppe had a brush in his hand and was sweeping away the dirt. He looked round at her and grinned. 'I sweep, Missis Boss! Veree good, yes?'

Mrs McBride stepped back and shut the door.

During the next few days Mrs McBride had not much time to worry about the Italian. As soon as Mary had gone she began to realize just how much work the glaikit creature had been able to do. She had always needed supervision; nevertheless, she had been able to do all the rough work which Mrs McBride now found she had to do herself. It was a scutter. 'I'm fair trachled to death,' she complained one evening to her husband. 'The quicker we get another maid the better.'

'Well, who's fault is it?' he said. 'Ye should ha'e thought aboot that afore ye gave the quaen her notice. What do ye think I would do if I was aye castin' oot wi' ma men? I would be in a bonnie like mess if I sent them packin' every time I had a few words wi' them.'

'Huh, there's one I would send packin' double quick, onywye,' she said. 'And that's that dirty Italian. I widna ha'e him aboot ma place.'

'What's wrong wi' him?' Mr McBride said. 'He's a very pleasant obliging childe. And he's a right guid worker.'

'Worker!' Mrs McBride sniffed. 'A fat lot o' work he does as far as I can see. He's aye fleein' aboot on that bike. Just caperin'. It's a peety nor he widna break his neck!'

'Noo listen to me, woman, just you leave Gee-up and his bike alone. It's the only pleasure that puir devil has.' Mr McBride chuckled as he lit his pipe. 'Man, he's just like a bairn wi' a toy,' he said, puffing vigorously to get the pipe alight. 'He's a right caution the way he cleans and oils at it. He attends til't better than many a woman attends til her bairns. I doot he'd be fair heart-broken if onythin' happened til that bike.'

Mrs McBride smiled sarcastically. 'I widna mind puttin' a spoke in his wheel!' she said. 'What's a prisoner needin' wi' a bike, onywye? It's chains he should ha'e, and it's chains he *would* ha'e if I had my way o't.'

'Ye're a right nasty bitch sometimes, Peg,' he said. 'Ye dinna like to see onybody enjoyin' theirsels. It's a guid job that everybody on the farm isna like you, or we widna be able to live.'

'Oh, are they no'?' she snorted. 'I bet they like the Tally as little as I do. Only they're feared to say it to ye. They ken ye're that soft-hearted.'

'I dinna ken aboot that,' he said. 'I had Jack Hutcheon at me the day, wonderin' if it would be a' right if he took the Tally to the pictures in the village.'

'Pictures!' Mrs McBride leaned back in her chair. 'Pictures! Well, I never heard the like! Wantin' to take a prisoner to the pictures! I must say I aye thought Jack Hutcheon had mair sense. I hope ye tellt him to ging hame and nae haver?'

'Ay, unfortunately,' Mr McBride sighed. 'I had to say that I didn't think the POW Camp would be very pleased aboot it if they heard. It's a pity, it would ha'e been a fine treat for him.'

'I'd treat him!' She stood up, preparing to go and get the supper. 'I'd treat him to a right guid wallop on the lug! It's a pity nor he hadna to dae some o' the hard work I have to dae – and a' because o' that glaikit cratur', Mary!'

It was when she was feeding the hens that Mrs McBride missed Mary most. The girl had always been there to run out in any kind of weather. And although she would hardly have admitted it to herself Mrs McBride sometimes found the heavy pails of mash just more than she could manage. But she struggled on with them. She was determined not to ask Mr McBride to get a woman from the cottar houses to help her; she knew that if she did the cottar women would gossip amongst themselves about it.

One morning a week after Mary had gone she was coming out of the back door with two heavy pails of mash when she met Guiseppe. She wished that she had not looked so trauchled. She was preparing to pass him, as she usually did, with her head in the air, but he stepped in front of her. 'Excuse, Missis Boss,' he said, smiling. 'I carry pail.'

'No, thank you,' she said coldly.

'Ah yes, yes!' he said, and he seized the pails. 'Veree heavy for *la padrona*.'

'I'll carry them myself,' she said, and she tried to pull them away from him. But he grinned and held tightly to them. 'Too heavy for woman,' he said. 'Guiseppe carry.'

Mrs McBride was thankful that none of the other men were about. What would they have thought! And what would they have gone home and told their wives! All the way to the hen-house she kept saying 'I'll manage fine myself', and she kept trying to take the pails away from him. But Guiseppe just grinned and shook his head. 'I carry, Missis Boss,' he said.

She was relieved when they got to the hen-house. She pulled the pails from him, muttered 'Thank you', and rushed inside.

The following morning when she went out with the pails he was waiting for her. He came forward, smiling, and took the pails. She protested as vigorously as she could, but he merely smiled and said: 'Too heavy for woman. Guiseppe carry.'

Mrs McBride did not know what to do about it. She had never been used to having men do things for her; men about farms were usually too busy to bother about courtesies. Frankie McBride had carried things for her only when they were courting and then in a shamefaced way. But all those foreigners were alike, she thought. There was something namby-pamby about them, aye running after women and slavering about them. It was just a lot of dirt!

'Ach, why should he nae do it?' she said to herself on the third morning when he came to the back door and stood waiting for the pails. 'It's just part o' his work.'

Mr McBride had known from the medallion on Guiseppe's wrist that he was a Roman Catholic, but he was surprised one day when the prisoner came and said: 'Boss! Please to listen to me, boss! Chapel in village, yes?'

'No,' Mr McBride said. 'No chapel.'

'Too bad,' Guiseppe said, laying his head almost on top of his right shoulder and spreading out his arms. 'I want confess. Go to Mass sometime. Mass in Campo, no Mass at Missis Hutcheon. Too bad.'

'I see.' Mr McBride scratched his chin. 'Well, there's a Chapel at Clovey, but it's ten miles awa'. Ye couldna very well ging there.'

'Bike,' Guiseppe said. 'Bike verree good.'

'Ach, it widna dae ava. He couldna ha'e ye cyclin' a' that distance.'

'Please, boss, I can manage fine.'

'Very well, if ye think ye can manage,' Mr McBride said, 'ye're welcome to try it.'

But after thinking it over Mr McBride thought that perhaps he'd better phone the Camp authorities before he allowed Guiseppe to go. After all the man was a prisoner and was in his care.

'It's impossible,' the Camp Labour Organizer said. 'It's ridiculous. The man shouldn't have a bike, anyway. You must take the bike away from him at once, Mr McBride. Didn't you get a notice to say that prisoners weren't to be allowed to ride on bikes?'

'Ay, I believe there was somethin' o' the kind came in,' Mr McBride said. 'But I dinna believe I ever read it right.'

'Good heavens, man, what do you think we send these notices out for?' The Camp Labour Organizer was raising his voice so much that

Mr McBride held the phone away from his ear, screwing up his face at the noise. 'Do you think we send these notices out for fun?'

'No, I just thought ye sent them to gi'e us puir farmers a lot o' work,' Mr McBride said. 'I have as many Government notices here as would paper a fair-sized room. Goodbye!'

'So that's that,' he said to his wife after dinner. 'If I dinna take the bike awa' frae him they'll take him awa' frae me.'

'Well!' Mrs McBride said.

She rattled the dirty dishes on to a tray. 'The idea!' she said. 'What a nerve thae fowk at the Camp have! Just a lot o' red tape, that's what it is. Tryin' to keep the poor Tally frae goin' to the kirk.'

She picked up the tray and held it like a shield in front of her. 'Frankie,' she said. 'Do we get petrol for goin' to the kirk?'

'Ay,' he said. 'We could if we wanted to.'

'What way?' he said, raising one eyebrow. Mrs McBride had not been through a church door for over three years. She had always maintained that it was unpatriotic to waste the nation's petrol on kirk-going, and that, speaking for herself, you could live a godly enough life at home without attending services.

She carried the tray to the door. 'Well, ye'd better apply for it right now,' she said. 'We're goin' to Clovey on Sunday. It's a long time since I was at the kirk and I dinna see why I shouldna get when other fowk ha'e the nerve to apply for petrol to go. We'll take Gee-up wi' us and he can ging to his Mass. That'll learn the Camp authorities for tryin' to take the poor Tally's bike awa' frae him!'

C. S. Forester

Indecision

THERE were medal ribbons across the Baron's chest, and there was a cross hanging from his buttonhole, and he wore the epaulets of a major-general, but what was more important was that he wore the crimson stripes of the general staff. Even to someone who did not know the Baron personally that would be the most important thing about him; anyone with good fortune and bulldog courage might rise to be a major-general, but it called for much rarer qualities to be appointed to the general staff. To pass the rigorous tests necessary a candidate had to be blessed both with brains and a capacity for hard work, and furthermore a suitable combination of these two, for a high proportion of either one would not compensate for a deficiency of the other. A certain quality of character was necessary too; not merely an unremitting diligence but a selfless kind of diligence that prompted the candidate regardless of his own future to devote all his efforts to making the German General Staff the finest in the world and the army that it directed necessarily the finest in the world as well. The watchful people in high positions in the general staff were always on the lookout for men with these qualities, and whoever was discovered to possess them was promptly rewarded, not necessarily with promotion, although that might be incidental, but with work and more work, responsibility and more responsibility. One other factor was desirable yet unnecessary, and that was noble descent. Plenty of people from bourgeois families had risen to high rank on the general staff, but it helped to be of blue blood, and the Baron's blood was the bluest of the blue. That was why he was called the Baron, *the* Baron, when there were thousands of barons in the army of the Reich; he had been called that ever since he was a subaltern, and although it was a nickname conferred by the accident of birth one could be prouder of it than of some of the other nicknames which had begun to be whispered in the ranks, like the 'Hitler-Youth General,' or the 'Yes-General,' or the 'Lackey-General.'

It was many years ago that the Baron had passed into the general staff. He was ageing now, and it was certain that he would retire (if he lived long enough) with no higher rank than his present one. He would never carry the baton of a field-marshal; he would never even be a full general, because he had been found wanting in other qualities. For a brief interval he had been entrusted with the command of a division in the field, and it had soon become apparent that he did not possess the bloody resolution, the dash, and the infectious personality necessary to a man commanding fighting forces; the staff needed him, and the field army emphatically did not. He had been brought back and re-established in his office, where he could do work that few others could do, and thereby influence the operations of the army, for good or evil, far more than any general commanding a division – more than any general commanding an army corps or even an army, for that matter.

Because the Baron was a man with a remarkable brain; it would have been remarkable in any man, and it was quite astonishing to find such mental powers in someone of blue blood; to anyone unacquainted with the conventions that ruled the German army it would be still more astonishing that the man with such a brain should go about with a shaven bullet-head that gave him a brutish look, and with a single eyeglass screwed into his right eye to flavour the brutishness with an appearance of vapidity.

There could be no doubting his powers, though. As a subaltern the Baron had enlivened dreary evenings in the mess by impressive little demonstrations – he could run swiftly through a pack of fifty-one cards and announce without hesitation which was the missing one. Long and complex tables of establishments were as familiar to him as the buttons of his uniform; admiring – and exasperated – subordinates used to say that he knew every nut and bolt necessary for the equipment of an armoured division and the weight of every tool allocated to a bridging company. With this remarkable memory was combined a logical and mathematical mind that could calculate the ultimate resultant from a host of converging factors.

It was in consequence of these abilities that the Baron had been in charge for a long time of the military management of the railways, the most complex and sensitive section of all the work of the general staff. From Bordeaux to Warsaw, from Copenhagen to Rome, not a train moved without an order for which the ultimate responsibility lay with the Baron. It was a task that gave full play to his co-ordinating abilities. He had to bear in mind not only the permanent factors, like the shortage of coal and of rolling stock, and the necessity of keeping the mine traffic ceaselessly on the move, but also the constantly fluctuating factors, such as the damage done by Allied air raids and the repairs that had been effected. The bottleneck of Ulsen, the complexities of Ham; he had been familiar with those for years, and at the same time he had always at his fingertips the details of the military demands of the Eastern front, for it was he who directed the torrent of men and materials thither – the torrent that like a river losing itself in the desert poured in that direction to evaporate amid the fiery heat of war. At one and the same time he might be faced with the demand for routing a couple of army corps to Bessarabia and the necessity of evacuating the civilian population of Hamburg, and it was the Baron's business to see that the two operations were economically performed even if fog or snow or flood came unexpectedly.

Today – a flaming summer day, although he was hardly aware of the fact – he had some delicate problems to solve. He sat at his desk in his office thinking them out. The walls were hung with maps, but he did not have to refer to them; they were there so that he could illustrate his orders to his subordinates or explain to other generals not as logistically-minded as he was the incompatibility of their several demands. A very large troop-transference had to be planned, for Fuehrer Headquarters was now coming round to the idea that the Anglo-American landing in Normandy was a serious invasion and not a mere feint designed to bring about the evacuation of some other sector of the European coast. If Fuehrer Headquarters did not change its mind (as it often did) the correct action to be taken would be to gather up all available divisions and fling them upon the invading army, to scrape together every man, every gun, and every tank that could be spared from other duties, to move them across the continent with the utmost rapidity, and to strike with the utmost force before the Allies could build up their strength.

There were German divisions in France not yet engaged; von Rundstedt and Rommel and Fuehrer Headquarters were deep in a triangular argument about the advisability of moving them, and where. The Baron had to calculate the chances of whose opinion would prevail – and then he had to superimpose the chances of the Allied air actions allowing those troops to move by rail at all. Yet allowance had to be made for rolling stock in case of sudden demand. Other things were more easily calculable; there were divisions earmarked as a mobile reserve in Norway and Denmark and Frisia, and even here in the environs of Berlin; pitifully few after the disasters in the East, and yet enough to make it a tricky business to thread them all through the network of worn-out railways already carrying as much traffic as exhausted equipment and personnel could handle. The problems involved were of exactly the type to suit the Baron's mind, and he was devoting himself to them with something of pleasure, and with the disinterestedness of a surgeon performing a delicate operation. The patient's wife might be sitting in the waiting-room weeping, waiting for the result, but the surgeon would give her no thought. The Reich might be torn to pieces, but that was not the Baron's business at the moment; he had to concentrate on moving certain divisions in a certain direction.

Moreover, there was a small but unusual complication. Mussolini, Il Duce, was on his way to pay a state visit to the Fuehrer. In extreme secrecy his special train was starting today, winding its slow way over the Brenner, carrying the Duce all the way across Europe from his puppet principality in Italy to Fuehrer Headquarters in East Prussia. Not only the secrecy but the precautions against assassination complicated the move. Routing the train and pilot engine to an exact rendezvous with the Fuehrer, across the lines of communication of the struggling Central Army Group, called for careful consideration.

So he was not too pleased when his office door opened and the Count came in. The Count was a lieutenant-general, and a lofty figure at the staff headquarters round the corner in the Bendlerstrasse, and he was a lifetime personal friend as well; the pleasure of seeing him nearly counterbalanced the irritation of being interrupted in his work. But it was possible that the Count had suggestions to make, or news to transmit, or orders to pass on, with an actual bearing on the problems in hand. The opening question seemed to indicate it.

'You have seen the new Fuehrer order?' asked the Count.

'Directive 112? Yes, I've seen it.'

'You're working on it now, I suppose,' said the Count.

'Yes,' said the Baron.

The Count turned to study one of the maps on the wall, so that when he spoke again his face was averted, which might account for a stilted hollowness of tone in what he said next.

'I see the Ninety-eighth Armoured comes under your orders.'

'Yes,' said the Baron.

The Ninety-eighth Armoured was a division that had been nearly destroyed in Russia during the spring, and had been brought home to Parchim to be reconstituted, re-equipped and remanned. It was almost ready for service now – Fuehrer Headquarters declared it quite ready and had detailed it for transfer to France.

'Are you routing it through Berlin?' asked the Count, still with his face averted.

'I haven't decided yet. But I don't expect so.'

Wittenberge would probably be a better route, although there was something to be said in favour of Berlin with the Hamburg network so badly crippled and all those ammunition trains heading east.

'I see old Keil is in command,' said the Count; he turned back from the map to face the Baron again.

'I didn't know that,' said the Baron. 'How is he?'

'Well enough,' answered the Count.

Keil was an old friend, too, dating back to the days of the Kriegsakademie.

'His wife's hair is red this year,' supplemented the Count, with a grin.

One half of the Count's face was less mobile than the other; the plastic surgeons had done amazingly good work after he had received that frightful shrapnel wound – there was no perceptible scarring, and they had given his face symmetry, but even their best efforts could not result in a completely natural appearance. There was something rather ghastly about his grin, which could hardly be due to the fact that they were talking about Wilhelmina Keil – Frau Generalleutnant Keil – whose amiable eccentricities were well known.

'What about Barbarossa?' asked the Count. 'They are under orders too?'

'Yes,' said the Baron.

'Fully equipped, I suppose? The cream of the new recruits? New Tiger tanks?'

'Of course,' answered the Baron.

Barbarossa was an SS armoured division, reconstituting itself in the same way as the Ninety-eighth; the SS nowadays managed to secure the best of everything available. With its headquarters at Nauen Barbarossa was within an easy day's march of Berlin.

'You'll be sending them first, then, I hope,' said the Count. 'Route them via Stendal. Give the old Ninety-eighth a chance.'

'The Tommies hit the railway bridge at Rathenow in the last raid. You ought to remember that,' said the Baron. 'Three more days before it'll carry any traffic.'

In ordinary circumstances it would be the natural route for the Barbarossa division travelling west from Nauen. As it was it would be more economical as well as quicker to send the Ninety-eighth ahead through the bottleneck.

'I'd forgotten that,' said the Count; it was remarkable how much concern he displayed over such a small detail as the relative times of arrival in action of the two divisions. 'The road bridge is still intact, though. Send Barbarossa by road as far as the river. It can entrain on the far side easily enough – all the ramps in the world in the sidings there.'

'That would be sensible,' said the Baron, 'but— You know as well as I do about the fuel situation.'

Coal and rolling stock might be in desperately short supply, but motor fuel and oil were scarcer still. No conscientious staff officer would move an armoured division by road when it was easily possible to move it by rail.

'Yes,' said the Count meditatively. That wound of his certainly gave the oddest expression to his face. Then came a burst of candour. 'You see, Baron, the first armour to arrive will undoubtedly go into Dietrich's corps. You know how old Keil stands with relation to Dietrich. Sepp will have him unstuck in two days – out of uniform, even, perhaps.'

SS General Sepp Dietrich was a hard man, and the Baron was vaguely aware of friction at some earlier period between Dietrich and Keil. It might be possible that Dietrich would take the opportunity of paying off an old score if he found Keil under his command. And Keil was, after all, one of the old army, while Dietrich was Dietrich.

'I see,' said the Baron.

'Send Barbarossa through first – Sepp will be glad to have only SS troops in his corps. Then Geyr von Schweppenburg will have Keil and the Ninety-eighth. Geyr and Keil are good friends.'

'I would like to,' said the Baron. 'It's a pity about the bridge.'

Even to do a good turn for Keil he could not issue orders that would mean wasting a whole day's fuel for an armoured division.

'Tommy's air force!' said the Count. 'Even Rommel couldn't escape them.'

'Rommel?' asked the Baron.

'Good God! Haven't you heard? They got Rommel in his car two hours ago – he's badly wounded; doubtful if he'll live. Didn't you know? Von Kluge is taking over personal command of Army Group B.'

'Rommel wounded!' said the Baron. The situation in the West might well be considered hopeless in that case. Rommel might have fought a good delaying action at least, but not fussy old von Kluge.

'You're so wrapped up in your damned trains,' said the Count, 'you have no thought for anything else. I don't believe you're human – I never have thought so. Even when we were young—'

'Rommel wounded!' repeated the Baron; his sick astonishment was proof that he was perfectly human. And yet as regards his personal duty it did not matter who was in command of Army Group B; what he had to do was to move the reinforcements earmarked by Fuehrer Headquarters into the sphere of command of the commander-in-chief west. Whether it was Rommel or von Kluge who handled them in action was none of his concern.

At this moment there was a distraction; Colonel Fink came into the room with a file.

'The Hamburg returns, sir,' he said, and then, after a glance at the Count, 'you've heard the news, sir?'

'About Rommel? Yes, I've heard it.'

The Baron was already fidgeting with the file. He had been waiting for it before completing his plans; Rommel wounded or Rommel in good health, those divisions had to be moved. And even though the news was disturbing, that logical brain of his was at work, adjusting time-tables one against another, and fretting because in the absence of the Hamburg data definite conclusions could not be reached. The Count had turned back to look at the map again.

'It's bad, sir,' said Fink, and it was quite an effort for the Baron to realize that Fink was still talking about Rommel's wound, so rapidly had his mind reverted to its own problems.

'Undoubtedly,' said the Baron. 'I'll be ready to give those orders in an hour, Colonel.'

'Very well, sir.'

Fink withdrew, and the Count turned to face the Baron again.

'You'll route Barbarossa via Stendal?' he asked.

'I don't see how I can,' replied the Baron, a little puzzled.

'Not even after the news?'

'I don't see how that affects it.'

The Count looked round the room with a hint of desperation; half his face revealed his emotion while the other half remained wooden. Then the Count looked round the room again; this time it was clear that he was not seeking inspiration but was making sure he would not be overheard. He came close to the desk and lowered his voice.

'Isn't this the time when we should try to save what is left?' he said in a low voice.

'If that were possible,' said the Baron, puzzled that the Count should make such a point regarding whether Keil should come under Sepp Dietrich's command or not, but also guarded because the Count was clearly being guarded as well.

The Count stepped back from the desk again; his monocle slipped from his eye – ever since his wound he had found difficulty in keeping it in place – and dangled by its ribbon. He replaced it carefully; seeing him do so was infectious like seeing someone else yawn, and the Baron put up his own hand to his own eyeglass, which was a mere rimless lens, devoid of ribbon or chain, fixed apparently permanently under his almost hairless eyebrow – people used to wonder if he slept with it in place. It occurred to the Baron that they might be two members of a secret society making the society's secret sign to each other, and then he realized that there was a tiny piece of truth in the idea, for the single eyeglass screwed into one eye was the almost exclusive prerogative of members of the nobility attached to the general staff – life would be hard for any bourgeois, at least until he reached the rank of full general, who ventured to wear a monocle. His brother officers would rend him with ridicule.

Fink came in again at this moment.

'Fuehrer Headquarters are coming on the wire, sir,' he said. 'The field-marshal will be through to you in three minutes.'

'Very well,' said the Baron.

'Then I'll leave,' said the Count.

The Baron rose and stood at attention, as was the due of an officer one grade higher than his own, even though he was a lifetime friend. Fink brought his heels together, and then, stiff as a ramrod, marched the two steps to the door to open it. The Count hesitated before he passed through.

'Remember what I said,' he said, and then he was gone.

The door had hardly closed before the telephone bell jangled, three times, abruptly, indicating that it was the left-hand desk telephone to be answered, the one on the direct wire to Rastenburg. The Baron picked up the receiver and announced himself. At the same time he nodded to Fink, who hastened to the auxiliary desk at the far end of the room and picked up the extension there, spreading his notebook to record the conversation for the Most Secret pages of the telephone log of the Railway Headquarters.

Keitel's hard metallic voice was clearly recognizable.

'The Fuehrer has decided to leave the Two Hundred and Second where it is,' said Keitel. 'But he will make the Four Hundred and Ninth available. All the other orders stand unchanged. Prepare the necessary routings – have you done so already?'

'Not yet, sir.'

'Then do so at once. Those divisions must be on the move tomorrow morning.'

'Yes, sir.'

'I shall want a full report,' went on Keitel. 'Stauffenberg is flying here on the 20th, the day after tomorrow. He can bring it with him. A full movement sheet and time-table. I want time to look through it before the Fuehrer Conference.'

'Yes, sir.'

'Staff officer, repeat those numbers.'

'Two–zero–two,' said Fink into his telephone, with the greatest care in his diction to eliminate all chance of mistake. 'Four–zero–nine.'

'Correct. Good-bye.'

Fink and the Baron replaced their telephones.

'I'll confirm the move-warnings, sir,' said Fink.

'Very well.'

Now the decision had to be made; that should be simple enough, for the Baron's mind had had some hours now in which to put all the data in place. Five minutes should suffice for him to decide everything – the substitution of the 409th from Rendsburg for the 202nd from Tondern actually simplified the problem. He might as well begin to dictate the directives at once. A few rapid sentences, and a hundred thousand men and nearly as many tons of equipment would begin to roll towards the West, cutting smoothly and cleanly without turbulence across the vast stream of drafts and munitions flowing daily to the East. But there was the Count's suggestion to be borne in mind. Or to be dismissed without further thought. No officer with a strict regard for his duty would contemplate using up a day's fuel just to preserve Keil from the attentions of Sepp Dietrich. The Baron had done little jobs often enough for those of his kind, but only when all the other circumstances had been in strict balance. When there was no concrete reason to prefer A to B the Baron had naturally decided in favour of A when there was a 'von' in front of A's name. Yet here there was a very concrete reason, and no friendship for Keil – not even that past but happy friendship with Wilhelmina Keil – could weigh against it. The strange thing was that the Count could even have thought it could, that he should have expended the time and trouble of making a personal appeal. He had really been urgent about it, quite pressing.

It could be done, of course. If he were to send Barbarossa by road across the river the keen minds of Fuehrer Headquarters – Keitel and Jodl – might dwell upon that clause in the orders for a moment, might spend one second questioning its advisability, but they would decide in the end – would decide at once – that the Baron could not be wrong; they would decide that his accurate judgment and weighing of all the pros and cons – whose significance they could not determine for themselves – must be relied upon. He could do it. He could move Keil through Berlin and Barbarossa through Stendal. Then – then – the Baron stirred uncomfortably in his chair. Then there would be a moment when there were no SS armoured troops, almost no SS troops at all, in the vicinity of Berlin, while Keil would be close at hand with the 98th Armoured. An interesting point. Very interesting indeed. That would be on the 20th of this month, the day after tomorrow. The 20th? The day after tomorrow? That was the day when Stauffenberg was to make his report at Fuehrer Headquarters. Stauffenberg! The Baron moved again in his chair. It was something more than the heat that made the palms of his hands wet so that he wiped them nervously on his handkerchief. Stauffenberg was of blue blood, like the Count. There were dozens of Stauffenbergs, all cousins – his own great-uncle had married into the family. But this was Claus Schenk von Stauffenberg, the fiery active member of the family, whose restless vigour had not even been curbed by the mutilations he had undergone after the explosion of a land mine in Africa. Stupid old Stieff had mentioned once Stauffenberg's restlessness and discontent as well as his ability. And then there was the link with that other group, those odd people who, descendants of the fighting heroes of previous wars, debated ethics or dogma or theories of government, barely existing under the strained toleration of the Fuehrer – Moltke and Yorek von Wartenburg and those others of famous names. There were ties of blood, of common discontent, between them and Stauffenberg, and through Stauffenberg

to the Count – and through the Count to Keil. He had heard that
Moltke had been arrested a short time ago. The tension must be
mounting to breaking point. So was it just coincidence that on the day
that Stauffenberg was due to report personally to the Fuehrer the Count
was trying to replace the SS troops in Berlin with an army division –
and an army division under Keil's command? Coincidence? The Baron's
hands were wet again. There were other discontented people in Berlin
at this moment. There were Beck and Witzleben, who had held the
highest positions in the army and had been retired. They still made
appearances at the Herrenklub and at the Ministry. Could it all be
coincidence? What was it the Count had said when he was leaving this
room a quarter of an hour ago? Something about 'trying to save what
was left.' Did that refer merely to trying to save the army from further
domination by the SS? The Count's expression, the Count's manner;
had they been quite normal? Yes? No?

The Baron, sitting solitary in his office, found himself confronted
with reality, more surely than if Death himself had stalked into the
room to stand before the desk with his bones gleaming in the sunshine.
Reality; the Baron was an office soldier, as his brief experience in the
field had proved. Those divisions that he moved about on his maps were
not assemblages of men, living men of flesh and blood, of lusts and
aspirations, of loves and hates and personal happiness and misery. They
were only 'divisions,' coloured pins on a map. When a division became
'battle-worn' that did not mean that ten thousand men had suffered
agony and death; it meant that a pin of another colour had to be stuck
into the map instead. The Baron had drifted entirely out of touch with
reality; perhaps that had been an advantage during his tenure of the
railway command. His remarkable mental powers had done nothing to
keep him in the world of reality; actually they had acted the other way
even when Stalingrad was lost, even when El Alamein was fought. But
now he was face to face with reality again, reality so intense that he had
to wipe the sweat from his hands and then from the hairless folds at the
back of his neck. Death, agonizing and humiliating, might be awaiting
him; the Baron had no illusions about the fate which an infuriated and
frightened Fuehrer would deal out to anyone involved in a conspiracy
against his rule. He had to decide what to do, and he had to decide
quickly – Fink was waiting in the other room for his orders. If he
brought Keil's division down to Berlin he would be making a contri-
bution to the success of the conspiracy – if there *were* a conspiracy. But
the conspiracy still might not succeed. In that case there would be the
strictest investigation, and his motives for ordering that particular move
would never withstand Himmler's pitiless analysis.

It would be safer to issue normal orders. Safer – yes, certainly, for
should the conspiracy succeed, should the régime be overthrown, he

could always say that it had never occurred to him that the Count had any special motive in making that request regarding Keil. Yet if he brought Keil down to Berlin the presence of the 98th Armoured might make the difference between failure and success for the conspiracy. The SS police would not dare move in that case, or if they did the 98th would exterminate them. The SS would be exterminated whether they moved or not; the streets of Berlin would run with blood – the Baron faced reality again.

If there were a conspiracy blood would run in rivers, in rivers if the conspiracy succeeded and in rivers if it failed. And some of it might be his own blood. Lives were at stake, perhaps including his own. Not lives represented by numbers written on a casualty return, either. The lives of the Satanic Fuehrer in the Rastenburg headquarters, of Keitel of the metallic voice, of Jodl and Himmler and Goebbels; those lives on the one hand, and on the other the lives of the Count, of Stauffenberg, of Beck and Witzleben, his friends. And his own life too; it was strange how difficult it was to make that fine brain of his really think about that matter. The Baron forced himself to imagine himself being led before a firing squad; he forced himself to think of a sudden pistol bullet into his stomach which would leave him writhing on the ground in agony. He simply could not bear to think of such things.

The thought of something happening that would bring the present régime to an end stirred even the mentally insulated Baron to the depths; it roused every emotion. Not only did it set his mind working fast, but it worked upon his bulky and lethargic body. He felt a quickening of his heartbeat and his respiration; he crossed and uncrossed his legs repeatedly, fidgeting in his chair. The thought was hideously attractive like some female vampire of old legend. To end the agony through which Germany was passing; to save the army – the most vital institution of all Germany – not only from the Russians and British and Americans but from the Fuehrer and his minions; that was something to be longed for with all the passion of which the Baron was capable. But the danger was terrifying. Even to think of that demoniac personality at Fuehrer Headquarters made a man shudder. Inhuman, merciless – and cunning; facile in every shift and subterfuge, suspicious, savage; who would dare even to cross his path, let alone rouse him to the paroxysm of insane rage that would be the inevitable result of a move counter to his ideals, threatening his authority, imperilling his life? Torture and death would be the fate of everyone involved, and for everyone related by blood to them. That was something no one could face. His mind shrank away from such thoughts, just as it shrank away from the unhappy memory of his divisional command in Poland.

Save for that dreadful episode his life during Germany's agony had strangely been a satisfactory one; as military administrator of railways he had been doing a difficult job well, better than anyone else could have done it. His active logical mind had always been fully employed, and the moments of weariness had been made happy by the knowledge that he had made no mistakes, had wasted nothing, had kept his head clear in face of a myriad complications. Now he was like a chess master looking up from a study of the board to see that the spectators were drawing daggers.

The door opened to admit Fink.

'The orders, sir?' asked Fink.

'Oh, God!' said the Baron. There were drops of sweat on his face which he mopped off.

Fink glanced just sufficiently obviously at his wristwatch to remind his chief of the passage of time.

'Very well then,' said the Baron, desperately. 'I'll dictate them now.'

On the afternoon of July 20th the Baron was at his desk as usual. It was an even hotter, more stifling day. His eyes were on the clock in the wall; he was looking at it as though mesmerized. The two hands were together, indistinguishable. It was an instant's calculation for his mind to work out that in that case it must be sixteen point four minutes past three o'clock. But the hands seemed to be not merely indistinguishable; they seemed to be inseparable. The minute hand did not seem to move, so slowly the seconds were passing. The Fuehrer conference was usually over by two o'clock. By two-thirty on most days or by three at the latest, he received his telephone call from headquarters. Keitel or Jodl or one of the junior staff officers at O.K.W. would transmit him his orders, telling him of the Fuehrer's decisions as far as they concerned him.

The wide strategic gestures the Fuehrer had made on the map were translated to the Baron in the form of directives, and he had to translate those into logistic terms – one careless sweep of the Fuehrer's pencil might mean reversing the direction of travel of two hundred trains. It was hardly ever later than three o'clock that the first call would come through, and now it was sixteen point four minutes past three – no, he could call it seventeen minutes past three now. Had Stauffenberg succeeded in whatever it was he had planned – if he had planned anything at all? The Baron's hand went out to the telephone, and then he drew it back again. He could not trust himself; he did not know what to say over the telephone that would not commit him one way or the other. To telephone might imply a guilty foreknowledge, but not to telephone might imply exactly the same. How hot it was! His clothes were sticking to him. Now it was half-past three; he would wait until a quarter to four, and then he would telephone.

Here was Fink, agitated and excited; his hurried entrance started the Baron's heart pounding wildly. Fink hardly gave himself time to clock his heels.

'If you please, sir—'

'Y-yes?'

'The Home Army has been alerted for immediate duty.'

Then something had certainly happened.

'By whose orders?' The Baron hoped his voice did not quaver.

'Orders of the Commander-in-Chief, Home Army.'

'You are sure of this?'

'I put a query through to the Bendlerstrasse, sir,' said Fink. 'The reply was: "All orders of the Commander-in-Chief, Home Army, are to be obeyed." '

'Who did you speak to?'

'Colonel von Stauffenberg, sir.'

Stauffenberg! Back from Fuehrer Headquarters?

'You're sure it was he?'

'Oh, yes, sir. I knew his voice.'

'If those are the orders from the Bendlerstrasse then they must be obeyed,' said the Baron at length.

'The Bendlerstrasse' was the universal term for the General Staff Headquarters, an eighth of a mile away from the Railway Headquarters. It was the source of all military authority in the absence of orders from the Fuehrer and O.K.W.

A knock at the door made both men jump. It was a junior officer, one of Fink's assistants, not privileged to enter without knocking.

'Fuehrer Headquarters coming through on the wire, sir!' he said.

The Baron grabbed for the telephone; the receiver beat against his ear with the shaking of his hand. Fink took up the extension telephone.

'Who is that?' said the earpiece instantly, in the hard unmistakable voice of Keitel. The Baron announced himself.

'This is Keitel. You know my voice?'

'Yes, sir.'

'You are to obey no orders from the Bendlerstrasse. None. You understand? None. And no orders from the Commander-in-Chief, Home Army, either. Understand?'

Y-yes, sir. If you please, what has happened?'

'Nothing serious. You are to disregard all orders that do not emanate from me personally.'

'Yes, sir.'

The telephone went dead instantly, leaving the Baron and Fink staring at each other, the instruments still in their hands.

'I don't understand, sir,' said Fink. 'Shall I get through to the Bendlerstrasse?'

'No. Yes. No.'

It was an incredibly serious matter to be told to disregard orders; an army that did so would fall into chaos, would melt into a formless mass like a wax figure in a furnace. Keitel was the direct representative of the Fuehrer; but the Bendlerstrasse was the direct representative of the army.

That knock at the door again; the junior officer reappeared.

'The Bendlerstrasse on the telephone, sir.'

'Who is it speaking?'

'Count von Stauffenberg, sir.'

'Very well.'

There could be no harm in answering the telephone; that did not necessitate obeying any orders that might come through on it from the Chief of Staff of the Home Army. The Baron and Fink picked up the instruments from their desks, and the Baron announced himself.

'Good afternoon, Baron,' said the telephone. It was Stauffenberg's voice, of normal pitch and modulation – perhaps there was a touch of light-heartedness in it, as there often was. 'No order from Fuehrer Headquarters is authentic. You are not to obey any such order.'

'I – I do not understand.'

'Field-Marshal von Witzleben is now in command. The Reich is in danger and the army has its duty to do.'

Witzleben! All possible doubt as to the existence of a crisis disappeared with that name. If there were such a thing as an opposition to the Fuehrer, von Witzleben would be at least the titular head of it. The mention of the name introduced another complication; Witzleben as field-marshal was senior to Keitel. If any military precept applied in the present situation, a soldier would obey von Witzleben rather than Keitel.

'Did you hear what I said, Baron?' asked von Stauffenberg's voice, as airily as ever.

'I heard,' said the Baron.

'Quite likely you will receive contradictory orders from Keitel,' went on Stauffenberg's voice. 'Field-Marshal Keitel has no authority. Is that quite clear, Baron?'

'Not – not quite.'

'It is a clear, definite order. You are to pay no attention to anything Keitel says. Lakaitel's day is over. So cheer up. Good-bye.'

The telephone went dead. If it were really true that the day of Lakaitel – the Lackey General – were over the army would rejoice. But clearly there was a clash in progress between the two forces, a clash that could only end in the death of every single supporter of the losing side. And it was impossible to guess from the data at present available which side would be the losing side. The Baron went back through his memory over his actions up to the present, and felt a momentary relief at deciding they had been entirely correct. But the Fuehrer was merciless – a creature without pity, with no more thought for his victims than a tiger. But Stauffenberg of the airy voice; he would be merciless too. That light manner concealed a will of steel and an unrelenting determination. The Baron thought of firing squads and torture chambers.

Then he recovered himself with the realization that Fink was still staring at him. The play of emotion over his face must have been quite obvious.

'Very well, Colonel,' he said, making every effort to speak with the polite curtness he always had employed towards his deputy.

Alone once more the Baron could mop his face again, with the handkerchief that was more than damp. The heat was dreadful. So was the strain. And time had fled by on wings; now it was past five o'clock on a glaring, brassy evening.

The telephone buzzed on his desk, and he picked it up.

'Major Schimpf is asking for orders, sir,' said Fink's voice.

'Who is he?'

'Chief of Staff to General Keil, sir.'

Keil of the 98th Armoured, the division which the Count had asked him to route through Berlin today.

'What does he want?' asked the Baron, desperately.

'You had better speak to him yourself, sir,' said Fink; he bleated the helpless reply like an old sheep. Yet even though he bleated, he acted; there was a click as the connection was transferred before the Baron could say more.

'What is it, Schimpf?' demanded the Baron as brusquely as he could manage.

'I am asking for confirmation of my orders, sir,' said a voice in the well-trained accent of the general staff.

'What are they?'

'They re-route the division via Berlin, sir.'

'Where are you?'

'Wittenberge, sir. The general and I arrived by road and found these orders awaiting us by teletype.'

'Where's your division?'

'The first train is due in half an hour.'

'And who signs these orders?'

'Chief of Staff, Home Army, sir.'

'Ah!' The Baron tried to make the monosyllable completely expressionless.

'It's a clear-the-road order,' said Schimpf. 'First priority.'

That order if obeyed would bring the first echelon of the 98th into Berlin two hours from leaving Wittenberge. The whole division could be detrained and ready for action in the city – unless an allied air raid imposed delay – before midnight. And only a few minutes ago the Baron had been congratulating himself that so far all his actions had been strictly correct. Now he was faced with the immediate necessity of taking sides, and Fink was listening on the extension. No! It was not quite an immediate necessity.

'Your first train due in half an hour, you say?'

'Yes, sir.'

'I'll confirm or countermand those orders within that time,' said the Baron, trying to pick his words with all the care he could. 'Telephone again five minutes before your first train is due.'

'But, sir! The priority—'

'That will do, Schimpf,' said the Baron, harshly, putting down the receiver.

The existence of a clear-the-road order between Wittenberge and Berlin would play havoc with the orderly flow of traffic. If it were going to be countermanded it should be done at once. Yet— what was he to say in twenty-five minutes from now?

The door opened to the sound of music. Light dance music! Fink was carrying in a portable radio.

'An announcement, sir,' he said. 'The Minister – Goebbels himself.'

'Very well.'

Fink put the instrument down on the desk, and the two of them looked at it as it ground out the frivolous tune; it might have been a ticking bomb. The reddening sunlight was pouring in through the windows. The music stopped in the middle of a bar, and an expressionless voice announced the Minister for Public Enlightenment. There was no mistaking Goebbels' voice following immediately after, that excellent speaking voice, impassioned or sarcastic, serious or sad at will. He wasted no time in getting to the heart of the matter.

'An attempt has been made on the life of our Fuehrer. He was very slightly injured, although several of his personal staff were killed or mortally wounded. His slight injury has in no way interrupted his performance of his onerous duties, and he is at present in conference with Il Duce, Signor Mussolini, our devoted ally, who arrived at Fuehrer Headquarters immediately after the dastardly attempt. The Fuehrer will address his devoted people over the radio tonight at midnight, when we will all be able to listen to his beloved voice and will be able to renew our vows of eternal allegiance to Fuehrer, People, and Reich. Our hearts go out to him in this solemn moment when we know that Providence has guarded him from a great danger, and we can rejoice to know that the dastardly attempt was the work only of a small group of disloyal officers of the general staff, seduced from their allegiance by international Jewry. Now there can be an end to the rumours which the

Jewish agents are circulating. We can all remain tranquil and loyal, paying no attention to any further attempts by international Jewry to disturb our peace and our allegiance, while we wait to hear that voice which we all know and love. We can all say, deep in our hearts, "Heil Hitler! Sieg Heil! Sieg Heil!" '

The blare of a band bursting into the *Horst Wessel* song followed instantly on Goebbels' last words, and the Baron and Fink were left, as so often before, looking at each other. Neither dared say a word, but the Baron's brain was hard at work. Undoubtedly that was Goebbels' voice. But if the Fuehrer were dead or under arrest Goebbels would be saying just the same things, playing for time while the Nazis gathered their forces to strike back at the army; it might be significant that the Fuehrer was delaying his broadcast until midnight, but then it might not. With Mussolini on his hands and with the most important speech of his life to prepare Hitler might well need time. Only one thing was certain, and that was that the Nazis still had possession of the broadcasting station; even that might be significant or it might not. Thank God he still had not committed himself, although – he looked at the clock – the minutes were now flying by.

The radio was still blaring, and suddenly through its din another noise was to be heard, a rumbling and roaring down below in the street which until now had been so quiet. The Baron hurried to the window; Fink snapped off the radio and followed him. A long column of trucks and lorries was rolling along the street towards the Bendlerstrasse; looking down on to each the Baron saw steel helmets, packed close together; the trucks were full of troops. At the machine guns mounted over the cabs and pointing out from behind were soldiers, braced and ready to fire. Soldiers! Not police, not SS, but soldiers!

'Wachtbataillon Grossdeutchland,' said Fink, reading the badges.

'Brought in from Doeberitz, then,' said the Baron.

It was one of the best of the battalions of guards, but the Baron had no knowledge as to who was its commanding officer. It occurred to him at that moment that if he had fallen in with the Count's suggestion it would not be one battalion in trucks, but Keil's whole division in tanks that would now be rumbling down the street. If – he looked at the clock again – in ten minutes' time he confirmed the Home Army's orders Keil would be here by midnight. It was desperately important to know if the battalion was acting under the orders of a living Hitler, or of a Goebbels fighting for his life with Hitler dead, or of von Witzleben the self-appointed commander-in-chief. Torture chambers and firing parties. The last truck of the column had vanished from sight now, round the corner to the Bendlerstrasse and all was deathly quiet again. Time was passing. Torture chambers and firing parties! And then, clear and loud through the sultry stillness, came the sound of a volley, rifle fire, half a dozen rifles fired not quite at the same moment. That was a firing squad, an execution, in the Bendlerstrasse. The Baron started to look over at Fink and then changed his mind, he could not trust himself to meet anyone's eyes, and he looked at the ceiling instead. Now another volley. The sweat inside the Baron's shirt was icy cold. It was hard to think. Who was shooting whom? Was von Witzleben making an example of officers who had not come over wholeheartedly to his side? Another volley. Who had died then? Some SS spy or some friend on the general staff? God, another volley! There was a massacre going on.

A massacre! That settled it. Von Witzleben would not order a massacre in the Bendlerstrasse. If von Witzleben were in power there might well be a massacre at Goebbels' house in the Hermann Goeringstrasse, or at the Gestapo Headquarters in the Prinz Albrechtstrasse, but not here. There was another volley, and another. Victims must be being dragged in rapid succession before the firing squads. Loud, shattering reports, announcing to the waiting city that order was being restored. There could be no doubt about it. Thank God he had not committed himself on the wrong side. Time was just up.

'Colonel Fink!'

'Sir!' Fink's heels came together with a click, his hands at the seams of his trousers.

'Telephone immediately to Fuehrer Headquarters. Tell them that the Ninety-eighth Armoured is entrained at Wittenberge ready for immediate transfer to Berlin if they think it necessary.'

'Very well, sir.'

Now the Baron could meet Fink's eyes with a steady glance. But as Fink put out his hand to open the door it opened to admit three SS officers, pistols in their hands.

'You are under arrest,' said the leader, and the Baron submitted to arrest with an easy mind; it would not take long to clear himself.

'And why did you plot with the Count?' asked the Gestapo officer for the twentieth time.

'I did not! I did not!' said the Baron. 'I swear it!'

The Gestapo officer nodded to one of his assistants, who opened the door of the cell and gave an order. Two hard-faced young men came in, dragging between them a wreck of a man, shrinking yet helpless. It was hard to recognize him as Fink. The two hard-faced young men propped him up between them, to face the Baron and the Gestapo officer.

'Did the Count come to call on the Baron in his office on the 18th?' asked the latter.

'Yes – oh, yes!' said Fink.

'You saw them together?'

'Yes!'

INDECISION

'Did they look like conspirators? Did they?'

'Yes!'

'You interrupted them conspiring?'

'Yes!'

Fink had come in to find them both adjusting their monocles – oh, God! The Baron remembered thinking that it might well have been a secret sign.

'Did the Count say anything as he left?'

'Yes!'

'What was it?'

Fink's pale grey eyes could not focus; they seemed to be unseeing as they passed over the Baron's face.

'What was it?'

'He said – he said— "Remember what I said," he said!'

'Now, Baron, what was it the Count had said?'

'But I didn't do it! I didn't do it! You can look at the orders.'

'What was it he asked you to do?'

The Count was dead, shot in the courtyard at the Bendlerstrasse. He could not be hurt further, not like the Baron. The Baron told, spluttering about the Count's request to route the 98th Armoured through Berlin.

'But I didn't do it. You can tell I didn't do it! I routed them through Wittenberge.'

'So? Did it not occur to you, Baron, that one telephone call to Fuehrer Headquarters, or to Gestapo Headquarters here, would have nipped the conspiracy in the bud? Was it not your duty to make that call?'

The Baron swallowed hard. To his credit it simply had not occurred to him that he might have betrayed his friends. Surprise delayed his answer, which should have been pat enough.

'But that wasn't the reason I was asked. It was because—'

The Baron rambled on explaining the personal relationships between Keil and Sepp Dietrich and Geyr von Schweppenburg.

'Send a message to France to have General Keil arrested wherever he is, at the front or anywhere else,' said the Gestapo officer to an assistant, and then he turned back to the Baron. 'Now why did you hesitate before you answered my question, Baron?'

The questioning went on. All the pettinesses, all the shiftinesses, were revealed. Schimpf had telephoned from Wittenberge. Why had he not instantly been told that all orders from the Bendlerstrasse had been countermanded by Fuehrer Headquarters? Why that delay? Why? Why? Why? And Stauffenberg, the man who had tried to blow up the Fuehrer, the man who had flown back to rouse Berlin to rebellion, was a cousin of the Baron's. Was that not so?

'No!'

The Gestapo officer referred to a notebook.

'There was a marriage in 1878,' he said, 'between a Countess von Stauffenberg and—'

That was the Baron's great-uncle.

'I never thought about that for one moment,' said the Baron.

No? And what about the Baron's membership in the Herrenklub? And what about—? The true and the partly true and the false, the relevant and the irrelevant – the latter strangely transmuted into matters of great importance – all were worked in together.

'No need for further questioning,' said the Gestapo officer at length, in a patronizing tone. All his contempt for blue blood, for great mental powers, was evident in his words. These pitiful gentlemen of the general staff who could not construct a watertight conspiracy!'

'You will appear before the Court of Honour tomorrow,' said the Gestapo officer, and the Baron looked at him stupidly. His emotions were all exhausted now. There was nothing left in him. And yet his mind was still ticking over slowly. The Court of Honour would cast him out of the army, so that the People's Court that would follow would not suffer the pain of finding an army officer guilty of treason. The People's Court – a blaring judge, a jeering prosecution, an inevitable sentence, and then a slow hanging. He could have made that telephone call and betrayed his friends, or he could have brought the 98th Armoured up to Berlin; but he had done neither.

Thomas Gilchrist

Daylight

As he dressed quickly but without hurry in response to the Second Mate's phone call, he glanced again at the incredible letter on his desk. He did not have to read it again. As if with a hammer-blow, it had been impressed indelibly upon his mind.

It had left all other action in a state of suspense, as if the war itself had ceased to be. It had left him with the conviction that his voyage was no longer important; that his first command was unimportant; that whether he returned or failed to return was of even less consequence.

For it seemed he had nothing left to return to. *She* had gone war-happy and had thrown him over for a soldier. A soldier, mind you! A Staff Captain. A chocolate soldier, he had called him once, with his thin moustache and his display of jungle knives and assorted revolvers and nothing but a pen to wield for the duration.

And now he was in convoy. Off Jap-held New Guinea, too. He was almost unconsciously clawing his way to the bridge through darkness and rain . . .

He remembered too keenly her elbow dimples, the sea-blue of her eyes; the light wrestling matches when she had the mood of a tomboy; the anxious kisses that followed when he hurt her a little bit; her . . .

He reached the bridge. He could feel the cool rain, but it was too hot for an oilskin. He fingered the wet rail and his eyes were already ahead. And he couldn't see a thing – not even the Second Mate alongside him.

'We seemed to be west of the convoy,' he heard the Second Mate say, a nervous tremor in his voice, 'so I hauled her over to starboard. She's back on her course now – three-fifty. Okay, sir?'

'Three-fifty?' he queried. 'But we were scheduled to alter to three-seventeen at 2 am.'

'Yes, sir,' the Second Mate said vaguely. 'That's why I called you. No execution orders from the escort. We're in position, though – I think.'

His position was 12 in the second column of a five-column convoy. He was one of two Army Transports. The rest were seventy-five landing craft of all shapes and tonnage, escorted by destroyers and PTs. A complete army division was afloat with him; and several thousand trucks, tanks and 'ducks', not to mention bombs, high explosive and perhaps a million gallons of 100-octane aviation spirit, half of which was right under his feet. He had a date with the carriers and cruisers for a landing operation in New Guinea.

He became aware of the Second Mate's voice again. 'We're okay, though,' he was saying. 'The one we're following is just on the starboard bow. See him?'

'Nope,' he told him, 'I can't. Is it the LST towing the little feller?'

'Yes, sir. You can see his wake, all right – just faintly luminous. Just there.'

'My eyes aren't used to the dark yet,' he murmured.

He could see the Second Mate now – or, rather, his face, as if it had no body. It was too dark to read his expression, but he sensed that the other was merely persuading himself.

The dark outline of the ship began to take shape: the foremast, fo'c'sle head, the Bofors 40 pointing hungrily skyward; the gun turrets over each wing of the bridge. And he became conscious of the shadows that were lookoutmen, gunners, a signalman.

Shadows. His world was darkly peopled by treacherous friends, a beautiful – cobra. And he couldn't get away from it. It held him in bondage. He could well imagine her as she wrote that letter, a hurt look in her eyes, pleading . . . she still thought an awful lot of him, she'd said . . . would be happier if only he weren't hurt too much . . . nice of her . . . nice of her indeed.

He stepped over to the wing of the bridge as if a change of position would change his thoughts. The sea murmured along the hull. The wind sighed in his face. His shirt and pants clung soddenly to his skin and a little, cool trickle navigated his spine on a southerly course.

The Second Mate was still chattering. 'It's been raining like hell, but it's clearing now. See the barge now, sir? The LST? You can hear her engines chugging.'

He turned his head to get the wind abaft his right ear. Yes, he could hear that. Which was something. That LST was phutt-phutting all day yesterday and up to the time he went to bed. He could see, at last, the faint luminosity that could be her wake.

'She's too close,' he said. 'Reduce ten revs.'

'Aye, aye, sir!'

He trained his binoculars. No good. The wind had risen again, the rain was slanting, the lenses were wet. There was nothing but black, ragged cloud and he could only hazard a guess at the horizon level. He could see nothing much better with the naked eye. The friendly phutt-phutting was dying out.

After a while the visibility improved a little.

'All right,' he told the Second Mate. 'I can see her now.'

There was a little black smudge just about ahead. But for reassurance he squelched over to the starboard wing.

'Can you see that craft fine on the starboard bow?' he asked a lookoutman.

'Yes – I think I can, sir.'

'Oh – you *think* you can. Can you hear her chugging?'

'I believe I can, sir. It's very faint.'

He sighed. I *think*. I *believe*. He was a little indignant. He walked back.

'We'd better keep within earshot, anyway,' he told the Second Mate. 'Phone the engine room – up fifteen revs.'

'Aye, aye, sir!'

'Keeping a steady course, helmsman?'

'Right on three-fifty all the time, sir.'

'Good.'

He glanced over his shoulder. The helmsman was invisible in his armour-plated wheelhouse. The visor over the thin slit hid even the faint glow from the binnacle.

And so everything was fine, he told himself. If we're all watching the guy ahead we can't go wrong. Soon his pupils would open wider and he'd be able to see some more of the convoy. A pity those landing craft weren't bigger, though. A big ship convoy is comparatively simple . . . A blue light would help but, of course, in enemy waters, with the Japs on the beaches just to the south'ard . . .

She was fond of the beach, he remembered. In fact, as soon as he would return from a trip she'd drag him right back to the sea for a swim. Bondi Beach. She would always take a teasing on that. And then there was her morning greeting, once: 'What will you have for breakfast, darling? We've only *got* eggs!' He'd smiled for a couple of years over that. And then he remembered the party and the chocolate soldier who'd become his 'friend' . . .

He became aware of another squall. He couldn't dodge behind the weather plate because he had to listen – to listen for other craft. His eyeballs took a drumming from the fingers of rain. It hissed malevolently on the sea. His pants flapped wetly in protest and the little trickle on his spine became a stream.

He wouldn't hear that chugging now, and he wouldn't see anything till it hit him. And he was acutely aware of what that would do to his bombs, high explosive and aviation spirit. He could practically see and hear the hot, screaming metal, and then—

'Down ten revs,' he ordered without alarm. Actually, he was not even greatly concerned, he assured himself. What the hell did it matter, anyway?

Presently the weather cleared somewhat. But he was still navigating through a chimney. He heard six bells strike. From the flying bridge he heard some footsteps, loud in the stillness, and then a gunner report:

'Two craft on the port bow, sir!'

'Fine,' he said with a sense of relief. That was exactly where they should be – part of the first column. He tried his binoculars again. He tried to dry them with a wet handkerchief. He gave up. But it was part of a good master's job to know when to check with other people's natural faculties. He was nearly content, though there were still only ragged, different shades of black aloft and alow and he couldn't distinguish substance from shadow . . .

Substance and shadow. 'It was so easy,' she'd said. So easy. Sure it was easy when a man had to go to sea for a living – and for hers. Well, maybe the soldier was a friend, at that. It was his grief now . . . But philosophy was easy enough to peddle, hopeless to acquire. If only . . .

He took a turn across the bridge; eased the sodden cap from his brow. A lookoutman was alongside him.

'I think that feller is abeam now, sir,' he heard him say.

'Which feller?'

'The one that was chugging, sir. He sounds abeam.'

He studied the blackness to starboard. He cocked his ear. The Second Mate was beside him now.

'Can you see that craft abeam?' he asked him.

The Second Mate looked; listened.

'Certainly *sounds* like her,' he said at last.

Humph! Overtaking her already? He knew there was something wrong . . . His revs. What had he done with his revs?

'Down ten,' he said. 'God knows what those other fellows are doing. Backing and filling . . . Port half-a-port, helmsman! Either she's out of line or we are.'

He felt for a cigarette but remembered he couldn't smoke until daylight. Anyway, his fingers encountered only a mushy pack. He hauled it out and threw it overboard.

'The Liberty ship's on the starboard quarter, sir!' a gunner shouted.

He wasn't concerned about her. He wished to God they were all Libertys in the convoy. He'd have stood a chance of seeing them.

'She's okay,' he said.

'There's the Liberty again!' the Second Mate yelled. 'Close-to on the starboard quarter, sir! See her?'

'Yes, yes,' he lied impatiently. 'And to hell with the Liberty and the starboard quarter and anything else abaft the beam,' he told him evenly. 'I'm interested in what's *before* the beam. Understand?'

'Very good, sir,' the Second Mate conceded.

But he'd noted the urgency, the alarm, in the other's voice, and on second thoughts he believed he'd better take a look at this Liberty they were all yelling about. Having said what he'd said, however, he waited at least twenty seconds before he squelched over to the starboard side.

And he saw a black mountain deliberately and ferociously bearing down upon him. A fleeting indignation ripped him; a deep resentment.

'Up twenty revs – twenty-five!' he shouted. 'Hard-a-starboard your wheel! . . . Are the fools blind?' he wanted to know.

No more so than a husband can be – blind fool that you are, yourself. A real husband . . .

Anxiously, he watched alternately ahead and astern. He'd either hit something ahead or be clouted from astern – or, more than likely, be rammed from either side.

'Steady your helm!'

Presently the mountain merged into the outer darkness and there was nothing again. It had been a close shave, but it made him feel better, somehow. He put the ship back on her normal course and speed. But he'd lost the bearing of the friendly phutt-phutt; or could he still hear it – abaft the beam now? Yes, quite distinctly, he thought.

After a while he settled down again. It was nearly 4 am. It would be dawn soon. There was just a trace of it to starboard. He knew it would be a late dawn on account of the weather. But then he would smoke and tell himself what a nut he was to imagine the whole convoy was jostling him just because it was dark and squally. He would find the other craft exactly as they were; one column to port, the line ahead, three columns to starboard and the fussy destroyers and cheeky little PTs all about.

In anticipation, he sent the boy down to make coffee and bring up a fresh packet of smokes.

Presently came the dawn. Once the day broke it came quickly. He wiped his binoculars and tried them again. There wasn't much light yet, but he could see quite distinctly the craft ahead. Which was most reassuring. Oh, yes. And now the world became a dirty grey. He was still watching the ship ahead and his eyes were growing rounder.

'Destroyer ahead, Captain!'

He recognized the voice of the Naval Ensign from the flying bridge.

'Yes,' he agreed. 'Laying across our bows, too! I guess he'll have something to say.'

'I expect so, sir. "Flags" is standing by.'

'Okay.'

The destroyer's blinker was winking now. The sending was a bit fast, but he thought he got the word 'rejoice' . . . Rejoice? No . . .

The winking stopped and the destroyer flounced around like a saucy damsel, cutting the water disdainfully. The Ensign looked over, smiling queerly.

'He says, Captain; *follow me to rejoin convoy.* The destroyer says,' he explained apologetically.

So. It was nearly daylight. He looked around and abaft the beam for the phutt-phutting LST. She wasn't there, but the phutt-phutt was. And it was what he had vaguely suspected all along – the phutt-phutt of the fan belt in his own engine room. He looked astern, he looked on both beams and then he raised his binoculars and revolved slowly, sweeping the horizon.

It was ten miles to any point on the horizon. And there wasn't another ship in sight; hadn't been, obviously, since he'd been called to the bridge.

So, as a concession to tradition, he blamed the Second Mate for losing the convoy and told him to follow the Navy. Then he lit a cigarette and descended to his cabin. And an odd sense of serenity was stealing over him, a new awareness of the preposterous claims of night, the distorted and crazily multiple shadows of one chocolate soldier; the significance of a new dawn.

He was smiling thoughtfully and there was a gentle sort of anticipatory stirring in his heart when he hauled the pad across his desk and wrote:

Dear Norma, You may go to hell. It is daylight.

Noël Coward

A Richer Dust

'—There shall be
In that rich earth a richer dust concealed;
A dust whom England bore, shaped, made aware,
Gave, once, her flowers to love, her ways to roam,
A body of England's, breathing English air,
Washed by the rivers, blest by suns of home.

Rupert Brooke

CHAPTER I

SIDNEY'S letter arrived on 12 May 1941, and Joe brought it down to the pool. Lenore was at the bar mixing two tomato-juice cocktails with an extra dash of Worcester sauce, as they both felt a bit liverish after Shirley's party and had made a mutual pact not to touch any hard liquor before sundown. Joe came shuffling down the white steps and Morgan felt irritated before he even saw the letter; the scraping of Joe's shoes set his teeth on edge; he snatched the letter from Joe's hand, recognized the handwriting and felt more irritable than ever. Joe went off again up the steps, still shuffling his feet. Morgan dried his hands on the corner of the towel and opened the letter, and when Lenore came out with the cocktails he had read it and was gazing out over the Beverly Hills to the sea with an expression of set exasperation. Lenore noted the expression and placed the tomato-juice gently beside him, then she sat down herself on the edge of the diving-board and rummaged in her bathing bag for her sunglasses. She was aware that she probably felt a bit better than he did because she had quite shamelessly cheated while mixing the tomato-juice and given herself a shot of rye; her stomach felt smoother and the sensation of nausea and dizziness which had been plaguing her all the morning had passed away.

Morgan continued to gaze out into the blue distance in silence. Lenore contemplated for an instant making a little joke such as – 'Cut – the scene stinks anyway!' or 'Is there anything wrong with the sound?' but thought better of it and kept quiet. She rubbed her sun-glasses with her handkerchief and put them on. The world immediately became cooler and less harsh; the sky took on a pinky glow and the light on the hills softened. Morgan's body looked even more tanned than it actually was; he never went very dark, just an even golden brown. It was certainly a fine body, long legs, strongly-developed chest tapering to a perfect waistline, hardly any hips and no bottom to speak of. She gave a little sigh and wistfully regretted that they had had a tumble that morning on waking – those 'over-in-a-flash' hangover tumbles were never really satisfactory, it would have been much more sensible to have saved it for later, now, for instance, in the hot sun. Obeying an overwhelming impulse she slid her hand along his thigh. Even as she did it she knew it was a mistake; he jumped violently, and said in a tone of bored petulance, 'Lay off me for one minute, can't you.' Discouraged, she withdrew her hand as requested, muttered, 'Pardon me for living,' and took a swig of tomato juice which brought tears to her eyes owing to the sharpness of the Worcester sauce. Morgan, his mood of retrospection shattered, gave a disagreeable grunt and went off into the change room to have a shower. Lenore picked up the letter. The handwriting was neat and clear, and the address at the top was H.M.S. *Tagus*, c/o G.P.O. London. It started 'Dear Les' – she smiled at this, he hated being called Les and very few people in Hollywood knew that it was his name. She turned the page over and saw that it was signed – 'Your affectionate brother, Sid'. Then, still smiling, she read it through.

DEAR LES,

I expect you'll be surprised to hear from me after so long, but I've been at sea now for several months. You'll see where I am by the postmark and we're moving along in your direction in a few days time all being well. So expect me when you see me and hang out the holly and get the old calf fatted up because I shall probably get forty-eight hours leave. Mum and Dad and Sheila were all well when last heard from. One of my mates wants to meet some film lovelies in the following order – Betty Grable, Loretta Young, Paulette Goddard and Marlene Dietrich, failing these he doesn't mind settling for Shirley Temple at a pinch as he likes them young. I just want to see you and a nice big steak, done medium, with chips.

Your affectionate brother
SID.

In the change room Morgan had a shower and dried himself with grim efficiency; he then emptied some toilet water, tactfully labelled 'For Men Only', into the palms of his hands and rubbed it over his chest and under his arms. The long mirror reflected his expression which was still set in exasperation; he stared at himself, for once almost without enthusiasm, and lit a cigarette; his mouth felt tacky and unpleasant and the cigarette did nothing to improve it. 'Dear Les' – 'Your affectionate brother, Sid'. 'Les and Sid' – he shuddered and slowly pulled on a pair of dark red linen trousers and a sweater. The awful thing was that 'Your affectionate brother, Sid' was true. Ever since they were tiny kids trudging home from school across Southsea Common Sid had been affectionate, much more so than Sheila really, although it was generally supposed to be sisters who lavished adoration and hero-worship on their elder brothers. Sheila, however, had never been the hero-worshipping type; plain and practical, she had always, even when very young, refused to be impressed. Sid, on the other hand, had been a push-over from the word go; whatever Morgan, or rather 'Les', said or did was perfection. There were so many occasions that Morgan could remember when Sid had taken the rap for him. During the roof-climbing phase for instance, when seventeen slates had been broken and gone crashing down into Mrs Morpeth's back garden – Sid had taken all the blame for that and, what's more, been punished for it. Then there was the ringing door-bells and running away episode when Morgan, who had instigated the whole affair, had managed to hop over somebody's garden wall and lie panting in a shrubbery while Sid was captured and led off to the police station. Sid, with admirable *Boy's Own Paper* gallantry, had resolutely refused to divulge the name of his accomplice. The policeman had finally brought him home where, after a big family scene during which Morgan remained ignobly silent, Sid was whacked by Dad and sent to bed supperless. There were many other like instances, through child-hood and adolescence and right on until they were grown men. Sid certainly had the right to sign himself 'Your affectionate brother', and the strange thing was that through all the years this steady, undemanding affection had merely served to annoy the recipient of it, sometimes quite intolerably. Perhaps deep down beneath the armoured shell of Morgan's self-esteem there were remnants of a conscience which had not quite atrophied, perhaps, who knows, there were moments every now and then when in his secret private heart he was ashamed? Whether this was so or not, the presence or even the thought of Sid invariably made him ill at ease and irritable. Now Sid was going to appear in his life again; six years had passed since they had seen each other. Six eventful years for the world and even more eventful for Morgan, for in course of time he had climbed from being a small-part English actor to being one of the biggest film stars in Hollywood.

CHAPTER II

IN 1933, aged nineteen, Leslie Booker was a floor-walker in the novelty department of Hadley's. This position was procured for him through the civic influence of his Uncle Edward, who, owing to certain connections on various Boards and Committees, knew Fred Cartwright, one of the Directors of Hadley's. Uncle Edward privately thought no great shakes of his nephew but being strong in family conscience and devoted to his sister Nell, who was Leslie's mother, he decided to do what he could for the boy. His misgivings about Leslie were based more on intuition than actual knowledge of his character. This intuition told him that Leslie was idle, over good-looking, excessively pleased with himself and flash, and that his younger brother Sid was worth twenty of him any day of the week; however, he was Nell's eldest and he couldn't ride about the countryside indefinitely on a second-hand motor-cycle with a series of tartish young ladies in flannel slacks riding pillion behind him with their arms clasped tightly round his stomach, so something had to be done. Mr Cartwright was invited to the 'Queen's', given an excellent lunch and, when sufficiently mellowed by Hock and two double Martell Three Star brandies, was finally persuaded to give Leslie a three months' trial in the shop.

The three months passed swiftly and proved little beyond the fact that Leslie was idle, over good-looking, excessively pleased with himself and flash. However, he did more or less what was required of him, which was mostly to smile and look amiable and tactfully coax the customers to buy things that they didn't really want and so he was re-engaged for a further six months with a vague promise of a raise in salary if he did well. It was during these six months further probation that Adele Innes arrived in Portsmouth to play a week's try-out of a new farce which was due to open in the West End. Adele was a conscientious young actress with good legs and little talent. In the farce she played the heroine's best friend who made a lot of pseudo-sophisticated wisecracks and was incapable of sitting down without crossing her legs ostentatiously and loosening her furs. On the Monday of the try-out week, after a tiring dress-rehearsal, she popped into Hadley's on her way home to the digs to buy a few roguish little first-night gifts for her friends in the Company. Leslie Booker helped her assiduously to choose a china Pierrot scent-burner, two green elephant book-ends, a cunning replica of an apple made of china which could be used, Leslie assured her, either as a paper-weight or a door stop, and a small scarlet leather book-shelf containing four minute dictionaries which were virtually illegible owing to the smallness of print. Having made these purchases she lingered a little, chatting nonchalantly with the affable young salesman. She was a democratic girl quite uninhibited by any sense of class distinction, so uninhibited indeed that she deliberately allowed her hand to rest against his while he was totting up the bill. During the ensuing week they had morning coffee twice at the Cadena, went to Gosport and back three times on the ferry in between the matinée and evening performances on the Wednesday, which was early closing day; and went to bed together once in her digs between the matinée and evening performance on the Saturday which, although not early closing day, was perfectly convenient as the shop shut at six and she didn't have to be in the theatre again until eight. A few weeks later, after some impassioned correspondence, Leslie abandoned Hadley's novelty department for ever and arrived in London with seventeen pounds ten shillings; nine pounds of which were savings and the rest borrowed from brother Sid. According to pre-arranged plan he went directly to Adele's flat just off the Fulham Road which she shared with a girl friend who was at present away on tour. Thus comfortably established with bed and board and convivial company he managed, through Adele's influence, to get into the chorus of the current revue at the Caravel Theatre which, as he was without theatrical experience and could neither sing nor dance, said a great deal for Adele's influence.

By 1934 the revue at the Caravel had closed and he was sharing the flat of a husky-voiced singer called Diana Grant in St John's Wood. Diana was large, possessive, generous, exceedingly bad-tempered and had a rooted objection to going to bed before five a.m., and rising before noon. Leslie's brief but tempestuous association with her depleted his natural vitality to such a degree that when he was offered, through a friend of a friend of hers, a general understudy and small part job in a repertory company in Dundee, he accepted it from sheer self-preservation.

By 1936 he had played several insignificant parts in several insignificant productions both in the Provinces and in London and was playing a young dope fiend in a thriller called *Blood on the Stairs*. In this piece he had one of those sure-fire scenes in Act Three in which he had to break down under relentless cross-examination and confess to a murder. The breakdown entailed all the routine gurglings and throat clutchings which never fail to impress the dramatic critics, and so consequently he received glowing tributes from the *Daily Mirror*, the *Daily Express* and the *Star*, an honourable mention in the *Daily Telegraph* and an admonition against over-acting in *Time and Tide* which he immediately ascribed to personal jealousy and wrote a dignified letter of protest to the Editor. *Blood on the Stairs* was a fatuous, badly-written little melodrama, which, having received enthusiastic notices, closed after a run of seven and a half weeks, but as far as Leslie Booker was concerned it achieved some purpose, for during its brief run he was sent for and interviewed by a visiting American manager at the Savoy Hotel who was on the lookout for a clean English type to play a young dope fiend in a mystery murder play he was presenting in New York in the fall. The visiting American manager's name was Sol Katsenberg and he prided himself, generally inaccurately, upon his unique flair for discovering new talent. He was noisy and friendly and gave Leslie two double whiskies and sodas which he described as highballs and which contained too much ice, too much whisky and too little soda. He also gave him a graphic description of the super-efficiency of the American Theatre as opposed to the English. He said 'Christ Almighty' a great many times but without religious implication and by the end of the interview Leslie, slightly dizzy, had signed a contract for three hundred dollars a week and had agreed to change his name, for, as Sol explained, Leslie Booker sounded too Christ Almighty dull. The name agreed upon after a great deal of discussion was Morgan Kent, a name, had they but known it, that was destined to flash over all the movie screens of the world.

The Sol Katsenberg production of *Blood Will Tell* opened in Long Branch on 17 September 1936, and closed, after three changes of cast and two changes of author, on 29 October in Pittsburgh. The name Morgan Kent rang no urgent tocsin in the stony hearts of the American out-of-town critics which was odd because, in the last act of the play, he had a scene in which, crazed by dope, he had to break down under relentless cross-examination and confess to a murder. He gurgled and clutched his throat with even more abandon than he had exhibited in *Blood on the Stairs* but to no avail. Nobody cared, not even *Variety* which merely listed him among the minor players and spelled his name Kant instead of Kent. Reeling under this blow to his pride, Leslie, or rather Morgan, was driven to sharing a small apartment in West 31st Street, New York City with Myra Masters, a statuesque red-haired ex-show girl who had played a vampire in the deceased *Blood Will Tell*. Myra was a cheerful, open-hearted girl with what is known as 'contacts'. These contacts were mostly square-looking business men from Detroit and points Middle West who cherished tender memories of her in George White's *Scandals* and Earl Carroll's *Vanities*. One of them, fortunately for Morgan, was in Advertising, and before Christmas had cast its pall of goodwill over Manhattan, magazine readers were being daily tantalized by photographs of Morgan Kent (nameless) discussing with another young man (also nameless) the merits of 'Snugfit' men's underwear. Both young men in the photograph were depicted practically nude in the change room of a country club where presumably they had been swimming or playing polo or doing something equally virile; but whereas one was wearing what appeared to be rather baggy old-fashioned underpants, the other, Morgan, was pointing proudly to his groin which was adorned with none other than the new 'Snugfit'. The dialogue beneath the photograph, although uninspired, proved its point.

1st Y.M.: 'Gee, Buddy – don't you find that those little old pants you're wearing spoil your game?'

2nd Y.M.: 'Well, Chuck, as a matter of fact they do.'

1st Y.M. (*triumphantly*): 'Well, you old son of a gun, why not follow my example and try SNUGFIT!'

The result of this well-paid but unromantic publicity was as inevitable as the March of Time. Morgan was traced through Myra Masters, sent for and interviewed brusquely by a film agent in an ornate office in

Rockefeller Plaza. The film agent, Al Tierney, had astute eyes jockeying for position over a long ponderous nose, a gentle rather high voice and a sapphire and platinum ring. He explained to Morgan that his fortune was in his face and figure and that if he would sign a contract authorizing him, Al Tierney, to deal exclusively with his affairs within the year he would be on the up and up and saving thousands of dollars a week.

In due course Morgan bade farewell to Myra and set out for Hollywood.

CHAPTER III

THE first months in Hollywood were conventionally difficult. Morgan virtually starved, waited in queues outside casting offices, wandered up and down the boulevards homesick and weary; lived on inadequate sandwiches in snack bars; made innumerable tests; made a few casual friends on the same plane of frustration and failure as himself and lived in celibate squalor in a pseudo-Mexican apartment-house in a side street off Willshire Boulevard in which he had one room with shower and could, when desperate and his financial circumstances permitted, have a blue plate dinner in a teeming restaurant on the ground floor for seventy-five cents, service included.

Al Tierney, his exclusive agent, remained exclusively in New York; occasionally his Hollywood representative Wally Newman granted Morgan an interview, in course of which he outlined in glowing colours the lucky breaks and golden opportunities there were waiting just round the corner; in addition to these optimistic flights of fancy he contrived now and then to get him a few days crowd work which was of more practical value although less heartening. In these dreary months Morgan deteriorated in looks owing to malnutrition but gained perceptibly in moral stature, it being a well-known fact that just as travel broadens the mind, so a little near-starvation frequently broadens the spirits. Leslie Booker alias Morgan Kent, the assured, charming, flash young salesman from Southsea, the complacent, attractive, promising young actor from London, had suddenly time, far too much time, to reflect; to look at himself, into himself and around himself, to discover bitterly that a handsome face, wide shoulders and small hips were not enough in this much-publicized land of opportunity. Day after day he waited about in casting offices with dozens of handsome young men with as wide if not wider shoulders and as small if not smaller hips. Women, who had hitherto been his solace both physically and financially in times of stress, were, in Hollywood, either too tough, too blasé or too pre-occupied with their own ambitions to devote their time and energy to a, by now, only comparatively good-looking young film extra. Morgan was forced to face the unpalatable truth that masculine good looks in the outer fringes of the movie industry were as monotonously prevalent as the eternal sunshine, the painted mountains and the cellophane-wrapped sandwiches. Had this dismal state of affairs continued much longer; had his self-esteem received just a few more kicks in the teeth; had his shrinking ego shuddered under just a few more bludgeonings of Fate, who knows what might have happened? He might conceivably have given up the struggle, begged, borrowed, earned or stolen enough money to get himself back to New York or London and started again playing small parts and learning to become a good actor. He might have given up all idea of either stage or screen and worked his way home on a freighter or even as a steward on a liner in which capacity he would have done very well. There are a thousand things he might have done had not Fate suddenly relented and whisked him from penury and frustration into such flamboyant notoriety that he was dazzled, bewildered and lost for ever.

It all came about, as usual, through hazard, chance, an accident, somebody else's misfortune. The somebody else was a young man called Freddie Branch and the accident occurred on number seven stage in the M.G.M. lot when they were in course of shooting a big ballroom scene which purported to be taking place in one of the stately homes of England. The set was impressive. There was a Tudor staircase at the top of which stood the stand-in for the hostess wearing white satin and a tiara and elbow-length gloves. At the foot of the stairs stretched the vast ballroom flanked by footmen in powdered wigs; there were also heraldic shields, suits of armour, Gothic windows and two immense Norman fireplaces, one on each side, in which gargantuan logs were waiting to flicker realistically. The floor, rather erratically, was made of composition black marble and upon it were grouped hundreds of extras cunningly disguised as members of the effete British Aristocracy. The accident which was negligible happened to poor Freddie Branch after he had been standing quite still clasping his hostess's hand for three hours and four minutes. The whistles blew for a rehearsal, bejewelled ladies and eccentrically be-uniformed and be-tailed gentlemen stiffened to attention and proceeded, as previously rehearsed, to revolve like automatons. Freddie Branch retreated to the foot of the stairs and proceeded, as previously rehearsed, to walk up them again. Upon gaining the top step he suddenly felt an overwhelming desire to be sick, grabbed frenziedly at his collar, murmured 'Jesus' in audible tones and fainted dead away. Morgan, whose proud task it was to follow him, jumped nimbly aside and watched his inert body roll and sprawl to the bottom of the stairs. There was an immediate uproar; more whistles blew, the unconscious Freddie was carried off the set and Morgan was detailed to take over his business.

That was Fate's gesture to Morgan Kent – the striking down of the wretched Freddie Branch, who had barely had time to come to from his faint before Morgan was ascending those shining stairs in his place. He continued to ascend them at intervals for the rest of the morning. Miss Carola Blake, the star, finally emerged from her dressing-room and took over from her stand-in and the scene was taken. It was taken at 2 o'clock, at 2.20, at 2.45, at 3.10, at 3.40, at 4.15 and, owing to hitch in the sound, at 8, 8.30 and 9 onwards during the following morning. By the following evening, Miss Carola Blake had shaken Morgan's hand – plus rehearsals – forty-seven times and become aware in the process that he had fine eyelashes, an excellent physique, although a little on the thin side, and a deep and attractive speaking voice. (Having spent the thirty years of her life in Illinois and California her ear was naturally oblivious to any subtle Cockney intonations and, to do Morgan justice, these were becoming increasingly rare.) When the ballroom scene had been packed away in the can, Morgan together with the other extras was paid off. Only a few days later he received a peremptory call to report at the casting office. To his surprise he was greeted with a welcoming smile from the outer secretary, arch friendliness by the inner secretary and downright effusiveness by the casting director himself. It appeared, after some casual conversation and the offer and refusal of a cigar, that the sharp-eyed observers on the set had noted his charm, poise and talent and that he was to be tested for a scene in a speed-boat – Miss Carola Blake, the casting director added with an oblique look, had actually consented to do the test with him herself. Later on the same day Morgan, wearing abbreviated swimming trunks, spent three and a half hours with Miss Carola Blake, also scantily clad, sitting in the built-up bows of a speed boat with, behind them, a back projection screen upon which were monotonously depicted the swirling waters of the Caribbean.

Five weeks later he moved unostentatiously into Carola Blake's elaborate house in Beverly Hills.

A little later still they were married.

CHAPTER IV

BY the autumn of 1938, while the English Prime Minister was shuttling back and forth between England and Germany, two things of considerable importance had happened to Morgan Kent. The first was his sensational success in a picture called *Loving Rover* in which he played an eighteenth-century pirate who, after many nautical and amorous vicissitudes, finally evaded death by a hair's breadth, and found true love in the arms of a beautiful New England girl with a pronounced Middle Western accent. The second was his divorce from Carola Blake on the grounds of mental cruelty. The publicity of the latter almost surpassed that of the former with the result that his fan mail reached unheard of proportions and he signed a new seven years' starring contract, the terms of which were published inaccurately in every newspaper in the United States. Throughout 1939 and the beginning of 1940 he made no less than seven successful pictures, one of which was quite good. He bought a delightful house in the hills behind Hollywood which commanded a spectacular view of the town especially at night, when the myriad lights blazed from Sunset Boulevard to the sea. Here he enjoyed a carefree bachelor existence with, in order of their appearance and disappearance, Jane Fleming, Beejie Lemaire, Dandy Lovat, Glory Benson and Brenda Covelin.

In the spring of 1940, at the time of the evacuation of the British Expeditionary Force from the beaches of Dunkirk, he had just completed a grim but exciting war picture entitled *Altitude*, in which he portrayed to perfection a taciturn but gallant fighter pilot whose ultimate death for the sake of his fiancée and his best friend created on the screen a dramatic climax hitherto unparalleled in the art of film-making. While making *Altitude* he met for the first time Lenore Fingal who was cast as his fiancée. Their meeting was described by all observers as an absolute and concrete example of love at first sight and before the picture was half finished they had flown together over the border into Mexico on a Saturday, been married on the Sunday and flown back again in time for work on Monday. A little later he gave up his bachelor establishment and they moved into a larger and more convenient house in Beverly Hills.

CHAPTER V

LENORE FINGAL, at the time of her marriage to Morgan Kent, was twenty-five years old. She was small and dark, with a good figure, an attractive husky voice and very lovely grey-blue eyes. These eyes were undoubtedly her best feature but they were deceptive. There was an appealing expression in them, a tender naïveté, a trusting friendly generosity which, although effective in 'close-ups', was actually at variance with her character. Lenore was neither tender, naïve, trusting, nor particularly generous. The exigencies of her life in the treacherous shallows of the motion picture industry had not allowed her much time for the development of these qualities. She was hard, calculating, and although occasionally sentimental, never emotional. In course of her journey from the slums of Los Angeles to the heights of Beverly Hills she had, once or twice, permitted herself the luxury of a love affair, that is to say she had consciously directed her will into an emotional channel in order, presumably, to discover what it was all about but, as her heart had never seriously been involved, she had discovered very little. She had played a few stormy scenes, shed a few tears, and emerged unscathed and tougher than ever. It is doubtful that she even imagined herself in love with Morgan. He was physically attractive to her and, in the dazzling light of his rise to stardom, an excellent matrimonial proposition. Now, in the spring of 1941, they had been married for a year, a professionally successful year for them both. He had made three pictures and was in process of making a fourth. She had made two apart from him and one with him in which she had portrayed a gallant British Red Cross nurse who rescued her lover (Morgan) from the beaches of Dunkirk by rowing out from Dover in a dinghy. The picture when shown in New York and London had had a disappointing reception from the critics and so it had been decided, for the time being anyhow, that it would be wiser to cast Lenore and Morgan separately, and wiser still to keep Lenore away from the perils of English pronunciation and allow her to exhibit her undoubted talent securely enclosed in her own idiom. Domestically their first year of marriage had also been fairly successful. They had quarrelled a good deal, naturally enough, and had once come to blows, but the blows given and received had not been violent and the original cause of the row swiftly lost for ever in a haze of alcohol.

The arrival of the letter from brother Sid, coming as it did on the morning of a hangover, had both irritated and depressed Morgan considerably, and the arrival of brother Sid himself a few days later irritated and depressed him still more. They were all sitting round the pool drinking 'Old Fashioneds' before going over to dinner at Beejie's: Morgan, Lenore, Coral Leroy, Sammy Feisner, Charlie Bragg and Doll Hartley. Sammy was just reaching the point of a long story about a scene between Hester Norbury and Louis B. Mayer when there was a loud 'Hallo there' from the upper terrace and Sid came bounding down the steps, followed by another sailor who was red-haired and covered with freckles. Sammy stopped abruptly on the verge of his story's denouement; Morgan rose from a canvas chair, leaving on it the dark imprint of his damp swimming trunks, and, with a valiant smile masking his annoyance, advanced to meet his brother.

Sid, in appearance, temperament and character, was everything Morgan was not. Whereas Morgan was tall, lithe and dark, Sid was short, square and fair. Whereas Morgan's temperament was naturally solemn, Sid's was ebullient and permanently cheerful. Sid was trusting, kind and uninhibited; Morgan was suspicious, egocentric and, since his early Hollywood struggles, frequently a prey to misgivings. Sid had none. It would never have occurred to him that he wasn't immediately welcome wherever he went. He flung his arms affectionately round Morgan and banged him heartily on the back. 'My God, Les,' he said, 'I've been looking forward to this for months!' The word 'Les' went through Morgan's heart like a poisoned spear and he shuddered. Lenore, who had also got up to greet the new arrivals, noticed and giggled. Morgan, with an excellent display of brotherly affection, introduced Sid to everyone. Sid introduced his friend, Pete Kirkwall, who shyly shook hands all round; Charlie Bragg got up to mix fresh drinks; there was a lot of shifting of chairs and finally Sid found himself ensconced between Morgan and Lenore on a striped swing seat which creaked plaintively whenever any of them moved. Morgan realized with a sinking heart that Sid and his friend would not only have to be offered the best guest-room but would have to be taken with the others to dinner at Beejie's. They would also without doubt expect a personally-conducted tour of the studios the next day and a glamorous lunch in the commissariat. It was not that he was ashamed of Sid. There was nothing to be ashamed of in a reasonably nice-looking sailor brother, but there was, as there always is in such circumstances, a wide gulf to be bridged. None of his friends either at the studio or at Beejie's would have much in common with Sid and Pete. In envisaging the social strain involved, the effort he would have to make not to shudder when called 'Les', nor flush at Sid's over-British naval repartee and, above all, not to betray to anybody the fact that he devoutly wished that his brother had never been born, almost overwhelmed him. He knew that Lenore was watching, waiting for a chance to sneer, to get in a crack at him. He also knew that she would extract from Sid as much information as possible about his early years and fling it in his face the next time an opportunity offered. Sid on the other hand, sublimely unaware of the conflict raging in his brother's heart, was perfectly happy and at ease. He kept a weather eye open to see that Pete was doing all right and was relieved to see that he was thawing out a bit and exchanging 'Player's' cigarettes for 'Lucky Strikes' with a blonde woman, whose breasts seemed about to burst exuberantly from a tightly-stretched bandana handkerchief. He had already taken a fancy to Lenore whom he considered to be on the skinny side but friendly and attractive. Charlie Bragg handed him an Old-Fashioned, and called him 'Pal', Les – good old Les – asked him how long his leave was, and said of course he and Pete must stay in the house and that he'd take them round some studios the next day. Everything in fact had turned out as well as, if not better than, he had hoped. After a few more drinks and a swim in the pool, during which he churned up and down doing a rather clumsy 'crawl' and treating the water as though it were a personal enemy, he squeezed himself back into his 'Tiddley' suit which, being his best, was moulded tightly to his stocky figure, and, with bell-bottomed trousers flapping and vitality unimpaired, climbed into a blue Packard with Lenore, Sammy Feisner and Coral Leroy. Pete was with Morgan and the others in a beige Chrysler convertible.

Beejie's house was in another canyon which entailed a sharp and tortuous descent from Morgan's house and a sharper and more tortuous ascent on the other side of the valley. Sid, who was sitting next to

Lenore in the front seat, was both fascinated and alarmed at the firm assurance with which her small brown hands gripped the wheel. During the drive she gave him a few hints as to what he was to expect from the evening.

'It isn't that Beejie isn't all right,' she explained. 'Beejie's as right as rain, but don't go outside with her after she's had more than three drinks.'

'If you take my advice,' interposed Coral from the back seat, 'you won't go outside with her at all, drink or no drink. She's the biggest rip-snorting Nympho between here and Palm Springs!'

'Maybe the sailor would like to have a few passes made at him,' said Sammy. 'After all he's only got forty-eight hours.'

'He's my brother-in-law—' Here Lenore swerved sharply round a curve. 'My baby brother-in-law – and so help me God I'm going to protect him from evil if it kills me!'

Sid laughed loudly at this and was rewarded by an affectionate pat on the thigh. He gathered in course of the drive that his imminent hostess had been married four times; had made a smash hit some years before in a picture called *Honey Face*, but had never really had a success since; that her present husband was a surgeon whose speciality was the quasi-miraculous removal of gall-bladders, and that in 1939 she had had a brief but tempestuous affair with Morgan. This neither shocked nor surprised him. He had always viewed Les's sexual promiscuities with tolerant good-humour not entirely devoid of admiration. Good old Les had always been a quick worker even way back in the old days in Southsea. He recounted with brotherly pride an episode in Morgan's adolescence which concerned a chemist's daughter called Dodo Platt and her official fiancé who was in the Wool business. As a story it wasn't perhaps extravagantly amusing but Coral, Sammy and Lenore laughed satisfactorily and Lenore made a mental note of Dodo Platt. Encouraged by this and the general atmosphere of warm conviviality, Sid obliged with a few more light-hearted anecdotes about Morgan's early youth, all of which were rapturously received. At last, with a screeching of brakes, the car swirled through a pink plaster archway and drew up before what looked like a Spanish Sanatorium.

The phrase 'Hollywood Party' has become synonymous in the public mind with drink, debauch, frequent violence and occasional murder. This is both unjust and inaccurate, but the reason for it is not far to seek and lies, obviously enough, in the publicity value of the hosts, or the guests, or both. The movie colony lives, breathes and functions in a blaze of publicity. Many members of it make a point of leading quiet lives and evading the limelight as much as possible, and in the old days, when the various social strata were more clearly defined, it was easier for certain groups of the upper hierarchy to move about unobtrusively

among themselves, to give little dinners and to visit each other's houses
without the world at large being informed of it. But during the last few
years this has become increasingly difficult owing to the misguided
encouragement of a new form of social parasite, the gossip columnist.
This curious phenomenon has insinuated itself into the life-stream not
only of Hollywood but of the whole of America, and what began as a
minor form of local social and professional scandal-mongering has now
developed into a major espionage system, the power of which, aided
and abetted by the radio, has reached fabulous proportions. It would
not, I think, be incorrect to say that today the minds of millions of
citizens of the United States are affected by it. A column of inconsequential gossip is written daily by Mr So-and-So or Miss Such-and-
Such. This column, in addition to being printed in the newspaper for
which it is written, is syndicated throughout the country. Mr So-and-So
and Miss Such-and-Such also – as a rule – have a weekly, or sometimes
daily, half an hour on the radio, during which they recapitulate what
they have already written and give pointers as to what they are going to
write. The effect of this widespread assault upon the credulity of an
entire nation must inevitably be confusing. It would not be so were the
information given checked and counter-checked and based on solid
truth, but unfortunately it seldom is, therefore anybody who has the
faintest claims to celebrity is likely to have his character, motives and
private and public actions cheerfully misrepresented to an entire
continent. This is not done, except on rare occasions, with any particular
malicious intent, but merely to gratify one of the least admirable
qualities of human nature: vulgar curiosity. The accuracy of what is
written, stated, listened to and believed is immaterial. The monster
must be fed, and the professionally employed feeder of it is highly paid
and acquires a position of power in the land which would be ridiculous
were it not so ominous. In Hollywood, where this epidemic first began
to sap the nation's mental vitality, no large, and very few small, social
gatherings can take place without one or several potential spies being
present. An exchange of views between two directors; a light argument
between two leading ladies; a sharp word, spoken perhaps only jokingly,
by a young husband to his young wife, will, by the next day, have been
misquoted, distorted, magnified, read and believed by several million
people. This reprehensible state of affairs concerns our story vitally
because at Beejie Lemaire's party, in the regretted absence of Miss
Louella Parsons and Miss Hedda Hopper, there was present an up-and-
coming young lady journalist called Ruthie Binner, who ran a column
in a locally-read magazine, *Hollywood Highlights*. The column was
headed 'Nest Eggs' and consisted of a series of staccato mis-statements
purporting to have been whispered to Ruthie by a little bird. The

inventive capacities of Ruthie's little bird could have found no parallel in the annals of ornithology.

To describe Beejie's party as 'informal' would be an understatement. It began hilariously with one of her ex-husbands, Peppo Ragale, falling down three steps in the bar with a plate of cheese appetizers and breaking his ankle. Her present husband, Grant Lawrence, who, apart from his deft manipulation of gall-bladders, could also reset bones and apply compresses, dealt with the matter with gay efficiency and the party went on from there. Morgan drank steadily throughout the evening and became more and more depressed. Lenore drank too, but not to excess as she was anxious not to miss anything that was going on. Sid and Pete were received enthusiastically by Beejie and everyone present. Soon after the buffet dinner Pete retired into the garden with Doll Hartley and was not retrieved until it was time to go home. Sid enjoyed every moment. He had seven Old-Fashioneds before dinner and a number of Scotch highballs after dinner. He answered questions about the war, the British Navy, 'dear old London', and, volubly, about his brother. He had an unproductive but enjoyable interlude with Beejie on a chintz-covered divan in what she laughingly described as 'The Library'. He helped Beejie's husband to scramble eggs in the kitchen at 2 a.m. At 2.20 a.m. he was beckoned alluringly to a seat at the edge of the swimming pool by a vivacious dark girl who said her name was Ruthie. He found her outspoken, amusing and sincerely concerned about the progress of the war. He was also touched and charmed by her evident devotion to 'Les' and his career. They talked cosily for a long while and finally returned to the house to find Lenore rounding up her party to go home.

On the following morning Morgan, who was not working, stayed in bed and turned Sid and Pete over to Lenore who took them on to several of the M.G.M. stages and showed them Joan Crawford, Jeanette Macdonald and Myrna Loy in the distance and Mickey Rooney, Spencer Tracy, Judy Garland and Nelson Eddy close to. They lunched in the cafeteria and consumed vast glasses of milk and cartwheel slices of tomato on acres of hygienic lettuce. They were then shown some convulsive rough-cuts of incomplete movies in a projection room, where they sprawled in gargantuan armchairs flanked by ash-trays and cuspidors so that they could sleep and smoke and spit whenever they so desired. In the evening, after a merry cocktail gathering down by the pool, they were taken by Morgan and Lenore to a much grander dinner party than Beejie's. This was given by Arch Bowdler, one of the most prominent Hollywood executives, in a resplendent house that had been furnished with the utmost care. Attired as they were in the usual 'Square-Rig' of British Ordinary Seamen, they caused a mild sensation except among the English actors present, who of course recognized it immediately.

After a suitable sojourn in a cocktail bar laboriously decorated to represent an open-air café in the Place Pigalle, they were ushered into a large, pale-green room where they were placed at little tables for dinner. Sid found himself opposite a dim English actor who asked him a few lachrymose questions about New Malden, where apparently he had been born, and then lapsed into a gloomy silence, and between two ladies of outstanding glamour. One was Mae Leitzig, who had been whisked by the host from under the iron heel of the Nazis in Vienna and was about to star in a picture about Charlotte Corday, and the other, Zenda Hicks, a tough little blonde, who had recently won an award for the best minor performance of February 1941. She explained to Sid during the meal that it was just 'one of those crazy things' and that no one had been more surprised than she was. On the whole he got along better with her than with Mae Leitzig, who was rather sombre and seemed to be worried about something. Zenda obviously was not worried about anything. She told him all about her first marriage and divorce and also about her present husband who was Mexican and terribly jealous. She told him the entire story of the picture she was working in at the moment and gave her free and unprejudiced opinion of her director, who had a knowledge of life and humanity in general which was nothing short of 'dreamy'. He also, it appeared, thought very highly of her own talents and was in the habit of sitting up to all hours in the morning with her asking her advice about his unhappy marriage, discussing world affairs and occasionally breaking into uncontrollable sobs at the sheer hopelessness of everything. These nocturnal but strictly platonic interludes had been the cause of many bitter quarrels between her and Juano, but as Juano was apparently nothing but a big baby anyway, everyone was as friendly as could be and there was no harm done. She was just about to describe her early life in Omaha, Nebraska, when there was a sharp call for silence and the host rose to his feet. He was a round man with very small hands and black hair. He made a long speech bidding everyone welcome to his house and board, and then, to Sid's slight embarrassment, launched forth into an impassioned eulogy of England and the British war effort. He sat down at last amid loud applause having called upon Robert Bailey, one of the leading British actors present, to respond. Robert Bailey spoke well and slowly with an underlying throb of patriotism in his voice. He paused once or twice to find a word and it was obvious to all that he was making a brave effort to restrain his emotion. He was followed by an English character actress of high repute who waved her arms a good deal and talked about the women of England and how staunchly they had behaved during the blitzes. She concluded by reading a letter from her married sister in St John's Wood upon which it appeared bombs had been raining incessantly for months. By this time Sid was getting restless, bored and a little sleepy. He roused himself, however, when Morgan was called upon to speak. Morgan rose shyly to his feet and stood in silence for a moment, twisting the stem of his champagne glass. His speech was mercifully brief, but in every word of it pulsated a love of his native land which was intensely moving. Sid was genuinely surprised having no idea that 'Les' thought of the Old Country in those terms. He was still more surprised and utterly shattered when 'Les' finished up by asking everyone to join with him in drinking the health of – 'My sailor brother and The British Navy'. There were resounding cheers at this and everyone rose solemnly and clinked glasses. Sid, sweating with embarrassment, was forced to stand up and make a brief response. He cleared his throat, wishing devoutly that he was safely in his ship and at the other side of the world and said:

'On behalf of my friend and I – thanks a lot for making us so welcome here tonight and for giving us such a good time. When we tell our shipmates about all the wonderful people we've seen they'll be green with envy and that's no lie.' Here he paused for a moment and cleared his throat again. 'As you are all aware . . .' Realizing that he was speaking rather loudly he lowered his voice. 'As you are all aware, the Navy is known as "The Silent Service", so you will not expect from an ordinary seaman such as I myself am – anything high-falutin in the way of a speech, speech-making not being much in my line as you might say. But I would like to say, on behalf of the Old Country which I proudly belong to and the fleet in which I serve – thanks a lot for all the kind things that have been said here tonight and, as far as the war goes, Down with old Hitler and Musso and God Save the King.' He sat down abruptly amid tumultuous applause; someone shouted 'Good old England' and an Irish actress who had been playing 'bit' parts for thirteen years burst into loud sobs.

After this everyone was shepherded into an enormous blue room, the walls of which were lined with sets of the classics bound in different colours. Here trays of highballs were handed round, a movie screen rose noiselessly from the floor, and the party settled down to a preview of Clyde Oliver in *The Eagle Has Wings*. The screen titles, which were printed in glittering white against a background of moving planes and clouds, proclaimed that the story was a simple human document concerning a New York Playboy who found his true self in the crucible of war, and that the producer was Arch Bowdler, the associate producers, Josh Spiegal and Chuck Mosenthal; the director, Bud Capelli, and the cameraman, Vernon Chang. The titles further stated that the story was by Norma and Perce Fennimore adapted from the novel by Cynthia Stein; that the screen play was by Max

322

THE BEST WAR STORIES

Macgowan and Eloise Hunt with additional dialogue by Olaf Hansen and Benny Zeist, and that the music had been specially composed by Gregor Borowitz with orchestrations and vocal arrangements by Otto von Stollmeyer. Then came a long list of lesser people who had operated the sound; supervised the make-up; designed the hair styles; organized the publicity, and supplied extra effects. As an afterthought it was explained that the whole thing was a 'Bowdler-L.N.G.-Peerless Production'.

It took one hour and fifty-five minutes for the hero to find his true self in the crucible of war because before doing so he was constrained to find a great many other things as well. These included a tough friend with a hairy chest who cried on the least provocation; a drunk Canadian sergeant-pilot with a heart of gold who crashed in flames half-way through the picture; a lovable but brusque British peeress who lived in some Tudor tea-rooms on the Yorkshire moors; and last, but unfortunately not least, an adorable American girl of great courage and vivacity who was continually hiding herself in the cockpits of Eagle Squadron bombers. Finally, after a moving scene in a hospital run by some over made-up nuns, all misunderstandings were straightened out and the picture ended with the hero and heroine walking up a steep hill to the deafening accompaniment of a celestial choir.

When the lights went up several members of the party were discovered to be in tears. Pete was fast asleep with his head resting on the bare breast of his dinner partner. Morgan and Lenore were bickering in a corner and Sid was utterly exhausted and wished to go home.

The next day, Sunday, was passed peacefully. A few people came over for drinks before lunch and stayed until three. After lunch everyone slept, either in the house or by the pool, and at seven o'clock, fortified by some Old Fashioneds and peanut butter appetizers, Sid and Pete were dispatched to their ship in Morgan's car. When they had gone Morgan and Lenore continued the squabble they had begun the night before and went on with it intermittently for the rest of the evening. The gist of it was, of course, Sid. Actually Lenore had found him rather boring but she spoke of him constantly with enthusiastic admiration in order to irritate Morgan. In this she succeeded easily. He rose to the bait every time. Finally, towards the end of dinner, he got up from the table violently and retired to the pool where he remained for an hour by himself, leaving Lenore in lonely triumph with the strawberry shortcake.

The visit of the two sailors had undoubtedly been a great success. Neither of them had behaved badly nor said anything shaming. Sid, of the two, had been the more popular because of his natural ease, lack of shyness and vitality, but they had both made a good impression on everyone they had met and had been pressed on all sides to return for further hospitality should their ship ever again be in the vicinity.

Morgan was not much given to introspection, nor was he particularly adept at analysing his own feelings. In his early years when his ego was more easily satisfied and assuaged by sexual promiscuity, and his ambition was goading him to succeed, he had had little time to sift, weigh and evaluate his motives. Perhaps if he had, the impact of his sudden fame might have steadied him instead of confusing him. As it was he was in a muddle, and somewhere, deep in his subconscious, he knew it. He was aware, dimly, that he had changed; that his reactions were less gay, less volatile than they used to be; that his capacity for enjoyment seemed to have dwindled and that with the increasing burden of his stardom he was considerably less happy than he had been before. He was also aware, not dimly but very clearly, that he was much to be envied. He was young, successful, immensely publicized and sought after. Big executives argued and fought for the loan of his services; his financial position was assured and his contract with C.R.P.I. (Cinesound Radiant Pictures Incorporated) was watertight with automatic raises of salary for the next four years. True he was sick of Lenore, but she was still physically satisfactory and, when not determined to be bitchy, fairly good company.

The arrival of Sid had disturbed him by bringing into his mind something that for years he had been striving to shut out: memory of the past, concern for his family, perhaps – who knows – even a little concern for his country. During the last years he had written home occasionally; dutifully remembered his mother's and Sheila's birthdays and sent them presents at Christmas. Sid he had ignored. Sid had always been a thorn in his flesh. He knew that there was no reason for this. Sid was devoted to him; was loyal, affectionate and true, whereas he, Morgan, was none of these things and wasn't even sure that he wanted to be. Sid was the trouble all right. Sid was the weight on his conscience. Ordinary Seaman Sidney Booker, brother of Morgan Kent – sailor brother of Morgan Kent. What the hell had Sid wanted to join the Navy for in the first place, and having joined it why the hell couldn't he have stayed with the Home Fleet and not come dashing romantically out to the Pacific in a destroyer? Sitting gloomily by the pool while Lenore amused herself up in the house with the radio, Morgan was compelled to face one fact honestly and without compromise, and that was that he wished his good-humoured, loyal, affectionate sailor brother dead and at the bottom of the sea. He crushed down this unedifying reflection as soon as it seared across his mind but it remained there dormant until the next morning when it re-emerged with even greater force. Lenore wandered into his bedroom wearing peach-coloured pyjamas. She had a glint in her eye and *Hollywood Highlights*, which was published with dreadful regularity every Monday, in her hand.

'Well, "Les",' she said cheerfully, 'our Ruthie's little bird certainly worked overtime at Beejie's the other night. Just cast those dway big violet eyes over this.' She threw the magazine lightly on to his chest and lit a cigarette.

Morgan, with dry mouth and a sinking heart, read Ruthie's column, flung the magazine on to the floor, stamped into the bathroom and slammed the door. Lenore languidly picked it up and read it again with a quizzical smile. 'A very cute little bird talked to Ruthie the other evening – the cutest little bird you've ever seen, with curly fair hair, blue eyes and bell-bottomed pants – now don't try to guess, girls, because you never will. It was our Morgan Kent's sailor brother and was our Morg's face red when S.B. called him "Les", because, girls, "Les" is what his name really is. Les Booker from Southsea, England. There had been a lot of bombs falling on Southsea lately, so it's nice to think that at least one of the Booker boys is out trying to stop them.'

CHAPTER VI

IN the December following Sid's visit to Hollywood the Japanese, to the astonishment of a great many people, dropped a number of bombs on Pearl Harbor, an American Naval Base on the island of Oahu. The reverberations of those bombs echoed across the Western World, and that lesser world bounded by Los Angeles in the East and Santa Monica in the West was shaken to its foundations. Enemy invasion was expected hourly; vital and momentous decisions were made; the course of many a contract was drastically changed and several important projects abandoned. One of these was a Technicolor Musical with a Japanese setting entitled provisionally, *Get Yourself a Geisha*, which was to have been a starring vehicle for Linda Lakai, a new Hungarian soprano with tiny eyes and an enormous range. A quarter of the picture had been shot and so its sudden abandonment caused acute financial anxiety, until fortunately one of the script writers conceived the brilliant idea of altering the locale from Japan to China, a gallant country with which everyone was in sympathy. This change was immediately put into effect and, with only minor alterations to the costumes, the picture ultimately emerged as *Pekin Parade* starring Laurine Murphy. There were of course other equally momentous but more personal upheavals in the movie colony, among them the sudden discovery, by careful X-ray, of an ulcer in Morgan Kent's duodenum. This unforeseen disaster, although not directly attributable to Oriental treachery, must certainly have been aggravated by it and it entailed immediate and radical changes in Morgan's professional and private life as well as in his diet. His alcohol consumption was grimly rationed to two Scotch highballs a day and no Old Fashioneds at all. He was obliged to withdraw from a 'Period' picture he had only just begun called *Hail Hannibal* and retire sadly to a rented bungalow in Palm Springs for a prolonged rest. Here Lenore visited him occasionally for week-ends, bringing with her the gossip of the town and a few friends to cheer his loneliness. The gossip of the town at that time was rich in surmise and agitation. Nation-wide conscription was inevitable; Robert Bailey had flown to Canada to enlist but had been invalided out after three weeks training on account of an undescended testicle, an embarrassment which hitherto had been unsuspected by his friends. Ross Cheeseman, Sonny Blake and Jimmy Clunes were on the verge of being drafted, and Joan Ziegler, obsessed by the fear of Japanese invasion, had had a nervous collapse, left poor Charlie, and fled to her mother's home in Iowa with the three children. Dear old Paul Newcombe had been absolutely splendid and was organizing vast projects for British War Relief, and Lulu Frazer had volunteered to make a tour of personal appearances for the Red Cross and had designed for herself two uniforms, one for day work and one for night work, and both in sharkskin. There were many other titbits of news fo relieve the tedium of Morgan's enforced seclusion, but happily, after three months, Doc Mowbray – who was a personal friend as well as a physician and had originally diagnosed the ulcer and arranged the X-ray – announced that the patient had so much improved in his general condition that, provided that he took things easily and remained true to his diet, he could come back and start work on a new picture.

The next year was a successful one for Morgan. He happened to be given two good scripts one after the other and both of them were completed pictures within seven months. In November he was loaned to the 'Arch Bowdler-L.N.G. Studios' to play the much-coveted rôle of Jumbo in *Jumbo R.A.F.*, a story based on the sensationally successful novel of the same name and which, as everyone in the industry had already prophesied, would certainly be the Picture of the Year and had as good as won the critics' award before the first reel was in the can. This, being an 'Epic' production, took a long time to make and it wasn't until June 1943 that it was finished, sneak-previewed and finally given its world première at Grauman's Chinese Theatre. Of all premières given in that great theatre since war had cast its shadow over American life, none had approached within a thousand miles of the brilliance and distinction of this one. To begin with, the picture had been discussed and publicized over a long period. There had also been trouble with the Hays Office over certain scenes which were considered to be too realistic and outspoken, notably one in which a tough but good-hearted squadron leader said to the hero, 'By God, Jumbo, in spite of your crazy flying, you're a lovable bastard!' This phrase had of course been viewed with slight scepticism at the preliminary script conferences, but, as it was the climax of one of the most memorable scenes in the original book, it had been left, in the hope that it would get by. The Hays Office, however, its ears protectively attuned to the fragile sensibilities of the American movie-going public, was inexorable and the line had to be changed to: 'By Gosh, Jumbo, in spite of your crazy flying, you're a fine kid.' This, together with some other similar assaults upon national decency, necessitated retakes which put several weeks extra time on to the production schedule. Also, as the whole Hays episode had been widely discussed in the press, public anticipation had been worked up to fever pitch.

The première itself was attended by everyone of note in the motion picture industry and by a great many who weren't. Special cordons of police were employed to beat back the eager crowds; arc lamps bathed the occasion in shrill blue light; the immaculately shod feet of certain stars were pressed into wet cement and the imprints duly autographed and every celebrity upon arrival was led to a microphone in the lobby where, amid the whirring and clicking of cameras, he or she gave his or her message of goodwill to an expectant radio public of several millions.

The auditorium of the theatre had been draped with R.A.F. flags and on the stage was grouped the Los Angeles Civic Choir in its entirety appropriately dressed in R.A.F. uniforms. When finally the audience was seated and the choir had rendered 'Oh for the Wings of a Dove' and 'There'll Always be an England', a British Ministry of Information 'Documentary' was shown which, although a little slow in tempo, proved conclusively that London really had been bombed. This was followed by an inaudible speech from the British Consul and a 'Donald Duck' cartoon. Then at last – at long last – came the picture itself, which, on the whole, was very good. There were of course a few minor anachronisms here and there; a Brittany fisher-girl who spoke French with a pronounced Hessian accent; a scene in a blossom-laden English orchard in June at the end of which the hero's humble mother, wearing a tea-gown, presented her son's fiancée with a large bunch of chrysanthemums; and an amusing but unconvincing episode between the hero and a cockney greengrocer who, late at night in the spring of 1942, happened to be wheeling a barrow down Piccadilly piled with Sunkist oranges. Apart from these insignificant errors which only a carping mind would have noted, the story moved along to its climax with gathering emotional strength and commendable speed. Some of the air battle sequences were magnificent and the escape of the hero from a Nazi prison camp was breath-taking. Morgan Kent as 'Jumbo' gave unquestionably his finest performance of his career. He played his love scenes with sincerity and beautifully restrained passion, and his portrayal of grim determination mixed with terror when he was forced to bale out of a blazing plane brought forth a spontaneous burst of applause. When it was all over there was prolonged cheering from the audience, and Morgan was almost torn to pieces by the crowd outside who unhappily had not been able to see the picture at all.

There was a party afterwards at the Arc de Triomphe night club which had been taken over for the occasion by Arch Bowdler, and it wasn't until 3.30 a.m. that Morgan and Lenore, tired but exalted, let themselves into their house and found, propped up on the bar, a telegram. Lenore opened it while Morgan was fixing a 'night-cap' – she said, 'My God!' under her breath, and handed it to him. He read it and slowly put the bottle of Bourbon he was holding back on the shelf. It said, 'Sid reported missing presumably killed. Mother terribly upset. Please cable. Love. Sheila.'

CHAPTER VII

IN the months following, Morgan, on the advice of the Studio Publicity Department, went out very little and wore a black armband. People were wonderfully kind and sympathetic and he received many letters of condolence. Arch Bowdler indeed was so profoundly moved when he heard the news that he suggested organizing a memorial service for Morgan's sailor brother in the Sweetlawn Baptist Temple on Sunset Boulevard. Upon reflection, however, the idea was abandoned, but he did give a small dinner party for twenty-eight people in Morgan's honour, at which Sid's memory was toasted reverently before the party adjourned to the Blue Room to see the new L.N.G. Musical, starring Glenda Crane and Bozo Browning.

Morgan, who had cabled his mother immediately upon receiving the telegram and flogged himself into writing a long letter of commiseration, accepted the attitude of his friends and acquaintances with dignity and restraint and it was evident to all that he was bearing his loss with the utmost fortitude. Another effect of his bereavement was the strange lessening of friction in his home life. Lenore, softened, perhaps by the passing wings of the Angel of Death, became kinder in her everyday manner, drank a little less and made fewer sarcastic wisecracks. Life went on much as usual except that in the autumn of 1943 both of them, Morgan and Lenore, together with a group of other stars, went on a flying tour through the United States and Canada in order to make personal appeals for a great War Bond drive. This was publicly a great success and privately not without its rewards. They had a special plane to take them from place to place; they were entertained lavishly and photographed and interviewed ad nauseam; they had to sign thousands of autograph books which was of course dreadfully tiring, but they took it in their stride upheld by the reflection that they were working for a magnificent cause and doing something really worth while.

Morgan actually enjoyed the Canadian part of the tour a little less. His well rehearsed and beautifully delivered patriotic appeal was received politely but without quite the same vibrant acclaim that it had been in the States. In fact on one occasion, in an enormous cinema in Toronto, someone at the back shouted something apparently uncomplimentary. No one ever found out exactly what it was, but the tension of the moment was snapped and he found it difficult to recapture the audience's attention. The War Bond tour came to an end in Washington where they were all entertained at the White House and photographed still more; inside and outside and in the garden. Later on they were photographed again; outside the Capitol; outside the headquarters of the F.B.I.; and posed reverently in front of the Lincoln Memorial. *Life* Magazine published a six-page photographic survey of the whole expedition and *Time* devoted an entire page to a eulogistic article uder the heading 'Stars Calling'.

CHAPTER VIII

IN November 1943 Morgan celebrated his thirtieth birthday by giving a party. This had to take place on a Saturday night because he was in the middle of a French Resistance picture called *Hidden Flames* and had to get up at six o'clock every morning excepting Sundays. The party was a great success up to a certain point. A large number of people came, most of them bearing gifts; there was an entertaining quarrel between Hester Roach and Lois Levine, two exquisitely proportioned young starlets who had unfortunately both fallen in love with the same agent; Tonio Lopez brought his guitar and sang Mexican folk songs for an hour and a half by the pool; the buffet supper was delicious; Gloria Marlow choked over a fishbone in the kedgeree and had to be taken to the bathroom to be sick; everyone drank a great deal and enjoyed themselves immensely. Morgan himself was at the top of his form and, in addition to being a perfect host and seeing that all his guests were looked after, contrived to have a brief but satisfactory affair with Opal Myers in the bath-house. He emerged with admirable suavity from this episode, leaving Opal to reappear a little later. Tonio was still singing his songs; the moon was shining and although it was cold by the pool, there were enough mink coats to go round and everyone seemed to be happy. From the house above, where Lenore was dispensing drinks in the bar, came a cheerful buzz of chatter and laughter. Morgan picked his way through the group of muffled figures lying about on the canvas furniture, their cigarettes glowing like red fireflies in the moonlight, and went up the steps. He was aware of contentment. Life was good and

God was in his heaven. It was at this moment, this instant of rare and perfect fulfilment, that Destiny elected to kick him violently in the stomach. There was a honking of a klaxon in the drive, and, coinciding with Morgan's arrival on the porch, a taxi drew up. Morgan, still serene, still swathed in physical satisfaction and mental ease, went forward hospitably to welcome the late-comers. There was, however, only one late-comer. The taxi stopped with a screech of brakes, there was a hearty roar of 'Les' from inside it, and Sid leapt out of it, bounded up the porch steps and clasped Morgan in his arms. It was a moment of extraordinary poignancy. Lenore, hearing the noise, came out of the bar with several others and gave a loud shriek. The distant murmur of Tonio's baritone down by the pool came to an abrupt stop; there was a babel of voices; Sid was hugged and kissed and slapped on the back and swept into the bar. With him was swept into bitter oblivion Morgan's peace of mind. His sudden, transient awareness of the joy of living turned brown at the edges, curled up and died. The moon went behind a cloud; the wind from the Pacific Palisades blew chill and his heart writhed with dreadful, unacknowledged dismay. From then on the party, for him, became a nightmare. The gay, excited clamour of his guests rasped his nerves; the very recent memory of Opal Myers' surrender lay stately on his senses, and Lenore's fatuous, incredulous, welcoming screams irritated him to such an extent that he longed to bash her perfectly-capped teeth down her throat. To do him justice, however, his outward behaviour was beyond reproach. He installed Sid in a comfortable chair, plied him with drink and food and gave over the whole evening to him without stint and without betrayal. It must frankly be admitted that Sid accepted it wholeheartedly. He was looking ill and emaciated and was wearing creased khaki slacks and a stained tropical tunic, but his good spirits were in no way impaired. Before the party was over he had told the story of his escape four times, each time leavening its drama with impeccable British understatement. It was a thrilling, almost incredible story and was received by the assembled company with gasps and groans of excitement. To begin with, his ship had been sunk off the coast of Borneo in the summer of 1942. He had clung to a raft in shark-infested waters for eleven hours before being picked up by an armed Japanese trawler. He had escaped from a pestilential prison camp in Malaya with two comrades, both American, in July 1943. One of them was a big, husky fellow from Texas and the other a Jewish boy from Brooklyn who possessed qualities of courage and endurance which were nothing short of fantastic. The three of them, after terrible vicissitudes, managed to get to Ceylon in an open boat. From there, after weeks in hospital, they were sent in a transport plane to Honolulu via Australia, New Zealand, New Caledonia and Fiji. In Honolulu they parted company. Tex and Lew, the Brooklyn boy, remained in Schofield barracks awaiting leave while Sid, through the goodwill of an American Naval Intelligence officer, was given space in a bomber which was flying to San Francisco. In San Francisco he reported to the British Consul who had notified the Naval attaché in Washington, who in turn notified the Admiralty in London. After three days, during which he had lived in a small hotel on money supplied by the Consul who had been extremely decent to him, the order came through from London that he was to take a week's leave and report to H.M.S. *Taragon* which was refitting in Norfolk, Virginia. He had cabled his mother and Sheila, but had purposely not let Morgan know that he was alive and safe because he wanted it to be a surprise. Well, here he was and it was certainly a surprise. He was finally led to bed, happily drunk, and the party broke up.

The next three days, the duration of Sid's visit, were a perpetual embarrassment to Morgan. Of course he told himself repeatedly how delighted he was that Sid, instead of being missing and presumed killed, was alive and kicking and exuberantly cheerful, but the strain was considerable.

The Sunday following upon Sid's dramatic arrival was hectic beyond all bearing. The house was besieged by reporters and cameramen. Sid was photographed interminably; inside the house, outside the house, by the pool, on the porch, with Morgan, without Morgan, with Lenore, without Lenore, with Fred, the coloured butler, and alone, in the shower. The telephone rang incessantly; sheaves of telegrams arrived; Arch Bowdler called personally and insisted on giving a dinner for Sid that very night. It was enormous, noisy and successful. Everybody, as usual, made speeches and for once no movie was shown, the emergence of Morgan's sailor brother from the jaws of death being a far greater attraction than any preview.

On the Monday, Ruthie's column in *Hollywood Highlights* was one long scream of hero-worship. All the other papers also were plastered with photographs of Sid, articles on Sid, anecdotes about Sid and interviews with Sid. Louella Parsons flung her arms round him in The Brown Derby and burst into tears and Hedda Hopper, looking extremely chic, appeared at a cocktail party wearing a new toque made entirely of palm fronds and white ensigns. To do Sid justice all this embarrassed him almost as much as it embarrassed Morgan, but for different reasons. Morgan's reactions, entangled as they were with family conscience, subconscious jealousy and an agitated inferiority complex, were difficult to define accurately. Sid's were quite simple. He was glad to be alive; delighted to see 'Old Les' again; pleased up to a point with all the fuss that was being made of him but aware in his heart that it was perhaps a bit overdone, and impatient, above all else, to get home – via Norfolk, Virginia – as soon as possible.

A RICHER DUST

Fortunately on the second day of his visit, Gareth Gibbons, a new and handsome L.N.G. 'Heart-throb' was arrested for driving a car while under the influence of alcohol, and attempting to rape a sixteen-year-old waitress in a milk bar in Brentwood Heights. This happily deflected the full blaze of publicity away from Sid, and his departure, on the Wednesday, was achieved, much to his relief, almost without comment.

The repercussions of his visit, however, were apparent for a long while. Morgan's behaviour had been exemplary throughout and most people had taken his carefully adjusted acceptance of Sid's reflected glory at its face value. Hollywood, however, is a strange place. It is filled with charming and talented people who work hard and do much to alleviate the miseries and troubles of the world. It is climatically amiable and steady; scenically it has much to offer; beautiful mountains surround it, efficient clear-cut architecture adorns it and blue skies, as a rule, smile down upon it. In spite of these advantages and a great many more besides, there is, as in all highly sensitive communities, an inevitable streak of cruelty and personal envy lying just below the radiant surface. There are, the fact must be frankly admitted, a few hard-boiled, over-sophisticated, unkind characters abroad whose pleasure it is to strike down the successful, undermine the contented and distort, whenever possible, the pure motives of human behaviour. These minds, it must also be frankly admitted, are frequently employed by the newspapers, for is it not from the newspapers that we first receive intimations that all is not well with our friends? In Morgan's case it was Ruthie's little bird that first started the trouble. The ungenerous innuendo made by that feathered scavenger two years before had been quickly forgotten, but now, reinforced by Sid's second and far more spectacular arrival in the colony, it chirped again and again with increasingly malicious effect. Presently, in the columns of larger, more revered periodicals than *Hollywood Highlights* unpleasant paragraphs about Morgan began to appear. Several of his magnanimous gestures towards the war effort were deprecated and questioned. His successful War Bond tour of the preceding year was alleged to have been mere publicity-hunting; his duodenal ulcer, which had been troubling him acutely since Sid's visit, was mocked at and above all the fact that he had large-heartedly given his entire salary for *High Adventure* to the British War Relief was smeared with the suggestion that, as this picture was one over his schedule for the year, he evaded a great deal of super-tax by doing so. All this of course was unmannerly and reprehensible, but alas, in public life it is often necessary to take the rough with the smooth, and occasionally with the rough. This Morgan was temperamentally incapable of doing. His spirits were not particularly resilient and his morale crumbled easily. As the insidious attacks upon his integrity increased and spread he became more and more nervy, irritable and morose. Lenore, to her eternal credit, stood by him loyally. On one occasion she even went so far as to slap Mona Melody's face in The Beachcomber when that lady unequivocally stated that Morgan's moving-picture career was shot to hell. But in spite of his wife's steadfastness and the devotion of his friends, things went from bad to worse.

High Adventure opened simultaneously in New York, Chicago and Hollywood, and was unanimously voted by the critics to be the worst picture to come out of Hollywood since the war. Morgan's personal notices were insulting and occasionally downright vituperative. He was torn to pieces with all the gleeful savagery that only well-established, perennially successful stars can ever inspire. Al Tierney, his agent, flew especially to the coast from New York and grave consultations ensued between him, the Studio Publicity Department, Lenore and Morgan himself. It was finally decided that he must publicly renounce his next two contracted pictures and go immediately on a tour of the war areas under the aegis of U.S.O. Morgan protested against this decision at first on the reasonable grounds that, being unable either to sing or dance, there was little that he could contribute to the entertainment of troops. He ultimately gave in, however; on the assurance that his rôle would be that of Master of Ceremonies and that all that would be required of him would be to talk nonchalantly into a microphone, tell a few funny stories, and introduce the more musical artists supporting him.

In March 1944 the party set forth across the Atlantic in a transport plane. They all wore khaki uniforms with U.S.O. 'flashes' on their shoulders and had a farewell party given for them at the Stork Club in New York on the eve of their departure.

The tour was strenuous but triumphant. They played Gibraltar, Oran, Algiers, Tunis, Tripoli, Malta and Cairo. Then, after a few days rest, they went on to Sicily, Naples and Rome. The show, being speedy, efficient and abundantly noisy, was received enthusiastically almost everywhere. Morgan had been paralysed with nerves at the first few performances but he gradually became more relaxed and began to enjoy himself. He discovered that the less effort he made, the more the troops liked him. He had been supplied with a few good stories before leaving and these he interspersed with impromptu comments of his own, some of which brought forth gratifying roars of laughter. The company consisted of Zaza Carryl, a slumbrous 'Blues' singer, who moaned lugubriously into the microphone and was invariably cheered to the echo; Ella Rosing, a very small starlet with a piercing coloratura, who went on first and sang 'Je Suis Titania' and 'The Bells of St Mary's'; Gus Gruber, who did card tricks interlarded with rather suggestive patter and finished up by playing a ukelele and singing and dancing at the same time; and Okie Wood and Buzzie Beckman, a vaudeville act who had the star position at the end of the programme and monotonously tore the place up. Lenore had been left behind in Beverly Hills, and Morgan, after a few half-hearted approaches to Ella Rosing, who was not really his type, finally settled on Zaza Carryl as the partner of his private pleasures. She was an amiable, uncomplicated creature and they got on very well.

Upon arrival in Rome towards the end of July, orders came through that when their week there was over they were to proceed to England. This caused a lot of discussion in the troupe and a great many jokes were made about food rationing, Doodlebugs and Rocket Bombs. Morgan, naturally enough, was tremendously excited at the thought of returning to his homeland after so many years absence and in such circumstances. He realized, without cynicism but with sheer common sense, that, from the publicity angle alone, it would be an excellent thing to do. Imagine therefore his bitter disappointment when, three days before they were due to leave he collapsed in agony half-way through a performance they were giving at an air base in the Campagna. He was hurried immediately into hospital, examined by several doctors, and X-rayed. Nothing definite appeared in the X-ray, but as his pains, although sporadic, were intense, and he was also in a bad state of nervous exhaustion, it was deemed wiser to fly him directly back to the States rather than let him risk continuing the tour.

His plane was met at Los Angeles by Lenore, Arch Bowdler, the deputy head of the Studio Publicity Department, Doc Mowbray, and an ambulance in which he was whisked off to a clinic where he stayed for three weeks undergoing various tests and gradually regaining his strength. The publicity accruing from his misfortune was, on the whole, innocuous. Even Ruthie's little bird, although a trifle sceptical, was forced to admit that Morgan's tour of the battle areas had been an unqualified success and that he had done a fine job and been popular with the 'Boys'.

CHAPTER IX

IN the autumn of 1945 Morgan's dream of returning home to England at last came true. During the defeat of the Nazis in Europe and the dropping of the Atomic Bomb on Hiroshima he had made two immensely successful pictures. His position now was more unassailable than it had ever been even in the year of his first meteoric rise to stardom. Only one thing marred the joy and gratification of his spectacular 'comeback' into public favour, and that was Lenore's unexpected and crude announcement that she was sick to death of him, was passionately in love with Tonio Lopez, and wished for a divorce as soon as it conveniently could be arranged. There were some violent scenes and much bitter recrimination during which the names of Opal

Myers and Zaza Carryl were hurled at his head with, it must be admitted, certain justification. Finally, with the assistance of two lawyers and the Studio Publicity Department and a lot of bickering, it was arranged that Lenore should divorce him on the grounds of mental cruelty and acute incompatibility of temperament. Soon after this Lenore unostentatiously left the house and retired, for discretion's sake, to her married sister's home in Salt Lake City. Morgan meanwhile, oppressed by a sense of matrimonial failure, was dispatched, in a blaze of publicity, to attend a Royal Command Performance of his latest picture *The Boy from the Hills* at the Empire Theatre, Leicester Square, London.

His reception in England surpassed not only his own but the Studio Publicity Department's wildest dreams. From the moment he stepped ashore from the *Queen Elizabeth* at Southampton he was mobbed by wildly cheering crowds. Sid, wearing inconspicuous civilian clothes, met him at the dock. His mother and Sheila remained at home on the advice of the English representative of the Studio Publicity Department who had organized for Morgan a triumphant return to Southsea on the coming Saturday and wished the long-awaited reunion of mother and son to be handled in the proper manner at the proper time.

At Waterloo Station Morgan was nearly trampled underfoot by his English fans and the expectant crowd outside Claridge's was so vast that special mounted police had to be deployed to keep it in order and deflect the traffic. The première at the Empire the next evening was, to Morgan, the accolade of his whole career. He received an ovation upon entering the theatre; was presented, with others, to the King and the Queen, and cheered with heartwarming enthusiasm at the end when he stepped on to the stage to make his personal appearance.

His return to his home-town of Southsea on the Saturday was even more tumultuous and, although not graced by the presence of Royalty, almost equally moving. The streets were hung with banners and flags; his mother and Sheila and the Mayor greeted him on the steps of the Town Hall, and it wasn't until after a reception at the Queen's Hotel, at which he was called upon to make one speech for the news-reels and another for the B.B.C., that he was allowed to relax in the bosom of his family. Even then the street remained thronged with adolescent enthusiasts for quite a while. His first impression on entering the familiar sitting-room was that it was much smaller than he remembered it to be. Sheila, married now and with two children, was as brusque and downright as ever. His mother had aged a good deal but her eyes were glistening with excitement and she was inclined to be tearful. After tea, conversation flagged a bit. All family news had been exhausted. Father's death and funeral in 1943 had been described in detail, also Sheila's wedding, the birth of both her children and Sid's intended marriage to a Miss Doris Solway in a few months' time. Strangely enough the devastation of the town in the early years of the war was hardly mentioned. Even the fact that Hadley's, where Morgan had once worked as a salesman, was now nothing but a mound of grass-covered rubble was only once lightly commented upon by Sheila.

Morgan found himself glancing furtively at his watch and hoping that the studio car would soon arrive to drive him back to London. It is sad to reflect how many family reunions are spoiled by anti-climax. The excitement and anticipation have been so strong; the moment so often and so gloriously pre-envisaged that the human heart seems unable to sustain the joy of actuality. Morgan's homecoming was naturally poignant and touching and happy. Not only this but it was publicly spectacular into the bargain. And yet, inevitably, when the first greetings were over, the occasion wilted and became soggy; little nervous jokes were made and there were unexplained silences. Presently the car arrived and Morgan got up to go. He kissed Sheila, wrung Sheila's husband's hand and banged Sid on the back. There was suddenly a renewed burst of conversation as though everything was perfectly normal. Morgan's mother, after a swift, appealing glance at Sheila, went out with him into the hall. He took her in his arms and was aware of a genuine surge of emotion. She felt frail and old and somehow pathetic. She stood away from him and gave her hair a little pat. 'Come back soon, Les,' she said, and then with a tremor in her voice, 'We didn't know anything about the ulcer, dear, it must have been dreadful.'

Morgan squeezed her arm affectionately. 'That's all over now, Mum, don't worry.'

'It isn't that . . .' she seemed to be speaking with an effort – 'But if anyone mentions your tubercular lung – do remember that we *had* to say something.'

Laurens van der Post

A Bar of Shadow

As we walked across the fields we hardly spoke. I, myself, no longer had the heart to try and make conversation. I had looked forward so eagerly to this Christmas visit of John Lawrence and yet now that he was here, we seemed incapable of talking to each other in a real way. I had not seen him for five years; not since we said goodbye at our prison gates on release at the end of the war, I to return to my civilian life, he to go straight back to the Army on active service. Until then for years he and I had walked as it were hand in hand with the danger of war and endured the same bitter things at the hands of the Japanese in prison. Indeed, when our release came we found that our experience, shared in the embattled world about us, fitted like a measured garment to the great and instinctive coincidence of affection we felt for each other. That moment of rounded nearness had stayed with me. There was no separation in it for me, no distance of purple leagues between him and me. I knew only too tell the cruel and unnecessary alliance (unnecessary because either one of them is powerful enough) that time and distance contract for waging their war against our brief and brittle human nearnesses. But if I had managed to stay close, why should he have been set so far apart? For that is precisely what I felt. Although he was so near to me that I had but to half-stretch out a hand to take his arm, never in five years of separation had he seemed so far away as now.

I stole a quick glimpse of him. The suit of pre-war tweeds which still fitted him perfectly, sat on his tall broad frame more like service uniform than becoming country garments and he was walking like a somnambulist at my side, with an odd unconscious deliberation and purposefulness, a strange, tranced expression on his face. His large grey eyes, set well apart under that fine and wide brow in a noble head, were blue with the distance between us. Even the light of that contracting December afternoon, receding from the day like the grey tide of a stilled sea from a forgotten and forlorn foreshore fuming silently in the gathering mists of time, glowed in his eyes not like a light from without so much as the fading tones of a frozen wintry moment far back in some calendar of his own within. Their focus clearly was not of that moment and that place and the irony of it was almost more than I could bear without protest.

I don't know what I would have done if something unknown within me, infinitely wiser and more knowledgeable than my conscious self marching at his side in bitter judgement over this resumption that was not a resumption of our relationship, had not suddenly swept into command and ordered me to ask: 'You have not by any chance run into "Rottang" Hara again?'

The question was out before I even knew I was going to ask it and instantly I felt a fool at having put it, so irrelevant and remote from that moment did it seem. But to my amazement, he stopped short in his tracks, turned to me and, like someone released from an emotion too tight for him, said with obvious relief:

'It is curious you asking me that! For I was thinking of him just then.' He paused slightly and then added with an apologetic laugh, as if he feared being misunderstood: 'I have been thinking of him all day. I can't get him out of my mind.'

My relief matched his, for instantly I recognized a contact that could bridge his isolation. Here was a pre-occupation I could understand and follow a long way even if I could not share it to the end. Just the thought of Hara and the mention of his name was enough to bring the living image of the man as clearly to my senses as if I had only just left him and as if at any moment now behind me that strange, strangled, nerve-taut, solar-plexus voice of his which exploded in him when he was enraged, would shriek '*Kura!*' – the rudest of the many rude ways in Japanese of saying: 'Come here, you!'

At the thought the hair on the back of my neck suddenly became sensitive to the cold air and involuntarily I looked over my shoulder as if I really expected to see him standing at the gate by the Long Barn beckoning us with an imperious arm stretched out straight in front of him, and one impatient hand beating the air like the wings of a large yellow butterfly in its last desperate flutter before metamorphosis into a creeping and crawling thing on earth. But the field behind us, of course, was empty, and the great, grey piece of winter, the tranquil and tranced benediction of a rest well earned by eager earth long wooed and well-beloved by man, lay over the tired and sleeping land. The scene indeed in that gently shrinking moment of daylight stood over itself as if it were an inner dream in the inmost sleep of itself, as if circumstances had contrived to make it conform absolutely to that vision which had made England a blessed thought of heaven on earth to us when we were in prison under Hara, and a rush of bitterness, rudely brushing aside the relief I had felt, went straight to my heart that Hara's twisted, contorted shape should still be able to walk this intimate and healing scene with us.

I said 'in prison under Hara' for though he was not the Commandant he was by far the greatest of the powers that ruled our prison world. He himself was only a third-class sergeant in His Imperial Japanese Majesty's forces and nominally we had a young subaltern in charge, but that slight young man more resembled an elegant character out of the novels of the great Murasaki or the pillow book of her hated rival than a twentieth-century Samurai. We seldom saw him and his interest in us seemed focused only on the extent to which we could add in variety and number to his collection of wrist-watches. John Lawrence, who had once been assistant military attaché in Tokyo, said he was certain our commandant was not born in the great hereditary military classes of Japan but was probably a second-class Customs official from Kobe or Yokohama who could therefore not be dishonoured as a real soldier would have been by an ignominious appointment to command a camp of despised prisoners of war. But Hara, he said, was the real thing, not of the officer class, but the authentic feudal follower, unhesitatingly accompanying his master and overlords into battle. He had served his masters long and well, had fought in Korea, Manchuria, China, and this unexacting job now, presumably, was his reward.

I don't know how right Lawrence was, but one thing stood out: Hara had no inferiority complex about his officer. One had only to see them together to realize which was authentic, predestined military material and which merely deriving colour and benefit from war. Scrupulously correct as Hara was in his outward behaviour to his officer, we had no doubt that inwardly he felt superior. He never hesitated to take command of a situation when he thought it necessary. I have seen him on inspections walk rudely in between the Commandant and our ranks, haul out someone who had unwittingly transgressed his mysterious code of what was due on these occasions, and in a kind of semi-conscious epilepsy of fury beat the poor fellow nearly to death with anything that came to hand, while his disconcerted officer took himself and his refined-Custom-house senses off to a more tranquil part of the parade-ground. No! Not he but Hara ruled us with a cold, predetermined, carefully conditioned and archaic will of steel as tough as the metal in the large, two-handed sword of his ancestors dangling on his incongruous prehistoric hip.

It was he, Hara, who decided how much or rather how little we had to eat. He ordained when we were driven to bed, when we got up, where and how we paraded, what we read. It was he who ordered that every book among the few we possessed wherein the word 'kiss' or mention of 'kissing' appeared, should be censored by having the offending pages torn out and publicly burned as an offence against

'Japanese morality'. It was he who tried to 'purify' our thinking by making us in our desperately undernourished condition go without food for two days at a time, confined in cramped and over-crowded cells, forbidden even to talk so that we could contemplate all the better our perverse and impure European navels. It was he who beat me because a row of beans that he had made my men plant had not come up and he put the failure down to my 'wrong thinking'. It was he who, when drunk, would babble to me endlessly about Greta Garbo and Marlene Dietrich whose faces haunted him. He who questioned me for hours about Knights of the Round Table, '606', Salvarsan and the latest drugs for curing syphilis. He mounted and controlled our brutal Korean guards, gave them their orders and made them fanatical converts, more zealous than their only prophet, to his outlook and mood. He made our laws, judged us for offences against them, punished us and even killed some of us for breaking them.

He was indeed a terrible little man, not only in the way that the great Tartar Ivan was terrible but also in a peculiarly racial and demonic way. He possessed the sort of terribleness that thousands of years of littleness might seek to inflict on life as both a revenge and a compensation for having been so little for so long. He had an envy of tallness and stature which had turned to an implacable hatred of both, and when his demon – an ancient, insatiable and irresistibly *compelled* aspect of himself that lived somewhere far down within him with a great yellow autonomy and will of its own – stirred in him I have seen him beat-up the tallest among us for no other reason save that they were so much taller than he. Even his physical appearance was both a rejection and a form of vengeance on normality, a vaudeville magnification and a caricature of the Japanese male figure.

He was so short that he just missed being a dwarf, so broad that he was almost square. He hardly had any neck and his head, which had no back to it, sat almost straight on his broad shoulders. The hair on his head was thick and of a midnight-blue. It was extremely coarse and harsh in texture and, cut short, stood stark and stiff like the bristles on a boar's back straight up in the air. His arms were exceptionally long and seemed to hang to his knees but his legs by contrast were short, extremely thick and so bowed that the sailors with us called him 'Old Cutlass-legs'. His mouth was filled with big faded yellow teeth, elaborately framed in gold, while his face tended to be square and his forehead rather low and simian. Yet he possessed a pair of extraordinarily fine eyes that seemed to have nothing to do with the rest of his features and appearance. They were exceptionally wide and large for a Japanese and with the light and polish and warm, living, luminous quality of the finest Chinese jade in them. It was extraordinary how far they went to redeem this terrible little man from caricature. One looked into his eyes and all desire to mock vanished, for then one realized that this twisted being was, in some manner beyond European comprehension, a dedicated and utterly selfless person.

It was John Lawrence, who suffered more at Hara's hands than any of us except those whom he killed, who first drew our attention to his eyes. I remember so clearly his words one day after a terrible beating in prison.

'The thing you mustn't forget about Hara,' he had said, 'is that he is not an individual or for that matter even really a man.' He had gone on to say that Hara was the living myth, the expression in human form, the personification of the intense, inner vision which, far down in their unconscious, keeps the Japanese people together and shapes and compels their thinking and behaviour. We should not forget two thousand and seven hundred full cycles of his sun-goddess's rule burnt in him. He was sure no one could be more faithful and responsive to all the imperceptible murmurings of Japan's archaic and submerged racial soul than he. Hara was humble enough to accept implicitly the promptings of his national spirit. He was a simple, uneducated country lad with a primitive integrity unassailed by higher education, and really believed all the myths and legends of the past so deeply that he did not hesitate to kill for them. Only the day before he had told Lawrence how in Manchuria the sun-goddess had once lifted a train full of soldiers over an undetected Chinese mine laid for them on the track and put them all down again safely on the other side.

'But just look in his eyes,' Lawrence had said: 'there is nothing ignoble or insincere there: only an ancient light, refuelled, quickened and brightly burning. There is something about the fellow I rather like and respect.'

This last sentence was such heresy among us at the time that I protested at once. Nothing Lawrence could say or explain could wash our *bête noir blanc* or even *jaune* for that matter, and I would have none of it.

'The troops do not call him "Rottang" for nothing,' I had reminded him severely. 'Rottang' is the Malay for the kind of cane Hara was seldom without. The troops christened him that because he would at times, seemingly without cause, beat them over the head and face with it.

'He can't help himself,' John Lawrence had said. 'It is not he but an act of Japanese gods in him, don't you see? You remember what the moon does to him!'

And indeed I remembered. The attraction, both the keen conscious and the deep, submerged attraction that all the Japanese feel for the moon seemed to come to a point in Hara. If ever there was a moon-swung, moon-haunted, moon-drawn soul it was he. As the moon waxed – and how it waxed in the soft, velvet sky of Insulinda, how it grew and seemed to swell to double its normal gold and mystically burning proportions in that soft, elastic air; how it swung calmly over the great volcanic valleys like a sacred lamp, while the ground mist, mingling with the smell of cloves, cinnamon and all the fragrant spices of Insulinda drifted among the soaring tree trunks like incense round the lacquered columns of a sequined temple – Yes! as this unbelievable moon expanded and spread its gold among the blacknessses of our jungle night, we saw it draw a far tide of mythological frenzy to the full in Hara's blood. Seven days, three days before and three days after and on the day of the full moon itself, were always our days of greatest danger with Hara. Most of his worst beatings and all his killings took place then. But once the beating was over and the moon waning, he would be, for him, extraordinarily generous to us. It was as if the beating and killing had purged him of impurities of spirit, of madness and evil in some strange way and made him grateful to them. In fact, the morning after he had cut off the head of one of us, I remembered seeing him talking to Lawrence and being struck by the fact that he had an expression of purified, of youthful and almost springlike innocence on his face, as if the sacrifice of the life of an innocent British aircraftman the night before, had redeemed him from all original as well as private and personal sin, and appeased for the time the hungry bat-like gods of his race.

All this passed through my mind like a dream with the speed and colour of a dream and it was almost as a man half-asleep that I heard Lawrence continue: 'Yes. It is curious that you too should think of him just then; for I have an anniversary of Hara in me today, that I am not allowed to forget, try as I may. Have I ever told you?'

He had not, and eager to consolidate any contact between us, even this grim, precarious bridge, I said quickly: 'No! Please tell me.'

Well, it was exactly seven years ago, he said, seven years within an hour or so, allowing for differences of Insulinda and Greenwich mean time. He was lying in a dream beyond the deep, raw, physical pain in his bruised and outraged body, when far away, like a bird perched on the daylight rim of a deep well into which he might have been thrown, he heard the first chee-chak call. Yes, that was it: a chee-chak, one of those agile, translucent little lizards that lived in every hut, house and even deepest dungeons in Insulinda. There were two of them in his cell and he loved them dearly. They had shared his solitary confinement from the beginning and in his affection for them he fancied he could tell them apart, the male from the female, just by the sound of their voices. They were the only living things not Japanese or Korean, not an active, aggressive enemy that he had seen for many weeks. So real had they become to him that he christened them Patrick and Patricia. He knew instantly when he heard the sound, that the sound came from Patricia, and at once he was out of the dream that had consoled and drugged his pain, and back on the damp stone floor with his bruised, stiff, aching and tired body, so tired that it could hardly take note even of the dismay which clutched at his heart the moment Patricia called. For she called like that only when it was well and truly dark, only when the jungle outside had closed its ranks and fallen back on its own black shadows between the purple volcanoes, the better to withstand that sheer, utter obliteration of outline and shape brought about by the overwhelming invasion of the moonless tropical night in the valley outside. It was as if then Patricia herself was afraid and wanted Patrick quickly to rejoin and reassure her that this great black nothingness abolished only the vision of the nearness of her mate and not the nearness itself. There! Patrick had answered her, and Lawrence knew his fear was justified. For this was the hour at which the Japanese usually came for him; this was the time of night when they usually did their torturing. Yes, the details of it were not important, he said, but for weeks they had been torturing him, and the interesting thing was they did it always at night.

I might smile and think him fanciful as I did about his belief that Hara was an embodiment of a myth more than a conscious individual being, even though I had seen for myself how moon-swung Hara and his countrymen were. But that was by no means all there was to it. That was only the elementary beginning of it all. The more complete truth was: they were all still deeply submerged like animals, insects and plants in the succession of the hours, the movement of day into night and of the days into their lunar months and the months into their seasons. They were subject to cosmic rhythm and movement and ruled by cosmic forces beyond their control to an extent undreamt of in the European mind and philosophy. He would have more to say of that presently, but all he had to stress at the moment was this: it was only at night that people so submerged in the raw elements of nature could discover sufficiently the night within themselves – could go down far enough with the sun and sunlight into that deep, deep pit of blackness in time and themselves to the bottom of their own unlit natures, where torture was not only natural but inevitable, like the tides of the sea. I may not recognize it, he said, but Patricia and Patrick knew in the nerves and very swish of their tidal tails that a moment of great and ancient dread in the movement of the spheres had come. And hardly had they called, when he heard the jack-booted steps, untidy and slurred as if the boots were mounted on an orang-utan and not a man, coming down the corridor towards his cell.

'Our Father which art in heaven,' his lips moved instinctively. 'Once more please be thou my shepherd.'

As he said this prayer for the third time to himself, the door was unlocked and a Korean guard called out, in a mixture of the crudest Japanese and Malay and in the most arrogant and insolent tone: '*Kura!* You there, come here! *Lakas!* Quick!'

He got up slowly. He could not in his condition do otherwise, but it was too slow for the guard who jumped into the cell, pulled Lawrence angrily to his feet and pushed him out into the corridor, prodding him with the butt of his rifle and saying again and again: '*Lakas! Lakas!*' and 'Quick! Quick!' as well as making other strange irritated abdominal noises at him. In a few minutes he was marched into the Commandant's office and there sitting at the Commandant's desk was not that girlish young subaltern, but Hara himself with a section of the guard, hat in hand and rifles at the side standing respectfully behind him. Lawrence, his eyes hurting as if stung by bees in that fierce electric light, looked round the room for the rest of the inquisition as he called them, that expert band from the Kempeitai, the headquarters of the secret police, who did the real torturing, but there was not a sign of any of them.

For the first time a feeling of hope so keen and unnerving that his conscious mind would not allow it, assailed him fiercely. True, Hara was one of the band but not the worst. He joined in too but only when that deep sense of an almost mystical necessity to participate in all that a group or herd of his countrymen did, forced him to identify himself with what was going on. It was as if they were incapable of experiencing anything individually; as if a thought or deed in one was instantly contagion to the rest and the fated plague of cruel-doing like a black or yellow death killed their individual resistances in an instant. Hara, after all, was the Japanese of the Japanese among them and he too would have to join in the torturing. But he never started it and Lawrence knew somehow that he would have preferred killing outright to protracted torture. With all this in his mind he looked at Hara more closely and noticed that his eyes were unusually bright and his cheeks flushed.

'He has been drinking,' he thought, for there was no mistaking in Hara's cheeks the tell-tale pink that drink brings so easily to the Japanese face. 'And that accounts for the glitter in his eye. I had better watch out.'

He was right about the flush in Hara's cheeks but wrong about the light in his eyes, for suddenly Hara said, with a curl of the lip that might have been a smile strangled at birth: 'Rorensu-san: do you know Fazeru Kurïsumasu?'

The unexpected use of the polite 'san' to his name so nearly unnerved Lawrence that he could hardly concentrate on the mysterious 'Fazeru Kurïsumasu' in Hara's question, until he saw the clouds of incomprehension at his slowness, which usually preluded frenzy, gathering over Hara's impatient brow. Then, he got it.

'Yes, Hara-san,' he said slowly. 'I know of Father Christmas.'

'Heh-to!' Hara exclaimed, hissing with polite gratification between his teeth, a gleam of gold sparkling for a moment between his long lips. Then sitting far back in his chair, he announced: 'Tonight I am Fazeru Kurïsumasu!' Three or four times he made this astonishing statement, roaring with laughter.

Lawrence joined in politely without any idea what it really meant. He had been lying there in his cell alone, under sentence of death, for so long that he hardly knew the hour of the night beyond the fact that it was normal torture hour, and he had no idea of the date or month; he certainly had no idea that it was Christmas.

Hara enjoyed his announcement and Lawrence's obvious perplexity so much that he would have gone on prolonging his moment of privileged and one-sided merriment, had not a guard presented himself at that moment in the doorway and ushered in a tall, bearded Englishman, in the faded uniform of a Group-Captain in the R.A.F.

Hara stopped laughing instantly and an expression of reserve, almost of hostility came over his features at the sight of Hicksley-Ellis's elongated frame in the doorway.

I could see Hara clearly, as Lawrence spoke; could see him stiffen at the R.A.F. officer's entrance, for of all of us he hated the tall, lisping Hicksley-Ellis, I think, by far the most.

'This Air Force Colonel,' he told Lawrence in Japanese, waving his hand disdainfully at the Group-Captain, 'is Commander of the prisoners in my camp; you can go with him now.'

Lawrence hesitated, not believing his ears, and Hara, confirmed in his own sense of the magnanimity of his gesture by the unwilled expression of disbelief on Lawrence's face, sat back and laughed all the more. Seeing him laugh like that again, Lawrence at last believed him and walked over to join the Group-Captain. Together, without a word, they started to go but as they got to the door, Hara in his fiercest parade voice called: 'Rorensu!'

Lawrence turned round with a resigned despair. He might have known it, known that this transition was too sudden, too good to be true; this was but part of the torture; some psychologist secret police must have put the simple Hara up to it. But one look at Hara's face reassured him. He was still beaming benevolently, a strange twisted smile, between a quick, curling lip and yellow teeth framed in gold on his twilight face. With an immense, hissing effort, as he caught Lawrence's eye, he called out, 'Rorensu: Merry Kurïsumasu!'

'Merry' and 'Fazeru Kurïsumasu' were the only English words Lawrence ever heard him use and he believed Hara knew no others. Hara went pinker still with the effort of getting them out, before he relaxed, purring almost like a cat, in the Commandant's chair.

'But he knew something about Christmas, all the same,' I interrupted

Lawrence. 'It was most extraordinary, you know. When the Padre, Hicksley-Ellis and I, thought of organizing some celebration of our first Christmas in gaol, we never thought for a moment a thug like Hara would allow it. But the curious thing was when we asked him, he exclaimed at once, so our interpreter said: "The feast of Fazeru Kurïsumasu!' When the interpreter answered "Yes", Hara agreed at once. No argument or special plea was needed. He said "Yes" firmly, and his orders went out accordingly. In fact, he was himself so taken by the idea that he went to the other camps that were also in his Officers command, camps with non-Christian Chinese, animistic Menadonese and Moslem Javanese in them and forced them all to celebrate Christmas whether they liked it or not. The interpreter told us, in fact, that Hara even beat up the Chinese commandant. When Hara asked him who Fazeru Kurïsumasu was, the unsuspecting man quite truthfully said he had no idea. Whereupon Hara called him a liar, a crime in his code equal to "wrong thinking" and "wilfulness", said all the world knew who "Fazeru Kurïsumasu" was, and at once flew into one of his frenzies. It was odd, very odd, the value he attached to Christmas; we never found out where he got it from. Did you?'

'I am afraid not,' Lawrence answered, 'but odder still it saved my life.'

'You never told us!' I exclaimed, amazed.

'No, I did not, for I didn't know it myself at the time, though I expected it of course from my own sentence. But I saw my papers after the war and they were actually going to kill me on December 27. But your putting the idea of Christmas into Hara's head saved me. He substituted a Chinaman for me and let me out as a gesture to "Fazeru Kurïsumasu." But to continue . . .'

He had followed Hicksley-Ellis out of Hara's office and joined up with me again in the common prison. Suddenly he smiled at me, a gentle, reminiscent and tenderly grateful smile as the relief of his release came back to him. Did I remember the moment? He could not but be amused in his recollection, for although we were all incarcerated in a Dutch colonial gaol for murderers and desperate criminals, so relative had our concept of freedom become, that we rushed up to him and congratulated him on his liberation without a trace on our part, or a suspicion on his, of the irony implicit in it.

Then not long afterwards Hara suddenly left us. He was put in charge of a draft of R.A.F. officers and men under Hicksley-Ellis, and sent to build aerodromes in the outer islands. We did not see him again until near the end, when he returned with only one-fifth of the original draft left alive. Our men looked like ghosts or drought-stricken cattle when they arrived back. We could see their shoulder-blades and ribs through their thread-bare tunics. They were so weak that we had to carry most of them in stretchers from the cattle-trucks wherein they had travelled, trucks which stank of urine and diseased excretions. For not only were they so starved that just a faint pulse of life fluttering with a rapidly regressive spirit was left in them, but also they all had either dysentery, malignant malaria or both. One-fifth was all that remained; the rest were dead and Hicksley-Ellis had terrible things to tell of their treatment by the Japanese officers and N.C.O.s and their Korean underlings, and above all about Hara. Again, Hara was at the centre, the primordial Japanese core of this weird inspiration of distorted circumstances. It was he who was again *de facto* if not *de jure* ruler of their world; he who beat dying men saying there was nothing wrong with them except their 'spirit', their 'evil thinking', their 'wayward wilfulness of heart' which made them deliberately ill in order to retard the Japanese war effort. It was he, Hara, who cut off the heads of three Aircraftmen because they had crept through a fence at night to buy food in a village, and after each head rolled on the ground brought his sword to his lips thanking it for having done its work so cleanly. It was he who day after day in the tropical sun drove a horde of men ailing and only half alive to scrape an aerodrome out of coral rock with inadequate tools until they were dying and being thrown to the sharks in the sea at the rate of twenty or thirty a day. But Hara himself appeared untouched by his experience, as if he had foreseen and presuffered it all in his mother's womb, as if life could neither add to nor diminish the stark wine in his legendary cup. He came back to us burnt black by the sun; that was all. For the rest he naturally took up the steely thread of Command where he left it as if he had never been away, and drove us again with the same iron hand.

Even at the end when the prison was full of rumours and the treacherous, unstable Korean guards, scenting a change in the wind of time, were beginning to fawn and make-up to our men for past misdeeds, were even whining to them about their own suppression under the Japanese, when the ground under the feet of Hara's war lords was cracking and reverberating from the shock of the explosions at Hiroshima and Nagasaki and when the legendary twilight of the submerged racial soul of Japan must have been dark and sagging under the weight of the wings of dragons coming home to roost, Hara never trembled nor wavered once. He must have known as well as anybody what was going on, but in that tide of rumour and wild emotion running free before the wind of change, he stood like a rock.

Only three days before the end there was a terrible scene with Lawrence. Lawrence had found a Korean sentry, one of the worst, prodding a dying man with his bayonet, trying to make the Aircraftman stand up to salute him. Lawrence had seized the sentry's rifle with both hands, pushed the bayonet aside and forced himself between the sentry and the sick man. He was immediately marched off to the guardroom, arriving there just as Hara returned from a tour of inspection. The sentry told Hara what had happened and Hara, much as he liked Lawrence, would not overlook this insult to the arms of his country. He beat-up Lawrence with his cane over the face and head so thoroughly that I hardly recognized him when he joined us again.

Three days later the end came and we all went our inevitable ways. Lawrence did not see Hara again for nearly two years. When he saw Hara then it was in dock at his trial. Yes! Hadn't I heard? Hara was sought out and brought to trial before one of our War Crimes Tribunals. It was largely Hicksley-Ellis's doing of course. I could have no idea how bitter that mild, lisping, sensitive fellow had become. It was understandable, of course, after what he had suffered, that he should be truly, implacably and irretrievably bitter and vengeful, and he gave his evidence at the trial with such a malign relish and fury that Hara never had a hope of a mitigated sentence, let alone acquittal. But what was not so understandable was the bitterness of the official prosecution, for bitter as Hicksley-Ellis was, his temper was more than matched by that of the war-crimes sleuths.

'And that,' Lawrence exclaimed, incomprehension on his broad brow, 'was very odd to me. After all, none of them had suffered under the Japanese. As far as I know, not one of the particular bunch on Hara's trail had even been on active service but they were none-the-less a bloodthirsty lot. They were more vengeful on behalf of our injuries than I myself could ever be.'

He said all this in such a way that I gathered he had tried to plead for Hara and had failed. It certainly seemed highly significant to me that when Lawrence held his hand out after the trial to say goodbye, Hicksley-Ellis had refused to take it and silently turned a neat, tense Air Force back on him. I could not resist asking therefore:

'Did you tell the Court that Hara saved your life?'

'Indeed I did,' he replied, surprised that I should have found the question necessary. 'I did that and the judge-advocate looked me up and down over a pair of the most unmilitary glasses and said in a slow, precise voice, each syllable as distinct and pointed as a letter pen-pricked on a blank sheet of paper, a trace of ponderous irony, for which I can't blame him, in his voice: "That, of course, Colonel Lawrence, is a valuable consideration – most valuable, indeed hardly less valuable to this court than it must be to you; but it must not be overlooked that there are many others for whom life would have been no less valuable who are not here today as a direct result of the accused's actions." '

No, there was obviously nothing to be done. Hara was inevitably condemned to be hanged.

'How did he take it?' I asked with the memory of the way others had marched to the fall of Hara's keen two-headed sword on the backs of their necks as fresh in my mind as if it were a picture painted that morning.

'Without a tremor or change of expression, as you would have expected,' Lawrence said. 'After all, he had pleaded guilty from the start, said, as that hopelessly inadequate interpreter told the Court: "I am wrong for my people and ready to die!" He made no effort to defend himself except to say that he tried never to do more or less than his duty. He called no witnesses, asked no questions even of me, and just went on standing silently and rigidly to attention in the box right to the end. Besides, all that too had been foreseen.'

'Foreseen?' I asked, surprised.

Yes! He explained Hara had never expected anything except death of some kind in the war. In fact, in an unconscious way, perhaps he had even longed for death. I must please not be too sceptical but try and follow what he was trying to say with intuition rather than with conscious understanding. This was the other half of what he'd been trying to say in the beginning. It was most important, most relevant and the one foundation whereon his understanding either stood erect or fell . . . He had always felt even when he was in Japan that the Japanese were a people in a profound, inverse, reverse, or if I preferred it, even perverse sense, more in love with death than living. As a nation they romanticized death and self-destruction as no other people. The romantic fulfilment of the national ideal, of the heroic thug of tradition, was often a noble and stylized self-destruction in a selfless cause. It was as if the individual at the start, at birth even, rejected the claims of his own individuality. Henceforth he was inspired not by individual human precept and example so much as by his inborn sense of the behaviour of the corpuscles in his own blood dying every split second in millions in defence of the corporate whole. As a result they were socially not unlike a more complex extension of the great insect societies in life. In fact in the days when he lived in Japan, much as he liked the people and country, his mind always returned involuntarily to this basic comparison: the just parallel was not an animal one, was not even the most tight and fanatical horde, but an insect one: collectively they were a sort of super-society of bees with the Emperor as a male queen-bee at the centre. He did not want to exaggerate these things but he knew of no other way of making me realize how strangely, almost cosmically, propelled like an eccentric and dying comet on an archaic, anti-clockwise and foredoomed course, Hara's people had been. They were so committed, blindly and mindlessly entangled in their real and imagined past that their view of life was not synchronized to our urgent time. Above all they could not respond to the desperate twentieth-century call for greater and more precise individual differentiation. Their view of life refused to be individual and to rise above their own volcanic and quaking earth, as if there was always a dark glass or the shadow of the dragon's wings of their submerged selves between them and the light of individual mind, a long blackness of their own spinning globe between them and the sun, darkening the moon for which they yearned so eagerly, and some of the finest stars. He was sorry if it sounded fantastic but he could put it no other way. Unless . . .

He paused and looked at the simple spire of the village church just appearing in a dip in the fold of the fields in front of us, as if its precise and purposeful shape presiding so confidently over the trusting and sleeping land, rebuked the shapeless, unformed and dim-lit region wherein his imagination moved so like a lone sleep-walker at midnight. Thereupon, he broke off the apparent continuity of his thought at once and asked me if I knew how the Japanese calculated the age of an individual? I said 'No' and he explained that at birth they added nine months to a person's life, counted in all the days between his conception and emergence from the womb. Didn't I see the significance of that? Didn't I realize that such a system of reckoning life was not just an artless and naïve accident of minds more primitive than ours? If I paused to reflect how biology clearly establishes that we recapture and relive in the womb the whole evolution of life from amoeba to pithecanthropus erectus, surely I too would recognize implicit in this system of reckoning a clear instinctive acknowledgement of the importance of the dim past to the Japanese character. He certainly looked at it that way and until now he had been forced to think of them as a people whose spiritual and mental umbilical cord with the past was uncut; as a people still tied by the navel to the mythical mother and begetter of their race, the great sun-goddess Ama-terasu. Even in that they were characteristically perverse, reverse and inside out, for to most races in the past the sun was a bright and shining masculine deity, but to them only a great, darkly glittering mother. While the moon, so beloved and eternally feminine to the rest of mankind, was male and masculine to them. Perhaps it was that inside-out, upside-down subjection to the past which gave them their love of death.

If I had ever attended a feast of the dead in Japan as he had often done I would not be surprised at his use of so strange a word as love to illustrate his meaning. That feast was the gayest and most cheerful of all Japanese celebrations. Their dead were happy, cheerful, contented and benevolent spirits. Why? Because the living, one felt, really preferred dying to living as they had to live; not only preferred it but also thought it nobler to die than to live for their country. Not life but death was romantic to them and Hara was no exception. He had all this and more, deeply ingrained in him, underneath and beyond conscious thinking; he had more because above all he was a humble, simple and believing country fellow as well.

'I shall never forget one night in prison,' Lawrence continued, picking up yet another thread of our prison yesterdays, and weaving it as if it were something new and freshly made into this pattern of Hara in his mind until my heart was heavy that so much should remain for him apparently immune to time. 'Hara sent for me. He had been drinking and greeted me uproariously but I knew his merriment was faked. He always behaved like that when his heart and mind were threatening to join in revolt against his long years of exile from Japan. I could see that the drink had failed to blur the keen edge of nostalgia that was like a knife-stab in the pit of his stomach. He wanted someone to talk to about his country and for some hours I walked Japan from end to end with him through all four of its unique and dramatic seasons. The mask of cheerfulness got more and more threadbare as the evening wore on and at last Hara tore it from his face.

' "Why, Rorensu," he exclaimed fiercely at last. "Why are you alive? I would like you better if you were dead. How could an officer of your rank ever have allowed himself to fall alive in our hands? How can you bear the disgrace? Why don't you kill yourself?" '

'Yes. He asked me that too once,' I interrupted, more with the object of letting Lawrence know how closely I was following him than of telling him something he didn't know. 'In fact he taunted us all so much with it that in time the Koreans picked up the habit, too, but what did you say in reply?'

'I admitted the disgrace, if he wished to call it that,' Lawrence replied. 'But said that in our view disgrace, like danger, was something which also had to be bravely borne and lived through, and not run away from by a cowardly taking of one's own life. This was so novel and unexpected a point of view to him that he was tempted to dismiss it as false and made himself say: "No! no! no! it is fear of dying that stops you all." He spat disdainfully on the floor and then tapping on his chest with great emphasis added: "I am already dead. I, Hara, died many years ago."

'And then it came out, of course. The night before he left home to join the army at the age of seventeen, that is after nine months in the womb and sixteen years and three months on earth, he had gone to a little shrine in the hills nearby to say goodbye to life, to tell the spirits of his ancestors that he was dying that day in his heart and spirit for his country so that when death came to claim him in battle it would be a mere technicality, so that far from being surprised he would greet it either like a bosom friend, long expected and overdue, or merely accept it as formal confirmation of a state which had long existed. To hear him one would have thought that this bow-legged boy, with his blue-shaven head, yellow face and shuffling walk, had gone to report to his ancestors his decision to enter one of the grimmer monastic orders like the Grande Chartreuse, rather than to announce his banal intention of joining a regiment of infantry. But you see what I mean, when I say the end too had been foreseen?'

I nodded silently, too interested to want to speak, and Lawrence went steadily on. Even that evening in prison Lawrence was conscious of a content, a sort of extra-territorial meaning to the moment that did not properly belong to it. It was as if Hara's end was drinking his wine with him, as if far down at some inexpressible depth in their minds the ultimate sentence was already pronounced. Looking back now, he found it most significant, that towards the end of the evening, Hara began to try his hand at composing verses in that tight, brief and extremely formal convention in which the popular hero of the past in Japan inevitably said farewell to the world before taking his own life. He remembered Hara's final effort well: roughly translated it ran:

'When I was seventeen looking over the pines at Kurashiyama, I saw on the full yellow moon, the shadow of wild-geese flying South. There is no shadow of wild-geese returning on the moon rising over Kurashi-yama tonight.'

'Poor devil: as I watched and listened to him trying to break into verse, suddenly I saw our roles reversed. I saw as if by a flash of lightning in the darkness of my own mind that I was really the free man and Hara, my gaoler, the prisoner. I had once in my youth in those ample, unexacting days before the war when the coining of an epigram had looked so convincingly like a discovery of wisdom, defined individual freedom to myself as freedom to choose one's own cage in life. Hara had never known even that limited freedom. He was born in a cage, a prisoner in an oubliette of mythology, chained to bars welded by a great blacksmith of the ancient gods themselves. And I felt an immense pity for him. And now, four years later, Hara was our kind of prisoner as well and in the dock for the last time, with sentence of death irrevocably pronounced.'

So unsurprised, so unperturbed was Hara, Lawrence said, that as his escort snapped the handcuffs on him and ordered him to step down to his cell below, he stopped on the edge of the concealed stair, turned round with the utmost self-composure, sought out Lawrence and Hicksley-Ellis who were sitting side by side next to the prosecuting officer. When his eyes met theirs, he raised his manacled hands above his head, clasped them together like those of a boxer who had just won the world championship and waved gaily to the two of them, grinning a golden smile from ear to ear as he did so.

How clearly I saw him do it: that gesture was all of a piece with the character also as I knew it, for whatever it was that held Hara together,

I too knew that he could never fail it. Suddenly I was glad, almost grateful to him that he had taken it like that, gone from our view with a gay, triumphant gesture of farewell, for somehow, I imagined, that would make it easier for us now to have done with his memory.

'So that was how he went,' I remarked, not without a certain unwilled relief, 'that then was Hara's that.'

'No, not at all,' Lawrence said quickly, a strange new ring in his voice, a passionate and surprisingly emotional undertone for so calm and contemplative a person. 'That by no means was his "that". As far as I am concerned "that" was only the end of the beginning of the "that" . . .'

It came out then that the night before he was hanged, Hara got a message through, begging Lawrence to come and see him. Hara had made the request – his last – many days before but it was not surprising to anyone who knew the 'usual official channels' as well as we did that the request did not reach Lawrence until ten o'clock on the night before the morning set for the execution. Lawrence got his car out as fast as he could; his chivalrous nature outraged by the thought that the condemned man would now most certainly have given up all hope of seeing him, and be preparing to die with the bitter conviction that even his last slight request had been too much. Hara's prison was on the far side of the island and he could not, with the best of luck, get there before midnight.

The evening was very still and quiet, rather as if it had caught its own breath at the beauty and brilliance of the night that was marching down on it out of the East like a goddess with jewels of fire. An immense full moon had swung itself clear over the dark fringe of the jungle bound, like a ceremonial fringe of ostrich plumes designed for an ancient barbaric ritual, to the dark brow of the land ahead. In that responsive and plastic tropical air the moon seemed magnified to twice its normal size and to be quick-silver wet and dripping with its own light. To the north of the jungle and all along its heavy feathered fringes the sea rolled and unrolled its silver and gold cloak on to the white and sparkling sand, as lightly and deftly as a fine old far-eastern merchant unrolling bales of his choicest silk. The ancient, patient swish of it all was constantly in Lawrence's ears. But far out on the horizon, the sea too went dark, seemed shrunk into a close defensive ring, in face of the thunder and lightning hurled against it by curled, curved and jagged peaks of cloud which stood revealed on the uttermost edge by the intermittent electric glow imperative in purple and sullen in gold. It was the sort of night and the kind of setting in a half-way moment between the end of one day and the beginning of the other, in which Lawrence's articulate knowledge seemed to hold the same urgent, spasmodic, and intermittent quality as the electricity and lightning quivering along the horizon; yet his inarticulate, inexpressible awareness of the abiding meaning, beauty and richness of life was as great as the vast, eager-footed and passionate night striding overhead like a queen to a meeting with a royal lover. All that we had been through, the war, the torture, the long hunger, all the grim and tranced years in our sordid prison, he found light and insignificant weighed in the golden scales of that moment. The thought that yet another life should be sacrificed to our discredited and insufficient past, seemed particularly pointless and repugnant and filled him with a sense of angry rebellion. In this mood and manner he arrived at the prison just before midnight. He found he was expected and was taken at once to Hara's cell.

Like all condemned persons Hara was alone in the cell. When the door opened to let Lawrence in, although there was a chair at hand Hara was standing by the window, his face close to the bars, looking at the moonlight, so vivid and intense by contrast to the darkness inside that it was like a sheet of silver silk nailed to the square window. He had obviously given up all idea of visitors and was expecting, at most, only a routine call from one of his gaolers. He made no effort to turn round or speak. But as the guard switched on the light he turned to make a gesture of protest and saw Lawrence. He stiffened as if hit by a heavy blow in the back, came to attention and bowed silently and deeply to his visitor in a manner which told Lawrence that he was moved beyond words. As he bowed Lawrence saw that his head had been freshly shaven and that the new scraped skin shone like satin in the electric light. Lawrence ordered the sentry to leave them for a while, and as the door once more closed he said to Hara who was coming out of his low bow:

'I'm very sorry I am so late. But I only got your message at nine o'clock. I expect you gave me up as a bad job long ago and thought I'd refused to come.'

'No, Rorensu-san,' Hara answered. 'No, not that. I never thought you would refuse to come, but I was afraid my message, for many reasons, might not be delivered to you. I am very grateful to you for coming and I apologize for troubling you. I would not have done so if it hadn't been so important. Forgive me please, but there is something wrong in my thinking and I knew you would understand how hard it would be for me to die with wrong thoughts in my head.'

Hara spoke slowly and deliberately in a polite, even voice, but Lawrence could tell from its very evenness that his thought was flowing in a deep fast stream out to sea, flowing in a deeper chasm of himself than it had ever flowed before.

'Poor, poor devil, bloody poor devil,' he thought, 'even now the problem is "thinking", always his own or other people's "thinking" at fault.'

'There is nothing to forgive, Hara-san,' he said aloud. 'I came at once when I got your message and I came gladly. Please tell me what it is and I'll try and help you.'

From the way Hara's dark, slanted, child-of-a-sun-goddess's eyes lit up at the use of the polite 'san' to his name, Lawrence knew that Hara had not been spoken to in that manner for many months.

'Rorensu-san,' he answered eagerly, pleading more like a boy with his teacher than a war-scarred sergeant-major with an enemy and an officer, 'it is only this: you have always, I felt, always understood us Japanese. Even when I have had to punish you, I felt you understood it was not I, Hara, who wanted it, but that it had to be, and you never hated me for it. Please tell me now: you English I have always been told are fair and just people: whatever other faults we all think you have; we have always looked upon you as a just people. You know I am not afraid to die. You know that after what has happened to my country I shall be glad to die tomorrow. Look, I have shaved the hair off my head, I have taken a bath of purification, rinsed my mouth and throat, washed my hands and drunk the last cupful of water for the long journey. I have emptied the world from my head, washed it off my body, and I am ready for my body to die, as I have died in my mind long since. Truly you must know, I do not mind dying, only, only, only, why must I die for the reason you give? I don't know what I have done wrong that other soldiers who are not to die have not done. We have all killed one another and I know it is not good, but it is war. I have punished you and killed your people, but I punished you no more and killed no more than I would have done if you were Japanese in my charge who had behaved in the same way. I was kinder to you, in fact, than I would have been to my own people, kinder to you all than many others. I was more lenient, believe it or not, than army rules and rulers demanded. If I had not been so severe and strict you would all have collapsed in your spirit and died because your way of thinking was so wrong and your disgrace so great. If it were not for me, Hicksley-Ellis and all his men would have died on the island out of despair. It was not my fault that the ships with food and medicine did not come. I could only beat my prisoners alive and save those that had it in them to live by beating them to greater effort. And now I am being killed for it. I do not understand where I went wrong, except in the general wrong of us all. If I did another wrong please tell me how and why and I shall die happy.'

'I didn't know what to say.' Lawrence turned to me with a gesture of despair. 'He was only asking me what I had asked myself ever since these damned war-trials began. I honestly did not understand myself. I never saw the good of them. It seemed to me just as wrong for us now to condemn Hara under a law which had never been his, of which he had never even heard, as he and his masters had been to punish and kill us for transgressions of the code of Japan that was not ours. It was not as if he had sinned against his own lights: it ever a person had been true to himself and the twilight glimmer in him, it was this terrible little man. He may have done wrong for the right reasons but how could it be squared by us now doing right in the wrong way. No punishment I could think of could restore the past, could be more futile and more calculated even to give the discredited past a new lease of life in the present than this sort of uncomprehending and uncomprehended vengeance! I didn't know what the hell to say!'

The distress over his predicament became so poignant in this recollection that he broke off with a wave of his hand at the darkening sky.

'But you did say something surely,' I said. 'You could not leave it at that.'

'Oh yes, I said something,' he said sadly, 'but it was most inadequate. All I could tell him was that I did not understand myself and that if it lay with me I would gladly let him out and send him straight back to his family.'

'And did that satisfy him?' I asked.

Lawrence shook his head. He didn't think so, for after bowing deeply again and thanking Lawrence, he looked up and asked: 'So what am I to do?'

Lawrence could only say: 'You can try to think only with all your heart, Hara-san, that unfair and unjust as this thing which my people are doing seems to you, that it is done only to try and stop the kind of things that happened between us in the war from ever happening again. You can say to yourself as I used to say to my despairing men in prison under you: "There is a way of winning by losing, a way of victory in defeat which we are going to discover." Perhaps that too must be your way to understanding and victory now.'

'That, Rorensu-san,' he said, with the quick intake of breath of a Japanese when truly moved, 'is a very Japanese thought!'

They stood in silence for a long while looking each other straight in the eyes, the English officer and the Japanese N.C.O. The moonlight outside was tense, its silver strands trembling faintly with the reverberation of inaudible and far-off thunder and the crackle of the electricity of lightning along the invisible horizon.

Hara was the first to speak. In that unpredictable way of his, he suddenly smiled and said irrelevantly: I gave you a good Kurïsumasu once, didn't I?'

'Indeed you did,' Lawrence answered unhappily, adding instinctively, 'You gave me a very, very, good Christmas. Please take that thought with you tonight!'

'Can I take it with me all the way?' Hara asked, still smiling but with something almost gaily provocative in his voice. 'Is it good enough to go even where I am going?'

'Yes: much as circumstances seem to belie it,' Lawrence answered, 'it is good enough to take all the way and beyond . . .'

At that moment the guard announced himself and told Lawrence he had already overstayed his time.

'Sayonara Hara-san!' Lawrence said, bowing deeply, using that ancient farewell of the Japanese 'If-so-it-must-be' which is so filled with the sense of their incalculable and inexorable fate. 'Sayonara and God go with you.'

'If so it must be!' Hara said calmly, bowing as deeply. 'If so it must be, and thank you for your great kindness and your good coming, and above all your honourable words.'

Lawrence stood up quickly not trusting his self-control enough to look at Hara again, and started to go, but as he came to the doorway, Hara called out: 'Rorensu!' just as he had once called it in the Commandant's office after Lawrence's weeks of torture. Lawrence turned and there was Hara grinning widely, faded yellow teeth and gold rims plainly showing as if he had never enjoyed himself more. As Lawrence's eyes met his, he called out gaily: 'Merry Kurïsumasu, Rorensu-san.'

But the eyes, Lawrence said, were not laughing. There was a light in them of a moment which transcends lesser moments wherein all earthly and spiritual conflicts tend to be resolved and unimportant, all partiality and incompletion gone, and only a deep sombre between-night-and-morning glow left. It transformed Hara's strange, distorted features. The rather anthropoidal, prehistoric face of Hara's looked more beautiful than any Lawrence had ever seen. He was so moved by it and by the expression in those archaic eyes that he wanted to turn back into the cell. Indeed he tried to go back but something would not let him. Half of himself, a deep, instinctive, natural, impulsive half, wanted to go back, clasp Hara in his arms, kiss him goodbye on the forehead and say: 'We may not be able to stop and undo the hard old wrongs of the great world outside, but through you and me no evil shall come either in the unknown where you are going, or in this imperfect and haunted dimension of awareness through which I move. Thus between us, we shall cancel out all private and personal evil, thus arrest private and personal consequences to blind action and reaction, thus prevent specifically the general incomprehension and misunderstanding, hatred and revenge of our time from spreading further.' But the words would not be uttered and half of him, the conscious half of the officer at the door with a critical, alert sentry at his side held him powerless on the threshold. So for the last time the door shut on Hara and his golden grin.

But all the way back to town that last expression on Hara's face travelled at Lawrence's side. He was filled with great regret that he had not gone back. What was this ignoble half that had stopped him? If only he had gone back he felt now he might have changed the whole course of history. For was not that how great things began in the tiny seed of the small change in the troubled individual heart? One single, lonely, inexperienced heart had to change first and all the rest would follow? One true change in one humble, obedient and contrite individual heart humble enough to accept without intellectual question the first faint stirring of the natural spirit seeking flesh and blood to express it, humble enough to live the new meaning before thinking it, and all the rest would have followed as day the night, and one more archaic cycle of hurt, hurt avenged and vengeance revenged would have been cut for ever. He felt he had failed the future and his heart went so dim and black on him that abruptly he pulled up the car by a palm-grove on the edge of the sea.

Sadly he listened to the ancient sound of the water lapping at the sands, and the rustle of the wind of morning in the palms overhead travelling the spring world and night sky like the endless questing spirit of God tracking its brief and imperfect container in man. He saw some junks go out to sea and the full moon come sinking down, fulfilled and weary, on to their black corrugated sails. The moon was now ever larger than when he had first seen it. Yes. Now Hara's last moon was not only full but also overflowing with a yellow, valedictory light. And as he was thinking, from a Malay village hidden in the jungle behind there suddenly rang out the crow of a cock, sounding the alarm of day. The sound was more than he could bear. It sounded like notice of the first betrayal joined to depravity of the latest and became a parody of Hara's call of 'Merry Christmas'. And although it was not Christmas and the land behind was not a Christian land, he felt that he had betrayed the sum of all the Christmases.

Quickly he turned the car round. He would get back to the gaol, see Hara and atone for his hesitation. He drove recklessly fast and reached the gates as the dawn, in a great uprush of passionate flaming red light, hurled itself at the prison towers above him.

'But of course I was too late,' Lawrence told me, terribly distressed. 'Hara was already hanged.'

I took his arm and turned with him for home. I could not speak and when he went on to ask, more of himself than of me or the darkening sky, 'Must we always be too late?' he asked the question, without knowing it, also for me. It hung like the shadow of a bar of a new prison between us and the emerging stars and my heart filled with tears.

James A. Michener

The Cave

IN those fateful days of 1942 when the Navy held on to Guadalcanal by faith rather than by reason, there was a P.T. Boat detachment stationed on nearby Tulagi. It was my fortune to be attached to this squadron during the weeks when P.T. Boats were used as destroyers and destroyers were used as battleships. I was merely doing paper work for Admiral Kester, but the urgency of our entire position in the Solomons was so great that I also served as mess officer, complaints officer, and errand boy for Lieut.-Comdr. Charlesworth, the Annapolis skipper.

The job of Charlesworth's squadron was to intercept anything that came down The Slot. Barges, destroyers, cruisers, or battleships. The P.T.'s went out against them all. The Japs sent something down every night to reinforce their men on Guadal. The P.T.'s fought every night. For several weeks, terrible crushing weeks of defeat, the defences of Guadalcanal rested upon the P.T.'s. And upon Guadal rested our entire position in the South Pacific.

I have become damned sick and tired of the eyewash written about P.T. Boats. I'm not going to add to that foolish legend. They were rotten, tricky little craft for the immense jobs they were supposed to do. They were inprovised, often unseaworthy, desperate little boats. They shook the stomachs out of many men who rode them, made physical wrecks of others for other reasons. They had no defensive armour. In many instances they were suicide boats. In others they were like human torpedoes. It was a disgrace, a damned disgrace that a naval nation like America should have had to rely upon them.

Yet I can understand their popularity. It was strictly newspaper stuff. A great nation was being pushed around the Atlantic by German submarines. And mauled in the Pacific by a powerful Jap fleet. Its planes were rust on Hickam Field and Clark Field. Its carriers were on the bottom. Americans were desperate. And then some wizard with words went to work on the P.T. Boat. Pretty soon everybody who had never seen a real Jap ship spitting fire got the idea our wonderful little

THE CAVE

P.T.'s were slugging it out with Jap battleships. Always of the Kongo Class.

Well, that crowd I served with on Tulagi in 1942 knew different. So far as I ever heard, none of my gang even sank a Jap destroyer. It was just dirty work, thumping, hammering, kidney-wrecking work. Even for strong tough guys from Montana it was rugged living.

The day I started my duty with the P.T. Boats we were losing the battle of Guadalcanal. Two American warships were sunk north of Savo that night. Eight of our planes were shot down over Guadal, and at least fifteen Jap barges reached Cape Esperance with fresh troops. Towards morning we were bombed both at Tulagi and at Purvis Bay. A concentration of Bettys. At dawn a grim bunch of men rose to survey the wreckage along the shore.

Lieut.-Comdr. Charlesworth met me at the pier. A stocky, chunky, rugged fellow from Butte, Montana. Stood about five feet nine. Had been an athlete in his day. I found him terribly prosaic, almost dull. He was unsure of himself around other officers, but he was a devil in a P.T. Boat. Didn't know what fear was. Would take his tub anywhere, against any odds. He won three medals for bravery beyond the call of duty. Yet he was totally modest. He had only one ambition: to be the best possible naval officer. Annapolis could be proud of Charlesworth. We were.

'We got by again,' he said as we studied the wreckage of the night before. 'Any damage to the gasoline on Gavutu?'

'None,' his exec replied.

'Looks like some bombs might have hit right there beside that buoy.'

'No, sir. One of the P.T.'s hit that last night. Tying up.'

Charlesworth shook his head. 'How do they do it?' he asked. 'They can hit anything but a Jap barge.'

'Sir!' an enlisted man called out from the path almost directly above us on the hillside. 'V.I.P. coming ashore!'

'Where?' Charlesworth cried. As an Annapolis man he was terribly attentive when any V.I.P.'s were about. He had long since learned that half his Navy job was to fight Japs. The other half was to please 'very important persons' when they chanced to notice him. Like all Annapolis men, he knew that a smile from a V.I.P. was worth a direct hit on a cruiser.

'In that little craft!' the man above us cried. Probably someone aboard the small craft had blinkered to the signal tower. Charlesworth straightened his collar, hitched his belt and gave orders to the men along the shore. 'Stand clear and give a snappy salute.'

But we were not prepared for what came ashore. It was Tony Fry! He was wearing shorts, only one collar insigne, and a little go-to-hell cap. He grinned at me as he threw his long legs over the side of the boat. 'Hallo, there!' he said. Extending a sweaty hand to Charlesworth he puffed, 'You must be the skipper. Y'get hit last night?'

'No, sir,' Charlesworth said stiffly. 'I don't believe I know you, sir.'

'Name's Fry. Tony Fry. Lieutenant. Just got promoted. They only had one pair of bars, so I'm a little lopsided.' He flicked his empty collar point. It was damp. 'Holy cow! It's hot over here!'

'What brings you over?' Charlesworth asked.

'Well, sir. It's secret business for the admiral. Nothin' much, of course. You'll get the word about as soon as I do, Commander,' Fry said. 'I hear you have a cave somewhere up there?'

'Yes, we do,' Charlesworth said. 'Right over those trees.' Above us we could see the entrance to the cave Fry sought. Into the highest hill a retreat, shaped like a U, had been dug. One entrance overlooked the harbour and Purvis Bay, where our big ships were hidden. The other entrance, which we could not see, led to a small plateau with a good view of Guadal and Savo, that tragic island. Beyond Savo lay The Slot, the island-studded passage leading to Bougainville, Rabaul, Truk, and Kuralei.

'I understand the cave's about ten feet high,' Tony mused.

'That's about right,' Charlesworth agreed.

'Just what we want,' Tony replied. He motioned to some men who were carrying gear in black boxes. 'Let's go, gang!' he called.

Charlesworth led the way. With stocky steps he guided us along a winding path that climbed steeply from the P.T. anchorage where Fry had landed. Hibiscus, planted by the wife of some British official years ago, bloomed and made the land as lovely as the bay below.

'Let's rest a minute!' Fry panted, the sweat pouring from his face.

'It's a bit of a climb,' Charlesworth replied, not even breathing hard.

'Splendid place, this,' Fry said as he surveyed the waters leading to Purvis Bay. 'Always depend upon the British to cook up fine quarters. We could learn something from them. Must have been great here in the old days.'

As we recovered our breath Charlesworth pointed to several small islands in the bay. 'That's where the Marines came ashore. A rotten fight. Those ruins used to be a girls' school. Native children from all over the islands came here.' I noticed that he spoke in rather stilted sentences, like a Montana farmer not quite certain of his new-found culture.

'It'll be a nice view from the cave,' Fry said. 'Well, I'm ready again.'

We found the cave a cool, moist, dark retreat. In such a gothic place the medieval Japs naturally located their headquarters. With greater humour we Americans had our headquarters along the shore. We reserved the cave for Tony Fry.

For once he saw the quiet interior with its grand view over the waters he said, 'This is for me.' He turned to Charlesworth and remarked, 'Now, Commander, I want to be left alone in this cave. If I want any of you P.T. heroes in here I'll let you know.'

Charlesworth, who was already irritated at having a mere lieutenant, a nobody and a reserve at that, listed as a V.I.P., snapped to attention. 'Lieut. Fry,' he began, 'I'm the officer-in-charge . . .'

'All right, Commander. All right,' Fry said rapidly. 'I'm going to give you all the deference due your rank. I know what the score is. But let's not have any of that Annapolis fol-de-rol. There's a war on.'

Charlesworth nearly exploded. He was about to grab Fry by the arm and swing him around when Tony turned and grinned that delightfully silly smirk of his. Sunlight from the plateau leaped across his wet face. He grinned at Charlesworth and extended a long hand. 'I'm new at this business, Commander,' he said. 'You tell me what to do, and I'm gonna do it. I just don't want any of your eager beavers messing around. They tell me over at Guadal that you guys'd take on the whole fleet if Halsey would let you.'

Charlesworth was astounded. He extended his hand in something of a daze. Tony grabbed it warmly. In doing so he engineered Charlesworth and me right out of the cave. 'Men bringin' in the stuff,' he explained.

This Fry was beyond description, a completely new type of naval officer. He didn't give a damn for anything or anybody. He was about thirty, unmarried. He had some money and although he loved the Navy and its fuddy ways, he ridiculed everything and everybody. He was completely oblivious to rank. Even admirals loved him for it. Nobody was ever quite certain what he was supposed to be doing. In time no one cared. The important thing was that he had unlimited resources for getting whisky, which he consumed in great quantities. I've been told the Army wouldn't tolerate Fry a week.

We were several days finding out what he was doing on Tulagi. Late that afternoon, for example, we heard a clattering and banging in the cave. We looked up, and Tony had two enlisted men building him a flower-box. That evening he was down in the garden of the old British residency digging up some flowers for his new home. A pair of Jap marauders came winging in to shoot the island up. Tony dived for a trench and raised a great howl.

'What's the matter with the air-raid system?' he demanded that night at chow. 'That's why I like the cave. It's safe! They'd have to lay a bomb in there with a spoon!'

It soon became apparent that Charlesworth and Fry would not get along. Tony delighted in making sly cracks at the 'trade-school boys.' Charlesworth, who worshipped the stones of Annapolis, had not the ready wit to retaliate. He took no pains to mask his feelings, however.

It was also apparent that Fry was rapidly becoming the unofficial commanding officer of the P.T. base. Even Charlesworth noticed that wherever Tony propped his field boots, that spot was headquarters. That was the officers' club.

Settled back, Tony would pass his whisky bottle and urge other men to talk. But if there was anything pompous, or heroic, or ultra-Annapolis in the conversation, Fry would mercilessly ridicule it and puncture the balloons. The P.T. captains delighted to invite him on their midnight missions.

'Me ride in those death traps? Ha, ha! Not me! I get paid to sit right here and think. That's all I'm in this man's Navy for. You don't get medals for what I do. But you do get back home!' Unashamedly he would voice the fears and cowardice that came close to the surface of all our lives. Men about to throw their wooden P.T.'s at superior targets loved to hear Fry express their doubts. 'Those sieves? Those kidney-wreckers? Holy cow! I'd sooner go to sea in a native canoe!'

But when the frail little craft warmed up, and you could hear Packard motors roaring through Tulagi, Tony would pull himself out of his chair in the cave, unkink a drunken knee, and amble off towards the waterfront. 'Better see what the heroes are doing,' he would say. Then, borrowing a revolver or picking up a carbine as he went, he would somehow or other get to where Charlesworth's P.T. was shoving off.

'Room for a passenger?' he would inquire.

'Come aboard, sir,' Charlesworth would say primly, as if he were back at San Diego.

Enlisted men were especially glad to see Tony climb aboard. 'He's lucky!' they whispered to one another. 'Guys like him never get killed.'

Tony, or God, brought the P.T.s luck one night. That was when Charlesworth got his second medal. His prowling squadron ran smack into some Jap A.K.A.s south of Savo. Charlesworth was a little ahead of the other P.T.s when the Japs were sighted. Without waiting a moment he literally rushed into the formation, sank one and hung on to another, dodging shells, until his mates could close in for the kill.

Tony was on the bridge during the action. 'You handle this tub right well, skipper,' he said.

'It's a good boat,' Charlesworth said. 'This is a mighty good boat. A man ought to be willing to take this boat almost anywhere.'

'You did!' Fry laughed.

In the bright morning, when Charlesworth led his P.T.s roaring home through the risky channel between Tulagi and Florida, Tony lay sprawled out forward, watching the spray and the flying fish. 'What a tub!' he grunted as he climbed ashore. 'There must be an easier way to earn a living!'

And if one of the enlisted men from Charlesworth's P.T. sneaked up to the cave later in the day, Fry would shout at him, 'Stay to hell out of here! If you want a shot of whisky that bad, go on down to my shack. But for God's sake don't let the commander see you. He'd eat my neck out.' Whether you were an enlisted man or an officer, you could drink Fry's whisky. Just as long as he had any.

We had almost given up guessing what Fry was doing when he woke Charlesworth and me one morning about five. 'This is it!' he whispered.

He led us up to the cave but made us stand outside. In a moment an enlisted radioman, Lazars, appeared. 'Any further word?' Fry asked.

'None, sir,' Lazars said.

'Something big's up,' Tony said in a low voice. We moved towards the cave. 'No,' Fry interrupted. 'We had the boys rig a radio for you over in that quonset,' he said. Dawn was breaking as he led us to a half-size quonset at the other side of the plateau. When we stepped inside the barren place Lazars started to tune a radio. He got only a faint whine. He kept twirling the dials. It was cool in the hut. The sun wasn't up yet.

'It may be some time,' Fry said. The sun rose. The hut became humid. We began to sweat. We could hear the metal expanding in little crackles. New men always thought it was rain, but it was the sun. Then you knew it was going to be a hot day.

Lazars worked his dials back and forth with patient skill. 'No signal yet,' he reported. Fry walked up and down nervously. The sweat ran from his eyes and dropped upon his thin, bare knees. Finally he stopped and wiped the moisture from his face.

'I think this is it, Charlesworth,' he said.

'What?' the commander asked.

'We sneaked a man ashore behind the Jap lines. Somewhere up north. He's going to try to contact us today. Imagine what we can do if he sends us the weather up there. News about the Jap ships! How'd you like to go out some night when you knew the Japs were coming down? Just where they were and how many. How would that be, eh?' Tony was excited.

Then there came a crackle, a faint crackling sound. It was different from the expansion of the burning roof. It was a radio signal! Fry put his finger to his lips.

From far away, from deep in the jungles near Jap sentries, came a human voice. It was clear, quiet, somewhat high-pitched. But it never rose to excitement. I was to hear that voice often, almost every day for two months. Like hundreds of Americans who went forth to fight aided by that voice, I can hear it now. It fills the room about me as it filled that sweating hut. It was always the same. Even on the last day it was free from nervousness. On this morning it said: 'Good morning, Americans! This is your Remittance Man. I am speaking from the Upper Solomons. First the weather. There are rain clouds over

Bougainville, the Treasuries, Choiseul, and New Georgia. I believe it will rain in this region from about 0900 to 1400. The afternoon will be clear. It is now 94 degrees. There are no indications of violent weather.'

The lonely voice paused. In the radio shack we looked at one another. No one spoke. Lazars did not touch the dials. Then the voice resumed, still high, still precise and slow:

'Surface craft have been in considerable motion for the last two days. I think you may expect important attempts at reinforcement tonight. One battleship, four cruisers, a carrier, eight destroyers and four oilers have been seen in this region. They are heading, I presume, towards Kolombangara rendezvous. In addition not less than nineteen and possibly twenty-seven troop barges are definitely on their way south. When I saw them they were making approximately eleven knots and were headed right down The Slot. I judge they will pass Banika at 2000 tonight. Landing attempts could be made near Esperance any time after 0200 tomorrow morning. You will be glad to know that the barges appear to be escorted by heavy warships this time. The hunting should be good.'

The speaker paused again. Charlesworth rubbed his chin and studied a map pasted on wallboard and hung from the sloping tin. No one spoke.

'And for you birdmen,' the voice continued. 'Four flights have set out for your territory. They are in rendezvous at present. North of Munda. I cannot see the types of planes at present. I judge them to be about forty bombers. Twenty fighters. If that proportion makes any sense. I'm not very good on aircraft. Ah, yes! This looks like a flight down from Kieta right above me. Perhaps you can hear the motors! Thirty or more fighter planes. Altitude ten thousand feet, but my distances are not too accurate. I'm rather new at this sort of thing, you know.'

The Remittance Man paused and then for the first time gave his closing comment which later became a famous rallying cry in the South Pacific: 'Cheerio, Americans. Good hunting, lads!'

As soon as the broadcast ended Charlesworth dashed from the quonset and started laying plans for that night's foray. At every subsequent broadcast it was the same way. No sooner would the Remittance Man finish speaking than Charlesworth would bound into action and move imaginary P.T.s all through the waters between Guadal and the Russells. For him the Remittance Man was an abstract, impersonal command to action.

But to Tony Fry the enigmatic voice from the jungle became an immense intellectual mystery. It began on this first morning. After Charlesworth had dashed down to the P.T.s Fry asked me, 'What do you make of it?'

THE CAVE

'Very clever intelligence,' I replied.

'Holy cow!' he snorted. 'I don't mean that! I mean this chap. This fellow up there in the jungles. Japs all around him. How can he do it?'

'He probably volunteered for it,' I replied.

'Of course he did!' Fry agreed with some irritation. 'But what I mean is, how does a guy get courage like that? I should think his imagination alone would drive him frantic.'

'He's probably some old duffer's been out in the islands all his life.'

'I know who he is,' Fry said, kicking at pebbles as we walked over to the cave. 'Chap named Anderson. Trader from Malaita. An Englishman. But why did he, of all the men out here, volunteer? How can he face that?' Tony gripped my arm. 'A single man goes out against an island of Japs? Why?'

We didn't see Tony that day. He ate canned soup and beer in the cave. That night the P.T.s went out without him. They did all right, thanks to the Remittance Man. The Japs came down exactly as he said. Charlesworth slipped in and chopped them up. The black year of 1942, the terrible year was dying. But as it died, hope was being born on Guadalcanal and Tulagi.

Next morning at 0700 all those who were not in sick-bay getting wounds and burns from the night before patched up were in the steaming quonset. Promptly on time the Remittance Man spoke. Fry stood close to the radio listening to the high-pitched voice extend its cheery greeting: 'Good morning, Americans! I have good news for you today. But first the weather.' He told us about conditions over Bougainville, Choiseul, and New Georgia. Flying weather was excellent.

'In fact,' he said, 'flying looks so good that you shall probably have visitors. Very heavy concentrations of bombers overhead at 1100 this morning. If I can judge aircraft, not less then ninety bombers and fighters are getting ready for a strike this morning. Some are in the air ready to leave. They appear to be at 12,000 feet. Don't bet on that, though. I can't say I've learned to use the estimating devices too well yet. Let's say not less than 10,000. Some fighters have moved in from Bougainville. Look at them! Rolling about, doing loops and all sorts of crazy things. There they go! It's quite a circus. This will be a fine day. Cheerio, Americans! Good hunting!' The radio clicked. There was silence.

Immediately, Charlesworth called his men together. 'They'll want some P.T.s for rescue work!' he snapped. 'If that man is right, this may be a big day. A very big day. We'll put B Squadron out. Shove. And don't come home till you comb every shore about here. Pick them all up! Get them all!' He hurried his men down to the shore.

A phone jangled. It was headquarters. 'Admiral Kester wants the P.T.s out for rescue,' intelligence said.

'They've already left,' I reported.

'This Remittance Man,' Tony said when the others had gone. 'Commander, where do you suppose he is?'

'I thought Bougainville,' I said.

'No. I was studying a map. He's on some peak from which he can see Munda.'

'Maybe you're right,' I said. 'He confuses his broadcasts nicely.'

'Don't be surprised if he was on Sant' Ysabel all the time,' Fry said.

But not then, nor at any other time, did he or any of us say what was in our minds: *How desperately the Japs must be searching for that man! How fitful his sleep must be! How he must peer into every black face he sees in the jungle, wondering, 'Is this my Judas?'*

Tony and I went out into the brilliant sunlight to watch the miracle below us. From the unbroken shoreline of Tulagi bits of green shrubbery pulled into the channel. Then camouflage was discarded. The P.T.s roared around the north end of the island. Off towards Savo. The P.T.s were out again.

'I've been trying to find out something about the man,' Tony continued. 'Just a man named Anderson. Nobody knows much about him. He came out here from England. Does a little trading for Burns Philp. Went into hiding when the Japs took Tulagi. Came over to Guadal and volunteered for whatever duty was available. Medium-sized chap. You've heard his voice.'

At 1100 the first Jap plane came into view. It was a Zero spinning wildly somewhere near the Russells. It flamed and lurched into the sea. The battle was on!

For an hour and ten minutes the sky above Guadal and Tulagi was a beautiful misery of streaming fire, retching planes, and pyres flaming out of the sea. The Japanese broke through. Nothing could stop them. We heard loud thunder from Purvis Bay. Saw high fires on Guadal. Eight times Jap fighters roared low over Tulagi. Killed two mechanics at the garage. But still we watched the breathless spectacle overhead.

Yes, the Japs broke through that day. Some of them broke through, that is. And if they had unlimited planes and courage, they could break through whenever they wished. But we grinned! God, we even laughed out loud. Because we didn't think the Japs had planes to waste! Or pilots either. And mark this! When Jap pilots plunged into the sea, The Slot captured them and they were seen no more. But when ours went down, P.T. boats sped here and there to pick them up.

So, we were happy that night. Not silly happy, you understand, because we lost a P.T. boat to strafers. And we could count. We knew how many Yank planes crashed and blew up and dived into the sea. But nevertheless we were happy. Even when Tony Fry came in slightly drunk and said, 'That guy up there in the jungles. How long can he keep going? You radio men. How long would it take American equipment to track down a broadcasting station?'

There was no reply. 'How long?' Fry demanded.

'Two days. At the most.'

'That's what I thought,' he said.

Next morning at seven the Remittance Man was happy, too. 'The Japanese Armada limped home,' he reported in subdued exultation as if he knew that he had shared in the victory. 'I myself saw seven planes go into the sea near here. I honestly believe that not more than forty got back. And now good news for one squadron. My little book tells me the plane with that funny nose is the P-40. One P-40 followed two crippled Jap bombers right into New Georgia waters. They were flying very low. He destroyed each one. Then the Nips jumped him and he went into the water himself. But I believe I saw him climb out of his plane and swim to an island. I think he made it safely.'

The distant speaker cleared his throat and apparently took a drink of water. 'Thank you, Basil,' he said. 'There will be something in The Slot tonight, I think. Four destroyers have been steaming about near Vella Lavella. Something's on! you can expect another landing attempt tonight. If you chappies only had more bombers you could do some pretty work up here today. Cheerio, Americans! Good hunting!'

Charlesworth was more excited than I had ever seen him before. Jap D.D.s on the move! His eyes flashed as he spread maps about the baking quonset. At 1500 Fry came down the winding path, dragging a carbine and a raincoat along the trail. 'Might as well see if you trade-school boys can run this thing,' he said as he climbed aboard.

At 2300 that night they made contact. But it was disappointing. The big stuff was missing. Only some Jap barges and picket boats. There was a long confused fight. Most of the Japs got through to Guadal. The P.T.s stayed out two more nights. On the last night they got in among some empty barges heading back to Munda. Got five of them. Fry shot up one with a Thompson when the torpedoes were used up. But the kill, the crushing blow from which the Japs would shudder back, that eluded them.

On the dreary trip home Fry asked Charlesworth if he thought the Remittance Man moved from one island to another in a canoe. 'Oh, damn it all,' Charlesworth said. 'Stop talking about the man. He's just a fellow doing a job.'

Tony started to reply but thought better of it. He went forward to watch the spray and the flying fish. As the boats straggled into Tulagi he noticed great activity along the shore.

A P.T. blinkered to Charlesworth: 'The coast-watcher says tonight's the night. Big stuff coming down!'

'What's he say?' Fry asked.

'We're going right out again,' Charlesworth said, his nostrils quivering.

Tony barely had time to rush up to the cave. He dragged me in after him. It was my first trip inside since he had taken charge. I was surprised. It looked much better than any of the quonsets. Spring mattresses, too. 'I told the men to fix it up,' Fry said, waving a tired hand about the place. 'Commander,' he asked quietly. 'What did the . . .' He nodded his head towards Bougainville.

'He was off the air yesterday,' I said. 'This morning just a sentence. "Destroyers definitely heading south." That was all.'

Tony leaned forward. He was sleepy. The phone rang. 'Holy cow!' Fry protested. 'You been out three nights runnin', skipper. You're takin' this war too hard.' There was a long pause. Then Fry added, 'Well, if you think you can't run it without me, O.K. But those Jap destroyers have guns, damn it. Holy cow, these guys'd shoot at you in a minute!'

They left in mid-morning sunlight, with great shafts of gold dancing across the waters of Tulagi bay. They slipped north of Savo in the night. They found nothing. The Japs had slipped through again. Halsey would be splitting a gut. But shortly after dawn there was violent firing over the horizon towards the Russells. Charlesworth raced over. He was too late. His exec had sighted a Jap destroyer! Full morning light. Didn't wait a second. Threw the P.T. around and blazed right at the D.C. On the second salvo the Jap blew him to pieces. Little pieces all over The Slot. The exec was a dumb guy, as naval officers go. A big Slav from Montana.

Charlesworth was a madman. Wanted to sail right into Banika channel and slug it out. He turned back finally. Kept his teeth clenched all the way home. When Fry monkeyed with the radio, trying to intercept the Remittance Man, Charlesworth wanted to scream at him. He kept his teeth clenched. A big thing was in his heart. His lips moved over his very white teeth. 'Some day,' he muttered to himself, 'we'll get us a D.D. That big Slav. He was all right. He was a good exec. My God, the fools can't handle these boats. They haven't had the training. Damn it, if that fool would only stop monkeying with that radio!'

Tony couldn't make contact. That was not his fault, because the Remittance Man didn't broadcast. Fry clicked the radio off and went forward to lie in the sun. When the P.T. hove to at its mooring he started to speak to Charlesworth, but the skipper suddenly was overwhelmed with that burning, impotent rage that sneaks upon the living when the dead were loved. 'By God, Fry. Strike me dead on this spot, but I'll get those Japs. You wait!'

Fry grinned. 'I ain't gonna be around, skipper. Not for stuff like that. No need for me to wait!' The tension snapped. Charlesworth blinked his eyes. The sun was high overhead. The day was glorious, and hot, and bright against the jungle. But against the shore another P.T. was missing.

Back in the quonset Tony studied his maps, half sleeping, half drunk. In the morning the cool voice of the Remittance Man reported the weather and the diminishing number of Jap aircraft visible these days. Fry strained for any hint that would tell him what the man was doing, where he was, what his own estimates of success were. Charlesworth sat morosely silent. There was no news of surface movements. It was a dull day for him, and he gruffly left to catch some extra sleep.

Tony, of course, stayed behind in the hot quonset, talking about the Remittance Man. 'This Basil he mentioned the other day? Who is he?' We leaned forward. For by this time Tony's preoccupation with the Englishman affected all of us. We saw in that lonely watcher something of the complexity of man, something of the contradictory character of ourselves. We had followed Tony's inquiries with interest. We were convinced that Anderson was an ordinary nobody. Like ourselves. We became utterly convinced that under similar circumstances we ordinary people would have to act in the same way.

Fry might ask, 'What makes him do that?' but we knew there was a deeper question haunting each of us. And we would look at one another. At Charlesworth, for example, who went out night after night in the P.T.s and never raised his voice or showed fear. We would ask ourselves: 'What makes him do it? We know all about him. Married a society girl. Has two kids. Very stuffy, but one of the best men ever to come from Annapolis. We know that. But what we don't know is how he can go out night after night.'

Tony might ask, in the morning, 'Where do you suppose he is now?' And we would ponder, not that question, but another: 'Last night. We knew Jap D.D.s were on the loose. But young Clipperton broke out of infirmary so he could take his P.T. against them. What?' And Clipperton, whose torpedoman was killed, would think, not of the Remittance Man, but of Fry himself: 'Why does a character like that come down to the pier each night, dragging that fool carbine in the coral?'

And so, arguing about the Remittance Man we studied ourselves and found no answers. The coast-watcher did nothing to help us, either. Each morning, in a high-pitched cheerful voice he gave us the weather, told us what the Japs were going to do, and ended, 'Cheerio, Americans! Good hunting!'

I noticed that Charlesworth was becoming irritated at Fry's constant speculation about the coast-watcher. Even Anderson's high voice began to grate upon the skipper's ears. We were all sick at the time. Malaria. Running sores from heavy sweating. Armpits gouged with little blisters that broke and left small holes. Some had open sores on their wrists.

The jungle rot. Most of us scratched all the time. It was no wonder that Charlesworth was becoming touchy.

'Damn it all, Fry,' he snapped one day. 'Knock off this chatter about the Remittance Man. You're getting the whole gang agitated.'

'Is that an order?' Fry said very quietly, his feet on the table.

'Yes, it is. You're bad for morale.'

'You don't know what morale is,' Fry grunted, reaching for the whisky bottle and getting to his feet. Charlesworth pushed a chair aside and rushed up to Tony, who ignored him and slumped lazily towards the door of the quonset.

'You're under quarters arrest, Fry! You think you can get away with murder around here. Well, you're in the Navy now.' The skipper didn't shout. His voice quivered. Sweat was on his forehead.

Fry turned and laughed at him. 'If I didn't know I was in the Navy, you'd remind me.' He chuckled and shuffled off towards the cave. We didn't see him in the quonset ever again.

But it was strange. As the tenseness on Tulagi grew, as word seeped down the line that the Japs were going to have one last mighty effort at driving us out of the Solomons, more and more of the P.T. skippers started to slip quietly into the cave. They went to talk with Tony. Behind Charlesworth's back. They would sit with their feet on an old soap-box. And they would talk and talk.

'Tony,' one of them said, 'That damn' fool Charlesworth is going to kill us all. Eight P.T.s blown up since he took over.'

'He's a good man,' Tony said.

'The enlisted men wish you'd come along tonight, Tony. They say you're good luck.'

'O.K. Wait for me at the Chinaman's wharf.' And at dusk Fry would slip out of the cave, grab a revolver, and shuffle off as if he were going to war. Next morning the gang would quietly meet in the cave. As an officer accredited directly to Charlesworth I felt it my duty to remain loyal to him, but even I found solace of rare quality in slipping away for a chat with Tony. He was the only man I knew in the Pacific who spoke always as if the destiny of the human soul were a matter of great moment. We were all deeply concerned with why we voyagers ended our travels in a cave in Tulagi. Only Fry had the courage to explore that question.

As the great year ended he said, 'The Remittance Man is right. The Japs have got to make one more effort. You heard what he said this morning. Ships and aircraft massing.'

'What you think's gonna happen, Tony?' a young ensign asked.

'They'll throw everything they have at us one of these days.'

'How you bettin'?'

'Five nights later they'll withdraw from Guadal!'

THE CAVE

The men in the cave whistled. 'You mean . . .'

'It's in the bag, fellows. In the bag.'

You know what happened! The Remittance Man tipped us off one boiling morning. 'Planes seem to be massing for some kind of action. It seems incredible, but I count more than two hundred.'

It was incredible. It was sickening. Warned in advance, our fighters were aloft and swept into the Jap formations like sharks among a school of lazy fish. Our Negro cook alone counted forty Zeros taking the big drink. I remember one glance up The Slot. Three planes plunging in the sea. Two Japs exploding madly over Guadal.

This was the high tide! This was to be the knockout blow at Purvis Bay and Guadal. This was to be the Jap revenge against Tulagi. But from Guadal wave after wave of American fighters tore and slashed and crucified the Japs. From Purvis our heavy ships threw up a wall of steel into which the heavy bombers stumbled and beat their brains out in the bay.

In the waters around Savo our P.T.s picked up twenty American pilots. Charlesworth would have saved a couple of Japs, too, but they fired at him from their sinking bomber. So he blasted it and them to pieces.

He came in at dusk that night. His face was lined with dirt, as if the ocean had been dusty. I met him at the wharf. 'Was it what it seemed like?' he asked. 'Out there it looked as if we . . .'

'Skipper,' I began. But one of the airmen Charlesworth had picked up had broken both legs in landing. The fact that he had been rescued at all was a miracle. Charlesworth had given him some morphine. The silly galoot was so happy to see land he kept singing the Marine song:

> Oh we asked for the Army at Guadalcanal
> But Douglas MacArthur said, 'No!'
> *He gave as his reason,*
> *'It's now the hot season,*
> Besides there is no U.S.O.'

'Take him up to sick-bay,' Charlesworth said, wiping his face.

The injured pilot grinned at us. 'That's a mighty nice little rowboat you got there, skipper!' he shouted. He sang all the way to sick-bay.

At dinner Charlesworth was as jumpy as an embezzler about to take a vacation during the check-up season. He tried to piece together what had happened, how many Japs had gone down. We got a secret dispatch that said a hundred and twelve. 'Pilots always lie,' he said gruffly. 'They're worse than young P.T. men.' He walked up and down his hut for a few minutes and then motioned me to follow him.

We walked out into the warm night. Lights were flashing over Guadal. 'The Japs have got to pull out of that island,' Charlesworth insisted as we walked up the hill behind his hut. When we were on the plateau he stopped to study the grim and silent Slot. 'They'll be coming down some night.' To my surprise he led me to the cave. At the entrance we could hear excited voices of young P.T. skippers. They were telling Tony of the air battles they had watched.

We stepped into the cave. The P.T. men were embarrassed and stood at attention. Tony didn't move, but with his foot he shoved a whisky bottle our way. 'It's cool in here,' Charlesworth said. 'Carry on, fellows.' The men sat down uneasily. 'Fry,' the commander blurted out, 'I heard the most astonishing thing this morning.'

'What was it?' Tony asked.

'This Remittance Man,' Charlesworth said. 'I met an old English trader down along the waterfront. He told me Anderson was married to a native girl. The girl broke her leg and Anderson fixed it for her. Then he married her, priest and all. A real marriage. And the girl is as black . . . as black as that wall.'

'Well, I'll be damned!' Fry said, bending forward. 'Where'd you meet this fellow! What was he like? Holy cow! We ought to look him up!'

'He said a funny thing. I asked him what Anderson was like and he said, "Oh, Andy? He was born to marry the landlady's daughter!" I asked him what this meant and he said, "Some fellows are born just to slip into things. When it comes time to take a wife, they marry the landlady's daughter. She happens to be there. That's all." '

The cave grew silent. We did not think of Jap planes crashing into The Slot, but of the Remittance Man, married to a savage, slipping at night from island to island, from village to hillside to treetop.

At 0700 next morning all of us but Fry were in the steaming quonset listening to the Remittance Man. We heard his quavering voice sending us good cheer. 'Good morning, Americans!' he began. 'I don't have to tell you the news. Where did they go? So many went south and so few came back! During the last hour I have tried and tried to avoid optimism. But I can't hide the news. I sincerely believe the Nips are planning to pull out! Yes, I have watched a considerable piling up of surface craft. And observe this. I don't think they have troops up here to fill those craft. It can mean only one thing. I can't tell if there will be moves tonight. My guess, for what it is worth, is this: Numerous surface craft will attempt to evacuate troops from Guadalcanal tonight. Some time after 0200.' There was a pause. Our men looked at one another. By means of various facial expressions they telegraphed a combined: 'Oh boy!' Then the voice continued:

'You may not hear from me for several days. I find a little trip is necessary. Planes are overhead. Not the hundreds that used to fly your way. Two only. They are looking for me, I think.'

From that time on the Remittance Man never again broadcast at

0700. He did, however, broadcast to us once more. One very hot afternoon. But by then he had nothing of importance to tell us. The Japanese on Guadal were knocked out by then. They were licking their wounds in Munda. They didn't know it at the time, but they were getting ready to be knocked out of Munda, too.

The Remittance Man guessed wrong as to when the Japs would evacuate Guadal. It came much later than he thought. When the attempt was made, we were waiting for them with everything we had. This time the P.T. boats were fortified by airplanes and heavy ships. We weren't fighting on a shoe-string this time.

I suppose you know it was a pretty bloody affair. Great lights flashed through the dark waters. Japs and their ships were destroyed without mercy. Our men did not lust after the killing. But when you've been through the mud of Guadal and been shelled by the Japs night after night until your teeth ached; when you've seen the dead from your cruisers piled up on Savo, and your planes shot down, and your men dying from foes they've never seen; when you see good men racked with malaria but still slugging it out in the jungle . . .

A young P.T. skipper told me about the fight. He said, 'Lots of them got away. Don't be surprised if Admiral Halsey gives everybody hell. Too many got away. But we'll get them some time later. Let me tell you. It was pitch black. We knew there were Japs about. My squadron was waiting. We were all set. Then a destroyer flashed by. From the wrong way! 'Holy God!' I cried. 'Did they slip through us after all?' But the destroyer flashed on its searchlights. Oh, man! It was one of ours! If I live to be a million I'll never see another sight like that. You know what I thought? I thought, "Oh, baby! What a difference! Just a couple of weeks ago, if you saw a destroyer, you knew it was a Jap!" ' The ensign looked at us and tried to say something else. His throat choked up. He opened his mouth a couple of times, but no words came out. He was grinning and laughing and twisting a glass around on the table.

Of course, one Jap destroyer did get through. As luck would have it, the D.D. came right at Charlesworth. That was when he got his third ribbon. It happened this way. We got a false scent and had our P.T.s out on patrol two days early. All of them. On the day the little boats ripped out of Hutchinson Creek and Tulagi Harbour Charlesworth stopped by the cave. 'The boys say you're good luck, Tony. Want to go hunting?'

'Not me!' Fry shuddered. 'There's going to be shooting tonight. Somebody's going to get killed.'

'We're shoving off at 1630.'

'Well, best of luck, skipper.'

Tony was there, of course, lugging that silly carbine. They say he and Charlesworth spent most of the first day arguing. Fry wanted to close Annapolis as an undergraduate school. Keep it open only as a professional school for training regular college graduates. You can imagine the reception this got from the skipper. The second day was hot and dull. On the third afternoon word passed that the Nips were coming down. Fourteen or more big transports.

'Those big transports have guns, don't they?' Tony asked at chow.

'Big ones.'

'Then what the hell are we doin' out here?'

'We'll stick around to show the others where the Japs are. Then we'll hightail it for home,' Charlesworth laughed.

'Skipper, that's the first sensible thing you've said in three days.'

That night the P.T.s were in the thick of the scramble. It was their last pitched battle in the Solomons. After that night their work was finished. There were forays, sure. And isolated actions. But the grand job, that hellish job of climbing into a plywood tug waving your arms and shouting, 'Hey fellows! Look at me! I'm a destroyer!' That job was over. We had steel destroyers, now.

You know how Charlesworth got two transports that night. Laid them wide open. He had one torpedo left at 0340. Just cruising back and forth over towards Esperance. With that nose which true Navy men seem to have he said to Fry and his crew, 'I think there's something over there towards Savo.'

'What are we waiting for?' his ensign asked. The P.T. heeled over and headed cautiously towards Savo. At 0355 the lookout sighted this Jap destroyer. You know that one we fished up from the rocks of Iron Bottom Bay for the boys to study? The one that's on the beach of that little cove near Tulagi? Well, the D.D. they sighted that night was the same class.

Tensely Charlesworth said, 'There she is, Tony.'

'Holy cow!' Fry grunted. 'That thing's got cannons!'

This remark was what the skipper needed. Something in the way Tony drew back as if mortally afraid, or the quaver in his voice, or the look of mock horror on his thin face was the encouragement Charlesworth wanted.

'Pull in those guts!' he cried. The P.T. jumped forward, heading directly at the destroyer.

At 2000 yards the first Jap salvo landed to port. 'Holy cow!' Fry screamed. 'They're shooting at us!'

At 1800 yards three shells splashed directly ahead of the P.T. One ricocheted off the water and went moaning madly overhead. At 1500 yards the P.T. lay over on its side in a hard turn to starboard. Jap shells landed in the wake. The P.T. resumed course. The final 500 yards was a grim race. Jap searchlights were on the P.T. all the time, but at about 950 Charlesworth nosed straight at the port side of the destroyer and let fly with his last torpedo.

THE CAVE

I wish that torpedo had smacked the Jap in the engine-room. Then we might have some truth to support all the nonsense they write about the P.T.s sinking capital ships. A little truth, at any rate. But the damned torpedo didn't run true. You'd think after all this time BuOrd could rig up a torpedo that would run true. This one porpoised. The Jap skipper heeled his tug way over, and the torpedo merely grazed it. There was an explosion, of course, and a couple of the enlisted men were certain the Jap ship went down. But Charlesworth knew different. 'Minor damage,' he reported. 'Send bombing planes in search immediately.' So far as we knew, our planes never found the Jap. We think it hid in some cove in the Russells and then beat it on up to Truk.

Back at Tulagi our officers and men tried to hide their feelings but couldn't. Nobody wanted to come right out and say, 'Well, we've licked the yellow bastards.' But we were all thinking it. Tulagi was exactly like a very nice Sunday School about to go on a picnic. Everybody behaved properly, but if you looked at a friend too long he was likely to break out into a tremendous grin. Fellows played pranks on one another. They sang! Oh, lord! How they sang. Men who a few days before were petty enemies now flopped their arms around each other's necks and made the night air hideous. Even the cooks celebrated and turned out a couple of almost decent meals. Of course, we starved for the next week, but who cared? The closest anyone came to argument was when Charlesworth's ensign ribbed a pilot we had fished from The Slot. 'If you boys had been on the job, you could have knocked over a Jap D.D.' A week earlier this would have started a fight. But this time the aviator looked at the red-cheeked ensign and started laughing. He rumpled the ensign's hair and cooed, 'I love you! I love you! You ugly little son-of-a-bitch!'

But there was a grim guest at all of our celebrations. Fry saw to that. He would come out of the cave at mealtime, or when we were drinking. And he would bring the Remittance Man with him. He dragged that ghostly figure into every bottle of beer. The coast-watcher ate every meal with us. Officers would laugh, and Fry would trail the ghost of that lonely voice across the table. The aviator would tell a joke, and Tony would have the silent broadcaster laughing at his side. He never mentioned the man, his name, or his duties. Yet by the look on Fry's face, we all knew that he was constantly wondering why the morning broadcasts had not been resumed.

One night Charlesworth and I followed Tony to the cave. 'Fry, goddam it,' the skipper began. 'You've got me doing it, too!'

'What?'

'This coast-watcher. Damn it all, Fry. I wish we knew what had happened to that chap.' The men sat on boxes in the end of the cave towards the bay.

'I don't know,' Tony said. 'But the courage of the man fascinates me. Up there. Alone. Hunted. Japs getting closer every day. God, Charlesworth, it gets under my skin.'

'Same way with me,' the skipper said. 'His name comes up at the damnedest times. Take yesterday. I was down at the waterfront showing some of the bushboys how to store empty gas drums. One of them was from Malaita. I got to talking with him. Found out who this Basil is that Anderson referred to one morning.'

'You did?' Fry asked eagerly.

'Yes, he's a murderer of some sort. There was a German trader over on his island. Fellow named Kesperson. Apparently quite a character. Used to beat the boys up a good deal. This chap Basil killed him one day. They hid in the bush. Well, you know how natives are. Always know things first. When word got around that Anderson was to be a coast-watcher this Basil appears out of the jungle and wants to go along. Anderson took him.'

'That's what I don't understand, skipper,' Fry commented. 'The things Anderson does don't add up to an ordinary man. Why would a good man like that come out here in the first place? How does he have the courage?'

Fry's insidious questions haunted me that night. Why do good men do anything? How does any man have the courage to go to war? I thought of the dead Japs bobbing upon the shorelines of The Slot. Even some of them had been good men. And might be again, if they could be left alone on their farms. And there was bloody Savo with its good men. All the men rotting in Iron Bottom Bay were good men, too. The young men from the *Vincennes*, the lean Australians from the *Canberra*, the cooks from the *Astoria* and those four pilots I knew so well . . . they were good men. How did they have the courage to prowl off strange islands at night and die without cursing and whimpers? How did they have the courage?

And I hated Tony Fry for having raised such questions. I wanted to shout at him, 'Damn it all! Why don't you get out of the cave? Why don't you take your whisky bottles and your lazy ways and go back to Noumea?'

But as these words sprang to my lips I looked across the cave at Tony and Charlesworth. Only a small light was burning. It threw shadows about the faces of the two men. They leaned towards one another in the semi-darkness. They were talking of the coast-watcher. Tony was speaking: 'I think of him up there pursued by Japs. And us safe in the cave.'

And then I understand. Each man I knew had a cave somewhere, a hidden refuge from war. For some it was love for wives and kids back home. That was the unassailable retreat. When bad food and Jap shells and the awful tropic diseases attacked, there was the cave of love. There a men found refuge. For others the cave consisted of jobs waiting, a farm to run, a business to establish, a tavern on the corner of Eighth and Vine. For still others the cave was whisky, or wild nights in the Pink House at Noumea, or heroism beyond the call of valour. When war became too terrible or too lonely or too bitter, men fled into their caves, sweated it out, and came back ready for another day or another battle.

For Tony and Charlesworth their cave was the contemplation of another man's courage. They dared not look at one another and say, 'Hell! Our luck isn't going to hold out much longer.' They couldn't say, 'Even P.T. boats get it sooner or later.' They dared not acknowledge, 'I don't think I could handle another trip like that one, fellow.'

No, they couldn't talk like that. Instead they sat in the cave and wondered about the Remittance Man. Why was he silent? Had the Japs got him? And every word they said was directed inward at themselves. The Englishman's great courage in those critical days of The Slot buoyed their equal courage. Like all of us on Tulagi, Tony and Charlesworth knew that if the coast-watcher could keep going on Bougainville, they could keep going in the P.T.s.

Then one morning, while Tony sat in the cave twisting the silent dials, orders came transferring him to Noumea. He packed one parachute bag. 'An old sea captain once told me,' he said at lunch, 'to travel light. Never more than twenty-five pieces of luggage. A clean shirt and twenty-four bottles of whisky!'

At this moment there was a peremptory interruption. It was Lazars. 'Come right away!' he shouted. 'The Remittance Man.'

The coast-watcher was already speaking when we reached the cave. '. . . and I judge it has been a great victory because only a few ships straggled back. Congratulations, Americans. I am sorry I failed you during the critical days. I trust you know why. The Nips are upon us. This time they have us trapped. My wife is here. A few faithful boys have stayed with us. I wish to record the names of these brave friends. Basil and Lenato from Malaita. Jerome from Choiseul. Morris and his wife Ngana from Bougainville. I could not wish for a stauncher crew. I do not think I could have had a better . . .'

There was a shattering sound. It could have been a rifle. Then another and another. The Remittance Man spoke no more. In his place came the hissing voice of one horrible in frustration: 'American peoper! You die!'

For a moment it was quiet in the cave. Then Fry leaped to his feet and looked distractedly at Charlesworth. 'No! No!' he cried. He returned to the silent radio. 'No!' he insisted, hammering it with his fist. He swung around and grabbed Charlesworth by the arm. 'I'm going over to see Kester,' he said in mumbling words.

'Fry! There's nothing you can do,' the skipper assured him.

'Do? We can get that man out of Bougainville!'

'Don't be carried away by this thing, Fry,' Charlesworth reasoned quietly. 'The man's dead and that's that.'

'Dead?' Tony shouted. 'Don't you believe it!' He ran out of the cave and started down the hill.

'Fry!' Charlesworth cried. 'You can't go over to Guadal. You have no orders for that.' Tony stopped amid the flowers of the old English garden. He looked back at Charlesworth in disgust and then ran on down the hill.

We were unprepared for what happened next. Months later Admiral Kester explained about the submarine. He said, 'When Fry broke into my shack I didn't know what to think. He was like a madman. But as I listened to him I said, "This boy's talking my language." A brave man was in trouble. Up in the jungle. Some damn' fools wanted to try to help him. I thought, "That's what keeps the Navy young. What's it matter if this fool gets himself killed. He's got the right idea." So there was a sub headed north on routine relief. The skipper would try anything. I told him to take Fry and the Fiji volunteer along.' The admiral knocked the ashes out of his pipe as he told me about it. 'It's that go-to-hell spirit you like about Tony Fry. He has it.'

The sub rolled into Tulagi Bay that afternoon. The giant Fiji scout stayed close to Tony as they came ashore. Whenever we asked the Fiji questions about the trip into the jungle he would pat his kinky hair and say in Oxford accents, 'Ah, yes! Ah, yes!' He was shy and afraid of us, even though he stood six feet seven.

I dragged my gear down to the shore and saw the submariners, the way they stood aloof and silent, watching their pigboat with loving eyes. They are alone in the Navy. I admired the P.T. boys. And I often wondered how the aviators had the courage to go out day after day, and I forgave their boasting. But the submariners! In the entire fleet they stand apart.

Charlesworth joined us, too. About dusk he and Fry went to the P.T. line and hauled out a few carbines. They gave me one. We boarded the sub and headed north. In the pigboat Tony was like the mainspring of a watch when the release is jammed. Tense, tight-packed, he sweated. Salt perspiration dripped from his eyebrows. He was lost in his own perplexing thoughts.

We submerged before dawn. This was my first trip down into the compressed, clicking, beehive world of the submariners. I never got used to the strange noises. A head of steam pounding through the pipes above my face would make me shudder and gasp for air. Even Charlesworth had trouble with his collar, which wasn't buttoned.

At midnight we put into a twisting cove south of Kieta on the north shore of Bougainville. I expected a grim silence, ominous with over-hanging trees along the dark shore. Instead men clanked about the pigboat, dropped a small rubber boat overboard, and swore at one another. 'Ah, yes!' the Fiji mused. 'This is the place. We were here four weeks ago. No danger here.' He went ashore in the first boatload.

While we waited for the rubber boat to return, the submariners argued as to who would go along with us as riflemen. This critical question had not been discussed on the way north. Inured to greater dangers than any jungle could hold, the submariners gathered in the blue light of a passageway and matched coins. Three groups of three played odd-man-out. Losers couldn't go.

'Good hunting,' one of the unlucky submariners called as we climbed into the boat. 'Sounds like a damned fool business to me. The guy's dead, ain't he?' He went below.

Ashore the Fiji had found his path. We went inland half a mile and waited for the dawn. It came quietly, like a purposeful cat stealing home after a night's adventure. Great trees with vine-ropes woven between them fought the sun to keep it out of the jungle. Stray birds, distant and lonely, shot through the trees, darting from one ray of light to another. In time a dim haze seeped through the vast canopy above us. The gloomy twilight of daytime filled the jungle.

As we struggled towards the hills we could see no more than a few feet into the dense growth. No man who has not seen the twisting lianas, the drooping parasites, the orchids, and the dim passages can know what the jungle is like, not oppressive and foreboding. A submariner dropped back to help me with my pack. 'How do guys from Kansas and Iowa fight in this crap?' he asked. He went eight steps ahead of me, and I could not see him, nor hear him, nor find any trace that a human had ever stood where I then stood. The men from Kansas and Iowa, I don't know how they cleaned up one jungle after another.

The path became steeper. I grew more tired, but Tony hurried on. We were dripping. Sweat ran down the bones at the base of my wrist and trickled off my fingers. My face was wet with small rivulets rising from the springs of sweat in my hair. No breath of air moved in the sweltering jungle, and I kept saying to myself, 'For a man already dead!'

The Fiji leaned his great shoulders forward and listened. 'We are almost there,' he said softly, like an English actor in a murder mystery. The pigboat boys grinned and fingered their carbines. The jungle path became a trail. The lianas were cut away. Some coconut husks lay by the side of a charred fire. We knew we were near a village of pretensions.

Fry pushed ahead of the Fiji. He relaxed his grip upon the carbine and dragged it along by the strap. He hurried forward.

'There it is!' he cried in a hoarse whisper. He started to run. The Fiji reached forward and grabbed him, like a mother saving an eager child.

The giant Negro crept ahead to study the low huts. Inch by inch we edged into the village square. We could see no one. Only the hot sun was there. A submariner, nineteen years old, started to laugh.

'Gosh!' he cried. 'Nobody here!' We all began to laugh.

And then I saw it! The line of skulls! I could not speak. I raised my arm to point, but my hand froze in half-raised position. One by one the laughing men saw the grim palisades, each pole with a human head on top. I was first to turn away and saw that Fry was poking his carbine into an empty hut.

'Hey!' he shouted. 'Here's where he was. This was his hut!'

'Tony!' I cried. My voice burst from me as if it had a will of its own.

'What do you know?' Tony called out from the hut. 'Here's the guy's stuff! I wouldn't be surprised if he . . .'

Fry rejoined us, carrying part of a radio set. The bright sun blinded him for a moment. Then he saw my face, and the row of skulls. He dropped his carbine and the rheostat. 'No!' he roared. 'God! No!' He rushed across the sun-drenched square. He rushed to the fifteen poles and clutched each one in turn. The middle, thickest and most prominent, bore the sign: 'American Marine You Die.'

Charlesworth and I crossed to the skull-crowned palisades. I remember two things. Fry's face was composed, even relaxed. He studied the middle pole with complete detachment. Then I saw why! Up the pole, across the Jap sign, and on up to the withering head streamed a line of jungle ants. They were giving the Remittance Man their ancient jungle burial.

Charlesworth's jaw grew tense. I knew he was thinking, 'When I get a Jap . . .' I can't remember what I thought, something about, 'This is the end of war . . .' At any rate, my soliloquy was blasted by an astonished cry from a submariner.

The skulls had shocked us. What we now saw left us horrified and shaken. For moving from the jungle was a native with elephantiasis. He was so crippled that he, of all the natives, could not flee at our approach.

I say he moved. It would be more proper to say that he crawled, pushing a rude wheelbarrow before him. In the barrow rested his scrotum, a monstrous growth that otherwise would drag along the ground. His glands were diseased. In a few years his scrotum had grown until it weighed more than seventy pounds and tied him a prisoner to his barrow.

We stepped back in horror as he approached. For not only did he have this monstrous affliction, but over the rest of his body growths the size of golf balls protruded. There must have been fifty of them. He, knowing of old our apprehensions, smiled. Tony Fry, alone among us, went forward to greet him and help him into the shade. The man dropped his barrow handles and shook hands with Tony. Fry felt the knobs and inwardly winced. To the man he made no sign. 'You talk-talk 'long me?' Tony asked. The man spoke a few words of pidgin.

Fry gave the man cigarettes and candy. He broke out some cloth, too, and threw it across the wheelbarrow. Without thinking, he placed his right foot on the barrow, too, and talked earnestly with the crippled native.

All that steaming midday, with the sun blazing overhead, Tony asked questions, questions, and got back fragments of answers in pidgin.

'Japoni come many time. Take Maries. Take banan'. Take young girls. Kill missi. One day white man come. Two bockis. Black string. There! There! There! Chief want to kill white man like Japoni say. Now chief he pinis. That one. That he skull.

'White man got 'long one Mary. Black allasame me. She say, "No killim." White man live in hut 'long me.' We were revolted at the thought of the Remittance Man and his wife living with the scrofulous man and his wheelbarrow. The dismal account droned on. 'One day Japoni come. Fin' white man. Break bockis. Tear down string. Shoot white man. White man he not die.'

Tony reached out and grabbed the man by his bumpy arm. The man recoiled. Fry turned to us and called in triumph, 'He isn't dead! They didn't kill him, did they?'

'Not killim,' the diseased man replied. 'Jus' here!' The man indicated his shoulder and tried to simulate blood running from a wound.

'Where did they take him?' Tony pressed, his voice low and quick.

'Bringim out here. Tie him to stick. Big fella b'long sword cut him many time.' With his cigarette the native made lunging motions. Finally he swished it across his own neck. 'Cut 'im head off.'

Tony wiped his long hand across his sweating forehead. He looked about him. The sun was slanting westwards and shone in his eyes. He turned his back on the barrow and studied the ants at their work. 'We'll bury the guy,' he said.

Immediately the native started to wail. 'Japoni say he killim all fella b'long village we stop 'im 'long ground. All fella b'long here run away you come, like Japoni say.' It was apparent the Japs had terrified the jungle villages. 'No takem skull. Please!'

We looked up at the whitening remnants. The ants, impervious to our wonder, hurried on. Fry raised his right hand to his waist and flicked a salute at the middle skull. He shook hands with the thankful native and gave him four packages of cigarettes. He gave him his knife, a penknife, his handkerchief, the last of his candy and two ends of cloth. Again he shook the knobby hand. 'Listen, Joe,' he said sharply, his eyes afire. 'We'll be back to get you one of these days. Won't be long. We fix you up. American doctors. They can cut that way. No pain. Good job. All those bumps. All gone. Joe! I've seen it done in Santo. We'll fix you up, good. All you got to do, Joe. Watch that one. Don't let it get lost. We'll be back. Not long now.'

In a kind of ecstasy Fry motioned us into the jungle. When we were half-way back to the submarine he stopped suddenly. He was excited. 'You heard what I told that guy. If any of you are around when we take Bougainville, come up here and get him. Haul him down to a hospital. A good doctor can fix that guy up in one afternoon. Remember. And when you're up here bury that skull.'

We plunged into the deepest part of the jungle and waited for the submarine to take us to whatever caves of refuge we had fashioned for ourselves. Fry hid in his atop Tulagi for the better part of a week, drunk and unapproachable. On the seventh day he appeared unshaven, gaunt, and surly.

'I'm gettin' to hell out of here,' he said. He went down to the bay and caught a small boat for Guadal.

I can't say he left us, though, for his fixation on the Remittance Man remained. We used to say, 'Who do you suppose that guy actually was?' We never found out. We found no shred of evidence that pointed to anything but a thoroughly prosaic Englishman. As I recall, we added only one fact that Fry himself hadn't previously uncovered. On the day that Charlesworth received notice of his third medal he rushed into the mess all excited. 'What do you know?' he cried. 'That fellow up in the jungle. At least I found out where he came from! A little town near London.'

Irwin Shaw

Retreat

THE column of trucks wound into the little square beside the Madeleine and stopped there, under the trees. They were furry with dust, the black cross almost indistinguishable even in the bright Paris sunlight under the harsh dry coat they had accumulated in the retreat from Normandy.

The engines stopped and suddenly the square was very quiet, the drivers and the soldiers relaxing on the trucks, the people at the little tables in the cafés staring without expression at the line of vehicles, bullet-scarred and fresh from war against the trees and Greek columns of the Madeleine.

A major at the head of the column slowly raised himself and got out of his car. He stood looking up at the Madeleine, a dusty, middle-aged figure, the uniform no longer smart, the lines of the body sagging and unmilitary. The major turned around and walked slowly toward the Café Bernard across the square, his face grimly and worn and expressionless, with the dust in heavy, theatrical lines in the creases of his face and where his goggles had been. He walked heavily, thoughtfully, past his trucks and his men, who watched him dispassionately and incuriously, as though they had known him for many years and there was nothing more to be learned from him. Some of the men got out of their trucks and lay down in the sunshine on the pavement and went to sleep, like corpses in a town where there has been a little fighting, just enough to produce several dead without doing much damage to the buildings.

The major walked over to the little sidewalk tables of the Café Bernard, looking at the drinkers there with the same long, cold, thoughtful stare with which he had surveyed the Madeleine. The drinkers stared back with the guarded, undramatic faces with which they had looked at the Germans for four years.

The major stopped in front of the table where Segal sat alone, the half-finished glass of beer in his hand. A little twist of a smile pulled momentarily at the German's mouth as he stood there, looking at Segal, small and pinned together with desperate neatness in his five-year-old suit, his shirt stitched and cross-stitched to hold it together, his bald head shining old and clean in the bright sun.

'Do you mind . . . ?' The major indicated the empty chair beside Segal with a slow, heavy movement of his hand.

Segal shrugged. 'I don't mind,' he said.

The major sat down, spread his legs out deliberately in front of him. '*Garçon*,' he said, 'two beers.'

They sat in silence and the major watched his men sleeping like corpses on the Paris pavement.

'For this drink,' the major said, in French, 'I wanted to sit with a civilian.'

The waiter brought the beers and set them down on the table and put the saucers in the middle, between them. The major absently pulled the saucers in front of him.

'To your health,' he said. He raised his glass. Segal lifted his and they drank.

The major drank thirstily, closing his eyes, almost finishing his glass before he put it down. He opened his eyes and licked the tiny scallop of froth from the beer off his upper lip, as he slowly turned his head, regarding the buildings around him. 'A pretty city,' he said. 'A very pretty city. I had to have one last drink.'

'You've been at the front?' Segal asked.

'Yes,' said the major. 'I have been at the front.'

'And you are going back?'

'I am going back,' the Major said, 'and the front is going back.' He grinned a little, sourly. 'It is hard to say which precedes which . . .' He finished his beer, then turned and stared at Segal. 'Soon,' he said, 'the Americans will be here. How do you feel about that?'

Segal touched his face uncomfortably. 'You don't really want a Parisian to answer a question like that,' he said, 'do you?'

'No.' The major smiled. 'I suppose not. Though, it's too bad the Americans had to meddle. However, it's too late to worry about that now.' Under the warlike dust his face now was tired and quiet and intellectual, not good-looking, but studious and reasonable, the face of a man who read after business hours and occasionally went to concerts without being pushed into it by his wife. He waved to the waiter. '*Garçon*, two more beers.' He turned to Segal. 'You have no objections to drinking another beer with me?'

Segal looked across at the armoured vehicles, the two hundred sprawling men, the heavy machine guns mounted and pointing toward the sky. He shrugged, his meaning cynical and clear.

'No,' said the major. 'I would not dream of using the German army to force Frenchmen to drink beer with me.'

'Since the Germans occupied Paris,' Segal said. 'I haven't drunk with one or conducted a conversation with one. Four years. As an experience, perhaps, I should not miss it. And now is the time to try it. In a little while it will no longer be possible, will it?'

The major disregarded the jibe. He stared across at his command stretched wearily and incongruously in front of the Greek temple Paris had faithfully erected in her midst. He never seemed to be able to take his eyes off the armour and the men, as though there was a connection there, bitter and unsatisfactory and inescapable, that could never really be broken, even for a moment, in a café, over a glass of beer. 'You're a Jew,' he said quietly to Segal, 'aren't you?'

The waiter came and put the two beers and the saucers on the table.

Segal put his hands into his lap, to hide the trembling and the terror in the joints of his elbows and knees and the despair in all the veins of the body that the word had given rise to in him, each time, every day, since the bright summer days of 1940. He sat in silence, licking his lips, automatically and hopelessly looking for exits and doorways, alleys and subway entrances.

The major lifted his glass. 'To your health,' he said. 'Come on. Drink.'

Segal wet his lips with the beer.

'Come on,' the major said. 'You can tell me the truth. If you don't talk, you know, it would be the easiest thing in the world to call over a sergeant and have him look at your papers . . .'

'Yes,' said Segal. 'I'm a Jew.'

'I knew it,' said the major. 'That's why I sat down.' He stared at his men with the same look of bondage, devoid of affection, devoid of warmth or loyalty or hope. 'There are several questions in my mind you can answer better than anyone.'

'What are they?' Segal asked uneasily.

'No rush,' said the major. 'They'll wait for a minute.' He peered curiously at Segal. 'You know, it's forbidden for Jews to enter a café in France . . . ?'

'I know,' said Segal.

'Also,' said the major, 'all Jews are instructed to wear the yellow star on their coats . . .'

'Yes.'

'You don't wear yours and I find you in a café in broad daylight.'

'Yes.'

'You're very brave.' There was a little note of irony in the major's voice. 'Is it worth it for a drink – to risk being deported?'

Segal shrugged. 'It isn't for the drink,' he said. 'Maybe you won't understand, but I was born in Paris. I've lived all my life in the cafés, on the boulevards.'

'What is your profession, Mr . . . Mr . . . ?'

'Segal.'

'What do you do for a living?'

'I was a musician.'

'Ah,' there was an involuntary little tone of respect in the German's voice. 'What instrument?'

'The saxophone,' said Segal, 'in a jazz orchestra.'

The major grinned. 'An amusing profession.'

'I haven't played in four years,' said Segal. 'Anyway, I was getting too old for the saxophone and the Germans permitted me to make a graceful exit. But imagine, for a jazz musician, the cafés are his life, his studio, his club, his places to make love, his library and place of business. If I am not free to sit down on a *terrasse* and have a *vin blanc* in Paris, I might just as well go to a concentration camp . . .'

'Every man,' said the major, 'to his own particular patriotism.'

'I think,' said Segal, starting to rise, 'that perhaps I'd better go now . . .'

'No. Sit down. I have a little time.' The German stared once more at his men. 'We will arrive in Germany a half hour later, if at all. It doesn't matter. Tell me something. Tell me about the French. We have not behaved badly in France. Yet, I feel they hate us. They hate us, most of them, almost as much as the Russians hate us . . .'

'Yes,' said Segal.

'Fantastic,' said the major. 'We have been most correct, within the bounds of military necessity.'

'You believe that. It's wonderful, but you really believe it.' Segal was beginning to forget where he was, whom he was talking to, the argument rising hot within him.

'Of course I believe it.'

'And the Frenchmen who have been shot . . . ?'

'The army had nothing to do with it. The SS, the Gestapo . . .'

Segal shook his head. 'How many times I have heard that!' he said. 'And all the dead Jews, too.'

'The army knew nothing about it,' the major said stubbornly. 'I, myself, have never lifted my hand, or done one bad thing against any Jew in Germany or Poland or here in France. At this point, it is necessary to judge accurately who did what . . .'

'Why is it necessary?' Segal asked.

'Let us face the facts.' The major looked around him suddenly, lowered his voice. 'It is very probable now that we are beaten . . .'

'It is probable,' Segal smiled. 'It is also probable that the sun will rise sometime about six o'clock tomorrow morning.'

'A certain amount of revenge – what you call justice, will be demanded. The army has behaved in a civilized manner and that must not be forgotten.'

Segal shrugged. 'I do not recall seeing the Gestapo in Paris until after the German army came in . . .'

'Ah, well,' said the major, 'you are not representative. You are a Jew, and naturally a little more bitter, although you seem to have done very well, I must say.'

'I've done very well,' said Segal. 'I am still alive. It is true that my two brothers are no longer alive, and my sister is working in Poland, and my people have been wiped out of Europe, but I have done very well. I have been very clever.' He took out his wallet and showed it to the major. The Star of David was tucked in so that it could be snapped out in a moment, and there was a needle already threaded, wound round a piece of yellow cardboard right next to it. 'In a tight spot,' said Segal, 'I could always take out the star and put it on. It took six stitches, exactly.' His hand trembled as he closed the wallet and put it away. 'Four years, major, imagine four years praying each moment you will have thirty seconds somewhere to sew in six stitches before they ask to look at your papers. I've done very well. I've always found the thirty seconds. And do you know where I slept at night, because I was clever? In the women's jail. So, when the Gestapo came to my house looking for me, I was comfortably locked in a cell among the whores and shoplifters. I could arrange that because my wife is Catholic and a nurse at the jail. Again, I've done very well. My wife decided finally she had had enough of me. I don't blame her, it's difficult for a woman. It's all right for a year, two years, but then the gesture wears out, you yearn not to have the millstone around your neck. So she decided to divorce me. A very simple procedure for a Christian. You merely go to court and say, "My husband is a Jew," and that's the end of it. We have three children, and I have not seen them for a year. Well enough. And the propaganda agencies, who also have no connection to the correct German army, also have done well. The French hate the Germans, but they have been fed the lies for four years and I think maybe they will never quite get over the lies about the Jews. The Germans have various accomplishments to their credit, and this is another one . . .'

'I think perhaps you're being too pessimistic,' the major said. 'People change. The world goes back to normal, people get tired of hatred and bloodshed.'

'You're getting tired of hatred and bloodshed,' said Segal. 'I can understand that, after all this time.'

'Myself,' said the major, 'I never wanted it. Look at me. Fundamentally, I'm not a soldier. Come to Germany after the war and I'll sell you a Citroen. I'm an automobile salesman, with a wife and three children, dressed in uniform.'

'Maybe,' said Segal. 'Maybe . . . Now we will hear that from many people. Fundamentally, I am not a soldier, I am an automobile salesman, a musician, a pet-fancier, a stamp-collector, a Lutheran preacher, a schoolteacher, anything . . . But in 1940 we did not hear that as you marched down the boulevards. There were no automobile salesmen then – only captains and sergeants, pilots, artillerists . . . Somehow, the uniform was not such an accident in 1940.'

They sat silent. A passing automobile backfired twice and one of the sleeping soldiers screamed in his sleep, the noise echoing strangely in the sunny square. One of the other soldiers woke the sleeping man and explained to him what had happened and the sleeper sat up against a truck wheel, wiped his face nervously with his hand, and went to sleep again, sitting up.

'Segal,' said the major, 'after this war is over, it will be necessary to salvage Europe. We will all have to live together on the same continent. At the basis of that, there must be forgiveness. I know it is impossible to forgive everyone, but there are the millions who never did anything . . .'

'Like you?'

'Like me,' said the German. 'I was never a member of the Party. I lived a quiet middle-class existence with my wife and three children.'

'I am getting very tired,' Segal said, 'of your wife and three children.'

The major flushed under the dust. He put his hand heavily on Segal's wrist. 'Remember,' he said, 'the Americans are not yet in Paris.'

'Forgive me,' said Segal. 'I believed you when you told me I could talk freely.'

The major took his hand off Segal's wrist. 'I mean it,' he said. 'Go ahead. I have been thinking about these things for a long time, I might as well listen to you.'

'I'm sorry,' said Segal. 'I have to go home and it's a long walk, to the other bank.'

'If you have no objection,' said the major, 'I'll drive you there.'

'Thank you,' said Segal.

The major paid and they walked together across the square, in front of the men, who stared at them both with the same incurious, hostile expressions. They got into the major's car and started off. Segal couldn't help enjoying his first ride in an automobile in four years and smiled a little as they crossed the Seine, with the river blue and pleasant below them.

The major barely looked at where they were going. He sat back wearily, an aging man who had been pushed beyond the limits of his strength, his face worn and gentle now with exhaustion as they passed in front of the great statues that guard the Chambre des Députés. He took off his cap and the fresh wind blew his sparse hair in thin curls.

'I am ready to face the fact,' he said, his voice soft and almost pleading, 'that there is a price to be paid for what could be called our guilt. We have lost and so we are guilty.'

Segal chuckled drily. By this time he was feeling exhilarated by the beer he had drunk, and the ride, and the sense of danger and victory that came with talking to the major in a town full of German troops.

'Perhaps,' said the major, 'even if we hadn't lost we would be guilty. Honestly, Mr Segal, for the last two years I have thought that. In the beginning, a man is swept up. You have no idea of the pressure that is applied when a country like Germany goes to war, to make a man join in with a whole heart, to try to succeed in the profession of soldiering. But even so, it wasn't the older ones like me . . . It was the young ones, the fanatics, they were like a flood, and the rest of us were carried along. You've seen for yourself . . .'

'I've seen the young ones myself,' said Segal. 'But also the older ones, sitting at the best restaurants, eating butter and steaks and white bread for four years, filling the theatres, wearing the pretty uniforms, signing orders to kill ten Frenchmen a day, twenty . . .'

'Weakness,' said the major. 'Self-indulgence. The human race is not composed of saints. Somewhere, forgiveness has to begin.'

Segal leaned over and touched the driver on the shoulder. 'Stop here, please,' he said in German. 'I have to get off.'

'Do you live here?' the major asked.

'No. Five streets from here,' said Segal. 'But with all due respect, major, I prefer not showing a German, any German, where I live.'

The major shrugged. 'Stop here,' he told the driver.

The car pulled over to the kerb and stopped. Segal opened the door and got out.

The major held his hand. 'Don't you think we've paid?' he asked harshly. 'Have you seen Berlin, have you seen Hamburg, were you at Stalingrad, have you any idea what the battlefield looked like at Saint Lô, at Mortain, at Falaise? Have you any notion of what it's like to be on the road with the American air force over you all the time and Germans trying to get away in wagons, on foot, on bicycles, living in holes like animals, like cattle in slaughter pens in an abattoir? Isn't that paying, too?' His face worked convulsively under the dust and it seemed to Segal that as though he might break into tears in a moment. 'Yes,' he said, 'yes, we're guilty. Granted, we're guilty. Some of us are more guilty than the rest. What are we to do now? What can I do to wash my hands?'

Segal pulled his arm away. For a moment, helplessly, he felt like comforting this aging, wornout, decent-looking man, this automobile salesman, father of three children, this weary, frightened, retreating soldier, this wavering, hopeless target on the straight, long roads of France. Then he looked at the rigid face of the driver, sitting at attention in the front of the car, with his machine pistol, small, and clever, well-oiled and ready for death in the sling under the windshield.

'What can I do?' the major cried again, 'to wash my hands?'

Segal sighed wearily, spoke without exultation or joy or bitterness, speaking not for himself, but for the first Jew brained on a Munich street long ago and the last American brought to earth that afternoon by a sniper's bullet outside Chartres, and for all the years and all the dead and all the agony in between. 'You can cut your throat,' he said, 'and see if the blood will take the stain out.'

The major sat up stiffly and his eyes were dangerous, cold with anger and defeat, and for a moment Segal felt he had gone too far, that after four years' successful survival, he was going to die now, a week before the liberation of the city, and for the same moment, looking at the set, angry, beaten face, he did not care. He turned his back and walked deliberately toward his home, the space between his shoulder blades electric and attendant, waiting tightly for the bullet. He had walked ten steps, slowly, when he heard the major say something in German. He walked even more slowly, staring, stiff and dry-eyed, down the broad reaches of the Boulevard Raspail. He heard the motor of the car start up, and the slight wail of the tyres as it wheeled around sharply, and he did not look back as the car started back toward the Seine and the Madeleine and the waiting troops sleeping like so many dead by their armoured cars before the Madeleine, back along the open, unforgiven road to Germany.

Nadine Gordimer

Oral History

THERE'S always been one house like a white man's house in the village of Dilolo. Built of brick with a roof that bounced signals from the sun. You could see it through the mopane trees as you did the flash of paraffin tins the women carried on their heads, bringing water from the river. The rest of the village was built of river mud, grey, shaped by the hollows of hands, with reed thatch and poles of mopane from which the leaves had been ripped like fish-scales.

It was the chief's house. Some chiefs have a car as well but this was not an important chief, the clan is too small for that, and he had the usual stipend from the government. If they had given him a car he would have had no use for it. There is no road: the army patrol Land Rovers come upon the people's cattle, startled as buck, in the mopane scrub. The village has been there a long time. The chief's grandfather was the clan's grandfathers' chief, and his name is the same as that of the chief who waved his warriors to down assegais and took the first bible from a Scottish Mission Board white man. *Seek and ye shall find*, the missionaries said.

The villagers in those parts don't look up, any more, when the sting-shaped army planes fly over twice a day. Only fish-eagles are disturbed, take off, screaming, keen swerving heads lifting into their invaded domain of sky. The men who have been away to work on the mines can read, but there are no newspapers. The people hear over the radio the government's count of how many army trucks have been blown up, how many white soldiers are going to be buried with *full military honours* – something that is apparently white people's way with their dead.

The chief had a radio, and he could read. He read to the headmen the letter from the government saying that anyone hiding or giving food and water to those who were fighting against the government's army would be put in prison. He read another letter from the government saying that to protect the village from these men who went over the border and came back with guns to kill people and burn huts, anybody who walked in the bush after dark would be shot. Some of the young men who, going courting or drinking to the next village, might have been in danger, were no longer at home in their fathers' care anyway. The young go away: once it was to the mines, now – the radio said – it was over the border to learn how to fight. Sons walked out of the clearing of mud huts; past the chief's house; past the children playing with the models of police patrol Land Rovers made out of twisted wire. The children called out, Where are you going? The young men didn't answer and they hadn't come back.

There was a church of mopane and mud with a mopane flagpole to fly a white flag when somebody died; the funeral service was more or less the same protestant one the missionaries brought from Scotland and it was combined with older rituals to entrust the newly-dead to the ancestors. Ululating women with whitened faces sent them on their way to the missionaries' last judgment. The children were baptized with names chosen by portent in consultation between the mother and an old man who read immutable fate in the fall of small bones cast like dice from a horn cup. On all occasions and most Saturday nights there was a beer-drink, which the chief attended. An upright chair from his house was brought out for him although everyone else squatted comfortably on the sand, and he was offered the first taste from an old decorated gourd dipper (other people drank from baked-bean or pilchard tins) – it is the way of people of the village.

It is also the way of the tribe to which the clan belongs and the subcontinent to which the tribe belongs, from Matadi in the west to Mombasa in the east, from Entebbe in the north to Empangeni in the south, that everyone is welcome at a beer-drink. No traveller or passer-by, poling down the river in his pirogue, leaving the snake-skin trail of his bicycle wheels through the sand, betraying his approach – if the dogs are sleeping by the cooking fires and the children have left their home-made highways – only by the brittle fragmentation of the dead leaves as he comes unseen through miles of mopane, is a presence to be questioned. Everyone for a long way round on both sides of the border near Dilolo has a black skin, speaks the same language and shares the custom of hospitality. Before the government started to shoot people at night to stop more young men leaving when no one was awake to ask, 'Where are you going?' people thought nothing of walking ten miles from one village to another for a beer-drink.

But unfamiliar faces have become unusual. If the firelight caught such a face, it backed into darkness. No one remarked the face. Not even the smallest child who never took its eyes off it, crouching down among the knees of men with soft, little boy's lips held in wonderingly over teeth as if an invisible grown-up hand were clamped there. The young girls giggled and flirted from the background, as usual. The older men didn't ask for news of relatives or friends outside the village. The chief seemed not to see one face or faces in distinction from any other. His eyes came to rest instead on some of the older men. He gazed and they felt it.

Coming out of the back door of his brick house with its polished concrete steps, early in the morning, he hailed one of them. The man was passing with his hobbling cows and steadily bleating goats; stopped, with the turn of one who will continue on his way in a moment almost without breaking step. But the summons was for him. The chief wore a frayed collarless shirt and old trousers, like the man, but he was never barefoot. In the hand with a big steel watch on the wrist, he carried his thick-framed spectacles, and drew down his nose between the fingers of the other hand; he had the authoritative body of a man who still has his sexual powers but his eyes flickered against the light of the sun and secreted flecks of matter like cold cream at the corners. After the greetings usual between a chief and one of his headmen together with whom, from the retreat in the mopane forest where they lay together in the same age-group recovering from circumcision, he had long ago emerged a man, the chief said, 'When is your son coming back?'

'I have no news.'

'Did he sign for the mines?'

'No.'

'He's gone to the tobacco farms?'

'He didn't tell us.'

'Gone away to find work and doesn't tell his mother? What sort of child is that? Didn't you teach him?'

The goats were tongue-ing three hunchback bushes that were all that was left of a hedge round the chief's house. The man took out a round tin dented with child's tooth-marks and taking care not to spill any snuff, dosed himself. He gestured at the beasts, for permission: 'They're eating up your house . . .' He made a move towards the necessity to drive them on.

'There is nothing left there to eat.' The chief ignored his hedge, planted by his oldest wife who had been to school at the mission up the river. He stood among the goats as if he would ask more questions. Then he turned and went back to his yard, dismissing himself. The other man watched. It seemed he might call after; but instead drove his animals with the familiar cries, this time unnecessarily loud and frequent.

Often an army patrol Land Rover came to the village. No one could predict when this would be because it was not possible to count the days in between and be sure that so many would elapse before it returned, as could be done in the case of a tax-collector or cattle-dipping officer. But it could be heard minutes away, crashing through the mopane like a frightened animal, and dust hung marking the direction from which it was coming. The children ran to tell. The women went from hut to hut. One of the chief's wives would enjoy the importance of bearing the news: 'The government is coming to see you.' He would be out of his house when the Land Rover stopped and a black soldier (murmuring towards the chief the required respectful greeting in their own language) jumped out and opened the door for the white soldier. The white soldier had learned the names of all the local chiefs. He gave greetings with white men's brusqueness: 'Everything all right?' And the chief repeated to him: 'Everything is all right.' 'No one been bothering you in this village?' 'No one is troubling us.' But the white soldier signalled to his black men and they went through every hut busy as wives when they are cleaning, turning over bedding, thrusting gun-butts into the pile of ash and rubbish where the chickens searched, even looking in, their eyes dazzled by darkness, to the hut where one of the old women who had gone crazy had to be kept most of the time. The white soldier stood beside the Land Rover waiting for them. He told the chief of things that were happening not far from the village; not far at all. The road that passed five kilometres away had been blown up. 'Someone plants land-mines in the road and as soon as we repair it they put them there again. Those people come from across the river and they pass this way. They wreck our vehicles and kill people.'

The heads gathered round weaved as if at the sight of bodies laid there horrifyingly before them.

'They will kill you, too – burn your huts, all of you – if you let them stay with you.'

A woman turned her face away: 'Aïe-aïe-aïe-aïe.'

His forefinger half-circled his audience. 'I'm telling you. You'll see what they do.'

The chief's latest wife, taken only the year before and of the age-group of his elder grandchildren, had not come out to listen to the white man. But she heard from others what he had said, and fiercely smoothing her legs with grease, demanded of the chief, 'Why does he want us to die, that white man!'

Her husband, who had just been a passionately shuddering lover, became at once one of the important old with whom she did not count and could not argue. 'You talk about things you don't know. Don't speak for the sake of making a noise.'

To punish him, she picked up the strong, young girl's baby she had borne him and went out of the room where she slept with him on the big bed that had come down the river by barge, before the army's machine guns were pointing at the other bank.

He appeared at his mother's hut. There, the middle-aged man on whom the villagers depended, to whom the government looked when it wanted taxes paid and culling orders carried out, became a son – the ageless category, no matter from which age-group to another he passed in the progression of her life and his. The old woman was at her toilet. The great weight of her body settled around her where she sat on a reed mat outside the door. He pushed a stool under himself. Set out was a small mirror with a pink plastic frame and stand, in which he caught sight of his face, screwed up. A large black comb; a little carved box inlaid with red lucky beans she had always had, he used to beg to be allowed to play with it fifty years ago. He waited, not so much out of respect as in the bond of indifference to all outside their mutual contact that reasserts itself when lions and their kin lie against one another.

She cocked a glance, swinging the empty loops of her stretched ear-lobes. He did not say what he had come for.

She had chosen a tiny bone spoon from the box and was poking with trembling care up each round hole of distended nostril. She cleaned the crust of dried snot and dust from her delicate instrument and flicked the dirt in the direction away from him.

She said: 'Do you know where your sons are?'

'Yes, I know where my sons are. You have seen three of them here today. Two are in school at the mission. The baby – he's with the mother.' A slight smile, to which the old woman did not respond. Her preferences among the sons had no connection with sexual pride.

'Good. You can be glad of all that. But don't ask other people about theirs.'

As often when people who share the same blood share the same thought, for a moment mother and son looked exactly alike, he old-womanish, she mannish.

'If the ones we know are missing, there are not always empty places,' he said.

She stirred consideringly in her bulk. Leaned back to regard him: 'It used to be that all children were our own children. All sons our sons. *Old-fashion*, these people here' – the hard English word rolled out of their language like a pebble, and came to rest where aimed, at his feet.

It was spring: the mopane leaves turn, drying up and dying, spattering the sand with blood and rust – a battlefield, it must have looked, from the patrol planes. In August there is no rain to come for two months yet. Nothing grows but the flies hatch. The heat rises daily and the nights hold it, without a stir, till morning. On these nights the radio voice carried so clearly it could be heard from the chief's house all through the village. Many were being captured in the bush and killed by the army – *seek and destroy* was what the white men said now – and many in the army were being set upon in the bush or blown up in their trucks and buried with full military honours. This was expected to continue until October because the men in the bush knew that it was their last chance before the rains came and chained their feet in mud.

On these hot nights when people cannot sleep anyway, beer-drinks last until very late. People drink more; the women know this, and brew more. There is a fire but no one sits close round it.

Without a moon the dark is thick with heat; when the moon is full the dark shimmers thinly in a hot mirage off the river. Black faces are blue, there are watermarks along noses and biceps. The chief sat on his chair and wore shoes and socks in spite of the heat; those drinking nearest him could smell the suffering of his feet. The planes of jaw and lips he noticed in moonlight molten over them, moonlight pouring moths broken from white cases on the mopane and mosquitoes rising from the river, pouring glory like the light in the religious pictures people got at the mission – he had seen those faces about lately in the audacity of day, as well. An ox had been killed and there was the scent of meat sizzling in the village (just look at the behaviour of the dogs, they knew) although there was no marriage or other festival that called for someone to slaughter one of his beasts. When the chief allowed himself, at least, to meet the eyes of a stranger, the whites that had been showing at an oblique angle disappeared and he took rather than saw the full gaze of the seeing eye: the pupils with their defiance, their belief, their claim, hold, on him. He let it happen only once. For the rest, he saw their arrogant lifted jaws to each other and warrior smiles to the girls, as they drank. The children were drawn to them, fighting one another silently for places close up. Towards midnight – his watch had its own glowing galaxy – he left his chair and did not come back from the shadows where men went to urinate. Often at beer-drinks the chief would go home while others were still drinking.

He went to his brick house whose roof shone almost bright as day. He did not go to the room where his new wife and sixth son would be sleeping in the big bed, but simply took from the kitchen, where it was kept when not in use, a bicycle belonging to one of his hangers-on, relative or retainer. He wheeled it away from the huts in the clearing, his village and grandfather's village that disappeared so quickly behind him in the mopane, and began to ride through the sand. He was not afraid he would meet a patrol and be shot; alone at night in the sand forest, the forested desert he had known before and would know beyond his span of life, he didn't believe in the power of a roving band of government men to end that life. The going was heavy but he had mastered when young the art of riding on this, the only terrain he knew, and the ability came back. In an hour he arrived at the army post, called out who he was to the sentry with a machine gun, and had to wait, like a beggar rather than a chief, to be allowed to approach and be searched. There were black soldiers on duty but they woke the white man. It was the one who knew his name, his clan, his village, the way these modern white men were taught. He seemed to know at once why the chief had come; frowning in concentration to grasp details, his mouth was open in a smile and the point of his tongue curled touching at back teeth the way a man will verify facts one by one on his fingers. 'How many?'

'Six or ten or – but sometimes it's only, say, three or one .... I don't know. One is here, he's gone; they come again.'

'They take food, they sleep, and off. Yes. They make the people give them what they want, that's it, eh? And you know who it is who hides them – who shows them where to sleep – of course you know.'

The chief sat on one of the chairs in that place, the army's place, and the white soldier was standing. 'Who is it—' the chief was having difficulty in saying what he wanted in English, he had the feeling it was not coming out as he had meant nor being understood as he had expected. 'I can't know who is it' – a hand moved restlessly, he held a breath and released it – 'in the village there's many, plenty people. If it's this one or this one—' He stopped, shaking his head with a reminder to the white man of his authority, which the white soldier was quick to placate. 'Of course. Never mind. They frighten the people; the people can't say no. They kill people who say no, eh; cut their ears off, you know that? Tear away their lips. Don't you see the pictures in the papers?'

'We never saw it. I heard the government say on the radio.'

'They're still drinking . . . How long – an hour ago?'

The white soldier checked with a look the other men, whose stance had changed to that of bodies ready to break into movement: grab weapons, run, fling themselves at the Land Rovers guarded in the dark outside. He picked up the telephone receiver but blocked the mouthpiece as if it were someone about to make an objection. 'Chief, I'll be with you in a moment. – Take him to the duty room and make coffee. Just wait—' he leaned his full reach towards a drawer in a cabinet on the left of the desk and, scrabbling to get it open, took out a half-full bottle of brandy. Behind the chief's back he gestured the bottle towards the chief, and a black soldier jumped obediently to take it.

The chief went to a cousin's house in a village the other side of the army post later that night. He said he had been to a beer-drink and could not ride home because of the white men's curfew.

The white soldier had instructed that he should not be in his own village when the arrests were made so that he could not be connected with these and would not be in danger of having his ears cut off for taking heed of what the government wanted of him, or having his lips mutilated for what he had told.

His cousin gave him blankets. He slept in a hut with her father. The deaf old man was aware neither that he had come nor was leaving so early that last night's moon, the size of the bicycle's reflector, was still shiny in the sky. The bicycle rode up on spring-hares without disturbing them, in the forest; there was a stink of jackal-fouling still sharp on the dew. Smoke already marked his village; early cooking fires were lit. Then he saw that the smoke, the black particles spindling at his face, were not from cooking fires. Instead of going faster as he pumped his feet against the weight of sand the bicycle seemed to slow along with his mind, to find in each revolution of its wheels the countersurge: to stop; not go on. But there was no way not to reach what he found. The planes only children bothered to look up at any longer had come in the night and dropped something terrible and alive that no one could have read or heard about enough to be sufficiently afraid of. He saw first a bloody kaross, a dog caught on the roots of an upturned tree. The earth under the village seemed to have burst open and flung away what it carried: the huts, pots, gourds, blankets, the tin trunks, alarm-clocks, curtain-booth photographs, bicycles, radios and shoes brought back from the mines, the bright cloths young wives wound on their heads, the pretty pictures of white lambs and pink children at the knees of the golden-haired Christ the Scottish Mission Board first brought long ago – all five generations of the clan's life that had been chronicled by each succeeding generation in episodes told to the next. The huts had staved in like broken anthills. Within earth walls baked and streaked by fire the thatch and roof-poles were ash. He bellowed and stumbled from hut to hut, nothing answered frenzy, not even a chicken rose from under his feet. The walls of his house still stood. It was gutted and the roof had buckled. A black stiff creature lay roasted on its chain in the yard. In one of the huts he saw a human shape transformed the same way, a thing of stiff tar daubed on a recognizable framework. It was the hut where the mad woman lived; when those who had survived fled, they had forgotten her.

The chief's mother and his youngest wife were not among them. But the baby boy lived, and will grow up in the care of the older wives. No one can say what it was the white soldier said over the telephone to his commanding officer, and if the commanding officer had told him what was going to be done, or whether the white soldier knew, as a matter of procedure laid down in his military training for this kind of war, what would be done. The chief hanged himself in the mopane. The police or the army (much the same these days, people confuse them) found the bicycle beneath his dangling shoes. So the family hanger-on still rides it; it would have been lost if it had been safe in the kitchen when the raid came. No one knows where the chief found a rope, in the ruins of his village.

ORAL HISTORY

The people are beginning to go back. The dead are properly buried in ancestral places in the mopane forest. The women are to be seen carrying tins and grain panniers of mud up from the river. In talkative bands they squat and smear, raising the huts again. They bring sheaves of reeds exceeding their own height, balanced like the cross-stroke of a majuscular T on their heads. The men's voices sound through the mopane as they choose and fell trees for the roof supports.

A white flag on a mopane pole hangs outside the house whose white walls, built like a white man's, stand from before this time.

ACKNOWLEDGEMENTS

The Publishers wish to thank the following for permission to reprint previously published material. Every effort has been made to locate all persons having any rights in the stories appearing in this book but appropriate acknowledgement has been omitted in some cases through lack of information. Such omissions will be corrected in future printings of the book upon written notification to the Publishers.

Jonathan Cape Ltd and Naomi Mitchison for 'Black Sparta' by Naomi Mitchison

Henry Holt & Company, Inc. and Robert Hale Ltd for 'The Taking of Montfaucon' from *The Baby in the Icebox and Other Short Fiction* by James M. Cain. Copyright © 1981 by Alice M. Piper.

John Murray Publishers Ltd for 'The Coward of the Legion' from *Good Gestes* by P.C. Wren.

Doubleday, a division of Bantam, Doubleday, Dell Publishing Group, Inc. for 'The Gardener' from *Debits and Credits* by Rudyard Kipling. Copyright © 1926 by Rudyard Kipling.

The Estate of Geoffrey Household for 'Tell These Men to Go Away' from *The Europe That Was* by Geoffrey Household.

The Marine Society for 'Out of the Depths' by Sid Gorell from *Twenty Singing Seamen* selected by Ronald Hope.

The Marine Society for 'Survivor's Leave' by William Venables from *Twenty Singing Seamen* selected by Ronald Hope.

George MacDonald Fraser and John Farquharson Ltd for 'Wee Wullie' from *The General Danced at Dawn*. Copyright © George MacDonald Fraser.

F.J. Salfeld for 'Fear of Death'. Also published in *Short Stories of the Second World War* ed. by D.M. Davin (OUP).

Fred Urquhart for 'The Prisoner's Bike'. First published in *Modern Reading* (1944). Also published in *Short Stories of the Second World War* ed. by D.M. Davin (OUP). Copyright © Fred Urquhart 1944.

The Peters Fraser and Dunlop Group Ltd for 'Indecision' from *The Nightmare* by C.S. Forester.

The Marine Society for 'Daylight' by Thomas Gilchrist from *Twenty Singing Seamen* selected by Ronald Hope.

Methuen, London and E.P. Dutton, a division of Penguin Books USA, Inc. for 'A Richer Dust' from *The Collected Stories of Noel Coward* by Noel Coward. Copyright © 1939, 1951, 1963, 1965, 1966, 1967, 1983 by the Estate of Noel Coward.

Laurens Van Der Post and The Hogarth Press for 'A Bar of Shadow' from *The Seed and the Sower* by Laurens Van Der Post.

The Macmillan Publishing Company for 'The Cave' from *Tales of the South Pacific* by James A. Michener. Copyright © 1947 by James A. Michener.

Jonathan Cape Ltd and Delacorte Press, a division of Bantam, Doubleday, Dell Publishing Group, Inc. for 'Retreat' from *Short Stories: Five Decades* by Irwin Shaw. Copyright © 1937, 1938, 1939, 1940, 1941, 1942, 1943, 1944, 1945, 1946, 1947, 1949, 1950, 1952, 1953, 1954, 1955, 1956, 1957, 1958, 1961, 1962, 1963, 1964, 1967, 1968, 1969, 1971, 1973, 1977, 1978 by Irwin Shaw.

Jonathan Cape Ltd and Viking Penguin, a division of Penguin Books USA, Inc. for 'Oral History' from *A Soldier's Embrace* by Nadine Gordimer. Copyright © 1975, 1977, 1980 by Nadine Gordimer.